By Richard K. Morgan

Altered Carbon

Broken Angels

Market Forces

Woken Furies

WOKeN FURIeS

WOKeN FURIeS

...

RICHARD K. MORGAN

DEL
REY

BALLANTINE BOOKS

NEW YORK

Copyright © 2005 by Richard Morgan

Published in the United States by Del Rey Books, an imprint of The Random House Publishing Group, a division of Random House, Inc., New York.

DEL REY is a registered trademark and the Del Rey colophon is a trademark of Random House, Inc.

Originally published in Great Britain by Gollancz, an imprint of Orion Publishing Group, London.

ISBN 0-345-47971-8

Printed in the United States of America on acid-free paper

www.delreybooks.com

2 4 6 8 9 7 5 3 1

First Edition

Book design by Susan Turner

This book is for my wife,
Virginia Cottinelli,
who knows of impediment

Fury (n):

1a intense, disordered and often destructive rage . . .

2   wild, disordered force or activity

3a any of the three avenging deities who in
    Greek mythology punished crimes

3b an angry or vengeful woman

The New Penguin English Dictionary, 2001

ACKNOWLeDGMeNTS

Most of this book I just went ahead and made up. In the few places where that wasn't possible, I'm indebted to the following people for their help:

Dave Clare provided invaluable climbing advice and expertise, both on the page and on the rock. Kem Nunn's excellent novel *Tapping the Source* and Jay Caselberg's e-mails both offered valuable insight into the world of surfing. And Bernard at Diving Fornells taught me to exist safely underwater. Anything I got wrong was me, not them.

Special thanks also to Simon Spanton and Carolyn Whitaker, who waited with endless patience, and never even hinted at deadlines.

WOKeN
FURIeS

PROLOGUe

The place they woke me in would have been carefully prepared.

The same for the reception chamber where they laid out the deal. The Harlan family don't do anything by halves and, as anyone who's been Received can tell you, they like to make a good impression. Gold-flecked black décor to match the family crests on the walls, ambient subsonics to engender a tear-jerking sense that you're in the presence of nobility. Some Martian artifact in a corner, quietly implying the transition of global custody from our long-vanished un-human benefactors to the firmly modern hand of the First Families oligarchy. The inevitable holosculpture of old Konrad Harlan himself in triumphal "planetary discoverer" mode. One hand raised high, the other shading his face against the glare of an alien sun. Stuff like that.

*So here comes Takeshi Kovacs, surfacing from a sunken bath full of tank gel, sleeved into who knows what new flesh, spluttering into the soft pastel light, and helped upright by demure court attendants in cutaway swimming costumes. Towels of immense fluffiness to clean off the worst of the gel and a robe of similar material for the short walk to the next room. A shower, a mirror—*better get used to that face, soldier*—a new set of clothes to go with the new sleeve, and then on to the audience chamber for an interview with a member of the family. A woman, of course. There was no way they'd use a man, knowing what they did about my background. Abandoned by an alcoholic father at age ten, raised alongside two younger sisters, a lifetime of sporadically psychotic reaction when presented with patriarchal authority figures. No, it was a woman. Some urbane executive aunt, a secret-service caretaker for the Harlan family's less public affairs. An understated beauty in a custom-grown clone sleeve, probably in its early forties, Standard Reckoning.*

"Welcome back to Harlan's World, Kovacs-san. Are you comfortable?"

"Yeah. You?"

Smug insolence. Envoy training conditions you to absorb and process environmental detail at speeds normal humans can only dream about. Looking around, the Envoy Takeshi Kovacs knows in split seconds, has known since the sunken bath awakening, that he's in demand.

"*I? You may call me Aiura.*" The language is Amanglic, not Japanese, but the beautifully constructed misunderstanding of the question, the elegant evasion of offense without resorting to outrage, traces a clean line back to the First Families' cultural roots. The woman gestures, equally elegantly. "*Though who I am isn't very important in this matter. I think it's clear to you whom I represent.*"

"*Yes, it's clear.*" Perhaps it's subsonics, perhaps just the woman's sober response to my levity that dampens the arrogance in my tone. Envoys soak up what's around them, and to some extent that's a contaminative process. You often find yourself taking to observed behavior instinctively, especially if your Envoy intuition grasps that behavior as advantageous in the current surroundings. "*So I'm on secondment.*"

Aiura coughs, delicately.

"*In a manner of speaking, yes.*"

"*Solo deployment?*" Not unusual in itself, but not much fun, either. Being part of an Envoy team gives you a sense of confidence you can't get from working with ordinary human beings.

"*Yes. That is to say, you will be the only Envoy involved. More conventional resources are at your disposal in great number.*"

"*That sounds good.*"

"*Let us hope so.*"

"*So what do you want me to do?*"

Another delicate throat-clearing. "*In due course. May I ask, once again, if the sleeve is comfortable?*"

"*It seems very.*" Sudden realization. Very smooth, response at impressive levels even for someone used to Corps combat custom. A beautiful body, on the inside at least. "*Is this something new from Nakamura?*"

"*No.*" Does the woman's gaze slant upward and left? She's a security exec, she's probably wired with retinal datadisplay. "*Harkany Neurosystems, grown under offworld license for Khumalo-Cape.*"

Envoys aren't supposed to suffer from surprise. Any frowning I did would have to be on the inside. "*Khumalo? Never heard of them.*"

"*No, you wouldn't have.*"

"*Excuse me?*"

"*Suffice it to say we have equipped you with the very best biotech available. I doubt I need to enumerate the sleeve's capacities to someone of your background. Should you wish detail, there is a basic manual accessible through the datadisplay in your left field of vision.*" A faint smile, maybe the hint of weariness. "*Harkany were not culturing specifically for Envoy use, and there has not been time to arrange anything customized.*"

"*You've got a crisis on your hands?*"

"*Very astute, Kovacs-san. Yes, the situation might fairly be described as critical. We would like you to go to work immediately.*"

"Well, that's what they pay me for."

"Yes." Will she broach the matter of exactly who is paying at this point? Probably not. "As you've no doubt already guessed, this will be a covert deployment. Very different from Sharya. Though you did have some experience of dealing with terrorists toward the end of that campaign, I believe."

"Yeah." After we smashed their IP fleet, jammed their data transmission systems, blew apart their economy, and generally killed their capacity for global defiance, there were still a few diehards who didn't get the Protectorate message. So we hunted them down. Infiltrate, befriend, subvert, betray. Murder in back alleys. "I did that for a while."

"Good. This work is not dissimilar."

"You've got terrorist problems? Are the Quellists acting up again?"

She makes a dismissive gesture. No one takes Quellism seriously anymore. Not for a couple of centuries now. The few genuine Quellists still around on the World have traded in their revolutionary principles for high-yield crime. Same risks, better paid. They're no threat to this woman, or the oligarchy she represents. It's the first hint that things are not as they seem.

"This is more in the nature of a manhunt, Kovacs-san. An individual, not a political issue."

"And you're calling in Envoy support." Even through the mask of control, this has to rate a raised eyebrow. My voice has probably gone up a little as well. "Must be a remarkable individual."

"Yes. He is. An ex-Envoy, in fact. Kovacs-san, before we proceed any farther, I think something needs to be made clear to you, a matter that—"

"Something certainly needs to be made clear to my commanding officer. Because to me this sounds suspiciously like you're wasting Envoy Corps time. We don't do this kind of work."

"—may come as something of a shock to you. You, ah, no doubt believe that you have been resleeved shortly after the Sharya campaign. Perhaps even only a few days after your needlecast out."

A shrug. Envoy cool. "Days or months—it doesn't make much difference to m—"

"Two centuries."

"What?"

"As I said. You have been in storage for a little under two hundred years. In real terms—"

Envoy cool goes out the window, rapidly. "What the fuck happened to—"

"Please, Kovacs-san. Hear me out." A sharp note of command. And then, as the conditioning shuts me down again, pared back to listen and learn, more quietly: "Later I will give you as much detail as you like. For now, let it suffice that you are no longer part of the Envoy Corps as such. You can consider yourself privately retained by the Harlan family."

Marooned centuries from the last moments of living experience you recall.

Sleeved out of time. A lifetime away from everyone and everything you knew. Like some fucking criminal. *Well, Envoy assimilation technique will by now have some of this locked down, but still—*

"How did you—"

"Your digitized personality file was acquired for the family some time ago. As I said, I can give you more detail later. You need not concern yourself too much with this. The contract I am here to offer you is lucrative and, we feel, ultimately rewarding. What's important is for you to understand the extent to which your Envoy skills will be put to the test. This is not the Harlan's World you know."

"I can deal with that." Impatiently. "It's what I do."

"Good. Now, you will of course want to know—"

"Yeah." Shut down the shock, like a tourniquet on a bleeding limb. Drag up competence and a drawled lack of concern once more. Grab on to the obvious, the salient point in all of this. "Just who the fuck is this ex-Envoy you so badly want me to catch?"

Maybe it went something like that.

Then again, maybe not. I'm inferring from suspicion and fragmented knowledge after the event. Building it up from what I can guess, using Envoy intuition to fill in the gaps. But I could be completely wrong.

I wouldn't know.

I wasn't there.

And I never saw his face when they told him where I was. Told him that *I was, and what he'd have to do about it.*

PART ONE

THIS IS WHO YOU ARe

Make it personal . . .

QUELLCRIST FALCONER
*Things I Should Have
Learned by Now*
Volume II

CHAPTeR ONe

D*amage.*
    The wound stung like fuck, but it wasn't as bad as some I'd had. The blaster bolt came in blind across my ribs, already weakened by the door plating it had to chew through to get to me. Priests, up against the slammed door and looking for a quick gut shot. Fucking amateur night. They'd probably caught almost as much pain themselves from the point-blank blowback off the plating. Behind the door, I was already twisting aside. What was left of the charge plowed a long, shallow gash across my rib cage and went out, smoldering in the folds of my coat. Sudden ice down that side of my body and the abrupt stench of fried skin-sensor components. That curious bone-splinter fizzing that's almost a taste, where the bolt had ripped through the biolube casing on the floating ribs.

Eighteen minutes later, by the softly glowing display chipped into my upper left field of vision, the same fizzing was still with me as I hurried down the lamplit street, trying to ignore the wound. Stealthy seep of fluids beneath my coat. Not much blood. Sleeving synthetic has its advantages.

"Looking for a good time, sam?"

"Already had one," I told him, veering away from the doorway. He blinked wave-tattooed eyelids in a dismissive flutter that said *your loss* and leaned his tightly muscled frame languidly back into the gloom. I crossed the street and took the corner, tacking between a couple more whores, one a woman, the other of indeterminate gender. The woman was an augment, forked dragon tongue flickering out around her overly prehensile lips, maybe tasting my wound on the night air. Her eyes danced a similar passage over me, then slid away. On the other side, the cross-gender pro shifted its stance slightly and gave me a quizzical look but said nothing. Neither was interested. The streets were rain-slick and deserted, and they'd had longer to see me coming than the doorway operator. I'd cleaned up since leaving the citadel, but something about me must have telegraphed the lack of business opportunity.

At my back, I heard them talking about me in Stripjap. I heard the word for *broke.*

They could afford to be choosy. In the wake of the Mecsek Initiative, business was booming. Tekitomura was packed that winter, thronging with salvage brokers and the deCom crews that drew them the way a trawler wake draws ripwings. *Making New Hok Safe for a New Century,* the ads went. From the newly built hoverloader dock down at the Kompcho end of town it was less than a thousand kilometers, straight-line distance, to the shores of New Hokkaido, and the 'loaders were running day and night. Outside of an airdrop, there is no faster way to get across the Andrassy Sea. And on Harlan's World, you don't go up in the air if you can possibly avoid it. Any crew toting heavy equipment—and they all were—was going to New Hok on a hoverloader out of Tekitomura. Those that lived would be coming back the same way.

Boomtown. Bright new hope and brawling enthusiasm as the Mecsek money poured in. I limped down thoroughfares littered with the detritus of spent human merriment. In my pocket, the freshly excised cortical stacks clicked together like dice.

There was a fight going on at the intersection of Pencheva Street and Muko Prospect. The pipe houses on Muko had just turned out and their synapse-fried patrons had met late-shift dockworkers coming up through the decayed quiet of the warehouse quarter. More than enough reason for violence. Now a dozen badly coordinated figures stumbled back and forth in the street, flailing and clawing inexpertly at each other while a gathered crowd shouted encouragement. One body already lay inert on the fused-glass paving, and someone else was dragging their body, a limb's length at a time, out of the fray, bleeding. Blue sparks shorted off a set of overcharged power knuckles; elsewhere light glimmered on a blade. But everyone still standing seemed to be having a good time, and there were no police as yet.

Yeah, part of me jeered. *Probably all too busy up the hill right now.*

I skirted the action as best I could, shielding my injured side. Beneath the coat, my hands closed on the smooth curve of the last hallucinogen grenade and the slightly sticky hilt of the Tebbit knife.

Never get into a fight if you can kill quickly and be gone.

Virginia Vidaura—Envoy Corps trainer, later career criminal and sometime political activist. Something of a role model for me, though it was several decades since I'd last seen her. On a dozen different worlds, she crept into my mind unbidden, and I owed that ghost in my head my own life a dozen times over. This time I didn't need her or the knife. I got past the fight without eye contact, made the corner of Pencheva, and melted into the shadows that lay across the alley mouths on the seaward side of the street. The timechip in my eye said I was late.

Pick it up, Kovacs. According to my contact in Millsport, Plex wasn't all that reliable at the best of times, and I hadn't paid him enough to wait long.

Five hundred meters down and then left into the tight fractal whorls of Belacotton Kohei Section, named centuries ago for the habitual content and the original owner-operator family whose warehouse frontages walled the curving maze of alleys. With the Unsettlement and the subsequent loss of New Hokkaido as any kind of market, the local belaweed trade pretty much collapsed and families like Kohei went rapidly bankrupt. Now the grime-filmed upper-level windows of their façades peered sadly across at each other over gape-mouthed loading bay entrances whose shutters were all jammed somewhere uncommitted between open and closed.

There was talk of regeneration, of course, of reopening units like these and retooling them as deCom labs, training centers, and hardware storage facilities. Mostly, it was still just talk—the enthusiasm had kindled on the wharfline units facing the hoverloader ramps farther west, but so far it hadn't spread farther in any direction than you could trust a wirehead with your phone. This far off the wharf and this far east, the chitter of Mecsek finance was still pretty inaudible.

The joys of trickledown.

Belacotton Kohei Nine Point Twenty-six showed a faint glow in one upper window, and the long restless tongues of shadows in the light that seeped from under the half-cranked loading bay shutter gave the building the look of a one-eyed, drooling maniac. I slid to the wall and dialed up the synthetic sleeve's auditory circuits for what they were worth, which wasn't much. Voices leaked out into the street, fitful as the shadows at my feet.

"—telling you, I'm not going to hang around for *that.*"

It was a Millsport accent, the drawling metropolitan twang of Harlan's World Amanglic dragged up to an irritated jag. Plex's voice, muttering below sense-making range, made soft provincial counterpoint. He seemed to be asking a question.

"How the fuck would I know that? Believe what you want." Plex's companion was moving about, handling things. His voice faded back in the echoes of the loading bay. I caught the words *kaikyo, matter,* a chopped laugh. Then again, coming closer to the shutter, "—matters is what the family believes, and they'll believe what the technology tells them. Technology leaves a trail, my friend." A sharp coughing and indrawn breath that sounded like recreational chemicals going down. "This guy is fucking late."

I frowned. *Kaikyo* has a lot of meanings, but they all depend on how old you are. Geographically, it's a strait or a channel. That's early-Settlement-years use, or just hypereducated, kanji-scribbling, First Families pretension. This guy didn't sound First Family, but there was no reason he couldn't have been *around* back when Konrad Harlan and his well-connected pals were turning Glimmer VI into their own personal backyard. Plenty of DH personalities still on stack from that far back, just waiting to be downloaded into a working sleeve. Come to that, you wouldn't need to resleeve more than half a dozen times, end-to-end, to live through the whole of Harlan's World's human history anyway. It's still not much over four centuries, Earth-standard, since the colony barges made planetfall.

Envoy intuition twisted about in my head. It felt wrong. I'd met men and women with centuries of continuous life behind them, and they didn't talk like this guy. This wasn't the wisdom of ages, drawling out into the Tekito-mura night over pipe fumes.

On the street, scavenged into the argot of Stripjap a couple of hundred years later, *kaikyo* means a contact who can shift stolen goods. A covert flow manager. In some parts of the Millsport Archipelago, it's still common usage. Elsewhere, the meaning is shifting to describe aboveboard financial consultants.

Yeah, and farther south it means a holy man possessed by spirits, or a sewage outlet. Enough of this detective shit. You heard the man—you're late.

I got the heel of one hand under the edge of the shutter and hauled upward, locking up the tidal rip of pain from my wound as well as the synthetic sleeve's nervous system would let me. The shutter ratcheted noisily to the roof. Light fell out into the street and all over me.

"Evening."

"Jesus!" The Millsport accent jerked back a full step. He'd been only a couple of meters away from the shutter when it went up.

"Tak."

"Hello, Plex." My eyes stayed on the newcomer. "Who's the *tan*?"

By then I already knew. Pale, tailored good looks straight out of some low-end experia flick, somewhere between Micky Nozawa and Ryu Bartok. Well-proportioned fighter's sleeve, bulk in the shoulders and chest, length in the limbs. Stacked hair, the way they're doing it on the bioware catwalks these days, that upward static-twisted thing that's meant to look like they just pulled the sleeve out of a clone tank. A suit bagged and draped to suggest hidden weaponry, a stance that said he had none he wasn't ready to use. Combat arts crouch that was more bark than readiness to bite. He still had the discharged micropipe in one curled palm, and his pupils were spiked wide open. Concession to an ancient tradition put illuminum-tattooed curlicues across one corner of his forehead.

Millsport yakuza apprentice. Street thug.

"You don't call me *tani*," he hissed. "You are the outsider here, Kovacs. *You* are the intruder."

I left him at the periphery of my vision and looked toward Plex, who was over by the workbenches, fiddling with a knot of webbing straps and trying on a smile that didn't want to be on his dissipated aristo face.

"Look, Tak—"

"This was strictly a private party, Plex. I didn't ask you to subcontract the entertainment."

The yakuza twitched forward, barely restrained. He made a grating noise deep in his throat. Plex looked panicked.

"Wait, I . . ." He put down the webbing with an obvious effort. "Tak, he's here about something else."

"He's here on my time," I said mildly.

"*Listen,* Kovacs. You fucking—"

"*No.*" I looked back at him as I said it, hoping he could read the bright energy in my tone for what it was. "You know who I am, you'll stay out of my way. I'm here to see Plex, not you. Now get out."

I don't know what stopped him, Envoy rep, late-breaking news from the citadel—*because they'll be all over it by now, you made such a fucking mess up there*—or just a cooler head than the cheap-suited punk persona suggested. He stood braced in the door of his own rage for a moment, then stood down and displaced it, all poured into a glance at the nails of his right hand and a grin.

"Sure. You just go ahead and transact with Plex here. I'll wait outside. Shouldn't take long."

He even took the first step toward the street. I looked back at Plex.

"What the fuck's he talking about?"

Plex winced.

"We, uh, we need to reschedule, Tak. We can't—"

"Oh no." But looking around the room I could already see the swirled patterns in the dust where someone had been using a grav lifter. "No, no, you told me—"

"I-I know, Tak, but—"

"I *paid* you."

"I'll give you the money—"

"I don't *want* the fucking money, Plex." I stared at him, fighting down the urge to rip his throat out. Without Plex, there was no upload. Without the upload—"*I want my fucking body back.*"

"It's cool, it's cool. You'll get it back. It's just right now—"

"It's just right now, Kovacs, we're using the facilities." The yakuza drifted back into my line of sight, still grinning. "Because to tell the truth, they were pretty much ours in the first place. But then Plex here probably didn't tell you that, did he?"

I shuttled a glance between them. Plex looked embarrassed.

You gotta feel sorry for the guy. Isa, my Millsport contact broker, all of fifteen years old, razored violet hair and brutally obvious archaic datarat plugs, working on world-weary reflective while she laid out the deal and the cost. *Look at history, man. It fucked him over but good.*

History, it was true, didn't seem to have done Plex any favors. Born three centuries sooner with the name *Kohei,* he'd have been a spoiled stupid younger son with no particular need to do more than exercise his obvious intelligence in some gentleman's pursuit like astrophysics or archaeologue science. As it was, the Kohei family had left its post-Unsettlement generations nothing but the keys to ten streets of empty warehouses and a decayed aristo charm that, in Plex's own self-deprecating words, made it easier than you'd think to get laid when broke. Pipe-blasted, he told me the whole shabby story on less than three days' acquaintance. He seemed to need to tell someone, and Envoys are good listeners. You listen, you file under local color, you soak it up. Later, the recalled detail maybe saves your life.

Driven by the terror of a single life span and no resleeve, Plex's newly impoverished ancestors learned to work for a living, but most of them weren't very good at it. Debt piled up; the vultures moved in. By the time Plex came along, his family were in so deep with the yakuza that low-grade criminality was just a fact of life. He'd probably grown up around aggressively slouched suits like this one. Probably learned that embarrassed, give-up-the-ground smile at his father's knee.

The last thing he wanted to do was upset his patrons.

The last thing I wanted to do was ride a hoverloader back to Millsport in this sleeve.

"Plex, I'm booked out of here on the *Saffron Queen.* That's four hours away. Going to refund me my ticket?"

"We'll flicker it, Tak." His voice was pleading. "There's another 'loader out to EmPee tomorrow evening. I've got stuff, I mean Yukio's guys—"

"—use my fucking *name,* man," yelped the yakuza.

"They can flicker you to the evening ride, no one's ever going to know." The pleading gaze turned on Yukio. "Right? You'll do that, right?"

I added a stare of my own. "Right? Seeing as how you're fucking up my exit plans currently?"

"You already fucked up your exit, Kovacs." The yakuza was frowning, head-shaking. Playing at *sempai* with mannerisms and a clip-on solemnity he'd probably copied directly from his own *sempai* not too far back in his apprenticeship. "Do you know how much heat you've got out there looking for you right now? The cops have put in sniffer squads all over uptown, and my guess is they'll be all over the 'loader dock inside an hour. The whole TPD is out to play. Not to mention our bearded stormtrooper friends from the citadel. Fuck, man, you think you could have left a little *more* blood up there."

"I asked you a question. I didn't ask for a critique. You going to flicker me to the next departure or not?"

"Yeah, yeah." He waved it away. "Consider it fucking done. What you don't appreciate, Kovacs, is that some people have got serious business to transact. You come up here and stir up local law enforcement with your mindless violence, they're liable to get all enthusiastic and go busting people we *need.*"

"Need for what?"

"None of your fucking business." The *sempai* impression skidded off and he was pure Millsport street again. "You just keep your fucking head down for the next five or six hours and try not to kill anyone else."

"And then what?"

"And then we'll call you."

I shook my head. "You'll have to do better than that."

"Better than." His voice climbed. "Who the *fuck* do you think you're talking to, Kovacs?"

I measured the distance, the time it would take me to get to him. The pain it would cost. I ladled out the words that would push him. "Who am I talking to? I'm talking to a whiff-wired *chimpira,* a fucking street punk up here from Millsport and off the leash from his *sempai,* and it's getting old, Yukio. Give me your fucking phone—I want to talk to someone with authority."

The rage detonated. Eyes flaring wide, hand reaching for whatever he had inside the suit jacket. Way too late.

I hit him.

Across the space between us, unfolding attacks from my uninjured side. Sideways into throat and knee. He went down choking. I grabbed an arm, twisted it, and laid the Tebbit knife across his palm, held so he could see.

"That's a bioware blade," I told him tightly. "Adoracion Hemorrhagic Fever. I cut you with this and every blood vessel in your body ruptures inside three minutes. *Is that what you want?*"

He heaved against my grip, whooped after breath. I pressed down with the blade, and saw the panic in his eyes.

"It isn't a good way to die, Yukio. *Phone.*"

He pawed at his jacket and the phone tipped out, skittered on the evercrete. I leaned close enough to be sure it wasn't a weapon, then toed it back toward his free hand. He fumbled it up, breath still coming in hoarse jags through his rapidly bruising throat.

"Good. Now punch up someone who can help, then give it to me."

He thumbed the display a couple of times and offered the phone to me, face pleading the way Plex's had a couple of minutes earlier. I fixed him with my eyes for a long moment, trading on the notorious immobility of cheap synth features, then let go of his locked-out arm, took the phone, and stepped back out of reach. He rolled over away from me, still clutching his throat. I put the phone to my ear.

"Who is this?" asked an urbane male voice in Japanese.

"My name is Kovacs." I followed the language shift automatically. "Your *chimpira* Yukio and I are having a conflict of interest that I thought you might like to resolve."

A frigid silence.

"That's sometime tonight I'd like you to resolve it," I said gently.

There was a hiss of indrawn breath at the other end of the line. "Kovacs-san, you are making a mistake."

"Really?"

"It would be unwise to involve us in your affairs."

"I'm not the one doing the involving. Currently I'm standing in a warehouse looking at an empty space where some equipment of mine used to be. I have it on pretty good authority the reason it's gone is that you took it."

More silence. Conversations with the yakuza are invariably punctuated with long pauses, during which you're supposed to reflect and listen carefully to what's not being said.

I wasn't in the mood for it. My wound ached.

"I'm told you'll be finished in about six hours. I can live with that. But I want your word that at the end of that time the equipment will be back here and in working order, ready for me to use. I want your word."

"Hirayasu Yukio is the person to—"

"Yukio is a *chimp*. Let us deal honestly with each other in this. Yukio's only job here is to make sure I don't slaughter our mutual service provider. Which, incidentally, is something he's not doing well. I was already short on patience when I arrived, and I don't expect to replenish my stock anytime soon. I'm not interested in Yukio. I want *your* word."

"And if I do not give it?"

"Then a couple of your front offices are going to end up looking like the inside of the citadel tonight. You can have *my* word on that."

Quiet. Then: "We do not negotiate with terrorists."

"Oh *please*. What are you, making speeches? I thought I was dealing at executive level. Am I going to have to do some damage here?"

Another kind of silence. The voice on the other end of the line seemed to have thought of something else.

"Is Hirayasu Yukio harmed?"

"Not so's you'd notice." I looked down coldly at the yakuza. He'd mastered breathing again and was beginning to sit up. Beads of sweat gleamed at the borders of his tattoo. "But all that can change. It's in your hands."

"Very well." Barely a handful of seconds before the response. By yakuza standards, it was unseemly haste. "My name is Tanaseda. You have my word, Kovacs-san, that the equipment you require will be in place and available to you at the time you specify. In addition, you will be paid for your trouble."

"Thank you. That—"

"I have not finished. You further have my word that if you commit any acts of violence against my personnel, I shall issue a global writ for your capture and subsequent execution. I am talking about a very unpleasant Real Death. Is that understood?"

"It seems fair. But I think you'd better tell the *chimp* to behave himself. He seems to have delusions of competence."

"Let me speak to him."

Yukio Hirayasu was sitting by now, hunched over on the evercrete, wheezing breathily. I hissed at him and tossed him the phone. He caught it awkwardly, one-handed, still massaging his throat with the other.

"Your *sempai* wants a word."

He glared up at me out of tear-smeared, hating eyes, but he put the phone to his ear. Compressed Japanese syllables trickled out of it, like someone riffing on a ruptured gas cylinder. He stiffened, and his head lowered. His answers ran bitten off and monosyllabic. The word *yes* featured a lot. One thing you've got to hand to the yakuza—they do discipline in the ranks like no one else.

The one-sided conversation ended and Yukio held the phone out to me, not meeting my eye. I took it.

"This matter is resolved," said Tanaseda in my ear. "Please arrange to be elsewhere for the remainder of the night. You may return six hours from now when the equipment and your compensation will both be waiting for you. We will not speak again. This. Confusion. Has been most regrettable."

He didn't sound that upset.

"You recommend a good place for breakfast?" I asked.

Silence. A polite static backdrop. I weighed the phone in my palm for a moment, then tossed it back to Yukio.

"So." I looked from the yakuza to Plex and back. "Either of *you* recommend a good place for breakfast?"

CHAPTeR TWO

Before Leonid Mecsek unleashed his beneficence on the struggling econo-
mies of the Saffron Archipelago, Tekitomura scraped a seasonal living out
of big-game bottleback charters for rich sportsmen across from Millsport or
the Ohrid Isles, and the harvest of webjellies for their internal oils. Biolumi-
nescence made these latter easiest to catch at night, but the sweeper crews
that did it tended not to stay out for more than a couple of hours at a time.
Longer and the webjellies' gossamer-fine stinging aerials got plastered so
thick over clothing and onboard surfaces that you could lose serious produc-
tivity to toxin inhalation and skin burns. All night long, the sweepers came in
so that crew and decks could be hosed clean with cheap biosolvent. Behind
the Angier lamp glare of the hosing station, a short parade of bars and eating
houses stayed open until dawn.

Plex, spilling apologies like a leaky bucket, walked me down through the
warehouse district to the wharf and into an unwindowed place called Tokyo
Crow. It wasn't very different from a low-end Millsport skipper's bar—mural
sketches of Ebisu and Elmo on the stained walls, interspersed with the standard votive plaques inscribed in kanji or Amanglic Roman: CALM SEAS,
PLEASE, AND FULL NETS. Monitors up behind the mirrorwood bar, giving out
local weather coverage, orbital behavior patterns, and global breaking news.
The inevitable holoporn on a broad projection base at the end of the room.
Sweeper crew members lined the bar and knotted around the tables, faces
blurred weary. It was a thin crowd, mostly male, mostly unhappy.

"I'll get these," said Plex hurriedly, as we entered.

"Too fucking right, you will."

He gave me a sheepish look. "Um. Yeah. What do you want, then?"

"Whatever passes for whiskey around here. Cask strength. Something
I'll be able to taste through the flavor circuits in this fucking sleeve."

He sloped off to the bar, and I found a corner table out of habit. Views to
the door and across the clientele. I lowered myself into a seat, wincing at the
movement in my blaster-raked ribs.

What a fucking mess.

Not really. I touched the stacks through the fabric of my coat pocket. *I got what I came for.*

Any special reason you couldn't just cut their throats while they slept?

They needed to know. They needed to see it coming.

Plex came back from the bar, bearing glasses and a tray of tired-looking sushi. He seemed unaccountably pleased with himself.

"Look, Tak. You don't need to worry about those sniffer squads. In a synth sleeve—"

I looked at him. "Yes. I know."

"And, well, you know. It's only six hours."

"And all of tomorrow until the 'loader ships out." I hooked my glass. "I really think you'd better just shut up, Plex."

He did. After a couple of brooding minutes, I discovered I didn't want that, either. I was jumpy in my synthetic skin, twitching like a meth come-down, uncomfortable with who I physically was. I needed distraction.

"You know Yukio long?"

He looked up, sulkily. "I thought you wanted—"

"Yeah. Sorry. I got shot tonight, and it hasn't put me in a great mood. I was just—"

"You were *shot*?"

"Plex." I leaned intently across the table. "Do you want to keep your *fucking* voice down."

"Oh. Sorry."

"I mean." I gestured helplessly. "How the fuck do you stay in business, man? You're supposed to be a criminal, for Christ's sake."

"It wasn't my choice," he said stiffly.

"No? How's that work, then? They got some kind of conscription for it up here?"

"Very funny. I suppose you *chose* the military, did you? At seventeen fucking standard years old?"

I shrugged. "I made a choice, yeah. Military or the gangs. I put on a uniform. It paid better than the criminal stuff I was already doing."

"Well, I was never *in* a gang." He knocked back a chunk of his drink. "The yakuza made sure of that. Too much danger of corrupting their investment. I went to the right tutors, spent time in the right social circles, learned to walk the walk, talk the talk, and then they plucked me like a fucking cherry."

His gaze beached on the scarred wood of the tabletop.

"I remember my father," he said bitterly. "The day I got access to the family datastacks. Right after my coming-of-age party, the next morning. I was still hung over, still fried, and Tanaseda and Kadar and Hirayasu in his office like fucking vampires. He cried that day."

"*That* Hirayasu?"

He shook his head. "That's the son. Yukio. You want to know how long I've known Yukio? We grew up together. Fell asleep together in the same kanji classes, got wrecked on the same *take,* dated the same girls. He left for Millsport about the time I started my DH/biotech practicals, came back a year later wearing that fucking stupid suit." He looked up. "You think I like living out my father's debts?"

It didn't seem to need an answer. And I didn't want to listen to any more of this stuff. I sipped some more of the cask-strength whiskey, wondering what the bite would be like in a sleeve with real taste buds. I gestured with the glass. "So how come they needed your de- and regear tonight. Got to be more than one digital human shunting set in town, surely."

He shrugged. "Some kind of fuckup. They had their own gear, but it got contaminated. Seawater in the gel feeds."

"Organized crime, huh."

There was a resentful envy in the way he stared at me. "You don't have any family, do you?"

"Not so's you'd notice." That was a little harsh, but he didn't need to know the close truth. Feed him something else. "I've been away."

"In the store?"

I shook my head. "Offworld."

"Offworld? Where'd you go?" The excitement in his voice was unmistakable, barely held back by the ghost of breeding. The Glimmer system has no habitable planets apart from Harlan's World. Tentative terraforming down the plane of the ecliptic on Glimmer V won't yield useful results for another century. Offworld for a Harlanite means a stellar-range needlecast, shrugging off your physical self and resleeving somewhere light-years distant under an alien sun. It's all very romantic, and in the public consciousness known needlecast riders are accorded a celebrity status somewhat akin to pilots back on Earth during the days of intrasystem spaceflight.

The fact that, unlike pilots, these latter-day celebrities don't actually have to *do* anything to travel the hypercaster, the fact that in many cases they have no actual skills or stature other than their hypercast fame itself, doesn't seem to impede their triumphant conquest of the public imagination. Old Earth is the real jackpot destination, of course, but in the end it doesn't seem to make much difference where you go, so long as you come back. It's a favorite boost technique for fading experia stars and out-of-favor Millsport courtesans. If you can just somehow scrape up the cost of the 'cast, you're more or less guaranteed years of well-paid coverage in the skullwalk magazines.

That, of course, doesn't apply to Envoys. We just used to go silently, crush the odd planetary uprising, topple the odd regime, and then plug in something UN-compliant that worked. Slaughter and suppression across the stars, for the greater good—*naturally*—of a unified Protectorate.

I don't do that anymore.

"Did you go to Earth?"

"Among other places." I smiled at a memory that was getting on for a century out of date. "Earth's a shithole, Plex. Static fucking society, hyper-rich immortal overclass, cowed masses."

He shrugged and poked morosely at the sushi with his chopsticks. "Sounds just like this place."

"Yeah." I sipped some more whiskey. There were a lot of subtle differences between Harlan's World and what I'd seen on Earth, but I couldn't be bothered to lay them out right now. "Now you come to mention it."

"So what are you. Oh *fuck!*"

For a moment I thought he was just fumbling the bottleback sushi. Shaky feedback on the holed synth sleeve, or maybe just shaky close-to-dawn weariness on me. It took me whole seconds to look up, track his gaze to the bar and the door, make sense of what was there.

The woman seemed unremarkable at first glance—slim and competent looking, in gray coveralls and a nondescript padded jacket, unexpectedly long hair, face pale to washed out. A little too sharp-edged for sweeper crew, maybe. Then you noticed the way she stood, booted feet set slightly apart, hands pressed flat to the mirrorwood bar, face tipped forward, body preternaturally immobile. Then your eyes went back to that hair and—

Framed in the doorway not five meters off her flank, a group of senior-caste New Revelation priests stood frigidly surveying the clientele. They must have spotted the woman about the same time I spotted them.

"Oh, *shit* fuck!"

"Plex, shut up." I murmured it through closed teeth and stilled lips. "They don't know my face."

"But she's—"

"Just. Wait."

The spiritual well-being gang advanced into the room. Nine of them, all told. Cartoon patriarch beards and close-shaven skulls, grim-faced and intent. Three officiators, the colors of the evangelical elect draped blackly across their dull ocher robes and the bioware scopes worn like an ancient pirate patch across one eye. They were locked in on the woman at the bar, bending her way like gulls on a downdraft. Across the room, her uncovered hair must have been a beacon of provocation.

Whether they were out combing the streets for me was immaterial. I'd gone masked into the citadel, synth-sleeved. I had no signature.

But rampant across the Saffron Archipelago, dripping down onto the northern reaches of the next landmass like venom from a ruptured webjelly and now, they told me, taking root in odd little pockets as far south as Millsport itself, the Knights of the New Revelation brandished their freshly regenerated gynophobia with an enthusiasm of which their Earth-bound

Islamo-Christian ancestors would have been proud. A woman alone in a bar was bad enough, a woman uncovered far worse, but *this*—

"Plex," I said quietly. "On second thoughts, I think you'd maybe better get out of here."

"Tak, listen—"

I dialed the hallucinogen grenade up to maximum delay, fused it, and let it roll gently away under the table. Plex heard it go and made a tiny yelping noise.

"Go on," I said.

The lead officiator reached the bar. He stood half a meter away from the woman, maybe waiting for her to cringe.

She ignored him. Ignored, for that matter, everything farther off than the bar surface under her hands and, it dawned on me, the face she could see reflected there.

I eased unhurriedly to my feet.

"Tak, it isn't *worth* it, man. You don't know wha—"

"I said go, Plex." Drifting into it now, into the gathering fury like an abandoned skiff on the edge of the maelstrom. "You don't want to play this screen."

The officiator got tired of being ignored.

"Woman," he barked. "You will cover yourself."

"Why," she enunciated back with bitten clarity, "don't you go and fuck yourself with something sharp."

There was an almost comical pause. The nearest barflies jerked around on a collective look that gaped *did she really say*—

Somewhere, someone guffawed.

The blow was already swinging in. A gnarled, loose-fingered backhander that by rights should have catapulted the woman off the bar and onto the floor in a little heap. Instead—

The locked-up immobility dissolved. Faster than anything I'd seen since combat on Sanction IV. Something in me was expecting it, and I still missed the exact moves. She seemed to flicker like something from a badly edited virtuality, sideways and gone. I closed on the little group, combat rage funneling my synthetic vision down to targets. Peripherally, I saw her reach back and fasten on the officiator's wrist. I heard the crack as the elbow went. He shrilled and flapped. She levered hard and he went down.

A weapon flashed out. Thunder and greasy lightning in the gloom at the bar rail. Blood and brains exploded across the room. Superheated globs of the stuff splattered my face and burned.

Mistake.

She'd killed the one on the floor, let the others alone for time you could measure. The nearest priest got in close, lashed out with power knuckles, and down she went, twisting, onto the ruined corpse of the officiator. The others closed in, steel-capped boots stomping down out of robes the color of dried blood. Someone back at the tables started cheering.

I reached in, yanked back a beard, and sliced the throat beneath it, back to the spine. Shoved the body aside. Slashed low through a robe and felt the blade bury itself in flesh. Twist and withdraw. Blood sluiced warm over my hand. The Tebbit knife sprayed droplets as it came clear. I reached again, dream-like. Root and grab, brace and stab, kick aside. The others were turning, but they weren't fighters. I laid open a cheek down to the bone, parted an outflung palm from middle finger to wrist, drove them back off the woman on the floor, grinning, all the time grinning like a reef demon.

Sarah.

A robe-straining belly offered itself. I stepped in and the Tebbit knife leapt upward, unzipping. I went eye-to-eye with the man I was gutting. A lined, bearded visage glared back. I could smell his breath. Our faces were centimeters apart for what seemed like minutes before the realization of what I had done detonated behind his eyes. I jerked a nod, felt the twitch of a smile in one clamped corner of my mouth. He staggered away from me, screaming, insides tumbling out.

Sarah—

"It's *him!*"

Another voice. Vision cleared, and I saw the one with the wounded hand holding his injury out like some obscure proof of faith. The palm was gouting crimson, blood vessels closest to the cut already rupturing.

"It's him! The Envoy! The transgressor!"

With a soft thud behind me, the hallucinogen grenade blew.

● ● ●

Most cultures don't take kindly to you slaughtering their holy men. I couldn't tell which way the roomful of hard-bitten sweeper crew might lean—Harlan's World never used to have much of a reputation for religious fanaticism, but a lot had changed while I was away, most of it for the worse. The citadel looming above the streets of Tekitomura was one of several I'd run up against in the last two years, and wherever I went north of Millsport, it was the poor and work-crushed who swelled the ranks of the faithful.

Best to play it safe.

The grenade blast shunted aside a table like a bad-tempered poltergeist, but alongside the scene of blood and fury at the bar it went pretty much unnoticed. It was half a dozen seconds before the vented molecular shrapnel got into lungs, decayed, and started to take effect.

Screams to drown the agony of the priests dying around me. Confused yelling, threaded with iridescent laughter. It's an intensely individual experience, being on the receiving end of an H-grenade. I saw men jerk and swat at invisible things apparently circling them at head height. Others stared bemused at their own hands or into corners, shuddering. Somewhere I heard hoarse weeping. My own breathing had locked up automatically on the blast, relic of decades in one military context or another. I turned to the woman and found her propping herself up against the bar. Her face looked bruised.

I risked breath to shout across the general uproar.

"Can you stand?"

A clenched nod. I gestured at the door.

"Out. Try not to breathe."

Lurching, we made it past the remains of the New Revelation commandos. Those who had not already started to hemorrhage from mouth and eyes were too busy hallucinating to present any further threat. They stumbled and slipped in their own blood, bleating and flapping at the air in front of their faces. I was pretty sure I'd gotten them all one way or another, but on the off chance I was losing count I stopped by one who showed no apparent wounds. An officiator. I bent over him.

"A light," he driveled, voice high-pitched and wondering. His hand lifted toward me. "A light in the heavens, the angel is upon us. Who shall claim *rebirth* when they would not, when they await."

He wouldn't know her name. What was the fucking point.

"The angel."

I hefted the Tebbit knife. Voice tight with lack of breath. "Take another look, officiator."

"The an—" And then something must have gotten through the hallucinogens. His voice turned suddenly shrill, and he scrabbled backward away from me, eyes wide on the blade. "No! I *see* the old one, the reborn. *I see the destroyer.*"

"Now you've got it."

The Tebbit knife bioware is encoded in the runnel, half a centimeter off the edge of the blade. Cut yourself accidentally, you probably don't go deep enough to touch it.

I slashed his face open and left.

Deep enough.

● ● ●

Outside, a stream of tiny iridescent skull-headed moths floated down out of the night and circled my head, leering. I blinked them away and drew a couple of hard, deep breaths. Pump that shit through. Bearings.

The wharfway that ran behind the hosing station was deserted in both directions. No sign of Plex. No sign of anyone. The emptiness seemed pregnant, trembling with nightmarish potential. I fully expected to see a huge pair of reptilian claws slit through the seams at the bottom of the building and lever it bodily out of the way.

Well, don't, Tak. You expect it in this state, it's going to fucking happen.
The paving . . .
Move. Breathe. Get out of here.

A fine rain had started to sift down from the overcast sky, filling up the glow of the Angier lamps like soft interference. Over the flat roof of the hosing station, the upper decks of a sweeper's superstructure slid toward me, jeweled with navigation lights. Faint yells across the gap between ship and wharf and the hiss-clank of autograpples firing home into their shoreside sockets. There was a sudden tilting calm to the whole scene, some unusually peaceful moment drifting up from memories of my Newpest childhood. My earlier dread evaporated, and I felt a bemused smile creep out across my face.

Get a grip, Tak. It's just the chemicals.

Across the wharf, under a stilled robot crane, stray light glinted off her hair as she turned. I checked once more over my shoulder for signs of pursuit, but the entrance to the bar was firmly closed. Faint noises leaked through at the lower limits of my cheap synth hearing. Could have been laughter, weeping, pretty much anything. H-grenades are harmless enough long-term, but while they last you do tend to lose interest in rational thought or action. I doubted anyone'd work out where the door was for the next half hour, let alone how to get through it.

The sweeper bumped up to the wharf, cranked tight by the autograpple cables. Figures leapt ashore, trading banter. I crossed unnoticed to the shadow of the crane. Her face floated ghost-like in the gloom. Pale, wolfish beauty. The hair that framed it seemed to crackle with half-seen energies.

"Pretty handy with that knife."

I shrugged. "Practice."

She looked me over. "Synth sleeve, biocode steel. You deCom?"

"No. Nothing like that."

"Well, you sure—" Her speculative gaze stopped, riveted on the portion of my coat that covered the wound. "Shit, they got you."

I shook my head. "Different party. Happened a while back."

"Yeah? Looks to me like you could use a medic. I've got some friends could—"

"It isn't worth it. I'm getting out of this in a couple of hours."

Brows cranked. "Resleeve? Well, okay, you got better friends than mine. Making it pretty hard for me to pay off my *giri* here."

"Skip it. On the house."

"On the *house*?" She did something with her eyes that I liked. "What are you, living some kind of experia thing? Micky Nozawa stars in? Robot samurai with the human heart?"

"I don't think I've seen that one."

"No? Comeback flick, 'bout ten years back."

"Missed it. I've been away."

Commotion back across the wharf. I jerked around and saw the bar door propped open, heavily clothed figures silhouetted against the interior lighting. New clientele from the sweeper, crashing the grenade party. Shouts, and high-pitched wailing boiled out past them. Beside me, the woman went quietly tense, head tilted at an angle that mingled sensual and lupine in some indefinable, pulse-kicking fashion.

"They're putting out a call," she said and her posture unlocked again, as rapidly and with as little fuss as it had tautened. She seemed to flow backward into the shadows. "I'm out of here. Look, uh, thanks. Thank you. Sorry if I spoiled your evening."

"It wasn't shaping up for much anyway."

She took a couple more steps away, then stopped. Under the vague caterwauling from the bar and the noise of the hosing station, I thought I could hear something massive powering up, tiny insistent whine behind the fabric of the night, sense of shifting potential, like carnival monsters getting into place behind a stage curtain. Light and shadow through the stanchions overhead made a splintered white mask of her face. One eye gleamed silver.

"You got a place to crash, Micky-san? You said a couple of hours. What do you plan to do until then?"

I spread my hands. Became aware of the knife, and stowed it.

"No plans."

"No plans, huh?" There was no breeze coming in off the sea, but I thought her hair stirred a little. She nodded. "No place, either, right?"

I shrugged again, fighting the rolling unreality of the H-grenade comedown, maybe something else besides. "That's about the size of it."

"So. Your plans are play tag with the TPD and the Beards for the rest of the night, try to see the sun come out in one piece. That it?"

"Hey, you should be writing experia. You put it like that, it sounds almost attractive."

"Yeah. Fucking romantics. Listen, you want a place to crash until your high-grade friends are ready for you, that I can do. You want to play Micky Nozawa in the streets of Tekitomura, well." She tilted her head again. "I'll 'trode the flick when they make it."

I grinned.

"Is it far?"

Her eyes shuttled left. "This way."

From the bar, the cries of the deranged, a single voice shouting murder and holy retribution.

We slipped away among the cranes and shadows.

CHAPTeR THRee

Kompcho was all light, ramp after sloping evercrete ramp aswarm with Angier lamp activity around the slumped and tethered forms of the hover-loaders. The vessels sprawled in their collapsed skirts at the end of the auto-grapples, like hooked elephant rays dragged ashore. Loading hatches gleamed open on their flaring flanks and illuminum-painted vehicles maneuvered back and forth on the ramps, offering up forklift arms laden with hardware. There was a constant backdrop of machine noise and shouting that drowned out individual voices. It was as if someone had taken the tiny glowing cluster of the hosing station four kilometers east and cultured it for massive, viral growth. Kompcho ate up the night in all directions with glare and sound.

We threaded our way through the tangle of machines and people, across the quay space behind the loader ramps. Discount hardware retailers piled high with aisles of merchandise shone neon pale at the base of the reclaimed wharf frontages, interspersed with the more visceral gleaming of bars, whore-houses, and implant clinics. Every door was open, providing step-up access in most cases as wide as the frontage itself. Knots of customers spilled in and out. A machine ahead of me cut a tight circle, backing up with a load of Pil-sudski ground profile smart bombs, alert blaring *watch* it, *watch* it, *watch* it. Someone stepped sideways past me, grinning out of a face half metal.

She took me in through one of the implant parlors, past eight work-chairs where lean-muscled men and women sat with gritted teeth, seeing themselves get augmented in the long mirror opposite and the banks of close-up monitors above. Probably not pain as such, but it can't be much fun watching the flesh you wear sliced and peeled and shoved aside to make room for whatever new internal toy your sponsors have told you *all* the deCom crews are wearing this season.

She stopped by one chair and looked in the mirror at the shaven-headed giant it barely held. They were doing something to the bones in the right shoulder—a peeled-back flap of neck and collar hung down on a blood-soaked towel in front. Carbon-black neck tendons flexed restlessly in the gore within.

"Hey, Orr."

"Hey! Sylvie!" The giant's teeth appeared to be ungritted, eyes a little vacant with endorphins. He raised a languid hand on the side that was still intact and knocked fists with the woman. "You doing?"

"Out for a prowl. You sure this is going to heal by the morning?"

Orr jerked a thumb. "Or I do the same to this scalpelhead before we leave. Without chemicals."

The implant operative smiled a tight little smile and went on with what he was doing. He'd heard it all before. The giant's eyes switched to me in the mirror. If he noticed the blood on me, it didn't seem to bother him. Then again, he was hardly spotless himself.

"Who's the synth?"

"Friend," said Sylvie. "Talk to you upstairs."

"Be up in ten." He glanced at the operative. "Right?"

"Half an hour," said the operative, still working. "The tissue bond needs setting time."

"Shit." The giant fired a glance at the ceiling. "Whatever happened to Urushiflash. That stuff bonds in seconds."

Still working. A tubular needle made tiny sucking sounds. "You asked for the standard tariff, sam. Military-issue biochem isn't available at that rate."

"Well, for fuck's sake what's it going to cost me to upgrade to deluxe then?"

"About fifty percent more."

Sylvie laughed. "Forget it, Orr. You're almost done. You won't even get to enjoy the 'dorphs."

"Fuck that, Sylvie. I'm bored rigid here." The giant spittled his thumb and held it out. "Swipe me up, you."

The implant operative looked up, shrugged minutely, and set down his tools on the operating palette.

"Ana," he called. "Get the Urushiflash."

While the attendant busied herself in a footlocker with the new biochemicals, the operative took a DNA reader from amid the clutter on the mirror shelf and rubbed the upsoak end across Orr's thumb. The machine's hooded display lit and shifted. The operative looked back at Orr.

"This transaction will put you in the red," he said quietly.

Orr glared. "Never fucking mind. I'm shipping out tomorrow, I'm good for it and you know it."

The operative hesitated. "It is *because* you are shipping out tomorrow," he began, "that—"

"Oh, for fuck's sake. Read the sponsor screen, will you. Fujiwara Havel. Making New Hok Safe for a New Century. We're not some goddamned bootstrap leverage outfit. I don't come back, the *enka* payment covers it. You know that."

"It isn't—"

The exposed tendons in Orr's neck tensed and lifted. "The *fuck* are you, my *accountant*?" He levered himself up in the chair and stared into the operative's face. "Just *put it through,* will you. And get me some of those mil-issue endorphins while you're about it. I'll take them later."

We stayed long enough to see the implant operative cave in, then Sylvie nudged me away toward the back.

"We'll be upstairs," she said.

"Yeah." The giant was grinning. "See you in ten."

Upstairs was a spartan set of rooms wrapped around a kitchen-lounge combination with windows out onto the wharf. The soundproofing was good. Sylvie shrugged off her jacket and slung it over the back of a lounger. She looked back at me as she moved to the kitchen space.

"Make yourself at home. Bathroom in the back over there if you need to clean up."

I took the hint, rinsed the worst of the gore off my hands and face in a tiny mirrored basin niche, and came back out to the main room. She was over at the kitchen counter, searching cabinets.

"Are you really with Fujiwara Havel?"

"No." She found a bottle and cracked it open, pinched up two glasses in her other hand. "We're a goddamned bootstrap leverage outfit. And then some. Orr just has a datarat tunnel into FH's clearance codes. Drink?"

"What is it?"

She looked at the bottle. "Don't know. Whiskey."

I held out my hand for one of the glasses. "Tunnel like that's got to cost in the first place."

She shook her head. "Fringe benefits of deCom. We're all wired better for crime than a fucking Envoy. Got electronic intrusion gear up the ass." She handed me the glass and poured for both of us. The neck of the bottle made a single tiny clink in the quiet of the room each time it touched down. "Orr's been out on the town for the last thirty-six hours, whoring and shooting chemicals on nothing but credit and *enka* payment promises. Same thing every time we ship out. Views it as an art form, I reckon. Cheers."

"Cheers." It was a very rough whiskey. "Uhh. You been crewing with him long?"

She gave me an odd look. "Long enough. Why?"

"Sorry, force of habit. I used to get paid to soak up local information." I raised the glass again. "Here's to a safe return, then."

"That's considered bad luck." She didn't lift her own glass. "You really have been away, haven't you."

"For a while."

"Mind talking about it?"

"Not if we sit down."

The furniture was cheap, not even automold. I lowered myself carefully into a lounger. The wound in my side seemed to be healing, to the extent that synth flesh ever did.

"So." She seated herself opposite me and pushed her hair away from her face. A couple of the thicker strands flexed and crackled faintly at the intrusion. "How long you been gone?"

"About thirty years, give or take."

"Pre-Beard, huh?"

Sudden bitterness. "Before this heavy stuff, yeah. But I've seen the same thing in a lot of other places. Sharya. Latimer. Parts of Adoracion."

"Oh. *Catch* those names."

I shrugged. "It's where I've been."

Behind Sylvie, an interior door unfolded crankily and a slight, cocky-looking woman wandered yawning into the room, wrapped in a lightweight black polalloy skinsuit half unseamed. She put her head on one side as she spotted me and came to lean on the back of Sylvie's lounger, scrutinizing me with unapologetic curiosity. There were kanji characters shaved into her stubble-length hair.

"Got company?"

"Glad to see you got those viewfinder upgrades at last."

"*Shut* up." She flicked idly at the other woman's hair with hard-lacquered fingernails, grinning when the tresses crackled and shifted away from the touch.

"Who is this? Bit late for shore-leave romances, isn't it?"

"This is Micky. Micky, meet Jadwiga." The slight woman winced at the full name, mouthed the single syllable *Jad*. "And Jad. We are not fucking. He's just crashing here."

Jadwiga nodded and turned away, instantly disinterested. From the back, the kanji on her skull read JUST DON'T FUCKING MISS. "We got any shiver left?"

"Think you and Las dropped it all last night."

"*All* of it?"

"Jesus, Jad. It wasn't my party. Try the box on the window."

Jadwiga walked spring-heeled dancer's steps across to the window and upended the box in question. A tiny vial fell out into her hand. She held it up to the light and shook it so the pale red liquid at the bottom quivered back and forth.

"Well," she said meditatively. "Enough for a couple of blinks. Ordinarily I'd offer it around, but—"

"But instead you're going to hog the whole lot yourself," predicted Sylvie. "That old Newpest hospitality thing. Just gets me right there every time."

"Oh look who's talking, bitch," said Jadwiga without heat. "How often, outside of mission time, you ever agree to hook us up to that mane of yours?"

"It isn't the sa—"

"No, it's *better*. You know, for a Renouncer kid, you're pretty fucking stingy with your capacity. Kiyoka says—"

"Kiyoka doesn't—"

"Guys, *guys*." I gestured for attention, broke the tightening cable of confrontation that was cranking Jadwiga back across the room toward Sylvie a couple of flexed steps at a time. "It's okay. I'm not up for any recreational chemicals right now."

Jad brightened. "See," she told Sylvie.

"Although if I could beg some of Orr's endorphins when he gets up here, I'd be grateful."

Sylvie nodded, not looking away from her standing companion. She was clearly still miffed, either over the breach of host etiquette or the mention of her Renouncer background. I couldn't work out which.

"Orr's got *endorphins*?" Jadwiga wanted to know loudly.

"Yes," said Sylvie. "He's downstairs. Getting cut."

Jad sneered. "Fucking fashion victim. He's never going to learn." She slipped a hand inside her unseamed suit and produced an eye-hypo. Fingers programmed by obvious habit screwed the mechanism onto the end of the vial; then she tipped her head back and with the same automatic deftness spread the eyelids of one eye and fired the hypo into it. Her tight-cabled stance slackened, and the drug's signature shudder dropped through her from the shoulders.

Shiver is pretty innocuous stuff—it's about six-tenths betathanatine analog, cut with a couple of *take* extracts that make everyday household objects dreamily fascinating and perfectly innocent conversational gambits sniggeringly hilarious. Fun if everyone in the room is dropping it, irritating for anyone left out. Mostly, it just slows you down, which I imagine was what Jad, in common with most deComs, was after.

"You're from Newpest," I asked her.

"Mm-mm."

"What's it like these days?"

"Oh. Beautiful." A badly controlled smirk. "Best-looking swamp town in the southern hemisphere. Well worth a visit."

Sylvie sat forward. "You from there, Micky?"

"Yeah. Long time ago."

The apartment door chimed and then unfolded to reveal Orr, still stripped to the waist, right shoulder and neck liberally smeared with orange tissue weld. He grinned as he saw Jadwiga.

"So you're up, are you?" Advancing into the room, dumping a fistful of clothing into the lounger beside Sylvie, who wrinkled her nose.

Jad shook her head and waved the empty vial at the giant. "Down. Definitely down. Chilled to flatline."

"Anyone ever tell you you've got a drug problem, Jad?"

The slight woman dribbled sniggering, as poorly suppressed as the earlier smirk. Orr's grin broadened. He mimed junkie trembling, a twitching, idiot face. Jadwiga erupted into laughter. It was infectious. I saw the smile on Sylvie's face and caught myself chuckling.

"So where's Kiyoka?" asked Orr.

Jad nodded back at the room she'd come out of. "Sleep."

"And Lazlo's still chasing that weapons chick with the cleavage, right?"

Sylvie looked up. "What's that?"

Orr blinked. "You know. Tamsin, Tamita, whatever her name was. The one from that bar on Muko." He pouted and squeezed his pectorals hard toward each other with the palms of both hands, then winced and stopped as the pressure touched his recent surgery. "Just before you pissed off on your own. Christ, you were *there*, Sylvie. I wouldn't have thought anyone could forget that rack."

"She's not equipped to register that kind of armament," grinned Jadwiga. "No consumer interest. Now *I*—"

"Any of you guys hear about the citadel?" I asked casually.

Orr grunted. "Yeah, caught the newscast downstairs. Some psycho offed half the head Beards in Tekitomura by the sound of it. They say there are stacks missing. Guy just carved them out of the spines like he'd been doing it all his life, apparently."

I saw Sylvie's gaze track down and across to the pocket of my coat, then up to meet my eyes.

"Pretty savage stuff," said Jad.

"Yeah, but pretty pointless." Orr acquired the bottle from where it stood on the kitchen bar countertop. "Those guys can't resleeve anyway. It's an article of faith for them."

"Fucking freaks." Jadwiga shrugged and lost interest. "Sylvie says you scored some 'dorphs downstairs."

"Yes, I did." The giant poured himself a glass of whiskey with exaggerated care. "Thanks."

"Ahhh, *Orr.* Come *on.*"

Later, with the lights powered down and the atmosphere in the apartment mellowed almost to comatose proportions, Sylvie shoved Jadwiga's slumped form out of the way on the lounger and leaned across to where I sat enjoying the lack of pain in my side. Orr had long ago slipped away to another room.

"You did that?" she asked quietly. "That stuff up at the citadel?"

I nodded.

"Any particular reason?"

"Yeah."

A small silence.

"So," she said finally. "It wasn't quite the Micky Nozawa rescue it looked like, huh? You were already cranked up."

I smiled, slightly stoned on the endorphin. "Call it serendipity."

"All right. Micky Serendipity, that's got a ring to it." She frowned owlishly into the depths of her glass, which, like the bottle, had been empty for a while. "Got to say, Micky, I like you. Can't put my finger on it. But I do. I like you."

"I like you, too."

She wagged a finger, maybe the one she couldn't quite put on my likable qualities. "This is not. Sex. You know?"

"I know. Have you seen the size of the hole in my ribs?" I shook my head muzzily. "Of course you have. Spectrochem vision chip, right?"

She nodded complacently.

"You really from a Renouncer family?"

A sour grimace. "Yeah. *From* being the operative word."

"They're not proud of you?" I gestured at her hair. "I'd have thought that qualifies as a pretty solid step on the road to Upload. Logically—"

"Yeah, logically. This is a religion you're talking about. Renouncers make no more fucking sense than the Beards when it comes down to it."

"So they're not in favor?"

"Opinion," she said with mock delicacy, "is divided on the matter. The aspirant hard-liners don't like it; they don't like anything that roots construct systems firmly to physical being. The preparant wing of the faith just want to play nice with everyone. They say any virtuality interface is, as you say, a step on the road. They don't expect Upload to come in their lifetime, anyway; we're all just handmaidens to the process."

"So which are your folks?"

Sylvie shifted her body on the lounger again, frowned, and gave Jadwiga another shove to make space.

"Used to be moderate preps, that's the faith I grew up in. The last couple of decades though, with the Beards and the whole antistack thing, a lot of moderates are turning into hard-line asps. My mother probably went that way. She was always the seriously pious one." She shrugged. "No idea really. Haven't been home in years."

"Like that, huh?"

"Yeah, like that. There's no fucking point. All they'd do is try and marry me off to some eligible local." She snorted with laughter. "As if that's going to happen while I'm carrying this stuff."

I propped myself up a little, groggy with the drugs. "What stuff?"

"*This.*" She tugged at a handful of hair. "This fucking stuff."

It crackled quietly around her grasp, tried to writhe away like thousands of tiny snakes. Under the crinkled black-and-silver mass of it, the thicker cords moved stealthily, like muscles under skin.

DeCom command datatech.

I'd seen a few like her before—a prototype variant back on Latimer, where the core of the new Martian machine interface industry was boiling into R&D overdrive. A couple more used as minesweepers in the Hun Home system. It never takes long for the military to bastardize cutting-edge technology for their own use. Makes sense. As often as not, they're the ones paying for the R&D anyway.

"That's not unattractive," I said carefully.

"Oh *sure.*" She raked through the tresses and separated out the central cord until it hung clear of the rest, an ebony snake gripped in her fist. "That's attractive, right? Because, after all, *any* red-blooded male's just going to love a twice-prick-length member flopping around in bed at head height, right? Fucking competition anxiety and creeping homophobia, all in one."

I gestured. "Well, women—"

"Yeah. Unfortunately, I'm straight."

"Oh."

"Yeah." She let the cord fall and shook her head so the rest of the silvered mane rearranged itself as it had been. "Oh."

A century ago they were harder to spot. Military systems officers might have extensive virtual training in how to deploy the racks of interface hardware built into their heads, but the hardware was internal. Externally, machine interface pros never looked much different from the next human sleeve—a bit sick around the gills maybe when they'd been in the field for too long, but that's the same for any datarat with overexposure. You learn to ride it, they say.

The archaeologue finds just outside the Latimer system changed all that. For the first time in nearly six hundred years of scratching around across the Martians' interstellar backyard, the Guild finally hit the jackpot. They found ships. Hundreds, quite possibly thousands of ships, locked into the cobwebbed quiet of ancient parking orbits around a tiny attendant star called Sanction. Evidence suggested they were the remains of a massive naval engagement and that some of them at least had faster-than-light stardrive capacity. Other evidence, notably the vaporization of an entire Archaeologue Guild research habitat and its seven-hundred-odd crew, suggested the vessels' motive systems were autonomous and very much awake.

Up to that point, the only genuinely autonomous machines the Martians had left us were Harlan's World's very own orbital guardians, and no one was getting near them. Other stuff was automated but not what you'd call smart.

Now here the archaeologue systems specialists were suddenly being asked to take on interface with crafty naval command intelligences an estimated half a million years old.

Some form of upgrade was in order. Definitely.

Now that upgrade was sitting across from me, sharing a military-issue endorphin rush and staring into an empty whiskey glass.

"Why'd you sign up?" I asked her, to fill the quiet.

She shrugged. "Why does anyone sign up for this shit? The money. You figure you'll make back the sleeve mortgage in the first couple of runs, and then it's all pure credit stacking up."

"And it isn't?"

A wry grin. "No, it is. But you know, there's a whole lifestyle comes with it. And then, well, servicing costs, upgrades, repairs. Weird how fast the money spends itself. Stack it up, burn it down again. Kind of hard to save enough to ever get out."

"The Initiative can't last forever."

"No? Lot of continent still to clean up over there, you know. We've barely pushed a hundred klicks out of Drava in some places. And even then you've got to do constant housecleaning everywhere you've been, keep the mimints from creeping back in. They're talking about another decade minimum before they can start resettlement. And I'll tell you, Micky, personally I think even that's crabshit optimism, strictly for public consumption."

"Come on. New Hok isn't so big."

"Well, spot the fucking offworlder." She stuck out her tongue in a gesture that had more Maori challenge about it than childishness. "Might not be big by your standards—I'm sure they've got continents fifty thousand klicks across where you've been. Around here it's a little different."

I smiled. "I'm *from* here, Sylvie."

"Oh yeah. Newpest. You said. So don't tell me New Hok's a small continent. Outside of Kossuth, it's the biggest we've got."

In actual fact, there was more landmass contained in the Millsport Archipelago than either Kossuth or New Hokkaido, but as with most of the island groups that made up the bulk of Harlan's World's available real estate, a lot of it was hard-to-use, mountainous terrain.

You'd think, given a planet nine-tenths covered in water and a solar system with no other habitable biospheres, that people would be *careful* with that real estate. You'd think they'd develop an intelligent approach to land allocation and use. You'd think they wouldn't fight stupid little wars over large areas of useful terrain, wouldn't deploy weaponry that would render the theater of operations useless to human habitation for centuries to come.

Well, *wouldn't* you?

"I'm going to bed," slurred Sylvie. "Busy day tomorrow."

I glanced across at the windows. Outside, dawn was creeping up over the Angier lamp glow, soaking it out on a blotter of pale gray.

"Sylvie, it is tomorrow."

"Yeah." She got up and stretched until something cracked. On the lounger, Jadwiga mumbled something and unkinked her limbs into the space Sylvie had vacated. " 'Loader doesn't lift till lunchtime, and we're pretty much stowed with the heavy stuff. Look, you want to crash, use Las's room. Doesn't look like he's coming back. Left of the bathroom."

"Thanks."

She gave me a faded smile. "Hey, Micky. Least I can do. G'night."

" 'Night."

I watched her wander to her room, checked my timechip, and decided against sleep. Another hour, and I could go back to Plex's place without disturbing whatever Noh dance his yakuza pals were wound up in. I looked speculatively at the kitchen space and wondered about coffee.

That was the last conscious thought I had.

Fucking synth sleeves.

CHAPTeR FOUR

The sound of hammering woke me. Someone chemically too far gone to remember how to operate a flexdoor, reverting to Neanderthal tactics.
Bang, bang, bang. I blinked eyes gone gummy with sleep and struggled upright in the lounger. Jadwiga was still stretched out opposite, still comatose
by the look of it. A tiny thread of spit ran out of the corner of her mouth and
dampened a patch on the lounger's worn belacotton covering. Across at the
window, bright sunlight streamed into the room and turned the air in the
kitchen space hazy with luminescence. Late morning, at least.

Shit.

Bang, *bang.*

I stood, and pain flashed rustily up my side. Orr's endorphins seemed to
have leached out while I slept.

Bang, bang, bang.

"*Fuck* is that?" yelled someone from an inner room.

Jadwiga stirred on the lounger at the sound of the voice. She opened one
eye, saw me standing over her, and thrashed rapidly into some kind of combat guard, then relaxed a little as she remembered me.

"Door," I said, feeling foolish.

"Yeah, yeah," she grumbled. "I hear it. If that's fucking Lazlo forgotten
his code again, he's looking for a boot in the crotch."

The banging at the door had stopped, presumably at the sound of voices
from within. Now it started up again. I felt a jagged twinge in the side of my
head.

"Will *someone* fucking *answer that!*" It was a female voice, but not one
I'd heard before. Presumably Kiyoka, awake at long last.

"*Got it,*" Jadwiga yelled back, stumbling across the room. Her voice
dropped back to a mutter. "Did anyone go down and check in with embarkation yet? No, course not. Yeah, yeah. *Coming.*"

She hit the panel, and the door folded itself up and away.

"You got some kind of fucking motor dysfunction?" she inquired acidly
of whoever was outside. "We heard you the first ninety-seven ti— *Hey!*"

There was a brief scuffle, and then Jadwiga bounced back into the room, struggling not to fall. Following her in, the figure who'd dealt the blow scanned the room with a single trained sweep, acknowledged my presence with a barely perceptible nod, and wagged an admonishing finger at Jad. He wore an ugly grin full of fashionably jagged teeth, a pair of smoked-yellow enhanced-vision lenses barely a centimeter from top to bottom, and spreading wings of tattoo work across both cheekbones.

It didn't take much imagination to guess what was coming next.

Yukio Hirayasu stepped through the door. A second thug followed him in, clone-identical to the one who'd shoved Jad aside except he wasn't smiling.

"Kovacs." Yukio had just spotted me. His face was a tight mask of throttled-back anger. "What exactly the *fuck* do you think you're doing here?"

"I'd have thought that was my line."

Peripheral vision gave me a tiny flinch across Jadwiga's face that looked like internal transmission.

"You were *told,*" snapped Yukio, "to stay out of the way until we were ready for you. To stay out of trouble. Is that so fucking difficult to do?"

"These your high-powered friends, Micky?" It was Sylvie's voice, drawling from the door to my left. She stood wrapped in a bathrobe and gazed curiously at the new arrivals. Proximity sense told me that Orr and someone else had made appearances elsewhere, behind me. I saw the movement reflected in the EV lenses of Yukio's muscle clones, saw it registered with minute tautening of their faces beneath the smoked glass.

I nodded. "You might say that."

Yukio's eyes flickered to the woman's voice and he frowned. Maybe the reference to Micky had thrown him; maybe it was just the five-to-three disadvantage he'd walked into.

"You know who I am," he began. "So let's not complicate matters any—"

"I don't know who the fuck you are," said Sylvie evenly. "But I know you're in our place without an invitation. So I think you'd better just leave."

The yakuza's face flared disbelief.

"Yeah, get the *fuck* out of here." Jadwiga threw up both hands in something midway between a combat guard and a gesture of obscene dismissal.

"Jad—" I started, but by then it had all already tipped too far.

Jad was already swinging forward, chin jutting, clearly bent on shoving the yak muscleman tit-for-tat back to the door. The muscle reached, still grinning. Jad dummied him, *very* fast, left him reaching, and took him down with a judo trick. Someone yelled, behind me. Then, without fuss, Yukio produced a tiny black particle blaster and shot Jad with it.

She dropped, freeze-lit by the pale flash of the blast. The odor of roasted meat rolled out across the room. Everything stopped.

I must have been moving forward, because the second yak enforcer blocked me, face gone shocked, hands filled with a pair of Szeged slug guns.

I froze, lifted empty warding hands in front of me. On the floor, the other thug tried to get up and stumbled over the remains of Jad.

"Right." Yukio looked around the rest of the room, wagging the blaster mainly in Sylvie's direction. "That's enough. I don't know what the fuck's going on here, but you—"

Sylvie spat out a single word.

"Orr."

Thunder detonated in the confined space again. This time, it was blinding. I had a brief impression of looping gouts of white fire, past me and branching, buried in Yukio, the enforcer in front of me, the man still halfway up from the floor. The enforcer flung out his arms, as if embracing the blast that drenched him from the chest down. His mouth gaped wide. His sun-lenses flashed incandescent with reflected glare.

The fire inked out, collapsing afterimages soaking across my vision in tones of violet. I blinked through it, groping at detail.

The enforcer was two severed halves steaming up at me from the floor, Szeged still gripped in each fist. Excess discharge had welded his hands to the weapons.

The one getting up had never made it. He was down next to Jad again, gone from the chest up.

Yukio had a hole through him that had removed pretty much every internal organ he owned. Charred rib ends protruded from the upper half of a perfectly oval wound in which you could see the tiled floor he lay on like a cheap experia special effect.

The room filled with the abrupt reek of voided bowels.

"Well. That seemed to work."

Orr stepped past me, peering down at what was apparently his handiwork. He was still stripped to the waist, and I saw where the discharge vents had blown open in a vertical line up one side of his back. They looked like massive fish gills, still rippling at the edges with dissipating heat. He went straight to Jadwiga and crouched over her.

"Narrow beam," he diagnosed. "Took out the heart and most of the right lung. Not much we can do for her here."

"Someone close the door," suggested Sylvie.

● ● ●

As a council of war, it was pretty headlong. The deCom team had a couple of years of close-wired operational time behind them, and they communicated in a flickering shorthand that owed as much to internal tannoy and compressed symbol gesture as it did to actual speech. Envoy-conditioned intuition at full stretch gave me just enough of an edge to keep up.

"Report this?" Kiyoka, a slight woman in what had to be a custom-grown

Maori sleeve, wanted to know. She kept looking at Jadwiga on the floor and biting her lip.

"To?" Orr flipped her a rapid thumb-and-little-finger gesture. His other hand traced tattooing across his face.

"Oh. And him?"

Sylvie did something with her face, gestured low. I missed it, guessed and grabbed.

"They were here for me."

"Yeah, no shit." Orr was looking at me with something that grazed open hostility. The vents in his back and chest had closed up, but looking at the massive muscled frame it wasn't hard to imagine them ripping open for another blast. "Some nice friends you've got."

"I don't think they would have gotten violent if Jad hadn't jumped the goon. It was a misunderstanding."

"Misunder— *fuck.*" Orr's eyes widened. "Jad is *dead,* you asshole."

"She's not Really Dead," I said doggedly. "You can excise the stack and—"

"Excise?" The word came out lethally soft. He trod closer, looming. "You want me to *cut up* my friend?"

Playing back the position of the gunmetal discharge tubes from memory, I guessed most of his right side was prosthetic, charging the five vents from a power pack buried somewhere in the lower half of his rib cage. Given recent advances in nanotech, you could get large blotches of energy to go pretty much anywhere you wanted over a limited distance. The nanocon shepherd fragments just rode the blast like surfers, sucking power and tugging the containment field wherever the launch data had them headed.

I made a mental note, if I had to hit him, to go left.

"I'm sorry. I don't see another solution right now."

"You—"

"Orr." Sylvie made a sideways chopping gesture. "Tats, this place, *time.*" She shook her head. Another sign, thumb and forefinger forced apart by the fingers of the other hand. From the look on her face, I got the sense she was emitting data through the team net as well. "Cache, the same. Three days. Puppetry. Torch and wipe, *now.*"

Kiyoka nodded. "Sense, Orr. Las? Oh."

"Yeah, we can do that." Orr wasn't plugged all the way into this. He was still angry, speaking slowly. "Yeah, I mean. Okay."

" 'Ware?" Kiyoka again, some complex counting off from one hand, an inclination of her head. "Jet?"

"No, there's time." Sylvie made a flat-palmed motion. "Orr and Micky. Easy. You run blank. This, this, maybe this. Down."

"Got it." Kiyoka was checking out a retinal screen as she spoke, eyes up and left to skim the data Sylvie had shot her. "Las?"

"Not yet. I'll flag you. *Go.*"

The Maori-sleeved woman disappeared back into her room, emerged a second later pulling on a bulky gray jacket, and let herself out the main door. She allowed herself a single backward look at Jadwiga's corpse, then she was gone.

"Orr. Cutter." A thumb at me. *"Guevara."*

The giant gave me a final smoldering look and went to a case in the corner of the room, from which he took a heavy-bladed vibroknife. He came back and stood in front of me with the weapon, deliberately enough for me to tauten up. Only the obvious—that Orr didn't need a knife to grease me—kept me from jumping him. My physical reaction must have been pretty obvious, because it got a derisive grunt out of the giant. Then he spun the knife in his hand and presented it to me grip-first.

I took it. "You want me to do it?"

Sylvie moved across to Jadwiga's corpse and stood looking down at the damage.

"I want you to dig out the stacks on your two friends there, yes. I think you've had the practice for it. Jad you can leave."

I blinked.

"You're leaving her?"

Orr snorted again. The woman looked at him and made a spiraling gesture. He compressed a sigh and went to his room.

"Let me worry about Jad." Her face was clouded with distance, engaged at levels I couldn't sense. "Just get cutting. And while you're at it, you want to tell me who exactly we've killed here?"

"Sure." I went to Yukio's corpse and manhandled it onto what was left of its front. "This is Yukio Hirayasu—local yak, but he's someone important's son apparently."

The knife burred into life in my hand, vibrations backing up unpleasantly as far as the wound in my side. I shook off a teeth-on-edge shiver, placed one cupped palm on the back of Yukio's skull to steady it, and started cutting into the spine. The mingled stink of scorched flesh and shit didn't help.

"And the other one?" she asked.

"Disposable thug. Never seen him before."

"Is he worth taking with us?"

I shrugged. "Better than leaving him here, I guess. You can toss him over the side halfway to New Hok. This one I'd keep for ransom, if I were you."

She nodded. "What I thought."

The knife bit down through the last millimeters of spinal column and sliced rapidly into the neck below. I switched off, changed grip, and started a new cut, a couple of vertebrae lower down.

"These are heavyweight yakuza, Sylvie." My guts were chilling over as I recalled my phone conversation with Tanaseda. The *sempai* had cut a deal with me purely on the strength of Yukio's value in one piece. And he'd been pretty explicit about what would happen if things didn't stay that way. "Millsport-connected, probably with First Family links. They're going to come after you with everything they've got."

Her eyes were unreadable. "They're going to come after you, too."

"Let me worry about that."

"That's very generous of you. However—" She paused as Orr came back out of his room fully dressed and headed out the door with a curt nod. "—I think we have this handled. Ki is off wiping our electronic traces now. Orr can torchblast every room in this place in about half an hour. That leaves them with nothing but—"

"Sylvie, this is the yakuza we're talking about."

"Nothing but eyewitnesses, peripheral video data, and besides which we'll be on our way to Drava in about two hours' time. And no one's going to follow us there." There was a sudden, stiff pride in her voice. "Not the yakuza, not the First Families, not even the fucking Envoys. No one wants to fuck with the mimints."

Like most bravado, it was misplaced. For one thing, I'd had it from an old friend six months back that Envoy Command *had* tendered for the New Hokkaido contract—they just hadn't been cheap enough to suit the Mecsek government's freshly rediscovered faith in unfettered market forces. A sneer across Todor Murakami's lean face as we shared a pipe on the ferry from Akan to New Kanagawa. Fragrant smoke on the winter air of the Reach, and the soft grind of the maelstrom as backdrop. Murakami was letting his cropped Corps haircut grow out, and it stirred a little in the breeze off the water. He wasn't supposed to be there, talking to me, but it's hard to tell Envoys what to do. They know what they're worth.

Hey, fuck Leo Mecsek. We told him what it'd cost. He can't afford it, whose problem is that supposed to be? We're supposed to cut corners and endanger Envoy lives so he can hand the First Families back some more of the tax they pay? Fuck that. We're not fucking locals.

You're a local, Tod, I felt driven to point out. *Millsport-born and -bred.*

You know what I mean.

I knew what he meant. Local government don't get to punch keys on the Envoy Corps. The Envoys go where the Protectorate needs them, and most local governments pray to whatever gods they give house room that they'll never be found wanting enough for that contingency to be invoked. The aftermath of Envoy intervention can be very unpleasant for all concerned.

This whole tendering angle's fucked anyway. Todor plumed fresh smoke out over the rail. *No one can afford us, no one trusts us. Can't see the point, can you?*

I thought it was about offsetting nonoperational costs while you guys were sitting on your asses undeployed.

Oh yeah. Which is when?

Really? I heard it was all pretty quiet right now. Since Hun Home, I mean. Going to tell me some covert insurgency tales?

Hey, sam. He passed me the pipe. *You're not on the team anymore. Remember?*

I remembered.

Innenin!

It bursts on the edges of memory like a downed marauder bomb going up distant, but not far enough off to be safe. Red laser fire and the screams of men dying as the Rawling virus eats their minds alive.

I shivered a little and drew on the pipe. With Envoy-tuned sensitivity, Todor spotted it and shifted subject.

So what's this scam about? Thought you were hanging out with Radul Segesvar these days. Hometown nostalgia and cheap organized crime.

Yeah. I looked at him bleakly. *Where'd you hear that, then?*

A shrug. Around. You know how it is. So why you going up north again?

The vibroknife broke through into flesh and muscle again. I switched it off and started to lever the severed section of spine out of Yukio Hirayasu's neck.

Yakuza gentry, dead and destacked. Courtesy of Takeshi Kovacs, because that was the way the label was going to read, whatever I did now. Tanaseda was going to be looking for blood. Hirayasu senior, too, presumably. Could be he saw his son as the lipslack fuckup he evidently was, but somehow I doubted it. And even if he did, every rule of obligation the Harlan's World yakuza girded themselves with was going to force him to make it right. Organized crime is like that. Radul Segesvar's Newpest *haiduci* mafia or the yak, north or south, they're all the fucking same. Fucking blood-tie junkies.

War with the yakuza.

Why you going up north again? I looked at the excised spinal segment and the blood on my hands. It wasn't what I'd had in mind when I caught the hoverloader up to Tekitomura three days ago.

"Micky?" For a moment, the name meant nothing to me. "Hey, Mick, you okay?"

I looked up. She was watching me with narrow concern. I forced a nod. "Yeah. I'm fine."

"Well, do you think you could pick it up a bit? Orr'll be back and he'll want to get started."

"Sure." I turned to the other corpse. The knife burred back into life. "I'm still curious what you plan to do about Jadwiga."

"You'll see."

"Party trick, huh?"

She said nothing, just walked to the window and stared out into the light and clamor of the new day. Then, as I was starting the second spinal incision, she looked back into the room.

"Why don't you come with us, Micky?"

I slipped and buried the knife blade up to its hilt. "What?"

"Come with us."

"To *Drava*?"

"Oh, you're going to tell me you've got a better chance running against the yak here in Tekitomura?"

I freed the blade and finished the incision. "I need a new body, Sylvie. This one's in no state for meeting the mimints."

"What if I could set that up for you?"

"Sylvie." I grunted with effort as the bone segment levered upward. "Where the fuck are you going to find me a body on New Hokkaido? Place barely permits human life as it is. Where are you going to find the facilities?"

She hesitated. I stopped what I was doing, Envoy intuition wakening to the realization that there was something here.

"Last time we were out," she said slowly, "we turned up a government command bunker in the hills east of Sopron. The smart locks were too complex to crack in the time we had, we were way too far north anyway and it's bad mimint territory, but I got in deep enough to run a basic inventory. There's a full medlab facility, complete resleeving unit, and cryocap clone banks. About two dozen sleeves, combat biotech by the signature traces."

"Well, that'd make sense. That's where you're taking Jadwiga?"

She nodded.

I looked pensively at the chunk of spine in my hand, the ragged-lipped wound it had come out of. I thought about what the yakuza would do to me if they caught up with me in this sleeve.

"How long are you going over for?"

She shrugged. "Long as it takes. We're provisioned for three months, but last time we filled our quota in half that time. You could come back sooner if you like. The 'loaders run out of Drava all the time."

"And you're sure this stuff in the bunker is still functional?"

She grinned and shook her head.

"What?"

"It's New Hok, Micky. Over there, *everything's* still functional. That's the whole problem with the fucking place."

CHAPTeR FIVe

The hoverloader *Guns for Guevara* was exactly what she sounded like—a low-profile, heavily armored shark of a vessel, spiking weaponry along her back like dorsal spines. In marked contrast with the commercial 'loaders that plied the routes between Millsport and the Saffron Archipelago, she had no external decks or towers. The bridge was a snubbed blister on the forward facings of the dull gray superstructure, and her flanks swept back and out in smooth, featureless curves. The two loading hatches, open on either side of her nose, looked built to disgorge flights of missiles.

"You sure this is going to work?" I asked Sylvie as we reached the downward slope of the docking ramp.

"Relax," growled Orr, behind me. "This isn't the Saffron Line."

He was right. For an operation that the government claimed was being run under stringent security guidelines, deCom embarkation struck me as sloppy in the extreme. At the side of each hatch, a steward in a soiled blue uniform was taking *hardcopy* documentation and running the authorization flashes under a reader that wouldn't have looked much out of place in a Settlement-years experia flick. The ragged queues of embarking personnel snaked back and forth across the ramp, ankle deep in carry-on baggage. Bottles and pipes passed back and forth in the cold, bright air. There was highly strung hilarity and mock-sparring up and down the lines, repeated jokes over the antique reader. The stewards smiled back repeatedly, wearily.

"And where the fuck is Las?" Kiyoka wanted to know.

Sylvie shrugged. "He'll be here. He always is."

We joined the back of the nearest queue. The little knot of deComs ahead of us glanced around briefly, spent a couple of measured looks on Sylvie's hair, then went back to their bickering. She wasn't unusual among this crowd. A tall black sleeve a couple of groups down had a dreadlocked mane of similar proportions, and there were others less imposing here and there.

Jadwiga stood quiet beside me.

"This thing with Las is pathological," Kiyoka told me, looking anywhere but at Jad. "He's always fucking late."

"It's wired into him," said Sylvie absently. "You don't get to be a career wincefish without a tendency toward brinkmanship."

"Hey, *I'm* a wincefish, and I turn up on time."

"You're not a lead wincefish," said Orr.

"Oh *right*. Listen we're all—" She glanced at Jadwiga and bit her lip. "Lead's just a player position. Las is wired no different from me or—"

Looking at Jad, you'd never have guessed she was dead. We'd cleaned her up in the apartment—beam weapons cauterize, there's not often much in the way of blood—rigged her in a tight marine-surplus combat vest and jacket that covered the wounds, fitted heavy black EV lenses over her shocked open eyes. Then Sylvie got in through the team net and fired up her motor systems. I'd guess it took a little concentration, but nothing to the focus she'd have to have online when she deployed the team against the mimints on New Hok. She got Jad walking at her left shoulder, and we formed a phalanx around them. Simple commands to facial muscles clamped the dead deCom's mouth shut, and the gray pallor—well, with the EV lenses on and a long gray sealwrap bag slung over one shoulder, Jad looked no worse than she should have done on a shiver comedown with added endorphin crash. I don't suppose the rest of us looked too hot, either.

"Authorization, please."

Sylvie handed over the sheaf of hardcopy, and the steward set about passing it through the reader one sheet at a time. She must have sent a tiny jolt through the net to the muscles in Jadwiga's neck at the same time, because the dead woman tilted her head, a little stiffly, as if scanning the 'loader's armored flank. Nice touch, very natural.

"Sylvie Oshima. Crew of five," said the steward, looking up to count. "Hardware already stowed."

"That's right."

"Cabin allocation." He squinted at the reader's screen. "Sorted. P-nineteen to -twenty-two, lower deck."

There was a commotion back up near the top of the ramp. We all looked back, apart from Jadwiga. I spotted ocher robes and beards, angry gesticulating, and voices raised.

"What's going on?" asked Sylvie casually.

"Oh—Beards." The steward shuffled the scanned documentation back together. "They've been prowling up and down the waterfront all morning. Apparently they had a run-in last night with a couple of deComs someplace way east of here. You know how they are about that stuff."

"Yeah. Fucking throwbacks." Sylvie took the paperwork and stowed it in her jacket. "They got descriptions, or will any two deComs do?"

The steward smirked. "No vid, they say. Place was using up all its capacity on holoporn. But they got a witness description. A woman. And a man. Oh, yeah, and the woman had hair."

"Christ, that could be *me*," laughed Sylvie.

Orr gave her a strange look. Behind us, the clamor intensified. The steward shrugged.

"Yeah, could be any of a couple of dozen command heads I passed through here this morning. Hey, what I want to know is, what are a bunch of priests doing in a place runs holoporn anyway?"

"Jerking off?" suggested Orr.

"Religion," said Sylvie, with a sudden click in her throat as if she were going to vomit. At my side, Jadwiga swayed unsteadily and twisted her head more abruptly than people generally do. "Has it occurred to anybody that—"

She grunted, gut deep. I shot a glance at Orr and Kiyoka, saw their faces go tight. The steward looked on, curious, not yet concerned.

"—that every human sacrament is a cheap evasion, that—"

Another choked sound. As if the words were being wrenched up out of somewhere buried in hard-packed silt. Jadwiga's swaying worsened. Now the steward's face began to change as he picked up the scent of distress. Even the deComs in the queue behind us were shifting their attention from the brawl at the top of the ramp, narrowing in on the pale woman and the speech that came sputtering up out of her.

"—that the *whole of human history* might just be some *fucking excuse* for the inability to provide *a decent female orgasm.*"

I trod on her foot, hard.

"Quite."

The steward laughed nervously. Quellist sentiments, albeit early poetic ones, were still marked HANDLE WITH CARE in the Harlan's World cultural canon. Too much danger that any enthusiasm for them might spill over into her later political theory and, of course, practice. You can name your hoverloaders for revolutionary heroes if you want, but they need to be far enough back in history that no one can remember what they were fighting for.

"I—" said Sylvie, puzzled. Orr moved to support her.

"Let's have this argument later, Sylvie. We'd better get stowed first. Look." He nudged her. "Jad's *dead on her feet,* and I don't feel much better. Can we—"

She caught it. Straightened and nodded.

"Yeah, later," she said. Jadwiga's corpse stopped swaying, even lifted the back of one hand realistically to its brow.

"Comedown blues," I said, winking at the steward. His nervousness ironed out and he grinned.

"Been there, man."

Jeering from the top of the ramp. I heard the shouted word *abomination*, then the sound of electrical discharge. Probably power knuckles.

"Think they've reeled in more than they can stow up there," said the steward, peering past us. "Should have come heavy, they're going to mouth off like that to a dock full of deCom. Okay, that's us. You can go through."

We made it through the hatch without further stumbling from anybody, and went down metal-echoing corridors in search of the cabins. At my back, Jad's corpse kept mechanical pace. The rest of the team acted like nothing had happened.

●●●

"So what the fuck was that?"

I finally got around to asking the question about half an hour later. Sylvie's crew stood around in her cabin, looking uncomfortable. Orr had to stoop below the reinforcing joists of the ceiling. Kiyoka stared out of the tiny one-way porthole, finding something of great interest in the water outside. Jadwiga lay facedown on a bunk. Still no sign of Lazlo.

"It was a glitch," said Sylvie.

"A glitch." I nodded. "Does this kind of glitch happen often?"

"No. Not often."

"But it has happened before."

Orr ducked under a joist to loom over me. "Why don't you give it a rest, Micky. No one forced you to come along. You don't like the terms, you can just fuck off, can't you."

"I'm just curious to know what we do if Sylvie drops out of the loop and starts spouting Quellisms in the middle of a mimint encounter, that's all."

"Let us worry about the mimints," said Kiyoka tonelessly.

"Yeah, Micky." Orr sneered. "It's what we do for a living. You just sit back and enjoy the ride."

"All I want to—"

"You shut the fuck up if you—"

"Look." She said it very quietly, but Orr and Kiyoka both hooked around toward the sound of her voice. "Why don't you two leave me and Micky alone to talk about this?"

"Ah, Sylvie, he's just—"

"He's got a right to know, Orr. Now, you want to give us some space?"

She watched them out, waited for the cabin door to fold, then went past me back to her seat.

"Thanks," I said.

"Look." It took me a moment to realize she meant it literally this time. She reached into the mass of her hair and lifted the center cord. "You know how this works. There's more processing capacity in this than in most city databases. Has to be."

She let the cord go and shook her hair across it. A small smile flickered around her mouth. "Out there, we can get a viral strike flung at us hard enough to scrape out a human mind like fruit pulp. Or just mimint interactive codes trying to replicate themselves, machine intrusion systems, construct personality fronts, transmission flotsam, you name it. I have to be able to contain all that, sort it, use it, and not let anything leak through into the net. It's what I do. Time and time again. And no matter how good the housecleaning you buy afterward, some of that shit stays. Hard-to-kill code remnants, traces." She shivered a little. "Ghosts of things. There's stuff bedded down there, beyond the baffles, that I don't want to even think about."

"Sounds like it's time for some fresh hardware."

"Yeah." She grinned sourly. "I just don't have that much loose change right now. Know what I mean?"

I did know. "Recent tech. It's a fucker, huh?"

"Yeah. Recent tech, fucking indecent pricing. They take the Guild subsidies, the Protectorate defense funding, and then pass on the whole fucking cost of the Sanction labs' R and D to people like me."

I shrugged. "Price of progress."

"Yeah, saw the ad. Assholes. Look, what happened back there is just gunge in the works, nothing to worry about. Maybe something to do with trying to hotwire Jad. That's something I don't do usually, it's unused capacity. And that's usually where the data management systems dump any trace junk. Running Jad's CNS must have flushed it out."

"Do you remember what you were saying?"

"Not really." She rubbed at the side of her face, pressed fingertips against one closed eye. "Something about religion? About the Beards?"

"Well, yeah. You lifted off from there, but then you started paraphrasing early Quellcrist Falconer. Not a Quellist, are you?"

"Fuck, no."

"Didn't think so."

She thought about it for a while. Under our feet, the *Guns for Guevara*'s engines began to thrum gently. Departure for Drava, imminent.

"Could be something I caught off a dissemination drone. There's still a lot of them out in the east—not worth the bounty to decommission, so they get left alone unless they're fucking up local comlinks."

"Would any of them be Quellist?"

"Oh yeah. At least four or five of the factions who fucked up New Hok were Quellist-inspired. Shit, from what I hear she was fighting up there herself back when the Unsettlement kicked off."

"That's what they say."

The door chimed. Sylvie nodded at me, and I went to open it. Out in the faintly shuddering corridor stood a short, wiry figure with long black hair bound back in a ponytail. He was sweating heavily.

"Lazlo," I guessed.

"Yeah. Who the fuck are you?"

"Long story. You want to talk to Sylvie?"

"That'd be nice." The irony was ladled on. I stood aside and let him in. Sylvie gave him a weary top-to-toe look.

"Got in the life-raft launcher," Lazlo announced. "Couple of bypass jolts and a seven-meter crawl up a polished steel chimney. Nothing to it."

Sylvie sighed. "It's not big, Las, it's not clever, and someday you'll miss the fucking boat. What are we going to do for a lead then?"

"Well, looks to me like you're already lining up replacements." A cocked glance in my direction. "Who is this, exactly?"

"Micky, Lazlo." An idle gesture back and forth between us. "Lazlo, meet Micky Serendipity. Temporary traveling companion."

"Did you get him aboard with my flashes?"

Sylvie shrugged. "You never use them."

Lazlo spotted Jadwiga's form on the bed, and a grin lit up his bony face. He strode across the cabin and slapped her on one buttock. When she didn't respond, he frowned. I shut the door.

"Jesus, what did she take last night?"

"She's dead, Las."

"Dead?"

"For the moment, yes." Sylvie looked across at me. "You've missed rather a lot of the dance since yesterday."

Lazlo's eyes followed Sylvie's gaze across the cabin. "And it all has something to do with tall, dark, and synthetic there, right?"

"Right," I said. "Like I said, it's a long story."

Lazlo went across to the basin niche and ran water into his cupped hands. He lowered his face into the water and snorted. Then he wiped the surplus water back through his hair, straightened up, and eyed me in the mirror. He turned pointedly toward Sylvie.

"All right, skipper. I'm listening."

CHAPTeR SIX

It took a day and a night to get to Drava.

From about midway across the Andrassy Sea, *Guns for Guevara* ran throttled back, sensor net spread as wide as it would go, weapons systems at standby. The official line from the Mecsek government was that the mimints had all been designed for a land war and so had no way of getting off New Hok. On the ground, deCom crews reported seeing machines there were no descriptors for in the Military Machine Intelligence archive, which suggested at least some of the weaponry still prowling the continent had found ways to evolve beyond its original program parameters. The whispered word was that experimental nanotech had run wild. The official line said nanotech systems were too crude and too poorly understood at the time of the Unsettlement to have been deployed as weapons. The whispered word was dismissed as antigovernment scaremongering, the official line was derided everyplace you could find intelligent conversation. Without satellite cover or aerial support, there was no way to prove the thing either way. Myth and misinformation reigned.

Welcome to Harlan's World.

"Hard to believe," muttered Lazlo as we cruised the last few kilometers up the estuary and through Drava's deserted dockyards. "Four centuries on this fucking planet and we still can't go up in the air."

Somehow he'd blagged entry to one of the open-air observation galleries the hoverloader had sprouted from its armored spine once we were inside the Drava base scanning umbrella. Somehow else, he'd chivied us into going up there with him, and now we all stood shivering in the damp cold of early morning as the silent quays of Drava slid by on either side. Overhead, the sky was an unpromising gray in all directions.

Orr turned up the collar on his jacket. "Anytime you come up with a way to deCom an orbital, Las, just let us know."

"Yeah, count me in," said Kiyoka. "Bring down an orbital, they'd make Mitzi Harlan give you head every morning for the rest of your life."

It was common talk among the deCom crews, an analog of the fifty-meter bottleback stories charter boat skippers told in the Millsport bars. No matter how big the bounty you hauled back from New Hok, it was all *human* scale. No matter how hostile the mimints, ultimately they were things we'd built ourselves and they were barely three centuries old. You couldn't compare that with the lure of hardware the Martians had apparently left in orbit around Harlan's World approximately five hundred thousand years ago. Hardware that, for reasons best known to itself, would carve pretty much anything airborne out of the sky with a lance of angelfire.

Lazlo blew on his hands. "They could have brought them down before now if they'd wanted to."

"Oh man, here we go again." Kiyoka rolled her eyes.

"There's a lot of crabshit talked about the orbitals," said Lazlo doggedly. "Like how they'll hit anything bigger or faster than a helicopter, but somehow four hundred years ago we managed to land the colony barges okay. Like—"

Orr snorted. I saw Sylvie close her eyes.

"—how the government has these big hyperjets they keep under the pole, and nothing ever touches *them* when they fly. Like all the times the orbitals take out something surface-based, only they don't like to talk about that. Happens *all the time,* man. Bet you didn't hear about that dredger they found ripped apart yesterday off Sanshin Point—"

"I did hear that one," said Sylvie irritably. "Caught it while we were waiting for you to turn up yesterday morning. Report said they ran aground on the point. You're looking for conspiracy when all you've got is incompetence."

"Skipper, they *said* that, sure. They *would* say that."

"Oh for fuck's sake."

"Las, old son." Orr dropped a heavy arm around the lead wincefish's shoulders. "If it'd been angelfire, there wouldn't have been anything left to find. You know that. And you know damned well there's a fucking hole in the coverage down around the equator big enough to drive a whole fleet of colony barges through if you do the math right. Now, why don't you give the conspiracy shit a rest and check out the scenery you dragged us all up here to see."

It was an impressive enough sight. Drava, in its day, was both trade gateway and naval port for the whole New Hokkaido hinterland. The waterfront saw shipping from every major city on the planet, and the sprawl of architecture behind the docks reached back a dozen kilometers into the foothills to provide homes for almost five million people. At the height of its commercial powers, Drava rivaled Millsport for wealth and sophistication, and the navy garrison was one of the strongest in the northern hemisphere.

Now we cruised past rows of smashed-in Settlement-years warehouses, containers and cranes tumbled across the docks like children's toys and merchant vessels sunk at anchor end-to-end. There were lurid chemical stains on the water around us, and the only living things in view were a miserable-looking clutch of ripwings flapping about on the canted, corrugated roof of a warehouse. One of them flung back its neck and uttered a clattering challenge as we went past, but you could tell its heart wasn't in it.

"Want to watch out for those," said Kiyoka grimly. "They don't look like much but they're smart. Most places on this coast they've already polished off the cormorants and the gulls, and they've been known to attack humans, too."

I shrugged. "Well, it's their planet."

The deCom beachhead fortifications came into view. Hundreds of meters of razor-edged livewire crawling restlessly about inside its patrol parameters, jagged rows of crouched spider blocks on the ground and robot sentries perched brooding on the surrounding rooftops. In the water, a couple of automated mini subs poked conning towers above the surface, bracketing the curve of the estuary. Surveillance kites flew at intervals, tethered to crane stacks and a communications mast in the heart of the beachhead.

Guns for Guevara cut power and drifted in broadside between the two subs. On the dockside, a few figures paused in what they were doing, and voices floated across the closing gap to the new arrivals. Most of the work was done by machines, silently. Beachhead security interrogated the hoverloader's navigational intelligence and gave clearance. The autograpple system talked to the sockets on the dock, agreed trajectory, and fired home. Cables cranked tight and pulled the vessel in. An articulated boarding corridor flexed itself awake and nuzzled up to the dockside loading hatch. Buoyancy antigrav kicked over to mooring levels with a shiver. Doors unlatched.

"Time to go," said Lazlo, and disappeared below like a rat down a hole. Orr made an obscene gesture in his wake.

"What you bring us up here in the first place for, you're in such a fucking hurry to get off?"

An indistinct answer floated back up. Feet clattered on the companionway.

"Ah, let him go," said Kiyoka. "No one rolls till we talk to Kurumaya anyway. There'll be a queue around the 'fab."

Orr looked at Sylvie. "What are we going to do about Jad?"

"Leave her here." The command head was gazing out at the ugly gray bubblefab settlement with a curiously rapt expression on her face. Hard to believe it was the view—maybe she was listening to the machine systems talk, senses open and lost in the wash of transmission traffic. She snapped out of it abruptly and turned to face her crew. "We've got the cabins till noon. No point in moving her till we know what we're doing."

"And the hardware?"

Sylvie shrugged. "Same applies. I'm not carting that lot around Drava all day while we wait for Kurumaya to give us a slot."

"Think he'll ramp us again?"

"After last time? Somehow I doubt it."

Belowdecks, the narrow corridors were plugged up with jostling de-Coms, carry-on gear slung across shoulders or portered on heads. Cabin doors stood folded open, occupants within rationalizing baggage prior to launching themselves into the crush. Boisterous shouts ricocheted back and forth over heads and angled cases. Motion was sludgily forward and port, toward the debarkation hatch. We threaded ourselves into the crowd and crept along with it, Orr in the lead. I hung back, protecting my wounded ribs as much as I could. Occasional jolts got through. I rode it with gritted teeth.

What seemed like a long time later, we spilled out the end of the debarkation corridor and stood amid the bubblefabs. The deCom swarm drifted ahead of us, through the 'fabs and toward the center mast. Partway there, Lazlo sat waiting for us on a gutted plastic packing crate. He was grinning.

"What kept you?"

Orr feinted at him with a growl. Sylvie sighed.

"At least tell me you got a queue chip."

Lazlo opened his hand with the solemnity of a conjuror and presented a little fragment of black crystal on his palm. The number fifty-seven resolved itself from a blurred point of light inside. A string of muttered curses smoked off Sylvie and her companions at the sight.

"Yeah, it'll be a while." Lazlo shrugged. "Leftovers from yesterday. They're still assigning the backlog. I heard something serious went down inside the Cleared Zone last night. We may as well eat."

He led us across the encampment to a long silver trailer backed up against one of the perimeter fences. Cheap molded tables and chairs sprouted in the space around the serving hatch. There was a scattering of clientele, sleepy-faced and quiet over coffees and foil-plated breakfast. In the hatch, three attendants moved back and forth as if on rails. Steam and the smell of food boiled out toward us, pungent enough to trigger even the meager taste/scent sense on the synthetic sleeve.

"Misos and rice all around?" asked Lazlo.

Grunts of assent from the deComs as they took a couple of tables. I shook my head. To synthetic taste buds, even good miso soup tastes like dishwater. I went up to the hatch with Lazlo to check what else was on offer. Settled for coffee and a couple of carbohydrate-heavy pastries. I was reaching for a credit chip when Lazlo put out his hand.

"Hey. On me, this."

"Thanks."

"No big deal. Welcome to Sylvie's Slipins. Guess I forgot to say that yesterday. Sorry."

"Well, there was a lot going on."

"Yeah. You want anything else?"

There was a dispenser on the counter selling painkiller dermals. I pulled a couple of strips out and waved them at the attendant. Lazlo nodded, dug out a credit chip of his own, and tossed it onto the counter.

"So you got tagged."

"Yeah. Ribs."

"Thought so, from the way you were moving. Our friends yesterday?"

"No. Before that."

He raised an eyebrow. "Busy man."

"Like you wouldn't believe." I tore a dosage off one of the strips, pushed up a sleeve, and thumbed the dermal into place. Warm wash of chemical well-being up my arm. We gathered up the food on trays and carried it back to the tables.

The deComs ate in a focused silence at odds with their earlier bickering. Around us, the other tables started to fill up. A couple of people nodded at Sylvie's crew in passing, but mostly the deCom norm was standoffish. Crews kept to their own little knots and gatherings. Shreds of conversation wisped past, rich in specs and the same sawn-off cool I'd picked up in my companions over the last day and a half. The attendants yelled order numbers and someone got a receiver tuned to a channel playing Settlement-years jazz.

Loose and painless from the dermal wash, I caught the sound and felt it kick me straight back to my Newpest youth. Friday nights at Watanabe's place—old Watanabe had been a big fan of the Settlement-years jazz giants, and played their stuff incessantly, to groans from his younger patrons that swiftly became ritualized. Spend enough time at Watanabe's and whatever your own musical preferences, it wore you down. You ended up with an engraved liking for the tipped-out-of-kilter rhythms.

"This is old," I said, nodding at the trailer-mounted speakers.

Lazlo grunted. "Welcome to New Hok."

Grins and a trading of finger-touch gestures.

"You like this stuff, huh?" Kiyoka asked me through a mouthful of rice.

"Stuff like it. I don't recognize—"

"Dizzy Csango and Great Laughing Mushroom," said Orr unexpectedly. " 'Down the Ecliptic.' But it's a cover of a Blackman Taku float, originally. Taku never would have let the violin in the front door."

I shot the giant a strange look.

"Don't listen to him," Sylvie told me, scratching idly under her hair. "You go back to early Taku and Ide stuff, they've got that gypsy twang scribbled all over the place. They only phased it out for *Millsport Sessions.*"

"That isn't—"

"Hey, Sylvie!" A youngish-looking command head with hair static-stacked straight up paused at the table. There was a tray of coffees balanced on his left hand and a thick coil of livecable slung over his right shoulder, twitching restlessly. "You guys back already?"

Sylvie grinned. "Hey Oishii. Miss me?"

Oishii made a mock-bow. The tray on his splayed fingers never shifted. "As ever. More than can be said for Kurumaya-san. You plan on seeing him today?"

"You don't?"

"Nah, we're not going out. Kasha caught some counterint splash last night, it'll be a couple of days before she's up and about. We're kicking back." Oishii shrugged. " 'S paid for. Contingency funding."

"Fucking *contingency* fund?" Orr sat up. "What happened here yesterday?"

"You guys don't know?" Oishii looked around the table, eyes wide. "About last night. You didn't hear?"

"No," said Sylvie patiently. "Which is why we're asking you."

"Oh, okay. I thought everyone would know by now. We've got a co-op cluster on the prowl. Inside the Cleared Zone. Last night it started putting together artillery. Self-propelled gun, a big one. Scorpion chassis. Kurumaya had to scramble everybody before we got shelled."

"Is there anything left?" asked Orr.

"They don't know. We took down the primary assemblers along with the gun, but a lot of the smaller stuff scattered. Drones, secondaries, shit like that. Someone said they saw karakuri."

"Oh crab*shit*," Kiyoka snorted.

Oishii shrugged again. "Just what I heard."

"Mech puppets? No fucking way." Kiyoka was warming to her theme. "There haven't been any karakuri in the CZ for better than a year."

"Haven't been any co-op machines either," pointed out Sylvie. "Shit happens. Oishii, you think there's any chance we'll get assigned today?"

"You guys?" Oishii's grin reappeared. "No way, Sylvie. Not after last time."

Sylvie nodded glumly. "That's what I thought."

The jazz track faded out on a lifting note. A voice surged into place behind it, throaty, female, insistent. There was an archaic lilt to the words it used.

"And there Dizzy Csango's push on the classic 'Down the Ecliptic,' new light shed on an old theme, just in the manner Quellism illuminates those ancient iniquities of the economic order we have carried with us all the darkened way from the shores of Earth. Naturally, Dizzy was a confirmed Quellist all his life, and as he many times said—"

Groans went up from the gathered deComs.

"Yeah, fucking methhead junkie all his life, too," yelled someone.

The propaganda DJ warbled on amid the jeers. She'd been singing the same hardwired song for centuries. But the deCom complaints sounded comfortable, habit as well worn as our protests had been at Watanabe's place. Orr's detailed knowledge of Settlement-years jazz began to make some sense.

"Got to hop," said Oishii. "Maybe catch up with you in the Uncleared, yeah?"

"Maybe, yeah." Sylvie watched him leave, then leaned in Lazlo's direction. "How we doing for time?"

The wincefish dug in his pocket and displayed the queue chip. The numbers had shifted to fifty-two. Sylvie blew a disgusted breath.

"So what are karakuri?" I asked.

"Mech puppets." Kiyoka was dismissive. "Don't worry, you aren't going to see any around here. We cleaned them out last year."

Lazlo stuck the chip back in his pocket. "They're facilitator units. Come in all shapes and sizes. Little ones start about the size of a ripwing, only they don't fly. Arms and legs. Armed, sometimes, and they're fast." He grinned. "Not a lot of fun."

A sudden, impatient tightening from Sylvie. She got up.

"I'm going to talk to Kurumaya," she announced. "I think it's time to volunteer our services for cleanup."

General protest, louder than the propaganda DJ had elicited.

"—can*not* be serious."

"Cleanup pays shit, skipper."

"Fucking grubbing about door-to-door—"

"Guys." She held up her hands. "I don't care, all right. If we don't jump the queue, we're not getting out of here till tomorrow. And that's no fucking good. In case any of you've forgotten, pretty soon Jad is going to start smelling antisocial."

Kiyoka looked away. Lazlo and Orr muttered into the dregs of their miso soup.

"Anyone coming with me?"

Silence and averted gazes. I glanced around, then propped myself upright, luxuriating in the new absence of pain.

"Sure. I'll come. This Kurumaya doesn't bite, does he?"

● ● ●

In fact, he looked as if he might.

On Sharya there was a nomad leader I once had dealings with, a sheikh with wealth stacked away in databases all over the planet who chose to spend his days herding semi-domesticated genetically adapted bison back and forth across the Jahan steppe and living out of a solar-powered tent. Directly and indirectly, nearly a hundred thousand hardened steppe nomads owed him allegiance under arms, and when you sat in council with him in that tent, you felt the command coiled inside him.

Shigeo Kurumaya was a paler edition of the same figure. He dominated the command 'fab with the same closemouthed, hard-eyed intensity, for all that he was seated behind a desk laden with monitoring equipment and surrounded by a standing phalanx of deComs awaiting assignment. He was a command head like Sylvie, gray- and black-streaked hair braided back to reveal the central cord bound up in a samurai style a thousand years out of date.

"Special dep, coming through." Sylvie shouldered a path for us through the other deComs. "Coming through. Special dep. Goddamn it, give me some space here. Special *dep*."

They gave ground grudgingly, and we got to the front. Kurumaya barely looked up from his conversation with a team of three deComs sleeved in the slim-young-thing look I was starting to identify as wincefish-standard. His face was impassive.

"You're on no special deployment that I know of, Oshima-san," he said quietly, and around us the deComs exploded in angry reaction. Kurumaya stared back and forth at them and the noise quieted.

"As I said—"

Sylvie made a placatory gesture. "I know. Shigeo, I know I don't *have* it. I *want* it. I'm volunteering the Slipins for karakuri cleanup."

That got some surf, but subdued this time. Kurumaya frowned.

"You're *asking* for cleanup?"

"I'm asking for a pass. The guys have run up some heavy debt back home, and they want to get earning six hours ago. If that means door-to-door, we'll do it."

"Get in the motherfucking queue, bitch," said someone behind us.

Sylvie stiffened slightly, but she didn't turn around. "I might have guessed you'd see it like that, Anton. Going to volunteer, too, are you? Take the gang on house-to-house. Don't see them thanking you for that, somehow."

I looked back at the gathered deComs and found Anton, big and blocky looking beneath a command mane dyed half a dozen violently clashing colors. He'd had his eyes lensed so the pupils looked like steel bearings, and there were traceries of circuitwork under the skin of his Slavic cheekbones. He twitched a little, but he made no move toward Sylvie. His metallic-dull eyes went to Kurumaya.

"Come on, Shigeo." Sylvie grinned. "Don't tell me these people are all queuing up for cleaning duty. How many old hands are going to volunteer for this shit. You're sending the sprogs out on this one, because nobody else will do it for the money. I'm offering you a gift here, and you know it."

Kurumaya looked her up and down, then nodded the three wincefish aside. They stepped back with sullen expressions. The holomap winked out. Kurumaya leaned back in his chair and stared at Sylvie.

"Oshima-san, the last time I ramped you ahead of schedule, you neglected your assigned duties and disappeared north. How do I know you won't do the same thing this time?"

"Shig, you sent me to look at *wreckage*. Someone got there before us, there was nothing left. I told you that."

"When you finally resurfaced, yes."

"Oh be reasonable. How was I supposed to deCom what's already been trashed? We lit out, because there was nothing fucking there."

"That doesn't answer my question. How can I trust you this time?"

Sylvie gave out a performance sigh. "Jesus, Shig. You've got the excess-capacity ponytail, you do the math. I'm offering you a favor in return for the chance to make some quick cash. Otherwise, I've got to wait to clear the queue sometime day after tomorrow, you get nothing but sprog sweepers, everybody loses. What's the fucking point of that?"

For a long moment, no one moved. Then Kurumaya glanced aside at one of the units on the desk. A datacoil awoke above it.

"Who's the synth?" he asked casually.

"Oh." Sylvie made *may-I-present* gestures. "New recruit. Micky Serendipity. Ordnance backup."

Kurumaya raised an eyebrow. "Since when does Orr need or want help from anybody?"

"It's just a tryout. My idea." Sylvie smiled brightly. "Way I see it, you never can be too backed up out there."

"That may be so." Kurumaya turned his gaze on me. "But your new friend here is carrying damage."

"It's just a scratch," I told him.

Colors shifted in the datacoil. Kurumaya glanced sideways, and figures coalesced near the apex. He shrugged.

"Very well. Be at the main gate in an hour, bring your gear. You'll get standard maintenance rate per day plus ten percent seniority increment. That's the best I can do. Bonus for any kills you make, MMI chart value."

She gave him another brilliant smile. "That'll do fine. We'll be ready. Nice doing business with you again, Shigeo. Come on, Micky."

As we turned to go, her face twitched with incoming traffic. She jerked back around to look at Kurumaya, irritated.

"Yes?"

He smiled gently at her. "Just so we're clear, Oshima-san. You'll be webbed into a sweep pattern with the others. If you do try and slide out again, I'll know. I'll pull your authorization and I'll have you brought back in, if I have to deploy the whole sweep to do it. You want to be arrested by a bunch of sprogs and then frog-marched back here, you just try me."

Sylvie produced another sigh, shook her head sorrowfully, and walked out through the throng of queuing deComs. As we passed Anton, he showed his teeth.

"Maintenance rate, Sylvie," he sneered. "Looks like you found your level at last."

Then he flinched, his eyes fluttered upward, and his expression blanked as Sylvie reached in and twisted something inside his head. He swayed and the deCom next to him had to grab his arm to steady him. He made a noise like a freak fighter taking a heavy punch. Slurred voice, thick with outrage.

"Fucking—"

"Back off, swamp boy." It trailed out behind her, laconic, as we left the 'fab.

She hadn't even looked in his direction.

CHAPTeR SeVeN

The gate was a single slab of gray alloy armoring six meters across and ten high. Antigrav lifters at either edge were railed onto the inner surfaces of two twenty-meter towers topped with robot sentry gear. If you stood close enough to the gray metal, you could hear the restless scratching of livewire on the other side.

Kurumaya's cleanup volunteers stood about in small knots before the gate, muttered conversation laced with brief flares of loud bravado. As Sylvie had predicted, most were young and inexperienced, both qualities telegraphed clearly in the awkwardness with which they handled their equipment and gawked around them. The sparse assortment of hardware they had was none too impressive, either. Weaponry looked to be largely obsolete military surplus, and there couldn't have been more than a dozen vehicles all told—transport for maybe half of the fifty-odd deComs present, some of it not even grav effect. The rest, it seemed, were doing the sweep on foot.

Command heads were few and far between.

"How it's done," said Kiyoka complacently. She leaned back on the nose of the grav bug I was riding and folded her arms. The little vehicle rocked slightly on its parking cushion, and I upped the field to compensate. "See, most sprogs got no money to speak of, they come into the game practically systems-blind. Try and earn cash for the upgrades with cleanup work and maybe some easy bounty on the edges of the Uncleared. If they get lucky, they do good work and someone notices them. Maybe some crew with losses takes them on."

"And if not?"

"Then they go grow their own hair." Lazlo grinned up from the opened pannier he was rifling through on one of the other two bugs. "Right, skipper?"

"Yeah, just like that." There was a sour edge in Sylvie's voice. Stood near the third bug with Orr for company, she was once again trying to make Jadwiga look like a living human being, and the strain was showing. I wasn't enjoying the process much myself—we'd gotten the dead deCom mounted on one of the bugs, but piloting the vehicle secondhand was beyond Sylvie's control options, so Jad rode pillion behind me. It would have looked pretty strange if I'd gotten off while we waited and she'd stayed sitting there, so I stayed aboard, too. Sylvie had the corpse drape one arm affectionately on my shoulder and left the other resting on my thigh. From time to time, Jadwiga's head swiveled and her sunlensed features flexed in something approximating a grin. I tried to look casual about it.

"You don't want to listen to Las," Kiyoka advised me. "Not one in twenty sprogs is going to have what it takes to make command. Sure, they could wire the stuff into your head, but you'd just go insane."

"Yeah, like the skipper here." Lazlo finished with the pannier, resealed it, and wandered around to the other side.

"What happens," said Kiyoka patiently. "You look for someone who can stand the heat and you form a co-op. Pool funds till you can pay for them to get the hair plus basic plug-in for everybody else, and there you go. Brand-new crew. What're you looking at?"

This last to a young deCom who'd wandered over to stare enviously at the grav bugs and the equipment they mounted. He backed up a little at Kiyoka's tone, but the hunger in his face stayed.

"Dracul line, right?" he said.

"That's right." Kiyoka rapped knuckles on the bug's carapace. "Dracul Forty-one series, only three months off the Millsport factory lines and *every-thing* you heard about it is one hundred percent true. Cloaked drives, internally mounted EMP and particle beam battery, fluid response shielding, integrated Nuhanovic smart systems. You name it, they built it in."

Jadwiga twisted her head in the young deCom's direction, and I guessed the dead mouth was trying on its grin again. Her hand moved off my shoulder and down my side. I shifted slightly in the seat.

"What'd it cost?" asked our new fan. Behind him, a small crowd of like-minded hardware enthusiasts was gathering.

"More than any of you'll earn this year." Kiyoka gestured airily. "Basic package starts at a hundred and twenty grand. And this is *not* the basic package."

The young deCom took a couple of steps closer. "Can I—"

I speared him with a look. "No you can't. I'm sitting on this one."

"Come over here, kid." Lazlo rapped on the carapace of the bug he was messing about with. "Leave the lovebirds alone—they're both too hung over for manners. I'll show you this one. Give you something to aspire to next season."

Laughter. The little group of sprogs drifted in toward the invitation. I exchanged relieved glances with Kiyoka. Jadwiga patted my thigh and nestled her head on my shoulder. I glared across at Sylvie. Behind us, an address system cleared its throat.

"Gate release in five minutes, ladies and gentlemen. Check your tags."

●●●

Whine of grav motors, minute scrape of poorly aligned rail runners. The gate lifted jerkily to the top of its twenty-meter run and the deComs trudged or rode, according to their finances, through the space beneath. The livewire coiled and snaked back from the clean field our tags threw down, building itself into restless hedges over head height. We moved along a cleared path whose sides undulated like something out of a bad *take* dream.

Farther out, the spider blocks shifted on their multiple haunches as they detected the approaching tag fields. When we got closer, they heaved their massive polyhedral bodies up off the cracked evercrete and scuttled aside in reverse imitation of their programmed block-and-crush function. I rode between them with wary attention. One night on Hun Home, I'd sat behind the fortifications of the Kwan Palace and listened to the screams as machines like these wiped out an entire assault wave of insurgent techninjas. For all their bulk and blind sluggishness, it hadn't taken them very long.

Fifteen carefully negotiated minutes later, we cleared the beachhead's defenses and spilled untidily out into the streets of Drava. The dock surfacing gave way to rubble-strewn thoroughfares and sporadically intact apartment buildings averaging twenty stories high. The style was Settlement-years utilitarian standard—this close to the water, accommodation had been thrown up to serve the fledgling port, with little thought for aesthetics. Rows of small, recessed windows peered myopically out toward the sea. The raw evercrete walls were scarred from bombardment and worn from centuries of neglect. Bluish gray patches of lichen marked the places where the antibac sheathing had failed.

Overhead, watery sunlight was leaking through the cloud cover and filtering down into the silent streets ahead. A gusting wind blew in off the estuary, seeming to hurry us forward. I glanced back and saw the livewire and spider blocks reknit behind us like a healing wound.

"Better get on with it, I suppose." Sylvie's voice, at my shoulder. Orr had ridden the other bug up parallel and the command head was seated behind him, head weaving back and forth as if seeking a scent. "At least it's not raining."

She touched a control on the coms jacket she wore. Her voice leapt out in the quiet, reverberated off the deserted façades. The deComs turned at the sound, keyed up and expectant as a pack of hunting dogs.

"All right, friends. Listen up. Without wishing to take unseemly command here—"

She cleared her throat. Whispered.

"But someone, if not I then—"

Another cough.

"*Someone* has to fucking do something. This is not another exercise in, in." She shook her head slightly. Her voice gathered strength, echoed off the walls again. "This is not some fucking political masturbation fantasy we're fighting for, these are facts. Those in power have formed their alliances, shown their allegiance or lack of it, made their choices. And our choices in turn have been taken from us. I don't want, I *don't* want—"

She choked off. Head lowered.

The deComs stood still, waiting. Jadwiga slumped against my back, then started to slide out of the pillion seat. I grabbed backward with one arm and stopped her. Flinched as pain sparkled through the soft woolen gray of the painkillers.

"*Sylvie!*" I hissed it across the space between us. "Get a fucking grip, Sylvie. Pull out of there."

She looked up at me through the tangled mess of her hair, and for a long moment it was as if I were a total stranger.

"Get a grip," I repeated softly.

She shuddered. Sat up and cleared her throat again. Waved one arm airily.

"Politics," she declaimed, and the waiting crowd of deComs laughed. She waited it out. "*Not* what we are here for, ladies and gentlemen. I'm aware that I'm not the only hairhead among us, but I think I probably rank the rest of you in terms of experience, so. For those of you who aren't too sure how this works, here's what I suggest. Radial search pattern, splitting off at every junction until each motorized crew has a street to itself. The rest of you can follow who you like but I'd advise no less than half a dozen in each search line. Motorized crews lead on each street, those of you unlucky enough to be on foot get to check the buildings. Long pause at each building search, motorized guys *don't* get ahead of the pattern, indoor guys call in backup from the riders outside if you see *anything* that might be mimint activity. Anything at all."

"Yeah, what about the bounty?" yelled someone.

A surging murmur of agreement.

"What I take down is mine, ain't here for sharing it out," agreed someone else loudly.

Sylvie nodded.

"You will find." Her amplified voice trod down the dissent. "That successful deCom has three stages. First you take down your mimint. Then you register the claim for it. *Then* you have to live long enough to get back to the beachhead and pick up the money. The last two stages of that process are *es-*

pecially hard to do if you're lying back there in the street with your guts spilled and your head gone. Which is more than likely what'll happen if one of you tries to take down a karakuri nest without help. The word *crew* has connotations. Those of you who aspire to be in a *crew* at some stage, I suggest you meditate upon that."

The noise fizzled out into muttering. Behind me, Jadwiga's corpse straightened up and took the weight off my arm. Sylvie surveyed her audience.

"Right. Now the radial pattern is going to fan us out pretty fast, so keep your mapping gear online at all times. Tag every street when you're done, stay in contact with each other, and be prepared to double back to cover the gaps as the pattern opens up. Spatial analysis. Remember, the mimints are fifty times as good as us at this. If you leave a gap they'll spot it and use it."

"If they're there at all," came another voice from the crowd.

"If they're there at all," agreed Sylvie. "Which they may or may not be. Welcome to New Hok. Now." She stood up on the grav bug's running boards and looked around. "Does anyone have anything *constructive* to say?"

Quiet. Some shuffling.

Sylvie smiled. "Good. Then let's get on with this sweep, shall we. Radial search, as agreed. *Scan up.*"

A ragged cheer went up and fists brandished hardware. Some moron fired a blaster bolt into the sky. Whoops followed, volcanic enthusiasm.

"... kick some motherfucking mimint ass ..."

"Going to make a *pile,* man. A fucking pile."

"Drava, baby, here we *come!*"

Kiyoka cruised up on my other flank and winked at me.

"They're going to need all of that," she said. "And then some. You'll see."

● ● ●

An hour in, I knew what she meant.

It was slow, frustrating work. Move fifty meters down a street at webjelly pace, skirting fallen debris and dead ground cars. Watch the scans. Stop. Wait for the foot sweepers to penetrate the buildings on either side and work their way up twenty-odd levels one creeping step at a time. Listen to their structure-skewed coms transmission. Watch the scans. Tag the building clear. Wait for the foot sweepers to come down. Watch the scans. Move on, another halting fifty-meter stretch. Watch the scans. Stop.

We found nothing.

The sun fought a losing battle against the cloud cover. After a while, it started to rain.

Watch the scans. Move on up the street. Stop.

"Not all it's cracked up to be in the ads, eh?" Kiyoka sat beneath the magical splatter of rain off her bug's invisible screens and nodded at the foot sweepers as they disappeared into the latest façade. They were already drenched, and the tense, flicker-eyed excitement of an hour ago was fading fast. "Opportunity and adventure in the fallow land of New Hok. Bring an umbrella."

Seated behind her, Lazlo grinned and yawned. "Knock it off, Ki. Everyone's got to start somewhere."

Kiyoka leaned back in the seat, looking over her shoulder. "Hey, Sylvie. How much longer are we going to—"

Sylvie made a sign, one of the terse coded gestures I'd seen in action in the aftermath of the firefight with Yukio. Envoy focus gave me the quiver of one eyelid from Kiyoka as she ate up data from the command head. Lazlo nodded contentedly to himself.

I tapped the comset they'd given me in lieu of a direct line into the command head's skull.

"Something going on I should know about, Sylvie?"

"Nah." Orr's voice came back, dismissive. "We'll cut you in when you need to know something. Right, Sylvie?"

I looked back at her. "Right, Sylvie?"

She smiled a little wearily. "Now isn't the time, Micky."

Watch the scans. Move along the rain-damp, damaged streets. The screens on the bugs made shimmering oval umbrellas of rainsplash over our heads; the foot sweepers cursed and got wet.

We found nothing.

By midday, we were a couple of kilometers into the city and operational tension had given way to boredom. The nearest crews were half a dozen streets away on either side. Their vehicles showed up on the mapping equipment in lazily slewed parking formations, and if you tuned to the general channel you could hear the foot sweepers grumbling their way up and down buildings, all trace of the earlier make-a-killing enthusiasm gone from their voices.

"Oh look," rumbled Orr suddenly.

The thoroughfare we were working doglegged right and then opened immediately onto a circular plaza lined with pagoda-style terracing and blocked at the far end by a multileveled temple supported on broadly spaced pillars. Across the open space, rain lay in broad pools where the paving had taken damage. Aside from the massive tilted wreckage of a burned-out scorpion gun, there was no cover.

"Is that the one they killed last night?" I asked.

Lazlo shook his head. "Nah, been there for years. Besides, the way Oishii told it, last night's never built beyond the chassis before it got fried. That one

out there was a walking, talking self-prop mimint motherfucker before it
died."

Orr shot him a frowning glance.

"Better get the sprogs downstairs," said Kiyoka.

Sylvie nodded. Over the local channel, she hurried the sweepers out of
the last buildings and got them assembled behind the grav bugs. They wiped
rain out of their faces and stared resentfully out across the plaza. Sylvie stood
up on the running boards at the rear of the bug and cued the coms jacket.

"All right, listen," she told them. "This looks pretty safe, but there's no
way to be sure, so we're taking a new pattern. The bugs will cruise across to
the far side and check the temple's lower level. Say ten minutes. Then one
bug backs up and maintains a sentry point while the other two work their way
back around on either side of the plaza. When they get back to you safely,
everybody comes across in a wedge and the foot sweepers go up to check the
upper levels of the temple. Has everybody got that?"

Sullen wave of assent up and down the line. They couldn't have cared
less. Sylvie nodded to herself.

"Good enough. So let's do it. Scan up."

She twisted about on the bug and seated herself once more behind Orr.
As she leaned into him, I saw her lips move, but the synth sleeve wasn't up to
hearing what she said. The murmur of the bug's drives lifted fractionally, and
Orr drifted them out into the plaza. Kiyoka nudged the bug she and Lazlo
were riding into a flanking position on the left and followed. I bent to my own
controls and picked up the right flank.

After the relative press of the debris-choked streets, the plaza felt at once
less oppressive and more exposed. The air seemed lighter, the rainsplash on
the bug shield less intense. Over the open ground, the bugs actually picked
up some speed. There was an illusory sensation of progress—

and risk

The Envoy conditioning, scratching for attention. Trouble, just over the
perceptual horizon. Something getting ready to blow.

Hard to tell what gleanings of subconscious detail might have triggered
it this time. Envoy intuitive functions are a temperamental set of faculties at
the best of times, and the whole city had felt like a trap since we left the beachhead.

But you don't dismiss that stuff.

You don't dismiss it when it's saved your life half a thousand times before, on worlds as far apart and different as Sharya and Adoracion. When it's
wired into the core of who you are, deeper than the memory of your childhood.

My eyes ran a constant peripheral scan along the pagoda terracing. My
right hand rested lightly on the weapons console.

Coming up on the wrecked scorpion gun.

Almost halfway.

There!

Flare of adrenaline analog, rough through the synth system. My hand skittered on the fire control—

No.

Just the nodding flower heads on a stand of plant life sprouting up through the shattered carapace of the gun. Rain splatter knocking each flower gently down against the spring of its stalk.

My breathing eased back into action. We passed the scorpion gun and the halfway mark. The sense of impending impact stayed.

"You okay, Micky?" Sylvie's voice in my ear.

"Yeah." I shook my head." 'S nothing."

At my back, Jadwiga's corpse clutched me a little closer.

We made the shadows of the temple without incident. The angled stonework bulked over our heads, leading the eye upward toward huge statues of *daiko* drummers. Steep-leaning load-bearing support structures like drunken pillars, merging seamlessly with the fused-glass floor. Light fell in from side vents and rainwater from the roof in incessant clattering streams farther back in the gloom. Orr pushed his bug inward with what seemed to me a lack of due care.

"This'll do," Sylvie called, voice loud enough to echo in the space we'd entered. She stood, leaned on Orr's shoulder, and twisted herself lithely to the floor beside the bug. "Make it quick, guys."

Lazlo vaulted from the back of Kiyoka's bug and prowled about for a while, apparently scanning the supporting structure of the temple. Orr and Kiyoka started to dismount.

"What are we—" I started, and stopped at the muffled sense of a dead comlink in my ear. I braked the bug, tugged the comset off, and stared at it. My gaze flickered to the deComs and what they were doing. "*Hoy!* Someone want to tell me what the fuck's going on here?"

Kiyoka offered me a busy smile in passing. She was carrying a webbing belt strapped with enough demolition charges to—

"Sit tight, Micky," she said easily. "Be done in a moment."

"Here," Lazlo was saying. "Here. And here. Orr?"

The giant waved a hand from the other side of the deserted space. "In hand. Maps just like you figured, Sylvie. Couple more, max."

They were placing the charges.

I stared up at the propped and vaulted architecture.

"Oh no. Oh no, you've got to be fucking *kidding* me." I moved to get off, and Jadwiga's dead grip wrapped around my chest. "Sylvie!"

She looked up briefly from where she knelt before a black satcheled unit on the glass floor. Hooded displays showed piles of multicolored data, shifting as her fingers moved on the deck.

"Just a couple of minutes, Mick. 'S all we need."

I jerked a thumb backward at Jadwiga. "Get this fucking thing off me before I break it, Sylvie."

She sighed and got up. Jadwiga let go of me and sagged. I twisted in the bug saddle and caught her before she could topple to the floor. Sylvie reached me about the same time. She nodded to herself.

"Okay. Want to be useful?"

"I want to know what the fuck this is about."

"Later. Right now, you can take that knife I gave you back in Tekitomura and cut the stack out of Jad's spine for me. Seems to be a core skill for you, and I don't know that any of the rest of us want the duty."

I looked down at the dead woman in my arms. She'd flopped facedown, and the sunlenses had slipped. One dead eye caught the faint light.

"*Now* you want to do the excision?"

"Yes, now." Her eyes swiveled up to check a retinal display. We were on a clock. "In the next three minutes, because that's about all we have."

"All done this side," called Orr.

I climbed off the bug and lowered Jadwiga to the fused glass. The knife came to my hand as if it belonged there. I cut through the corpse's clothing at the nape and peeled the layers back to reveal the pale flesh beneath. Then switched on the blade.

Across the temple floor, the others looked up involuntarily at the sound. I stared back, and they looked away.

Under my hands, the top of Jad's spine came out with a pair of deft slices and a brief levering motion. The smell that came with it wasn't pleasant. I wiped the knife on her clothing and stowed it, examined the tissue-clogged vertebrae as I straightened up. Orr reached me with long strides and held out his hand.

"I'll take that."

I shrugged. "My pleasure. Here."

"We're all set." Back at the satchel unit, Sylvie folded something closed with a gesture that reeked of finality. She stood up. "Ki, you want to do the honors?"

Kiyoka came and stood beside me, looking down at Jad's mutilated corpse. There was a smooth gray egg in her hand. For what seemed like a long time, we all stood there in silence.

"Running short, Ki," Lazlo said quietly.

Very gently, Kiyoka knelt at Jadwiga's head and placed the grenade in the space I'd cut in her nape. As she got up again, something moved in her face.

Orr touched her gently on the arm.

"Be good as new," he told her.

I looked at Sylvie. "So you guys want to share your plans now?"

"Sure." The command head nodded at the satchel. "Escape clause. Datamine there blows in a couple of minutes, blips everybody's coms and scanners out. Couple of minutes more, the noisy stuff goes up. Bits of Jad everywhere, then the house comes down. And we're gone. Out the back door. Shielded drives, we can ride out the EMP and by the time the sprogs get their scanners back online we'll be peripheral, invisible. They'll find enough of Jad to make it look like we tripped a karakuri nest or a smart bomb and got vaporized in the blast. Leaving us free agents once more. Just the way we like it."

I shook my head. "That is the worst fucking plan I have ever heard. What if—"

"Hey." Orr gave me an unfriendly stare. "You don't like it, you can fucking stay here."

"Skipper." Lazlo again, an edge in his voice this time. "Maybe instead of talking about this, we could just *do* it, you know? In the next two minutes? What do you reckon?"

"Yeah." Kiyoka glanced at Jadwiga's sprawled corpse and then away. "Let's get out of here. Now."

Sylvie nodded. The Slipins mounted up, and we cruised in formation toward the sound of falling water at the back of the temple.

No one looked back.

CHAPTeR eIGHT

As far as anybody could tell, it worked perfectly.

We were a good five hundred meters the other side of the temple when it blew. There was a muffled series of detonations, and then a rumbling that built to a roar. I twisted in my seat—with Jadwiga now in Orr's pocket instead of riding pillion, the view was unobstructed—and in the narrow frame of the street we had taken I saw the whole structure slump undramatically to the ground amid a boiling cloud of dust. A minute later, an underpass took us below street level and I lost even that fractional view.

I rode level with the other two bugs. "You had this all mapped out?" I asked. "All the time, you knew this was what you were going to do?"

Sylvie nodded gravely in the dim light of the tunnel. Unlike the temple, here the effect was unintended. Decayed illuminum paneling overhead cast a last-gasp bluish glow over everything, but it was less than you'd get on a triple-moon night with clear sky. Navigation lights sprang up on the bugs in response. The underpass angled right and we lost the wash of daylight from the mouth of the tunnel behind us. The air started to turn chilly.

"Been through here half a hundred times before," drawled Orr. "That temple's been a bolt-hole dream every time. Just we never had anyone to run away from before."

"Yeah, well, thanks for sharing."

A ripple of deCom mirth in the blue gloom.

"Thing is," Lazlo said. "Couldn't really let you in on the loop without real-time auditory communication, and that's clumsy. The skip clued us and cued us in about fifteen seconds through the crew net. You we would have had to tell, you know, with words. And the amount of state-of-the-art coms gear floating around the beachhead, no way to know who's listening in."

"We had no choice," said Kiyoka.

"No choice," echoed Sylvie. "Bodies burned, and screaming skies, and they tell me, I tell myself—" She cleared her throat. "Sorry, guys. Fucking slippage again. Really got to get this sorted when we're back south."

I nodded back the way we'd come. "So how long before those guys get their scan systems back up?"

The deComs looked at each other. Sylvie shrugged.

"Ten, fifteen minutes, depends what fail-safe software they had."

"Too bad if the karakuri show up in the meantime, huh?"

Kiyoka snorted. Lazlo raised an eyebrow.

"Yeah, that's right," rumbled Orr. "It's too bad. Life in New Hok, better get used to it."

"Anyway, look." Kiyoka, patiently reasonable. "There are no bloody karakuri in Drava. They wouldn't—"

Metallic flailing, up ahead.

Another taut exchange of glances. The weapons consoles on all three bugs lit across, tugged to readiness, presumably by Sylvie's command-head override, and the little convoy jolted to a halt. Orr straightened up in his seat.

Ahead of us, an abandoned vehicle hulked in the gloom. No sign of movement. The frantic clashing sounds bounced past it from somewhere beyond the next bend in the tunnel.

Lazlo grinned tightly in the low light. "What were you saying, Ki?"

"Hey," she said weakly. "I'm open to contrary evidence."

The flailing stopped. Repeated.

"The fuck is that?" murmured Orr.

Sylvie's face was unreadable. "Whatever it is, the datamine should have gotten it. Las, you want to start earning your wincefish pay?"

"Sure." Lazlo winked at me and swung off his seat behind Kiyoka. He laced his fingers and pushed them outward until the knuckles cracked. "You powered up there, big man?"

Orr nodded, already dismounting. He cracked the bug's running-board storage space and dragged out a half-meter wrecking bar. Lazlo grinned again.

"Then, ladies and gentlemen, fasten your seat belts and stand well back. *Scan up.*"

And he was gone, loping along the curved wall of the tunnel, hugging the cover it offered until he reached the wrecked vehicle, then flitting sideways, seeming in the dim light to have no more substance than the shadow he cast. Orr stalked after him, a brutal apeman figure with the wrecking bar held low in his left hand. I glanced back to the bug where Sylvie sat crouched forward, eyes hooded, face blanked in the curious mix of intent and absent that signaled net engagement.

It was poetry to watch.

Lazlo grabbed part of the wreckage with one hand and hauled himself, monkey-casual, up onto the vehicle's roof. He froze into immobility, head cocked slightly. Orr hung back at the curve. Sylvie muttered inaudibly to herself, and Lazlo moved. A single leap, straight back to the floor of the tunnel, and he landed running. Diagonally, across the curve toward something I couldn't see. Orr stepped across, arms spread for balance, upper body held rigid facing the way the wincefish had gone. Another split second, half a dozen rapid, deliberate steps forward, and then he, too, was out of line-of-sight.

Seconds decayed. We sat and waited in the blue gloom.

Seconds decayed.

And—

"... so what the fuck is ... ?"

Sylvie's voice, puzzled. Sliding up in volume as she emerged from the linkup and gave her real-world senses dominance again. She blinked a couple of times and looked sideways at Kiyoka.

The slight woman shrugged. Only now, I realized she'd been part of it, tuned into the ballet I'd just watched at standby, her body slightly stiff in the saddle of the bug while her eyes rode with the rest of the crew on Lazlo's shoulder.

"Fucked if I know, Sylvie."

"All right." The command head's gaze turned on me. "Seems safe. Come on, let's go have a look."

We rode the bugs cautiously up around the bend in the tunnel and dismounted to stare at what Lazlo and Orr had found.

The kneeling figure in the tunnel was only humanoid in the vaguest terms. There was a head, mounted on the main chassis, but the only reason it bore resemblance to a man was that something had ripped the casing apart and left a more delicate structure beneath partially exposed. At the uppermost point, a wide bracing ring had survived, halo-like, to hover on a skeletal framework over the rest of the head.

It had limbs, too, in approximately the positions you'd expect on a human being, but enough of them to suggest insect rather than mammalian life. On one side of the main body mass, two of the available four arms were inert, hanging limp and in one case scorched and shredded to scrap. On the other side, one limb had been torn entirely off, with massive damage to the surrounding body casing, and two more were clearly beyond useful function. They kept trying to flex but at every attempt, sparks ripped savagely across the exposed circuitry until the movement spasmed and froze. The flaring light threw spastic shadows on the walls.

It wasn't clear if the thing's four lower limbs were functional or not, but it didn't try to get up as we approached. The three functioning arms merely redoubled their efforts to achieve something indefinable in the guts of the metal dragon laid out on the tunnel floor.

The machine had four powerful-looking side-mounted legs ending in clawed feet, a long, angular head full of multibarrel ancillary weaponry, and a spiked tail that would gouge into the ground to give added stability. It even had wings—a webbed framework of upward-curving launch cradles designed to take the primary missile load.

It was dead.

Something had torn huge parallel gashes in the left flank, and the legs below the damage had collapsed. The launch cradles were twisted out of alignment, and the head was wrenched to one side.

"Komodo launcher," said Lazlo, skirting the tableau warily. "And karakuri caretaker unit. You lose, Ki."

Kiyoka shook her head. "Doesn't make any fucking sense. What's it doing down here? What's it fucking *doing*, come to that?"

The karakuri cocked its head at her. Its functional limbs crept out of the gash in the dragon's body and hovered over the damage in a gesture that looked weirdly protective.

"Repairs?" I suggested.

Orr barked a laugh. "Yeah. Karakuri are caretakers to a point. After that, they turn scavenger. Something this badly hit, they'd dismember it for a co-op cluster to make into something new. Not try and *repair* it."

"And that's another thing." Kiyoka gestured around. "The mech puppets don't get out that much on their own. Where's the rest of them? Sylvie, you're getting nothing, right?"

"Nothing." The command head looked up and down the tunnel pensively. Blue light glinted off strands of silver in her hair. "This is all there is."

Orr hefted his wrecking bar. "So we going to switch it off or what?"

"Worth fuck-all bounty anyway," grumbled Kiyoka. "Even if we could claim it, which we can't. Why not just leave it for the sprogs to find?"

"I am not," said Lazlo, "walking the rest of this tunnel with that thing still on ops behind me. Turn it off, big man."

Orr looked questioningly at Sylvie. She shrugged and nodded.

The wrecking bar swung. Inhumanly swift, into the eggshell remnants of the karakuri's head. Metal grated and tore. The halo ripped loose, bounced on the tunnel floor, and rolled away into the shadows. Orr pulled the bar clear and swung again. One of the machine's arms came up, fending—the bar flattened it into the ruins of the head. Eerily silent, the karakuri struggled to rise on lower limbs that I now saw were irretrievably mangled. Orr grunted, lifted one booted foot, and stomped down hard. The machine went over, thrashing at the damp tunnel air. The giant moved in, wielding the bar with the economical savagery of experience.

It took a while.

When he was done, when the sparks had bled dry amid the wreckage at his feet, Orr straightened and wiped his brow. He was breathing hard. He glanced at Sylvie again.

"That do?"

"Yeah, it's off." She went back to the bug they were sharing. "Come on, we'd better get cracking."

As we all mounted up again, Orr caught me watching him. He flexed his brows good-naturedly at me and puffed out his cheeks.

"Hate it when you've got to do them by hand," he said. " 'Specially after just paying out all that cred on new blaster upgrades."

I nodded slowly. "Yeah, that's tough."

"Ah, be better when we hit the Uncleared, you'll see. Plenty of room to deploy the hardware, no need to hide the splash. Still." He pointed at me with the wrecking bar. "If we do have to do another by hand, you're aboard now. You can turn off the next one."

"Thanks."

"Hey, no big deal." He handed the bar back over his shoulder to Sylvie, who stowed it. The bug quivered under his hands and drifted forward, past the wreckage of the fallen karakuri. The flexed brows again, and a grin. "Welcome to deCom, Micky."

PART TWO

THIS IS
SOMeONe eLSe

Pull on the new flesh like borrowed gloves
And burn your fingers once again

BAY CITY GRAFFITO
On a bench outside the
Central Penal Storage Facility

CHAPTeR NINe

Static hiss. The general channel was wide open.

"Look," said the scorpion gun reasonably. "There's no call for this. Why don't you just leave us alone."

I sighed and shifted cramped limbs slightly in the confines of the overhang. A cold polar wind hooted in the eroded bluffs, chilling my face and hands. The sky overhead was a standard New Hok gray, the miserly northern winter daylight already past its best. Thirty meters below the rock face I was clinging to, a long trail of scree ran out to the valley floor proper, the river bend and the small cluster of archaic rectangular prefabs that formed the abandoned Quellist listening post. Where we'd been an hour ago. Smoke was still rising from one smashed structure where the self-propelled gun had lobbed its last smart shell. So much for programming parameters.

"Leave us alone," it repeated. "And we'll do you the same favor."

"Can't do that." Sylvie murmured, voice gentle and detached as she ran the crew linkup at combat standby and probed for chinks in the artillery co-op's system. Mind cast out in a gossamer net of awareness that settled over the surrounding landscape like a silk slip to the floor. "You know that. You're too dangerous. Your whole system of life is inimical to ours."

"Yeah." Jadwiga's new laugh was taking some getting used to. "And besides which, we want the fucking land."

"The essence of empowerment," said the dissemination drone from somewhere safe upstream, "is that land should not find ownership outside the parameters of the common good. A commonweal economic constitution . . ."

"*You* are the aggressors here." The scorpion gun cut across the drone with a hint of impatience. It had been hardwired with a strong Millsport accent that reminded me vaguely of the late Yukio Hirayasu. "We ask only to exist as we have for the last three centuries, undisturbed."

Kiyoka snorted. "Oh *come* off it."

"Doesn't work that way," rumbled Orr.

It certainly didn't. In the five weeks since we'd crept out of the Drava suburbs and into the Uncleared, Sylvie's Slipins had taken down a total of four co-op systems and over a dozen individual autonomous mimints of varying shapes and sizes, not to mention tagging the array of mothballed hardware we'd turned up in the command bunker that had yielded my new body. The call-in bounty Sylvie and her friends had amassed was huge. Provided they could ride out Kurumaya's semi-allayed suspicions, they'd made themselves temporarily rich.

So, after a fashion, had I.

". . . those who enrich themselves through the exploitation of that relationship cannot permit the evolution of a truly representative democratic . . ."

Drone's the right fucking word.

I cranked up my neurachem eyes and scanned the valley floor for signs of the co-op. The new sleeve's enhancements were basic by modern standards—there was, for example, no vision-chip time display of the sort that now came as standard on even the cheapest synth sleeves—but they worked with smooth power. The Quellist base leapt into focus at what felt like touching distance. I watched the spaces between the prefabs.

". . . in a struggle that has surfaced again and again everyplace the human race finds a foothold because in every such place are found the rudiments of—"

Movement.

Hunched-up bundles of limbs, like huge, self-conscious insects. The karakuri advance guard, scuttling. Levering back doors and windows on the prefabs with can-opener strength, slipping inside and back out again. I counted seven. About a third strength—Sylvie had estimated the co-op's offensive strength ran to nearly a score of mech puppets, along with three spider tanks, two of them cobbled together out of spares, and of course the core self-propelled weapon, the scorpion gun itself.

"Then you leave me no choice," it said. "I shall be forced to neutralize your incursion with immediate effect."

"Yeah," said Lazlo through a yawn. "You'll be forced to try. So let's get to it, my metal friend."

"I am already about it."

Faint shiver, as I thought of the murderous weapon crawling up the valley toward us, heatseeker eyes casting about for our traces. We'd been stalking the mimint co-op through these mountains for the last two days, and it was an unpleasant turnaround to find ourselves abruptly the hunted. The hooded stealth suit I wore would shut out my body's radiance, and my face and hands were liberally daubed with a chameleochrome polymer that had much the same effect, but with the domed overhang above and a straight twenty-meter drop under my barely ledged boots, it was hard not to feel cornered.

Just the fucking vertigo, Kovacs. Hold it down.

It was one of the less amusing ironies of my new life in the Uncleared. Along with the standard combat biotech, my recently acquired sleeve— Eishundo Organics, whoever they once were—came equipped with gecko-gene enhancement in palms and soles of the feet. I could—assuming I actually fucking wanted to—scramble up a hundred meters of cliff face with no more effort than most people needed to climb a ladder. In better weather I could do it in bare feet, and double my grip, but even like this I could hang here pretty much indefinitely. The million tiny gene-engineered spines in my hands were bedded solidly in the rock, and the perfectly tuned, fresh-from-the-tank muscle system required only occasional shifts in posture to beat the cramping tiredness of long strain. Jadwiga, resleeved out of the tank next to mine and twitchy with the changeover, had vented an earsplitting whoop as she discovered the genetech and then proceeded to crawl around on the walls and ceiling of the bunker like a lizard on tetrameth for the rest of the afternoon.

Personally, I don't like heights.

On a world where no one goes up in the air much for fear of angelfire, it's a common enough condition. Envoy conditioning will shut down the fear with the smooth power of a massive hydraulic crusher, but it doesn't take away the myriad tendrils of caution and dislike we use to cushion ourselves against our phobias on a day-to-day basis. I'd been up on the rock face for nearly an hour, and I was almost ready to give myself away to the scorpion gun if the resulting firefight would get me down.

I shifted my gaze, peered across to the north wall of the valley. Jad was up there somewhere, waiting. I found I could almost picture her. Equally stealthed up, considerably more poised, but still lacking the internal wiring that would have linked her in tight with Sylvie and the rest of the crew. Like me, she was making do with an induction mike and a security-scrambled audio channel patched into Sylvie's crew net. Not much chance that the mimints would be able to crack it—they were two hundred years behind us in cryptographics and hadn't had to deal with the codes of human speech at all for the bulk of that time.

The scorpion gun stalked into view. Running the same khaki drab as the karakuri, but massive enough to be clearly visible even without my racked-up vision. Still a kilometer off the Quellist base, but it had crossed the river and was prowling the high ground on the south side with clear line-of-sight on the hasty cover positions the rest of the team had taken downriver. The tail-end primary weapons pod that had earned the machine its name was flexed for horizontal fire.

I chinned the scrambled channel and muttered into the induction rig. "Contact, Sylvie. We're going to need to do this now, or fall back."

"Take it easy, Micky," she drawled back. "I'm on my way in. And we're well covered for the moment. It isn't going to start shooting up the valley at random."

"Yeah, it wasn't going to fire on a Quellist installation, either. Programmed parameters. Remember *that*?"

A brief pause. I heard Jadwiga making chicken noises in the background. On the general channel, the dissemination drone burbled on.

Sylvie sighed. "So I misjudged their political hardwiring. You know how many rival factions there were fighting up here during the Unsettlement? All fucking squabbling with each other at the end when they should have been fighting the government forces. You know how hard it is to tell some of them apart at a rhetorical code level? This has got to be some captured government armor, rewired by some fucking para-Quellist splinter movement after Alabardos. November Seventeenth Protocol Front, maybe, or the Drava Revisionists. Who the fuck knows?"

"Who the fuck cares?" echoed Jadwiga.

"We would have," I pointed out. "If we'd been eating our breakfast two prefabs to the left an hour ago."

It was unfair—if the smart shell had missed us, we had our command head to thank for it. Behind my eyes, the scene played back in perfect recall. Sylvie slammed abruptly to her feet at the breakfast table, face blank, mind flung out, reaching for the thin electronic squeal of the incoming that only she had picked up. Deploying viral tinsel transmissions at machine speed. Whole seconds later, I heard the shrill whistle of the smart shell's descent through the sky above us.

"Correct!" she'd hissed at us, eyes empty, voice a scream robbed of amplification and razed to inhuman cadence. It was sheer blind reflex, speech centers in the brain spewing an analog of what she was pumping out at transmission levels, like a man gesturing furiously on an audio-phone link. *"Correct your fucking parameters."*

The shell hit.

Muffled crump as the primary detonation system blew, rattle of light debris on the roof above our heads, and then—nothing. She'd locked out the shell's main payload, isolated it from the detonator with emergency shutdown protocols stolen out of its own rudimentary brain. Sealed it shut and killed it with deCom viral plug-ins.

We scattered across the valley like belaweed seed from the pod. A ragged approximation of our drilled ambush configuration, wincefish spread wide in front while Sylvie and Orr hung back at the apex of the pattern with the grav bugs. Mask up and hide and wait, while Sylvie marshaled the weaponry in her head and reached out for the approaching enemy.

". . . our warriors will emerge from the foliage of their ordinary lives to tear down this structure that for centuries has . . ."

Now, on the far side of the river, I could make out the first of the spider tanks. Turret questing left and right, poised in the fringe of vegetation at the water's edge. Set against the scorpion gun's ponderous bulk, they were flimsy-looking machines, smaller even than the manned versions I'd murdered on worlds like Sharya and Adoracion, but they were aware and alert in a way that a human crew could never be. I wasn't looking forward to the next ten minutes.

Deep in the combat sleeve, the chemistry of violence stirred like a snake and called me a liar.

A second tank, then a third, stepping delicately into the swift flow of the river. Karakuri scuttling along the bank beside them.

"Here we go, people." A sharp whisper, for Jadwiga's and my benefit. The rest would already know, advised on the internal net in less time than it takes to form a conscious human thought. "Through the primary baffles. Move on my command."

The self-propelled gun was past the little huddle of prefabs now. Lazlo and Kiyoka had taken up positions close to the river not two kilometers downstream of the base. The karakuri advance guard had to be almost on top of them by now. The undergrowth and long silver grass along the valley twitched in a dozen places with their passing. The rest kept pace with the bigger machines.

"Now!"

Fire bloomed, pale and sudden amid the trees downstream. Orr, cutting loose against the first of the mech puppets.

"Go! Go!"

The lead spider tank staggered slightly in the water. I was already moving, a route down the rock I'd mapped out a couple of dozen times while I was waiting under the overhang. Cascading seconds, the Eishundo sleeve took over and put my hands and feet in place with engineered poise. I jumped the last two meters and hit the scree slope. An ankle tried to turn on the uneven footing—emergency sinew servos yanked taut and stopped it. I stood and sprinted.

A spider turret swiveled. The scree shattered into shale where I'd been. Splinters stung the back of my head and ripped into my cheek.

"Hey!"

"Sorry." The strain was in her voice like unshed tears. "On it."

The next shot went way over my head, maybe homing in on some seconds-decayed image of my scramble down the rock face that she'd stabbed into the sighting software, maybe just a blind shot in the machine equivalent of panic. I snarled relief, drew the Ronin shard blaster from the sheath on my back, and closed with the mimints.

Whatever Sylvie had done to the co-op's systems was brutally effective. The spider tanks were swaying drunkenly, loosing fire at random into the sky and the upper crags of the valley's sides. Around them, karakuri ran about like rats on a sinking raft. The scorpion gun stood in the midst of it all, apparently immobilized, low on its haunches.

I reached the gun in under a minute, pushing the sleeve's biotech to its anaerobic limits. Fifteen meters off, a semi-functional karakuri stumbled into my path, upper arms waving confusedly. I shot it left-handed with the Ronin, heard the soft cough of the blast and saw the storm of monomolecular fragments rip it apart. The shard gun clanked another round into the chamber. Against the small mimints, it was a devastating weapon, but the scorpion gun was heavily armored and its internal systems would be hard to damage with directional fire.

I got up close, slapped the ultravibe mine against one towering metal flank, then tried to get out of the way before it blew.

And something went wrong.

The scorpion gun lurched sideways. Weapons systems on its spine woke to sudden life and swiveled. One massive leg flexed and kicked out. Intended or not, the blow grazed my shoulder, numbed the arm below it, and dumped me full-length into the long grass. I lost the shard blaster from fingers gone abruptly nerveless.

"Fuck."

The gun moved again. I got to my knees, saw peripheral movement. High up on the carapace, a secondary turret was trying to bring its machine guns to bear on me. I spotted the blaster lying in the grass and dived after it. Combat-custom chemicals squirted in my muscles, and feeling fizzed back down the numbed arm. Above me on the self-propelled weapon's bodywork, the machine-rifle turret triggered and slugs ripped the grass apart. I grabbed up the blaster and rolled frantically back toward the scorpion gun, trying to get under the angle of fire. The machine-rifle storm tracked me, showering ripped-up earth and shredded undergrowth. I shielded my eyes with one arm, threw up the Ronin right-handed, and fired blind at the sound of the guns. Combat conditioning must have put the shot somewhere close—the hail of slugs choked off.

And the ultravibe mine came to life.

It was like a swarm of Autumn Fire beetles in feeding frenzy, amplified for some bug's-eye experia documentary. A shrilling, chittering explosion of sound as the bomb shattered molecular bonds and turned a meter-broad sphere of armored machinery into iron filings. Metallic dust fountained out of the breach where I'd slapped the mine. I scrabbled backward along the scorpion gun's flank, unstrapping a second bomb from the bandolier. They're not much bigger than the ramen bowls they very closely resemble, but if you get caught in the blast radius, you're paste.

The scream of the first mine cut off as its field collapsed inward and it turned itself to dust. Smoke boiled out of the massive gash it had left. I snapped the fuse on the new mine and pitched it into the hole. The gun's legs flexed and stamped, uncomfortably close to where I was crouched, but it looked spasmodic. The mimint seemed to have lost directional sense of where the attack was coming from.

"Hey, Micky." Jadwiga, on the covert channel, sounding a little puzzled. "You need any help there?"

"Don't think so. You?"

"Nah, just you should see—" I lost the rest in the shriek as the new mine cut in. The breached hull vomited fresh dust and violet electrical discharge. Across the general channel, the scorpion gun began a high-pitched electronic weeping as the ultravibe chewed deeper into its guts. I felt every hair on my body rise at the sound.

In the background, someone was shouting. Sounded like Orr.

Something blew in the scorpion gun's innards, and it must have knocked out the mine because the chittering insect scream shut off almost the same instant. The weeping died away like blood soaking into parched earth.

"Say again?"

"I *said*," yelled Orr, "command head down. Repeat, Sylvie is *down*. Get the fuck out of there."

Sense of something massive tumbling—

"Easier said than done, Orr." There was a tight, high-tension grin in Jad's voice. "We're a little fucking pressed right now."

"Seconded," gritted Lazlo. He was using the audio link—Sylvie's collapse must have taken out the crew net. "Get the heavy ordnance up here, big man. We could use—"

Kiyoka broke in. "Jad, you just hang—"

Something flashed at the corner of my vision. I whipped about just as the karakuri came at me with all eight arms crooked to grab. No confused lurching to it this time, the mech puppet was up and running at capacity. I got my head out of the way just in time to miss a scything upper limb and pulled the shard blaster's trigger point-blank. The shot blew the karakuri backward in pieces, lower section shredded. I shot the upper half again to make sure, then swung about and skirted the dead bulk of the scorpion gun, Ronin cradled tight in both hands.

"Jad, where are you?"

"In the fucking river." Short, crunching explosions behind her voice on the link. "Look for the downed tank and the million fucking karakuri that want it back."

I ran.

●●●

I killed four more karakuri on the way to the river, all of them far too fast moving to be corrupted. Whatever had floored Sylvie hadn't left her time to finish the intrusion run.

On the audio link, Lazlo yelped and cursed. It sounded like damage. Jadwiga shouted a steady stream of obscenities at the mimints, counterpoint for the flat reports of her shard blaster.

I winced past the tumbling wreckage of the last mech puppet and sprinted flat-out for the bank. At the edge, I jumped. Drenching impact of icy water splashed to groin height and suddenly the swirling sound of the river. Mossed stones underfoot and a sensation like hot sweat in my feet as the genetech spines tried instinctively to grip inside my boots. Grab after balance. I nearly went over, didn't quite. Flexed like a tree in a high wind, beat my own momentum barely and stayed upright, knee deep. I scanned for the tank.

Near the other bank, I found it, collapsed in what looked like about a meter of fast-flowing water. Cranked-up vision gave me Jadwiga and Lazlo huddled in the lee of the wreck, karakuri crawling on the riverbank but seemingly not keen to trust themselves to the current the river was running. A couple had jumped to the tank's hull but didn't seem able to get much purchase. Jadwiga was firing at them one-handed, almost at random. Her other arm was wrapped around Lazlo. There was blood on both of them.

The range was a hundred meters—too far for effective shooting with the shard blaster. I plowed into the river until it reached chest height and was still too far off. The current tried to knock me down.

"Motherfucking—"

I kicked off and swam awkwardly, Ronin held to my chest with one arm. Instantly the current started tugging me away downstream.

"Fuuuck—"

The water was freezing, crushing my lungs closed against the need to breathe, numbing the skin on face and hands. The current felt like a living thing, yanking insistently at my legs and shoulders as I thrashed about. The weight of the shard blaster and the bandolier of ultravibe mines tried to drag me under.

Did drag me under.

I flailed to the surface of the water, sucked for air, got half and half, went under again.

Get a grip, Kovacs.

Think.

Get a fucking grip.

I kicked for the surface, forced myself up, and filled my lungs. Took a bearing on the rapidly receding wreck of the spider tank. Then I let myself be dragged down, reached for the bottom, and grabbed hold.

The spines gripped. I found purchase with my feet as well, braced myself against the current, and started to crawl across the riverbed.

It took longer than I'd have liked.

In places the stones I chose were too small or too poorly embedded, and they ripped loose. In other places my boots couldn't gouge enough purchase. I gave up seconds and meters of ground each time, flailed back again. Once I nearly lost the shard blaster. And anaerobic enhancement or not, I had to come up every three or four minutes for air.

But I made it.

After what seemed like an eternity of grabbing and rooting around in the stabbing, cramping cold, I stood up in waist-high water, staggered to the bank, and hauled myself panting and shaking out of the river. For a couple of moments, it was all I could do to kneel there, coughing.

Rising machine hum.

I staggered to my feet, trying to hold the shard blaster somewhere close to still in both trembling hands. My teeth were chattering as if something had short-circuited in my jaw muscles.

"Micky."

Orr, seated astride one of the bugs, a long-barrel Ronin of his own in one raised hand. Stripped to the waist, blast discharge vents still not fully closed up in the right-hand side of his chest, heat rippling the air around them. Face streaked with the remnants of stealth polymer and what looked like carbonized dust. He was bleeding a little from karakuri slashes across his chest and left arm.

He stopped the bug and stared at me in disbelief.

"Fuck happened to you? Been looking for you everywhere."

"I, I, I, the kara, kara, the kara—"

He nodded. "Taken care of. Jad and Ki are cleaning up. Spiders are out too, both of them."

"And ssssSylvie?"

He looked away.

CHAPTER TeN

"How is she?"

Kiyoka shrugged. She drew the insulating sheet up to Sylvie's neck and cleaned the sweat off the command head's face with a biowipe.

"Hard to tell. She's running a massive fever, but that's not unheard of after a gig like this. I'm more worried about that."

A thumb jerked at the medical monitors beside the bunk. A datacoil holodisplay wove above one of the units, shot through with violent colors and motion. Recognizable in one corner was a rough map of electrical activity in a human brain.

"That's the command software?"

"Yeah." Kiyoka pointed into the display. Crimson and orange and bright gray raged around her fingertip. "This is the primary coupling from the brain to the command net capacity. It's also the point where the emergency decoupling system sits."

I looked at the multicolored tangle. "Lot of activity."

"Yeah, far too much. Postrun, most of that area should be black or blue. The system pumps in analgesics to reduce swelling in the neural pathways, and the coupling pretty much shuts down for a while. Ordinarily, she'd just sleep it off. But this is." She shrugged again. "I haven't seen anything like this before."

I sat down on the edge of the bed and stared at Sylvie's face. It was warm inside the prefab, but my bones still felt chilled in my flesh from the river.

"What went wrong out there today, Ki?"

She shook her head. "I don't know. At a guess, I'd say we ran up against an antiviral that already knew our intrusion systems."

"In three-hundred-year-old software? Come off it."

"I know."

"They say the stuff is evolving." Lazlo stood in the doorway, face pale, arm strapped up where the karakuri had laid it open down to the bone. Behind him, the New Hok day was decaying to dark. "Running totally out of control. That's the only reason we're up here now, you know. To put a stop to it. See, the government had this top-secret AI-breeding project—"

Kiyoka hissed through her teeth. "Not now, Las. For fuck's sake. Don't you think we've got a few bigger things to worry about?"

"—and it got out of hand. This *is* what we've got to worry about, Ki. Right now." Lazlo advanced into the prefab, gesturing at the datacoil. "That's black clinic software in there, and it's going to eat Sylvie's mind if we don't find a blueprint for it. And that's bad news, because the original architects are all *back in fucking Millsport.*"

"And *that,*" shouted Kiyoka, *"is fucking bullshit."*

"Hoy!" To my amazement, they both shut up and looked at me. "Uh, look. Las. I don't see how even evolved software is going to map on to our particular systems just like that. I mean, what are the odds?"

"Because it's the *same people,* Mick. Come on. Who writes the stuff for deCom? Who designed the whole deCom program? And who's buried to the fucking balls in developing secret black nanotech? The fucking Mecsek administration, that's who." Lazlo spread his hands, gave me a world-weary look. "You know how many reports there are, how many people I know, I've talked to, who've seen mimints there are no fucking archive descriptors for? This whole continent's an experiment, man, and we're just a little part of it. And the skipper there just got dumped in the rat's maze."

More movement at the door—Orr and Jadwiga, come to see what all the shouting was about. The giant shook his head.

"Las, you really got to buy yourself that turtle farm down in Newpest you're always talking about. Go barricade yourself in there and talk to the eggs."

"Fuck you, Orr."

"No, fuck you, Las. This is serious."

"She no better, Ki?" Jadwiga crossed to the monitor and dropped a hand on Kiyoka's shoulder. Like mine, her new sleeve was grown on a standard Harlan's World chassis. Mingled Slavic and Japanese ancestry made for savagely beautiful cheekbones, epicanthic folds to the pale jade eyes, and a wide slash of a mouth. Combat biotech requirements hauled the body toward long-limbed and muscular, but the original gene stock brought it out at a curiously delicate ranginess. Skin tone was brown, faded out with tank pallor and five weeks of miserable New Hok weather.

Watching her cross the room was almost like walking past a mirror. We could have been brother and sister. Physically, we *were* brother and sister—the clone bank in the bunker ran to five different modules, a dozen sleeves grown off the same genetic stem in each. It had turned out easiest for Sylvie to hotwire only the one module.

Kiyoka reached up and took Jadwiga's new, long-fingered hand, but it was a conscious movement, almost hesitant. It's a standard problem with resleeves. The pheremonal mix is never the same, and entirely too much of most sex-based relationships is built on that stuff.

"She's fucked, Jad. I can't do anything for her. I wouldn't know where to start." Kiyoka gestured at the datacoil again. "I just don't know what's going on in there."

Silence. Everybody staring at the storm of color in the coil.

"Ki." I hesitated, weighing the idea. A month of shared operational deCom had gone some way to making me part of the team, but Orr at least still saw me as an outsider. With the rest, it depended on mood. Lazlo, usually full of easy camaraderie, was prone to occasional spasms of paranoia in which my unexplained past suddenly made me shadowy and sinister. I had some affinity with Jadwiga, but a lot of that was probably the close genetic match on the sleeves. And Kiyoka could sometimes be a real bitch in the mornings. I wasn't really sure how any of them would react to this. "Listen, is there any way we can fire the decoupler?"

"What?" Orr, predictably.

Kiyoka looked unhappy. "I've got chemicals that might do it, but—"

"You are not fucking taking her hair."

I got up from the bed and faced the giant. "And if what's in there kills her? You'd prefer her long-haired and dead, would you?"

"You shut your fucking m—"

"Orr, he's got a point." Jadwiga moved smoothly between us. "If Sylvie's caught something off the co-op and her own antivirals won't fight it, then that's what the decoupler's for, isn't it?"

Lazlo nodded vigorously. "Might be her only hope, man."

"She's been like this before," said Orr stubbornly. "That thing at Iyamon Canyon last year. She was out for hours, fever through the roof, and she woke up *fine*."

I saw the look swoop among them. *No. Not fine exactly.*

"If I induce the decoupler," said Kiyoka slowly, "I can't tell what damage it'll do her. Whatever's going on in there, she's fully engaged with the command software. That's how come the fever—she should be shutting down the link and she isn't."

"Yeah. And there's a reason for that." Orr glared around at us. "She's a fucking fighter, and she's in there, still fighting. She wanted to blow the coupling, she'd have done it herself."

"Yeah, and maybe whatever she's fighting won't let her." I turned back to the bed. "Ki, she's backed up, right? The cortical stack's nothing to do with the command software?"

"Yeah, it's security-buffered."

"And while she's like this, the stack update is locked out, right?"

"Uh, yeah, but . . ."

"Then even if decoupling does damage her, we've got her in one piece on stack. What update cycle do you guys run?"

Another exchange of glances. Kiyoka frowned. "I don't know, it'll be near to standard, I guess. Every couple of minutes, say."

"Then—"

"Yeah, that'd suit you, wouldn't it, Mister fucking Serendipity." Orr jabbed a finger in my direction. "Kill the body, cut out the life with your little knife. How many of those fucking cortical stacks are you carrying around by now? What's that about? What are you planning to do with them all?"

"That's not really the issue here," I said mildly. "All I'm saying is that if Sylvie comes out of the decouple damaged, we can salvage the stack before it updates and then go back to the bunker and—"

He swayed toward me. *"You're talking about fucking killing her."*

Jadwiga pushed him back. "He's talking about saving her, Orr."

"And what about the copy that's living and breathing right here and now. You want to slit her throat *just because she's brain-damaged and we've got a better copy backed up?* Just like you've done with all these other people you don't want to talk about?"

I saw Lazlo blink and look at me with newly suspicious eyes. I lifted my hands in resignation. "Okay, forget it. Do what you want, I'm just working my passage here."

"We can't do it anyway, Mick." Kiyoka was wiping Sylvie's brow again. "If the damage was subtle, it'd take us more than a couple of minutes to spot it and then it's too late, the damage gets updated to the stack."

You could kill this sleeve, anyway, I didn't say. *Cut your losses, cut its throat right now and excise the stack for—*

I looked back at Sylvie and bit down on the thought. Like looking at Jadwiga's clone-related sleeve, it was a kind of mirror, a flash glimpse of self that caught me out.

Maybe Orr was right.

"One thing's sure," said Jadwiga somberly. "We can't stay out here in this state. With Sylvie down, we're running around the Uncleared with no more survivability than a bunch of sprogs. We've got to get back to Drava."

More silence, while the idea settled in.

"Can she be moved?" I asked.

Kiyoka made a face. "She'll have to be. Jad's right, we can't risk staying out here. We've got to pull back, tomorrow morning at the latest."

"Yeah, and we could use some cover coming in," muttered Lazlo. "It's better than six hundred klicks back, no telling what we're going to run into. Jad, any chance we could dig up some friendlies en route? I know it's a risk."

A slow nod from Jadwiga. "But probably worth it."

"Going to be the whole night," said Lazlo. "You got any meth?"

"Is Mitzi Harlan straight?"

She touched Kiyoka's shoulder again, hesitant caress turning to business-like clap on the back, and left. With a thoughtful backward glance at me, Lazlo followed her out. Orr stood over Sylvie, arms folded.

"You don't fucking touch her," he warned me.

● ● ●

From the relative safety of the Quellist listening post, Jadwiga and Lazlo spent the rest of the night scanning the channels, searching the Uncleared for signs of friendly life. They reached out across the continent with delicate electronic tendrils, sat sleep-deprived and chemically wired in the backwash glow of their portable screens, looking for traces. From where I stood and watched, it looked a lot like the submarine hunts you see in old Alain Marriott experia flicks like *Polar Quarry* and *The Deep Chase*. It was in the nature of the work that deCom crews didn't do much long-range communication. Too much risk of being picked up by a mimint artillery system or a marauding pack of karakuri scavengers. Electronic transmission over distance was slashed to an absolute minimum of needlecast squirts, usually to register a kill claim. The rest of the time, the crews ran mostly silent.

Mostly.

But with skill you could feel out the whisper of local net traffic among the members of a crew, the flickering traces of electronic activity that the deComs carried with them like the scent of cigarettes on a smoker's clothes. With more skill, you could tell the difference between these and mimint spoor and, with the right scrambler codes, you could open communication. It took until just before dawn, but in the end Jad and Lazlo managed to get a line on three other deCom crews working the Uncleared between our position and the Drava beachhead. Coded needlecasts sang back and forth, establishing identity and clearance, and Jadwiga sat back with a broad tetrameth grin on her face.

"Nice to have friends," she said to me.

Once briefed, all three crews agreed, albeit with varying degrees of enthusiasm, to provide cover for our retreat within their own operational range. It was pretty much an unwritten rule of deCom conduct in the Uncleared to offer that much succor—you never knew when it might be you—but the competitive standoffishness of the trade made for grudging adherence. The positions of the first two crews forced us into a long, crooked path of withdrawal, and both were grumpily unwilling to move either to meet us or to provide escort south. With the third we got lucky. Oishii Eminescu was camped 250 kilometers northwest of Drava with nine heavily armed and equipped colleagues. He offered immediately to move up and fetch us from the previous crew's cover radius, and then to bring us all the way back to the beachhead.

● ● ●

"Truth is," he told me, as we stood at the center of his encampment and watched the daylight leach out of another truncated winter afternoon, "we can use the break. Kasha's still carrying some splash damage from that emergency deal we worked in Drava night before you guys got in. She says she's fine, but you can feel it in the wires when we're deployed that she's not. And the others are pretty tired, too. Plus we've done three clusters and twenty-odd autonomous units in the last month. That'll do us for now. No point in pushing it till it breaks."

"Seems overly rational."

He laughed. "You don't want to judge us all by Sylvie's standards. Not everybody's that driven."

"I thought driven came with the territory. DeCom to the max and all that."

"Yeah, that's the song." A wry grimace. "They sell it to the sprogs that way, and then yeah, the software, it naturally inclines you to excess. That's how come the casualty rates. But in the end, it's just software. Just wiring, sam. You let your wiring tell you what to do, what kind of human being does that make you?"

I stared at the darkening horizon. "I don't know."

"Got to think past that stuff, sam. Got to. It'll kill you if you don't."

On the other side of one of the bubblefabs, someone went past in the thickening gloom and called something out in Stripjap. Oishii grinned and yelled back. Laughter rattled back and forth. Behind us, I caught the scent of wood smoke as someone kindled a fire. It was a standard deCom camp—temporary 'fabs blown and hardened from stock that would dissolve down just as rapidly as soon as it was time to move on. Barring occasional stopovers in abandoned buildings like the Quellist listening post, I'd been living in similar circumstances with Sylvie's crew for most of the last five weeks. Still, there was a relaxed warmth around Oishii Eminescu that was at odds with most of the deComs I'd run into so far. A lack of the usual racing-dog edginess.

"How long you been doing this?" I asked him.

"Oh, a while. While longer than I'd like, but—"

A shrug. I nodded.

"But it pays. Right?"

He grinned sourly. "Right. I've got a younger brother studying Martian artifact tech in Millsport, parents both coming up on needing resleeves they can't afford. Way the economy's going right now, nothing else I could do would pay enough to cover the outlay. And the way Mecsek's butchered the education charter and the sleeve pension system, these days you don't pay, you don't get."

"Yeah, they've really fucked things up since I was last here."

"Been away, huh?" He didn't push the point the way Plex had. Old-style Harlan's World courtesy—if I wanted to tell him I'd been doing time in storage, he probably figured I'd get around to it. And if I didn't, well, then, what business was it of his anyway.

"Yeah, about thirty, forty years. Lot of changes."

Another shrug. "Been coming for longer than that. Everything the Quellists squeezed out of the original Harlan regime, those guys have been chipping away at ever since it happened. Mecsek's just the late-stage bad news."

"This enemy you cannot kill," I murmured.

He nodded and finished the quote for me. *"You can only drive it back damaged into the depths and teach your children to watch the waves for its return."*

"So I guess someone's not been watching the waves very carefully."

"That isn't it, Micky." He was looking away toward the failing light in the west, arms folded. "Times have changed since she was around, that's all. What's the point of toppling a First Families regime, here or anywhere else, if the Protectorate are just going to come in and unload the Envoys on you for your trouble?"

"You got a point there."

He grinned again, more real humor in it this time. "Sam, it's not *a* point. It's *the* point. It's the single big difference between then and now. If the Envoy Corps had existed back in the Unsettlement, Quellism would have lasted about six months. You can't fight those fuckers."

"They lost at Innenin."

"Yeah, and how often have they lost since? Innenin was a minor glitch, a blip on the scope, strictly."

Memory roared briefly down on me. *Jimmy de Soto screaming and clawing at the ruins of his face with fingers that have already scooped out one eye and look like getting the other if I don't . . .*

I locked it down.

Minor glitch. Blip on the scope.

"Maybe you're right," I said.

"Maybe I am," he agreed quietly.

We stood for a while in silence after that, watching the dark arrive. The sky had cleared enough to show a waning Daikoku spiked on mountains to the north and a full but distant Marikanon like a copper coin thrown high over our heads. Swollen Hotei still lay below the horizon to the west. Behind us, the fire settled in. Our shadows shaded into solidity amid flickering red glow.

When it started to get too hot to stand there comfortably, Oishii offered a mannered excuse and drifted away. I endured the heat across my back for another minute after he'd gone, then turned and stared blink-eyed into the flames. A couple of Oishii's crew crouched on the far side of the fire, warming their hands. Rippling, indistinct figures in the heated air and darkness. Low tones of conversation. Neither of them looked at me. Hard to tell if that was old-style courtesy like Oishii's or just the usual deCom cliquishness.

What the fuck are you doing out here, Kovacs?

Always the easy questions.

I left the fire and picked my way through the bubblefabs to where we'd pitched three of our own, diplomatically separate from Oishii's. Smooth cold on my face and hands as my skin noticed the sudden lack of warmth. Moonglow on the 'fabs made them look like breaching bottlebacks in a sea of grass. When I reached the one where Sylvie was bedded down, I noticed brighter light splintering out around the closed flap. The others were in darkness. Alongside, two bugs leaned at canted angles on their parking racks, steering gear and weapons stands branching against the sky. The third was gone.

I touched the chime patch, pulled open the flap, and went in. On one side of the interior, Jadwiga and Kiyoka sprang hastily apart on a tangle of bedding. Opposite them, beside a muffled illuminum night-lamp, Sylvie lay corpse-like in her sleeping bag, hair combed carefully back from her face. A portable heater glowed at her feet. There was no one else in the 'fab.

"Where's Orr?"

"Not here." Jad rearranged her clothing crossly. "You might have fucking knocked, Micky."

"I did."

"Okay, you might have fucking knocked *and waited*, then."

"Sorry, it's not what I was expecting. So where's Orr?"

Kiyoka waved an arm. "Gone on the bug with Lazlo. They volunteered for perimeter watch. Got to show willing, we figured. These people are going to carry us home tomorrow."

"So why don't you guys use one of the other 'fabs?"

Jadwiga looked across to Sylvie. "Because someone's got to keep watch in here, too," she said softly.

"I'll do it."

They both looked at me uncertainly for a moment, then at each other. Then Kiyoka shook her head.

"Can't. Orr'd fucking kill us."

"Orr isn't here."

Another exchange of glances. Jad shrugged.

"Yeah, fuck it, why not." She stood up. "C'mon, Ki. Watch won't change for another four hours. Orr's not going to be any the wiser."

Kiyoka hesitated. She leaned over Sylvie and put a hand on her forehead. "All right, but if anything—"

"Yeah, I'll call you. Go on, get out of here."

"Yeah, Ki—come *on*." Jadwiga chivied the other woman to the door-flap. As they were stepping out, she paused and grinned back at me. "And Micky. I've seen the way you look at her. No peeking and prodding, eh? No squeezing the fruit. Keep your fingers out of pies that don't belong to you."

I grinned back. "Fuck you, Jad."

"Yeah, you wish. In your dreams, man."

Kiyoka mouthed a more conventional *thanks,* and they were gone. I sat down beside Sylvie and stared at her in silence. After a couple of moments, I reached out and stroked her brow in an echo of Kiyoka's gesture. She didn't move. Her skin was hot and papery dry.

"Come on, Sylvie. Pull out of there."

No response.

I took back my hand and stared at the woman some more.

What the fuck are you doing out here, Kovacs?

She's not Sarah. Sarah's gone. What the fuck are you—

Oh, shut up.

It's not like I had another choice, is it?

Recall of the final moments in Tokyo Crow came and demolished that one. The safety of the table with Plex, the warm anonymity, and the promise of a ticket out tomorrow—I remembered standing up and walking away from it all, as if in answer to a siren song. Into the blood and fury of the fight.

In retrospect it was a moment so hinged, so loaded with implications of shifting fate, that it should have creaked at me as I moved to step through it.

But in retrospect they always are.

Got to say, Micky, I like you. Her voice blurred with the early hours and the drugs. Morning creeping up on us somewhere beyond the apartment windows. *Can't put my finger on it. But I do. I like you.*

That's nice.

But it's not enough.

My palms and fingers itched lightly, gene-programmed longing for a rough surface to grasp and climb. I'd noticed it a while ago on this sleeve; it came and went but manifested itself mostly around moments of stress and in-activity. Minor irritation, part of the download dues. Even a clone-new sleeve comes with a history. I clenched my fists a couple of times, put a hand in my pocket, and found the cortical stacks. They clicked through my fingers slickly, gathered together in my palm with the smooth weight of high-value machined components. Yukio Hirayasu and his henchman's added to the collection now.

Along the slightly manic search-and-destroy path we'd carved across the Uncleared in the last month, I'd found time to clean up my trophies with chemicals and a circuitboard scrubber. As I opened my hand in the illuminum lamplight, they gleamed, all trace of bone and spinal tissue gone. Half a dozen shiny metallic cylinders like laser-sliced sections of a slimline writing implement, their perfection marred only by the tiny spiking of filament microjacks at one end. Yukio's stack stood out among the others—precise yellow stripe wrapped around it at the midpoint, etched with the manufacturer's hardware coding. Designer merchandise. Typical.

The others, the yakuza henchman's included, were standard, state-installed product. No visible markings, so I'd carefully wrapped the yak's in black insulating tape to distinguish it from those I'd taken in the citadel. I wanted to be able to tell the difference. The man had no bargaining value the way Yukio might, but I saw no reason to consign a common gangster to the place I was taking the priests. I wasn't sure what I was going to do with him instead, but at the last moment something in me had rebelled at my previous suggestion to Sylvie to toss him into the Andrassy Sea.

I put him and Yukio back in my pocket, looked down at the other four gathered in my palm and wondered.

Is this enough?

Once, on another world around a star you couldn't see from Harlan's World, I'd met a man who made his living from trading cortical stacks. He bought and sold by weight, measuring the contained lives out like heaps of spice or semi-precious gems, something that local political conditions had conspired to make very profitable. To frighten the competition, he'd styled himself as a local version of Death personified and, overblown though the act was, it had stayed with me.

I wondered what he'd think if he could see me now.

Is this—

A hand closed on my arm.

The shock leapt up through me like current. My fist snapped closed around the stacks. I stared at the woman in front of me, now propped up in the sleeping bag on one elbow, desperation struggling with the muscles of her face. There was no sign of recognition in her eyes. Her grip on my arm was like a machine's.

"You," she said in Japanese, and coughed. "Help me. *Help me.*"

It was not her voice.

CHAPTeR eLeVeN

There was snow in the sky by the time we got into the hills overlooking Drava. Visible flurries at intervals, and the ever-present bite of it in the air between. The streets and the tops of buildings in the city below were dusted as if with insect poison, and thick cloud was piling up from the east with the promise of more. On one of the general channels, a pro-government dissemination drone was issuing microblizzard warnings and blaming the bad weather on the Quellists. When we went down into the city and the blast-torn streets, we found frost on everything and puddles of rainwater already frozen. In among the snowflakes, there was an eerie silence drifting to the ground.

"Merry fucking Christmas," muttered one of Oishii's crew.

Laughter, but not much of it. The quiet was too overpowering, Drava's gaunt snow-shrouded bones too grim.

We passed newly installed sentry systems on the way in. Kurumaya's response to the co-op incursion six weeks ago, they were single-minded robot weapons well below the threshold of machine intelligence permitted under the deCom charter. Still, Sylvie flinched as Orr guided the bug past each crouched form, and when one of them flexed upright slightly, running the make on our clear tags a second time with a slight chittering, she turned her hollow-eyed gaze away and hid her face against the giant's shoulder.

Her fever hadn't broken when she woke. It just receded like a tide, leaving her exposed and damp with sweat. And at the distant edge of the ground it had given up, tiny and almost soundless; you could see how the waves still pounded at her. You could guess at the minuscule roar it must still be making in the veins at her temples.

It wasn't over. Not nearly.

Through the tangled, abandoned streets of the city. As we drew closer to the beachhead, my new sleeve's refined senses picked up the faint scent of the sea under the cold. Mingling of salts and various organic traces, the ever-present tang of belaweed and the sharp plastic stink of the chemicals spilled across the surface of the estuary. I realized for the first time how stripped down the synthetic's olfactory system had been—none of this had made it through to me on the inward journey from Tekitomura.

The beachhead defenses flexed awake as we arrived. Spider blocks heaved themselves sideways; livewire swayed back. Sylvie hunched her shoulders as we passed between, lowered her head, and shivered. Even her hair seemed to have shrunk closer to her skull.

Overexposure, Oishii's crew medic opined, squinting into his imaging set while Sylvie lay impatiently still under the scanner. *You're not out of the breakers yet. I'd recommend a couple of months laid-back living somewhere warmer and more civilized. Millsport maybe. Get to a wiring clinic, get a full checkup.*

She seethed. *A couple of* months*? Fucking* Millsport*?*

A detached deCom shrug. *Or you'll blank out again. At a minimum, you've got to go back to Tekitomura and get checked out for viral trace. You can't stay out to play in this state.*

The rest of the Slipins concurred. Sylvie's sudden return to consciousness notwithstanding, we were going back.

Burn some of that stored credit, grinned Jadwiga. *Party on down. Tek'to nightlife, here we come.*

The beachhead gate juddered up for us, and we passed through into the compound. In comparison with the last time I'd seen it, the place seemed almost deserted. A few figures wandered about between the bubblefabs, carting equipment. Too cold to be out for anything else. A couple of surveillance kites fluttered madly from the coms mast, knocked about by wind and snow. It looked as if the rest had been taken down in anticipation of the blizzards. Visible over the tops of the 'fabs, the superstructure of a big hoverloader showed snow-coated at the dock, but the cranes that served it were stilled. There was a desolate sense of battening down across the encampment.

"Better go talk to Kurumaya right away," Oishii said, dismounting from his own use-battered solo bug as the gate came back down. He glanced around at his crew and ours. "See about some bunks. My guess is there won't be a lot of space. I can't see any of today's arrivals deploying until this weather clears. Sylvie?"

Sylvie drew her coat tighter around her. Her face was haggard. She didn't want to talk to Kurumaya.

"I'll go, skipper," offered Lazlo. He leaned on my shoulder awkwardly with his undamaged arm and jumped down from the bug we were sharing. Frosted snow crunched under his feet. "Rest of you go get some coffee or something."

"Cool," said Jadwiga. "And don't let old Shig give you a hard time, Las. He doesn't like our story, he can go fuck himself."

"Yeah, I'll tell him that." Lazlo rolled his eyes. "Not. Hey, Micky, want to come along and give me some moral support?"

I blinked. "Uh, yeah. Sure. Ki, Jad? One of you want to take the bug?"

Kiyoka slid off her pillion seat and ambled over. Lazlo joined Oishii and looked back at me. He inclined his head toward the center of the camp.

"Come on then. Let's get this over with."

●●●

Kurumaya, perhaps predictably, was less than happy to see members of Sylvie's crew. He made the two of us wait in a poorly heated outer chamber of the command 'fab while he processed Oishii and allocated billets. Cheap plastic seats were racked along the partition walls, and a corner-mounted screen gave out global news coverage at backdrop volume. A low table held an open-access datacoil for detail junkies, an ashtray for idiots. Our breath clouded faintly in the air.

"So what did you want to talk to me about?" I asked Lazlo, blowing on my hands.

"What?"

"Come on. You need moral support like Jad and Ki need a dick. What's going on?"

A grin surfaced on his face. "Well, you know I always wonder about those two. Sort of thing that keeps a man awake at night."

"Las."

"Okay, okay." He leaned on his good elbow in the chair, dumped his feet on the low table. "You were there with her when she woke up, right."

"Right."

"What did she say to you? Really."

I shifted around to look at him. "Like I told you all last night. Nothing you could quote. Asking for help. Calling for people who weren't there. Gibberish. She was delirious for most of it."

"Yeah." He opened his hand and examined the palm as if it might be a map of something. "See, Micky, I'm a wincefish. A lead wincefish. I stay alive by noticing peripheral stuff. And what I notice peripherally is that you don't look at Sylvie like you used to."

"Really?" I kept my tone mild.

"Yeah, really. Until last night when you looked at her, it was like you were hungry and you thought she might taste good. Now, well." He turned to meet my eyes. "You've lost your appetite."

"She isn't well, Las. I'm not attracted to sickness."

He shook his head. "Won't scan. She was ill all the way back from the listening-post gig, but you still had that hunger. Softer maybe, but it was still there. Now you look at her like you're waiting for something to happen. Like she's some kind of bomb."

"I'm worried about her. Just like everybody else."

And beneath the words, the thought ran like a thermocline. *So noticing this stuff keeps you alive, does it, Las? Well, just so you know, talking about it like this is likely to get you killed. Under different circumstances with me, it already would have.*

We sat side by side in brief silence. He nodded to himself.

"Not going to tell me, huh?"

"There's nothing to tell, Las."

More quiet. On the screen, breaking news unreeled. Accidental death (stack-retrievable) of some minor Harlan heirling in the Millsport wharf district, hurricane building in the Gulf of Kossuth, Mecsek to slash public health spending by end of year. I watched it without interest.

"Look, Micky." Lazlo hesitated. "I'm not saying I trust you, because I don't really. But I'm not like Orr. I'm not jealous about Sylvie. For me, you know, she's the skipper and that's it. And I do trust you to look after her."

"Thanks," I said drily. "And to what do I owe this honor?"

"Ah, she told me a little about how the two of you met. The Beards and everything. Enough to figure that—"

The door flexed back and Oishii emerged. He grinned and jerked a thumb back the way he'd come.

"All yours. See you in the bar."

We went in. I never found out what Lazlo had figured out or how far off the truth he might have been.

Shigeo Kurumaya was at his desk, seated. He watched us come in without getting up, face unreadable and body locked into a stillness that telegraphed his anger as clearly as a yell. Old school. Behind him, a holo made the illusion of an alcove in the 'fab wall where shadows and moonlight crawled back and forth around a barely visible scroll. On the desk, the datacoil idled at his elbow, casting stormy patterns of colored light across the spotless work surface.

"Oshima's ill?" he asked flatly.

"Yeah, she caught something off a co-op cluster in the highlands." Lazlo scratched his ear and looked around the empty chamber. "Not much going on here, huh? Locked down for the microbliz?"

"The highlands." Kurumaya wasn't going to be drawn. "Nearly seven hundred kilometers north of where you agreed to operate. Where you *contracted* to work cleanup."

Lazlo shrugged. "Well, look, that was the skipper's call. You'd have to—"

"You were under contract. More importantly, under obligation. You owed *giri* to the beachhead, and to me."

"We were under fire, Kurumaya-san." The lie came out, Envoy-smooth. Swift delight as the dominance conditioning took flight—it had been a while since I'd done this. "Following the ambush in the temple, our command software was compromised, we'd taken severe organic damage, to myself and another team member. We were running blind."

Quiet opened up in the wake of my words. Beside me, Lazlo twitched with something he wanted to say. I shot him a warning glance, and he stopped. The beachhead commander's eyes flickered between the two of us, settled finally on my face.

"You are Serendipity?"

"Yes."

"The new recruit. You offer yourself as spokesman?"

Tag the pressure point, go after it. "I, too, owe *giri* in this circumstance, Kurumaya-san. Without my companions' support, I would have died and been dismembered by karakuri in Drava. Instead, they carried me clear and found me a new body."

"Yes. So I see." Kurumaya looked down briefly at his desk and then back to me. "Very well. So far you have told me no more than the report your crew transmitted from within the Uncleared, which is minimal. You will please explain to me why, running blind as you were, you chose not to return to the beachhead."

This was easier. We'd batted it back and forth around campfires in the Uncleared for over a month, refining the lie. "Our systems were scrambled, but still partly functional. They indicated mimint activity behind us, cutting off our retreat."

"And presumably therefore threatening the sweepers you had undertaken to protect. Yet you did nothing to aid them."

"Jesus, Shig, we were fucking *blinded.*"

The beachhead commander turned his gaze on Lazlo. "I didn't ask for your interpretation of events. Be quiet."

"But—"

"We fell back to the northeast," I said, with another warning glance at the wincefish beside me. "As far as we could tell, it was a safe zone. And we kept moving until the command software came back online. By that time, we were almost out of the city, and I was bleeding to death. Of Jadwiga, we had only the cortical stack. For obvious reasons, we took a decision to enter the Uncleared and locate a previously mapped and targeted bunker with clone bank and sleeving capacity. As you know from the report."

"We? You were involved in that decision?"

"I was bleeding to death," I repeated.

Kurumaya's gaze turned downward again. "You may be interested to know that following the ambush you describe, there were no further sightings of mimint activity in that area."

"Yeah, that's 'cause we brought the fucking house down on them," snapped Lazlo. "Go dig that temple up, you'll find the pieces. Less a couple we had to take down hand-to-fucking-hand in a tunnel on our way out."

Again, Kurumaya favored the wincefish with a cold stare.

"There has not been time or manpower to excavate. Remote sensing indicates traces of machinery within the ruins, but the blast you triggered has conveniently obliterated most of the lower-level structure. If there—"

"*If*? Fucking *if*?"

"—were mimints as you claim, they would have been vaporized. The two in the tunnel have been found, and seem to corroborate the story you transmitted to us once you were safely removed to the Uncleared. In the meantime, you may also be interested to know that the sweepers you left behind *did* encounter karakuri nests several hours later and two kilometers farther west. In the ensuing suppression, there were twenty-seven deaths. Nine of them real, stack unrecovered."

"That is a tragedy," I said evenly. "But we would not have been able to prevent it. Had we returned with our injured and our damaged command systems, we would only have been a burden. Under the circumstances, we looked for ways to return to full operational strength as rapidly as possible instead."

"Yes. Your report says that."

He brooded for a few moments. I flickered another look at Lazlo, in case he was about to open his mouth again. Kurumaya's eyes lifted to meet mine.

"Very well. You are billeted along with Eminescu's crew for the time being. I will have a software medic examine Oshima, for which you will be billed. Allowing that her condition is stable, there will be a full investigation into the temple incident as soon as the weather clears."

"What?" Lazlo took a step forward. "You expect us to fucking hang around here while you dig up that mess? No fucking way, man. We're gone. Back to Tek'to on that fucking 'loader out there."

"Las—"

"I do not *expect* you to stay in Drava, no. I am ordering it. There is a command structure here, whether you like it or not. If you attempt to board the *Daikoku Dawn,* you will be stopped." Kurumaya frowned. "I would prefer not to be so direct, but if you force me to, I will have you confined."

"Confined?" For a couple of seconds, it was as if Lazlo hadn't heard the word before and was waiting for the command head to explain it to him. "Fucking *confined*? We take down five co-ops in the last month, over a dozen autonomous mimints, render safe an entire bunker full of nasty hardware, and *this* is the fucking thanks we get coming back in?"

Then he yelped and stumbled back, open palm jammed to one eye as if Kurumaya had just poked him in it. The command head got to his feet behind the desk. His voice was sibilant with suddenly uncapped rage.

"No. This is what happens when I can no longer trust the crews I am held responsible for." He jerked a glance at me. "You. Serendipity. Get him out of here, and convey my instructions to the rest of your companions. I do not expect to have this conversation again. Out, both of you."

Las was still clutching at his eye. I put a hand on his shoulder to guide him out, and he angrily shrugged it away. Muttering, he lifted a trembling finger to point at Kurumaya, then seemed to think better of it and turned on his heel. He made for the door in strides.

I followed him out. At the doorway, I looked back at the command head. It was hard to read anything in the taut face, but I thought I caught a waft of it coming off him nonetheless—rage at disobedience, worse still remorse at the failure to control both situation and self. Disgust at the way things had degenerated, in the command 'fab right here, right now, and maybe in the market free-for-all of the whole Mecsek Initiative. Disgust, for all I knew, at the way things were sliding for the entire damned planet.

Old school.

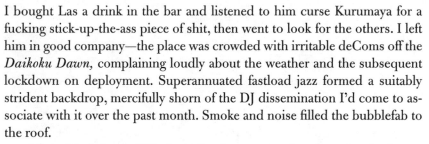

I bought Las a drink in the bar and listened to him curse Kurumaya for a fucking stick-up-the-ass piece of shit, then went to look for the others. I left him in good company—the place was crowded with irritable deComs off the *Daikoku Dawn,* complaining loudly about the weather and the subsequent lockdown on deployment. Superannuated fastload jazz formed a suitably strident backdrop, mercifully shorn of the DJ dissemination I'd come to associate with it over the past month. Smoke and noise filled the bubblefab to the roof.

I found Jadwiga and Kiyoka sitting in a corner, deep in each other's eyes and a conversation that looked a little intense to try to join. Jad told me, impatiently, that Orr had stayed with Sylvie in the accommodation 'fab and that Oishii was around somewhere, at the bar maybe, talking to someone last time she, anyway, somewhere over in the direction of her vaguely waving arm. I took the multiple hints and left the two of them to it.

Oishii wasn't really in the direction Jadwiga had pointed, but he was at the bar and he was talking to a couple of other deComs, only one of whom I recognized as being on his crew. He welcomed me with a grin and a lifted glass. Voice pitched over the noise.

"Get a grilling, did you?"

"Something like that." I lifted my hand to get attention behind the bar. "I get the impression Sylvie's Slipins have been pushing the line for a while now. You want a refill?"

Oishii looked judiciously at the level of his drink. "No, I'm okay. Pushing the line, you could say that. Not the most community-minded crew around, for sure. Still, they top the boards a lot of the time. You can live on that for a while, even with a guy like Kurumaya."

"Nice to have a reputation."

"Yeah, which reminds me. There's someone looking for you."

"Oh?" He was looking into my eyes as he told me. I quelled reaction and raised an eyebrow to go with the elaborately casual interest in my voice. Ordered a Millsport single malt from the barman and turned back to Oishii. "You get a name?"

"Wasn't me who spoke to him." The command head nodded at his non-crew companion. "This is Simi, lead wince for the Interruptors. Simi, that guy was asking around about Sylvie and her new recruit, you get a name?"

Simi squinted sideways for a moment, frowning. Then his face cleared and he snapped his fingers.

"Yeah, got it. Kovacs. Said his name was Kovacs."

CHAPTeR TWeLVe

Everything seemed to stop.

It was as if all the noise in the bar had abruptly frozen to arctic sludge in my ears. The smoke stopped moving; the pressure of the people behind me at the bar seemed to recede. It was a shock reaction I hadn't had from the Eishundo sleeve, even when locked in combat with the mimints. Across the dreamy quiet of the moment, I saw Oishii watching me intently, and I lifted the glass to my lips on autopilot. The single malt went down, burning, and as the warmth hit the pit of my stomach the world started up again just as suddenly as it had stopped. Music, noise, the shifting crush of people around me.

"Kovacs," I said. "Really?"

"You know him?" asked Simi.

"Heard of him." There wasn't much point in going for the deep lie. Not with the way Oishii was watching my face. I sipped at my drink again. "Did he say what he wanted?"

"Nah." Simi shook his head, clearly not that interested. "He was just asking where you were, if you'd gone out with the Slipins. Was a couple of days back, so I told him, yeah, you were all out in the Uncleared. He—"

"Did he—" I stopped myself. "Sorry, you were saying?"

"He seemed pretty concerned to talk to you. Persuaded someone, think it was Anton and the Skull Gang, to take him out into the Uncleared for a look. So you know this guy, right? He a problem for you?"

"Of course," said Oishii quietly. "Might not be the same Kovacs *you* know. It's a common enough name."

"There's that," I admitted.

"But you don't think so?"

I manufactured a shrug. "Seems unlikely. He's looking for me, I've heard of him. Most probable thing is, we've got some shared history."

Oishii's crew colleague and Simi both nodded dismissive, boozed-up assent. Oishii himself seemed more closely intrigued.

"And what have you heard about him, this Kovacs?"

This time the shrug was easier. "Nothing good."

"Yeah," Simi agreed sweepingly. "That's right. Seemed like a real hard-assed psycho motherfucker to me."

"Did he come alone?" I asked.

"Nah, whole squad of enforcer types with him. 'Bout four, five of them. Millsport accents."

Oh good. So this wasn't a local matter anymore. Tanaseda was living up to his promise. *A global writ for your capture.* And from somewhere they'd dug up—

You don't know that. Not yet.

Oh, come on. It has to be. Why use the name? Whose sense of humor does that sound like to you?

Unless—

"Simi, listen. He didn't ask for me by name, did he?"

Simi blinked at me. "Dunno, what is your name?"

"Okay. Never mind."

"Guy was asking after Sylvie," explained Oishii. "Her name, he knew. Knew the Slipins, seems like. But he really seemed interested in some new recruit Sylvie might have had in her team. And that name, he didn't know. Right, Simi?"

" 'S about it, yeah." Simi peered into his empty glass. I signaled the barman and got refills all around.

"So. These Millsport types. Any of them still around, you reckon?"

Simi pursed his lips. "Could be. Don't know, I didn't see the Skull Gang go out, don't know how much extra weight they were carrying."

"But it'd make sense," said Oishii softly. "If this Kovacs did his research, he'll know how hard it is to track movement in the Uncleared. It'd make sense to leave a couple of guys behind in case you came back." He paused, watching my face. "And to needlecast the news if you did."

"Yeah." I drained my glass and shivered slightly. Got up. "Think I need to talk to my crewmates. If you gentlemen will excuse me."

I shouldered my way back through the crowd until I reached Jadwiga and Kiyoka's corner again. They'd wrapped each other up in a passionate mouth-to-mouth embrace, oblivious to their surroundings. I slid into the seat next to them and tapped Jadwiga on the shoulder.

"Stop that, you two. We've got problems."

"Well," rumbled Orr. "I think you're full of shit."

"Really?" I kept a grip on my temper with an effort, wishing I'd just gone for full Envoy-effect persuasion instead of trusting my deCom colleagues with the use of their own decision-making faculties. "This is the yakuza we're talking about."

"You don't know that."

"Do the math. Six weeks ago we were collectively responsible for the death of a high-ranking yakuza's son and his two enforcers. And now there's someone looking for us."

"No. There's someone looking for *you*. Whether he's looking for the rest of us remains to be seen."

"Listen. All of you." Inclusive glance around the windowless billet they'd found for Sylvie. Spartan single berth, integral storage lockers in the walls, a chair in one corner. With the command head curled up on the bunk and her crew stood around, it was a tense, cramped space. "They know Sylvie, they've tied her to me. Oishii's pal said as much."

"Man, we wiped that room cleaner than—"

"I know, Jad, but it wasn't enough. They got witnesses who saw the two of us, peripheral video maybe, maybe something else. The point is, I know this Kovacs, and believe me, if we wait around for him to catch up with us, you're going to find out that it doesn't much matter whether he's looking for me, or Sylvie, or both of us. The man is an ex-Envoy. He'll take down everybody in this room, just to keep it simple."

That old Envoy terror—Sylvie was asleep, out on recuperative chemicals and sheer exhaustion, and Orr was too fired up with confrontation, but the rest of them flinched. Beneath the armored deCom cool, they'd grown up on the horror stories from Adoracion and Sharya, just like everybody else. The Envoys came and they tore your world apart. It wasn't that simple, of course; the truth was far more complex, and ultimately far more scary. But who in this universe wants the truth?

"What about we spike this ahead of time?" wondered Jadwiga. "Find Kovacs's holdout buddies in the beachhead and shut them down before they can transmit out."

"Probably too late, Jad." Lazlo shook his head. "We've been in a couple of hours. Anybody who wants to knows about it by now."

Gathering momentum. I stayed silent and watched it roll the way I wanted. Kiyoka weighed in, frowning.

"Anyway, we got no way to find these fuckers. Millsport accents and hard faces are plankton-standard around here. At a minimum, we'd need to case the beachhead datastack and"—she indicated Sylvie's fetal form—"we're in no position to do that."

"Even with Sylvie online, we'd be pushed," said Lazlo gloomily. "Way Kurumaya feels about us right now, he'll jump if we clean our teeth at the wrong voltage. I suppose that thing's intrusion-proofed."

He nodded at the personal space resonance scrambler perched on the chair. Kiyoka nodded back, slightly wearily I thought.

"State of the art, Las. Really. Picked it up in Reiko's Straight-to-Street before we shipped out. Micky, the point is, we're under virtual lockdown here. You say this Kovacs is coming for us. What do you suggest we do?"

Here we go.

"I suggest I get out of here tonight on the *Daikoku Dawn,* and I suggest I take Sylvie with me."

Quiet rocked the room. I tracked glances, gauged emotion, estimated where this was going.

Orr rolled his head on his neck, like a freak fighter warming up.

"You," he said deliberately, "can go fuck yourself."

"Orr—" said Kiyoka.

"No fucking way, Ki. No *fucking* way does he take her anywhere. Not on my watch."

Jadwiga looked at me narrowly. "What about the rest of us, Micky? What are we supposed to do when Kovacs turns up looking for blood?"

"Hide," I told her. "Pull some favors, get yourselves out of sight either somewhere in the beachhead or out in the Uncleared with someone else's crew if you can persuade them. Shit, you could even get Kurumaya to arrest you, if you trust him to keep you locked up safe."

"Hey, fuckhead, we can do all of that without handing Sylvie over to y—"

"Can you, Orr?" I locked gazes with the giant. "*Can you?* Can you wade back out into the Uncleared with Sylvie the way she is now? Who's going to carry her out there? What crew? What crew can afford the dead-weight?"

"He's right, Orr." Lazlo shrugged. "Even Oishii isn't going to go back out there with that on his back."

Orr looked around him, eyes flickering cornered.

"We can hide her here, in the—"

"Orr, you're not listening to me. Kovacs will tear this place apart to get to us. *I know him.*"

"Kurumaya—"

"Forget it. He'll go through Kurumaya like angelfire, if that's what it takes. Orr, there's only one single thing that'll stop him, and that's knowing that Sylvie and I are gone. Because then he won't have time to piss about looking for the rest of you. When we arrive in Tek'to, we make sure the news gets back to Kurumaya, and by the time Kovacs is here it'll be common knowledge around the beachhead that we skipped. That'll be enough to kick him out of here on the next 'loader."

More quiet, this time like something counting down. I watched them buy in, one by one.

"Makes sense, Orr." Kiyoka clapped the giant on the shoulder. "It isn't pretty, but it scans."

"At least this way, the skipper's out of the firing line."

Orr shook himself. "I don't fucking believe you people. Can't you see he's *trying* to scare you all?"

"Yeah, he's *succeeding* in scaring me," snapped Lazlo. "Sylvie's down. If the yakuza are hiring Envoy assassins, we're severely outclassed."

"We need to keep her safe, Orr." Jadwiga was staring at the floor as if digging a tunnel might be a good next move. "And we can't do it here."

"Then I'm going, too."

"I'm afraid that isn't going to be possible," I said quietly. "I figure Lazlo can get us in one of the life-raft launchers, the way he came aboard in Tek'to. But with the hardware you're carrying, the power source, penetrate the hull unauthorized, you're going to set off every leakage alarm the *Daikoku Dawn* has."

It was inspired guesswork, a blind leap off the rapid scaffolding of Envoy intuition, but it seemed to hit home. The Slipins looked back and forth at each other, and finally Lazlo nodded.

"He's right, Orr. No way can I get you up that chute quietly."

The ordnance giant stared at me for what seemed like a long time. Finally, he looked away, at the woman on the bed.

"If you hurt her in any way at all—"

I sighed. "The best way I know to hurt her, Orr, is to leave her here. Which I don't plan to do. So save the attitude for Kovacs."

"Yeah," said Jadwiga grimly. "And this is a promise. As soon as Sylvie's back online, we take that motherfucker and we—"

"Admirable," I agreed. "But a little premature. Plan your revenge later, okay? Right now let's just all concentrate on surviving."

● ● ●

Of course, it wasn't quite as easy as that.

When pressed, Lazlo admitted that security around the 'loader ramps at Kompcho was lax verging on laughable. At the Drava beachhead, with mimint assault a constant fear, the dockside would be sewn up tight with electronic intrusion countermeasures.

"So." I tried for patient calm. "You've never actually done this life-raft chute thing in Drava?"

"Well, yeah, once." Lazlo scratched his ear. "But I had some jamming help from Suki Bajuk."

Jadwiga snorted. "That little trollop."

"Hey, jealous. She's a fucking good command deCom. Even whiffed off her head, she greased the entry codes like—"

"Not all she greased that weekend, from what I hear."

"Man, just because she isn't—"

"Is she *here*?" I asked loudly. "Now, in the beachhead?"

Lazlo went back to scratching his ear. "Dunno. We could check, I guess, but—"

"It'll take forever," predicted Kiyoka. "And anyway, she may not be up for another code greasing, if she finds out what this is about. Helping you get your kicks is one thing, Las. Bucking Kurumaya's lockdown might not appeal so much, you know what I mean?"

"She doesn't have to know," said Jadwiga.

"Don't be a bitch, Jad. I'm not putting Suki in the firing line without—"

I cleared my throat. "What about Oishii?"

They all looked around at me. Orr's brow furrowed. "Maybe. He and Sylvie go back to the early days. Hired on as sprogs together."

Jadwiga grinned. "Sure, he'll do it. If Micky asks him."

"What?"

There were grins appearing on everyone's mouths now, it seemed. Welcome release to the building tension. Kiyoka sniggered behind a hand pressed to her nose. Lazlo looked elaborately at the ceiling. Stifled snorts of hilarity. Only Orr was too angry to join in the fun.

"Didn't you *notice* over the last couple of days, Micky?" Jadwiga, playing this one until it creaked. "Oishii likes you. I mean, he *really* likes you."

I looked around the cramped room at my companions and tried to match Orr for deadpan lack of amusement. Mostly, I was irritated at myself. I *hadn't* noticed, or at least hadn't identified the attraction for what—Jadwiga said—it was. For an Envoy, that was a serious failure to perceive exploitable benefit.

Ex-Envoy.

Yeah, thanks.

"That's good," I said evenly. "I'd better go talk to him, then."

"Yeah," Jadwiga managed, straight-faced. "See if he wants to give you a hand."

The laughter erupted, explosive in the confined space. An unwanted grin forced its way onto my mouth.

"You motherfuckers."

It didn't help. The hilarity scaled upward. On the bed, Sylvie stirred and opened her eyes at the sound. She propped herself up on one elbow and coughed painfully. The laughter drained out of the room as rapidly as it had come.

"Micky?" Her voice came out weak and rusty.

I turned to the bed. Caught out of the corner of one eye the venomous glare Orr fired at me. I leaned over her.

"Yeah, Sylvie. I'm here."

"What are you laughing for?"

I shook my head. "That's a very good question."

She gripped my arm with the same intensity as that night in Oishii's encampment. I steeled myself for what she might say next. Instead, she just shivered and stared at her fingers where they sank into the arm of the jacket I was wearing.

"I," she muttered. "It *knew* me. It. Like an old friend. Like a—"

"Leave her alone, Micky." Orr tried to shoulder me aside, but Sylvie's grip on my arm defeated the move. She looked at him uncomprehendingly.

"What's going on?" she pleaded.

I glanced sideways at the giant.

"You want to tell her?"

CHAPTeR THIRTeeN

Night fell across Drava in swathes of snow-chipped gloom, settling like a well-worn blanket around the huddled 'fabs of the beachhead and then the higher, angular ruins of the city itself. The microblizzard front came and went with the wind, brought the snow in thick, swirling wraps that plastered your face and got inside the neck of your clothing, then whirled away, thinning out to almost nothing, and then back again to dance in the funneled glare of the camp's Angier lamps. Visibility oscillated, went down to fifty meters and then cleared, went down again. It was weather for staying inside.

Crouched in the shadow of a discarded freight container at one end of the wharf, I wondered for a moment how the other Kovacs was coping, out in the Uncleared. Like me, he'd have the standard Newpest native's dislike for the cold, like me he'd be—

You don't know that, you don't know that's who he—

Yeah, right.

Look, where the fuck are the yakuza going to get hold of a spare personality copy of an ex-Envoy? And why the fuck would they take the risk? Under all that Old Earth ancestor crabshit veneer, in the end they're just fucking criminals. There's no way—

Yeah, right.

It's the itch we all live with, the price of the modern age. *What if?* What if, at some nameless point in your life, they copy you. What if you're stored somewhere in the belly of some machine, living out who knows what parallel virtual existence or simply asleep, waiting to be released into the real world.

Or already unleashed and out there somewhere. Living.

You see it in the experia flicks, you hear the urban myths of friends of friends, the ones who through some freak machine error end up meeting themselves in virtual or, less often, reality. Or the Lazlo-style conspiracy horror stories of military-authorized multiple sleeving. You listen, and you enjoy the existential shiver it sends up your spine. Once in a very long time, you hear one you might even believe.

I'd once met and had to kill a man who was double-sleeved.

I'd once met myself, and it hadn't ended well.

I was in no hurry to do it again.

And I had more than enough else to worry about.

Fifty meters down the dock, the *Daikoku Dawn* bulked dimly in the blizzard. She was a bigger vessel than the *Guns for Guevara,* by the look of her an old commercial 'loader, taken out of mothballs and regeared for deCom haulage. A whiff of antique grandeur hung about her. Light gleamed cozily from portholes and clustered in colder white and red constellations on the superstructure above. Earlier, there'd been a desultory trickle of figures up the gangways as the outgoing deComs went aboard, and lights at the boarding ramps, but now the hatches were closing up and the hoverloader stood isolated in the chill of the New Hok night.

Figures through the muffling swirl of white on black to my right. I touched the hilt of the Tebbit knife and cranked up my vision.

It was Lazlo, leading with a wincefish flex in his stride and a fierce grin on his snow-chilled face. Oishii and Sylvie in tow. Chemical functionality troweled across the woman's features, a more intense control in the other command head's demeanor. They crossed the open ground along the quayside and slipped into the shelter of the container. Lazlo scrubbed at his face with both hands and shook the melting snow from splayed fingers. He'd strapped his healing arm with a combat servosplint and didn't seem to be feeling any pain. I caught the blast of alcohol on his breath.

"Okay?"

He nodded. "Anyone who's interested, and a few who probably weren't, now knows Kurumaya's got us locked down. Jad's still in there, being loudly pissed off to anyone who'll listen."

"Oishii? You set?"

The command head regarded me gravely. "If you are. Like I said, you'll have five minutes max. All I can do without leaving traces."

"Five minutes is fine," said Lazlo impatiently.

Everybody looked at Sylvie. She managed a wan smile under the scrutiny.

"Fine," she echoed. "Scan up. Let's do it."

Oishii's face took on the abrupt inwardness of net time. He nodded minutely to himself.

"They're running the navigational systems at standby. Drives and systems test in two hundred and twenty seconds. You'd better be in the water by the time it kicks in."

Sylvie scraped up some hollow-eyed professional interest and a stifled cough.

"Hull security?"

"Yeah, it's on. But the stealth suits should throw back most of the scan.

And when you get down to water level, I'm going to pass you off as a couple of ripwings waiting for easy fish in the wake turbulence. Soon as the system test cycle starts, get up that chute. I'll vanish you on the internal scanners, and the navgear will assume it lost the rips in the wake. Same for you coming out, Lazlo. So stay in the water until she's well down the estuary."

"Great."

"You get us a cabin?" I asked.

The corner of Oishii's mouth twitched. "Of course. No luxury spared for our fugitive friends. Starboard lower are mostly empty, S-thirty-seven is all yours. Just push."

"Time to go," hissed Lazlo. "One at a time."

He flitted out of the cover of the container with the same accomplished wincefish lope I'd seen deployed in the Uncleared, was a moment exposed to view along the quay, and then swung himself lithely off the edge of the wharf and was gone again. I glanced sideways at Sylvie and nodded.

She went, less smoothly than Lazlo, but with an echo of the same grace. I thought I heard a faint splash this time. I gave her five seconds and followed, across the blizzard-shrouded open space, crouch to grab the top rung of the inspection ladder, and down, hand-over-rapid-hand, to the chemical stink of the estuary below. When I was immersed to the waist I let go and fell back into the water.

Even through the stealth suit and the clothes I wore over it, the shock of entry was savage. The cold stabbed through, clutched at my groin and chest, and forced the air out of my lungs through gritted teeth. The gecko-grip cells in my palms flexed their filaments in sympathy. I drew in a fresh breath and cast about in the water for the others.

"Over here."

Lazlo gestured from a corrugated section of the dock where he and Sylvie were clinging to a corroded cushioning generator. I slipped through the water toward them and let my genetech hands grip me directly to the evercrete. Lazlo breathed in jerkily and spoke through chattering teeth.

"Get ttto the stttern and tttread water between the dock and the hull. You'll sssee the launchers. Dddddon't dddrink the water, eh."

We traded clenched grins and kicked off.

It was hard work, swimming against a body reflex that wanted nothing more than to curl up tight against the cold and shudder. Before we'd gone halfway, Sylvie was falling behind and we had to go back for her. Her breath was coming in harsh bursts, her teeth were gritted, and her eyes were starting to roll.

"Cccan't hold it tttogether," she muttered as I turned in the water and Lazlo helped haul her onto my chest. "Dddon'ttt tell me we're whu-whu-wwinning, whu-winning fffucking wh-what?"

"Be okay," I managed through my own clamped jaws. "Hold on. Las, you keep going."

He nodded convulsively and flailed off. I struck out after him, awkward with the burden on my chest.

"Is there no other fucking choice?" she moaned, barely above a whisper.

Somehow I got us both to the rising bulk of the *Daikoku Dawn*'s stern where Lazlo was waiting. We paddled around into the crevice of water between the 'loader's hull and the dock, and I slapped a hand against the ever-crete wall to steady myself.

"Lllless thththan a mmminute," said Lazlo, presumably from reference to a retinal time display. "Lllet's hope Oishii'ssss ppplugged well in."

The hoverloader awoke. First the deep thrum as the antigrav system shifted from buoyancy to drive, then the shrill whining of the air intakes and the frrr-frump along the hull as the skirts filled. I felt the sideways tug of water swirling around the vessel. Spray exploded from the stern and showered me. Lazlo offered me one more wide-eyed grin and pointed.

"Up there," he yelled over the engine noise.

I followed the direction of his arm and saw a battery of three circular vents, hatches sliding out of the way in spiral petals. Maintenance lights showed inside the chutes, a chain-link inspection ladder up the 'loader's skirt to the lip of the first opening.

The note of the engines deepened, settling down.

Lazlo went first, up the rungs of the ladder and onto the scant, down-curving ledge offered by the top of the skirt. Braced against the hull above, he gestured down at me. I shoved Sylvie toward the ladder, yelled in her ear to climb, and saw with relief that she wasn't too far gone to do it. Lazlo grabbed her as soon as she got to the top, and after some maneuvering the two of them disappeared inside the shaft. I went up the ladder as fast as my numbed hands would pull me, ducked inside the chute and out of the noise.

A couple of meters above me I saw Sylvie and Lazlo, limbs splayed between protrusions on the inside of the launch tube. I remembered the wincefish's casual boast the first time I met him—*a seven-meter crawl up a polished steel chimney. Nothing to it.* It was a relief to see that, like a lot of Lazlo's talk, this had been an exaggeration. The tube was far from polished smooth, and there were numerous handholds built into the metal. I gripped experimentally at a scooped-out rung over my head and found I could haul myself up the incline without too much effort. Higher up. I found smoothly rounded bumps in the metal where my feet could take some of my body's weight. I rested against the faintly shuddering surface of the tube for a moment, recalled Oishii's five-minute maximum, and got moving again.

At the top of the chute, I found a bedraggled Sylvie and Lazlo braced on a finger-thin rim below an open hatchway filled with sagging orange canvasynth. The wincefish gave me a weary look.

"This is it." He thumped the yielding surface above his head. "This is the bottom-level raft. First to drop. You squeeze in here, get on top of the raft, and you'll find an inspection hatch that leads to the crawl space between levels. Just pop the nearest access panel and you're out in a corridor somewhere. Sylvie, you'd better go first."

We worked the canvasynth raft back from one edge of the hatchway, and warm, stale air gusted through into the chute. I laughed with sheer involuntary pleasure at the feel of it. Lazlo nodded sourly.

"Yeah, enjoy. Some of us are going back in the fucking water now."

Sylvie squeezed through, and I was about to follow when the wincefish tugged at my arm. I turned back. He hesitated.

"Las? Come on, man, we're running out of time."

"You." He lifted a warning finger. "I'm trusting you, Micky. You look after her. You keep her safe till we can get to you. Till she's back online."

"All right."

"I'm trusting you," he repeated.

Then he turned, unlatched his hold on the hatch, and was sliding rapidly down the curve of the launcher chute. As he disappeared at the bottom, I heard a faint whoop come floating back up.

I stared after him for what seemed like far too long, then turned and forced my way irritably through the canvasynth barrier between myself and my newly acquired responsibilities.

The memory rolled back over me.

In the bubblefab—

"You. Help me. Help me!"

Her eyes pin me. Muscles of her face taut with desperation, mouth slightly open. It's a sight that sends a deep and unlooked-for sense of arousal bubbling through my guts. She's thrown back the sleeping bag and leaned across to grab at me, and in the low light from the muffled illuminum lamp, under the reaching arm, I can see the slumped mounds her breasts make across her chest. It isn't the first time I've seen her like this—the Slipins don't suffer from coyness, and after a month of close-quarters camping across the Uncleared I could probably draw most of them naked from memory—but something about Sylvie's face and posture is suddenly deeply sexual.

"Touch me." The voice that is not hers rasps and prickles the hairs on my neck erect. "Tell me you're fucking real."

"Sylvie, you're not—"

Her hand shifts, from my arm to my face.

"I think I know you," she says wonderingly. "Black Brigade elect, right. Tetsu battalion. Odisej? Ogawa?"

The Japanese she's using is archaic, centuries out of date. I fight down the ghost of a shiver and stay in Amanglic. "Sylvie, listen to me—"

"Your name's Silivi?" Face racked with doubt. She shifts languages to meet me. "I don't remember, I, it's, I can't—"

"Sylvie."

"Yeah, Silivi."

"No," I say through lips that feel numb. "Your name's Sylvie."

"No." There's a sudden panic in her now. "My name's. My name's. They call me, they called me, they—"

Her voice stops up and her eyes flinch sideways, away from mine. She tries to get up out of the sleeping bag. Her elbow skids on the slick material of the lining, and she slips over toward me. I put out my arms and they're suddenly full of her warm, tightly muscled torso. The fist I snapped closed when she spoke opens involuntarily and the cortical stacks crushed inside it spill onto the floor. My palms press against taut flesh. Her hair moves and brushes at my neck and I can smell her, warmth and female sweat welling up out of the opened sleeping bag. Something trips again in the pit of my stomach, and maybe she can feel it, too, because she makes a low moaning sound into the flesh of my throat. Lower down in the confines of the bag, her legs shift around impatiently and then part for my hand as it slides down over one hip and between her thighs. I'm stroking her cunt before I realize what I'm doing, and she's damp to the touch.

"Yes." It gusts out of her. "Yes, that. There."

This time when her legs shift, her whole body tilts from the hips upward and her thighs spread as wide as the sleeping bag will allow. My fingers slip into her and she makes a tight hissing noise, pulls back from the clasp on my neck, and glares at me as if I've just stabbed her. Her fingers hook into my shoulder and upper arm. I rub long, slow ovals up inside her and feel her hips pump in protest at the deliberate pace of the motion. Her breath starts to come in shortening bursts.

"You're real," she mutters in between. "Oh, you're real."

And now her hands are moving over me, fingers tangling in the fastenings of my jacket, rubbing at my rapidly swelling crotch, gripping my face at the jaw. She seems unable to decide what to do with the body she's touching, and slowly the realization soaks through me that as she slides irretrievably into the crevasse of her orgasm, she's testing the assertion coming faster and faster across her lips you're real, you're real, you're fucking real, aren't you, you're real, oh, you're real, yes, you fucker, yes, yes, you're real you're fucking real—

Her voice locks up in her throat with her breath, and her stomach flexes her almost double with the force of the climax. She twines around me like the long lethal ribbons of belaweed out beyond Hirata's Reef, thighs clenched on my hand, body folded onto and over my chest and shoulder. From somewhere I know she's staring off that shoulder at the shadows on the far side of the bubblefab.

"My name is Nadia Makita," she says quietly.

And again, it's like current through my bones. Like the moment she grabbed my arm, the shock of the name. The litany kicks off in my head. It's not possible it's not—

I ease her loose from my shoulder, pull her back, and the motion dislodges a fresh wave of pheromones. Our faces are a couple of centimeters apart.

"Micky," *I mutter.* "Serendipity."

Her head darts forward like a bird's and her mouth fastens on mine, shutting off the words. Her tongue is hot and feverish, and her hands are working at my clothes again, this time with determined purpose. I struggle out of my jacket, unfasten the heavy canvasynth trousers, and her hand is burrowing in the gap as they open. Weeks in the Uncleared with barely the privacy to masturbate, a body kept on ice for centuries, it's all I can do to keep from coming as her hand closes around the shaft of my cock. She feels it and grins in the kiss, lips unsticking from mine, the faintest scrape of teeth on teeth and the grate of a chuckle deep in her throat. She kneels upright on the sleeping bag, balancing with one arm on my shoulder while the other stays between my legs, working. Her fingers are long and slim and hot and clammy with sweat, curling into a practiced grip and pumping gently up and down. I force the trousers down past my hips and lean backward to give her space. The ball of her thumb rubs back and forth against my glans like a metronome. I groan my lungs empty and instantly she slackens the pace almost to a halt. She presses her free hand flat on my chest, pushes me toward the floor while her grip on my hard-on tightens almost to crushing. Coiled muscle in my stomach keeps me flexed upright from the floor against the pressure she's exerting and damps down the pulsing need to come.

"Do you want to be inside me?" *she asks seriously.*

I shake my head. "Whatever, Sylvie. Whatever—"

A hard tug on the root of my cock. "My name is not Sylvie."

"Nadia. Whatever." *I grasp her by one curved ass cheek, one long hard thigh, and drag her forward onto me. She takes the hand from my chest, reaches down and spreads herself, then sinks slowly onto my cock. Our gasps blend at the contact. I search inside myself somewhere for a little Envoy control, settle my hands at her hips, and help her lift herself up and down. But this isn't going to last long. She reaches for my head and draws it down to one swollen breast, presses my face into the flesh, and guides me to the nipple. I suck it in and grip the other breast in one hand while she rises on her knees and rides us both to a climax that dims out my vision as it explodes through us.*

We collapse onto each other in the dimly lit bubblefab, slick with sweat and shuddering. The heater throws a reddish glow across our tangled limbs and tight-pressed bodies and there's a tiny sound in the gloom that could be this woman weeping or maybe just the wind outside, trying to find a way in.

I don't want to look her in the face to find out which.

● ● ●

In the bowels of the steadily thrumming *Daikoku Dawn,* we levered our-selves up from the crawl space into a corridor and made our dripping way to S37. As promised, the door flexed open at a push. Inside, lights sprang up in an unexpectedly luxurious space. I'd subconsciously been preparing myself for something along the lines of the spartan two-bunk accommodation we'd had on the *Guns for Guevara,* but Oishii had done us proud. The cabin was a well-appointed comfort class with an autoform bed space that could be pro-grammed to swell up as twin singles or a broad double. The fixtures showed wear, but a faint smell of mothball antibacterials clung to the air and made everything seem pristine.

"Vvvery nice," I chattered as I closed the door on lock. "Well done, Oishii. I appprove."

En-suite facilities were almost the size of another single cabin them-selves, complete with airblast dryer in the shower cabinet. We peeled naked and dumped our soaked clothing, then took turns rinsing the chill out of our bones first under a pummeling hail of hot water, then in a gently buffeting storm of warm air. It took a while, one at a time, but there was no hint of invi-tation in Sylvie's face as she stepped into the cabinet and so I stayed outside rubbing at my chilled flesh. At one point, watching her as she turned with water streaming down over her breasts and belly, trickling between her legs and tugging at a tiny tuft of drenched pubic hair, I felt myself beginning to harden. I moved quickly to pick up the jacket from my stealth suit and sat awkwardly with it covering my erection. The woman in the shower caught the movement and looked at me curiously, but she said nothing. No reason why she should. Last time I'd seen Nadia Makita, she'd been slipping into a postcoital drowse in a bubblefab out on the New Hok plains. Small, confi-dent smile on her lips, one arm wrapped loosely around my thigh. When I fi-nally pulled loose, she only turned over in the sleeping bag and muttered to herself.

She hadn't been back since.

And meanwhile you dressed and tidied up before the others got back, like a criminal trying to cover his tracks.

Met Orr's suspicious gaze with even Envoy deceit.

Slipped away with Lazlo to your own 'fab, to lie awake until dawn, disbe-lieving what you'd seen and heard and done.

Finally, Sylvie stepped out of the cabinet airblasted all but dry. With an effort I stopped myself staring at the suddenly sexualized landscape of her body and went to change places with her. She said nothing, just touched me on one shoulder with a loosely curled fist and frowned. Then she disap-peared into the cabin next door.

I stayed under the shower for nearly an hour, turning back and forth in water just below scalding, masturbating vaguely and trying not to think too much about what I was going to have to do when we got to Tekitomura. The *Daikoku Dawn* throbbed around me as she plowed southward. When I got out of the shower, I dumped our soaked clothing in the cabinet and left the airblast on full, then wandered through to the cabin. Sylvie was sleeping soundly beneath the coverlet of a bed space she'd programmed to mold as a double.

I stood and watched her sleep for a long time. Her mouth was open and her hair in chaotic disarray around her face. The ebony central cord had twisted so that it lay phallically across one cheek. Imagery I didn't need. I smoothed it back with the rest of the hair until her face was clear. She muttered in her sleep and moved the same loosely curled fist she'd punched me with up to touch her mouth. I stood and watched her some more.

She's not.

I know *she's not. It's not possi—*

What, just like it's not possible there's another Takeshi Kovacs out there hunting you? Where's your sense of wonder, Tak?

I stood and watched.

And in the end I shrugged irritably and climbed into the bed space beside her, and tried to sleep.

It took a while.

CHAPTeR FOURTeeN

The crossing back to Tekitomura was far faster than our trip out had been with the *Guns for Guevara*. Flogging steadily through the icy sea away from the New Hok coast, the *Daikoku Dawn* was constrained by none of the caution her sister ship had shown going in, and ran at full speed for the bulk of the voyage. According to Sylvie, we raised Tekitomura on the horizon not long after the sun came up and woke her through windows we'd forgotten to blank. Less than an hour after that we were crowding the ramps at Kompcho.

I woke to a sunlit cabin, stilled engines, and Sylvie, dressed and staring at me over arms folded across the backrest of a chair she'd straddled beside the bed space. I blinked at her.

"What?"

"What the fuck were you doing last night?"

I propped myself upright beneath the covers and yawned. "You want to expand on that a little? Give me some idea what you're talking about?"

"What I'm talking about," she snapped, "is waking up with your dick jammed against my spine like a fucking shard blaster barrel."

"Ah." I rubbed at one eye. "Sorry."

"Sure you are. Since when are we sleeping together?"

I shrugged. "Since you decided to mold the bed space as a double, I guess. What was I supposed to do, sleep on the floor like a fucking seal?"

"Oh." She looked away. "I don't remember doing that."

"Well, you did." I moved to get out of bed, noticed suddenly that the offending hard-on was still very much in evidence, and stayed where I was. I nodded at what she was wearing. "Clothes are dry, I see."

"Uhm, yeah. Thanks. For doing that." Hurriedly, maybe guessing my physical state, "I'll get yours for you."

We left the cabin and found our way up to the nearest debarkation hatch without meeting anyone. Outside in brilliant winter sunlight, a handful of security officers stood around on the ramp talking bottleback fishing and the waterfront property boom. They barely gave us a glance as we passed. We made the top of the ramp and slipped into the ebb and flow of the Kompcho morning crowds. A couple of blocks on and three streets back from the wharf run, we found a flophouse too seedy to have surveillance and rented a room that looked onto an internal courtyard.

"We'd better get you covered up," I told Sylvie, cutting a swath from one of the tatty curtains with the Tebbit knife. "No telling how many religious maniacs are still on the streets around here with a picture of you close to their hearts. Here, try this on."

She took the makeshift headscarf and examined it with distaste. "I thought the idea was to leave traces."

"Yeah, but not for the citadel's thugs. Let's not complicate our lives unnecessarily, eh."

"All right."

The room boasted one of the most battered-looking datascreen terminals I'd ever seen, sealed into a table over by the bed. I fired it up and killed the video option at my end, then placed a call to the Kompcho harbormaster. Predictably, I got a response construct—a blond woman in an early-twenties sleeve, fractionally too well groomed to be real. She smiled for all the world as if she could see me.

"How may I help you?"

"I have vital information for you," I told her. They'd print the voice for sure, but on a sleeve three centuries unused what were the chances of a trace? Even the company that built the damned thing didn't exist anymore. And with no face to work with, they'd have a hard time tracking me from incidental video footage. It ought to keep the trail cold enough to be safe for a while. "I have reason to believe that the recently arrived hoverloader *Daikoku Dawn* was infiltrated by two unauthorized passengers before departure from Drava."

The construct smiled again. "That's impossible, sir."

"Yeah? Then go check out cabin S-thirty-seven." I cut the call, turned off the terminal, and nodded at Sylvie, who was struggling to get the last of her riotous hair stuffed inside the curtain-cloth headscarf.

"Very becoming. We'll make a God-fearing maiden of modest demeanor out of you yet."

"Fuck off." The natural spring in the command-head mane was still pushing the edges of the scarf forward and out. She attempted to smear the cloth backward, out of the way of her peripheral vision. "You think they'll come here?"

"Eventually. But they've got to check the cabin, which they'll be in no hurry to do, crank call like that. Then check back with Drava, then trace the call. It'll be the rest of the day, maybe longer."

"So we're safe leaving this place untorched?"

I glanced around at the shabby little room. "Sniffer squad won't get much off what we've touched that isn't blurred with the last dozen occupants. Maybe just enough to confirm against the cabin traces. Not worth worrying about. Anyway, I'm short on incendiaries right now. You?"

She nodded at the door. "Get them anywhere on Kompcho wharf for a couple of hundred a crate."

"Tempting. Bit rough on the other guests, though."

A shrug. I grinned.

"Man, wearing that thing's really pissing you off, isn't it. Come on, we'll break the trail somewhere else. Let's get out of here."

● ● ●

We went down canted plastic stairs, found a side exit, and slipped into the street without checking out. Back into the pulsing flow of deCom commerce and stroll. Groups of sprogs clowning around on corners for attention, crew packs ambling along in the subtly integrated fashion I'd started to notice at Drava. Men, women, and machines carrying hardware. Command heads. Dealers of knocked-off chemicals and small novelty devices working from laid-out plastic sheets that shimmered in the sun. The odd religious maniac declaiming to passing jeers. Street entertainers aping the local trends for laughs, running cheap holo storytell and cheaper puppet shows, collection trays out for the sparse shower of near-exhausted credit chips and the hope that not too many spectators would fling the totally exhausted variety. We cut back and forth in it for a while, surveillance evasion habit on my part and a vague interest in some of the acts.

"—the bloodcurdling story of Mad Ludmila and the Patchwork Man—"

"—hardcore footage from the deCom clinics! See the latest in surgery and body testing to the *limits,* ladies and gentlemen, to the very *limits*—"

"—the taking of Drava by heroic deCom teams in full color—"

"—God—"

"—pirated full-sense repro. *One hundred percent* guaranteed genuine! Josefina Hikari, Mitzi Harlan, Ito Marriott, and many more. Get wet with the most beautiful First Family bodies in surroundings that—"

"—deCom souvenirs. Karakuri fragments—"

On one corner, a listing illuminum sign said WEAPONS in kanjified Amanglic lettering. We pushed through curtaining strung with thousands of minute shells and into the air-conditioned warmth of the emporium. Heavy-duty slug throwers and power blasters were mounted on walls alongside blown-up holo schematics and looping footage of battle joined with mimints in the bleak landscapes of New Hok. Reefdive ambient music bumped softly from hidden speakers.

Behind a high counter near the entrance, a gaunt-faced woman with command-head hair nodded briefly at us and went back to stripping down an aging plasmafrag carbine for the sprog who seemed to want to buy it.

"Look, you yank this back as far as it'll go and the reserve load drops. Right? Then you've got about a dozen shots before you have to reload. Very handy in a firefight. You go up against those New Hok karakuri swarms, you're going to be grateful you've got that to fall back on."

The sprog muttered something inaudible. I wandered about, looking for weapons you could conceal easily, while Sylvie stood and scratched irritably at her headscarf. Finally the sprog paid up and left with his purchase slung under one arm. The woman turned her attention to us.

"See anything you like?"

"Not really, no." I went up to the counter. "I'm not shipping out. Looking for something that'll do organic damage. Something I can wear to parties, you know."

"Oho. Fleshkiller, huh." The woman winked. "Well, that's not as unusual as you'd think around here. Let's see now."

She swung out a terminal from the wall behind the counter and punched up the datacoil. Now that I looked closely, I saw that her hair was lacking the central cord and some of the thicker associated tresses. The rest hung lank and motionless against her pallid skin, not quite hiding a long, looping scar across one corner of her forehead. The scar tissue gleamed in the light from the terminal display. Her movements were stiff and stripped of the deCom grace I'd seen in Sylvie and the others.

She felt me looking and chuckled without turning from the screen.

"Don't see many like me, eh? Like the song says—*see the deCom stepping lightly.* Or not stepping at all, right? Thing is, the ones like me, I guess we don't generally like to hang around Tek'to and be reminded what it was like to be whole. Got family, you go back to them, got a hometown you go back to it. And if I could *remember* if I had either or where it was, then I'd go." She laughed again, quietly, like water burbling in a pipe. Her fingers worked the datacoil. "Fleshkillers. Here we go. How about a shredder? Ronin MM-eighty-six. Snub-barrel shard blaster, turn a man to porridge at twenty meters."

"I said something I could wear."

"So you did. So you did. Well, Ronin don't make much smaller than the eighty-six in the monomol range. You want a slug gun maybe?"

"No, the shredder's good, but it's got to be smaller than that. What else have you got?"

The woman sucked at her upper lip. It made her look like a crone. "Well, there *are* some of the Old Home brands as well—H and K, Kalashnikov, General Systems. It's mostly preowned, see. Sprog trade-ins for mimint smasher gear. Look. Do you a GS Rapsodia. Scan-resistant and very slim, straps flat under clothing, but the butt's automold. Reacts to body heat, swells to fit your grip. How's that?"

"What's it ranged at?"

"Depends on dispersal. Tightened up I'd say you could take down a target at forty, fifty meters if your hands don't shake. On widespread, you don't get much range at all, but it'll clean out a room for you."

I nodded. "How much?"

"Oh, we can come to some arrangement on that." The woman winked clumsily. "Is your friend buying, too?"

Sylvie was on the other side of the emporium, half a dozen meters away. She heard and glanced across at the datacoil.

"Yeah, I'll take that Szeged squeeze gun you're listing there. Is that all the ammunition you've got for it?"

"Ah . . . yes." The older woman blinked at her, then back at the display. "But it'll take a Ronin SP-nine load, too, they made them compatible. I can throw in two or three clips if you—"

"Do that." Sylvie met my eyes with something in her face I couldn't read. "I'll wait outside."

"Good idea."

No one spoke again until Sylvie had brushed through the shell curtains and out. We both stared after her for a couple of moments.

"Knows her datacode," chirped the woman finally.

I looked at the lined face and wondered if there was anything behind the words. As a blatant demonstration of the deCom power her head had been scarfed to disguise, Sylvie reading detail off the datacoil at distance pretty much screamed for attention. But it wasn't clear what capacity this other woman's mind was running on, or if she cared about anything much beyond a quick sale. Or if she'd even remember us in a couple of hours' time.

"It's a trick," I said weakly. "Shall we, um, talk about price?"

● ● ●

Out in the street, I found Sylvie stood at the edges of a crowd that had gathered in front of a holoshow storyteller. He was an old man, but his hands were nimble on the display controls and a synth system taped to his throat modulated his voice to fit the different characters of his tale. The holo was a pale orb full of indistinct shapes at his feet. I heard the name *Quell* as I tugged at Sylvie's arm.

"Jesus, you think you could have been a bit *more* fucking obvious in there?"

"Ssh, shut up. Listen."

"Then Quell came out of the house of the belaweed merchant and she saw a crowd had gathered on the wharfside and were *shouting* and *gesturing furiously*. She couldn't see very clearly what was happening. Remember, my friends, this was on *Sharya* where the sun is a *violent actinic glare* and—"

"And where there's no such thing as belaweed," I muttered in Sylvie's ear.

"Sssh."

"—so she squinted and squinted but, well." The storyteller set aside his controls and blew on his fingers. In the holodisplay, his Quell figure froze and the scene around her began to dim. "Perhaps I will end here today. It is very cold and I am no longer a young man, my bones—"

A chorus of protests from the gathered crowd. Credit chips cascaded into the upturned webjelly sieve at the storyteller's feet. The man smiled and picked up the controls again. The holo brightened.

"You are very kind. Well, see then, Quell went among the shouting crowd and in the middle what did she see but a young whore, clothing all ripped and torn so that her *perfect, swollen, cherry-nippled breasts* stood *proudly* in the warm air for all to see and the soft dark hair between her *long, smooth thighs* was like a tiny frightened animal beneath the stoop of a *savage ripwing*."

The holo shifted for an obliging close-up. Around us, people stood on tiptoe. I sighed.

"And standing over her, *standing over her* were two of the *infamous* black-clad religious police, *bearded priests* holding *long knives*. Their eyes *gleamed* with bloodlust and their teeth *glinted* in their beards as they grinned at the *power* they held over this *helpless* woman's *young flesh*.

"But Quell placed herself between the points of those knives and the *exposed flesh* of the young whore and she said in a ringing voice: *what is this?* And the crowd fell silent at her voice. Again she asked: *what is this, why are you persecuting this woman,* and again all were silent, until finally one of the two black-clad priests stated that the woman had been caught in the sin of *whoring,* and that by the laws of Sharya she must be *put to death, bled* into the desert sand and her carcass thrown into the sea."

For just a second, the grief and rage flickered at the edges of my mind. I locked it down and breathed out, hard. The listeners around me were pressing closer, ducking and craning for a better view of the display. Someone crowded me, and I hooked an elbow back savagely into their ribs. A yelp, and aggrieved cursing that someone else hushed at.

"So Quell turned to the crowd and asked *who among you have not sinned with a whore at one time or another,* and the crowd grew quieter and would not meet her eyes. But one of the priests rebuked her angrily for her interference in a matter of holy law, and so she asked him directly *have you never been with a whore* and many in the crowd who knew him laughed so that he had to admit that he had. *But this is different,* he said, *for I am a man. Then,* said Quell, *you are a hypocrite,* and from her long gray coat she took a heavy-caliber revolver and she shot the priest in *both kneecaps.* And he collapsed to the ground *screaming.*"

Two tiny bangs and small, shrill shrieks from the holodisplay. The storyteller nodded and cleared his throat.

"*Someone take him away,* Quell commanded, and at this two of the crowd lifted the priest up and carried him off, still screaming. And I would guess that they were glad of the chance to leave because now these people were quiet and afraid when they saw the weapon in Quell's hand. And as the screaming died away in the distance, there was a silence broken only by the *moaning* of the seawind along the wharf, and the *whimpering* of the *comely whore* at Quell's feet. And Quell turned herself to the second priest and pointed the heavy-caliber revolver at him. *Now you,* she said. *Will you tell me that you have never been with a whore?* And the priest drew himself up and looked her back in the eye, and he said *I am a priest, and I have been with no woman in my life for I would not soil the sacredness of my flesh.*"

The storyteller struck a dramatic pose and waited.

"He's pushing his luck with this stuff," I murmured to Sylvie. "Citadel's only up the hill."

But she was oblivious, staring down at the little globe of the holodisplay. As I watched, she swayed a little.

Oh shit.

I grabbed at her arm, and she shook me off irritably.

"Well, Quell looked back at this black-clad man, and as she stared into his *hot jet eyes* she knew that he spoke the truth, that he was a man of his word. So she looked at the revolver in her hand and then back at the man. And she said *then you are a fanatic and cannot learn,* and she shot him in the face."

Another report, and the holodisplay splattered vivid red. Close-up on the ruined face of the priest. Applause and whoops among the crowd. The storyteller waited it out with a modest smile. At my side, Sylvie stirred like someone waking up. The storyteller grinned.

"Well now, my friends, as you can probably imagine, this *comely young whore* was *most* grateful to her rescuer. And when the crowd had carried the second priest's body away, she invited Quell to her *home* where she—" The storyteller set down his controls once more and wrapped his arms around himself. He gave a performance shudder and rubbed both hands on his upper arms. "But it really is too cold to continue, I fear. I could not—"

Amid a new chorus of protest, I took Sylvie by the arm again and led her away. She said nothing for the first few paces; then vaguely she looked back at the storyteller and then at me.

"I've never been to Sharya," she said in a puzzled voice.

"No, and I'm willing to bet neither has he." I looked her carefully in the eyes. "And Quell certainly never got to go there, either. But it makes a good story, right?"

CHAPTeR FIFTeeN

I bought a pack of disposable phones from an alcove dealer on the waterfront and used one of them to call Lazlo. His voice came through wavery with the squabble of antique jamming and counterjamming that floated over New Hok like smog from some early-millennium city on Earth. The wharfside noises around me didn't help much. I pinned the phone hard against my ear.

"You'll have to speak up," I told him.

"... *said* she's still not well enough to use the net, then?"

"She says not. But she's holding up okay. Listen, I've set the traces. You can expect a very pissed-off Kurumaya to come battering down your door later today. Better start practicing your alibis."

"Who, me?"

I grinned despite myself. "Any sign of this Kovacs then?"

His reply was inaudible behind a sudden thicket of static and flutter.

"Say again?"

"... in this morning, said he saw the Skull Gang up near Sopron yesterday with some faces he didn't know, looked li— ... south at speed. Probably get in sometime tonight."

"All right. When Kovacs does show up, you watch yourselves. The man is a dangerous piece of shit. You keep it tight. Scan up."

"Will do." A long, static-laced pause. "Hey, Micky, you're taking good care of her, right?"

I snorted. "No, I'm about to scalp her and sell off the spare capacity to a data brokerage. What do *you* think?"

"I know you ca—" Another wave of distortion squelched his voice. "... f not, then get her to someone who can help."

"Yeah, we're working on that."

"... Millsport?"

I guessed at content. "I don't know. Not yet, at any rate."

"If that's what it takes, man." His voice was fading out now, faint with distance and wrenched with the jamming. "*Whatever* it takes."

"Las, I'm losing you. I've got to go."

". . . an up, Micky."

"Yeah, you, too. I'll be in touch."

I cut the connection, took the phone away from my ear, and weighed it in my hand. I stared out to sea for a long time. Then I dug out a fresh phone and dialed another number from decades-old memory.

●●●

Like a lot of the towns on Harlan's World, Tekitomura clung to the skirts of a mountain range up to its waist in the ocean. Available space for building on was scarce. Back around the time that Earth was gearing up for the Pleistocene ice age, it seems that Harlan's World suffered a rapid climatic change in the opposite direction. The poles melted to ragged remnants, and the oceans rose to drown all but two of the little planet's continents. Mass extinctions followed, among them a rather promising race of tusked shore dwellers who, there's some evidence to suggest, had developed rudimentary stone tools, fire, and a religion based on the complicated gravitational dance of Harlan's World's three moons.

It wasn't enough to save them, apparently.

The colonizing Martians, when they arrived, didn't seem to have a problem with the limited terrain. They built intricate, towering eyries directly into the rock of the steepest mountain slopes and largely ignored the small nubs and ledges of land available at sea level. Half a million years later, the Martians were gone but the ruins of their eyries endured for the new wave of human colonizers to gawp at and leave mostly alone. Astrogation charts unearthed in abandoned cities on Mars had brought us this far, but once we arrived we were on our own. Unwinged, and denied much of our usual skygoing technology by the orbitals, humanity settled for conventional cities on two continents, a sprawling multi-islanded metropolis at the heart of the Millsport Archipelago, and small, strategically located ports elsewhere to provide linkage. Tekitomura was a ten-kilometer strip of densely built waterfront, backed up as far as the brooding mountains behind would allow and thereafter thinning out to nothing. On a rocky foothill, the citadel glowered over the skyline, perhaps aspiring in its elevation toward the semi-mystical status of a Martian ruin. Farther back, the narrow mountain tracks blasted by human archaeologue teams threaded their way up to the real thing.

There were no archaeologues working the Tekitomura sites anymore. Grants for anything not related to cracking the military potential of the orbitals had been cut to the bone, and those Guild Masters not absorbed by the military contracting had long since shipped out to the Latimer system on the hypercast. Pockets of stubborn and largely self-funding wild talent held out at a few promising sites near Millsport and points south, but on the mountainside above Tekitomura, the dig encampments sat forlorn and empty, as abandoned as the skeletal Martian towers they had been built next to.

"Sounds too good to be true," I said as we bought provisions in a water-front straight-to-street. "You're sure we're not going to be sharing this place with a bunch of teenage lovebirds and wirehead derelicts?"

For answer, she gave me a significant look and tugged at a single lock of her hair that had escaped from the cling of the headscarf. I shrugged.

"All right then." I hefted a sealpack of amphetamine cola. "Cherry-flavored okay?"

"No. It tastes like shit. Get the plain."

We bought packs to carry the provisions, picked an upward-sloping street out of the wharf district more or less at random, and walked. In under an hour, the noise and buildings began to fade out behind us and the incline grew steeper. I kept glancing across at Sylvie as our pace slacked off and our steps became more deliberate, but she showed no sign of wavering. If any-thing, the crisp air and cold sunlight seemed to be doing her good. The tense frown that had flitted on and off her face all morning ironed out, and she even smiled once or twice. As we climbed higher, the sun glinted off exposed min-eral traces in the surrounding rocks, and the view became worth stopping for. We rested a couple of times to drink water and gaze out over the shoreline sprawl of Tekitomura and the sea beyond.

"Must have been cool to be a Martian," she said at one point.

"I suppose."

The first eyrie crept into view on the other side of a vast rock buttress. It towered the best part of a kilometer straight up, all twists and swellings that were hard to look at comfortably. Landing flanges rolled out like tongues with slices cut out of them; spires sported wide, vented roofing hung with roost-bars and other less identifiable projections. Entrances gaped, an anarchic va-riety of oval-derived openings from long, slim, vaginal to plumped-up heart shape and everything between. Cabling dangled everywhere. You got the fleeting but repeating impression that the whole structure would sing in a high wind, and maybe somehow revolve like a gargantuan wind chime.

On the approach track, the human structures huddled small and solid, like ugly puppies at the feet of a fairy-tale princess. Five cabins in a style not much more recent than the relics on New Hok, all showing the faint blue in-terior light of damped-down automated systems. We stopped at the first one we came to and dumped our packs. I squinted back and forth at angles of fire, tagging potential cover for any attackers and thinking about delivery solu-tions that would beat it. It was a more or less automatic process, the Envoy conditioning killing time the way some people whistle through their teeth.

Sylvie ripped off her headscarf and shook her hair free with obvious relief.

"Be a minute," she said.

I considered my semi-instinctive assessment of the dig site's defensibility. On any planet where you could go up in the air easily, we'd be a sitting target. But on Harlan's World, the normal rules don't apply. Top mass limit on flying machines is a six-seat helicopter running an antique rotor-motor lift, *no* smart systems and *no* mounted beam weaponry. Anything else gets turned into midair ash. Likewise individual fliers in antigrav harnesses or nanocopters. The angelfire restrictions are, it appears, as much about a level of technology as physical mass. Add to that a height limit of about four hundred meters, which we were already well above, and it was safe to assume that the only way anyone would be approaching us was on foot up the path. Or climbing the sheer drop alongside, which they were very welcome to do.

Behind me, Sylvie grunted in satisfaction, and I turned to see the cabin door flex itself open. She gestured ironically.

"After you, Professor."

The blue standby light flickered and blinked up to white as we carried our packs inside, and from somewhere I heard the whisper of aircon kicking in. A datacoil spiraled awake on the table in one corner. The air reeked of antibacterials, but you could smell that it was shifting as the systems registered occupancy. I shoved my pack into a corner, peeled off my jacket, and grabbed a chair.

"Kitchen facilities are in one of the others," Sylvie said, wandering about and opening internal doors. "But most of this stuff we bought is self-heating anyway. And everything else we need, we've got. Bathroom there. Beds in there, there, and there. No automold, sorry. Specs I ran into when I was doing the locks say it sleeps six. Datasystems wired in, linked directly into the global net through the Millsport University stack."

I nodded and passed my hand idly through the datacoil. Opposite me, a severely dressed young woman shimmered into sudden existence. She made a quaint formal bow.

"Professor Serendipity."

I glanced at Sylvie. "Very funny."

"I am Dig Three-oh-one. How may I help you?"

I yawned and looked around the room. "Does this place run any defensive systems, Dig?"

"If you are referring to weapons," said the construct delicately, "I am afraid not. Discharge of projectiles or ungoverned energy so close to a site of such xenological significance would be unpardonable. However, all site units do lock on a coding system that is extremely hard to break."

I shot another glance at Sylvie. She grinned. I cleared my throat.

"Right. What about surveillance? How far down the mountain do your sensors reach?"

"My awareness range covers only the site and ancillary buildings. However, through the totality of the global datalink, I can access—"

"Yeah, thanks. That'll be all."

The construct winked out, leaving the room behind looking momentarily gloomy and still. Sylvie stepped across to the main door and thumbed it closed. She gestured around.

"Think we'll be safe here?"

I shrugged, remembering Tanaseda's threat. *A global writ for your capture.* "As safe as anywhere else I can think of right now. Personally, I'd be heading out for Millsport tonight, but that's exactly why—"

I stopped. She looked at me curiously.

"Exactly why what?"

Exactly why we're sticking with an idea you came up with and not me. Because anything I come up with, there's a good chance he's *going to come up with, too.*

"Exactly what they'll expect us to do," I amended. "If we're lucky they'll skip right past us on the fastest transport south they can arrange."

She took the chair opposite me and straddled it.

"Yeah. Leaving us to do what in the meantime?"

"Is that a proposition?"

It was out before I realized I'd said it. Her eyes widened.

"You—"

"Sorry. I'm sorry, that was. A joke."

As a lie, it would have got me thrown out of the Envoys to howls of derision. I could almost see Virginia Vidaura shaking her head in disbelief. It wouldn't have convinced a Loyko monk shot up with credence sacrament for Acceptance Fortnight. And it certainly didn't convince Sylvie Oshima.

"Look, Micky," she said slowly. "I know I owe you for that night with the Beards. And I like you. A lot. But—"

"Hey, seriously. It was a joke, okay. A bad joke."

"I'm not saying I haven't thought about it. I think I even dreamed about it a couple of nights ago." She grinned and something happened in my stomach. "You believe that?"

I manufactured another shrug. "If you say so."

"It's just." She shook her head. "I don't know you, Micky. I don't know you any better than I did six weeks ago, and that's a little scary."

"Yeah, well; changed sleeves. That can—"

"No. That's not it. You're locked up, Micky. Tighter than anyone I've ever met, and believe me I've met some fucked-up cases in this business. You walked into that bar, Tokyo Crow, with nothing but that knife you carry and you killed them all like it was a habit. And all the time, you had this little smile." She touched her hair, awkwardly it seemed to me. "This stuff, I get pretty much total recall when I want it. I saw your face, I can still see it now. You were smiling, Micky."

I said nothing.

"I don't think I want to go to bed with someone like that. Well," she smiled a little herself. "That's a lie. Part of me does, part of me *really* wants to. But that's a part I've learned not to trust."

"Probably very wise."

"Yeah. Probably." She shook hair back from her face and tried on a firmer smile. Her eyes hit mine again. "So you went up to the citadel and you took their cortical stacks. What for, Micky?"

I smiled back. Got up from the chair. "You know, Sylvie, part of me really wants to tell you. But—"

"All right, all right—"

"—it's a part of me I've learned not to trust."

"Very witty."

"I try. Look, I'm going to go check a couple of things outside before it starts getting dark. Be back in a while. You think you still owe me for the Beards, do me a small favor while I'm gone. Try to forget I came on quite as crass as I did just now. I'd really appreciate that."

She looked away, at the datacoil. Her voice was very quiet.

"Sure. No problem."

No, there's a problem. I bit back the words as I made my way to the door. *There really fucking is. And I still have no idea what to do about it.*

The second call picks up almost at once. A brusque male voice, not interested in talking to anyone.

"Yeah?"

"Yaroslav?"

"Yeah." Impatiently. "Who's this?"

"A little blue bug."

Silence opens like a knife wound behind the words. Not even static to cover it. Compared with the connection I had with Lazlo, the line is crystal clear. I can hear the shock at the other end.

"Who is this?" His voice has shifted completely. Hardened like sprayed evercrete. "Enable the videofeed, I want to see a face."

"Wouldn't help you much. I'm not wearing anything you'd recognize."

"Do I know you?"

"Let's just say you didn't have much faith in me when I went to Latimer, and I lived up to that lack of faith perfectly."

"You! You're back on the World?"

"No, I'm calling from orbit. What the fuck do you think?"

Long pause. Breathing on the line. I look up and down the Kompcho wharf with reflexive caution.

"What do you want?"

"You know what I want."

Another hesitation. "She's not here."

"Yeah, right. Put her on."

"I mean it. She left." There's a catch in the throat as he says it—enough to believe him. "When did you get back?"

"A while ago. Where's she gone?"

"I don't know. If I had to guess . . ." His voice dies off in breath blown through slack lips. I shoot a glance at the watch I ransacked from the bunker in the Uncleared. It's been keeping perfect time for three hundred years, indifferent to human absence. After years of chipped-in time displays, it still feels a little odd, a little archaic.

"You do have to guess. This is important."

"You never told anyone you were coming back. We thought—"

"Yeah, I'm not much for homecoming parties. Now guess. Where's she gone?"

I can hear the way his lips tighten. "Try Vchira."

"Vchira Beach? Oh come on."

"Believe what you like. Take it or leave it."

"After all this time? I thought—"

"Yeah, so did I. But after she left, I tried to—" He stops. Click in his throat as he swallows. "We still had joint accounts. She paid hard-class passage south on a Kossuth speed freighter, bought herself a new sleeve when she got there. Surfer specs. Cleaned out her account to make the price. Burned it all. She's, I know she's down there with fucking—"

It chokes off. Thick silence. Some corroded vestige of decency makes me wince. Keeps my voice gentle.

"So you think Brasil's still around, huh?"

"What changes on Vchira Beach?" he asks bitterly.

"All right, Yaros. That's all I need. Thanks, man." A cranked eyebrow at my own words. "You take it easy, huh."

He grunts. Just as I'm about to kill the connection, he clears his throat and starts to speak.

"Listen, if you see her. Tell her . . ."

I wait.

"Ah, fuck it." And he hangs up.

Daylight fading.

Below me, lights were starting to come on across Tekitomura as night breathed in from the sea. Hotei sat fatly on the western horizon, painting a dappled orange path across the water toward the shore. Marikanon hung coppery and bitten at one edge overhead. Out to sea, the running lights of sweepers already studded the deeper gloom. Faintly, the sounds of the port floated up to me. No sleep at deCom.

I glanced back toward the archaeologue cabin, and the Martian eyrie caught at the corner of my eye. It rose massive and skeletal into the darkening sky on my right, like the bones of something long dead. The copper-orange mix of moonlight fell through apertures in the structure and emerged at sometimes surprising angles. There was a cold breeze coming in with the night, and the dangling cables stirred idly on it.

We avoid them because we can't make much use of them on a world like this, but I wonder if that's the whole story. I knew an archaeologue once who told me human settlement patterns avoid the relics of Martian civilization like this on every world in the Protectorate. *It's instinctive,* she told me. *Atavistic fear. Even the dig towns start to die as soon as the excavations stop. No one stays around from choice.*

I stared into the maze of shattered moonlight and shadow made by the eyrie, and I felt a little of that atavistic fear seeping into me. It was all too easy to imagine, in the failing light, the slow-paced strop of broad wings and a spiral of raptor silhouettes turning against the evening sky above, bigger and more angular than anything that had flown on Earth in human memory.

I shrugged off the thought, irritably.

Let's just focus on the real problems we've got, eh, Micky? It's not like there aren't enough of them.

The door of the cabin flexed open and light spilled out, making me abruptly aware of how chilly the air had turned.

"You coming in to eat something?" she asked.

CHAPTeR SIXTeeN

Time on the mountain did nothing much to help.
The first morning I slept in, but it left me headachy and vague when I finally ventured out of the bedroom. Eishundo Organics didn't design their sleeves for decadence, it seemed. Sylvie was not around, but the table was littered with breakfast items of one sort or another, tabs mostly pulled. I poked around in the debris and found an unused coffee canister, tabbed it, and drank it standing at the window. Half-recalled dreams skittered about in the back of my head, mostly cell-deep stuff about drowning. Legacy of the overlong time the sleeve had been tanked—I'd had the same thing at the beginning in the Uncleared. Mimint engagement and the rapid flow of life with Sylvie's Slipins had damped it out in favor of more conventional flight-and-fight scenarios and reconstituted gibberish from the memories of my own overlaid consciousness.

"You are awake," said Dig 301, glimmering into existence at the edges of my vision.

I glanced over at her and raised my coffee canister. "Getting there."

"Your colleague left a message for you. Would you like to hear it?"

"I suppose."

"Micky, I'm going for a walk into town." Sylvie's voice came out of the construct's mouth without a corresponding shift in visuals. In my fragile state of wakefulness, it hit me harder than it should have. Spikily incongruous, and an unwelcome reminder of my central problem. *"Bury myself in the datawash down there. I want to see if I can get the net up and running, maybe use it to call through to Orr and the others. See what's going on over there. I'll bring back some stuff.* Message ends."

The sudden reemergence of the construct's own voice made me blink. I nodded and carried my coffee to the table. Cleared some of the breakfast litter away from the datacoil and brooded on it for a while. Dig 301 hovered at my back.

"So I can get into Millsport University through this, right? Search their general stack?"

"It will be quicker if you ask me," said the construct modestly.

"All right. Do me a précis search on," I sighed. "Quellcrist F—"

"Commencing." Whether out of boredom at the years of disuse or just poor intonation recognition, the construct was already off and running. The datacoil brightened and expanded. A miniature copy of Dig 301's head and shoulders appeared near the top and started in on the précis. Illustrative images tumbled into the space beneath. I watched, yawning, and let it run. "Found, one, Quellcrist, also Qualgrist, native Harlan's World amphibious weed. Quellcrist is a species of shallow-water seaweed, ocher in color, found mostly in temperate zones. Though containing some nutrients, it does not compare well in this with Earth-origin or purpose-bred hybrid species and is not therefore considered a sufficiently economic food crop to cultivate."

I nodded. Not where I wanted to start, but—

"Some medicinal substances may be extracted from mature Quellcrist strands, but outside certain small communities in the south of the Millsport Archipelago, the practice is uncommon. Quellcrist is in fact remarkable only for its unusual life cycle. If and when stranded in waterless conditions for long periods of time, the plant's pods dry out to a black powder, which can be carried by the wind over hundreds of kilometers. The remainder of the plant dies and decays, but the Quellcrist powder, upon coming into contact with water once more, reconstitutes into microfronds from which a whole plant may grow in a matter of weeks.

"Found, two, Quellcrist Falconer, *nom de guerre* of Settlement-years insurgent leader and political thinker Nadia Makita, born Millsport, April eighteenth, forty-seven (Colonial Reckoning), died October thirty-third, one-oh-five. Only child of Millsport journalist Stefan Makita and marine engineer Fusako Kimura. Makita studied demodynamics at Millsport University and published a controversial master's thesis, 'Gender Role Leakage and the New Mythology,' as well as three collections of verse in Stripjap, which quickly attained cult status among the Millsport literati. In later life—"

"Can you give me a little closer focus here, Dig?"

"In the winter of sixty-seven, Makita left academia, reputedly turning down both a generous offer of a research post within the faculty of social sciences and literary patronage from a leading member of the First Families. Between October sixty-seven and May seventy-one, she traveled widely on Harlan's World, supported partly by her parents and partly through a variety of menial jobs including belaweed cutter and ledgefruit harvester. It is generally thought that Makita's experiences among these workers helped to harden her political convictions. Pay and conditions for both groups were uniformly poor, with debilitating illnesses common on the belaweed farms and fall fatalities high among the ledgefruit workers.

"In any event, by the beginning of sixty-nine, Makita was publishing articles in the radical journals *New Star* and *Sea of Change* in which a clear departure can be traced from the liberal reformist tendency she had evinced as a student (and to which her parents both subscribed). In its place, she proposed a new revolutionary ethic that borrowed from existing strands of extremist thought but was remarkable for the vitriol with which said strands were themselves savagely critiqued almost as much as ruling-class policy. This approach did nothing to endear her to the radical intelligentsia of the period, and she found herself, though recognized as a brilliant thinker, increasingly isolated from the revolutionary mainstream. Lacking a descriptor for her new political theory, she named it Quellism via the article 'The Occasional Revolution,' in which she argued that modern revolutionaries *must when deprived of nourishment by oppressive forces blow away across the land like Quellcrist dust, ubiquitous and traceless but bearing within them the power of revolutionary regeneration where- and whensoever fresh nourishment may arise.* It is generally accepted that her own adoption of the name *Quellcrist* followed shortly after and derives from this same source of inspiration. The origin of the surname *Falconer,* however, remains in dispute.

"With the outbreak of the Kossuth belaweed riots in May seventy-one and the resulting crackdown, Makita made her first appearance as a guerrilla in—"

"Hold it." The canister coffee wasn't great and the steady march of comfortably familiar fact had grown hypnotic as I sat there. I yawned again and got up to toss the canister. "Okay, maybe not that close-focused after all. Can we skip farther forward?"

"A revolution," said Dig 301 obligingly, "which the newly ascendant Quellists could not hope to win while holding down internal opposition from—"

"Farther than that. Let's get to the second front."

"Fully twenty-five years later, that seemingly rhetorical boast now at last came to fruition as a working axiom. To use Makita's own imagery, the Quellcrist powder that Konrad Harlan's self-described harrowing storm of justice had blown far and wide in the aftermath of the Quellist defeat now sprouted new resistance in a dozen different places. Makita's second front began exactly as she had predicted it would, but this time the insurgency dynamic had shifted beyond recognition. In the context of . . ."

Digging around in the packs for more coffee, I let the narrative wash over me. This, too, I knew. By the time of the second front, Quellism was no longer the new fish on the reef. A generation of quiet incubation under the heel of the Harlanite crackdown had made it the only radical force left on the World. Other tendencies brandished their guns or sold their souls and were taken down all the same, stripped back to a bitter and disillusioned rump of has-beens by Protectorate-backed government forces. The Quellists meanwhile simply slipped away, disappeared, abandoned the struggle, and got on with living their lives as Nadia Makita had always argued they should be prepared to do. *Technology has given us access to time scales of life our ancestors could only dream of—we must be prepared to use that time scale, to live on that time scale, if we are to realize our own dreams.* And twenty-five years later, back they came, careers built, families formed, children raised, back to fight again, not so much aged but seasoned, wiser, tougher, stronger, and fed at core by the whisper that persisted at the heart of each individual uprising; the whisper that Quellcrist Falconer herself was back.

If the semi-mythical nature of her twenty-five-year existence as a fugitive had been difficult for the security forces to get to grips with, Nadia Makita's return was worse. She was fifty-three years old but sleeved in new flesh, impossible even for intimate acquaintances to identify. She stalked through the ruins of the previous revolution like a vengeful ghost, and her first victims were the backbiters and betrayers from within the ranks of the old alliance. This time, there would be no factional squabbles to diffract the focus, hamstring the Quellist lead, and sell her out to the Harlanites. The neoMaoists, the Communitarians, the New Sun Path, the Parliament Gradualists, and the Social Libertarians: she sought them out as they sat in their dotage, muttering over their respective fumbled grabs at power, and she slaughtered them all.

By the time she turned on the First Families and their tame assembly, it was no longer a revolution.

It was the Unsettlement.

It was a war.

Three years, and the final assault on Millsport.

I tabbed the second coffee and drank it while Dig 301 read the story to its close. As a kid, I'd heard it countless times and always hoped each telling for a last-minute reversal, a reprieve from the inevitable tragedy.

"With Millsport firmly in the hands of government forces, the Quellist assault broken, and a moderate compromise being brokered in the assembly, Makita perhaps believed that her enemies would have other more pressing matters to attend to before hunting her down. She had above all believed in their love of expediency, but faulty intelligence led her to misjudge the vital role her own capture or elimination had to play in the peace accord. By the time the error was realized, flight was all but impossible . . ."

Scratch the *all but.* Harlan sent more warships to ring the Alabardos Crater than had been deployed in any single naval engagement of the war. Crack helicopter pilots flew their craft at the upper edges of the four-hundred-meter limit with semi-suicidal brinkmanship. Spec ops snipers crammed inside, armed with weapons as heavy as it was thought the orbitals' parameters would permit. Orders were to bring down any escaping aircraft by all and any means including, if necessary, midair collision.

"In a final, desperate attempt to save her, Makita's followers risked a high-level flight in a stripped-down jetcopter that it was believed the orbital platforms might ignore. However—"

"Yeah, okay, Dig. That'll do." I drained my coffee. However, they fucked up. However, the plan was flawed (or possibly a deliberate betrayal). However, a lance of angelfire lashed down from the sky over Alabardos and carved the jetcopter into a flash-burned midair image of itself. However, Nadia Makita floated gently down to the ocean as randomized organic molecules among metallic ash. I didn't need to hear it again. "What about the escape legends?"

"As with all heroic figures, legends about Quellcrist Falconer's secret escape from Real Death are rife." Dig 301's voice seemed faintly tinged with reproach, but that might have been my groggy imagination. "There are those who believe she never entered the jetcopter in the first place and that later she slipped away from Alabardos disguised among the occupying ground troops. More credible theories derive from the idea that at some point before her death, Falconer's consciousness was backed up and that she was revived once the postwar hysteria had died down."

I nodded. "So where would they have stored her?"

"Beliefs vary." The construct raised one elegant hand and extended slim fingers in sequence. "Some claim she was needlecast offworld, either to a deep-space datavault—"

"Oh yeah, that's likely."

"—or to another of the Settled Worlds where she had friends. Adoracion and Nkrumah's Land are the favorites. Another theory suggests that she was stored after sustaining a combat injury in New Hokkaido from which she was expected to die. That when she recovered, her followers abandoned or forgot the copy—"

"Yep. As you would with your honored hero-leader's consciousness."

Dig 301 frowned at the interruption. "The theory presupposes widespread, chaotic fighting, extensive sudden deaths, and a breakdown of overall communication. Such salients did occur at various stages in the New Hokkaido campaigns."

"Hmm."

"Millsport is another theorized location. Historians of the period have argued that the Makita family was sufficiently elevated among the middle class to have had access to discreet storage facilities. Many data brokerage firms have successfully fought legal battles to maintain the anonymity of such stacks. The total discreet storage capacity in the Millsport metropolitan zone is estimated at over—"

"So which theory do you believe?"

The construct stopped so abruptly her mouth stayed open. A ripple blinked through the projected presence. Tiny machine-code specs shimmered briefly into existence at her right hip, left breast, and across her eyes. Her voice took the flattened tone of rote.

"I am a Harkany Datasystems service construct, enabled at basic interactional level. I cannot answer that question."

"No beliefs, huh?"

"I perceive only data and the probability gradients it provides."

"Sounds good to me. Do the math. What's the majority probability here?"

"The highest-likelihood outcome from the data available is that Nadia Makita was aboard the Quellist jetcopter at Alabardos, was vaporized with it by orbital fire, and no longer exists."

I nodded again and sighed.

"Right."

●●●

Sylvie came back a couple of hours later, carrying fresh fruit and a hotbox full of spiced shrimpcakes. We ate without talking much.

"Did you get through?" I asked her at one point.

"No." She shook her head, chewing. "There's something wrong. I can feel it. I can feel them out there, but I can't pin down enough for a transmission link."

Her eyes lowered, creased in a frown that looked like pain.

"There's something wrong," she repeated quietly.

"You didn't take the scarf off, did you?"

She looked at me. "No. I didn't take the scarf off. That doesn't affect functionality, Micky. It just pisses me off."

I shrugged. "You and me both."

Her eyes tracked to the pocket where I habitually kept the excised cortical stacks, but she said nothing.

We stayed out of each other's way for the rest of the day. Sylvie sat at the datacoil most of the time, periodically inducing shifts in the colored display without touching it or speaking. At one point, she went into her bedroom and lay there for an hour, staring at the ceiling. Glancing in on my way past to the bathroom, I saw her lips moving silently. I took a shower, stood by the window, ate fruit, and drank coffee I didn't want. Eventually I went outside and wandered around the margins of the eyrie's base, talking desultorily to Dig 301 who, for some reason, had taken it upon herself to tag along. Maybe she was there to make sure I didn't deface anything.

An undefined tension sat in the cold mountain air. Like sex unperformed, like bad weather coming in.

We can't stay like this forever, I knew. *Something has to give.*

But instead it got dark, and after another monosyllabic meal we went to our separate beds early. I lay in the deadened quiet of the cabin's soundproofing, imagining night sounds that mostly belonged to a climate much farther south. It hit me suddenly that I should have been there nearly two months back. Envoy conditioning—focus on your immediate surroundings and cope—had kept me from thinking about it much over the past several weeks, but whenever I had time my mind slipped back to Newpest and the Weed Expanse. It wasn't like anyone would be missing me exactly, but appointments had been made and now broken, and Radul Segesvar would be wondering if my silent disappearance might in fact signify detection and capture, with all the associated grief that could bring home to him on the Expanse. Segesvar owed me, but it was a debt of arguable worth and with the southern mafias, it doesn't do to push that angle too hard. The *haiduci* don't have the ethical discipline of the yakuza. And at a couple of months silently overdue, I was pushing it to the limit.

My hands were itching again. Gene-twitch of the desire to grab a rock surface and scale it the fuck out of here.

Face it, Micky. It's time to cut loose from this. Your deCom days are over. Fun while it lasted, and it got you a new face and these gecko hands, but enough's enough. It's time to get back on track. Back to the job in hand.

I turned on my side and stared at the wall. On the other side, Sylvie would be lying in the same quiet, the same isolation. Maybe the same harbor chop of distressed sleep as well.

What am I supposed to do? Leave her?

You've done worse.

I saw Orr's accusatory stare. *You don't fucking touch her.*

Heard Lazlo's voice. *I'm trusting you, Micky.*

Yeah, my own voice jeered through me. *He's trusting Micky. Takeshi Kovacs, he hasn't met yet.*

And if she is who she says she is?

Oh, come on. Quellcrist Falconer? You heard the machine. Quellcrist Falconer got turned into airborne ash at seven hundred meters above Alabardos.

Then who is she? The ghost, the one in the stack. Maybe she's not Nadia Makita, but she sure as hell thinks she is. And she sure as fuck isn't Sylvie Oshima. So who is she?

No idea. Is that supposed to be your problem?

I don't know, is it?

Your problem is that the yakuza have hired your own sweet self out of some archive stack to take you down. Very fucking poetic and you know what, he'll probably do not a bad job for them. He'll certainly have the resources—a global writ, remember. And you can bet the incentive scheme has a real fucking edge on it. You know the rules on double-sleeving.

And at the moment the only thing linking all this to that sleeve you're wearing is the woman next door and her low-grade mercenary pals. So the sooner you cut loose from them, head south, and get on with the job at hand, the better for all concerned.

The job at hand. Yeah, that'll solve all your problems, Micky.

And stop fucking calling me that.

Impatiently, I threw off the cover and got out of bed. I cracked the door and saw an empty room beyond. The table and the weaving datacoil, bright in the darkness, the bulk of our two packs leaning together in a corner. Hotei light painted the shapes of the windows in pale orange on the floor. I trod naked through the moonsplash and crouched by the packs, rooting around for a can of amphetamine cola.

Fuck sleep.

I heard her behind me and turned with a cold, unfamiliar unease feathering my bones. Not knowing whom I'd be face-to-face with.

"You, too, huh?"

It was Sylvie Oshima's voice, Sylvie Oshima's slightly quizzical lupine look as she stood facing me with arms wrapped around herself. She was naked as well, breasts gathered up and pressed in the V of her arms like a gift she planned to give me. Hips tilted in midstep, one curved thigh slightly behind the other. Hair in tangled disarray around her sleep-smudged face. In the light from Hotei, her pale skin took on tones of warm copper and fireglow. She smiled uncertainly.

"I keep waking up. Feels like my head's running on overdrive." She nodded at the cola can in my hand. "That isn't going to help, you know."

"I don't feel like sleeping." My voice came out a little hoarse.

"No." The smile inked out to sudden seriousness. "I don't feel like sleeping, either. I feel like doing what you wanted before."

She unfolded her arms, and her breasts hung free. A little self-consciously, she raised her arms and pushed back the mass of her hair, pressing her hands to the back of her head. She shifted her legs so that her thighs brushed together. Between the angles of her lifted elbows, she was watching me carefully.

"Do you like me like this?"

"I." The posture raised and modeled her breasts higher on her chest. I could feel the blood rushing into my cock. I cleared my throat. "I like you like that very much."

"Good."

And she stood without moving, watching me. I dropped the cola can on top of the pack it had come from and took a step toward her. Her arms unlinked and draped themselves around my shoulders, tightening across my back. I filled one hand with the soft weight of her breast, reached down with the other to the juncture of her thighs and the remembered dampness that—

"No, wait." She pushed the lower hand away. "Not there, not yet."

It was a tiny jarring moment, a jolt to expectations mapped out in the bubblefab two days earlier. I shrugged it off and gathered both hands to the breast I held, squeezing the nipple forward and sucking it into my mouth. She reached down and took my erection in her hand, stroking it back and forth with a touch that seemed forever on the point of letting go. I frowned, remembering a harder, more confident grip from before, and closed her hand tighter with my own. She chuckled.

"Oh sorry."

Stumbling a little, I pushed her to the edge of the table, pulled loose of her grip, and knelt on the floor in front of her. She murmured something deep in her throat and spread her legs a little, leaning back and bracing herself on the tabletop with both hands.

"I want your mouth on me," she said thickly.

I ran spread hands up her thighs and pressed the ball of each thumb either side of her cunt. A shiver ran through her and her lips parted. I bent my head and slid my tongue inside her. She made a tight, caught-up sound and I grinned. She felt the smile somehow and one hand slapped me across the shoulder.

"Bastard. Don't you fucking stop, you bastard."

I pushed her legs wider and went to work in earnest. Her hand came back to knead at my shoulder and neck and she shifted restlessly on the edge of the table, hips tilting back and forth with the motion of my tongue. The hand moved to tangle in my hair. I managed another split grin against the pressure she was exerting but this time she was too far gone to say anything coherent. She started to murmur, whether to me or herself I couldn't tell. At first it was simply the repeated syllables of assent, but as she tightened toward climax, something else began to emerge. Lost in what I was doing, it took me time to recognize it for what it was. In the throes of orgasm, Sylvie Oshima was chanting a skein of machine code.

She finished with a hard judder and two hands crushing my head into the juncture of her thighs. I reached back and gently prised her grip away, rose to my feet against her, grinning.

And found myself face-to-face with another woman.

It was impossible to define what had changed, but Envoy sense read it out for me and the absolute knowledge behind was like an elevator dropping through my stomach.

Nadia Makita was back.

She was there in the narrowing of the eyes and the deep quirk in one corner of her mouth that didn't belong to any expression Sylvie Oshima owned. In a kind of hunger that licked around her face like flames, and in breath that came in short, harsh bursts as if the orgasm, once spent, was now creeping back in some mirror-image replay.

"Hello there, Micky Serendipity," she husked.

Her breathing slowed and her mouth twisted into a grin to replace the one that had just melted off my own face. She slipped off the table, reached down, and touched me between the legs. It was the old, confident grasp I remembered, but I'd lost a lot of my erection with the shock.

"Something wrong?" she murmured.

"I—" She was using both hands on me like someone gently gathering in rope. I felt myself swelling again. She watched my face.

"Something *wrong*?"

"Nothing's wrong," I said quickly.

"Good."

She slid elegantly down on one knee, eyes still locked on mine, and took the head of my cock into her mouth. One hand stayed on the shaft, stroking, while the other found its way to my right thigh and curled around the muscle there, gripping hard.

This is fucking insane, a cold, mission-time shard of Envoy selfhood told me. *You need to stop this right now.*

And her eyes still on me, as her tongue and teeth and hand drove me into the explosion.

CHAPTeR SeVeNTeeN

Later, we lay draped wetly across each other in my bed, hands still loosely linked from the last frantic clasping. Our skins were sticky in patches with the mixed juices we'd spilled, and repeated climaxes had stung our muscles into lax submission. Flash images of what we'd done to and with each other kept replaying behind my eyes. I saw her crouched on top of me, crossed hands flat on my chest, pressing down hard with each movement. I saw myself slamming into her from behind. I saw her cunt descending onto my face. I saw her writhing under me, sucking wildly on the central cord of her own hair while I thrust between legs she had crooked over my hips like a vise. I saw myself taking the cord, wet with her saliva, into my own mouth as she laughed into my face and came with a powerful clenching of muscles that dragged me down after her.

But when she started talking to me, the altered lilt of her Amanglic sent an instant shiver down my spine.

"What?" She must have felt the shudder go through me.

"Nothing."

She rolled her head to face me. I could feel her stare pinned to the side of my face like heat. "I asked you a question. What's the matter?"

I closed my eyes briefly.

"Nadia, right?"

"Yes."

"Nadia Makita."

"Yes."

I glanced sideways at her. "How the fuck did you get here, Nadia?"

"What is that, a metaphysical question?"

"No. Technological." I propped myself up on one arm and gestured at her body. Envoy response conditioning or not, most of me was amazed at the detached sense of calm I was managing. "You can't be unaware of what's going on here. You live in the command software, and sometimes you get out. From what I've seen, I'd guess you come up through the basic instinct channels, riding the surge. Sex, maybe fear or fury, too. Stuff like that blots out a lot of the conscious mind's functions, and that'd give you the space. But—"

"You're some kind of expert, are you?"

"Used to be." I watched her for reaction. "I was an Envoy once."

"A what?"

"Doesn't matter. What I want to know is while you're here, what's happened to Sylvie Oshima?"

"Who?"

"You're wearing her fucking body, Nadia. Don't get obtuse on me."

She rolled onto her back and stared at the ceiling. "I don't really want to talk about this."

"No, you probably don't. And you know what, neither do I. But sooner or later, we're going to have to. You know that."

Long quiet. She opened her legs and rubbed absently at a patch of flesh on her inner thigh. She reached across and squeezed my shrunken prick. I took her hand and pushed it gently away.

"Forget it, Nadia. I'm wrung out. Even Mitzi Harlan couldn't get another hard-on out of me tonight. It's time to talk. Now where is Sylvie Oshima?"

She rolled away from me again.

"I'm supposed to be this woman's keeper?" she asked bitterly. "You think I'm in control of this?"

"Maybe not. But you've got to have some idea."

More quiet, but this time it quivered with tension. I waited. Finally, she rolled back to face me, eyes desperate.

"I *dream* this fucking Oshima, do you know that," she hissed. "She's a fucking *dream*, how am I supposed to know where she goes when I wake up?"

"Yeah, she dreams you, too, apparently."

"Is that supposed to make me feel better?"

I sighed. "Tell me what you dream."

"Why?"

"Because, Nadia, I'm trying to fucking help."

The eyes flared.

"All right," she snapped. "I dream that you scare her. How's that? I dream that she wonders where the fuck you're going with the souls of so many dead priests. That she wonders who the fuck Micky Serendipity really is, and whether he's safe to be around. Whether he'll fuck her over at the soonest opportunity. Or just fuck her and leave her. If you were thinking of getting your dick up this woman, Micky, or whoever the fuck you really are, I'd forget it. You're better off sticking with me."

I let that one soak out in silence for a moment. She flexed a smile at me.

"This the kind of thing you wanted to hear?"

I shrugged. "It'll do to be going on with. Did you push her into the sex? To get access?"

"Wouldn't you like to know."

"I can probably find out from her."

"You're assuming she'll be back." Another smile, more teeth this time. "I wouldn't do that if I were you."

And on like that. We snapped and snarled at each other for a while longer, but beneath the weight of postcoital chemistry none of it came to anything. In the end, I gave up and sat on the outer edge of the bed, staring out toward the main room and the Hotei-lit panels on the floor. A few minutes later, I felt her hand on my shoulder.

"I'm sorry," she said quietly.

"Yeah? For what?"

"I just realized I asked for this. I mean, I asked you what you were thinking about. If I didn't want to know, why ask, right?"

"There is that."

"It's just." She hesitated. "Listen, Micky, I'm getting sleepy here. And I lied back there, I've got no way of knowing if or when Sylvie Oshima's coming back. I don't know if I'll wake up tomorrow morning or not. That's enough to make anyone edgy, right?"

I stared at the orange-stained floor in the other room. A momentary sense of vertigo came and went. I cleared my throat.

"There's always the amphetamine cola," I said roughly.

"No. Sooner or later, I'll have to sleep. It might as well be now. I'm tired, and worse than that I'm happy and relaxed. Feels like if I've got to go, this'll do. It's only chemical, I know, but I can't hold out against it forever. And I think I will be back. Something's telling me that. But right now I don't know when, and I don't know where I'm going. And that scares me. Could you." Another pause. I heard the click as she swallowed in the quiet. "Would you mind holding me while I go under?"

Orange moonlight on a worn and darkened floor.

I reached back for her hand.

● ● ●

Like most of the combat custom I'd ever worn, the Eishundo sleeve came fitted with an internal wake-up. At the hour I'd fixed in my head, whatever dreams I was having coalesced into the rising rim of a tropical sun over quiet waters. Scent of fruit and coffee drifting from somewhere unseen and the cheerful murmur of voices far off. The cool of sand at early morning under my naked feet, and a faint but persistent breeze in my face. Sound of breakers

Vchira Beach? Already?

My hands were balled in the pockets of faded surfslacks, traces of sand in the lining of the pockets that—

The sense impressions vanished abruptly as I woke up. No coffee, and no beach to drink it on. No sand under my feet or my uncurling fingers. There was sunlight, but it was altogether thinner than in the wake-up imaging, strained colorlessly through the windows in the other room and into a gray, downward-pressing quiet.

I turned over gingerly and looked at the face of the woman sleeping next to me. She didn't move. I remembered the fear in Nadia Makita's eyes the night before as she let herself slide fractions at a time into sleep. Increments of consciousness slipping like taut rope through her hands and away, and then stopped as she flinched and blinked herself awake again. And then the moment, abrupt and unawaited, when she let go completely and didn't come back. Now I lay and watched the peace on her face as she slept, and it didn't help.

I slid out of bed and dressed quietly in the other room. I didn't want to be around when she woke up.

I certainly didn't want to wake her myself.

Dig 301 shaded into existence opposite me and opened her mouth. Combat neurachem got there first. I made a slicing gesture across my own throat and jerked a thumb back at the bedroom. Swept up my jacket from the back of a chair, shouldered my way into it, and nodded at the door.

"Outside," I murmured.

Outside, the day was shaping up better than its first impressions. The sun was wintry, but you could get warm if you stood in its rays directly, and the cloud cover was starting to break up. Daikoku stood like the ghost of a scimitar blade to the southwest and there was a column of specks circling slowly out over the ocean, ripwings at a guess. Down below, a couple of vessels were visible at the limits of my unaided vision. Tekitomura made a backdrop mutter in the still air. I yawned and looked at the amphetamine cola in my hand, then tucked it into my jacket. I was as awake as I wanted to be right now.

"So what did you want?" I asked the construct beside me.

"I thought you would like to know that the site has visitors."

The neurachem slammed online. Time turned to sludge around me as the Eishundo sleeve went to combat aware. I was staring sideways in disbelief at Dig 301 when the first blast cut past me. I saw the flare of disrupted air where it came through the construct's projected presence and then I was spinning away sideways as my jacket caught fire.

"Motherfu—"

No gun, no knife. I'd left them both inside. No time to reach the door, and Envoy instinct kicked me away from it anyway. Later, I'd realize what the situational intuition already knew—going back inside was a bolt-hole suicide. Jacket still in flames, I tumbled into the cover of the cabin wall. The blaster beam flashed again, nowhere near me. They were firing at Dig 301 again, misreading her for a solid human target.

Not exactly ninja-grade combat skills flashed through my mind. *These guys are the local hired help.*

Yeah, but they have guns and you don't.

Time to change arenas.

Fire-retardant material in my jacket had the flames down to smoke and heat across my ribs. The scorched fibers oozed damping polymer. I drew one hard breath and sprinted.

Yells behind me, boiling instantly from disbelief to anger. Maybe they thought they'd taken me down with the first shot; maybe they just weren't all that bright. It took them a pair of seconds to start shooting. By then I was almost to the next cabin. Blaster fire crackled in my ears. Heat flared close to my hip and my flesh cringed. I flinched sideways, got the cabin at my back, and scanned the ground ahead.

Three more cabins, gathered in a rough arc on the ground quarried out by the original archaeologues. Beyond them, the eyrie lifted off into the sky from massive cantilevered supports, like some vast premillennial rocket poised for launch. I hadn't been inside the day before; there was altogether too much abrupt space underfoot and a straight drop five hundred meters to the slanted mountainside below. But I knew from previous experience what the alien perspectives of Martian architecture could do to human perceptions, and I knew the Envoy conditioning would hold up.

Local hired help. Hold that thought.

They'd come in after me hesitantly at best, confused by the dizzying swoop of the interior, maybe even spiked with a little superstitious dread if I was lucky. They'd be off balance, they'd be afraid.

They'd make mistakes.

Which made the eyrie a perfect killing ground.

I bolted across the remaining open space, slipped between two of the cabins, and made for the nearest outcropping of Martian alloy, where it rose out of the rock like a tree root five meters thick. The archaeologues had left a set of metal steps bolted into the ground beside it. I took them three at a time and stepped onto the outcropping, boots slithering on alloy the color of bruises. I steadied myself against a bas-relief technoglyph facing that formed the side of the closest cantilever support as it extended outward into the air. The support was at least ten meters high, but a couple of meters to my left there was a ladder epoxied to the bas-relief surface. I grabbed a rung and started climbing.

More shouts from back among the cabins. No shooting. It sounded as if they were checking corners, but I didn't have the time to crank up the neu-rachem and make sure. Sweat jumped from my hands as the ladder creaked and shifted under my weight. The epoxy hadn't taken well to the Martian alloy. I doubled my speed, reached the top, and swung off with a tiny grunt of relief. Then I lay flat on top of the cantilever support, breathing and listening. Neurachem brought me the sounds of a badly organized search thrashing about below. Someone was trying to shoot the lock off one of the cabins. I stared up at the sky and thought about it for a moment.

"Dig? You there?" Voice a murmur.

"I am in communication range, yes." The construct's words seemed to come out of the air beside my ear. "You need speak no louder than you are. I assume from the situational context you do not wish me to become visible in your vicinity."

"You assume right. What I would like you to do is, on my command, be-come visible inside one of the locked-up cabins down there. Better yet, more than one if you can handle multiple projections. Can you do that?"

"I am enabled for one-to-one interaction up to and including every member of the original Dig Three-oh-one team at any given time, plus a guest potential of seven." It was hard to tell at this volume, but there seemed to be a trace of amusement in the construct's voice. "This gives me a total capacity of sixty-two separate representations."

"Yeah, well, three or four should do for now." I rolled with painstaking care onto my front. "And, listen, can you project as me?"

"No. I can choose among an index of personality projections, but I am not able to alter them in any way."

"You have any males?"

"Yes, though fewer options than—"

"All right, that's fine. Just choose a few out of the index that look like me. Male, about my build."

"When do you wish this to commence?"

I got my hands positioned under me.

"Now."

"Commencing."

It took a couple of seconds, and then chaos erupted among the cabins below. Blaster fire crackled back and forth, punctuated with shouts of warn-ing and the sound of running feet. Fifteen meters above it all, I pushed hard with both hands, came up in a crouch, and then exploded into the sprint.

The cantilever arm ran out fifty-odd meters over empty space, then buried itself seamlessly in the main body of the eyrie. Wide oval entrances gaped at the join. The dig team had attempted to attach a safety rail along the top of the arm, but as with the ladder the epoxy hadn't done well over time. In places the cabling had torn loose and now hung over the sides; elsewhere it was simply gone. I grimaced and narrowed focus to the broad flange at the end where the arm joined the main structure. Held the sprint.

Neurachem reeled in a voice shouting above the others—

"—pid motherfuckers, cease fire! Cease fire! *Cease fucking fire!* Up there, he's *up there!*"

Ominous quiet. I put on desperate increments of speed. Then the air was ripped through with blast beams. I skidded, nearly went over a gap in the rail. Flung myself forward again.

Dig 301 at my ear, thunderous under neurachem amp.

"Portions of this site are currently considered unsafe—"

My own wordless snarl.

Blast heat at my back and the stink of ionized air.

The new voice below again, neurachem'd in close. "Fucking give me that, will you. I'll show you how to—"

I threw myself sideways across the flange. The blast I knew was coming cut a scorching pain across my back and shoulder. Pretty sharp shooting at that range with a weapon that clumsy. I went down, rolled in approved fashion, came up, and dived for the nearest oval opening.

Blaster fire chased me inside.

● ● ●

It took them nearly half an hour to come in after me.

Holed up in the swooping Martian architecture, I strained with the neurachem and followed the argument as best I could. I couldn't find a vantage point this low in the structure that would give me a view of the outside— *fucking Martian builders*—but peculiar funneling effects in the eyrie's internal structure brought me the sound of voices in gusts. The gist of what was said wasn't hard to sort out. The hired help wanted to pack up and go home; their leader wanted my head on a stick.

You couldn't blame him. In his place, I wouldn't have been any different. You don't go back to the yakuza with half a contract fulfilled. And you certainly don't turn your back on an Envoy. He knew that better than anyone there.

He sounded younger than I'd expected.

"—believe you're fucking scared of this place. For Christ's sake, you all grew up just down the hill. It's only a fucking *ruin.*"

I glanced around at the billowing curves and hollows, felt the gentle but insistent way their lines sucked focus upward until your eyes started to ache. Hard morning light fell in from unseen vents overhead, but somehow on the way down it softened and changed. The clouded bluish alloy surfaces seemed to suck it in, and the reflected light that came back was oddly muted.

Below the mezzanine level I'd climbed to, patches of gloom alternated with gashes and holes in flooring where no sane human architect would have put them. A long way below that, the mountainside showed gray rock and sparse vegetation.

Only a ruin. Right.

He *was* younger than I'd expected.

For the first time, I started to wonder constructively exactly how young. At an absolute minimum, he was certainly short a couple of formative experiences I'd had around Martian artifacts.

"Look, he's not even fucking *armed*."

I pitched my voice to carry outside.

"Hoy, Kovacs! You're so fucking confident, why don't you come in and get me yourself?"

Sudden silence. Some muttering. I thought I caught a muffled guffaw from one of the locals. Then his voice, raised to match mine.

"That's good eavesdropping gear they fitted you with."

"Isn't it."

"You planning to give us a fight, or just listen in and shout cheap abuse?"

I grinned. "Just trying to be helpful. But you can have a fight if you want it—come on in. Bring the hired help, too, if you must."

"I've got a better idea. How about I let my hired help run an open-all-orifices train on your traveling companion, as long as it takes you to come out? You could use your neurachem to listen in on that as well if you like. Although, to be honest, the sound'll probably carry enough without. They're enthusiastic, these boys."

The fury spiked up through me, too fast for rational thought. Muscles in my face skipped and juddered, and the frame of the Eishundo sleeve cabled rigid. For two sluggish heartbeats, he had me. Then the Envoy systems came soaking coldly through the emotion, bleaching it back out for assessment.

He isn't going to do that. If Tanaseda traced you through Oshima and the Slipins, it's because he knows she's implicated in Yukio Hirayasu's death. And if he knows that, he'll want her intact. Tanaseda is old school and he's promised an old-school execution. He isn't going to want damaged goods.

And besides, this is you we're talking about. You know what you're capable of and it isn't this.

I was younger then. Now. I am. I wrestled the concept in my head. *Out there. I'm younger out there. There's no telling—*

Yes there is. This is Envoy bluff and you know it, you've used it enough yourself.

"Nothing to say about that?"

"We both know you won't do it, Kovacs. We both know who you're working for."

This time the pause before he called back was barely noticeable. Good recovery, very impressive.

"You seem remarkably well informed for a man on the run."

"It's my training."

"Soak up the local color, huh?"

Virginia Vidaura's words at Envoy induction, a subjective century ago. I wondered how long ago she'd said it to him.

"Something like that."

"Tell me something, man, 'cause I'd genuinely like to know. With all that training, how come you end up a cut-rate sneak assassin for a living? As a career move, I got to say it puzzles me."

A cold knowledge crept up through me as I listened. I grimaced and shifted my position slightly. Said nothing.

"Serendipity, right? It's Serendipity?"

"Well, I have got another name," I shouted back. "But some fuckhead stole it. Until I get it back, Serendipity's fine."

"Maybe you won't get it back."

"Nah, it's good of you to worry, but I know the fuckhead in question. He isn't going to be a problem for much longer."

The twitch was tiny, barely a missed beat. Only the Envoy sense picked it up, the anger, shut down as rapidly as it flared.

"Is that so?"

"Yeah, like I said. Real fuckhead. Strictly a short-lived thing."

"That sounds like overconfidence to me." His voice had changed fractionally. Somewhere in there, I'd stung him. "Maybe you don't know this guy as well as you like to think."

I barked a laugh. "Are you kidding? I taught him every fucking thing he knows. Without me—"

And *there*. The figure I'd known was coming. The one I couldn't listen for with neurachem while I traded veiled insults with the voice outside. A crouched, black-clad form sliding in through the opening five meters under me, some kind of spec ops eyemask-and-sensor gear turning the head insectile and inhuman. Thermographic imaging, sonic locater, motion alert, at a probable minimum—

I was already falling. Pushed off from the ledge, boot heels aligned to hit the neck below the masked head and snap it.

Something in the headgear warned him. He jumped sideways, looking up, twisting the blaster toward me. Beneath the mask, his mouth jerked open to yell. The blast cut through air I'd just dropped out of. I hit the floor crouched, a handbreadth off his right elbow. Blocked the swing of the blaster barrel as it came around. The yell came out of his mouth, shivery with the shock. I struck upward into his throat with the blade of one hand and the sound choked to retching. He staggered. I straightened, went after him, and chopped again.

There were two more of them.

Framed in the opening, side by side. The only thing that saved me was their incompetence. As the lead commando dropped strangling to death at my feet, either one could have shot me—instead, they both tried at the same time and tangled. I sprinted directly at them.

There are worlds I've been where you can gun down a man holding a knife at ten meters and claim it as self-defense. The legal argument is that it doesn't take very long to close that gap and stab.

That much is true.

If you really know what you're doing, you don't even need the knife.

This was five meters or less. I got in a flurry of blows, stamping down at shin and instep, blocked weapons however I could, hooking an elbow around hard into a face. A blaster came loose and I fielded it. Triggered it in a savage close-quarters arc.

Muffled shrieks and a short-lived explosion of blood as flesh seared open and then cauterized. Steam wisped, and their bodies tumbled away from me. I had time for a hard breath, a glance down at the weapon in my hands—*piece-of-shit Szeged Incandess*—and then another blaster beam flared off the alloy surface beside my head. They were coming in force.

With all that training, how come you end up a cut-rate sneak assassin for a living?

Just fucking incompetent, I guess.

I backed up. Someone poked a head into the oval opening and I chased them away with a barely aimed burst of fire.

And too fucking fascinated with yourself for your own good.

I grabbed a projection one-handed and hauled myself up, hooking my legs onto the wide, spiraling ramp that led back to my initial hiding place on the mezzanine. The Eishundo sleeve's gecko grip failed on the alloy. I slipped, grabbed again in vain, and fell. Two new commandos burst through a gap to the left of the one I was covering. I fired randomly and low with the Szeged, trying to get back up. The beam chopped a foot off the commando on the right. She screamed and stumbled, clutched at her injured leg, toppled gracelessly, and fell through a gash in the floor. Her second scream floated back up through the gap.

I came up off the ground and flung myself at her companion.

It was a clumsy fight, both of us hampered by the weapons we held. I lunged with the butt of the Szeged; he blocked and tried to level his own blaster. I smashed it aside and kicked at a knee. He turned the blow with a shin kick of his own. I got the Szeged butt under his chin and rammed upward. He dropped his weapon and punched me hard simultaneously in the side of the throat and the groin. I reeled back, hung on somehow to the Szeged, and suddenly had the distance to use it. Proximity sense screamed a warning at me through the pain. The commando ripped out a sidearm and pointed it. I flinched aside, ignoring the pain and the proximity warning in my head, leveled the blaster.

Sharp splatter from the gun in the commando's hand. The cold wrap of a stunblast.

My hand spasmed open and the Szeged clattered away somewhere.

I staggered backward and the floor vanished under my feet.

—*fucking Martian builders*—

I dropped out of the eyrie like a bomb, and fell wingless away from the rapidly contracting iris of my own consciousness.

CHAPTeR eIGHTeeN

"Don't open your eyes, don't open your left hand, don't move at all."

It was like a mantra, like an incantation, and someone seemed to have been singing it to me for hours. I wasn't sure if I could have disobeyed it anyway—my left arm was an icy branch of numbness from fist to shoulder and my eyes seemed gummed shut. My shoulder felt wrenched, maybe dislocated. Elsewhere, my body throbbed with the more general ache of a stunblast hangover. I was cold everywhere.

"Don't open your eyes, don't open your left hand, don't—"

"I heard you the first time, Dig." My throat felt clogged. I coughed and an alarming dizziness swung through me. "Where am I?"

A brief hesitation. "Professor Serendipity, perhaps that information would be better dealt with later. Don't open your left hand."

"Yeah, got it. Left hand, don't open it. Is it fucked?"

"No," said the construct reluctantly. "Apparently not. But it is the only thing holding you up."

Shock, like a stake in the chest. Then the rolling wave of false calm as the conditioning kicked in. Envoys are supposed to be good at this sort of thing—waking up in unexpected places is part of the brief. You don't panic, you just gather data and deal with the situation. I swallowed hard.

"I see."

"You can open your eyes now."

I fought the stunblast ache and got my eyelids apart. Blinked a couple of times to clear my vision and then wished I hadn't. My head was hanging down on my right shoulder and the only thing I could see under it was five hundred meters of empty space and the bottom of the mountain. The cold and the dizzy swinging sensation made abrupt sense. I was dangling like a hanged man from the grip of my own left hand.

The shock fired up again. I shelved it with an effort and twisted my head awkwardly to look upward. My fist was wrapped around a loop of greenish cable that disappeared seamlessly at both ends into a smoke-gray alloy cowling. Oddly angled buttresses and spires of the same alloy crowded me on all

sides. Still groggy from the stunblast, it took me a couple of moments to identify the underside of the eyrie. Apparently, I hadn't fallen very far.

"What's going on, Dig?" I croaked.

"As you fell, you took hold of a Martian personnel cable, which, in line
with what we understand of its function, retracted and brought you up into a
recovery bay."

"Recovery bay?" I cast about among the surrounding projections for
some sign of a safe place to stand. "So how does that work?"

"We are not sure. It would appear that from the position you now oc-
cupy, a Martian, an adult Martian at least, would be comfortable using the
structure you see around you to reach openings on the underside of the eyrie.
There are several within—"

"All right." I stared grimly up at my closed fist. "How long have I been
out?"

"Forty-seven minutes. It appears your body is highly resistant to neuronic
frequency weapons. As well as being designed for survival in high-altitude,
high-risk environments."

No shit.

How Eishundo Organics had ever gone out of business was beyond me.
They could have had an endorsement out of me on demand. I'd seen sub-
conscious survival programming in combat sleeves before, but this was a
piece of sheer biotech brilliance. Vague memory of the event stirred in my
stun-muddied recollection. The desperate terror of vertigo at full pitch and
the realization of the fall. Grabbing at something half seen as the stun-blast effects folded around me like a freezing black cloak. A final wrench as consciousness winked out. Saved, by some lab full of biotech geeks and their
project enthusiasm three centuries ago.

A weak grin faded as I tried to guess what nearly an hour of locked-
muscle grip and load-bearing strain might have done to the sinews and joints
of my arm. I wondered if there'd be permanent damage. If, for that matter, I'd
be able to get the limb to work at all.

"Where are the others?"

"They left. They are now beyond my sensor radius."

"So they think I fell all the way."

"It appears so. The man you referred to as Kovacs has detailed some of
his employees to begin a search at the base of the mountain. I understand
they will try to recover your body along with that of the woman you mutilated
in the firefight."

"And Sylvie? My colleague?"

"They have taken her with them. I have recorded footage of—"

"Not right now." I cleared my throat, noticing for the first time how
parched it felt. "Look, you said there are openings. Ways back into the eyrie
from here. Where's the nearest?"

"Behind the triflex downspire to your left, there is an entry port ninety-three centimeters in diameter."

I craned my neck and spotted what I assumed Dig 301 was talking about. The downspire looked very much like a two-meter inverted witch's hat that massive fists had crumpled badly in three different places. It was surfaced in uneven bluish facets that caught the shadowed light beneath the eyrie and gleamed as if wet. The lowest deformation brought its tip almost horizontal and offered a saddle of sorts that I thought I might be able to cling to. It was less than two meters from where I hung.

Easy. Nothing to it.

If you can make the jump with one arm crippled, that is.

If your trick hand grips better on Martian alloy than it did an hour ago upstairs.

If—

I reached up with my right arm and took hold of the loop of cable, close to my other hand. Very gently, I took up the tension and began to lift myself on the new grip. My left arm twinged as the weight came off it, and a jagged flash of heat spiked through the numbness. My shoulder creaked. The heat branched out across abused ligaments and started turning into something resembling pain. I tried to flex my left hand but got nothing outside a sparking sensation in the fingers. The pain in my shoulder swelled and began to soak down through the muscles of the arm. It felt as if, when it finally got going, it was going to hurt a lot.

I tried again with the fingers of my left hand. This time the sparking gave way to a bone-deep, pulsing ache that brought tears squirting into my eyes. The fingers would not respond. My grip was welded in place.

"Do you wish me to alert emergency services?"

Emergency services: the Tekitomura police, closely followed by deCom security with tidings of Kurumaya's displeasure, tipped-off local yakuza with the new me at their grinning head, and, who knew, maybe even the Knights of the New Revelation, if they could afford the police bribes and had been keeping up on current events.

"Thanks," I said weakly. "I think I'll manage."

I glanced up at my clamped left hand, back at the triflex downspire, down at the drop. I drew a long hard breath. Then, slowly, I worked my right hand along the cable until it was touching its locked-up mate. Another breath and I hinged my body upward from the waist. Barely recovered nerve tissue in my stomach muscles sputtered protest. I hooked with my right foot, missed, flailed and hooked again. My ankle lodged over the cable. More weight came off my left arm. The pain began in earnest, racking explosions through the joints and down the muscles.

One more breath, one more glance d—

No, don't *fucking look down.*

One more breath, teeth gritted.

Then I began, with thumb and forefinger, to unhinge my paralyzed fingers one at a time from the cable.

● ● ●

I left the swooping bluish gloom of the eyrie's interior half an hour later, still on the edge of a persistent manic giggle. The adrenaline humor stayed with me all the way along the cantilever arm, down the shaky archaeologue ladder—not easy with one arm barely functional—then the steps. I hit solid ground still smirking stupidly, and picked my way between the cabins with ingrained caution and tiny explosive snorts of hilarity. Even when I got back to the cabin we'd used, even inside and staring at the empty bed I'd left Sylvie in, I could feel the trace of the comedown grin twitching on and off my lips and the laughter still bubbled faintly in my stomach.

It had been a close thing.

Ungripping my fingers from the cable hadn't been much fun, but compared with the rest of the escapade, it was a joy. Once released, my left arm dropped and hung at the end of a shoulder socket that ached like a bad tooth. It was as much use to me as a deadweight slung around my neck. A sustained minute of cursing before I could bring myself to then unsling my right foot, swing free by my right hand, and use the momentum to make an ungainly leap sideways at the downspire. I grabbed, clawed, found that the Martians for once had built in a material that offered something approaching decent friction, and clamped myself panting into the saddle at the bottom. I stayed like that for a good ten minutes, cheek pressed to the cold alloy.

Careful exploratory leaning and peering showed me the floor hatch Dig 301 had promised, within grasping distance if I stood up on the tip of the downspire. I flexed my left arm, got some response above the elbow, and reckoned it might serve, if nothing else, as a wedge in the hatch. From that position, I could probably lever my legs up and inside.

Another ten minutes and I was sweatily ready to try.

A tense minute and a half after that and I was lying on the floor of the eyrie, cackling quietly to myself and listening to the trickle of echoes in the alien architecture that had saved my life.

Nothing to it.

Eventually, I got up and made my way out.

In the cabin they'd kicked open every internal door that might hide a threat, and in the bedroom Sylvie and I had shared there were some signs of a struggle. I looked around the cabin, massaging my arm at the shoulder. The lightweight bedside unit overturned, the sheets twisted and trailing from the bed to the floor. Elsewhere, they'd touched nothing.

There was no blood. No pervasive scent of weapons discharge.

On the floor in the bedroom, I found my knife and the GS Rapsodia. Smashed from the surface of the bedside unit as it went over, skittering off into separate corners. They hadn't bothered with them.

In too much of a hurry.

Too much of a hurry for what? To get down the mountain and pick up a dead Takeshi Kovacs?

I frowned slightly as I gathered up the weapons. Strange they hadn't turned the place inside out. According to Dig 301, someone had been de- tailed to go down and recover my broken body, but that didn't take the whole squad. It would have made sense to conduct at least a cursory search of the premises up here.

I wondered what kind of search they were conducting now, at the base of the mountain. I wondered what they'd do when they couldn't find my body, how long they'd keep looking.

I wondered what *he* would do.

I went back into the main living space of the cabin and sat at the table. I stared into the depths of the datacoil. I thought the pain in my left elbow might be loosening a little.

"Dig?"

She fizzled into being on the other side of the table. Machine-perfect as ever, untouched by the events of the last couple of hours.

"Professor Serendipity?"

"You said you had footage of what happened here? Does that cover the whole site?"

"Yes, input and output run off the same imaging system. There are microcams for every eight cubic meters of the site. Within the eyrie com- plexes, recording is sometimes of poor—"

"Never mind that. I want you to show me Kovacs. Footage of everything he did and said here. Run it in the coil."

"Commencing."

I laid the Rapsodia and the Tebbit knife carefully on the table by my right hand.

"And Dig? Anyone else comes up that path, you tell me immediately they get in range."

He had a good body.

I skipped about in the footage for the best shots, got one as the intruders came up the mountain path toward the cabin. Froze it on him and stared for a while. He had some of the bulk you expect from battlefield custom, but there was a lilt to it, a way of stepping and standing that leaned more toward

Total Body theater than combat. Face a smooth blend of more racial variants than you'd usually get on Harlan's World. Custom-cultured, then. Gene codes brought in from offworld. Skin tanned the color of worn amber, eyes a startling blue. Broad, protruding cheekbones, a wide, full-lipped mouth, and long, crinkled black hair bound back with a static braid. Very pretty.

And very pricey, even for the yakuza.

I quelled the faint scratching of disquiet and got Dig 301 to pan about a bit among the intruders. Another figure caught my eye. Tall and powerful, rainbow-maned. The site microcams yanked in a close-up of steel-lensed eyes and subcutaneous circuitry in a grim, pale face.

Anton.

Anton and at least a couple of slim wincefish types who preceded him up the path with the loose, in-step coordination of deCom operational pitch. One of them was the woman whose foot I'd shot off in the eyrie. Two, no three, more came behind the command head, standing out clearly from the rest of the party now that I was looking for that characteristic scattered-but-meshed pattern.

Somewhere in me, a faint gray sense of loss readied itself for recognition at the sight.

Anton and the Skull Gang.

Kovacs had brought his New Hok hunting dogs back with him.

I thought back to the confusion of the firefight amid the cabins and the eyrie, and it made some more sense. A boatload of yakuza enforcers and a deCom crew, mingled and getting in each other's way. Very poor logistics for an Envoy. No way I would have made that mistake at his age.

What are you talking about? You just did make that mistake at his age. That's you out there.

A faint shiver coiled down my spine.

"Dig, move it up to the bedroom again. Where they pull her out."

The coil jumped and shimmered. The woman with the tangled hyper-wired hair blinked awake among twisted sheets. The crash of gunfire outside had woken her. Eyes wide as she registered what it was. Then the door burst open and the room filled with bulky forms brandishing hardware and yelling. When they saw what they had, the shouting powered down to chuckles. Weapons were put up and someone reached for her. She punched him in the face. A brief struggle flared and guttered out as weight of numbers squashed her speed reflexes. Sheets torn away, efficient disabling blows administered to thigh and solar plexus. While she wheezed on the floor, one grinning thug grabbed at a breast, groped between her legs, and made pumped-hip rutting motions over her. A couple of his companions laughed.

I was seeing it for the second time. Still, the rage leapt up through me like flames. In my palms, the gecko spines sweated awake.

A second enforcer appeared in the doorway, saw what was going on, and bellowed in furious Japanese. The thug leapt away from the woman on the floor. He made a nervous bow, a stammered apology. The newcomer stepped in close and backhanded the man three times with shattering force. The thug cowered against the wall. More yelling from the newcomer. Amid some of the more colorful insults I'd ever heard in Japanese, he was telling someone to bring clothes for the captive.

By the time Kovacs got back from overseeing the hunt for himself, they had her dressed and seated on a chair in the center of the cabin's main living space. Her hands rested in her lap, wrists bound neatly, one over the other with a restraint patch you couldn't see. The yakuza stood at a careful distance from her, weapons still out. The would-be romantic sulked in a corner, disarmed, one side of his mouth swollen, upper lip split. Kovacs's eyes flickered over the damage, and he turned to the enforcer at his side. A muttered exchange the microcams were not amped to pick up. He nodded, looked again at the woman before him. I read a curious hesitation in his stance.

Then he turned back to the cabin door.

"Anton, you want to come in here?"

The Skull Gang command head stepped into the room. When the woman saw him, her mouth twisted.

"You fucking sellout piece of shit."

Anton's lip curled, but he said nothing.

"You know each other, I believe." But there was a faint question in Kovacs's voice, and he was still watching the woman before him.

Sylvie tipped her gaze at him. "Yeah, I know this asshole. And? Got something to do with you, has it, fuckhead?"

He stared at her, and I tensed in my chair. This segment was first time through for me, and I didn't know what he'd do. What would I have done at that age? No, scratch that. What was I about to do at that age? My mind fled back through the silted-up decades of violence and rage, trying to anticipate.

But he only smiled.

"No, Mistress Oshima. It has nothing to do with me anymore. You are a package I have to deliver in good condition, that's all."

Someone muttered; someone else guffawed. Still cranked tight, my neurachem hearing caught a crude joke about packages. In the coil, my younger self paused. His eyes flickered to the man with the broken lip.

"You. Come here."

The enforcer didn't want to. You could see it in his stance. But he was yakuza, and in the end it's all face with them. He straightened up, met Kovacs's eyes, and stepped forward with a filed-tooth sneer. Kovacs looked back at him neutrally and nodded.

"Show me your right hand."

The yakuza tipped his head to one side, gaze still locked on Kovacs's eyes. It was a gesture of pure insolence. He flipped up his hand, extended fingers, making it a loosely bent blade. He inclined his head again, the other way, still staring deep into this *tani* piece of shit's eyes.

Kovacs moved like whiplash on a broken trawler cable.

He snatched the offered hand at the wrist and twisted downward, blocking the other man's response options with his body. He held the captured arm straight out and his other hand arced over the wrestling lock of both bodies, blaster pointed. A beam flared and sizzled.

The enforcer shrieked as his hand went up in flames. The blaster must have been powered down—most beam weapons will take a limb clean off, vaporized across the width of the blast. This one had only burned away skin and flesh to the bone and tendon. Kovacs held the man a moment longer, then turned him loose with an elbow-strike cuff across the side of the head. The enforcer collapsed across the floor with his scorched hand clamped under his armpit and his trousers visibly stained. He was weeping uncontrollably.

Kovacs mastered his breathing and looked around the room. Stony faces stared back. Sylvie had turned hers away. I could almost smell the stench of cooked flesh.

"Unless she attempts to escape, you do not touch her, you do not speak to her. Any of you. Is that clear? In this scheme of things, you matter less than the dirt under my fingernails. Until we get back to Millsport, this woman is a *god* to you. *Is that clear?*"

Silence. The yakuza captain bellowed in Japanese. Muttered assent crept out in the wake of the dressing-down. Kovacs nodded and turned to Sylvie.

"Mistress Oshima. If you'd like to follow me, please."

She stared at him for a moment, then got to her feet and followed him out of the cabin. The yakuza filed after them, leaving their captain and the man on the floor. The captain stared at his injured enforcer for a moment, then booted him savagely in the ribs, spat on him, and stalked out.

Outside, they'd loaded the three men I'd killed in the eyrie onto a fold-down grav stretcher rack. The yakuza captain detailed a man to drive it, then took point ahead of a protective phalanx around Kovacs and Sylvie. Beside and behind the stretcher rack, Anton and the four remaining members of the Skull Gang formed up into a lax rear guard. Dig's outdoor microcams followed the little procession out of sight along the path down to Tekitomura.

Stumbling fifty meters behind them all, still nursing his ruined and as-yet-untreated hand, came the disgraced enforcer who had dared to touch Sylvie Oshima.

I watched him go, trying to make sense of it.

Trying to make it fit.

I was still trying when Dig 301 asked if I was finished, if I wanted to see something else. I told her no, absently. In my head, Envoy intuition was already doing what needed to be done.

Setting fire to my preconceptions and burning them to the ground.

CHAPTeR NINeTeeN

The lights were all out in Belacotton Kohei Nine Point Twenty-six when I got there, but in a unit half a dozen bays down on the right, the upper-level windows glowed fitfully, as if the place were on fire inside. There was a frenetic hybrid reefdive-neojunk rhythm blasting out into the night, even through the cranked-down loading bay shutter, and three thickset figures stood around outside in dark coats, breathing steam and flapping their arms against the cold. Plex Kohei might have the floor space to throw big dance parties, but it didn't look as if he could afford machine security on the door. This was going to be easier than I'd expected.

Always assuming Plex was actually there.

Are you kidding me? Isa's fifteen-year-old Millsport-accented scorn down the line when I phoned her late that afternoon. *Of* course *he'll be in. What day is it?*

Uh. I estimated. *Friday?*

Right, Friday. So what do the local yokels do up there on a Friday?

Fuck should I know, Isa? And don't be such a metrosnob.

Uh, Friday? Hello? Fishing community? Ebisu night?

He's having a party.

He's cranking some credit out of cheap floor space and good take *connections, is what he's doing,* she drawled. *All those warehouses. All those family friends in the yak.*

Don't suppose you'd know which warehouse exactly?

Stupid question. Picking my way through the fractal street planning of the warehouse district hadn't been my idea of fun, but once I hit Belacotton Kohei Section, it hadn't been hard to find my way to the party—you could hear the music across half a dozen alleys in every direction.

Don't suppose I would. Isa yawned down the line. I guessed she'd not been out of bed that long. *Say, Kovacs. You been pissing people off up there?*

No. Why?

Yeah, well, I probably shouldn't really be telling you this for nothing. But seeing as how we go back.

I stifled a grin. Isa and I went back all of a year and a half. When you're fifteen I guess that's a long time.

Yeah?

Yeah, been a lot of big heat down here, asking after you. Paying big for answers, too. So if you're not already, I'd start looking over the shoulder of that deep-voiced new sleeve you've got yourself there.

I frowned and thought about it. *What kind of big heat?*

If I knew that, you'd have to pay me for it. But as it happens, I don't. Only players talked to me were bent Millsport PD, and them you can buy for the price of an Angel Wharf blowjob. Anybody could have sent them.

And I don't suppose you told them anything about me.

Don't suppose I did. You planning on soaking up this line much longer, Kovacs? Only, I'm not like you. I have a social life.

No, I'm gone. Thanks for the newsflash, Isa.

She grunted. *My clit-tingling pleasure. You stay in one piece, maybe we get to do some more business I can charge you for.*

I pressed the sealseam of my newly acquired coat closed to the collar, flexed my hands inside the black polalloy gloves—spike of brief agony from the left—and poured gangster attitude into my stride as I came around the curve of the alley. Think Yukio Hirayasu at his most youthfully arrogant. Ignore the fact the coat wasn't hand-tailored—straight-to-street off-the-rack branded was the best I could do at short notice, a garment the real Hirayasu wouldn't have been seen dead in. But it was a rich matte black to match the sprayon gloves and, in this light, it should pass. Envoy deceit would do the rest.

I'd thought briefly about crashing Plex's party the hard way. Going in heavy against the door, or maybe scaling the back of the warehouse and cracking a skylight entry. But my left arm was still a single throbbing ache from fingertip to neck, and I didn't know how far I could trust it to do what I wanted in a critical situation.

The door detail saw me coming and drew together. Neurachem vision calibrated them for me at distance—cheap, wharf-front muscle, maybe some very basic combat augmentation in the way they moved. One of them had a tactical marine tattoo across his cheek, but that could have been a knockoff, courtesy of some parlor with army-surplus software. Or, like a lot of tacs, he could just have fallen on postdemob hard times. Downsizing. The universal catchall and catechism on Harlan's World these days. Nothing was more sacred than cost cutting, and even the military weren't entirely safe.

"Hold it, sam."

It was the one with the tattoo. I cut him a withering glance. Halted, barely.

"I have an appointment with Plex Kohei. I don't expect to be kept waiting."

"Appointment?" His gaze lifted and slipped left, checking a retinal guest list. "Not tonight you don't. Man's busy."

I let my eyes widen, built the volcanic pressure of fury the way I'd seen it from the yak captain in Dig 301's footage.

"Do you know who I am?" I barked.

The tattooed doorman shrugged. "I know I don't see your face on this list. And around here, that means you don't get in."

At my side, the others were looking me up and down with professional interest. Seeing what they could break easily. I fought down the impulse to take up a fighting stance and eyed them with mannered disdain instead. Launched the bluff.

"Very well. You will please inform your employer that you have turned Yukio Hirayasu from his door, and that thanks to your *diligence* in this matter, he will now speak to me in *sempai* Tanaseda's presence tomorrow morning, unadvised and thus unprepared."

Gazes flew back and forth between the three of them. It was the names, the whiff of authentic yakuza clout. The spokesman hesitated. I turned away. Was only midway through the motion when he made up his mind, and broke.

"All right. Hirayasu-san. Just one moment please."

The great thing about organized crime is the level of fear it likes to maintain among its minions and those who associate with them. Thug hierarchy. You can see the same pattern on any of a dozen different worlds—the Hun Home triads, Adoracion's *familias vigilantes,* the Provo Crews on Nkrumah's Land. Regional variations, but they all sow the same crop of respect through terror of retribution. And all reap the same harvest of stunted initiative in the ranks. No one wants to take an independent decision, when independent action runs the risk of reinterpretation as a lack of respect. Shit like that can get you Really Dead.

Better, by far, to fall back on hierarchy. The doorman dug out his phone and punched up his boss.

"Listen, Plex, we've—"

He listened a moment himself, face immobile. Angry insect sounds from the phone. I didn't need neurachem to work out what was being said.

"Uh, yeah, I know you said that, man. But I've got Yukio Hirayasu out here wanting a word, and I—"

Another break, but this time the doorkeep seemed happier. He nodded a couple of times, described me and what I'd just said. At the other end of the line, I could hear Plex dithering. I gave it a couple of moments, then snapped my fingers impatiently and gestured for the phone. The doorman caved in and handed it over. I mustered Hirayasu's speech patterns from memory a couple of months old, colored in what I didn't know with standard Millsport gangster idiom.

"Plex." Grim impatience.

"Uh. Yukio? That really you?"

I went for Hirayasu's yelp. "No, I'm a fucking *ledgedust* dealer. What do you think? We've got some serious business to transact, Plex. Do you know how close I am to having your security taken on a little dawn ride here? You don't fucking keep me waiting at the gate."

"Okay, Yukio, okay. It's cool. It's just. Man, we all thought you were *gone*."

"Yeah, well. Fucking streetflash. I'm back. But then Tanaseda probably didn't tell you that, did he?"

"Tana—" Plex swallowed audibly. "Is Tanaseda here?"

"Never mind Tanaseda. My guess is we've got about four or five hours before the TPD are all over this."

"All over what?"

"All over *what*?" I cranked the yelp again. "What do you fucking think?"

I heard his breathing for a moment. A female voice in the background, muffled. Something surged in my blood for a moment, then slumped. It wasn't Sylvie, or Nadia. Plex snapped something irritable at her, whoever she was, then came back to the phone.

"I thought they—"

"Are you going to fucking let me in or what?"

The bluff took. Plex asked to talk to the doorkeep, and three monosyllables later the man keyed open a narrow hatch cut into the metal shutter. He stepped through and gestured me to follow.

Inside, Plex's club looked pretty much the way I'd expected. Cheap echoes of the Millsport *take* scene—translucent alloy partitions for walls, mushroom-trip holos scribbled into the air over a mob of dancers clad in little more than bodypaint and shadow. The fusion sound drowned the whole space with its volume, stuffed its way into ears and made the translucent wall panels thrum visibly on the beat. I could feel it vibrate in my body cavities like bombing. Over the crowd, a couple of Total Body wannabes flexed their perfectly toned flesh in the air, choreographed orgasm in the way they dragged splayed hands across themselves. But when you looked carefully, you saw they were held up by cabling, not antigrav. And the trip holos were obvious recordings, not the direct cortical sampling you got in the Millsport *take* clubs. Isa, I guessed, would not have been impressed.

A bodysweep team of two propped themselves unwillingly upright from battered plastic chairs set against the containing wall. With the place packed to capacity, they'd obviously thought they were done for the night. They eyed me grumpily and brandished their detectors. Behind them, through the translucence, some of the dancers saw and mimicked the gestures with wide, tripped-out grins. My escort got both men seated again with a curt nod and we pushed past, around the end of the wall panel and into the thick of the dancing. The temperature climbed to blood-warm. The music got even louder.

We forged through the tightly packed dance space without incident. A couple of times, I had to shove hard to make progress but never got anything back beyond smiles, apologetic or just blissed-out vacant. The *take* scene is pretty laid-back wherever you go on Harlan's World—careful breeding has placed the most popular strains firmly in the euphoric part of the psychotropic spectrum, and the worst you can expect from those under the influence is to be hugged and slobbered on amid incoherent professions of undying love. There are nastier hallucinogenic varieties to be had, but generally nobody outside the military wants them.

A handful of caresses and a hundred alarmingly wide smiles later, we made the foot of a metal ramp and tramped upward to where a pair of dockyard containers had been set up on scaffolding and fronted in mirrorwood paneling. Reflected light from the holos smashed off their chipped and dented surfaces. My escort led me to the left-hand container, pressed a hand to a chime pad, and opened a previously invisible mirrored door panel. Really opened, like the hatch that opened onto the street. No flexportals here, it seemed. He stood aside to let me pass.

I stepped in and surveyed the scene. Foreground, a flushed Plex, dressed to the waist and struggling into a violently psychedelic silk blouse. Behind him, two women and a man lolled on a massive automold bed. They were all physically very young and beautiful; wore uniformly blank-eyed smiles, badly smeared bodypaint, and not much else. It wasn't hard to work out where Plex had gotten them from. Monitors for sweep-and-swoop microcams in the club outside were lined along the back wall of the container space. A constant shift of dance space image marched through them. The fusion beat came through the walls, muffled but recognizable enough to dance to. Or whatever.

"Hey, Yukio, man. Let me get a look at you." Plex came forward, raised his arms. He grinned uncertainly. "That's a nice sleeve, man. Where'd you get that? Custom-grown?"

I nodded at his playmates. "Get rid of them."

"Uh, sure." He turned back to the automold and clapped his hands. "Come on, boys and girls. Fun's over. Got to talk some business with the sam here."

They went, grudgingly, like small children denied a late night. One of the women tried to touch my face as she passed. I twitched irritably away, and she pouted at me. The doorman watched them out, then cast a querying glance at Plex. Plex echoed the look to me.

"Yeah, him, too."

The doorman left, shutting out some of the music blast. I looked back at

Plex, who was moving toward a low interior-lit hospitality module set against the sidewall. His movements were a curious mix of languid and nervous, *take* and situational jitters fighting it out in his blood. He reached into the glow of the module's upper shelf, hands clumsy among ornate crystal vials and delicate paper parcels.

"Uh, you want a pipe, man?"

"Plex." I played the last twist of the bluff for all it was worth. "Just what the *fuck* is going on?"

He flinched. Stuttered.

"I, uh, I thought Tanaseda would have—"

"*Fuck* that, Plex. Talk to me."

"Look, man, it's not my fault." His tone worked toward aggrieved. "Didn't I tell you guys right from the beginning she was fucked in the head? All that *kaikyo* shit she was spouting. Did any of you fucking listen? I *know* biotech, man, and I know when it's fucked up. And that cable-headed bitch was *fucked up.*"

So.

My mind whipped back two months to the first night outside the warehouse, sleeved synthetic, hands stained with priests' blood and a blaster bolt across the ribs, eavesdropping idly on Plex and Yukio. *Kaikyo*—a strait, a stolen-goods manager, a financial consultant, a sewage outlet. And a holy man possessed by spirits. Or a woman maybe, possessed by the ghost of a revolution three centuries past. Sylvie, carrying Nadia. Carrying Quell.

"Where'd they take her?" I asked quietly.

It wasn't Yukio's tone anymore, but I wasn't going to get much farther as Yukio anyway. I didn't know enough to sustain the lie in the face of Plex's lifelong acquaintance.

"Took her to Millsport, I guess." He was building himself a pipe, maybe to balance out the *take* blur. "I mean, Yukio, has Tanaseda really not—"

"Where in Millsport?"

Then he got it. I saw the knowledge soak through him, and he reached suddenly under the module's upper shelf. Maybe he had some neurachem wiring somewhere in that pale, aristocratic body he wore, but for him it would have been little more than an accessory. And the chemicals slowed him down so much it was laughable.

I let him get a hand on the gun, let him get it halfway clear of the shelf it was webbed under. Then I kicked his hand away, knocked him back onto the automold with a backfist, and stamped down on the shelf. Ornate glassware splintered, paper parcels flew, and the shelf cracked across. The gun fell out on the floor. Looked like a compact shard blaster, big brother to the GS Rapsodia under my coat. I scooped it up and turned in time to catch Plex scrambling for some kind of wall alarm.

"Don't."

He froze, staring hypnotized at the gun.

"Sit down. Over there."

He sank back into the automold, clutching at his arm where I'd kicked it. He was lucky, I thought with a brutality that almost instantly seemed too much effort, that I hadn't broken it for him.

Fucking set fire to it or something.

"Who." His mouth worked. "Who are you? You're not Hirayasu."

I put a splayed hand to my face and mimed taking off a Noh mask with a flourish. Bowed slightly.

"Well done. I am not Yukio. Though I do have him in my pocket."

His face creased. "What the fuck are you talking about?"

I reached into my jacket and pulled out one of the cortical stacks at random. In fact it wasn't Hirayasu's yellow-striped designer special, but from the look on Plex's face I judged the point made.

"Fuck. Kovacs?"

"Good guess." I put the stack away again. "The original. Accept no imitations. Now, unless you want to be sharing a pocket with your boyhood pal here, I suggest you go on answering my questions the way you were when you thought I was him."

"But, you're." He shook his head. "You're never going to get away with this, Kovacs. They've got. They've got *you* looking for you, man."

"I know. They must be desperate, right?"

"It isn't funny, man. He's fucking psychotic. They're still counting the bodies he left in Drava. They're Really Dead. Stacks gone, the works."

I felt a brief spike of shock, but it was almost distant. Behind it there was the grim chill that had come with my sight of Anton and the Skull Gang in Dig 301's recorded footage. Kovacs had gone to New Hok and he'd done the groundwork with Envoy intensity. He'd brought back what he needed. Corollary. What he couldn't use he'd left in smoking ruin behind him.

"So who'd he kill, Plex?"

"I. I don't know, man." He licked his lips. "A lot of people. All her team, all the people she—"

He stopped. I nodded, mouth tight. Detached regret for Jad, Kiyoka, and the others clamped and tamped down where it wouldn't get in the way.

"Yes. Her. Next question."

"Look, man, I can't help you. You shouldn't even—"

I shifted toward him, impatiently. Raging at the edges like lit paper. He flinched again, worse than he had when he thought I was Yukio.

"All right, all right. I'll tell you. Just leave me alone. What do you want to know?"

Go to work. Soak it up.

"First of all I want to know what *you* know, or think you know, about Sylvie Oshima."

He sighed. "Man, I told you not to get involved. Back in that sweeper bar. I warned you."

"Yeah, me and Yukio both, it seems. Very public-spirited of you, running around warning everybody. Why'd she scare you so much, Plex?"

"You don't know?"

"Let's pretend I don't." I raised a hand, displacement gesture as the anger threatened to get out. "And let's also pretend that if you try to lie to me, I'll torch your fucking head off."

He swallowed. "She's, she says she's Quellcrist Falconer."

"Yeah." I nodded. "So is she?"

"Fuck, man, how would I know?"

"In your professional opinion, could she be?"

"I don't know." He sounded almost plaintive. "What do you want from me? You went with her to New Hok, you know what it's like up there. I suppose, yeah, I suppose she *could* be. She might have stumbled on a cache of backed-up personalities. Gotten contaminated somehow."

"But you don't buy it?"

"It doesn't seem very likely. I can't see why a personality store would be set up to leak virally in the first place. Doesn't make any sense, even for a bunch of fuckwit Quellists. Where's the value? And least of all a backup of their precious fucking revolutionary wet-dream icon."

"So," I said tonelessly. "Not a big fan of the Quellists, then?"

For the first time I could remember, Plex seemed to shed his shield of apologetic diffidence. A choked snort came out of him—someone with less breeding would have spit, I guessed.

"Look around you, Kovacs. You think I'd be living like this if the Unsettlement hadn't hit the New Hok weed trade the way it did? Who do you think I've got to thank for that?"

"That's a complex historical question—"

"Like fuck it is."

"—that I'm not really qualified to answer. But I can see why you'd be pissed off. It must be tough having to trawl your playmates out of second-rate dance halls like this one. Not being able to afford the dress code on the First Families party circuit. I feel for you."

"Ha fucking ha."

I felt the way my own expression chilled over. Evidently he saw it, too, and the sudden rage leaked back out of him almost visibly. I talked to stop myself hitting and hurting him.

"I grew up in a Newpest slum, Plex. My mother and father worked the belaweed mills, everybody did. Temp contracts, day rate, no benefits. There were times we were lucky if we ate twice a day. And this wasn't any fucking trade slump, either, it was business as usual. Motherfuckers like you and your family got rich off it." I drew a breath and cranked myself back down to a dead irony. "So you're going to have to forgive my lack of sympathy for your tragically decayed aristo circumstances, because I'm a little short right now. 'Kay?"

He wet his lips and nodded.

"Okay. Okay, man, it's cool."

"Yeah." I nodded back. "Now. No reason for a stored copy of Quell to be set on viral deploy, you said."

"Yeah. Right, that's right." He was stumbling over himself to get back to safe ground. "And, anyway, look, she's, Oshima's loaded to the eyes with all sorts of baffles to stop viral stuff soaking through the coupling. That deCom command shit is state of the art."

"Yeah, so that brings us back to where we started. If she isn't really Quell, why are you so scared of her?"

He blinked at me. "Why am I—? Fuck, man, because whether she is Quell or whether she isn't, she *thinks* she is. That's a major psychosis. Would you put a psychotic in charge of that software?"

I shrugged. "From what I saw in New Hok, half of deCom would qualify for the same ticket. They're not overly balanced as a profession."

"Yeah, but I doubt many of them think they're the reincarnation of a revolutionary leader three centuries dead. I doubt they can quote—"

He stopped. I looked at him.

"Quote what?"

"Stuff. You know." He looked away, twitchily. "Old stuff from the war, the Unsettlement. You must have heard the way she talks sometimes, that period-flick Japanese she comes out with."

"Yeah, I have. But that's not what you were going to say, Plex. Is it."

He tried to get up from the automold. I stepped closer and he froze. I looked down at him with the same expression I'd had when I talked about my family. Didn't even lift the shard gun.

"Quote what?"

"Man, Tanaseda would—"

"Tanaseda isn't here. I am. Quote. What?"

He broke. Gestured weakly. "I don't even know if you'd understand what I'm talking about, man."

"Try me."

"Well, it's complicated."

"No, it's simple. Let me help you get started. The night I came to collect my sleeve, you and Yukio were talking about her. At a guess, you'd been doing some business with her, at a second guess you'd met her in that sweeper dock dive you took me to for breakfast, right?"

He nodded reluctantly.

"Okay. So the only thing I can't work out is why you were so surprised to see her there."

"I didn't think she'd come back," he muttered.

I remembered my first view of her that night, the entranced expression on her face as she stared at herself in the mirrorwood bar. Envoy recall dug out a fragment of conversation from the Kompcho apartment, later. Orr, talking up Lazlo's antics:

. . . still chasing that weapons chick with the cleavage, right?

And Sylvie: *What's that?*

You know. Tamsin, Tamita, whatever her name was. The one from that bar on Muko. Just before you pissed off on your own. Christ, you were there, Sylvie. I wouldn't have thought anyone could forget that rack.

And Jad: *She's not equipped to register that kind of armament.*

I shivered. No, not equipped. Not equipped to remember anything much, wandering around in the Tekitomura night torn between Sylvie Oshima and Nadia Makita, aka Quellcrist fucking Falconer. Not equipped to do anything except maybe navigate by dredged-up fragments of recall and dream, and fetch up in some vaguely remembered bar where, just as you were trying to put yourself back together, some hard-faced gang of bearded scum with a license to kill from God came to grind your face in the assumed inferiority of your gender.

I remembered Yukio when he burst into the Kompcho apartment the next morning. The fury in his face.

Kovacs, what exactly the fuck *do you think you're doing here?*

And his words to Sylvie when he saw her.

You know who I am.

Not a passing reference to his evident membership of the yakuza. *He thought she knew him.*

And Sylvie's even response. *I don't know who the fuck you are.* Because at that moment, she didn't. Envoy recall froze frame for me on the disbelief in Yukio's face. Not offended vanity after all. He was genuinely shocked.

In the scant seconds of the confrontation, in the seared flesh and blood of the aftermath, it hadn't occurred to me to wonder why he was so angry. Anger was a constant. The constant companion of the last two years and longer, rage in myself and the rage reflecting from those around me. I no longer questioned it, it was a state of being. Yukio was angry because he was. Because he was an asshole male with delusions of status just like Dad, just like the rest of them, and I'd humiliated him in front of Plex and Tanaseda. Because he was an asshole male just like the rest of them, in fact, and rage was the default setting.

Or:

Because you just wandered into the midst of a complicated deal with a

*dangerously unstable woman with a head full of state-of-the-art battletech soft-
ware and a direct line back to—*

What?

"What was she selling, Plex?"

The breath came out of him. He seemed to crumple with it.

"I don't know, Tak. Really, I don't. It was some kind of weapon, something from the Unsettlement. She called it the Qualgrist Protocol. Something
biological. They took it away from me as soon as I hooked her up with them.
Soon as I told them the preliminary data checked out." He looked away
again, this time with no trace of nerves. His voice took on a slurred bitterness. "Said it was too important for me. Couldn't trust me to keep my mouth
shut. They brought in specialists from Millsport. Fucking Yukio came with
them. They cut me out."

"But you were there. You'd seen her that night."

"Yeah, she was giving them stuff on blanked deCom chips. Pieces at a
time, you know, 'cause she didn't trust us." He coughed out a laugh. "No
more than we trusted her. I was supposed to go along each time and check
the prelim scrollup codes. Make sure they were genuine antiques. Everything
I okayed, Yukio took and handed on to his pet fucking EmPee team. I never
saw any of it. And you know who fucking found her in the first place? I did.
She came to me first. And all I get is flushed out with a finder's fee."

"How'd she find you?"

A dejected shrug. "Usual channels. She'd been asking around Tekitomura for weeks, apparently. Looking for someone to move this stuff for her."

"But she didn't tell you what it was?"

He picked moodily at a smear of bodypaint on the automold. "Nope."

"Plex, come on. She made a big enough splash with you that you called
in your yak pals, but she never showed you what it was she had."

"She asked for the fucking yak, not me."

I frowned. "*She* did?"

"Yeah. Said they'd be interested, said it was something they could use."

"Oh, that's *crabshit*, Plex. Why would the yakuza be interested in a
biotech weapon three centuries old? They're not fighting a war."

"Maybe she thought they could sell it on to the military for her. For a percentage."

"But she didn't say that. You just told me she said it would be something
they could *use*."

He stared up at me. "Yeah, maybe. I don't know. I'm not wired for that
fucking Envoy total-recall shit like you. I don't remember what she said, exactly. And I don't fucking care. Like they said, it's got nothing to do with me
anymore."

I stepped away from him. Leaned back on the container wall and examined the shard gun absently. Peripheral vision told me he wasn't moving from his slump on the automold. I sighed and it felt like weight shifting off my lungs, only to settle in again.

"All right, Plex. Just a couple more questions, easy ones, and I'm out of your hair. This new edition of me they've got, it was chasing Oshima, right? Not me?"

He clicked his tongue, barely audible above the fusion beat outside.

"Both of you. Tanaseda wants your head on a stick for what you did to Yukio, but you're not the main attraction."

I nodded bleakly. For a while I'd thought Sylvie must have somehow given herself away down in Tekitomura yesterday. Talked to the wrong person, been caught on the wrong surveillance cam, done something to bring the pursuit team crashing down on us like angelfire. But it wasn't that. It was simpler and worse—they'd vectored in on my own unshielded blunder through the Quellcrist Falconer archives. Must have had a global watch on the dataflows since this whole fucking mess blew up.

And you walked right into it. Nice going.

I grimaced. "And is Tanaseda running this?"

Plex hesitated.

"No? So who's reeling his line in then?"

"I don't—"

"Don't back up on me, Plex."

"Look, I don't fucking know. I don't. But it's up the food chain, I know that. First Families is what I hear, some Millsport court spymistress."

I felt a qualified sense of relief. Not the yakuza, then. Nice to know my market value hadn't fallen *that* far.

"This spymistress got a name?"

"Yeah." He got up abruptly and went to the hospitality module. Stared down into the smashed interior. "Name of Aiura. Real hardcase by all accounts."

"You haven't met her?"

He poked about in the debris I'd left, found an undamaged pipe. "No. I don't even get to see Tanaseda these days. No way I'd be let inside something at First Families level. But there's stuff about this Aiura on the court gossip circuit. She's got a reputation."

I snorted. "Yeah, don't they all."

"I'm serious, Tak." He fired up the pipe and looked reproachfully at me through the sudden smoke. "I'm trying to help you here. You remember that mess about sixty years ago, when Mitzi Harlan wound up in a Kossuth skullwalk porn flick?"

"Vaguely." I'd been busy at the time, stealing bioware and offworld data-bonds in the company of Virginia Vidaura and the Little Blue Bugs. High-yield criminality masquerading as political commitment. We watched the news for word of the police efforts at pursuit, not much else. There hadn't been a lot of time to worry about the incessant scandals and misdemeanors of Harlan's World's aristo larvae.

"Yeah, well, the word is that this Aiura ran damage limitation and clean-up for the Harlan family. Closed down the studio with extreme prejudice, hunted down everyone involved. I heard most of them got the skyride. She took them up to Rila Crags at night, strapped them to a grav pack each, and just flipped the switch."

"Very elegant."

Plex drew his lungs full of smoke and gestured. His voice came out squeaky.

"Way she is, apparently. Old school, you know."

"You got any idea where she got the copy of me from?"

He shook his head. "No, but I'd guess Protectorate military storage. He's young, a lot younger than you. Are now, I mean."

"You've met him?"

"Yeah, they hauled me in for an interview last month when he first got up here from Millsport. You can tell a lot about someone from the way they talk. He's still calling himself an Envoy."

I grimaced again.

"He's got an energy to him as well, it feels as if he can't wait to get things done, to get started on everything. He's confident, he's not scared of anything, nothing's a problem. He laughs at everything—"

"Yeah, all right, he's young. Got it. Did he say anything about me?"

"Not really, mostly he just asked questions and listened. Only." Plex drew on the pipe again. "I got the impression he was, I don't know, disappointed or something. About what you were doing these days."

I felt my eyes narrow. "He said that?"

"No, no." Plex waved the pipe, trickled smoke from his nose and mouth. "Just an impression I got, 's all."

I nodded. "Okay, one last question. You said they took her to Millsport. Where?"

Another pause. I shot him a curious look.

"Come on, what have you got to lose now? Where are they taking her?"

"Tak, let it go. This is just like the sweeper bar, all over again. You're getting involved in something that doesn't—"

"I'm already involved, Plex. Tanaseda's taken care of that."

"No, listen. Tanaseda will deal. You've got Yukio's stack, man. You could negotiate for its safe return. He'll do it, I *know* him. He and Hirayasu senior go back a century or more. He's Yukio's *sempai,* he's practically his adoptive uncle. He'll have to cut a deal."

"And you think this Aiura's going to let it go at that?"

"Sure, why not." Plex gestured with the pipe. "She's got what she wants. As long as you stay out of—"

"Plex, think about it. I'm double-sleeved. That's a UN rap, big-time penalties for all involved. Not to mention the issue of whether they're even entitled to hold a stored copy of a serving Envoy in the first place. If the Protectorate ever finds out about this, Aiura the spymistress is going to be looking at some serious storage, First Families connections or not. The sun'll be a fucking red dwarf by the time they let her out."

Plex snorted. "You think so? You really think the UN are going to come out here and risk upsetting the local oligarchy for the sake of one double-sleeving?"

"If it's made public enough, yes. They'll have to. They can't be seen to do anything else. Believe me, Plex, I know, I used to do this for a living. The whole Protectorate system hangs together on an assumption that no one dare step out of line. As soon as someone does, and gets away with it, no matter how small that initial transgression, it'll be like the first crack in the dam wall. If what's been done here becomes common knowledge, the Protectorate will have to demand Aiura's cortical stack on a plate. And if the First Families don't comply, the UN will send the Envoys, because a refusal by local oligarchy to comply can only be read one way, as insurrection. And insurrections get put down, wherever they are, at whatever cost, without fail."

I watched him, watched it sink in as it had sunk into me when I first heard the news in Drava. The understanding of what had been done, the step that had been taken, and the sequence of inevitability that we were all now locked into. The fact that there was no way back from this situation that didn't involve someone called Takeshi Kovacs dying for good.

"This Aiura," I said quietly, "has backed herself into a corner. I would love to know why, I would love to know what it was that was so fucking important it was worth this. But in the end it doesn't matter. One of us has to go, me or him, and the easiest way for her to make that happen is to keep sending him after me until either he kills me or I kill him."

He looked back at me, pupils blasted wide with the mix of whiff and mushrooms, pipe forgotten and trailing faint fumes from the cupped bowl of his hand. Like it was all too much to take in. Like I was a piece of *take* hallucination that refused to morph into something more pleasant or just go away.

I shook my head. Tried to get Sylvie's Slipins out of it.

"So like I said, Plex, I need to know. I *really* need to know. Oshima, Aiura, and Kovacs. Where do I find these people?"

He shook his head. "It's no good, Tak. I mean, I'll tell you. You really want to know, I'll tell you. But it isn't going to help. There's nothing you can do about this. There's no way you can—"

"Why don't you just tell me, Plex. Get it off your chest. Let me worry about the logistics."

So he told me. And I did the logistics, and worried at it.

All the way out, I worried at it, like a wolf at a limb caught in a trap. All the way out. Past the stoned and strobe-lit dancers, the recorded hallucinations and the chemical smiles. Past the throbbing translucent panels where a woman stripped to the waist met my eyes and smeared herself against the glass for me to look at. Past the cheap door muscle and detectors, the last tendrils of club warmth and reefdive rhythm, and out into the chill of the warehouse district night, where it was starting to snow.

PART THREE

THAT WAS A
WHILe AGO

That Quell, sure, man, she got something going on,
something you gotta think about. Thing is, some things last,
some things don't, but sometimes you got something don't
last won't be because it's gone, be because it's waiting for its
time to come again, maybe waiting on a change. Music's like
that, and so is life, man, so is life.

DIZZY CSANGO
from an interview for *New Sky Blue* magazine

CHAPTeR TWeNTY

There were storm warnings all the way south.

On some planets I've been to, they manage their hurricanes. Satellite tracking maps and models the storm system to see where it's going and, if necessary, associated precision beam weaponry can be used to rip its heart out before it does any damage. This is not an option we have on Harlan's World, and either the Martians didn't think it was worth programming that kind of thing into their own orbitals way back when, or the orbitals themselves have just stopped bothering since. Maybe they're sulking obscurely at being left behind. In any case, it leaves us back in the Dark Ages with surface-based monitoring and the odd low-level helicopter scout. Meteorological AIs help with prediction, but three moons and 0.8 G home gravity make for some seriously tumbled weather systems, and storms have been known to do some very odd things. When a Harlan's World hurricane gets into its stride there's really very little you can do but get well out of the way and stay there.

This one had been building for a while—I remembered newscasts about it the night we slipped out of Drava—and those who could move were moving. All across the Gulf of Kossuth, the urbrafts and seafactories were hauling keels west at whatever speed they could manage. Trawlers and rayhunters caught too far east sought anchorage in the relatively protected harbors among the Irezumi Shallows. Hoverloader traffic coming down from the Saffron Archipelago was rerouted out around the western cup of the Gulf. It put an extra day on the trip.

The skipper of the *Haiduci's Daughter* took it philosophically.

"Seen worse," he rumbled, peering into hooded displays on the bridge. "Back in the nineties, storm season got so bad we had to lay up in Newpest for more than a month. No safe traffic north at all."

I grunted noncommittally. He squinted away from the display at me.

"You were away then, right?"

"Yeah, offworld."

He laughed raspingly. "Yeah, that's right. All that exotic travel you been doing. So when do I get to see your pretty face on KossuthNet, then? Got a one-to-one lined up with Maggie Sugita when we get in?"

"Give me time, man."

"More time? Haven't you had enough *time* yet?"

It was the line of banter we'd maintained all the way down from Tekitomura. Like quite a few freight skippers I'd met, Ari Japaridze was a shrewd but relatively unimaginative man. He knew next to nothing about me, which, he told me, was the way he liked things to stay with his passengers, but he was nobody's fool. And it didn't take an archaeologue to work out that if a man comes aboard your raddled old freighter an hour before it leaves and offers as much for a cramped crewroom berth as you'd pay for a Saffron Line cabin—well, that man probably isn't on friendly terms with law enforcement. For Japaridze, the holes he'd turned up in my knowledge of the last couple of decades on Harlan's World had a very simple explanation. I'd been away, in the time-honored criminal sense of the word. I countered this assumption with the simple truth about my absence and got the rasping laugh every time.

Which suited me fine. People will believe what they want to believe—look at the fucking Beards—and I got the distinct impression that there was some storage time in Japaridze's past. I don't know what he saw when he looked at me, but I got an invite up to the bridge on our second evening out of Tekitomura, and by the time we left Erkezes on the southernmost tip of the Saffron Archipelago we were swapping notes on preferred Newpest drinking holes and how best to barbecue bottleback steaks.

I tried not to let the time chafe at me.

Tried not to think about the Millsport Archipelago and the long westward arc we were cutting away from it.

Sleep was hard.

The nighttime bridge of the *Haiduci's Daughter* provided a viable alternative. I sat with Japaridze and drank cheap Millsport blended whiskey, watching as the freighter plowed her way south into warmer seas and air that was fragrant with the scent of belaweed. I talked, as automatic as the machines that kept the vessel on her curving course, stock tales of sex and travel, memories of Newpest and the Kossuth hinterlands. I massaged the muscles of my left arm where they still ached and throbbed. I flexed my left hand against the pain it gave me. Beneath it all, I thought about ways to kill Aiura and myself.

By day, I prowled the decks and mingled with the other passengers as little as possible. They were an unappealing bunch anyway, three burned-out and bitter-talking deComs heading south, maybe for home, maybe just for the sun; a hard-eyed webjelly entrepreneur and his bodyguard, accompanying an oil shipment to Newpest; a young New Revelation priest and his carefully wrapped wife, who joined ship at Erkezes. Another half a dozen less memorable men and women who kept to themselves even more than I did and looked away whenever they were spoken to.

A certain degree of social interaction was unavoidable. *Haiduci's Daughter* was a small vessel, in essence not much more than a tug welded onto the nose of four duplex freight pods and a powerful hoverload driver. Access gantries ran at two levels from the forward decks between and alongside the pods and back to a narrow observation bubble bolted onto the rear. What living space there was felt crowded. There were a few squabbles early on, including one over stolen food that Japaridze had to break up with threats of putting people off at Erkezes, but by the time we left the Saffron Archipelago behind, everybody had pretty much settled down. I had a couple of forced conversations with the deComs over meals, trying to show interest in their hard-luck stories and life-in-the-Uncleared bravado. From the webjelly oil merchant I got repetitive lectures on the economic benefits that would emerge from the Mecsek regime's austerity program. The priest I didn't talk to at all, because I didn't want to have to hide his body afterward.

We made good time from Erkezes to the Gulf, and there was no sign of a storm when we got there. I found myself crowded out of my usual brooding spots as the other passengers came out to enjoy the novelty of warm weather and sun strong enough to tan. You couldn't blame them—the sky was a solid blue from horizon to horizon, Daikoku and Hotei both showing clear and high up. A strong breeze out of the northeast kept the heat pleasant and lifted spray from the ruffled surface of the sea. Westward, waves broke white and just audible on the great curving reefs that heralded the eventual rise of the Kossuth Gulf coastline farther south.

"It's beautiful, isn't it?" said a quiet voice beside me at the rail.

I glanced sideways and saw the priest's wife, still scarfed and robed despite the weather. She was alone. Her face, what I could see of it, tilted up at me out of the tightly drawn circle of the scarf that covered her below the mouth and above the brow. It was beaded with sweat from the unaccustomed heat but didn't seem unconfident. She had scraped her hair back so that not a trace made it past the cloth. She was very young, probably not long out of her teens. She was also, I realized, several months pregnant.

I turned away, mouth suddenly tight.

Focused on the view beyond the deck rail.

"I've never traveled this far south before," she went on, when she saw I wasn't going to take her up on her first gambit. "Have you?"

"Yeah."

"Is it always this hot?"

I looked at her again, bleakly. "It isn't hot, you're just inappropriately dressed."

"Ah." She placed her gloved hands on the rail and appeared to examine them. "You do not approve?"

I shrugged. "It's got nothing to do with me. We live in a free world, didn't you know? Leo Mecsek says so."

"Mecsek." She made a small spitting sound. "He is as corrupt as the rest of them. As all the materialists."

"Yeah, but give him his due. If his daughter ever gets raped, he's unlikely to beat her to death for dishonoring him."

She flinched.

"You are talking about an isolated incident, this is not—"

"Four." I held out my fingers, rigid in front of her face. "I'm talking about *four* isolated incidents. And that's just this year."

I saw color rise in her cheeks. She seemed to be looking down at her own slightly protruding belly.

"The New Revelation is not always most honestly served by those most active in its advocacy," she murmured. "Many of us—"

"Many of you cringe along in compliance, hoping to peel something of worth from the less psychotic directives of your gynocidal belief system because you don't have the wit or nerve to build something entirely new. I know."

Now she was flushing to the roots of her painstakingly hidden hair.

"You misjudge me." She touched the scarf she wore. "I have chosen this. Chosen it freely. I believe in the Revelation, I have my faith."

"Then you're more stupid than you look."

An outraged silence. I used it to crank the flurry of rage in my own chest back under control.

"So I'm stupid? Because I choose modesty in womanhood, I'm stupid. Because I don't display and cheapen myself at every opportunity like that whore Mitzi Harlan and her kind, because—"

"Look," I said coldly. "Why don't you exercise some of that modesty and just shut your womanly little mouth? I really don't care what you think."

"See," she said, voice turned slightly shrill. "You lust after her like all the others. You give in to her cheap sensual tricks and—"

"Oh *please.* For my money, Mitzi Harlan's a stupid, superficial little trollop, but you know what? At least she lives her life as if it belongs to her. Instead of abasing herself at the feet of any fucking baboon who can grow a beard and some external genitalia."

"Are you calling my husband a—"

"No." I swung on her. It seemed I didn't have it cranked down after all. My hands shot out and grasped her by the shoulders. "No, I'm calling *you* a gutless betrayer of your sex. I can see your husband's angle, he's a man, he's got everything to gain from this crabshit. But *you*? You've thrown away centuries of political struggle and scientific advance so you can sit in the dark and mutter your superstitions of unworth to yourself. You'll let your life, the most precious thing you have, be stolen from you hour by hour and day by day as long as you can eke out the existence your males will let you have. And then, when you finally die, and I hope it's soon, sister, I *really* do, then at the last you'll spite your own potential and shirk the final power we've won for ourselves to come back and try again. You'll do all of this because of your fucking faith, and if that child in your belly is female, then you'll condemn her *to the same fucking thing*."

Then there was a hand on my arm.

"Hey, man." It was one of the deComs, backed up by the entrepreneur's bodyguard. He looked scared but determined. "That's enough. Leave her alone."

I looked at his fingers, where they hung on my elbow. I wondered briefly about breaking them, locking out the arm behind them and—

A memory flared to life inside me. My father shaking my mother by the shoulders like a belaweed rack that wouldn't come loose of its mooring, screaming abuse and whiskey fumes into her face. Seven years old, I'd gone for his arm and tried to tug it away.

He'd clouted me almost absently that time, across the room and into a corner. Gone back to her.

I unlocked my hands from the woman's shoulders. Shook off the deCom's grip. Mentally shook myself by the throat.

"Now back off, man."

"Sure," I said it quietly. "Like I said, sister. 'S a free world. Got nothing to do with me."

● ● ●

The storm clipped us around the ear a couple of hours later. A long trailing scarf of bad weather that darkened the sky outside my porthole and caught the *Haiduci's Daughter* broadside-on. I was flat on my back in my bunk at the time, staring at the metal-gray ceiling and giving myself a furious lecture on undesirable involvement. I heard the engine thrum kick up a notch and guessed Japaridze was pulling more buoyancy from the grav system. A couple of minutes later the narrow cabin space seemed to lurch sideways; on the table opposite a glass slid a couple of centimeters before the antispill surface gripped it in place. The water it held slopped alarmingly and splashed over the edge. I sighed and got off the bunk, bracing myself across the cabin and leaning down to peer out the porthole. Sudden rain slapped the glass.

Somewhere in the freighter, an alarm went off.

I frowned. It seemed an extreme response to what wasn't much more than some choppy water. I shouldered my way into a light jacket I'd bought from one of the freighter's crew members, stowed Tebbit knife and Rapsodia beneath it, and slipped out into the corridor.

Getting involved again, are we?

Hardly. If this tub is going to sink, I want advance warning.

I followed the alarms up to main deck level and out into the rain. A member of the crew passed me, hefting a clumsy long-barrel blaster.

" 'S going on?" I asked her.

"Search me, sam." She spared me a grim look, jerked her head aft. "Main board's showing a breach in cargo. Maybe a ripwing trying to get in out of the storm. Maybe not."

"You want a hand?"

She hesitated, suspicion swimming momentarily on her face, then made a decision. Maybe Japaridze had said something to her about me, maybe she just liked my recently acquired face. Or maybe she was just scared and could use the company.

"Sure. Thanks."

We worked our way back toward the cargo pods and along one of the gantries, bracing ourselves each time the freighter rolled. Rain whipped in at odd, wind-driven angles. The alarm shrilled querulously over the weather. Ahead, in the sudden, sullen gloom of the squall, a row of red lights pulsed on and off along one section of the left-hand freight pod. Below the flashing alert signals, pale light showed from the edge of a cracked hatch. The crewwoman hissed and gestured with the blaster barrel.

"That's it." She started forward. "Someone's in there."

I shot her a glance. "Or something. Ripwings, right?"

"Yeah, but it takes a pretty sharp ripwing to figure out the buttons. Usually they'll just short the system with a beakbutt and hope it lets them in. And I don't smell anything burning."

"Me neither." I calibrated the gantry space, the rise of the cargo pods over us. Drew the Rapsodia and dialed it to maximum dispersal. "Okay, so let's do this sensibly. Let me go in there first."

"I'm supposed—"

"Yeah, I'm sure you are. But I used to do this for a living. So how about you have this one on me. Stay here, shoot anything that comes out of that hatch unless you hear me call it first."

I moved to the hatch as carefully as I could on the unstable footing and examined the locking mechanism. There didn't appear to be any damage. The hatch hung outward a couple of centimeters, maybe tipped that way by the pitch of the freighter in the squall.

After whichever pirate ninja opened it had cracked the lock, that is.

Thanks for that.

I tuned out the squall and the alarm. Listened for motion on the other side, cranked the neurachem tight enough to pick up heavy breathing.

Nothing. No one there.

Or someone with stealth combat training.

Will you shut up.

I fitted one foot against the edge of the hatch and gave it a cautious shove. The hinges were balanced to a hair—the whole thing swung weightily outward. Without giving myself time to think, I twisted into the gap, Rapsodia tracking for a target.

Nothing.

Waist-high steel barrels stood in shiny ranks across the cargo space. The gaps between were too thin to hide a child, let alone a ninja. I crossed to the nearest and read the label. FINEST SAFFRON SEAS LUMINESCENT XENOMEDUSAL EXTRACT, COLD PRESS FILTERED. Webjelly oil, designer-branded for added value. Courtesy of our entrepreneurial expert on austerity.

I laughed and felt the tension puddle back out of me.

Nothing but—

I sniffed.

There was a scent, fleeting on the metallic air in the cargo pod.

And gone.

The New Hok sleeve's senses were just acute enough to know it was there, but with the knowledge and the conscious effort, it vanished. Out of nowhere, I had a sudden flash recollection of childhood, an uncharacteristically happy image of warmth and laughter that I couldn't place. Whatever the smell was, it was something I knew intimately.

I stowed the Rapsodia and moved back to the hatch.

"There's nothing in here. I'm coming out."

I stepped back into the warm splatter of the rain and heaved the hatch closed again. It locked into place with a solid thunk of security bolts, shutting in whatever trace scent of the past I'd picked up on. The pulsing reddish radiance over my head died out and the alarm, which had settled to an unnoticed background constant, was abruptly silent.

"What were you doing in there?"

It was the entrepreneur, face tense closing on angry. He had his security in tow. A handful of crew members crowded behind. I sighed.

"Checking on your investment. All sealed and safe, don't worry. Looks like the pod locks glitched." I looked at the crew-woman with the blaster. "Or maybe that extra-smart ripwing showed up after all and we scared it off. Look, this is a bit of a long shot I know, but is there a sniffer set anywhere aboard?"

"*Sniffer* set? Like, for the police you mean?" She shook her head. "I don't think so. You could ask the skipper."

I nodded. "Yeah, well, like I said—"

"I asked you a question."

The tension in the entrepreneur's features had made it all the way to anger. At his side, his security glared supportively.

"Yeah, and I answered it. Now, if you'll excuse me—"

"You're not going anywhere. Tomas."

I cut the bodyguard a glance before he could act on the command. He froze and shifted his feet. I shifted my eyes to the entrepreneur, fighting a strong urge to push the confrontation as far as it would go. Since my run-in with the priest's wife, I'd been twitchy with the need to do violence.

"If your tuskhead here touches me, he's going to need surgery. And if you don't get out of my way, so will you. I already told you, your cargo's safe. Now suppose you step aside and save us both an embarrassing scene."

He looked back at Tomas, and evidently read something instructive in his expression. He moved.

"Thank you." I pushed my way through the gathered crew members behind him. "Anybody seen Japaridze?"

"On the bridge, probably," said someone. "But Itsuko's right, there's no sniffer gear on the *'Duci*. We're not fucking *seacops*."

Laughter. Someone sang the signature tune to the experia show of the same name, and the rest took it up for a couple of bars. I smiled thinly and shouldered my way past. As I left, I heard the entrepreneur demanding loudly that the hatch be opened again immediately.

Oh well.

I went to find Japaridze anyway. If nothing else, at least he could provide me with a drink.

The squall passed.

I sat on the bridge and watched it fade away eastward on the weather scanners, wishing the knot inside me would do the same. Outside, the sky brightened and the waves stopped knocking the *Haiduci's Daughter* about. Japaridze slacked off the emergency drive to the grav motors, and the freighter settled back into her former stability.

"So tell me the truth, sam." He poured me another shot of Millsport blended and settled back in the chair across the navigation table. There was no one else on the bridge. "You're casing the webjelly consignment, right?"

I lifted an eyebrow. "Well, if I am, that's a pretty unhealthy question to ask me."

"Nah, not really." He winked and knocked his drink back in one. Since it had become clear that the weather was going to leave us alone, he'd let himself get slightly drunk. "That fucking prick, for me you can have his cargo. Just so long as you don't try and lift it while it's on the *'Duci.'*"

"Right." I raised my glass to him.

"So who is it?"

"I'm sorry?"

"Who you running radar for? The yak? Weed Expanse gangs? Thing is—"

"Ari, I'm serious."

He blinked at me. "What?"

"Think about it. If I'm a yak research squad, you go asking questions like that, it's going to get you Really Dead."

"Ah, crabshit. You ain't going to kill me." He got up, leaned across the table toward me, and peered into my face. "You don't got the eyes for it. I can tell."

"Really."

"Yeah, besides." He sank back into his seat and gestured untidily with his glass. "Who's going to sail this tub into Newpest harbor if I'm dead. She's not like those Saffron Line AI babies, you know. Every now and then, she needs the human touch."

I shrugged. "I guess I could scare someone on the crew into it. Show them your smoldering corpse for an incentive."

"That's good thinking." He grinned and reached for the bottle again. "I hadn't thought of that. But like I said, I don't see it in your eyes."

"Met a lot like me, have you?"

He filled our glasses. "Man, I *was* one like you. I grew up in Newpest just like you and I was a pirate, just like you. Used to work route robberies with the Seven Percent Angels. Crabshit stuff, skimmer cargo coming in over the Expanse." He paused and looked me in the eyes. "I got caught."

"That's too bad."

"Yeah, it was too bad. They took the flesh off me and they dumped me in the store for three decades, near enough. When I got out, all they had to sleeve me in was some wired-for-shit methhead's body. My family had all grown up, or moved away, or, you know, died or something. I had a daughter, seven years old when I went in, she was ten years older than the sleeve I was wearing by the time I got out. She had a life and a family of her own. Even if I had known how to relate to her, she didn't want to know me. I was just a thirty-year gap in her eyes. Likewise her mother, who'd found some other guy, had kids, well, you know how it goes." He sank his drink, shivered and stared at me through suddenly teared eyes. He poured himself another. "My brother died in a bug crash a couple of years after I went away, no insurance, no way to get a resleeve. My sister was in the store, she'd gone in ten years after me, wasn't getting out for another twenty. There'd been another brother, born a couple of years after I went away, I didn't know what to say to him. My father and mother were separated—he died first, got his resleeve policy through, and went off somewhere to be young, free, and single again. Wouldn't wait for her. I went to see her but all she did was stare out of the window with this smile on her face, kept saying *soon, soon, it'll be my turn soon.* Gave me the fucking creeps."

"So you went back to the Angels."

"Good guess."

I nodded. It wasn't a guess, it was a riff on the lives of a dozen acquaintances from my own Newpest youth.

"Yeah, the Angels. They had me back, they'd gone up a notch or two in the scheme of things. Couple of the same guys I used to run with. They were knocking over hoverloaders on the Millsport runs from the inside. Good money, and with a meth habit to support I needed that. Ran with them for about two, three years. Got caught again."

"Yeah?" I made an effort, tried to look mildly surprised. "How long this time?"

He grinned, like a man in front of a fire. "Eighty-five."

We sat in silence for a while. Finally, Japaridze poured more whiskey and sipped at his drink as if he didn't really want it.

"This time, I lost them all for good. Whatever second life my mother got, I missed that. And she'd opted out of a third time around, just had herself stored with instructions for rental resleeve on a list of family occasions. Release of her son Ari from penal storage wasn't on that list, so I took the hint. Brother was still dead, sister got out of the store while I was in, went north decades before I got out again, I don't know where. Maybe looking for her father."

"And your daughter's family?"

He laughed and shrugged. "Daughter, grandkids. Man, by then I was another two generations out of step with them, I didn't even try to catch up. I just took what I had and I ran with it."

"Which was what?" I nodded at him. "This sleeve?"

"Yeah, this sleeve. I got what you might call lucky. Belonged to some rayhunter captain got busted for hooking out of a First Families marine estate. Good solid sleeve, well looked after. Some useful seagoing software racked in, and some weird instinctive shit for weather. Sort of painted a career for me all on its own. I got a loan on a boat, made some money. Got a bigger boat, made some more. Got the *'Duci.* Got a woman back in Newpest now. Couple of kids I'm watching grow up."

I raised my glass without irony. "Congratulations."

"Yeah, well, like I said. I got lucky."

"And you're telling me this because?"

He leaned forward on the table and looked at me. "You know why I'm telling you this."

I quelled a grin. It wasn't his fault, he didn't know. He was doing his best.

"All right, Ari. Tell you what, I'll lay off your cargo. I'll mend my ways, give up piracy, and start a family. Thanks for the tip."

He shook his head. "Not telling you anything you don't already know, sam. Just reminding you, is all. This life is like the sea. There's a three-moon tidal slop running out there and if you let it, it'll tear you apart from everyone and everything you ever cared about."

● ● ●

He was right, of course.

As a messenger, he was also a little late.

Evening caught up with the *Haiduci's Daughter* on her westward curve a couple of hours later. The sun split like a cracked egg either side of a rising Hotei, and reddish light soaked out across the horizon in both directions. The low rise of Kossuth's Gulf coastline painted a thick black base for the picture. High above, thin cloud cover glowed like a shovel full of heated coins.

I avoided the forward decks, where the rest of the passengers had gathered to watch the sunset—I doubted I'd be welcome among them given my various performances today. Instead I worked my way back along one of the freight gantries, found a ladder, and climbed it to the top of the pod. There was a narrow walkway there, and I settled cross-legged onto its scant breadth.

I hadn't lived quite the idiotic waste of youth Japaridze had, but the end result wasn't much different. I beat the traps of stupid crime and storage at an early age, but only just. By the time I hit my late teens, I'd traded in my Newpest gang affiliations for a commission in the Harlan's World tactical marines—if you're going to be in a gang, it might as well be the biggest one on the block, and no one fucked with the tacs. For a while, it seemed like the smart move.

Seven uniformed years down that road, the Corps recruiters came for me. Routine screening put me at the top of a shortlist, and I was invited to volunteer for Envoy conditioning. It wasn't the kind of invitation you turned down. A couple of months later I was offworld, and the gaps started opening up. Time away, needlecast into action across the Settled Worlds, time laid down in military storage and virtual environments between. Time speeded up, slowed down, rendered meaningless anyway by interstellar distance. I began to lose track of my previous life. Furlough back home was infrequent and brought with it a sense of dislocation each time that discouraged me from going as often as I could have. As an Envoy, I had the whole Protectorate as a playground—*might as well see some of it,* I reasoned at the time.

And then Innenin.

When you leave the Envoys, there are a very limited number of career options. No one trusts you enough to lend you capital, and you're flat-out forbidden under UN law to hold corporate or governmental posts. Your choices, apart from straight-up poverty, are mercenary warfare or crime. Crime is safer, and easier to do. Along with a few colleagues who'd also resigned from the Corps after the Innenin debacle, I ended up back on Harlan's World running rings around local law enforcement and the petty criminals they played tag with. We carved out reputations, stayed ahead of the game, went through anyone who opposed us like angelfire.

An attempted family reunion started out badly, plunged downhill from there. Ended in shouting and tears.

It was my fault as much as anyone's. My mother and sisters were unfamiliar semi-strangers already, memories of the bonds we'd once had blurred indistinct alongside the sharp shining functions of my Envoy recall. I'd lost track, didn't know where they were in their lives. The salient novelty was my mother's marriage to a Protectorate recruiting executive. I met him once, and wanted to kill him. The feeling was probably mutual. In my family's eyes, I'd crossed a line somewhere. Worse still, they were right—all we disagreed on was where that line had been. For them it was neatly epoxied to the boundary between my military service to the Protectorate and my step into unsanctioned for-personal-profit criminality. For me, it had come less specifically at some unnoticed moment during my time in the Corps.

But try explaining that to someone who hasn't been there.

I did try, briefly. The immediate and obvious pain it caused my mother was enough to make me stop. It was shit she didn't need.

On the horizon, the sun was gone to molten leavings. I looked southeast where the dark was gathering, approximately toward Newpest.

I wouldn't be dropping in to see anyone on my way through.

Leathery flap of wings past my shoulder. I glanced up and spotted a ripwing banking about over the freight pod, black turning iridescent shades of green in the last rays of the sun. It circled me a couple of times, then came in to land on the walkway an insolent half a dozen meters away. I edged around to watch it. Down around Kossuth they flock less and grow bigger than the ones I'd seen in Drava, and this specimen was a good meter from webbed talons to beak. Big enough to make me glad I was armed. It folded its wings with a rasp, lifted one shoulder in my direction, and regarded me unblinkingly from a single eye. It seemed to be waiting for something.

"Fuck are you looking at?"

For a long moment the ripwing was silent. Then it arched its neck, flexed its wings, and screeched at me a couple of times. When I didn't move, it settled down and cocked its head at a quizzical angle.

"I'm not going to see them," I told it after a while. "So don't try talking me into it. It's been too long."

But still, in the fast-growing gloom around me, that itch of family I'd felt in the pod. Like warmth from the past.

Like not being alone.

The ripwing and I sat hunched six meters apart, watching each other in silence while darkness fell.

CHAPTeR TWeNTY-ONe

Wpulled into Newpest harbor a little after noon the next day and crept to a mooring with painstaking care. The whole port was jammed up with hoverloaders and other vessels fleeing the threat of heavy weather in the eastern Gulf, and the harbormaster software had arranged them according to some counterintuitive mathematical scheme that the *Haiduci's Daughter* didn't have an interface for. Japaridze took the con on manual, cursing machines in general and the Port Authority AI in particular as we wound our way through the apparently random thickets of shipping.

"Fucking upgrade this, upgrade that. If I'd wanted to be a fucking tech-head, I would have gotten a job with deCom."

Like me, he had a slight but insistent hangover.

We said our farewells on the bridge, and I went down to the foredeck. I tossed my pack ashore while the autograpples were still cranking us in, and leapt the closing gap to the wharf from the rail. It got me a couple of glances from bystanders but no uniformed attention. With a circling storm out on the horizon and a harbor packed to capacity, port security had other things to worry about than reckless disembarkation. I picked up the pack, slung it on one shoulder, and drifted into the sparse flow of pedestrians along the wharf. The heat settled on me wetly. In a couple of minutes I was off the waterfront, streaming sweat and flagging down an autocab.

"Inland harbor," I told it. "Charter terminal, and hurry."

The cab made a U-turn and plunged back into the main crosstown thoroughfares. Newpest unfolded around me.

It's changed a lot in the couple of centuries I've been coming back to it. The town I grew up in was low lying, like the land it was built on, sprawling in stormproofed snub profile units and superbubbles across the isthmus between the sea and the great clogged lake that would later become the Weed Expanse. Back then Newpest carried the fragrance of belaweed and the stink of the various industrial processes it was subject to like the mix of perfume and body odor on a cheap whore. You couldn't get away from either without leaving town.

So much for youthful reminiscence.

As the Unsettlement receded into history, a return to relative prosperity brought new growth, out along the inner shore of the Expanse and the long curve of the coastline, and upward into the tropical sky. The height of the buildings in central Newpest soared, rising on the back of increased confidence in storm management technology and a burgeoning, moneyed middle class who needed to live near their investments but didn't want to have to smell them. By the time I joined the Envoys, environmental legislation had started to take the edge off the air at ground level and there were skyscrapers downtown to rival anything you could find in Millsport.

After that my visits were infrequent, and I wasn't paying enough attention to notice when exactly the trend started to reverse and why. All I knew was that now there were quarters of the southern city where the stink was back, and the brave new developments along the coast and the Expanse were collapsing, kilometer by kilometer, into creeping shantytown decay. In the center, there were beggars on the streets and armed security outside most of the large buildings. Looking out of the side window of the autocab, I caught an echo of irritated tension in the way people moved that hadn't been there forty years before.

We crossed the center in a raised priority lane that sent the digits on the cab meter spinning into a blur. It didn't last long—aside from one or two glossy limos and a scattering of cabs, we had the vaulted road to ourselves, and when we picked up the main Expanse highway on the other side, the charge count settled down to a reasonable rate. We curled away from the high-rise zone and out across the shanties. Low-level housing, pressed up close to the carriageway. This story I already knew from Segesvar. The cleared embankment space on either side of the road had been sold off while I was away and previous health and safety restrictions waived. I caught a glimpse of a naked two-year-old child gripping the wire fence around a flat roof, mesmerized by the blastpast of the traffic two meters from her face. On another roof farther along, two kids not much older hurled makeshift missiles that missed and fell bouncing in our wake.

The inland harbor exit sprang on us. The autocab took the turn at machine velocity, drifted across a couple of lanes, and braked to a more human speed as we rode the spiral curve through the shanty neighborhood and down to the fringes of the Weed Expanse. I don't know why the program ran that way—maybe I was supposed to be admiring the view; the terminal itself was pretty to look at anyway—steel-boned and up-jutting, plated in blue illuminum and glass. The carriageway ran through it like thread through a fishing float.

We drew up smoothly inside and the cab presented the charge in brilliant mauve numerals. I fed it a chip, waited for the doors to unlock, and climbed out into vaulted, air-conditioned cool. Scattered figures wandered back and forth or sat about the place either begging or waiting for something. Charter company desks were ranked along one wall of the building, backed and crowned with a range of brightly colored holos that in most cases included a virtual customer service construct. I picked one with a real person, a boy in his late teens who sat slumped over the counter fiddling with the quickplant sockets in his neck.

"You for hire?"

He turned lackluster eyes on me without lifting his head.

"Mama."

I was about to slap him when it hit me that this wasn't some obscure insult. He was wired for internal tannoy, he just couldn't be bothered to subvocalize. His eyes switched momentarily out to the middle distance as he listened to a response, then he looked at me again with fractionally more focus.

"Where you want to go?"

"Vchira Beach. One-way passage, you can leave me there."

He smirked. "Yeah, Vchira Beach—it's seven hundred klicks from end to end, sam. *Where* on Vchira Beach?"

"Southern reach. The Strip."

"Sourcetown." His gaze flickered doubtfully over me. "You a surfer?"

"Do I look like a surfer?"

Evidently there wasn't a safe answer to that. He shrugged sullenly and looked away, eyes fluttering upward as he hit the internal wire again. A couple of moments after that a tough-looking blond woman in weed-farm cutoffs and a faded T-shirt came in from the yard side of the terminal. She was in her fifties and life had frayed her around the eyes and mouth, but the cutoffs showed slim swimmer's legs and she carried herself erect. The T-shirt declared GIVE ME MITZI HARLAN'S JOB—I COULD DO IT LYING DOWN. There was a light sweat on her brow and traces of grease on her fingertips. Her handshake was dry and callused.

"Suzi Petkovski. This is my son, Mikhail. So you want me to run you out to the Strip?"

"Micky. Yeah, how soon can we leave?"

She shrugged. "I'm stripping down one of the turbines but it's routine. Say an hour, half if you don't care about security checks."

"An hour is fine. I'm supposed to be meeting someone before I go anyway. How much is it going to cost me?"

She hissed through her teeth. Looked up and down the long hall of competing desks and the lack of custom. "Sourcetown's a long haul. Bottom end of the Expanse and then some. You got baggage?"

"Just what you see."

"Do it for two hundred and seventy-five. I know it's one-way, but I got to come back even if you don't. And it's the whole day gone."

The price was a high shot, just begging to be haggled down under the 250 mark. But two hundred wasn't much more than I'd just paid for my priority cab ride across town. I shrugged.

"Sure. Seems very reasonable. You want to show me my ride?"

● ● ●

Suzi Petkovski's skimmer was pretty much the standard package—a blunt-nosed twenty-meter twin-turbine rig that deserved the name *hoverloader* more purely than did any of the huge vessels plying the sea-lanes of Harlan's World. There was no antigrav system to kick up the buoyancy, just the engines and the armored skirt, a variant on the basic machine they've been building since the pre-diaspora days on Earth. There was a sixteen-seat cabin forward and freight rack storage aft, railed walkways along either side of the superstructure from cockpit to stern. On the roof behind the pilot's cupola, a nasty-looking ultravibe cannon was mounted in a cheap autoturret.

"That get much use?" I asked, nodding up at the weapon's split snout.

She swung herself up onto the opened turbine mounting with accustomed grace, then looked back down at me gravely. "There are still pirates on the Expanse, if that's what you mean. But they're mostly kids, mostly methed to the eyes or"—an involuntary glance back toward the terminal building—"wirehead cases. Rehabilitation projects all folded with the funding cuts, we got a big street problem and it spills over into banditry out there. But they're not much to shout about, any of them. Usually scare off with a couple of warning shots. I wouldn't worry about it if I were you. You want to leave your pack in the cabin?"

"No, it's okay, it's not heavy." I left her to the turbine and retreated to a shaded area at the end of the wharf where empty crates and canisters had been piled without much care. I seated myself on one of the cleaner ones and opened my pack. Sorted through my phones and found an unused one. Dialed a local number.

"Southside Holdings," said an androgynous synth voice. "Due to—"

I reeled off the fourteen-digit discrete coding. The voice sank into static hiss and then silence. There was a long pause, then another voice, human this time. Male and unmistakable. The bitten-off syllables and squashed vowels of Newpest-accented Amanglic, as raw as they had been when I first met him on the streets of the city a lifetime ago.

"Kovacs, where the *fuck* have you been?"

I grinned despite myself. "Hey, Rad. Nice to talk to you, too."

"It's nearly three fucking months, man. I'm not running a pet hotel down here. Where's my money?"

"It's been *two* months, Radul."

"It's been more than two."

"It's been nine weeks—that's my final offer."

He laughed down the line, a sound that reminded me of a trawl winch cranking at speed. "Okay, Tak. So how was your trip? Catch any fish?"

"Yes, I did." I touched the pocket where I'd stowed the cortical stacks. "Got some for you right here as promised. Canned for ease of carriage."

"Of course. Hardly expect you to bring it fresh. Imagine the stink. Especially after three months."

"Two months."

The trawler winch again. "Nine weeks, I thought we agreed. So are you in town, finally?"

"Near enough, yeah."

"You coming out to visit?"

"Yeah, see, that's the problem. Something's come up and I can't. But I wouldn't want you to miss out on the fish—"

"No, nor would I. Your last consignment hasn't kept well. Barely fit for consumption these days. My boys think I'm crazy still serving it up, but I told them. Takeshi Kovacs is old school. He pays his debts. We do what he asks, and when he surfaces *finally,* he will do what is right."

I hesitated. Calibrated.

"I can't get you your money right now, Rad. I daren't go near a major credit transaction. Wouldn't be good for you any more than for me. I'll need time to sort it out. But you can have the fish, if you send someone to collect in the next hour."

The silence crawled back onto the line. This was pushing the elastic of the debt to failure point, and we both knew it.

"Look, I got four. That's one more than expected. You can have them now, all of them. You can serve them up without me, use them how you like, or not at all if my credit's really out."

He said nothing. His presence on the line was oppressive, like the wet heat coming off the Weed Expanse. Envoy sense told me this was the break, and Envoy sense is rarely wrong.

"The money's coming, Rad. Hit me with a surcharge, if that's what it takes. As soon as I'm done with this other shit, we're back to business as usual. This is strictly temporary."

Still nothing. The silence was beginning to sing, the tiny lethal song of a cable snagged and under stress. I stared out across the Expanse, as if I could find him and make eye contact.

"He would have gotten you," I said bluntly. "You know that."

The silence lasted a moment longer, then snapped across. Segesvar's voice rang with false boisterousness.

"What you talking about, Tak?"

"You know what I'm talking about. Our meth-dealing friend, back in the day. You ran with the others, Rad, but the way your leg was, you wouldn't have had a chance. If he'd come through me, he would have caught you up. You know that. The others ran, I stayed."

On the other end of the line I heard him breathe out, like something uncoiling.

"So," he said. "A surcharge. Shall we say thirty percent?"

"Sounds reasonable," I lied, for both of us.

"Yes. But I think your previous fish will have to be taken off the menu now. Why don't you come here to give your traditional valediction, and we'll discuss the terms of this. Refinancing."

"Can't do that, Rad. I told you, I'm only passing through. An hour from now I'm gone again. Be a week or more before I can get back."

"Then." I could almost see him shrug. "You will miss the valediction. I would not have thought you would want that."

"I don't." This was punishment, another surcharge on top of my volunteered thirty percent. Segesvar had me worked out; it's a core skill in organized crime, and he was good at his trade. The Kossuth *haiduci* might not have the cachet and sophistication of the yakuza farther north, but it's essentially the same game. If you're going to make a living out of extortion, you'd better know how to get to people. And how to get to Takeshi Kovacs was painted all over my recent past like blood. It couldn't have taken a lot of working out.

"Then come," he said warmly. "We will get drunk together, maybe even go to Watanabe's for old times' sake. Old times' *sake*, heheh? And a pipe. I need to look you in the eyes, my friend. To know that you have not changed."

Out of nowhere, Lazlo's face.

I'm trusting you, Micky. You look after her.

I glanced across to where Suzi Petkovski was lowering the canopy back over the turbine.

"Sorry, Rad. This is too important to juggle. You want your fish, send someone out to the inland harbor. Charter terminal, ramp seven. I'll be here for an hour."

"No valediction?"

I grimaced. "No valediction. I don't have the time."

He was quiet for a moment.

"I think," he said finally, "that I would like very much to look in your eyes right now, Takeshi Kovacs. Perhaps I will come myself."

"Sure. Be good to see you. Just make it inside the hour."

He hung up. I gritted my teeth and smashed a fist against the crate beside me.

"Fuck. *Fuck.*"

You look after her, right. You keep her safe.

Yeah, yeah. All right.

I'm trusting you, Micky.

All right, I fucking hear you.

The chime of a phone.

For a moment, I held the one I was using stupidly to my ear. Then it hit me that the sound came from the opened pack beside me. I leaned over and pushed aside three or four phones before I found the one with the lit display. It was one I'd used before, one with a broken seal.

"Yeah?"

Nothing. The line was open but there was no sound on it. Not even static. Perfect black silence yawned into my ear.

"Hello?"

And something whispered up out of the dark, just barely more audible than the tension I'd felt in the previous call.

hurry

And then there was only the silence again.

I lowered the phone and stared at it.

I'd made three calls in Tekitomura, used three phones from the pack. I'd called Lazlo, I'd called Yaroslav, I'd called Isa. It could have been any of the three who had just rung. To know for sure, I'd need to check the log to see whom the phone had connected with before.

But I didn't need to.

A whisper out of dark silence. A voice over distance you couldn't measure.

hurry

I knew which phone it was.

And I knew who was calling me.

CHAPTeR TWeNTY-TWO

Segesvar was as good as his word. Forty minutes after he hung up, a garish red-and-black open-top sports skimmer came howling off the Expanse and into the harbor at illegal speed. Every head on the wharf turned to watch it arrive. It was the kind of boatcraft that on the seaward side of Newpest would have occasioned an instant Port Authority override 'cast and an ignominious stall in the water there and then. I don't know whether the inland harbor was ill equipped, if Segesvar had expensive counterjamming software installed in his rich-kid toy, or if the Weed Expanse gangs just had the Inland PA in their pocket. In any event, the Expansemobile didn't stall out. Instead it banked about, raising spray, and made a fast line for the gap between ramps six and seven. A dozen meters out, it cut its motors and swept in on momentum. Behind the wheel, Segesvar spotted me. I nodded and raised one hand. He waved back.

I sighed.

This stuff trails out behind us across the decades, but it isn't like the spray Radul Segesvar's arrival was cutting from the water in the harbor. It doesn't fall tracelessly back. It just hangs there instead, like the raised dust you get in the wake of a Sharyan desert cruiser, and if you turn about and head back into your own past, you find yourself coughing on it.

"Hey, *Kovacs.*"

It was a shout, maliciously loud and cheerful. Segesvar was standing up in the cockpit, still steering. Broad, gull-wing-frame sunshades covered his eyes in conscious rejection of the Millsport fashion for ultra-engineered finger-width lenses. A paper-thin, hand-sanded iridescent swamp-panther-skin jacket draped his frame. He waved again and grinned. From the bow of the vessel a grapple line fired with a metallic bang. It was harpoon-headed, unrelated to any of the sockets along the ramp edge, and it chewed a hole in the evercrete facing of the wharf half a meter below the point where I stood. The skimmer cranked itself in and Segesvar leapt out of the cockpit to stand on the bow, looking up at me.

"You want to bellow my name a couple more times?" I asked him evenly. "In case someone didn't get it first time around."

"Oops." He cocked his head at an angle and raised his arms wide in a gesture of apology that wasn't fooling anybody. He was still angry with me. "Just my naturally open nature, I guess. So what are we calling you these days?"

"Forget it. You going to stand down there all day?"

"I don't know, you going to give me a hand up?"

I reached down. Segesvar grasped the offered hand and levered himself up onto the wharf. Twinges ran down my arm as I lifted him, subsiding to a fiery ache. Still paying for my arrested fall back under the eyrie. The *haiduci* straightened his immaculately tailored jacket and ran a fastidious hand through shoulder-length black hair. Radul Segesvar had made it far enough early enough to finance clone copies of the body he'd been born in, and the face he wore beneath the sunlenses was his own—pale despite the climate, narrow and hard-boned, no visible trace of Japanese ancestry. It topped an equally slim body that I guessed was in its late twenties. Segesvar generally lived each clone through from early adulthood until, in his own words, it couldn't fuck or fight like it ought to. I didn't know how many times he'd resleeved because in the years since our shared youth in Newpest, I'd lost track of how long he'd actually lived. Like most *haiduci*—and like me—he'd had his share of time in storage.

"Nice sleeve," he said, pacing a circle around me. "Very nice. What happened to the other one?"

"Long story."

"Which you're not going to tell me." He completed his circuit and took off the sunlenses. Stared into my eyes. "Right?"

"Right."

He sighed theatrically. "This is disappointing, Tak. Very disappointing. You're getting as closemouthed as all those slit-eyed fucking northerners you spend your time with."

I shrugged. "I'm half slit-eyed fucking northerner myself, Rad."

"Ah yes, so you are. I forgot."

He hadn't. He was just pushing. In some ways nothing much had changed since our days hanging out at Watanabe's. He was always the one who got us into fights back then. Even the meth dealer had been his idea originally.

"There's a coffee machine inside. Want to get some?"

"If we must. You know, if you'd come out to the farm, you could have had real coffee and a seahemp spliff, hand-rolled on the thighs of the best holo-porn actresses money can buy."

"Some other time."

"Yeah, you're always so fucking driven, aren't you? If it's not the Envoys or the neoQuells, it's some fucking private revenge scheme. You know, Tak, it isn't really my business, but someone needs to tell you this and looks like I get the job. You need to stop and smell the weed, man. Remember that you're living." He put his sunlenses back on and jerked his head toward the terminal. "All right, come on then. Machine coffee, why not. It'll be a novelty."

Back in the cool, we sat at a table near glass panels that gave a view out onto the harbor. Half a dozen other spectators sat in the same area with their associated baggage, waiting. A wasted-looking man in rags was doing the rounds among them, holding out a tray for credit chips and a hard-luck story for anyone who was interested. Most weren't. There was a faint odor of cheap antibacterial in the air that I hadn't noticed before. The cleaning robots must have been by.

The coffee was grim.

"See," said Segesvar, setting his aside with an exaggerated scowl. "I should have your legs broken just for making me drink that."

"You could try."

For a moment, our eyes locked. He shrugged.

"It was a joke, Tak. You're losing your sense of humor."

"Yeah, I'm putting a thirty percent surcharge on it." I sipped at my own coffee, expressionless. "Used to be my friends could get it for nothing, but times change."

He let that lie for a moment, then cocked his head and looked me in the eye again.

"You think I'm treating you unfairly?"

"I think you're conveniently forgetful of the real meaning behind the words *you saved my ass back there, man.*"

Segesvar nodded as if he'd expected no less. He looked down at the table between us.

"That is an old debt," he said quietly. "And a questionable one."

"You didn't think so at the time."

It was too far back to summon easily to mind. Back before the Envoy conditioning went in, back where things get blurred with the passing decades. Most of all, I remembered the stink in the alley. Alkaline precipitates from the belaweed-processing plant and dumped oil from the hydraulic systems on the compression tanks. The meth dealer's curses and the glint of the long bottleback gaff as he slashed it through the damp air toward me. The others were gone, their youthful thug enthusiasm for the robbery evaporating in swift terror as that honed steel hook came out and ripped open Radul Segesvar's leg from kneecap to thigh. Gone yelling and sprinting away into the night like exorcised sprites, leaving Radul dragging himself one yelping meter at a time along the alley after them, leaving me, sixteen years old, facing the steel with empty hands.

Come 'ere, you little fuck. The dealer was grinning at me in the gloom, almost crooning as he advanced, blocking my escape. *Try to tumble me on my own patch, will you. I'm going to open you up and feed you your own fucking guts, my lad.*

And for the first time in my life, I realized with a sensation like cold hands on my young neck that I was looking at a man who was going to kill me if I didn't stop him.

Not batter me like my father, not cut me up like one of the inept gang thugs we squabbled with daily on the streets of Newpest. Kill me. Kill me, and then probably rip out my stack and toss it into the scummed-up waters of the harbor where it would stay for longer than the life of anyone I knew or cared about. It was that image, that terror of being sunk and lost in poisoned water, that drove me forward, made me count the swing of the sharpened steel and hit him as he came off balance on the end of the downstroke.

Then we both went over in the muck and debris and ammoniac stink of the processing plant's leavings, and I fought him there for the gaff.

Took it from him.

Lashed out and, more by luck than judgment, ripped open his belly with it.

The fight went out of him like water down a sink. He made a loud gurgling, eyes wide and glued to mine. I stared back, rage and fear still punching through the veins in my temples, every chemical switch in my body thrown. I was barely aware of what I'd just done. Then he sank backward away from me and into the pile of muck. He sat down there as if it were an armchair he liked. I struggled off my knees, dripping alkaline slime from face and hair, still caught in his gaze, still gripping the handle of the gaff. His mouth made flapping motions, his throat gave up wet, desperate sounds. I looked down and I saw his innards still looped over the hook in my hand.

Shock caught me up. My hand spasmed open involuntarily and the hook fell out of it. I staggered away, spraying vomit. The weak, pleading sounds he made damped out beneath the hoarse rasp in my throat as my stomach emptied itself. The hot, urgent reek of fresh sick joined the general stench in the alley. I convulsed with the force of my heaving, and fell over in the mess.

I think he was still alive when I got back to my feet and went to help Segesvar. The sounds he was making followed me all the way out of the alley, and news reports the next day said he'd finally bled to death sometime close to dawn. Then again, the same sounds followed me around for weeks afterward, whenever I went anywhere quiet enough to hear myself think. For the best part of the next year, I woke up with them clotted in my ears as often as not.

I looked away from it. The glass panels of the terminal slid back into focus. Across the table, Segesvar was watching me intently. Maybe he was remembering, too. He grimaced.

"So you don't think I have a right to be angry about this? You disappear for nine weeks without a word, leave me holding your shit and looking like a fool in front of the other *haiduci*. Now you want to reschedule the finance? You know what I'd do to anyone else who pulled this shit?"

I nodded. Recalled with wry humor my own fury at Plex a couple of months back as I stood seeping synthetic body fluids in Tekitomura.

We, uh, we need to reschedule, Tak.

I'd wanted to kill him, just for saying it like that.

"You think thirty percent is unjust?"

I sighed.

"Rad, you're a gangster and I'm." I gestured. "No better. I don't think either of us knows much about what's just and unjust. You do what you like. I'll find you the money."

"All right." He was still staring at me. "Twenty percent. That fit your sense of commercial propriety?"

I shook my head, said nothing. I dug in my pocket for the cortical stacks, kept my fist closed as I leaned across with them. "Here. This is what you came for. Four fish. Do what you want with them."

He pushed my arm aside and jabbed an angry finger in my face.

"No, my friend. I do what *you* want with them. This is a service I'm providing you, and don't you fucking forget that. Now, I said twenty percent. Is that fair?"

The decision crystallized out of nowhere, so fast it was like a slap across the back of the head. Picking it apart later, I couldn't decide what triggered it, only that it felt like listening again to that tiny voice out of the darkness, telling me to hurry. It felt like a sudden prickle of sweat across my palms and the terror that I was going to be too late for something that mattered.

"I meant what I said, Rad. You decide. If this is costing you face with your *haiduci* pals, then drop it. I'll throw these over the side somewhere out on the Expanse and we can call time on the whole thing. You hit me with the bill, I'll find a way to pay it."

He threw up his hands in a gesture he'd copied when we were still young, from *haiduci* experia flicks like *Friends of Ireni Cozma* and *Outlaw Voices*. It was a fight not to smile as I saw it. Or maybe that was just the swiftly gathering sense of motion that had me now, the drug-like grip of a decision taken and what it meant. In the gravity of the moment, Segesvar's voice was suddenly a buzzing at the margins of relevance. I was tuning him out.

"All right, *fuck* it. *Fifteen* percent. Come on, Tak. That's fair. Any less, my own fucking people are going to take me out for mismanagement. Fifteen percent, right?"

I shrugged and held out my closed hand again. "All right, fifteen percent. Do you still want these?"

He brushed my fist with his palm, took the stacks with classic street sleight of hand, and pocketed them.

"You drive a hard fucking bargain, Tak," he growled. "Anybody ever tell you that?"

"That's a compliment, right?"

He growled again, wordless this time. Stood up and brushed off his clothes as if he'd been sitting on a baling dock. As I followed him to my feet, the ragged man with the begging tray vectored in on us.

"DeCom vet," he mumbled. "Got fried making New Hok safe for a new century, man, took down big co-op clusters. You got—"

"No, I haven't got any money," said Segesvar impatiently. "Look, you can have that coffee if you want it. It's still warm."

He caught my glance.

"What? I'm a fucking gangster, right? What do you expect?"

Out on the Weed Expanse, a vast quiet held the sky. Even the snarl of the skimmer's turbines seemed small-scale, soaked up by the emptied, flatline landscape and the piles of damp cloud overhead. I stood at the rail, hair plastered back by the speed of our passage, and breathed in the signature fragrance of raw belaweed. The waters of the Expanse are clogged with the stuff, and the passage of any vessel brings it roiling to the surface. We left behind a broad wake of shredded vegetation and muddied gray turbulence that would take the best part of an hour to settle.

To my left, Suzi Petkovski sat in the cockpit and steered with a cigarette in one hand, eyes narrowed against the smoke and the glare off the clouded sky. Mikhail was on the other walkway, slumped on the rail like a long sack of ballast. He'd been sullen for the whole voyage so far, eloquently conveying his resentment at having to come along but not much else besides. At intervals, he scratched morosely at the jackpoints in his neck.

An abandoned baling station flashed up on our starboard bow, this one not much more than a couple of bubblefab sheds and a blackened mirrorwood jetty. We'd seen more stations earlier, some still working, lit within and loading onto big automated barges. But that was while our trajectory still hugged the Newpest lakeside sprawl. Out this far, the little island of stilled industry only amped up the sense of desolation.

"Weed trade's been bad, huh?" I shouted over the turbines.

Suzi Petkovski glanced briefly in my direction.

"Say what?"

"The weed trade," I yelled again, gesturing back at the station as it fell behind. "Been bad recently, right?"

She shrugged. "Never secure, way the commodities market swings. Most of the independents got squeezed out a long time ago. Out here, KosUnity run these big mobile rigs, do all their own processing and baling right on board. Hard to compete with that."

It wasn't a new attitude. Forty years ago, before I went away, you could get the same phlegmatic responses to economic hardship from the Suzi Petkovskis of this world. The same clamped, chain-smoking capacity for endurance, the same grim shrug, as if politics were some kind of massive, capricious weather system you couldn't do anything about.

I went back to watching the skyline.

After a while, the phone in my left pocket rang. I hesitated for a moment then twitched irritably, fished it out still buzzing, and pressed it to my ear.

"Yeah, what?"

The murmuring ghosted up out of close-pressed electronic silence, a stirring of the quiet like a pair of dark wings beating in the stillness overhead. The hint of a voice, words riding a whisper into my ear

there isn't much time left

"Yeah, you said that. I'm going as fast as I can."

can't hold them back much longer . . .

"Yeah, I'm *working* on it."

working now . . . It sounded like a question.

"Yeah, I *said—*"

there are wings out there . . . a thousand wings beating and a whole world cracked . . .

It was fading out now, like a badly tuned channel, wavering, fluttering down into silence again

cracked open from edge to edge . . . it's beautiful, Micky . . .

And gone.

I waited, lowered the phone and weighed it in my palm. Grimaced and shoved it back into my pocket.

Suzi Petkovski glanced my way.

"Bad news?"

"Yeah, you could say that. Can we go any faster?"

She was already back to watching the water ahead. Kindling a new cigarette one-handed.

"Not safely, no."

I nodded and thought back through the communiqué I'd just had.

"And what's it going to cost me to be unsafe then?"

"About double?"

"Fine. Do it."

A grim little smile floated to her mouth. She shrugged, pinched out the cigarette and slid it behind one ear. She reached across the cockpit displays and jabbed a couple of screens. Radar images maximized. She yelled something to Mikhail in a Magyar street dialect that had slipped too much in the time I'd been away for me to catch more than skimmed gist. *Get below and keep your hands off* . . . something? He shot her a resentful look, then unslumped himself from the rail and made his way back into the cabin.

She turned back to me, barely looking away from the controls now.

"You, too. Better get yourself a seat back there. I speed up and we're liable to slosh about."

"I can hang on."

"Yeah, I'd rather you were back there with him. Give you someone to talk to, I'm going to be too busy."

I thought back to the equipment I'd seen stashed in the cabin. Navigational plug-ins, an entertainment deck, currentflow modifiers. Cables and jacks. I thought back, too, to the kid's demeanor and his scratching at the plugs in his neck, the slumped lack of interest in the whole world. It made a sense I hadn't really been paying attention to before.

"Sure," I said. "Always good to have someone to talk to, right?"

She didn't answer. Maybe she was already immersed in the darkly rainbowed radar images of our path through the Expanse, maybe just mired in something else. I left her to it and made my way aft.

Over my head, the turbines opened to a demented shriek.

CHAPTER TWeNTY-THRee

Eventually, time stands still on the Weed Expanse.

You start by noticing detail—the arched root system of a tepes thicket breaking the water like the half-decayed bones of some drowned giant humanoid, odd clear patches of water where the belaweed hasn't deigned to grow and you can see down to a pale emerald bed of sand, the sly rise of a mud bank, maybe an abandoned harvester kayak from a couple of centuries back, still not fully overgrown with Sakate's moss. But these sights are few and far between, and in time your gaze is drawn out to the great flat horizon, and after that, however many times you try to pull away to look at closer detail, it feels like there's a tide dragging your vision back out there.

You sit and listen to the cadences of the engines because there's nothing else to do. You watch the horizon and you sink into your own thoughts because there's nowhere else to go.

. . . hurry . . .

I'm trusting you, Micky. You look after her, her, her, her . . .

Her. Sylvie, maned in silver gray. Her face—

Her face, subtly changed by the woman who had crept out and stolen it from her. *Her* voice, subtly modulated . . .

I've got no way of knowing if or when Sylvie Oshima's coming back.

Nadia, I'm trying to fucking help.

She wonders who the fuck Micky Serendipity really is, and whether he's safe to be around. Whether he'll fuck her over at the soonest opportunity.

She wonders where the fuck you're going with the souls of so many dead priests.

Todor Murakami's lean, attentive features on the ferry. Pipe smoke, whipped away in the wind.

So what's this scam about? Thought you were hanging out with Radul Segesvar these days. Hometown nostalgia and cheap organized crime. Why you going up north again?

It's time to get back on track. Back to the job in hand.

The job in hand. Yeah, that'll solve all your problems, Micky.

Stop fucking calling me that.

And screams. And gaping holes cut in spines at neck height. And the weight of cortical stacks in my palm, still slick with clinging gore. And the hollow that would never be filled.

Sarah.

The job in hand.

I'm trying to fucking help.

. . . hurry . . .

I'm trusting you . . .

I'm trying to fucking . . .

. . . hurry . . .

I'm TRYING—

"Coastline." Suzi Petkovski's voice rinsed through the cabin speaker, laconic and firm enough to grab at. "Be hitting Sourcetown in fifteen."

I dumped my brooding and looked left where the Kossuth coast was slicing back toward us. It raised as a dark bumpy line on the otherwise featureless horizon, then seemed to leap in and resolve as a procession of low hills and the occasional flash of white dunes beyond and between. The backside of Vchira, the drowned nubs of an ancient mountain range worn down geological ages past to a seven-hundred-kilometer curve of marsh-fringed tidal barrier on one side and the same stretch of crystalline white sand on the other.

Someday, one of Sourcetown's long-term inhabitants had informed me nearly half a century ago, *the sea's going to break through all along here.* Break through and pour into the Weed Expanse like an invading army breaching a long-disputed frontier. Wear down the last remaining bastions and wreck the beach. *Some Day, man,* the Sourcetowner repeated slowly, and capitalized the phrase and grinned at me with what I'd already come to recognize as typical surfer detachment, *Some Day, but Not Yet. And until Yet, you just got to keep looking out to sea, man. Just keep looking out there, don't look behind you, don't worry what's keeping it all in place.*

Some Day, but Not Yet. Just look out to sea.

You could call it a philosophy, I suppose. On Vchira Beach, it often passed for one. Limited maybe, but then I've seen far worse ways of relating to the universe deployed elsewhere.

The sky had cleared up as we reached the southern fringes of the Expanse, and I started to see signs of habitation in the sunlight. Sourcetown isn't really a place, it's an approximation, a loose term for a 170-kilometer coastal strip of surfer support services and their associated infrastructure. In its most tenuous form, it comes into being as scattered tents and bubblefabs along the beach, generational fire circles and barbecue sites, roughly woven

belaweed shacks and bars. Settlement permanence increases and then de-
creases as the Strip approaches and then passes the places where the surf is
not merely good but phenomenal. And then, in the Big Surf zones, habitation
thickens to an almost municipal density. Actual streets appear on the hills behind the dunes, rooted street lighting along them and clusters of evercrete
platforms and jetties sprouting backward off the spine of land and into the
Weed Expanse. Last time I'd been here, there were five such accretions, each
with its gang of enthusiasts who swore that the best surf on the continent was
right fucking here, man. For all I knew, any one of them could have been correct. For all I knew, there'd be another five by now.

No less subject to flux were the inhabitants themselves. There were population cycles in lazy motion all the way along the Strip—some of them
geared to the turn of Harlan's World's five seasons, some to the complicated
rhythm of the trilunar tides, and some to the longer, languid pulse of a functional surfer sleeve's lifetime. People came and went and came back. Sometimes their locational loyalties to a part of the beach endured from cycle to
cycle, lifetime to lifetime; sometimes they shifted. And sometimes, that loyalty was never there to begin with.

Finding someone on the Strip was never going to be easy. In a lot of
cases, that was the reason people came here.

"Kem Point coming up." Petkovski's voice again, against a backdrop of
downwinding turbines. She sounded tired. "This good for you?"

"Yeah, as good as anywhere. Thanks." I peered out at the approaching
evercrete platforms and the low-rise tangle of buildings they held up over the
waters of the Expanse, the untidy sprawl of structure marching up the hill beyond. There were a handful of figures sitting in view on balconies or jetties,
but for the most part the little settlement looked emptied of life. I had no idea
if this was the right end of Sourcetown or not, but you've got to start somewhere. I grabbed a handstrap and hauled myself to my feet as the skimmer
banked left. Glanced across the cabin at my silent companion. "Nice talking
to you, Mikhail."

He ignored me, gaze pinned to the window. He'd said nothing the whole
time we'd shared the cabin space, just stared morosely out at the vast lack of
scenery around us. A couple of times, he'd caught me watching as he
scrubbed at his jack sockets, and stopped abruptly with a tightening look on
his face. But even then, he said nothing.

I shrugged, was about to swing out onto the railed decking, then thought
better of it. I crossed the cabin and propped myself against the glass, inter-
rupting Mikhail Petkovski's field of vision. He blinked up at me, momentarily surprised out of his self-absorption.

"You know," I said cheerfully. "You got lucky in the mother stakes. But
out there, it's all guys like me. And we don't give a flying fuck whether you

live or die. You don't get off your ass and start taking an interest, no one else is going to."

He snorted. "The fuck's it got to do with—"

Someone more street would have read my eyes, but this one was too washed out with the wirewant, too puffed up with maternal life support. I reached easily for his throat, dug in, and hauled him out of the seat.

"See what I mean? Who's going to stop me crushing your larynx now?"

He croaked. "Ma—"

"She can't hear you. She's busy up there, earning a living for you both." I gathered him in. "Mikhail, you are infinitely less important in the scheme of things than her efforts have led you to believe."

He reached up and tried to unpin my fingers. I ignored the feeble prisings and dug in deeper. He started to look genuinely frightened.

"The way you're headed," I told him in conversational tones, "you're going to end up on a spare-parts tray under low lighting. That's the only use you are to men like me, and no one else is going to get in our way when we come for you, because you've given no one a reason to care. Is that what you want to be? Spare parts and a two-minute rinse and flush?"

He jerked and flapped, face turning purple. Shook his head in violent denial. I held him a couple of moments longer, then loosened my grip and dumped him back in the chair. He gagged and coughed, eyes wide on me and flooded with tears. One hand crept up to massage his throat where I'd marked it. I nodded.

"All this, Mikhail? Going on all around you? This is life." I leaned closer over him and he flinched. "Take an interest. While you still can."

The skimmer bumped gently against something. I straightened up and went out onto the side deck into sudden heat and brightness. We were floating amid a crosswork of weathered mirrorwood jetties secured at strategic intervals by heavy evercrete mooring buttresses. The skimmer's motors kept up a low mutter and gentle pressure against the nearest landing stage. Late-afternoon sun glinted hard off the mirrorwood. Suzi Petkovski was standing up in the cockpit and squinting against the reflected light.

"That'll be double," she reminded me.

I handed over a chip and waited while she ran it. Mikhail chose not to emerge from the cabin. Maybe he was thinking things over. His mother handed me back the chip, shaded her eyes, and pointed.

"They got a place you can hire bugs cheap about three streets over. By that transmission mast you can see. The one with the dragon flags."

"Thanks."

"Sure. Hope you find what you're looking for here."

I skipped the bug hire, at least initially, and wandered up through the little town, soaking up my surroundings. Up to the crest of the hill, I could have been in any Expanse-side suburb of Newpest. The same utilitarian architecture predominated, the same frontage mix of waterware mech- and soft-shops mingling with eating houses and bars. The same stained and worn fused-glass streets, and the same basic smells. But from the top of the rise looking down, the resemblance ended like waking from a dream.

Below me, the other half of the settlement fell away downward in haphazard structures built out of every material you could readily bring to mind. Bubblefabs rubbed shoulders with wood-frame houses, driftwood shacks, and, toward the bottom, actual canvas tents. The fused-paving thoroughfares gave way to poorly laid evercrete slabs, then to sand, then finally to the broad, pale sweep of the beach itself. Here there was more movement on the streets than on the Expanse side, most of it semi-clad and drifting toward the shoreline in the late sun. Every third figure had a board slung under one arm. The sea itself was burnished a dirty gold in the low-angle light and flecked with activity, surfers floating astride their boards or upright and cutting casual slices across the gently flexing surface of the water. The sun and distance turned them all to anonymous black tin cutouts.

"Some fucking view, eh, sam?"

It was a high, child's voice, at odds with the words it uttered. I glanced around and saw a boy of about ten watching me from a doorway. Body rib-thin and bronzed in a pair of surfslacks, eyes a sun-faded blue. Hair a tangled mess from the sea. He was leaned in the door, arms folded nonchalantly across his bared chest. Behind him in the shop, I saw racked boards. Shifting screen displays for aquatech software.

"I've seen worse," I admitted.

"First time at Vchira?"

"No."

Disappointment notched his voice. "Not looking for lessons then?"

"No." I paused a moment, measuring advisability. "You been long on the Strip yourself?"

He grinned. "All my lives. Why?"

"I'm looking for some friends. Thought you might know them."

"Yeah? You a cop? Enforcer?"

"Not recently."

It seemed to be the right answer. His grin came back.

"They got names, these friends?"

"They did last time I was here. Brasil. Ado, Tres." I hesitated. "Vidaura, maybe."

His lips twisted and pursed and he sucked his teeth. It was all gesture learned in another, much older body.

"Jack Soul Brasil?" he asked warily.

I nodded.

"You a Bug?"

"Not recently."

"Multiflores crew?"

I drew breath. "No."

"BaKroom Boy?"

"Do you have a name?" I asked him.

He shrugged. "Sure. Milan. Around here they call me Gungetter."

"Well, Milan," I told him evenly. "You're beginning to irritate the fuck out of me. Now, are you going to be able to help me or not? You know where Brasil is, or are you just getting off on the rep vapor he trailed through here thirty years back?"

"Hey." The pale blue eyes narrowed. His arms unfolded, fists tensed to small hammers at his sides. "You know, I fucking *belong* here, sam. I *surf*. Been shooting curls at Vchira since before *you* were a fucking splatter up your mother's tube."

"I doubt that, but let's not quibble. I'm looking for Jack Soul Brasil. I'll find him with or without you, but you can maybe save me some time. Question is, are you going to?"

He stared back at me, still angry, stance still aggressive. In the ten-year-old sleeve, it was less than impressive.

"Question is, sam, what's it *worth* to help you?"

"Ah."

Paid, Milan was forthcoming in grudging fragments designed to disguise and eke out the very limited nature of his knowledge. I bought him rum and coffee in a street café across from the shop he was tending—*can't just close it up, sam, be more than my job's worth*—and waited out the storytelling process. Most of what he told me was readily identifiable as well-worn beach legend, but from a couple of things he said I decided he really had met Brasil a few times, maybe even surfed with him. The last encounter seemed to have been a decade or so back. Side-by-side empty-handed combat heroism in confrontation with a gang of encroaching Harlan Loyalist surfers a few klicks south from Kem Point. Facedown and general battery, Milan acquits himself with modestly understated savagery, collects a few wounds—*you should have seen the fucking scars on that sleeve, man, sometimes I still miss it*—but the highest praise is reserved for Brasil. *Like a fucking swamp panther, sam. Fuckers ripped him in the chest, he didn't even notice. He tore them all down. Just, like, nothing left when he was done. Sent them back north in pieces.* All followed by orgiastic celebration—bonfire glow and the cries of women in wild orgasm on a surf backdrop.

It was a standard picture, and I'd had it painted for me before by other

Vchira enthusiasts in the past. Looking past the more obvious embellish-ments, I panned out a little useful detail. Brasil had money—*all those years with the Little Blues, right. No way he has to scratch a living teaching wob-blies, selling boards, and training up some fucking Millsport aristo's spare flesh five years ahead of time*—but the man still didn't hold with clone reincar-nation. He'd be wearing good surfer flesh, but I wouldn't know his face. *Look for them fucking scars on his chest, sam.* Yes, he still wore his hair long. Cur-rent rumor had him holed up in a sleepy beach hamlet somewhere south. Ap-parently he was learning to play the saxophone. There was this jazzman, used to play with Csango junior, who'd told Milan . . .

I paid for the drinks and got up to go. The sun was gone and the dirty-gold sea all but tarnished through to base metal. Across the beach below us, lights were coming to firefly life. I wondered if I'd catch the bug-hire place before it shut.

"So this aristo," I said idly. "You teach his body to surf for five years, hone the reflexes for him. What's your end?"

Milan shrugged and sipped at what was left of his rum. He'd mellowed with the alcohol and the payment. "We trade sleeves. I get what he's wearing in return for this, age sixteen. So my end's a thirty-plus aristo sleeve, cosmetic alterations, and witnessed exchange, so I don't try to pass myself off as him, otherwise catalog-intact. Top-of-the-range clone stock, all the peripherals fit-ted as standard. Sweet deal, huh?"

I nodded absently. "Yeah, if he looks after what he's wearing, I guess. Aristo lifestyles I've seen can make for some pretty heavy wear and tear."

"Nah, this guy's in shape. Comes down here on and off to check on his investment, you know, swim and surf a bit. Would have been down this week but that Harlan limo thing put a lock on it. He's running a little extra weight he could do without, can't surf for shit of course. But that'll sort out easy enough when I—"

"Harlan limo thing?" Envoy awareness slithered along my nerves.

"Yeah, you know. Seichi Harlan's skimmer. This guy's real close with that branch of the family, had to—"

"What happened to Seichi Harlan's skimmer?"

"You didn't hear about this?" Milan blinked and grinned. "Where you been, sam? Been all over the net since yesterday. Seichi Harlan, taking his sons and daughter-in-law across to Rila, the skimmer just wiped out there in the Reach."

"Wiped out how?"

He shrugged. "They don't know yet. Whole thing just exploded, footage they showed looks like from the inside. Sank in seconds, what was left of it. They're still looking for the pieces."

They'd be lucky. The maelstrom made itself felt a long way in at this time of year, and the currents in the Reach were lethally unpredictable. Sinking fragments of wreckage might get carried for kilometers before they settled. The broken remains of Seichi Harlan and his family could end up in any of a dozen resting places amid the scattered islets and reefs of the Millsport Archipelago. Stack recovery was going to be a nightmare.

My thoughts fled back to Belacotton Kohei and Plex's *take*-soaked mutterings. *I don't know, Tak. Really, I don't. It was some kind of weapon, something from the Unsettlement.* He'd said biological, but on his own admission his knowledge was incomplete. He'd been shut out by high-level yakuza rank and the Harlan family retainer, Aiura. Aiura, who ran damage limitation and cleanup for the Harlan family.

Another wisp of detail settled into place in my mind. Drava wrapped in snow. Waiting in Kurumaya's antechamber, staring disinterestedly through the global news scrolldown. Accidental death of some minor Harlan heirling in the Millsport wharf district.

It wasn't a connection as such, but Envoy intuition doesn't work that way. It just goes on piling up the data until you start to see the shape of something in the mass. Until the connections make themselves for you. I couldn't see anything yet, but the fragments were singing to me like wind chimes in a storm.

That and the tiny insistent pulse of backbeat: *hurry, hurry, there isn't time.*

I traded a badly remembered Vchira handshake with Milan and set off back up the hill, hurrying.

●●●

The bug-hire place was still lit, and staffed by a bored-looking receptionist with surfer physique. He woke up around the eyes for long enough to find out that I wasn't a wave rider, aspiring or otherwise, and then settled into mechanical client service mode. Dayjob shielding around the briefly glimpsed inner core that kept him at Vchira, the heat of enthusiasm wrapped carefully back up again for when he could share it with someone who understood. But he set me up competently enough with a garishly colored single-seat speed bug and showed me the streetmap software with the return points I could use up and down the Strip. At request, he also provided me with a premolded polalloy crash suit and helmet, though you could see his already low opinion of me go through the floor when I asked for it. It seemed there were still a lot of people on Vchira Beach who couldn't tell risk and idiocy apart.

Yeah, maybe including you, Tak. Done anything safe yourself recently?

Ten minutes later, I was suited up and powering out of Kem Point behind a cone of headlamp glow in the gathering gloom of evening.

Somewhere south, listening for a badly played saxophone.

I'd had better sets of clues to follow, but there was one thing massively in my favor. I knew Brasil, and I knew that if he heard someone was looking for him, he wasn't likely to hide. He'd come out to deal with it the way you paddled up to a big wave. The way you faced down a spread of Harlan Loyalists.

Make enough noise, and I wouldn't have to find him.

He'd find me.

● ● ●

Three hours later, I pulled off the highway and into the cold bluish wash of bug-swarmed Angier lamps around an all-night diner and machine shop. Looking back a little wearily, I judged I'd made enough noise. My supply of low-value credit chips was depleted, I was lightly fogged from too much shared drink and smoke up and down the Strip, and the knuckles of my right hand still ached slightly from a badly thrown punch in a beachside tavern where strangers asking after local legends weren't well regarded.

Under the Angier lamps the night was pleasantly cool, and there were knots of surfers clowning about in the parking area, bottles and pipes in hand. Laughter that seemed to bounce off the darkened distance around the lampglow, someone telling a broken-board story in a high, excited voice. One or two more serious groups gathered around the opened innards of vehicles undergoing repair. Laser cutters flickered on and off, showering weird green or purple sparks off exotic alloys.

I got a surprisingly good coffee at the counter and took it outside to watch the surfers. It wasn't a culture I'd ever accessed during my youth in Newpest—gang protocols wouldn't permit a serious commitment to both scuba and wave riding, and the diving found me first. I never switched allegiances. Something about the silent world beneath the surface drew me. There was a vast, slow-breathing calm down there, a respite from all the street craziness and my own even more jagged home life.

You could bury yourself down there.

I finished the coffee and went back inside the diner. Ramen soup smells wreathed the air and tugged at my guts. It hit me suddenly that I hadn't eaten since a late ship's breakfast on the bridge of the *Haiduci's Daughter* with Japaridze. I climbed onto a counter stool and nodded at the same meth-eyed kid I'd bought my coffee from.

"Smells good. What have you got?"

He picked up a battered remote and thumbed it in the general direction of the autochef. Holodisplays sprang up over the various pans. I scanned them and chose a hard-to-spoil favorite.

"Give me the chilied ray. That's frozen ray, right?"

He rolled his eyes. "You expecting fresh, maybe? Place like this? At that price?"

"I've been away."

But it elicited no response in his meth-stunned face. He just set the autochef in motion and wandered away to the windows, staring out at the surfers as if they were some form of rare and beautiful sea life caught in an aquarium.

I was halfway through my bowl of ramen when the door opened behind me. No one said anything, but I knew already. I set down the bowl and turned slowly on the stool.

He was on his own.

It wasn't the face I remembered, not even close. He'd sleeved to fairer and broader features than the last time around, a tangled mane of blond traced with gray, and cheekbones that owed at least as much to Slavic genes as they did to his predilection for Adoracion custom. But the body wasn't much different—inside the loose coveralls he wore, he still had the height and slim breadth in chest and shoulders, the tapered waist and legs, the big hands. And his moves still radiated the same casual poise when he made them.

I knew him as certainly as if he'd torn open the coverall to show me the scars on his chest.

"I hear you're looking for me," he said mildly. "Do I know you?"

I grinned.

"Hello, Jack. How's Virginia these days?"

CHAPTeR TWeNTY-FOUR

"I still can't believe it's you, kid."

She sat on the slope of the dune at my side and traced triangles in the sand between her feet with a bottleback prod. She was still wet from the swim, water pearling on sun-darkened skin all over the surfer sleeve, razored black hair spiked damp and uneven on top of her head. The elfin face beneath was taking some getting used to. She was at least ten years younger than when I'd last seen her. Then again, she was probably having the same problem with me. She stared down at the sand as she spoke, features unreadable. She talked hesitantly, the same way she'd woken me in the spare room at dawn, asking if I wanted to go down to the beach with her. She'd had all night to get over the surprise, but she still looked at me in snatched glances, as if it weren't allowed.

I shrugged.

"I'm the believable part, Virginia. I'm not the one back from the dead. And don't call me *kid*."

She smiled a little. "We're all back from the dead at some point, Tak. Hazards of the profession, remember?"

"You know what I mean."

"Yeah." She stared away down the beach for a while, where the sunrise was still a blurred blood rumor through early-morning mist. "So do *you* believe her?"

"That she's Quell?" I sighed and scooped up a handful of sand. Watched it trickle away through my fingers and off the sides of my palm. "I believe *she* believes she is."

Virginia Vidaura made an impatient gesture. "I've met wireheads who believe they're Konrad Harlan. That isn't what I asked you."

"I know what you asked me, Virginia."

"Then deal with the fucking question," she said without heat. "Didn't I teach you anything in the Corps?"

"Is she Quell?" Trace moisture from the swim had left tiny lines of sand still clinging to my palms. I brushed my hands together brusquely. "How can she be, right? Quell's dead. Vaporized. Whatever your pals back at the house might like to wish for in their political wet dreams."

She looked over her shoulder, as if she thought they might hear us. Might have woken and come stretching and yawning down to the beach after us, rested and ready to take violent offense at my lack of respect.

"I can remember a time you might have wished for it, too, Tak. A time you might have wanted her back. What happened to you?"

"Sanction Four happened to me."

"Ah, yes. Sanction Four. Revolution called for a bit more commitment than you'd expected, did it?"

"You weren't there."

A small quiet opened up behind the words. She looked away. Brasil's little band were all nominally Quellists—or neoQuellists at least—but Virginia Vidaura was the only one among them with Envoy conditioning. She'd had the capacity for willful self-deception gouged out of her in a way that would permit no easy emotional attachment to legend or dogma. She'd have, I reasoned, an opinion worth listening to. She'd have perspective.

I waited. Down the beach, wavecrash kept up a slow, expectant backbeat.

"I'm sorry," she said finally.

"Skip it. We all get our dreams stamped on from time to time, right? And if it didn't hurt, what kind of second-rate dreams would they be?"

Her mouth quirked. "Still quoting her, though, I see."

"Paraphrasing. Look, Virginia, you correct me if I'm wrong, but there's no record of any backup of Nadia Makita ever made. Right?"

"There's no record of any backup of Takeshi Kovacs, either. Seems to be one out there, though."

"Yeah, don't remind me. But that's the fucking Harlan family, and you can see a rationale for why they'd do it. You can see the value."

She looked sidelong at me. "Well, it's good to see your time on Sanction Four didn't damage your ego."

"Virginia, come on. I'm an ex-Envoy, I'm a killer. I have *uses*. It's kind of hard to see the Harlan family backing up the woman who nearly tore their whole oligarchy apart. And anyway, how the hell does something like that, a copy of someone that historically vital, get dumped in the skull of a plankton-standard deCom artist."

"Hardly plankton-standard." She poked at the sand some more. The lull in the conversation stretched. "Takeshi, you know Yaros and I . . ."

"Yeah, spoke to him. He's the one told me you were down here. He said to say hello if I saw you. He hopes you're okay."

"Really?"

"Well, what he really said was *ah fuck it,* but I'm reading between the lines here. So it didn't work out?"

She sighed. "No. It didn't."

"Want to talk about it?"

"There's no point, it was all so long ago." A vicious jab at the sand with the bottleback prod. "I can't believe he's still hung up on it."

I shrugged. *"We must be prepared to live on time scales of life our ancestors could only dream of, if we are to realize our own dreams."*

This time the look she gave me was smeared with an ugly anger that didn't suit her fine new features.

"You trying to be fucking funny?"

"No, I'm just observing that Quellist thought has a wide range of—"

"Shut up, Tak."

The Envoy Corps was never big on traditional authority models, at least not as most humans would recognize them. But the habit, the assumption that my trainers were worth listening to was hard to break. And when you've had feelings that amount to—

Well, never mind.

I shut up. Listened to the waves.

A little while later, rusty saxophone notes started to float down to us from the house. Virginia Vidaura got up and looked back, expression softened somewhat, shading her eyes. Unlike a lot of the surfer crash pads I'd seen as I cruised this portion of the Strip the night before, Brasil's house was a built structure, not blown. Mirrorwood uprights caught the rapidly strengthening sunlight and glinted like huge edged weapons. The wind-worn surfaces between offered restful shades of washed-out lime and gray, but all the way up four stories of seaward-facing rooms the windows winked broadly at us.

An off note from the sax dented the halting melody out of shape.

"Ouch." I winced, perhaps exaggeratedly. The sudden softness in her face had caught me at an odd angle.

"At least he's trying," she said obscurely.

"Yeah. Well, I guess everyone's awake now, anyway."

She looked sideways at me, the same not-allowed glance. Her mouth quirked unwillingly.

"You're a real bastard, Tak. You know that?"

"I've been told once or twice. So what's breakfast like around here?"

● ● ●

Surfers.

You'll find them pretty much everywhere on Harlan's World, because pretty much everywhere on Harlan's World there's an ocean that throws waves to die for. And *to die for* has a couple of meanings here. Zero point eight G, remember, and three moons—you can ride a wave along some parts of Vchira for half a dozen kilometers at a time, and the height of the things some of these guys get up on has to be seen to be believed. But the low gravity and the trilunar tug has its flip side, and the oceans on Harlan's World run current systems like nothing ever seen on Earth. Chemical content, temperature, and flow all vary alarmingly, and the sea does bitchy, unforgiving things with very little warning. The turbulence theorists are still coming to grips with a lot of it, back in their modeled simulations. Out on Vchira Beach, they're doing a different kind of research. More than once I've seen the Young effect played out to perfection on a seemingly stable nine-meter face, like some Promethean myth in frame advance—the perfect rising shoulder of water eddies and stumbles drunkenly under the rider, then shatters apart as if caught by artillery frag fire. The sea opens its throat, swallows the board, swallows the rider. I've helped pull the survivors from the surf a few times. I've seen the dazed grins, the glow that seems to come off their faces as they say things like *I didn't think that bitch was* ever *going to get off my chest* or *man, did you see that shit come apart on me* or most often of all, urgently, *did you get my plank out okay, sam*. I've watched them go back out again, the ones who didn't have dislocated or broken limbs or cracked skulls from the wipeout, and I've watched the gnawing want in the eyes of the ones who have to wait to heal.

I know the feeling well enough. It's just that I tend to associate it with trying to kill people other than myself.

"Why us?" Mari Ado asked with the blunt lack of manners she obviously thought went with her offworld name.

I grinned and shrugged.

"Couldn't think of anyone else stupid enough."

She took a feline kind of offense at it, rolled a shrug of her own off one shoulder, and turned her back on me as she went to the coffee machine beside the window. It looked as if she'd opted for a clone of her last sleeve, but there was a down-to-the-bone restlessness about her that I didn't remember from forty years ago. She looked thinner, too, a little hollow around the eyes, and she'd drawn her hair back in a sawn-off ponytail that seemed to be pulling her features too tight. Her custom-grown Adoracion face had the bone structure to carry that; it just made the bent nose more hawkish, the dark liquid eyes darker, and the jaw more determined. But still, it didn't look good on her.

"Well, I think you've got some fucking nerve actually, Kovacs. Coming back here like this after Sanction Four."

Opposite me at the table, Virginia twitched. I shook my head minutely.

Ado glanced sideways. "Don't you think, Sierra?"

Sierra Tres, as was her tendency, said nothing. Her face was also a younger version of the one I remembered, features carved elegantly in the space between Millsport Japanese and the gene salons' idea of Inca beauty.

The expression it wore gave nothing away. She leaned against the blue color-washed wall beside the coffeemaker, arms folded across a minimal polalloy top. Like most of the recently woken household, she wore little more than sprayon swimwear and some cheap jewelry. A drained café-au-lait demitasse hung from one silver-ringed finger as if forgotten. But the look she danced between Mari and me was a requirement to answer.

Around the breakfast table, the others stirred in sympathy. With whom, it was hard to tell. I soaked up the responses with Envoy-conditioned blankness, filing it away for assessment later. We'd been through Ascertainment the night before; the stylized grilling disguised as conversational reminiscence was done, and I was confirmed in my new sleeve as who I claimed to be. That wasn't the problem here.

I cleared my throat.

"You know, Mari, you could always have come along. But then Sanction Four's a whole different planet, it has no tides and the ocean's as flat as your chest, so it's hard to see what fucking use you'd have been to me."

As an insult, it was as unjust as it was complex. Mari Ado, ex of the Little Blue Bugs, was criminally competent in a number of insurgency roles that had nothing to do with wavecraft, and for that matter no less well endowed physically than a number of the other female bodies in the room, Virginia Vidaura included. But I knew she was sensitive about her shape, and unlike Virginia or myself, she'd never been offworld. In effect I'd called her a local yokel, a surf nerd, a cheap source of sexual service, *and* sexually unappealing all in one. Doubtless Isa, had she been there to witness it, would have yipped with delight.

I'm still a little sensitive myself where Sanction IV's concerned.

Ado looked back across the table to the big oak armchair at the end. "Throw this motherfucker out, Jack."

"No." It was a low drawl, almost sleepy. "Not at this stage."

He sprawled almost horizontal in the dark wood seat, legs stretched out in front of him, face drooping forward, opened hands pressed loosely one on top of the other in his lap, almost as if he was trying to read his own palm.

"He's being rude, Jack."

"So were you." Brasil curled himself upright and forward in the chair. His eyes met mine. A faint sweat beaded his forehead. I recognized the cause. Fresh sleeve notwithstanding, he hadn't changed that much. He hadn't given up his bad habits.

"But she's got a point, Kovacs. Why us? Why would we do this for you?"

"You know damned well this isn't for me," I lied. "If the Quellist ethic isn't alive on Vchira, then tell me where the fuck else I go looking for it. Because time is short."

A snort from down the table. A young male surfer I didn't know. "Man, you don't even know if this *is* Quell we're talking about. Look at you, you don't even believe it yourself. You want us to go up against the Harlan family for the sake of a glitch in some deCom psychobitch's fucked-up head? No *way*, sam."

There were a couple of mutterings I took for assent. But the majority stayed silent and watched me.

I hooked the young surfer's gaze. "And your name is?"

"Fuck's it to you, sam?"

"This is Daniel," said Brasil easily. "He hasn't been here long. And yes, you're looking at his real age there. Listening to it, too, I'm afraid."

Daniel flushed and looked betrayed.

"Fact remains, Jack. We're talking about Rila Crags here. No one ever got inside there without an invitation."

A smile tripped like lightning from Brasil to Virginia Vidaura and on to Sierra Tres. Even Mari Ado chortled sourly into her coffee.

"What? Fucking what?"

I was careful not to join in the grinning as I looked across at Daniel. We might need him. "I'm afraid you are showing your age there, Dan. Just a little."

"Natsume," said Ado, as if explaining something to a child. "Name mean anything to you?"

The look she got back was answer enough.

"Nikolai Natsume." Brasil smiled again, this time for Daniel. "Don't worry about it, you're a couple of hundred years too young to remember him."

"That's a real story?" I heard someone mutter, and felt a strange sadness seep into me. "I thought it was a propaganda myth."

Another surfer I didn't know twisted in her seat to look at Jack Soul Brasil, protest in her face. "Hey, Natsume never got inside."

"Yeah, he did," said Ado. "You don't want to believe that crap they sell in school these days. He—"

"We can discuss Natsume's achievements later," said Brasil mildly. "For now it's enough that if we have to crack Rila, the precedent already exists."

There was a brief pause. The surfer who hadn't believed in Natsume's existence outside legend was whispering in Daniel's ear.

"Okay, that's fine," someone else said finally, "but if the Harlan family have this woman, whoever she is, is there any point in mounting a raid? Interrogation tech they've got up at Rila, they'll have cracked her by now."

"Not necessarily." Virginia Vidaura leaned forward across her cleared plate. Small breasts moved under her sprayon. It was strange seeing her in the surfer uniform, too. "DeCom are running state-of-the-art gear and more capacity than most AI mainframes. They're built as well as the wetware engineers know how. Supposed to be able to beat Martian naval intelligence systems, remember. I think even good interrogation software is going to look pretty sick against that."

"They could just torture her," said Ado, returning to her seat. "This is the Harlans we're talking about."

I shook my head. "If they try that, she can just withdraw into the command systems. And besides, they need her coherent at complicated levels. Inflicting short-term pain isn't going to get them there."

Sierra Tres lifted her head.

"You say she's talking to you?"

"I think so, yes." I ignored a couple more disbelieving noises from down the table. "At a guess, I'd say she's managed to use her deCom gear to hook into a phone I used to call one of her crew a while back. Probably a residual trace in the team net system, she could run a search for it. But he's dead now and it's not a good connection."

Hard laughter from a couple of the company, Daniel included. I memorized their faces.

Maybe Brasil noticed. He gestured for quiet.

"Her team are all dead, right?"

"Yes. That's what I was told."

"Four deComs, in a camp full of deComs." Mari Ado made a face. "Slaughtered just like that? Hard to believe, isn't it?"

"I don't—"

She talked over me. "That they'd let it happen, I mean. This, what's his name, Kurumaya was it? Old-school deCom big daddy, he's going to just let the Harlanites walk in and do that under his nose? And what about the rest of them? Doesn't say much for their *esprit de corps,* does it?"

"No," I said evenly. "It doesn't. DeCom runs as a competition-based nail-it-and-cash-in bounty dynamic. The crews are tight-knit internally. Outside of that, from what I saw there's not a lot of loyalty. And Kurumaya will have bowed to whatever oligarchy pressure was brought to bear, probably after the event. Sylvie's Slipins never did themselves any favors with him, certainly not enough for him to buck the hierarchy."

Ado curled her lip. "Sounds charming."

"Signs of the times," said Brasil unexpectedly. He looked at me. *"When you strip away all the higher loyalties, we inevitably fall back on fear and greed.* Right?"

In the wake of the quote, no one said anything. I scanned the faces in the room, trying to reckon support against dislike and the shades of gray between. Sierra Tres cranked one expressive eyebrow and stayed silent. Sanction IV, *fucking* Sanction IV, hung in the air about me. You could make a good case for my actions there being governed by fear and greed. Some of the faces I was watching already had.

Then again, none of them was there.

None of them was fucking there.

Brasil stood up. He searched the faces around the table, maybe for the same things I'd been looking at.

"Think about this, all of you. It will affect us all, one way or the other. Each one of you is here because I trust you to keep your mouth shut, and because if there's something to be done I trust you to help me do it. There'll be another meeting tonight at sundown. There'll be a vote. Like I said, give it some thought."

Then he picked up his saxophone from a stool by the window and ambled out of the room as if there were nothing more important going on in his life at that moment.

After a couple of seconds, Virginia Vidaura got up and went out after him. She didn't look at me at all.

CHAPTER TWENTY-FIVE

Brasil found me again later, on the beach.

He came trudging up out of the surf with the board slung under one arm, body stripped to shorts, scar tissue, and sprayon ankle boots, raking the sea out of his hair with his free hand. I lifted an arm in greeting, and he broke into a jog toward where I sat in the sand. No mean feat after the hours he'd had in the water. When he reached me, he was barely breathing heavily.

I squinted up at him in the sun. "Looks like fun."

"Try?" He touched the surfboard, angled it toward me. Surfers don't do that, not with a board they've owned any longer than a couple of days. And this one looked older than the sleeve that was carrying it.

Jack Soul Brasil. Even here on Vchira Beach, there was no one else much like him.

"Thanks, I'll pass."

He shrugged, dug the board into the sand, and flopped down beside me. Water sprang off him in droplets. "Suit yourself. Good swell out there today. Nothing too scary."

"Must be dull for you."

A broad grin. "Well, that's the trap, isn't it."

"Is it?"

"Yeah, it is." He gestured out to sea. "Get in the water, you do every wave for what it's worth. Lose that, you might as well go back to Newpest. Leave Vchira for good."

I nodded. "Get many like that?"

"The burnouts? Yeah, some. But leaving's okay. It's the ones who stay on that hurt to look at."

I glanced at the scar tissue on his chest.

"You're such a sensitive guy, Jack."

He smiled out at the sea. "Trying to be."

"That why you won't do the clone thing, huh? Wear every sleeve for what it's worth?"

"*Learn* every sleeve for what it's worth," he corrected me gently. "Yeah.

Plus you wouldn't believe what clone storage costs these days, even in New-pest."

"Doesn't seem to bother Ado or Tres."

He grinned again. "Mari's got an inheritance to spend. You know what her real name is, don't you?"

"Yeah, I remember. And Tres?"

"Sierra knows people in the trade. When the rest of us packed in the Bug stuff, she went on contracting for the *haiduci* for a while. She's owed some fa-vors up in Newpest."

He shivered slightly, let it run up to a shudder that twitched his shoul-ders. Sneezed suddenly.

"Still doing *that* shit, I see. Is that why Ado's so thin?"

He looked at me oddly. "Ado's thin because she wants to be thin. How she goes about it is her business, wouldn't you say?"

I shrugged. "Sure. I'm just curious. I figured you guys would have gotten bored with self-infection by now."

"Ah, but you never liked it in the first place, did you? I remember last time you were here, when Mari tried to sell you on that batch of HHF we had. You always were a little puritanical on the subject."

"I just never saw the point of making myself ill for fun. Thought as a trained medic, you'd be at least that smart, too."

"I'll remind you of that next time we're sharing a bad tetrameth come-down. Or a single-malt hangover."

"It's not the same."

"You're right." He nodded sagely. "That chemical shit is Stone Age stuff. I ran Hun Home flu against a spec-inhibited immune system for ten years and all I got was buzz and some really cool delirium dreams. Real wave-climbers. No headaches, no major organ damage, not even a runny nose once the inhibitors and the virus meshed. Tell me one drug you could do that with."

"Is that what you're running these days? HHF?"

He shook his head. "Not for a long time. Virginia got us some Adoracion custom a while back. Engineered spinal-fever complex. Man, you should see my dreams now. Sometimes I wake up screaming."

"I'm happy for you."

For a while, we both watched the figures in the water. A couple of times Brasil grunted and pointed out something in the way one of the surfers moved. None of it meant very much to me. Once he applauded softly as someone wiped out, but when I glanced at him there was no apparent mock-ery in his face.

A little later he asked me again, gesturing at the pegged board.

"You sure you don't want to try out? Take my plank? Man, that mothballed shit you're wearing looks practically made for it. Odd for military custom, come to think of it. Kind of light." He prodded idly at my shoulder with a couple of fingers. "In fact, I'd say that's near-perfect sports sleeve trim you're carrying. What's the label?"

"Ah, some defunct bunch, never heard of them before. Eishundo."

"Eishundo?"

I glanced at him, surprised. "Yeah, Eishundo Organics. You know them?"

"Fuck, yeah." He scooted back in the sand and stared at me. "Tak, that's a design classic you're wearing. They only ever built the one series, and it was a century ahead of its time at least. Stuff no one had ever tried before. Gecko grip, recabled muscle structure, autonomic survival systems like you wouldn't believe."

"No, I would."

He wasn't listening. "Flexibility and endurance through the roof, reflex wiring you don't start to see again until Harkany got started back in the early three hundreds. Man, they just don't build them like that anymore."

"They certainly don't. They went bust, didn't they?"

He shook his head vehemently. "Nah, that was politics. Eishundo was a Drava cooperative, set up in the eighties, typical Quiet Quellist types except I don't think they ever made any big secret of the fact. Would have been shut down probably, but everyone knew they made the best sports sleeves on the planet and they ended up supplying half the brats in the First Families."

"Handy for them."

"Yeah, well. Like I said, there was nothing to touch them." The enthusiasm leached from his face. "Then, with the Unsettlement, they declared for the Quellists. Harlan family never forgave them for that. When it was over they blacklisted everyone who'd ever worked for Eishundo, even executed a few of the senior biotech guys as traitors and terrorists. Providing arms to the enemy, all that tired line of shit. Plus, with the way things turned out at Drava, they were pretty fucked anyway. Man, I can't believe you're sitting there wearing that thing. It's a fucking piece of history, Tak."

"Well, that's good to know."

"You sure you don't want to—"

"Sell it to you? Thanks, no, I'll—"

"*Surf,* man. You sure you don't want to surf? Take the plank out and get wet? Find out what you can do in that thing?"

I shook my head. "I'll just live with the suspense."

He looked at me curiously for a while. Then he nodded and went back to watching the sea. You could feel the way just watching it did something for him. Balanced out the fever he'd set raging inside himself. I tried, a little grimly, not to feel envy.

"So maybe some other time," he said quietly. "When you're not carrying so much."

"Yeah. Maybe." It wasn't any other time I could usefully imagine, unless he was talking about the past, and I couldn't see any way to get back there.

He seemed to want to talk.

"You never did this stuff at all, did you? Even back in Newpest?"

I shrugged. "I know how to fall off a plank, if that's what you mean. Did the local beaches for a couple of summers when I was a kid. Then I started hanging out with a crew and they were strictly subaqua. You know how it goes."

He nodded, maybe remembering his own Newpest youth. Maybe remembering the last time we'd had this conversation, but I wouldn't count on it. The last time we'd talked about it was fifty-odd years back, and if you don't have Envoy recall that's a long time and a lot of conversations past.

"Fucking stupid," he muttered. "Who'd you run with?"

"Reef Warriors. Hirata chapter, mostly. *Dive Free, Die Free. Leave the Scum on the Surface.* We would have cut up guys like you as soon as look at you back then. What about you?"

"Me? Oh, I thought I was a real fucking free spirit. Storm Riders, Standing Wave, Vchira Dawn Chorus. Some others, I don't remember them all now." He shook his head. "*So* fucking stupid."

We watched the waves.

"How long have you been out here?" I asked him.

He stretched and tipped his head back toward the sun, eyes clenched shut. A sound like a cat purring made its way up out of his chest, broke finally into a chuckle.

"Here on Vchira? I don't know, I don't keep track. Got to be close to a century by now, I guess. On and off."

"And Virginia says the Bugs folded two decades back."

"Yeah, near enough. Like I said, Sierra still gets out and about occasionally. But most of the rest of us haven't been in worse than a beach brawl for ten, twelve years."

"Let's hope you haven't gotten rusty then."

He flipped another grin at me. "You take a lot for granted."

I shook my head. "No, I just listen carefully. *It will affect us all, one way or the other?* You got that right. You're going to go with this, whatever the others do. *You* think it's for real."

"Oh yeah?" Brasil lay back flat on the sand and closed his eyes. "Well, here's something you might want to think about then. Something you probably don't know. Back when the Quellists were fighting the First Families for continental dominance of New Hokkaido, there was a lot of talk about government death squads targeting Quell and the other Contingency Committee names. Sort of counterblow to the Black Brigades. So you know what they did?"

"Yeah, I know."

He squinted an eye open. "You do?"

"No. But I don't like rhetorical questions. You're going to tell me something, get on and tell me."

He closed his eyes again. I thought something like pain passed over his face.

"All right. Do you know what data shrapnel is?"

"Sure." It was an old term, almost outmoded. "Cheap virals. Stone Age stuff. Bits of cannibalized standard code in a broadcast matrix. You lob them into enemy systems, and they try to carry out whatever looped functions they were for originally. Clogs up the operating code with inconsistent commands. That's the theory, anyway. I hear it doesn't work all that well."

In fact, I knew the limitations of the weapon pretty well firsthand. Final resistance on Adoracion 150 years back had broadcast data shrapnel to slow down the Envoy advance across the Manzana Basin, because it was all they had left. It hadn't slowed us down all that much. The furious hand-to-hand fighting that followed in the covered streets of Neruda had hurt us far more. But Jack Soul Brasil, with his adopted name and passion for a culture whose planet he'd never seen, didn't need to hear about that right now.

He shifted his long body on the sand.

"Yeah, well, the New Hokkaido Contingency Committee didn't share your skepticism. Or maybe they were just desperate. Anyway, they came up with something similar based on digitized human freight. They built shell personalities for each committee member, just a surface assembly of basic memory and self—"

"Oh you are *fucking* kidding me!"

"—and loaded them into widecast datamines, to be deployed inside the Quellist sectors and triggered if they were overrun. No, I'm not kidding you."

I closed my own eyes.

Oh fuck.

Brasil's voice ticked onward, remorseless. "Yeah, plan was, in the event of a rout, they'd trigger the mines and leave a few dozen of their own defenders, maybe the vanguard units of the encroaching forces as well, each solidly convinced *they* were Quellcrist Falconer. Or whoever."

Sound of waves, and distant cries across the water.

Would you mind holding me while I go under?

I saw her face. I heard the changed voice that wasn't Sylvie Oshima.

Touch me. Tell me you're fucking real.

Brasil was still going, but you could hear him winding down. "Quite a smart weapon when you think about it. Widespread confusion, who the fuck do you trust, who do you arrest? Chaos, really. Maybe it buys time for the real Quell to get out. Maybe just. Creates chaos. The final blow. Who knows?"

When I opened my eyes again, he was sitting up and staring out to sea again. The peace and the humor in his face were gone, wiped away like makeup, like seawater dried off in the sun. Out of nowhere, inside the tight-muscled surfer physique, he looked suddenly bitter and angry.

"Who told you all that?" I asked him.

He glanced back at me, and the ghost of his former smile flickered.

"Someone you need to meet," he said quietly.

● ● ●

We took his bug, a stripped-down two-seater not much bigger than the single I'd rented but, as it turned out, far faster. Brasil took the trouble to pull on a battered-looking panther-skin crash suit, something else that marked him out as different from all the other idiots cruising up and down the highway in swimwear at speeds that would flay flesh to the bone if they spilled and rolled.

"Yeah, well," he said, when I mentioned it. "Some chances are worth taking. The rest is just death wish."

I picked up my polalloy helmet and molded it on. My voice came through the speaker tinnily.

"Got to watch that shit, huh?"

He nodded. "All the time."

He cranked the bug up, settled his own helmet, and then kicked us down the highway at an even two hundred kilometers an hour, heading north. Back along the path I'd already traced looking for him. Past the all-night diner, past the other stops and knots of population where I'd scattered his name like blood around a bottleback charter boat, back through Kem Point and farther. In daylight, the Strip lost a lot of its romance. The tiny hamlets of window light I'd passed going south the previous evening showed up as sun-blasted utilitarian low-rises and 'fabs. Neon and holosigns were switched off or bleached out to near invisibility. The dunetown settlements shed their cozy main-street-at-night appeal and became simple accretions of structure on either side of a detritus-strewn highway. Only the sound of the sea and the fragrances in the air were the same, and we were going too fast to register them.

Twenty kilometers north of Kem Point a small, badly paved side road led away into the dunes. Brasil throttled back for the turn, not as much as I would have liked, and took us off the highway. Sand boiled from under the bug, scoured out from around the irregular chunks of evercrete and off the bedrock the road had been laid over. With grav-effect vehicles, paving is often as much about signaling where the path goes as providing an actual surface. And just over the first line of dunes, whoever had laid this track had abandoned the effort in favor of illuminum and carbon-fiber marker poles driven into the ground at ten-meter intervals. Brasil let our speed bleed off, and we cruised sedately along the trail of poles as it snaked seaward through the sandscape. A couple of dilapidated bubblefabs appeared along the route, pitched at unlikely angles on the slopes around us. It wasn't clear if anyone was living in them. Farther on, I saw a combat-rigged skimmer parked under a tented dust canopy in a shallow defile. Spider-like watchdog systems like miniature karakuri flexed themselves awake on its upper surfaces at the sound of the bug's engine or maybe the heat we gave off. They raised a couple of limbs in our direction, then settled down again as we passed.

We crested the final set of dunes, and Brasil stopped the bug sideways-on to the sea. He lifted off his helmet, leaned forward on the controls, and nodded down the slope.

"There you go. Tell you anything?"

A long time ago, someone had driven an armored hoverloader up the beach until its nose rammed the line of dunes, and then apparently just left it there. Now the vessel sprawled in its collapsed skirt like a swamp panther that had crouched for approaching prey and then been slaughtered where it lay. The rear steerage vanes had blown around to an angle that suited the prevailing wind, and were apparently jammed there. Sand had crept into the jigsaw lines of the armoring and built up along the facing side of the skirt so the armored flanks of the 'loader seemed to be the upper surfaces of a much larger buried structure. The gunports on the side I could see offered blast barrels cranked to the sky, a sure sign that the hydraulic governors were shot. The dorsal hatches were blown back as if for evacuation.

On the side of the central fuselage, up near the blister of the bridge, I spotted traces of color. Black and red, wound together in a familiar pattern that touched me in the spine with a cold hand: the time-abraded traces of a stylized Quellcrist frond.

"Oh no way."

"Yeah." Brasil shifted in the bug's saddle. "That's right."

"Has this been here since ... ?"

"Yeah, pretty much."

We rode the bug down the dune and dismounted near the tail end. Brasil cut the power, and the vehicle sank to the sand like an obedient seal. The 'loader bulked above us, smart metal armor soaking up the heat of the sun so there was a faint chill close up. At three points along the pitted flank, access ladders led down from the edge of the skirt rail and buried their feet in the sand. The one at the rear, where the vessel had tilted toward the ground, was angled outward and almost horizontal. Brasil ignored it, grabbed at the skirt rail, and levered himself up onto the deck above with effortless grace. I rolled my eyes and followed suit.

The voice caught me as I straightened up.

"So is this him?"

I blinked in the sun and made out a slight figure ahead of us on the lightly canted deck. He stood about a head shorter than Brasil and wore a simple gray coverall whose sleeves were hacked off at the shoulders. From the features below the sparse white hair, he had to be in his sixties at least, but the exposed arms were ropey with muscle and ended in big, bony hands. And the soft voice had a corded strength behind it. There was a tension to the question that approached hostility.

I stepped forward to join Brasil. Mirrored the way the old man stood with his hands hanging at his sides like weapons he might need. Met his eyes incuriously.

"Yeah, I'm him."

His gaze seemed to flinch downward, but it wasn't that. He was looking me over. There was a moment of silence.

"You've spoken to her?"

"Yes." My voice softened a fraction. I'd misread the tension in him. It wasn't hostility. "I've spoken to her."

● ● ●

Inside the hoverloader, there was an unexpected sense of space and natural light. Combat vessels of this sort are usually pretty cramped, but Soseki Koi had had a lot of time to change all that. Bulkheads had been ripped out, and in places the upper-level deck had been peeled back to create five-meter light wells. The sun poured in through the few vision ports and the opened dorsal hatches, blasted its way elsewhere between cracked armoring that might have been battle damage or deliberate modification. A riot of plant life clustered about these opened areas, spilling out of hung baskets and twining up exposed struts in the skeleton of the fuselage. Illuminum paneling had been carefully replaced in some areas, left to decay in others. Somewhere not visible, waterflow over rocks chuckled in patient counterpoint to the bassline pounding of the surf outside.

Koi got us seated on padded matting around a low, formally set table at the bottom of one of the light wells. He served us with traces of old-school ceremony from the 'loader's autochef, which sat on a shelf behind him and still seemed to be working pretty well. To the selection of grilled meat and pan noodles, he added a pot of belaweed tea and fruit grown from the plants overhead—vine plums and thick, thirty-centimeter lengths of Kossuth chainberry. Brasil dug into everything with the enthusiasm of a man who'd been in the water all day. I picked at my food, took just enough to be polite apart from the chainberry, which was some of the best I'd ever tasted. Koi held himself rigidly back from questions while we ate.

Eventually, Brasil tossed the stripped threads of his last piece of chainberry onto his plate, wiped his fingers on a napkin, and nodded at me.

"Tell him. I gave him the highlights, but it's your story."

"I—" I looked across the table of devastated food and saw the hunger that sat there. "Well. It's a while back now. A few months. I was up in Tekitomura, on. Business. I was in this bar down on the waterfront, Tokyo Crow. She was—"

It felt strange, telling it. Strange and, if I was honest, very distant. Listening to my own voice now, I suddenly had a hard time myself believing the path I'd tracked from that night of splattered blood and screaming hallucinations, out across the machine-haunted wastes of New Hok and back south again, running from a doppelgänger. Quixotic chivalry in wharfside bars, frantic schizophrenic sex and repeated waterborne flight in the company of a mysterious and damaged woman with hair of living steel, mountainside gun battles with the shards of myself amid the ruins of our Martian heritage. Sylvie was right when she christened me Micky in the shadows of the crane. It was pure experia.

No wonder Radul Segesvar was having a hard time coming to terms with what I'd done. Told this tale of muddled loyalties and blown-off-course rerouting, the man who'd come to him two years previously for backing would have laughed out loud in disbelief.

No, you wouldn't have laughed.

You would have stared, cold with detachment as you barely listened, and thought about something else. About the next New Revelation slaughter, blood on the blade of a Tebbit knife, a steep-sided pit out in the Weed Expanse, and a shrill screaming that goes on and on . . .

You would have shrugged the story away, true or not, content with what you had instead.

But Koi drank it in without a word. When I paused and looked at him, he asked no questions. He waited patiently and once, when I seemed to have stalled, he made a single, gentle gesture for me to continue. Finally, when I was done, he sat for a while and then nodded to himself.

"You say she called you names when she first came back."

"Yes." Envoy recall lifted them from the depths of inconsequential memory for me. "Odisej. Ogawa. She thought I was one of her soldiers, from the Tetsu battalion. Part of the Black Brigades."

"So." He looked away, face indecipherable. Voice soft. "Thank you, Kovacs-san."

Quiet. I exchanged glances with Brasil.

The surfer cleared his throat. "Is that bad?"

Koi drew breath as if it hurt him.

"It isn't helpful." He looked at us again and smiled sadly. "I was in the Black Brigades. Tetsu battalion wasn't part of them, it was a separate front."

Brasil shrugged. "Maybe she was confused."

"Yes, maybe." But the sadness never left his eyes.

"And the names?" I asked him. "Do you recognize them?"

He shook his head. "*Ogawa*'s not an uncommon name for the north, but I don't think I knew anyone called that. It's hard to be sure after all this time, but it doesn't chime. And *Odisej,* well"—a shrug—"there's the kendo *sensei,* but I don't think she had a Quellist past."

We sat in silence for a little while. Finally, Brasil sighed.

"Ah, fuck."

For some reason, the tiny explosion seemed to animate Koi. He smiled again, this time with a gleam I hadn't seen in him before.

"You sound discouraged, my friend."

"Yeah, well. I really thought this might be it, you know. I thought we were really going to do this."

Koi reached for the plates and began to clear them onto the ledge behind his shoulder. His movements were smooth and economical, and he talked as he worked.

"Do you know what day it is next week?" he asked conversationally.

We both blinked at him.

"No? How unhealthy. How easily we wrap ourselves up in our own concerns, eh? How easily we detach from the wider scheme of life as it's lived by the majority." He leaned forward to collect the farthest dishes, and I handed them to him. "Thank you. Next week, the end of next week, is Konrad Harlan's birthday. In Millsport, celebration will be mandatory. Fireworks and festivities without mercy. The chaos of humans at play."

Brasil got it before me. His face lit up. "You mean . . . ?"

Koi smiled gently. "My friend, for all I know this might well really be *it,* as you rather cryptically describe it. But whether it is or not, I can tell you now we *are* really going to do this. Because we really have no other choice."

It was what I wanted to hear, but I still couldn't quite believe he'd said it. On the ride south, I'd imagined I might get Brasil and Vidaura, maybe another few of the neoQuell faithful, to weigh in on my side whatever the holes in their wish fulfillment. But Brasil's data shrapnel story, the way it fitted the New Hok detail, and the understanding that it came from someone who knew, who'd been there, the meeting with this small, self-contained man and his serious approach to gardening and food—all this was pushing me toward the vertiginous edge of a belief that I'd been wasting my time.

The understanding that I hadn't was almost as dizzying.

"Consider," said Koi, and something seemed to have changed in his voice. "Maybe this ghost of Nadia Makita is exactly that, a ghost. But is not a woken and vengeful ghost enough? Has it not already been enough for the oligarchs to panic and disobey the binding covenants of their puppet masters back on Earth? How then can we *not* do this? How can we *not* take back from their grip this object of their terror and rage?"

I traded another look with Brasil. Raised an eyebrow.

"This isn't going to be easy to sell," the surfer said grimly. "Most of the ex-Bugs will fight if they think it's Quell they're going to get, and they'll talk the others around. But I don't know if they'll do it for a woken ghost, however fucking vengeful."

Koi finished clearing the plates, took up a napkin, and examined his hands. He found a ribbon of chainberry juice caught around one wrist and cleaned it off with meticulous attention. His gaze was fixed on the task as he spoke. "I will speak to them, if you wish. But in the end, if they have no conviction of their own, Quell herself wouldn't ask them to fight, and neither will I."

Brasil nodded. "Great."

"Koi." Suddenly I needed to know. "Do *you* think this is a ghost we're chasing?"

He made a tiny sound, something between a chuckle and a sigh.

"We are all chasing ghosts, Kovacs-san. Living as long as we now do, how could we not be."

Sarah.

I forced it down, wondering if he saw the wince at the edges of my eyes as I did it. Wondering with sudden paranoia if he already somehow knew. My voice grated coming out.

"That isn't what I asked you."

He blinked and suddenly smiled again

"No, it isn't. You asked me if I believed, and I evaded your question. Forgive me. On Vchira Beach, cheap metaphysics and cheap politics rub shoulders and both are in frequent demand. With a little effort, a passable living can be made from dispensing them, but then the habit becomes hard to break." He sighed. "Do I believe we are dealing with the return of Quellcrist Falconer? With every fiber of my being I want to, but like any Quellist I am impelled to face the facts. And the facts do not support what I want to believe."

"It's not her."

"It's not likely. But in one of her less passionate moments, Quell herself once offered an escape clause for situations such as these. If the facts are against you, she said, but you cannot bear to cease believing—then at least suspend judgment. Wait and see."

"I'd have thought that mitigates pretty effectively against action."

He nodded. "Mostly it does. But in this case, the issue of what I want to be true has nothing to do with whether we act or not. Because this much I *do* believe: even if this ghost has no more than talismanic value, its time is here and its place is among us. One way or another, there is a change coming. The Harlanites recognize it as well as we do, and they have already made their move. It only remains for us to make ours. If in the end I have to fight and die for the ghost and memory of Quellcrist Falconer and not the woman herself, then that will be better than not fighting at all."

That stayed in my head like an echo, long after we left Soseki Koi to his preparations and rode the bug back along the Strip. That, and his simple question. The simple conviction behind it.

Is not a woken and vengeful ghost enough?

But it wasn't the same for me. Because this ghost I'd held, and I'd watched moonlight across the floor of a cabin in the mountains while she slipped away from me into sleep, not knowing if she'd be waking again.

If she could be woken again, I didn't want to be the one to tell her what she was. I didn't want to be there to watch her face when she found out.

CHAPTER TWENTY-SIX

After that, it went rapidly.

There is thought and there is action, a youngish Quell once said, stealing liberally, I later discovered, from Harlan's World's ancient samurai heritage. *Do not confuse the two. When the time comes to act, your thought must already be complete. There will be no room for it when the action begins.*

Brasil went back to the others and presented Koi's decision as his own. There was a splutter of dispute from some of the surfers who still hadn't forgiven me for Sanction IV, but it didn't last. Even Mari Ado dropped her hostility like a broken toy as it became clear I was peripheral to the real issue. One by one, in the sunset-painted shade and glow of the common living room, the men and women of Vchira Beach gave their assent.

It seemed that a woken ghost was going to be enough.

●●●

The component parts of the raid floated together with a speed and ease that for the more suggestible might have implied the favor of gods or agents of destiny. For Koi, it was simply the flow of historical forces, no more in question than the laws of gravity or thermodynamics. It was a confirmation that the time had come, that the political pot was boiling over. Of course it was going to spill, of *course* it was all going to fall in the same direction, onto the floor. Where else could it go?

I told him I thought it was luck, and he just smiled.

And it came together anyway.

Personnel:
The Little Blue Bugs. They barely existed anymore as an actual entity, but there were enough of the old crew around to form a core that corresponded roughly to legend. Newcomers drawn in over the years by the legend's gravitational pull sketched an outlined weight of numbers and claimed the

nomenclature by association. Over even more years, Brasil had learned to trust some of them. He'd seen them surf and he'd seen them fight. More importantly, he'd seen them all prove their ability to adopt Quell's maxim and get on with living a full life when armed struggle was inappropriate. Together, the old and the new, they were as close to a Quellist task force as it was possible to get without a time machine.

Weapons:
The casually parked military skimmer in Koi's backyard was emblematic of a tendency that ran the length and breadth of the Strip. The Bugs weren't the only heavy-heist types to have taken refuge on Vchira Beach. Whatever it was that drew Brasil and his kind to the waves, it was a general tug that manifested itself just as easily in an enthusiasm for lawbreaking of a dozen different stripes. Sourcetown was awash with retired thugs and revolutionaries, and it seemed none of them had ever felt like giving up their toys for good. Shake down the Strip and hardware tumbled out of it like vials and sex toys from the sheets of Mitzi Harlan's bed.

Planning:
Overrated as far as most of Brasil's crew were concerned. Rila Crags was almost as notorious as the old secret-police headquarters on Shimatsu Boulevard, the one Black Brigade member Iphigenia Deme brought down in smoking rubble when they tried to interrogate her in the basement and triggered her implanted enzyme explosives instead. The desire to do the same thing at Rila was a palpable prickle in the air of the house. It took a while to convince the more passionate among the newly reconfigured Bugs that an all-out assault on the Crags would be suicide of an infinitely less productive form than Deme's.

"Can't blame them," said Koi, his Black Brigade past suddenly glinting in the edge on his voice. "They've been waiting long enough for the chance to make someone pay."

"Daniel hasn't," I said pointedly. "He's barely been alive two decades."

Koi shrugged. "Rage at injustice is a forest fire—it jumps all divides, even those between generations."

I stopped wading and looked back at him. You could see how he might be getting carried away. We were both sea giants out of legend now, knee deep in a virtual ocean amid the islands and reefs of the Millsport Archipelago at one-to-two-thousand scale. Sierra Tres had called in some *haiduci* favors and gotten us time in a high-resolution mapping construct belonging to a firm of marine architects whose commercial management techniques wouldn't bear too much close legal scrutiny. They weren't overjoyed about the loan, but that's what happens when you cozy up with the *haiduci*.

"Have you ever actually seen a forest fire, Koi?"

Because they sure as hell aren't common on a world that's 95 percent ocean.

"No." He gestured. "It was a metaphor. But I have seen what happens when injustice finally triggers retribution. And it lasts for a long time."

"Yes, I know that."

I stared away toward the waters of the southern Reach. The construct had reproduced the maelstrom there in miniature, gurgling and grinding and tugging at my legs beneath the surface. If the depth of the water had been to the same scale as the rest of the construct, it probably would have dragged me off my feet.

"And you? Have you seen a forest fire? Offworld perhaps?"

"Seen a couple, yeah. On Loyko, I helped start one." I went on looking into the maelstrom. "During the Pilots' Revolt. A lot of their damaged vessels came down in the Ekaterina Tract, and they ran a guerrilla war from the cover for months. We had to burn them out. I was an Envoy then."

"I see." His voice showed no reaction. "Did it work?"

"Yeah, for a while. We certainly killed a lot of them. But like you said, that kind of resistance lives for generations."

"Yes. And the fire?"

I looked back at him again and smiled bleakly. "Took a long time to put out. Listen, Brasil's wrong about this gap. There's clear line of sight to the New Kanagawa security sweeps as soon as we round the headland here. Look at it. And the other side is reefed. We can't come in from that side, we'll get cut to pieces."

He waded across and looked.

"Assuming they're waiting for us, yes."

"They're waiting for something. They know me, they know I'll be coming for her. Fuck it, they've got me on tap. All they've got to do is fucking *ask* me, ask *him,* and he'll tell them what to expect, the little shit."

The sense of betrayal was raw and immense, like something ripped out of my chest. Like Sarah.

"Then will he not know to come here?" Koi asked softly. "To Vchira?"

"I don't think so." I reran my own second-guessing rationale as I boarded the *Haiduci's Daughter* in Tekitomura, hoping it sounded as convincing out loud. "He's too young to know anything about my time with the Bugs, and there's no official record they can feed him. Vidaura he knows, but for him she's still a trainer back in the Corps. He'll have no feel for what she might be doing now, or any postservice connection we might have. This Aiura bitch will give him what they've got on me, maybe on Virginia, too. But they don't have much, and what they do have is misleading. We're Envoys, we both covered our tracks and sewed the dataflows with tinsel every move we made."

"Very thorough of you."

I searched the lined face for irony, and found none apparent. I shrugged. "It's the conditioning. We're trained to disappear without trace on worlds we hardly know. Doing it somewhere you grew up is child's play. All these motherfuckers have got to work with is underworld rumor and a series of sentences in storage. That's not much to go on with a whole globe to cover and no aerial capacity. And the one thing he probably *thinks* he knows about me is that I'll avoid Newpest like the plague."

I shut down the updraft of family feeling that had stabbed through me on the *Haiduci's Daughter.* Let go a compressed breath.

"So where will he look for you?"

I nodded at the model of Millsport in front of us, brooding on the densely settled islands and platforms. "I think he's probably looking for me right there. It's where I always came when I wasn't offworld. It's the biggest urban environment on the planet, the easiest place to disappear if you know it well, and it's right across the bay from Rila. If I were an Envoy, that's where I'd be. Hidden, and in easy striking distance."

For a moment, my unaccustomed aerial viewpoint grew dizzying as I looked down on the wharf lines and streets, unfocused memory down the disjointed centuries blurring the old and new into a smudged familiarity.

And he's down there somewhere.

Come on, there's no way you can be sure of—

He's down there somewhere like an antibody, perfectly shaped to match the intruder he's looking for, asking soft questions in the flow of city life, bribing, threatening, levering, breaking, all the things that they taught us both so well. He's breathing deep as he does it, living it for its own dark and joyous sake like some inverted version of Jack Soul Brasil's philosophy of life.

Plex's words came trickling back to me.

He's got an energy to him as well, it feels as if he can't wait to get things done, to get started on everything. He's confident, he's not scared of anything, nothing's a problem. He laughs at everything—

I thought back along my train of associations in the last year, the people I might have endangered.

Todor Murakami, if he was still hanging around undeployed. Would my younger self know him? Murakami had joined the Corps almost the same time as I had, but we hadn't seen much of each other in the early days, hadn't deployed together until Nkrumah's Land and Innenin. Would Aiura's pet Kovacs make the connection? Would he be able to play Murakami successfully? Come to that, would Aiura let her newly double-sleeved creation anywhere near a serving Envoy? Would she dare?

Probably not. And Murakami, with the full weight of the Corps behind him, could look after himself.

Isa.

Oh shit.

Fifteen-year-old Isa, wearing tough-as-titanium woman-of-the-world like a panther-skin jacket over a soft and privileged upbringing among what was left of Millsport's middle class. Razor-sharp smart, and just as brittle. Like a pretend edition of little Mito, just before I left for the Envoys. If he found Isa, then—

Relax, you're covered. Only place she can put you is in Tekitomura. They get Isa, they've got nothing.

But—

It took me that long, that heartbeat, to care. The knowledge of the gap was a cold revulsion welling up through me.

But he'll break her in half if she gets in his way. He'll go through her like angelfire.

Will he? If she reminds you of Mito, isn't she going to remind him, too? It's the same sister for both of you. Isn't that going to stop him?

Isn't it?

I cast my mind back into the murk of operational days with the Corps, and didn't know.

"Kovacs!"

It was a voice out of the sky. I blinked and looked up from the modeled streets of Millsport. Over our heads, Brasil hung in the air of the virtuality clad in garish orange surf shorts and tatters of low-level cloud. With his physique and long fair hair blown back by stratospheric winds, he looked like a disreputable minor god. I raised a hand in greeting.

"Jack, you've got to come and look at this northern approach. It isn't going to—"

"Got no time for that, Tak. You need to bail out. Right now."

I felt a tightening around my chest. "What is it?"

"Company," he said cryptically, and vanished in a twist of white light.

The offices of Dzurinda Tudjman Sklep, marine architects and fluid dynamics engineers by appointment, were in north Sourcetown, where the Strip started to morph into resort complexes and beaches with safe surf. It wasn't a part of town any of Brasil's crew would have been seen dead in under normal circumstances, but they merged competently enough with the tourist hordes. Only someone who was looking for hardcore surfer poise would have spotted it beneath the violently mismatched high-color branded beachwear they'd adopted like camouflage. In the sober surroundings of a nilvibe conference chamber ten floors up from the promenade, they looked like an outbreak of some exotic anticorporate fungal infection.

"A priest, a fucking *priest*?"

"I'm afraid so," Sierra Tres told me. "Apparently alone, which I understand is unusual for the New Revelation."

"Unless they're borrowing tricks from the Sharyan martyr brigades," said Virginia Vidaura somberly. "Sanctified solo assassins against targeted infidels. What have you been up to, Tak?"

"It's personal," I muttered.

"Isn't it always." Vidaura grimaced and looked around at the assembled company. Brasil shrugged, and Tres showed no more emotion than usual. But Ado and Koi both looked angrily intent. "Tak, I think we have a right to know what's going on. This could jeopardize everything we're working for."

"It's got nothing to *do* with what we're working for, Virginia. It's irrelevant. These bearded fucks are too stupid incompetent to touch us. They're strictly the bottom of the food chain."

"Stupid or not," Koi pointed out, "one of them has succeeded in following you here. And is now asking after you in Kem Point."

"*Fine.* I'll go and kill him."

Mari Ado shook her head. "Not alone, you won't."

"Hey, this is *my* fucking problem, Mari."

"Tak, calm down."

"*I am fucking calm!*"

My shout sank into the nilvibe muffling like pain drowned in IV endorphin. No one said anything for a while. Mari Ado looked pointedly away, out of the window. Sierra Tres raised an eyebrow. Brasil examined the floor with elaborate care. I grimaced and tried again. Quietly.

"Guys, this is my problem, and I would like to deal with it myself."

"No." It was Koi. "There is no time for this. We have already spent two days that we can ill afford in preparation. We cannot delay further. Your private vendettas will have to wait."

"It isn't going to take—"

"I said *no*. By tomorrow morning your bearded friend will in any case be looking in entirely the wrong place for you." The ex–Black Brigade commando turned away, dismissing me the way Virginia Vidaura would sometimes do when we'd performed badly in Envoy training sessions. "Sierra, we'll need to up the real-time ratio on the construct. Though I don't imagine it ramps that high anyway, does it?"

Tres shrugged. "Architectural specs, you know how they are. Time's not usually the issue. Maybe get forty, fifty times real out of a system like that at full flog."

"That's fine." Koi was building an almost visible internal momentum as he talked. I imagined the Unsettlement, clandestine meetings in hidden back rooms. Scant light on scrawled plans. "It'll do. But we're going to need that running at two separate levels—the mapping construct and a virtual hotel suite with conference facilities. We need to be able to shuttle between the two easily, at will. Some kind of basic triggering gesture like a double blink. I don't want to have to come back to the real world while we're planning this."

Tres nodded, already moving. "I'll go tell Tudjman to get on it."

She ducked out of the nilvibe chamber. The door clumped gently shut behind her. Koi turned back to the rest of us.

"Now I suggest we take a few minutes to clear our heads because once this is up and running, we're going to live in virtual until we're done. With luck we can complete before tonight, real time, and be on our way. And Kovacs. This is only my personal opinion, but I think you owe at least some of us here an explanation."

I met his gaze, a sudden flood of dislike for his crabshit march-of-history politics giving me a handy frozen stare to do it with.

"You're so right, Soseki. That is your personal opinion. So how about you keep it to yourself?"

Virginia Vidaura cleared her throat.

"Tak, I think we should go down and get a coffee or something."

"Yeah, I think we should."

I gave Koi the last of my stare and made for the door. I saw Vidaura and Brasil exchange a look, and then she followed me out. Neither of us said anything as we rode the transparent elevator down through a light-filled central space to the ground. Halfway down, in a large, glass-walled office, I spotted Tudjman shouting inaudibly at an impassive Sierra Tres. Clearly the demand for a higher-ratio virtual environment wasn't being well received.

The elevator let us out into an open-fronted atrium and the sound of the street outside. I crossed the lobby floor, stepped out into the throng of tourists on the promenade, then hooked an autocab with a wave of my arm. Virginia Vidaura grabbed my other arm as the cab settled to the ground.

"Where do you think you're going?"

"You know where I'm going."

"No." She tightened up on me. "No, you're not. Koi's right, we don't have time for this."

"It isn't going to take long enough to worry about."

I tried to move toward the autocab's opening hatch, but short of hand-to-hand combat there was no way. And even that, against Vidaura, was a far-from-reliable option. I swung back toward her, exasperated.

"Virginia, let me *go.*"

"What happens if it goes wrong, Tak. What happens if this priest—"

"It isn't *going* to go wrong. I've been killing these sick fucks for over a year now and—"

I stopped. Vidaura's surfer sleeve was almost as tall as my own, and our eyes were only about a handbreadth apart. I could feel her breath on my mouth, and the tension in her body. Her fingers dug into my arm.

"That's it," she said. "Stand down. You talk to me, Tak. You stand down and you fucking talk to me about this."

"What is there to talk about?"

She smiles at me across the mirrorwood table. It isn't a face much like the one I remember—it's a good few years younger, for one thing—but there are echoes in the new sleeve of the body that died in a hail of Kalashnikov fire before my eyes, a lifetime ago. The same length of limb, the same sideways fall of raven hair. Something about the way she tips her head so that hair slides away from her right eye. The way she smokes. The way she still smokes.

Sarah Sachilowska. Out of storage, living her life.

"Well, nothing I guess. If you're happy."

"I am happy." She plumes smoke away from the table, momentarily irritated. It's a tiny spark of the woman I used to know. "I mean, wouldn't you be? Sentence commuted for cash equivalence. And the money's still flooding in, there'll be biocoding work for the next decade. Until the ocean settles down again, we've got whole new levels of flow to domesticate, and that's just locally. Someone's still got to model the impact where the Mikuni current hits the warm water coming up from Kossuth, and then do something about it. We'll be tendering as soon as the government funding clears. Josef says the rate we're going, I'll have paid off the whole sentence in another ten years."

"Josef?"

"Oh yeah, I should have said." The smile comes out again, wider this time. More open. "He's really great, Tak. You should meet him. He's running the project up there, he's one of the reasons I got out in the first wave. He was doing the virtual hearings, he was my project liaison when I got out and then we just, ah, you know."

She looked down at her lap, still smiling.

"You're blushing, Sarah."

"I am not."

"Yeah, you are." I know I'm supposed to feel happy for her, but I can't. Too many memories of her long, pale flanks moving against me in hotel-suite beds and seedy hideout apartments. "So he's playing for keeps, this Josef?"

She looks up quickly, pins me with a look. "We're both playing for keeps, Tak. He makes me happy. Happier than I've ever been, I think."

So why the fuck did you come and look me up, you stupid bitch?

"That's great," I say.

"And what about you?" she asks with arch concern. "Are you happy?"

I raise an eyebrow to gain some time. Slant my gaze to the side in a way that used to make her laugh. All I get this time is a maternal smile.

"Well, happy." I pull another face. "That's, ah, never been a trick I was very good at. I mean, yeah, I got out ahead of time like you. Full UN amnesty."

"Yeah, I heard about that. And you were on Earth, right?"

"For a while."

"And what about now?"

I gesture vaguely. "Oh, I'm working. Not anything as prestigious as you guys up there on the North arm, but it pays off the sleeve."

"Is it legal?"

"Are you kidding?"

Her face falls. "You know if that's true, Tak, I can't spend time with you. It's part of the resleeve deal. I'm still in parole time, I can't associate with . . ."

She shakes her head.

"Criminals?" I ask.

"Don't laugh at me, Tak."

I sigh. "I'm not, Sarah. I think it's great how things have worked out for you. It's just, I don't know, thinking of you writing biocode. Instead of stealing it."

She smiles again, her default expression for the whole conversation, but this time it's edged with pain.

"People can change," she says. "You should try it."

There's an awkward pause.

"Maybe I will."

And another.

"Look, I should really be getting back. Josef probably didn't—"

"No, come on." I gesture at our empty glasses, standing alone and apart on the scarred mirrorwood. There was a time we'd never willingly have left a bar like this one without littering the tabletop with drained tumblers and one-shot pipes. "Have you no self-respect, woman? Stay for one more."

So she does, but it doesn't really ease the awkwardness between us. And when she's finished her drink again, she gets up and kisses me on both cheeks and leaves me sitting there.

And I never see her again.

"Sachilowska?" Virginia Vidaura frowned in search of the memory. "Tall, right? Stupid hairstyle, like that, over one eye? Yeah. Think you brought her along to a party once, when Yaros and I were still living in that place on Ukai Street."

"Yeah, that's right."

"So she went off to the North arm, and you joined the Little Blue Bugs again, what, to spite her?"

Like the sunlight and the cheap metal fittings of the coffee terrace around us, the question glinted too brightly. I looked away from it, out to sea. It didn't work for me the way it seemed to for Brasil.

"It wasn't like that, Virginia. I was already plugged in with you guys by the time I saw her. I didn't even know she'd gotten out. Last I heard, when I got back from Earth, she was serving the full sentence. She was a cop killer, after all."

"So were you."

"Yeah, well that's Earth money and UN influence for you."

"Okay." Vidaura prodded at her coffee canister and frowned again. It hadn't been very good. "So you got out of storage at different times, and lost each other in the differential. That's sad, but it happens all the time."

Behind the sound of the waves, I heard Japaridze again.

There's a three-moon tidal slop running out there and if you let it, it'll tear you apart from everyone and everything you ever cared about.

"Yeah, that's right. It happens all the time." I turned back to face her across the filtered cool of the screen-shaded table. "But I didn't lose her in the differential, Virginia. I let her go. I let her go with that piece of shit, Josef, and I just walked away."

Understanding dawned across her face. "Oh, *okay.* So *that's* how come the sudden interest in Latimer and Sanction Four. You know, I always wondered back then why you changed your mind so suddenly."

"It wasn't just that," I lied.

"All right." Her face said never mind, she wasn't buying that one anyway. "So what happened to Sachilowska while you were gone that's got you slaughtering priests?"

"North arm of the Millsport Archipelago. Can't you guess?"

"They converted?"

"*He* fucking converted. She just got dragged along in the wake."

"Really? Was she that much of a victim?"

"Virginia, she was *fucking indentured!*" I stopped myself. The table screens cut out some heat and sound, but permeability was variable. Heads turned at other tables. I groped past the searing tower of fury for some Envoy detachment. My voice came out abruptly flat. "Governments change as well as people. They pulled the funding on the North arm projects a couple of years after she went up there. New antiengineering ethic to justify the cuts. Don't interfere with the natural balance of planetary biosystems. Let the Mikuni upheaval find its own equilibrium, it's a better, wiser solution. And a cheaper one of course. She still had another seven years of payments, and that was at the biocode consultancy rates she was earning before. Most of those villages had nothing *but* the Mikuni project lifting them out of poverty. Fuck knows what it was like when they all had to fall back on scratching an inshore fisherman's living all of a sudden."

"She could have left."

"*They had a fucking child, all right?*" Pause, breathe. Look out to sea. Crank it down. "They had a child, a daughter, only a couple of years old.

They had no money, suddenly. And they were both from the North arm originally, it's one of the reasons her name came out of the machine for parole in the first place. I don't know, maybe they thought they'd get by somehow. From what I hear, the Mikuni funding blipped on and off a couple of times before it got shut off for good. Maybe they just kept hoping there'd be another change."

Vidaura nodded. "And there was. The New Revelation kicked in."

"Yeah. Classic poverty dynamic, people clutch at anything. And if the choice is religion or revolution, the government's quite happy to stand back and let the priests get on with it. All of those villages had the old base faith anyway. Austere lifestyle, rigid social order, very male-dominated. Like something out of fucking Sharya. All it took was the NewRev militants and the economic downturn to hit at the same time."

"So what happened? She upset some venerable male?"

"No. It wasn't her, it was the daughter. She was in a fishing accident. I don't have the details. She was killed. I mean, stack-retrievable." The fury was flaring up again, freezing the inside of my head in icy splashes. "Except of course it's not *fucking* permitted."

The final irony. The Martians, once the scourge of the old Earth-bound faiths as knowledge of their million-year-old, prehuman, interstellar civilization cracked apart the human race's understanding of its place in the scheme of things. And now usurped by the New Revelation as angels: God's first, winged creations, and *no sign of anything resembling a cortical stack ever discovered in the few mummified corpses they left us.* To a mind sunk in the psychosis of faith, the corollary was inescapable. Resleeving was an evil spawned in the black heart of human science, a derailing of the path to the afterlife and the presence of the godhead. An abomination.

I stared at the sea. The words fell out of my mouth like ashes. "She tried to run. Alone. Josef was already fucked in the head with the faith, he wouldn't help her. So she took her daughter's body, alone, and stole a skimmer. Went east along the coast, looking for a channel she could cut through to get her south to Millsport. They hunted her down and brought her back. Josef helped them. They took her to a punishment chair the priests had built in the center of the village and they made her watch while they cut the stack from her daughter's spine and took it away. Then they did the same thing to her. While she was conscious. So she could appreciate her own salvation."

I swallowed. It hurt to do it. Around us, the tourist crowd ebbed and flowed like the multicolored idiot tide it was.

"Afterward, the whole village celebrated the freeing of their souls. New Revelation doctrine says a cortical stack must be melted to slag, to cast out the demon it contains. But they've got some superstitions of their own up on the North arm. They take the stacks out in a two-man boat, sealed in sonar reflective plastic. They sail fifty kilometers out to sea and somewhere along the way, the officiating priest drops the stacks overboard. He has no knowledge of the ship's course, and the helmsman's forbidden to know when the stacks have been dropped."

"That sounds like a pretty easily corrupted system."

"Maybe. But not in this case. I tortured both of them until they died, and they couldn't tell me. I'd have a better chance of finding Sarah's stack if Hirata's Reef had fucking tipped over on top of it."

I felt her gaze on me and, finally, turned to face it.

"So you've been there," she murmured.

I nodded. "Two years ago. I went to find her when I got back from Latimer. I found Josef instead, sniveling by her grave. I got the story out of him." My face twitched with the memory. "Eventually. He gave up the names of the helmsman and the officiator, so I tracked them down next. Like I said, they couldn't tell me anything useful."

"And then?"

"And then I went back to the village and I killed the rest of them."

She shook her head slightly. "The rest of who?"

"The rest of the village. Every motherfucker I could find who was an adult there the day she died. I got a datarat in Millsport to run population files for me, names and faces. Everyone who could have lifted a finger to help her and didn't. I took the list and I went back up there and I slaughtered them." I looked at my hands. "And a few others who got in my way."

She was staring at me as if she didn't know me. I made an irritable gesture.

"Oh, come on, Virginia. We've both done worse than that on more worlds than I can remember right now."

"You've got Envoy recall," she said numbly.

I gestured again. "Figure of speech. On seventeen worlds and five moons. And that habitat in the Nevsky Scatter. And—"

"You took their stacks?"

"Josef and the priests', yes."

"You destroyed them?"

"Why would I do that? It's exactly what they'd want. Oblivion after death. Not to come back." I hesitated. But it seemed pointless to stop now. And if I couldn't trust Vidaura, then there was no one else left. I cleared my throat and jabbed a thumb northward. "Back that way, out on the Weed Expanse, I've got a friend in the *haiduci*. Among other business ventures, he breeds swamp panthers for the fight pits. Sometimes, if they're good, he fits them with cortical stacks. That way, he can download injured winners into fresh sleeves and tip the odds."

"I think I see where this is going."

"Yeah. For a fee, he takes the stacks I give him, and loads their owners into some of his more over-the-hill panthers. We give them time to get used to the idea, then put them into the low-grade pits and see what happens. This friend can make good money running matches where it's known humans have been downloaded into the panthers; there's some kind of sick subculture built around it in fight circles apparently." I tipped my coffee canister and examined the dregs in the bottom. "I imagine they're pretty much insane by now. Can't be much fun being locked inside the mind of something that alien in the first place, let alone when you're fighting tooth and nail for your life in a mud pit. I doubt there's much conscious human mind left."

Vidaura looked down into her lap. "Is that what you tell yourself?"

"No, it's just a theory." I shrugged. "Maybe I'm wrong. Maybe there is some conscious mind left. Maybe there's a lot left. Maybe in their more lucid moments they think they've gone to hell. Either way suits me."

"How are you financing this?" she whispered.

I found a bared-teeth grin from somewhere and put it on. "Well, contrary to popular belief, some parts of what happened on Sanction Four worked out quite well for me. I'm not short of funds."

She looked up, face tightening toward anger. "You made *money* out of Sanction Four?"

"Nothing I didn't earn," I said quietly. .

Her features smoothed somewhat as she backed the anger up. But her voice still came out taut. "And are these funds going to be enough?"

"Enough for what?"

"Well." She frowned. "To finish this vendetta. You're hunting down the priests from the village but—"

"No, I did that last year. It didn't take me very long, there weren't that many. Currently, I'm hunting down the ones who were serving members of the Ecclesiastical Mastery when she was murdered. The ones who wrote the rules that killed her. That's taking me longer; there are a lot of them, and they're more senior. Better protected."

"But you're not planning to stop with them?"

I shook my head. "I'm not planning to stop at all, Virginia. They can't give her back to me, can they? So why would I stop?"

CHAPTeR TWeNTY-SeVeN

I don't know how much Virginia told the others once we got back inside the cranked-up virtuality. I stayed down in the mapping construct while the rest of them adjourned to the hotel-suite section, which somehow I couldn't help thinking of as upstairs. I don't know what she told them, and I didn't much care. Mostly, it was a relief just to have let someone else in on the whole story.

Not to be the only one.

People like Isa and Plex knew fragments, of course, and Radul Segesvar somewhat more. But for the rest, the New Revelation had hidden what I was doing to them from the start. They didn't want the bad publicity or the interference of infidel powers like the First Families. The deaths were passed off as accidents, monastery burglaries gone wrong, unfortunate petty muggings. Meanwhile, the word from Isa was that there were private contracts out on me at the Mastery's behest. The priesthood had a militant wing, but they obviously didn't place too much faith in it, because they'd also seen fit to engage a handful of Millsport sneak assassins. One night in a small town on the Saffron Archipelago, I let one of them get close enough to test the caliber of the hired help. It wasn't impressive.

I don't know how much Virginia Vidaura told her surfer colleagues, but the presence of the priest in Kem Point alone made it very clear that we could not return from a raid on Rila Crags and stay on the Strip. If the New Revelation could track me this far, so could others far more competent.

As a sanctuary, Vchira Beach was blown.

Mari Ado voiced what was probably a general feeling.

"You've fucked this up, dragging your personal crabshit into the harbor with you. *You* find us a solution."

So I did.

Envoy competence, one out of the manual—work with the tools to hand. I cast about in the immediate environment, summoned what I had that could be influenced, and saw it immediately. Personal shit had done the damage; personal shit would haul us out of the swamp, not to mention solve some more of my own more personal problems by way of a side effect. The irony of it grinned back at me.

Not everyone was so amused. Ado for one.

"Trust the fucking *haiduci*?" There was a well-bred Millsport sneer behind the words. "No thank you."

Sierra Tres raised an eyebrow.

"We've used them before, Mari."

"No, *you've* used them before. I steer well clear of scum like that. And anyway, this one you don't even know."

"I know of him. I've dealt with people who've dealt with him before, and from what I hear he's a man of his word. But I can check him out. You say he owes you, Kovacs?"

"Very much so."

She shrugged. "Then that should be enough."

"Oh, for fuck's sake, Sierra. You can't—"

"Segesvar is solid," I interrupted. "He takes his debts seriously in both directions. All it needs is the money. If you've got it."

Koi glanced at Brasil, who nodded.

"Yes," he said. "We can get it easily enough."

"Oh, happy fucking birthday, Kovacs!"

Virginia Vidaura nailed Ado with a stare. "Why don't you just shut the fuck up, Mari. It isn't your money. That's safely on deposit in a Millsport merchant bank, isn't it?"

"What's that supposed to—"

"Enough," said Koi, and everyone shut up. Sierra Tres went to make some calls from one of the other rooms down the corridor, and the rest of us went back to the mapping construct. In the speeded-up virtual environment, Tres was gone for the rest of the day—real-time equivalence in the outside world about ten minutes. In a construct, you can use the time differential to make three or four simultaneous calls, switching from one to the other in the minutes-long gaps that a couple of seconds' pause at the other end of the line will give you. When Tres came back, she had more than enough on Segesvar to confirm her original impression. He was old-style *haiduci,* at least in his own eyes. We went back up to the hotel suite and I dialed the discreet coding on speakerphone with no visual.

It was a bad line. Segesvar came on amid a lot of background noise, some of it real–virtual adjustment connection flutter, some of it not. The part that wasn't sounded a lot like someone or something screaming.

"I'm kind of busy here, Tak. You want to call me later?"

"How'd you like me to clear my slate, Rad? Right now, direct transfer through discreet clearing. And then a similar amount again on top."

The silence stretched into minutes in the virtuality. Maybe three seconds' hesitation at the other end of the line.

"I'd be very interested. Show me the money, and we'll talk."

I glanced at Brasil, who held up splayed fingers and thumb and left the room without a word. I made a rapid calculation.

"Check the account," I told Segesvar. "The money'll be there inside ten seconds."

"You're calling from a construct?"

"Go check your cash flow, Rad. I'll hold."

The rest was easy.

● ● ●

In a short-stay virtuality, you don't need sleep, and most programs don't bother to include the subroutines that would cause it. Long-term, of course, this isn't healthy. Hang around too long in your short-stay construct, and eventually your sanity will start to decay. Stay a few days, and the effects are merely . . . odd. Like bingeing simultaneously on tetrameth and a focus drug like Summit or Synagrip. From time to time your concentration freezes up like a seized engine, but there's a trick to that. You take the mental equivalent of a walk around the block, lubricate your thought processes with something unrelated, and then you're fine. As with Summit and Synagrip, you can start to derive a manic kind of enjoyment from the building focal whine.

We worked for thirty-eight hours solid, ironing out the bugs in the assault plan, running what-if scenarios, and bickering. Every now and then one of us would vent an exasperated grunt, fall backward into the knee-deep water of the mapping construct, and backstroke off out of the archipelago, toward the horizon. Provided you chose your angle of escape carefully and didn't collide with an unremembered islet or scrape your back on a reef, it was an ideal way to get away and unwind. Floating out there with the voices of the others grown faint with distance, you could feel your consciousness loosen off again, like a cramped muscle relaxing.

At other times, you could get a similar effect by blinking out completely and returning to the hotel-suite level. There was food and drink there in abundance and though neither ever actually reached your stomach, the subroutines for taste and alcoholic inebriation had been carefully included. You didn't need to eat in the construct any more than you needed to sleep, but the acts of consuming food and drink themselves still had a pleasantly soothing effect. So sometime past the thirty-hour mark, I was sitting alone, working my way through a platter of bottleback sashimi and knocking back Saffron sake, when Virginia Vidaura blinked into existence in front of me.

"There you are," she said, with an odd lightness of tone.

"Here I am," I agreed.

She cleared her throat. "How's your head?"

"Cooling off." I raised the sake cup in one hand. "Want some? Saffron Archipelago's finest *nigori*. Apparently."

"You've got to stop believing what you read on labels, Tak."

But she took the flask, summoned a cup directly into her other hand, and poured.

"*Kampai*," she said.

"*Por nosotros.*"

We drank. She settled onto the automold opposite me. "Trying to make me feel homesick?"

"Don't know. You trying to blend in with the locals?"

"I haven't been on Adoracion in better than a hundred and fifty years, Tak. This is my home now. I belong here."

"Yeah, you've certainly integrated into the local political scene well enough."

"And the beach life." She reclined a little on the automold and raised one leg sideways. It was sleekly muscled and tanned from life on Vchira, and the sprayon swimsuit she was wearing showed it off full-length. I felt my pulse pick up slightly.

"Very beautiful," I admitted. "Yaros said you'd spent everything you had on that sleeve."

She seemed to realize the overtly sexual nature of the pose then, and lowered her leg. She cupped her sake in both hands and leaned forward over it.

"What else did he tell you?"

"Well, it wasn't a long conversation. I was just trying to find out where you were."

"You were looking for me."

"Yeah." Something stopped me at that simple admission. "I was."

"And now that you've found me, what?"

My pulse had settled at an accelerated pounding. The edged whine of overstay in virtual was back. Images cascaded through my head. Virginia Vidaura, hard-eyed, hard-bodied, unattainable Envoy trainer, poised before us at induction, a dream of female competence beyond everyone's reach. Splinters of mirth in voice and eyes that might have kindled to sensuality in a less clearly defined set of relationships. A cringingly clumsy attempt at flirtation from Jimmy de Soto once in the mess bar, slapped down with brutal disinterest. Authority wielded with an utter lack of sexual tension. My own lurid undischarged fantasies, slowly flattening under an immense respect that went in at the same bone-deep level as the Envoy induction.

And then combat, the final dissipation of any romantic fumes that might have endured the training years. Vidaura's face in a dozen different sleeves on a dozen different worlds, sharpened with pain or fury or just the intense focus of mission time. The stink of her too-long-unwashed body in a cramped shuttle on the dark side of Loyko's moon, the slick feel of her blood on my hands one murderous night in Zihicce when she almost died. The look on her face when the orders to crush all resistance in Neruda came through.

I'd thought those moments had taken us beyond sex. They seemed to scoop out emotional depths that made fucking seem shallow by comparison. The last time I'd visited Vchira and seen the way Brasil leaned toward her—her Adoracion ancestry alone enough to strike sparks of desire off him—I'd felt a vague sort of superiority. Even with Yaroslav and the on-and-off long-term commitment they'd managed, I'd always believed that somehow he wasn't getting to the core of the woman I had fought beside in more corners of the Protectorate than most people would ever see.

I adopted a quizzical look that felt like taking cover.

"You think this is a good idea?" I asked.

"No," she said huskily. "Do you?"

"Uhm. In all honesty, Virginia, I'm rapidly beginning not to care. But I'm not the one attached to Jack Soul Brasil."

She laughed. "This isn't something that's going to bother Jack. This isn't even real, Tak. And anyway, he isn't going to know."

I looked around the suite. "He could pop up any minute. So could any of them for that matter. I'm not much for display sex."

"Me neither." She got up and offered me her hand. "Come with me."

She led me out of the suite and into the corridor. In both directions, identical doors mirrored each other across the anonymous gray carpeting and receded into a pale mist after a few dozen meters. We went, hand in hand, right up to the beginnings of the fade-out, feeling the faint cold that breathed out of it, and Vidaura opened the last door on the left. We slipped inside, hands already on each other.

It doesn't take long to peel off sprayons. Five seconds after the door closed, she had my surf shorts to my ankles and was rolling my rapidly hardening cock between her palms. I tugged free with an effort, got her swimsuit off her shoulders and skinned down to her waist, pressed the heel of one palm hard against the juncture of her thighs. Her breathing tautened and the muscles in her stomach flexed. I knelt and forced the suit down farther, over her hips and thighs until she could step easily out of it. Then I spread the lips of her cunt with my fingers, traced the opening lightly with my tongue, and stood up to kiss her on the mouth. Another tremor ran through her. She sucked my tongue in and bit it gently, then put both hands to my head and pulled back. I dragged my fingertips up the creases of her cunt again, found damp and heat, and pressed gently at her clitoris. She shivered and grinned at me.

"And now that you've found me," she repeated, eyes starting to defocus. "What?"

"Now," I told her, "I want to find out if the muscles in those thighs are as strong as they look."

Her eyes lit. The grin came back.

"I'll bruise you," she promised. "I'll crack your spine."

"You'll try, you mean."

She made a small, hungry noise and bit my lower lip. I hooked an arm under one of her knees and lifted. She grabbed at my shoulders and wrapped the other leg around my waist, then reached down for my cock and pressed it hard into the folds of her cunt. In the moments of conversation, she'd softened and moistened to readiness. With my free hand I spread her wider open and she sank onto me, gasping at the penetration and rocking back and forth against me from the waist up. Her thighs clamped around my waist with the promised bruising force. I swung us about to get a wall at my back and leaned against it. Got a measure of control.

It was short-lived. Vidaura hooked her grip deeper into my shoulders and began working herself back and forth on my erection, breath coming in short grunts of effort that went up in pitch and rapidity as her orgasm built. Not far behind her, I could feel the tension in my cock gathering heat all the way back to the root. I could feel the rub of her insides over my glans. I lost whatever control I'd had, grabbed at her ass with both hands, and rammed her harder onto me. Above my face, her closed eyes flew momentarily open and she grinned down at me. The tip of her tongue came out and touched her upper teeth. I laughed back, tight and locked up. Now it was a struggle, Vidaura arching her belly forward and hips back, working the head of my prick back to the mouth of her cunt and the tightly gathered nerve endings there, my hands ramming her back again and trying to bury myself in her to the hilt.

The fight dissolved in sensory avalanche.

Sweat building on our skin, slippery under our gripping hands—

Hard grins and kisses that were more like bites—

Breathing tipped frantically out of control—

My face, buried against the scant swelling of her breasts and the sweat-slick flat space between—

Her face rubbing sideways on the top of my head—

One agonizing moment when she held herself off me with all her force—

A yell, maybe hers, maybe mine—

—and then the liquid gushing of release, and collapse, juddering and sliding down the wall in a heap of splayed limbs and spasming bodies.

Spent.

After a long moment, I propped myself up sideways, and my flaccid cock popped slickly out of her. She moved one leg and moaned faintly. I tried to shift us both into a slightly more tenable position. She opened one eye and grinned.

"So, soldier. Wanted to do that for long, have you?"

I grinned back, weakly. "Only forever. You?"

"The thought had crossed my mind once or twice, yeah." She pushed against the wall with the soles of both feet and sat up, leaning on her elbows.

Her gaze flickered down the length of her body and then across at mine. "But I don't fuck the recruits. Jesus, look at the mess we made."

I reached a hand across to her sweat-smeared belly, trailed a finger down into the cleft at the start of her cunt. She twitched and I smiled.

"Want a shower then?"

She grimaced. "Yeah, I think we'd better."

We started to fuck again in the shower, but neither of us had the same manic strength that had imbued the first time and we couldn't stay braced. I carried her out to the bedroom and laid her down soaking wet on the bed instead. I knelt by her head, turned it gently and guided her mouth to my prick. She sucked, lightly at first then with gathering force. I lay backward alongside her slim muscled body, turned my own head and opened her thighs with my hands. Then I slid an arm around her hips, drew her cunt to my face, and went to work with my tongue. And the hunger came out all over again, like rage. The pit of my belly felt as if it was filled with sparking wires. Down the bed she made muffled noises, rolled her weight over, and crouched above me on elbows and spread knees. Her hips and thighs crushed down on me, her mouth worked the head of my prick, and her hand pumped at the shaft.

It took a long, slow, delirious time. Chemically unaided, we didn't know each other well enough for a truly synchronized orgasm, but the Envoy conditioning or maybe something else covered for the lack. When finally I came into the back of her throat, the force of it bent me up off the bed against her crouched body and in pure reflex I wrapped both arms tight around her hips. I dragged her down onto me, tongue frantic, so that she spat me out still spasming and leaking, and screamed with her own climax, and collapsed onto me shuddering.

But not long after, she rolled off, sat up cross-legged, and looked seriously at me, as if I were a problem she couldn't solve.

"I think that's probably enough," she said. "We'd better get back."

●●●

And later I stood on the beach with Sierra Tres and Jack Soul Brasil, watching the last rays of the sunset strike bright copper off the edge of a rising Marikanon, wondering if I'd made a mistake somewhere. I couldn't think straight enough to be sure. We'd gone into the virtuality with the physical feedback baffles locked closed, and for all the sexual venting I'd indulged in with Virginia Vidaura, my real body was still swamped with undischarged hormones. At one level at least, it might as well never have happened.

I glanced surreptitiously at Brasil and wondered some more. Brasil, who'd shown no visible reaction when Vidaura and I reentered the mapping construct within a couple of minutes of each other, albeit from different sides of the archipelago. Brasil, who'd worked with the same steady, good-natured, and elegant application until we'd wrapped the raid and the fallback after. Who'd placed one hand casually in the small of Vidaura's back and smiled faintly at me just before the two of them blinked out of the virtuality with a co-ordination that spoke volumes.

"You'll get your money back, you know," I told him.

Brasil twitched impatiently. "I know that, Tak. I'm not concerned about the money. We would have cleared your debt with Segesvar as simple payment, if you'd asked. We still can—you could consider it a bounty for what you've brought us if you like."

"That won't be necessary," I said stiffly. "I'm considering it a loan. I'll pay you back as soon as things have calmed down."

A stifled snort from Sierra Tres. I turned on her.

"Something amusing you?"

"Yeah. The idea that things are going to calm down anytime soon."

We watched the creep of night, across the sea in front of us. At the darkened end of the horizon, Daikoku crept up to join Marikanon in the western sky. Farther along the beach, the rest of Brasil's crew were building a bonfire. Laughter cracked around the gathering pile of driftwood, and bodies clowned about in dim silhouette. In defiance of any misgivings either Tres or I might have, there was a deep calm soaking into the evening, as soft and cool as the sand underfoot. After the manic hours of the virtuality, there seemed nothing that really needed to be done or said until tomorrow. And right now tomorrow was still rolling around the other side of the planet, like a wave out deep and building force. I thought that if I were Koi, I'd believe I could feel the march of history holding its breath.

"So I take it no one's going to get an early night," I said, nodding at the preparations for the bonfire.

"We could all be Really Dead in a couple of days," Tres said. "Get plenty of sleep then."

Abruptly, she tugged her T-shirt cross-armed up over her head. Her breasts lifted and then swung disconcertingly as she completed the movement. Not what I needed right now. She dumped the T-shirt in the sand and started down the beach.

"I'm going for a swim," she called back to us. "Anyone coming?"

I glanced at Brasil. He shrugged and went after her.

I watched them reach the water and plunge in, then strike out for deeper water. A dozen meters out, Brasil dived again, popped out of the water almost immediately, and called something to Tres. She eeled about in the water and listened to him for a moment, then submerged. Brasil dived after her. They were down for about a minute this time, and then both surfaced, splashing and chattering, now nearly a hundred meters from the shore. It was, I thought, like watching the dolphins off Hirata's Reef.

I angled right and set off along the beach toward the site of the bonfire.

People nodded at me; some of them even smiled. Daniel, of all people, looked up from where he sat in the sand with a few others I didn't know and offered me a flask of something. It seemed churlish to refuse. I knocked back the flask and coughed on vodka rough enough to be homemade.

"Strong stuff," I wheezed and handed it back.

"Yeah, nothing like it this end of the Strip." He gestured muzzily. "Sit down, have some more. This is Andrea, my best mate. Hiro. Watch him, he's a lot older than he looks. Been at Vchira longer than I've been alive. And this is Magda. Bit of a bitch, but she's manageable once you get to know her."

Magda cuffed him good-naturedly across the head and appropriated the flask. For lack of anything else to do, I settled onto the sand among them. Andrea leaned across and wanted to shake my hand.

"Just want to say," she murmured in Millsport-accented Amanglic. "Thanks for what you've done for us. Without you, we might never have known she was still alive."

Daniel nodded, vodka lending the motion an exaggerated solemnity. "That's right, Kovacs-san. I was out of line back there when you arrived. Fact, and I'm being honest now, I thought you were full of shit. Working some angle, you know. But now with Koi on board, man we are fucking rolling. We're going to turn this whole planet upside fucking down."

Murmured agreement, a little fervent for my tastes.

"Going to make the Unsettlement look like a wharf brawl," said Hiro.

I got hold of the flask again and drank. Second time around, it didn't taste so bad. Maybe my taste buds were stunned.

"What's she like?" asked Andrea.

"Uh." An image of the woman who thought she was Nadia Makita flickered through my mind. Face smeared in the throes of climax. The swilling cocktail of hormones in my system lurched at the thought. "She's. Different. It's hard to explain."

Andrea nodded, smiling happily. "You're so lucky. To have met her, I mean. To have talked to her."

"You'll get your chance," Daniel said, slurring a little. "Soon as we take her back from those motherfuckers."

A ragged cheer. Someone was lighting the bonfire.

Hiro nodded grimly. "Yeah. Payback time for the Harlanites. For all the First Family scum. Real Death, coming down."

"It'll be *so good*," said Andrea, as we watched the flames start to catch. "To have someone again who knows what to *do*."

PART FOUR

THIS IS ALL
THAT MATTERS

This much must be understood: Revolution requires
Sacrifice.

SANDOR SPAVENTA
Tasks for the Quellist Vanguard

CHAPTeR TWeNTY-eIGHT

Northeastward around the curve of the world from Kossuth, the Millsport Archipelago lies in the Nurimono Ocean, like a smashed plate. Once, eons ago, it was a massive volcanic system, hundreds of kilometers across, and the legacy still shows in the peculiarly curved outer edges of the rim islands. The fires that fueled the eruptions are long extinct, but they left a towering, twisted mountainscape whose peaks comfortably rode out the later drowning as the sea rose. In contrast with other archipelago chains on Harlan's World, the volcanic dribbling provided a rich soil base, and most of the land is thickly covered with the planet's beleaguered land vegetation. Later, the Martians came and added their own colonial plant life. Later still, humans came and did the same.

At the heart of the archipelago, Millsport itself sprawls in evercrete and fused-glass splendor. It's a riot of urban engineering, every available crag and slope forested with spires, extending out onto the water in broad platforms and bridges kilometers in length. Cities on Kossuth and New Hokkaido have grown to substantial size and wealth at various times over the last four hundred years, but there's nothing to match this metropolis anywhere on the planet. Home to over twenty million people, gateway to the only commercial spaceflight launch windows the orbital net will permit, nexus of governance, corporate power, and culture, you can feel Millsport sucking at you like the maelstrom from anywhere else on Harlan's World you care to stand.

"I hate the fucking place," Mari Ado told me as we prowled the well-to-do streets of Tadaimako looking for a coffeehouse called Makita's. Along with Brasil, she was throttling back on her spinal-fever complex for the duration of the raid, and the change was making her irritable. "Fucking metropolitan tyranny gone global. No single city should have this much influence."

It was a standard rant—one from the Quellist manual. They've been saying essentially the same thing about Millsport for centuries. And they're right, of course, but it's amazing how constant repetition can make even the most obvious truths irritating enough to disagree with.

"You grew up here, didn't you?"

"So?" She swung a glare on me. "Does that mean I've got to like it?"

"No, I guess not."

We continued in silence. Tadaimako buzzed primly about us, busier and more genteel than I remembered from thirty-plus years before. The old harbor quarter, once a seedy and faintly dangerous playground for aristo and corporate youth, had now sprouted a glossy new crop of retail outlets and cafés. A lot of the bars and pipe houses I remembered were gone to a relatively clean death; others had been made over into excruciating imagistic echoes of themselves. Every frontage on the street shone in the sun with new paint and antibac sheathing, and the paving beneath our feet was immaculately clean. Even the smell of the sea from a couple of streets farther down seemed to have been sanitized—there was no tang of rotting weed or dumped chemicals, and the harbor was full of yachts.

In keeping with the prevailing aesthetic, Makita's was a squeaky-clean establishment trying hard to look disreputable. Artfully grimed windows kept out most of the sun; inside, the walls were decorated with reprinted Unsettlement photography and Quellist epigrams in workman-like little frames. One corner held the inevitable iconic holo of the woman herself, the one with the shrapnel scar on her chin. Dizzy Csango was on the music system. *Millsport Sessions,* "Dream of Weed."

At a back booth, Isa sat and nursed a long drink, nearly down to the dregs. Her hair was a savage crimson today, and a little longer than it had been. She'd graysprayed opposing quadrants of her face for a harlequin effect, and her eyes were dusted with some hemoglobin-hungry luminescent glitter that made the tiny veins in the whites glow as if they were going to explode. The datarat plugs were still proudly on display in her neck, one of them hooked up to the deck she'd brought with her. A datacoil in the air above the unit kept up the fiction that she was a student doing some preexam catch-up. It also, if our last meeting was anything to go by, laid down a natty little interference field that would render conversation in the booth impossible to eavesdrop on.

"What took you so long?" she asked.

I smiled as I sat down. "We're fashionably late, Isa. This is Mari. Mari, Isa. So how are we doing?"

Isa took a long, insolent moment to check out Mari, then turned her head and unjacked with an elegant, much-practiced gesture that showed off the nape of her neck.

"We're doing well. And we're doing it silently. Nothing new on the Millsport PD net, and nothing from any of the private security outfits the First Families like to use. They don't know you're here."

I nodded. Gratifying though the news was, it made sense. We'd hit Millsport across the earlier part of the week, split into half a dozen separate groups, arrivals coordinated days apart. Fake ID at Little Blue Bug standards of impenetrability and a variety of different transport options ranging from cheap speed freighters to a Saffron Line luxury cruiser. With people streaming into Millsport from all over the planet for the Harlan's Day festivities, it would have been either very bad luck or very bad operational management if any of us had been picked up.

But it was still good to know.

"What about security up at the Crags?"

Isa shook her head. "Less noise out of there than a priest's wife coming. If they knew what you had planned, there'd be a whole new protocol layer, and there isn't."

"Or you haven't spotted it," said Mari.

Isa fixed her with another cool stare. "My dear, do you know *anything* at all about dataflow?"

"I know what levels of encryption we're dealing with."

"Yes, so do I. Tell me, how do you think I pay for my studies?"

Mari Ado examined her nails. "With petty crime, I assume."

"Charming." Isa shuttled her gaze in my direction. "Where *did* you get her, Tak? Madame Mi's?"

"Behave, Isa."

She gusted a long-suffering teenage sigh. "All right, Tak. For you. For you, I won't rip this mouthy bitch's hair out. And Mari, for your information, I am gainfully employed nights, under a pseudident, as a freelance security software scribe for more corporate names than you've probably given backstreet blowjobs."

She waited, tensed. Ado looked back at her with glittery eyes for a moment, then smiled and leaned forward slightly. Her voice rose no higher than a corrosive murmur.

"Listen, you stupid little virgin, if you think you're going to get a catfight out of me, you're badly mistaken. And lucky, too. In the unlikely event that you could push my buttons sufficient to piss me off that far, you wouldn't even see me coming. Now, why don't we discuss the business at hand, and then you can go back to playing at datacrime with your study partners and pretending you know something about the world."

"You fucking whor—"

"Isa!" I put a snap into my voice and a hand in front of her as she started to rise. "That's enough. She's right, she could kill you with her bare hands and not even break a sweat. Now behave, or I'm not going to pay you."

Isa shot me a look of betrayal and sat back down. Under the harlequin face paint, it was hard to tell, but I thought she was flushing furiously. Maybe the crack about virginity had touched a nerve. Mari Ado had the good grace not to look pleased.

"I didn't have to help you," Isa said in a small voice. "I could have sold you out a week back, Tak. Probably would have made more from that than you're paying me for this shit. Don't forget that."

"We won't," I assured her, with a warning glance at Ado. "Now, aside from the fact that no one thinks we're here, what else have you got?"

●●●

What Isa had, all loaded onto innocuous, matte-black datachips, was the backbone of the raid. Schematics of the security systems at Rila Crags, including the modified procedures for the Harlan's Day festivities. Up-to-date dynamic forecast maps of the currents in the Reach for the next week. Millsport PD street deployment and water traffic protocols for the duration of the celebrations. Most of all, she'd brought herself and her bizarre shadow identity at the fringes of the Millsport datacrime elite. She'd agreed to help, and now she was in deep with a role in the proceedings that I suspected was the main source of her current edginess and lost cool. Taking part in an assault on Harlan family property certainly constituted rather more cause for stress than her standard forays into illicit data brokerage. If I hadn't more or less dared her into it, I doubted she would have had anything to do with us.

But what fifteen-year-old knows how to refuse a dare?

I certainly didn't at her age.

If I had, maybe I'd never have ended up in that back alley with the meth dealer and his hook. Maybe—

Yeah, well. Who ever gets a second shot at these things? Sooner or later, we all get in up to our necks. Then it's just a question of keeping your face out of the swamp, one stumbling step at a time.

Isa covered it well enough to deserve applause. Whatever misgivings she had, by the time we'd finished the handover, her ruffled feathers had smoothed and she had her laconic Millsport drawl back in place.

"Did you find Natsume?" I asked her.

"Yeah, as it happens I did. But I'm not convinced you'll want to talk to him."

"Why not?"

She grinned. "Because he got religion, Kovacs. Lives in a monastery now, over on Whaleback and Ninth."

"Whaleback? That the Renouncer place?"

"Sure is." She struck an absurdly solemn, prayerful pose that didn't match her hair and face. "Brotherhood of the Awoken and Aware. Renounce henceforth all flesh, and the world."

I felt my mouth twitch. Beside me, Mari Ado sat humorless as a ripwing.

"I got no problem with those guys, Isa. They're harmless. Way I see it, they're stupid enough to shun female company, that's their loss. But I'm surprised someone like Natsume'd buy into something like that."

"Ah, but you've been away. They take women, too, these days."

"Really?"

"Yeah, started way back, nearly a decade ago. What I heard, they found a couple of covert females in their midst. Been there for years. Figures, right? Anyone who's resleeved could lie about their sex." Isa's voice picked up a beat as she hit her home turf running. "No one outside government's got the money to run datachecks on stuff like that. If you've lived in a male sleeve for long enough, even psychosurgery has a hard time telling the difference. So anyway, back at the Brotherhood, it was either go the NewRev single-sleeve-and-you're-out route, or come over all modern and desegregate. Lo and behold, the word from on high spake suddenly of change."

"Don't suppose they changed the name, too, did they?"

"Don't suppose they did. Still the Brotherhood. Brother embraces sister, apparently." A teenage shrug. "Not sure how the sisters feel about all that embracing, but that's entry-level dues for you."

"Speaking of which," said Mari Ado. "Are we permitted entry?"

"Yeah, they take visitors. You may have to wait for Natsume, but not so's you'd notice. That's the great thing about Renouncing the flesh, isn't it." Isa grinned again. "No inconvenient things like Time and Space to worry about."

"Good work, Issy."

She blew me a kiss.

But as we were getting up to leave, she frowned slightly and evidently came to a decision. She raised a hand and cupped her fingers to get us back closer.

"Listen, guys. I don't know exactly what you're after up at Rila, and to be honest with you, I don't want to know. But I can tell you this for nothing. Old Harlan won't be coming out of the pod this time around."

"No?" On his birthday, that was unusual.

"That's right. Bit of semi-covert court gossip I dipped yesterday. They lost another heirling down at Amami Sands. Hacked to death with a baling tine, apparently. They're not making it public, but the MPD are a bit sloppy with their encryption these days. I was cruising for Harlan-related stuff so, like that. Picked it out of the flow. Anyway, with that and old Seichi getting toasted in his skimmer last week, they're not taking any chances. They've called off half the family appearances altogether, and looks like even Mitzi Harlan's getting a doubled secret-service detachment. And Old Man Harlan stays unsleeved. That's for definite. Think they're planning to let him watch the celebrations through a virtual linkup."

I nodded slowly. "Thanks. That's good to know."

"Yeah, sorry if it's going to fuck up some spectacular assassination attempt for you. You didn't ask, so I wasn't going to say anything, but I'd hate for you to go all that way up there and find nothing to kill."

Ado smiled thinly.

"That's not what we're here for," I said quickly. "But thanks anyway. Listen Isa, you don't remember a couple of weeks back, some other Harlan small fry got himself killed in the wharf district?"

"Yep. Marek Harlan-Tsuchiya. Methed out of his head, fell off Karlovy Dock, banged his head, and drowned. Heartbreaking."

Ado made an impatient gesture. I held up a hand to forestall her.

"Any chance our boy Marek was helped over the edge, do you think?"

Isa pulled a face. "Could be, I guess. Karlovy's not the safest of places after dark. But they'll have resleeved him by now, and there's been nothing in the air about it being a murder. Then again—"

"Why should they let the general public in on it. Right." I could feel the Envoy intuition twitching, but it was too faint to make anything of. "Okay, Isa. Thanks for the newsflash. It doesn't affect anything at our end, but keep your ears tuned anyway, huh?"

"Always do, sam."

We paid the tab and left her there, red-veined eyes and harlequin mask and the coil of light weaving at her elbow like some domesticated demon familiar. She waved as I looked back, and I felt a brief stab of affection for her that lasted me all the way out into the street.

"Stupid little bitch," said Mari Ado as we headed down toward the waterfront. "I hate that fucking fake underclass thing."

I shrugged. "Well, rebellion takes a lot of different forms."

"Yeah, and that back there was none of them."

We took a real-keel ferry across the Reach to the platform suburb they're calling East Akan, apparently in the hope that people who can't afford the slopes of the Akan district itself will settle there instead. Ado went off to find some tea; I stayed by the rail, watching the water traffic and the changing perspectives as the ferry sailed. There's a magic to Millsport that's easy to forget while you're away, but get out on the waters of the Reach and the city seems to open to you. Wind in your face and the belaweed tang of the sea combine to scrub away the urban grimness, and you discover in its place a broad, seafarer's optimism that can sometimes stay with you for hours after you step back on land.

Trying not to let it go to my head, I squinted south to the horizon. There, shrouded to fading in seamist thrown up by the maelstrom, Rila Crags brooded in stacked isolation. Not quite the southernmost outcrop of the archipelago, but near enough, twenty klicks of open water back north to the nearest other settled piece of land—the tail end of New Kanagawa—and at least half that to the nearest piece of rock you could even stand on. Most of the First Families had staked out high ground in Millsport early on, but Harlan had trumped them all. Rila, beautiful in glistening black volcanic stone, was a fortress in all but name. An elegant and powerful reminder to the whole city of who was in charge here. An eyrie to supplant those built by our Martian predecessors.

We docked at East Akan with a soft bump that was like waking up. I found Mari Ado again, down by the debarkation ramp, and we threaded our way through the rectilinear streets as rapidly as was conducive to checking we weren't being followed. Ten minutes later, Virginia Vidaura was letting us into the as-yet-unfitted loft apartment space that Brasil had chosen as our base of operations. Her eyes passed across us like a clinical wipe.

"Go okay?"

"Yeah. Mari here didn't make any new friends, but what can you do?"

Ado grunted and shouldered past me, then disappeared off into the interior of the warehouse. Vidaura closed the door and secured it while I told her about Natsume.

"Jack'll be disappointed," she said.

"Yeah, not what I expected, either. So much for legends, eh? You want to come across to Whaleback with me?" I raised my eyebrows clownishly. "Virtual environment."

"I think that's probably not a good idea."

I sighed. "No, probably not."

CHAPTeR TWeNTY-NINe

The monastery on Whaleback and Ninth was a grim, blank-faced place. Whaleback islet, along with about a dozen other similar fragments of land and reclaimed reef, served as a commuting-distance settlement for workers in the docks and marine industries of New Kanagawa. Causeways and suspension spans provided ready access across the short expanse of water to Kanagawa itself, but the limited space on these satellite isles meant cramped, barracks-style apartments for the workforce. The Renouncers had simply acquired a hundred-meter frontage and nailed all the windows shut.

"For security," the monk who let us in explained. "We run a skeleton crew here, and there's a lot of valuable equipment. You'll have to hand over those weapons before we go any farther."

Beneath the simple gray coveralls of the order, he was sleeved in a basic, low-end Fabrikon synth that presumably ran built-in scanning gear. The voice was like a bad phone connection amplified, and the silicoflesh face was set in a detached expression that may or may not have reflected how he felt about us—small-muscle groups are never that great on the cheaper models. On the other hand, even cheap synths usually run machine levels of reflex and strength, and you could probably burn a blaster hole right through this one without doing much more than piss its wearer off.

"Seems fair," I told him.

I dug out the GS Rapsodia and handed it over butt-first. Beside me, Sierra Tres did the same with a blunt-looking blaster. Brasil spread his arms agreeably, and the synth nodded.

"Good. I'll return these when you leave."

He led us through a gloomy evercrete entry hall whose obligatory statue of Konrad Harlan had been unflatteringly masked in plastic, then into what must once have been a ground-floor apartment. Two rows of uncomfortable-looking chairs, as basic as the attendant's sleeve, were gathered facing a desk and a heavy steel door beyond. A second attendant was waiting for us behind the desk. Like her colleague, she was synth-sleeved and coveralled in gray, but her facial features seemed fractionally more animated. Maybe she was trying harder, working at full acceptance under the new unisex induction decrees.

"How many of you are requesting audience?" she asked, pleasantly enough given the limitations of her Fabrikon voice.

Jack Soul Brasil and I raised our hands; Sierra Tres stood pointedly to one side. The female attendant gestured to us to follow her and punched out a code on the steel door. It opened with an antique metallic grinding, and we stepped into a gray-walled chamber fitted with half a dozen sagging couches and a virtual transfer system that looked like it might still run on silicon.

"Please make yourselves comfortable in one of the couches and attach electrodes and hypnophones as in the instruction holo you will see at your right side."

Make yourselves comfortable was an ambitious request—the couches were not automold and didn't seem to have been made with comfort in mind. I was still trying to find a good posture when the attendant stepped across to the transfer control suite and powered us up. A sonocode murmured through the hypnophones.

"Please turn your head to the right and watch the holoform until you lose consciousness."

Transition, oddly enough, was a lot smoother than I'd expected from the surroundings. At the heart of the holosphere, an oscillating figure-eight formed and began cycling through the color spectrum. The sonocode droned counterpoint. In a few seconds the light show expanded to fill my vision, and the sound in my ears became a rushing of water. I felt myself tipping toward the oscillating figure, then falling through it. Bands of light flickered over my face, then shriveled to white and the blending roar of the stream in my ears. There was a tilting of everything under me, a sense of the whole world being turned 180 degrees, and suddenly I was deposited upright on a worn stone platform behind a waterfall in full flood. The remains of the oscillating spectrum showed up briefly as an edge of refracted light in faint mist, then faded like a dying note. Abruptly there were puddles around my feet, and cold, damp air on my face.

As I turned about, looking for a way out, the air beside me thickened and rippled into a sketched doll of light that became Jack Soul Brasil. The pitch of the waterfall jolted as he solidified, then settled down again. The oscillating spectrum raced through the air again, departed again. The puddles shimmered and reappeared. Brasil blinked and looked around him.

"It's this way, I think," I said, pointing to a set of shallow stone steps at one side of the waterfall.

We followed the steps around a rock bluff and emerged into bright sunlight above the waterfall. The steps became a paved path across a moss-grown hillside, and at the same moment I spotted the monastery.

It rose among gently rolling hills against a backdrop of jagged mountains that vaguely recalled parts of the Saffron Archipelago, seven levels and five towers of ornately worked wood and granite in classic pagoda style. The path up from the waterfall crossed the hillside and ended at a huge mirrorwood gate that shone in the sun. Other similar paths radiated out from the monastery in no particular pattern, leading away across the hills. One or two figures were visible walking them.

"Well, you can see why they went virtual," I said, mostly to myself. "It beats Whaleback and Ninth."

Brasil grunted. He'd been similarly uncommunicative all the way over from Akan. He still didn't seem to have gotten over the shock of Nikolai Natsume's renunciation of the world and the flesh.

We made our way up the hill and found the gate wedged open sufficiently to permit entry. Inside, a hall of polished Earthwood floors and beamed ceilings led through to a central garden and what looked like cherry trees in blossom. The walls on either side were hung with intricately colored tapestries, and as we moved into the center of the hall a figure from one of them unwove itself into a mass of threads that hung in the air, drifted downward, and became a man. He was dressed in the same monk's coveralls we'd seen on the Renouncers back in the real world, but the body beneath wasn't a synth.

"May I help you?" he asked gently.

Brasil nodded. "We're looking for Nik Natsume. I'm an old friend."

"Natsume." The monk bowed his head a moment, then looked up again. "He's currently working in the gardens. I've advised him of your presence. I imagine he will be here in a moment."

The last word was still leaving his mouth when a slim, middle-age man with a gray ponytail walked in at the far end of the hall. As far as I could see it was a natural appearance, but unless the gardens were hidden just around the corner, the speed of his arrival alone was a sign that this was still all subtly deployed systems magic in action. And there were no marks of water or soil on his coveralls.

"Nik?" Brasil moved forward to meet him. "Is that you?"

"Certainly, I would argue that it is, yes." Natsume glided closer across the wooden floor. Up close, there was something about him that reminded me painfully of Lazlo. The ponytail and the wiry competence in the way he stood; a hint of the same manic charm in his face. *Couple of bypass jolts and a seven-meter crawl up a polished steel chimney.* But where Lazlo's eyes had always shown the white-knuckled leash he had himself on, Natsume appeared to have beaten his inner ramping to an agreed peace. His gaze was intent and serious, but it demanded nothing of the world it saw. "Though I prefer to call myself Norikae these days."

He exchanged a brief series of honorific gestures with the other monk, who promptly drifted up from the floor, shredded into a mass of colored threads, and rewove himself into the tapestry. Natsume watched him go, then turned and scrutinized both of us. "I'm afraid I don't know either of you in those bodies."

"You don't know me at all," I reassured him.

"Nik, it's me, Jack. From Vchira."

Natsume looked at his hands for a moment, then up at Brasil again.

"Jack Soul Brasil?"

"Yeah. What are you *doing* in here, man?"

A brief smile. "Learning."

"What, you've got an ocean in here? Surf like at Four Finger Reef? Crags like the ones at Pascani? Come on, man."

"Actually, I'm learning at the moment to grow filigree poppies. Remarkably difficult. Perhaps you'd care to see my efforts so far?"

Brasil shifted awkwardly. "Look, Nik, I'm not sure we've got time for—"

"Oh, time here is." The smile again. "Flexible. I'll make time for you. Please, this way."

We left the hall and tracked left around the cherry-blossom quadrangle, then under an arch and across a pebbled courtyard. In one corner, two monks were knelt in meditation and did not look up. It was impossible to tell if they were human inhabitants of the monastery or functions of the construct like the doorkeeper. Natsume at least ignored them. Brasil and I caught each other's eye, and the surfer's face was troubled. I could read his thoughts as if they were printing out for me. This wasn't the man he'd known, and he didn't know if he could trust him anymore.

Finally, Natsume led us through an arched tunnel to another quadrangle and down a short set of Earthwood steps into a shallow pit of marshy grasses and weed bordered by a circular stone path. There, buoyed up amid the cobwebby gray scaffolding of their root systems, a dozen filigree poppies offered their tattered, iridescent purple and green petals to the virtual sky. The tallest wasn't much more than fifty centimeters high. Maybe it was impressive from a horticultural point of view; I wouldn't know. But it certainly didn't look like much of an achievement for a man who'd once fought off a full-grown bottleback with no weapon outside fists and feet and a short-burn chemical flare. For a man who'd once scaled Rila Crags without antigrav or ropes.

"Very nice," said Brasil.

I nodded. "Yes. You must be very pleased with those."

"Only moderately." Natsume circled his shred-petaled charges with a critical eye. "In the end I've succumbed to the obvious failing, as apparently most new practitioners do."

He looked expectantly up at us.

I glanced back at Brasil but got no help there.

"Are they a bit short?" I asked finally.

Natsume shook his head and chuckled. "No, in fact they're a good height for a base this moist. And—I'm so sorry—I see I've committed yet another common gardener's misdemeanor. I've assumed a general fascination with the subject of my personal obsessions."

He shrugged and joined us again on the steps, where he seated himself. He gestured out at the plants.

"They're too bright. An ideal filigree poppy is matte. It shouldn't glint like that, it's vulgar. At least, that's what the Abbot tells me."

"Nik . . ."

He looked at Brasil. "Yes."

"Nik, we need to. To talk to you about. Some stuff."

I waited. This had to be Brasil's call. If he didn't trust the ground, I wasn't going to walk ahead of him on it.

"Some stuff?" Natsume nodded. "What stuff would that be, then?"

"We." I'd never seen the surfer so locked up. "I need your help, Nik."

"Yes, clearly. But in what?"

"It's."

Suddenly, Natsume laughed. It was a gentle sound, light on mockery.

"Jack," he said. "This is me. Just because I grow flowers now, do you think it means you can't trust me? You think Renouncing means selling out your humanity?"

Brasil looked away at the corner of the shallow garden.

"You've changed, Nik."

"Of course I have. It's over a century, what did you expect?" For the first time, a faint rash of irritation marred Natsume's monkish serenity. He got up to better face Brasil. "That I'd spend my whole life on the same beach, riding waves? Climbing up suicidal hundred-meter pitches for thrills? Cracking locks on corporate bioware, stealing the stuff for quick cash on the black market, and calling it neoQuellism? The creeping bloody revolution."

"That's not—"

"Of *course* I've changed, Jack. What kind of emotional cripple would I be if I hadn't?"

Brasil came down a step toward him, abruptly. "Oh, you think *this* is better?"

He slung an arm at the filigree poppies. Their latticed roots seemed to quiver with the violence of the gesture.

"You crawl off into this fucking dream world, grow *flowers* instead of living, and you're going to accuse *me* of being emotionally crippled. Get fucked, Nik. You're the cripple, not me."

"What are you achieving out there, Jack? What are you doing that's worth so much more than this?"

"I was standing on a ten-meter wall four days ago." Brasil made an effort

to calm himself. His shout sank to a mutter. "That's worth all of this virtual shit twice over."

"Is it?" Natsume shrugged. "If you die under one of those waves out at Vchira, you got it written down somewhere that you don't want to come back?"

"That isn't the point, Nik. I'll come back, but I'll still have died. It'll cost me the new sleeve, and I'll have been through the gate. Out there in the real world you hate so much—"

"I don't hate—"

"Out *there,* actions have consequences. If I break something, I'll know about it because it'll fucking hurt."

"Yes, until your sleeve's enhanced endorphin system kicks in, or until you take something for the pain. I don't see your point."

"My point?" Brasil gestured at the poppies again, helplessly. *"None of this is fucking real, Nik."*

I caught a flicker of movement at the corner of my eye. Turned and spotted a pair of monks, drawn by the raised voices and hovering at the arched entrance to the quadrangle. One of them quite literally hovering. His feet were a clear thirty centimeters off the uneven paving.

"Norikae-san?" asked the other.

I shifted stance minutely, wondering idly if they were real inhabitants of the monastery or not, and, if not, what operating parameters they might have in circumstances like these. If the Renouncers ran internal security systems, our chances in a fight were zero. You don't wander into someone else's virtuality and brawl successfully unless they want you to.

"It's nothing, Katana-san." Natsume made a hurried and complicated motion with both hands. "A difference of perspective between friends."

"My apologies, then, for the intrusion." Katana bowed over fists gathered one into the other, and the two newcomers withdrew into the arched tunnel. I didn't see whether they walked away in real time or not.

"Perhaps," began Natsume quietly, then stopped.

"I'm sorry, Nik."

"No, you are right of course. None of this is real in the way we both used to understand it. But in here, *I* am more real than I ever was before. I define how I exist, and there is no harder challenge than that, believe me."

Brasil said something inaudible. Natsume resumed his seat on the wooden steps. He looked back at Brasil, and after a moment the surfer seated himself a couple of steps higher up. Natsume nodded and stared at his garden.

"There is a beach to the east," he said absently. "Mountains to the south. If I wish, they can be made to meet. I can climb anytime I wish, swim anytime I wish. Even surf, though I haven't so far.

"And in all of these things, I have choices to make. Choices of consequence. Bottlebacks in the ocean or not? Coral to scrape myself on and

bleed, or not? Blood to bleed with, come to that? These are all matters re-
quiring prior meditation. Full-effect gravity in the mountains? If I fall, will I
allow it to kill me? And what will I allow that to mean?" He looked at his
hands as if they, too, were a choice of some sort. "If I break or tear something,
will I allow it to hurt? If so, for how long? How long will I wait to heal? Will
I allow myself to remember the pain properly afterward? And then, from
these questions, the secondary—some would say the primary—issues raise
their heads from the swamp. Why am I really doing this? Do I *want* the pain?
Why would that be? Do I want to fall? Why would *that* be? Does it matter to
me to reach the top or simply to suffer on the way up? Who am I doing these
things for? Who was I ever doing them for? Myself? My father? Lara, perhaps?"

He smiled out at the filigree poppies. "What do you think, Jack? Is it
because of Lara?"

"That wasn't your fault, Nik."

The smile went away. "In here, I study the only thing that scares me anymore. Myself. And in that process, I harm no one else."

"And help no one else," I pointed out.

"Yes. Axiomatic." He looked around at me. "Are you a revolutionary,
too, then? One of the neoQuellist faithful?"

"Not as such."

"But you have little sympathy with Renouncing?"

I shrugged. "It's harmless. As you say. And no one has to play who doesn't
want to. But you kind of assume the rest of us are going to provide the powered
infrastructure for your way of life. Seems to me that's a basic failure in Renouncing, all on its own."

I got the smile back for that. "Yes, that is something of a test of faith for
many of us. Of course, ultimately we believe all humanity will follow us into
virtual. We are merely preparing the way. Learning the path, you might say."

"Yeah," snapped Brasil. "And meanwhile, outside the world falls apart
on the rest of us."

"It was always falling apart, Jack. Do you really think what I used to do
out there, the little thefts and defiances, do you really think all that made any
difference?"

"We're taking a team into Rila," said Brasil abruptly, decided. "That's
the difference we're going to make, Nik. Right there."

I cleared my throat. "With your help."

"Ah."

"Yeah, we need the route, Nik." Brasil got up and wandered off into a
corner of the quadrangle, raising his voice as if, now the secret was out, he
wanted even the volume of conversation to reflect his decision. "You feel like
giving it to us? Say, for old times' sake?"

Natsume got up and regarded me quizzically.

"Have you climbed a sea cliff before?"

"Not really. But the sleeve I'm wearing knows how to do it."

For a moment he held my eye. It was as if he were processing what I'd just said and it wouldn't load. Then, suddenly, he barked a laugh that didn't belong inside the man we'd been talking to.

"Your sleeve knows how?" The laughter shook out to a more governed chuckling and then a hard-eyed gravity. "You'll need more than that. You do know there are ripwing colonies on the top third of Rila Crags? Probably more now than there ever were when I went up. You do know there's an over-hanging flange that runs all the way around the lower battlements, and the Buddha alone knows how much updated anti-intrusion tech they've built into it since I climbed it. You *do know* the currents at the base of Rila will carry your broken body halfway up the Reach before they drop you anywhere."

"Well." I shrugged. "At least if I fall, I won't get picked up for inter-rogation."

Natsume glanced across at Brasil.

"How old is he?"

"Leave him alone, Nik. He's wearing Eishundo custom, which he *found,* he tells me, while wandering around New Hokkaido killing mimints for a liv-ing. You do know what a mimint is, don't you?"

"Yes." Natsume was still looking at me. "We've heard the news about Mecsek in here."

"It's not exactly news these days, Nik," Brasil told him, with evident glee.

"You're really wearing Eishundo?"

I nodded.

"You know what that's worth?"

"I've had it demonstrated to me a couple of times, yeah."

Brasil shifted impatiently on the stonework of the quadrangle. "Look, Nik, are you going to give us this route or not? Or are you just worried we're going to beat your record?"

"You're going to get yourselves killed, stack-irretrievable, both of you. Why should I help you to do that?"

"Hey, Nik—you've renounced the world and the flesh, remember. Why should how we end up in the real world bother you in here?"

"It bothers me that you're both fucking insane, Jack."

Brasil grinned, maybe at the obscenity he'd finally managed to elicit from his former hero. "Yeah, but at least we're still in the game. And you know we're going to do this anyway, with or without your help. So—"

"All right." Natsume held up his hands. "Yes, you can have it. Right now. I'll even talk you through it. For all the good it'll do you. Yeah, go on. Go and die on Rila Crags. Maybe that'll be *real* enough for you."

Brasil just shrugged and grinned again.

"What's the matter, Nik? You jealous or something?"

● ● ●

Natsume led us up through the monastery to a sparsely furnished suite of wood-floored rooms on the third floor, where he drew images in the air with his hands and conjured the Rila climb for us. Partly it was drawn direct from his memory as it now existed in the virtuality's coding, but the data functions of the monastery allowed him to check the mapping against an objective real-time construct of Rila. His predictions turned out to be on the nail—the rip-wing colonies had spread and the battlement flange had been modified, though the monastery's datastack could offer no more than visual confirmation of this last. There was no way to tell what else was up there waiting for us.

"But the bad news cuts both ways," he said, an animation in his voice that hadn't been there before he started sketching the route. "That flange gets in their way as well. They can't see down clearly, and the sensors get confused with the ripwing movement."

I glanced at Brasil. No point in telling Natsume what he didn't need to know—that the Crags' sensor net was the least of our worries.

"Over in New Kanagawa," I said instead, "I heard they're wiring ripwings with microcam systems. Training them, too. Any truth in that?"

He snorted.

"Yeah, they were saying the same thing a hundred and fifty years ago. It was paranoid crabshit then, and I guess it still is now. What's the point of a microcam in a ripwing? They never go near human habitation if they can avoid it. And from what I recall of the studies done, they don't domesticate or train easily. Plus more than likely the orbitals would spot the wiring and shoot them down on the wing." He gave me an unpleasant grin, not one from the Renouncer monk serenity suite. "Believe me, you've got quite enough to worry about climbing through a colony of *wild* ripwings, never mind some sort of domesticated cyborg variety."

"Right. Thanks. Any other helpful tips?"

He shrugged. "Yeah. Don't fall off."

But there was a look in his eyes that belied the laconic detachment he affected and later, as he uploaded the data for outside collection, he was quiet in a tightened way that had none of his previous monkish calm to it. When he led us back down through the monastery, he didn't speak at all. Brasil's visit had ruffled him like spring breezes coming in across the carp lakes in Danchi. Now, beneath the rippled surface, powerful forms flexed restlessly back and forth. When we reached the entrance hall, he turned to Brasil and started speaking, awkwardly.

"Listen, if you—"

Something screamed.

The Renouncer's construct rendering was good—I felt the minute prickle across my palms as the Eishundo sleeve's gecko reflexes got ready to grab rock and climb. Out of peripheral vision suddenly amped up, I saw Brasil tense—and behind him I saw the wall shudder.

"Move," I yelled.

At first, it seemed to be a product of the doorkeeper tapestries, a bulging extrusion from the same fabric. Then I saw it was the stonework behind the cloth that was bulging inward, warped under forces the real world would not have permitted. The screaming might have been some construct analog of the colossal strain the structure was under, or it might simply have been the voice of the thing that was trying to get in. There wasn't time to know. Split seconds later the wall erupted inward with a sound like a huge melon cracking, the tapestry tore down the center, and an impossible ten-meter-tall figure stepped down into the hall.

It was as if a Renouncer monk had been pumped so full of high-grade lubricant that his body had ruptured at every joint to let the oil out. A gray-coveralled human form was vaguely recognizable at the center of the mess, but all around it iridescent black liquid boiled out and hung on the air in viscous, reaching tendrils. The face of the thing was gone, eyes and nose and mouth ripped apart by the pressure of the extruding oil. The stuff that had done the damage pulsed out of every orifice and juncture of limb as if the heart within was still beating. The screaming emanated from the whole figure in time with each pulse, never quite dying away before the next blast of sound.

I found I'd dropped to a combat crouch that I knew was going to be worse than useless. All we could do now was run.

"Norikae-san, Norikae-san. Please leave the area now."

It was a chorus of cries, perfectly cadenced, as from the opposite wall a phalanx of doorkeepers threaded themselves out of the tapestries and arced gracefully over our heads toward the intruder, wielding curious, spiked clubs and lances. Their freshly assembled bodies were laced with an extrusion of their own that glowed with soft, crosshatched golden light.

"Please lead your guests to the exit immediately. We will deal with this."

The structured gold threads touched the ruptured figure, and it recoiled. The screaming splintered and mounted in volume and pitch, stabbing at my eardrums. Natsume turned to us, shouting above the noise.

"You heard them. There's nothing you can do about this. Get out of here."

"Yeah, how do we do that?" I shouted back.

"Go back to—" His words faded out as if he'd been turned down. Over his head, something punched a massive hole in the roof of the hall. Blocks of stone rained down, and the doorkeepers flinched about in the air, lashing out with golden light that disintegrated the debris before it could hit us. It cost two of them their existence as the black-threaded intruder capitalized on their distraction, reached out with thick new tentacles, and tore them apart. I saw them bleed pale light as they died. Through the roof—

"Oh, fuck."

It was another oil-exploded figure, this one double the size of the previous arrival, reaching in with human arms that had sprouted huge liquid talons from out of the knuckles and under the nails of each hand. A ruptured head squeezed through and grinned blankly down at us. Globules of the black stuff cascaded down like drool from the thing's torn mouth, splattering the floor and corroding it through to a fine silver filigree underlay. A droplet caught my cheek and scorched the skin. The splintered shrieking intensified.

"Through the waterfall," Natsume bellowed in my ear. "Throw yourself into it. Go."

Then the second intruder stamped down and the whole of the hall ceiling fell inward. I grabbed at Brasil, who was staring upward with numb awe, and dragged him in the direction of the wedged-open door. Around us, doorkeeper figures rallied and flung themselves upward to meet the new threat. I saw a fresh wave come out of the remaining tapestries, but half of them were grabbed up and shredded by the thing on the roof before they could finish assembling themselves. Light bled like rain onto the stone floor. Musical chords rang through the space of the hall and fractured apart on disharmonies. The black shredded things flailed about them.

We made it to the door with a couple more minor burns and I shoved Brasil through ahead of me. I turned back for a moment and wished I hadn't. I saw Natsume touched by a misshapen tendril of black and somehow heard him scream across the general shrieking. For a scant second it was a human voice; then it was twisted out of pitch as if by an impatient hand on a set of sound controls, and Natsume seemed to somehow swim away from his own solidity, thrashing back and forth like a fish trapped between compressing sheets of glass, all the time melting and shrieking in eerie harmony with the swooping rage of the two intruders.

I got out.

We sprinted for the waterfall. One more backflung glance showed me the whole side of the monastery punched apart behind us and the two black-tentacled figures growing in stature as they lashed at the doorkeepers swarming around them. The sky overhead was darkening as if for a storm, and the air had turned suddenly chilled. An indescribable hissing ran through the grass on either side of the path, like torrential rain, like leaking high-pressure gas. As we skidded down the winding path beside the waterfall, I saw savage interference patterns rip through the curtain of water and once, as we arrived on the platform behind the fall, the flow staggered altogether into a sudden bleakness of naked rock and open air, spluttered, then restarted.

I met Brasil's eye. He didn't look any happier than I felt.

"You go first," I told him.

"No, it's okay. You—"

A shrill, pealing howl from up the path. I shoved him in the small of the back and, as he disappeared through the thundering veil of water, I dived after him. I felt the water pour down onto my arms and shoulders, felt myself tip and—

—Jerked upright on the battered couch.

It was an emergency transition. For a couple of seconds, I still felt wet from the waterfall, could have sworn my clothes were drenched and my hair plastered down around my face. I drew one soggy breath, and then real-world perception caught up. I was dry. I was safe. I was tearing off hypno-phones and 'trodes, rolling off the couch, staring around me, heartbeat ripping belatedly upward as my physical body responded to signals from a consciousness that had only just slipped back into the adrenal driving seat.

Across the transfer chamber, Brasil was already on his feet, talking hastily to a grim-faced Sierra Tres who'd somehow reacquired both her own blaster and my Rapsodia. The room was full of a dusty-throated whoop from emergency sirens that hadn't seen use in decades. Lights flickered uncertainly. I met the female receptionist halfway across the chamber, where she'd just abandoned an instrument panel gone colorfully insane. Even on the poorly muscled face of the Fabrikon sleeve, shocked anger glared out at me.

"Did you bring it in?" she shouted. "Did you contaminate us?"

"No, of course not. Check your fucking instruments. Those things are still in there."

"What the fuck was that?" asked Brasil.

"At a guess, I'd say a sleeper virus." Absently, I took the Rapsodia from Tres and checked the load. "You saw the shape of it—part of those things used to be a monk, digitized human disguise wrapped around the offensive systems while they were dormant. Just waiting for the right trigger. The cover personality might not even have been aware what it was carrying until it blew."

"Yeah, but *why*?"

"Natsume." I shrugged. "They'd probably been tagging him since—"

The attendant was gaping at us as if we'd started gibbering in machine code. Her colleague appeared behind her at the door to the transfer chamber and pushed his way past. There was a small beige datachip in his left hand, and the cheap silicoflesh was stretched taut on his fingers where he gripped it. He brandished the chip at us and leaned in close to beat the noise of the sirens.

"You must leave now," he said forcefully, "I am requested by Norikae-san to give you this, but you must get out immediately. You are no longer either welcome or safe here."

"Yeah, no shit." I took the offered chip. "If I were you, I'd come with us.

Weld shut every dataport you've got into the monastery before you leave and then call a good viral cleanup crew. From what I saw back there, your door-keepers are outclassed."

The sirens whooped about us like methed-up partygoers. He shook his head, as if to clear it of noise. "No. If this is a test, we will meet it on Uploaded terms. We will not abandon our brothers."

"Or sisters. Well, suit yourself, that's very noble. But personally I think anyone you send in there at the moment is going to come out with their sub-conscious flayed to the bone. You badly need some real-world support."

He stared at me.

"You do not understand," he yelled. "This is our domain, not the flesh. This is the destiny of the human race, to Upload. We are at our strongest there, we will triumph there."

I gave up. I shouted back at him.

"Fine. Great. You let me know how that turns out. Jack, Sierra. Let's leave these idiots to kill themselves and get the fuck out of here."

We abandoned the two of them in the transfer room. The last I saw of either was the male attendant laying himself on one of the couches, staring straight up while the woman attached the 'trodes. His face was shiny with sweat, but it was rapt, too, locked in a paroxysm of will and emotion.

Out on Whaleback and Ninth, soft afternoon light was painting the blank-eyed walls of the monastery warm and orange, and the sounds of traffic hoot-ing in the Reach drifted up with the smell of the sea. A light westerly breeze stirred dust and dried-out spindrizzle spores in the gutters. Up ahead, a cou-ple of children ran across the street, making shooting noises and chasing a miniature robot toy made to resemble a karakuri. There was no one else about, and nothing in the scene to suggest the battle now raging back in the machine heart of the Renouncers' construct. You could have been forgiven for thinking the whole thing was a dream.

But down at the lower limits of my neurachem hearing as we walked away, I could just make out the cry of ancient sirens, like a warning, feeble and faint, of the stirring forces and the chaos to come.

CHAPTeR THIRTY

Harlan's Day.

More correctly, Harlan's Eve—technically, the festivities wouldn't commence until midnight rolled around, and that was a solid four hours away. But even this early in the evening, with the last of the day's light still high in the western sky, the proceedings had kicked off long since. Over in New Kanagawa and Danchi the downtown areas would already be a lurid parade of holodisplay and masked dance, and the bars would all be serving at state-subsidized birthday prices. Part of running a successful tyranny is knowing when and how to let your subjects off the leash, and at this the First Families were accomplished masters. Even those who hated them most would have had to admit that you couldn't fault Harlan and his kind when it came to throwing a street party.

Down by the water in Tadaimako, the mood was more genteel but festive still. Work had ceased in the commercial harbor around lunchtime, and now small groups of dockworkers sat on the high sides of real-keel freighters, sharing pipes and bottles and looking expectantly at the sky. In the marina, small parties were in progress on most of the yachts, one or two larger ones spilling out from vessels onto the jetties. A confused mishmash of music splashed out everywhere, and as the evening light thickened you could see where decks and masts had been sprayed with illuminum powder in green and pink. Excess powder glimmered scummily in the water between hulls.

A couple of yachts across from the trimaran we were stealing, a minimally clad blond woman waved giddily at me. I lifted the Erkezes cigar, also stolen, in cautious salute, hoping she wouldn't take it as an invitation to jump ship and come over. Isa had music she swore was fashionable thumping up from belowdecks, but it was a cover. The only thing going on to that beat was an intrusion run into the guts of the trimaran *Boubin Islander*'s onboard security systems. Uninvited guests trying to crash this particular party were going to meet Sierra Tres or Jack Soul Brasil and the business end of a Kalashnikov shard gun at the base of the companionway.

I knocked some ash off the cigar and wandered about in the yacht's stern seating area, trying to look as if I belonged there. Vague tension eeled through my guts, more insistent than I'd usually expect before a gig. It didn't take much imagination to work out why. An ache that I knew was psychosomatic twinged down the length of my left arm.

I very badly didn't want to climb Rila Crags.

Fucking typical. The whole city's partying, and I get to spend the night clinging to a two-hundred-meter sheer cliff face.

"Hello there."

I glanced up and saw the minimally clad blond woman standing at the gangplank and smiling brilliantly. She wobbled a little on exaggerated stiletto heels.

"Hello," I said cautiously.

"Don't know your face," she said with inebriated directness. "I'd remember a hull this gorgeous. You don't usually moor here, do you?"

"No, that's right." I slapped the rail. "First time she's been to Millsport. Only got in a couple of days ago."

For the *Boubin Islander* and her real owners at least, it was the truth. They were a pair of moneyed couples from the Ohrid Isles, rich by way of some state sell-off in local navigational systems, visiting Millsport for the first time in decades. An ideal choice, plucked out of the harbormaster datastack by Isa along with everything else we needed to get aboard the thirty-meter tri-maran. Both couples were unconscious in a Tadaimako hotel right now, and a couple of Brasil's younger revolutionary enthusiasts would make sure they stayed that way for the next two days. Amid the confusion of the Harlan's Day celebrations, it was unlikely anyone was going to miss them.

"Mind if I come aboard and take a look?"

"Uh, well, that'd be fine except, thing is, we're about to cast off. Couple more minutes, and we're taking her out into the Reach for the fireworks."

"Oh, that's fantastic. You know, I'd really love to do that." She flexed her body at me. "I go absolutely crazy for fireworks. They make me all, I don't know—"

"Hey, baby." An arm slipped around my waist and violent crimson hair tickled me under the jaw. Isa snuggling against me, stripped down to cutaway swimwear and some eye-opening embedded body jewelry. She glared balefully at the blond woman. "Who's your new friend?"

"Oh, we haven't, ah . . ." I opened an inviting hand.

The blond woman's mouth tightened. Maybe it was a competitive thing; maybe it was Isa's glittery, red-veined stare. Or maybe just healthy disgust at seeing a fifteen-year-old girl hanging off a man over twice her age. Resleeving can and does lead to some weird body options, but anyone with the money to run a boat like *Boubin Islander* doesn't have to go through them if they don't want to. If I was fucking someone who looked fifteen, either she *was* fifteen or

I wanted her to look like she was, which in the end comes to pretty much the same thing.

"I think I'd better get back," she said, and turned unsteadily about. Listing slightly every few steps, she made as dignified a retreat as was possible on heels that stupid.

"Yeah," Isa called after her. "Enjoy the party. See you around, maybe."

"Isa?" I muttered.

She grinned up at me. "Yeah, what?"

"Let go of me, and go put some fucking clothes back on."

●●●

We cast off twenty minutes later and cruised out of the harbor on a general guidance beam. Watching the fireworks from the Reach wasn't a stunningly original idea, and we weren't even close to the only yacht in Tadaimako harbor heading that way. For the time being, Isa kept watch from the belowdecks cockpit and let the marine traffic interface tug us along. There'd be time to break loose later, when the show started.

In the forward master cabin, Brasil and I broke out the gear. Stealth scuba suits, Anderson-rigged, courtesy of Sierra Tres and her *haiduci* friends, weaponry from the hundred personal arsenals on Vchira Beach. Isa's customized software for the raid patched into the suits' general-purpose processors, overlaid with a scrambler-rigged comsystem she'd stolen fresh from the factory that afternoon. Like the *Boubin Islander*'s comatose owners, it wouldn't be missed for a couple of days.

We stood and looked at the assembled hardware, the gleaming black of the powered-down suits, the variously scuffed and dented weapons. There was barely enough space on the mirrorwood floor for it all.

"Just like old times, huh?"

Brasil shrugged. "No such thing as an old wave, Tak. Every time, it's different. Looking back's the biggest mistake you can make."

Sarah.

"Spare me the cheap fucking beach philosophy, Jack."

I left him in the cabin and went aft to see how Isa and Sierra Tres were getting on at the con. I felt Brasil's gaze follow me out, and the taint of my own flaring irritation stayed with me along the corridor and up the three steps into the storm cockpit.

"Hey, baby," said Isa, when she saw me.

"Stop that."

"Suit yourself." She grinned unrepentantly and glanced across to where Sierra Tres was propped against the cockpit side panel. "You didn't seem to mind so much earlier on."

"Earlier on there was a—" I gave up. Gestured. "Suits are ready. Any word from the others?"

Sierra Tres shook her head slowly. Isa nodded at the comset datacoil.

"They're all online, look. Green glow, all the way across the board. For now, that's all we need or want. Anything more, it just means things have fucked up. Believe me, right now, no news is good news."

I twisted about awkwardly in the confined space.

"Is it safe to go up on deck?"

"Yeah, sure. This is a sweet ship, it runs weather-exclusion screens from generators in the rigging, I've got them up on partial opaque for incoming. Anyone out there nosy enough to be looking, like your little blond friend, say, your face is just going to be a blob in the scope."

"Good."

I ducked out of the cockpit, moved to the stern and heaved myself into the seating area, then up onto the deck proper. This far north, the Reach was running light and the trimaran was almost steady on the swell. I picked my way forward to the fair-weather cockpit, seated myself in one of the pilot chairs, and dug out a fresh Erkezes cigar. There was a whole humicrate of them below, I figured the owners could spare more than a few. Revolutionary politics—we all have to make sacrifices. Around me, the yacht creaked a little. The sky had darkened, but Daikoku stood low over the spine of Tadaimako and painted the sea with a bluish glow. The running lights of other vessels sat about, neatly separated from each other by the traffic software. Basslines thumped faintly across the water from the glimmering shore lights of New Kanagawa and Danchi. The party was in full swing.

Southward, Rila speared up out of the sea, distant enough to appear slim and weaponish—a dark, crooked blade, unlit but for the cluster of lights from the citadel at the top.

I looked at it and smoked in silence for a while.

He's up there.

Or somewhere downtown, looking for you.

No, he's there. Be realistic about this.

All right, he's there. And so is she. So for that matter is this Aiura, and a couple of hundred handpicked Harlan family retainers. Worry about stuff like that when you get to the top.

A launch barge slid past in the moonlight, on its way out to a firing position farther up the Reach. At the rear, the deck was piled high with tumbled packages, webbing, and helium cylinders. The sawn-off forward superstructure thronged with figures at rails, waving and firing flares into the night. A sharp hooting lifted from the vessel as it passed, the Harlan birthday hymn picked out in harsh collision alert blasts.

Happy birthday, motherfucker.

"Kovacs?"

It was Sierra Tres. She'd reached the cockpit without me noticing, which said either a lot for her stealth skills or as much for my lack of focus. I hoped it was the former.

"You okay?"

I considered that for a moment. "Do I not look okay?"

She made a characteristically laconic gesture and seated herself in the other pilot chair. For quite a long time, she just looked at me.

"So what's going on with the kid?" she asked finally. "You looking to recapture your long-lost youth?"

"No." I jerked a thumb southward. "My long-lost fucking youth is out there somewhere, trying to kill me. There's nothing going on with Isa. I'm not a fucking pedophile."

Another long, quiet spell. The launch barge slipped away into the evening. Talking to Tres was always like this. Under normal circumstances, I'd have found it irritating, but now, caught in the calm before midnight, it was curiously restful.

"How long do you think they had that viral stuff tagged to Natsume?"

I shrugged. "Hard to tell. You mean, was it long-term shadowing or a trap set specifically for us?"

"If you like."

I knocked ash off the cigar and stared at the ember beneath. "Natsume's a legend. Granted a dimly remembered one, but *I* remember him. So will the copy of me the Harlans have hired. He probably also knows by now that I talked to people back in Tekitomura, and that I know they're holding Sylvie at Rila. He knows what I'd do, given that information. A little Envoy intuition would do the rest. If he's in tune, then yeah, maybe he had them clip some viral watchdogs to Natsume, waiting for me to show up. With the backing he's got now, it wouldn't be hard to write a couple of shell personalities, have them wired in with faked credentials from one of the other Renouncer monasteries."

I drew on the cigar, felt the bite of the smoke, and let it up again.

"Then again, maybe the Harlan family had Natsume tagged from way back anyway. They're not a forgiving lot, and him climbing Rila like that made them look stupid, even if it wasn't much more than a Quellboy poster stunt."

Sierra was silent, staring ahead through the cockpit windshield.

"Comes to the same thing in the end," she said at last.

"Yes, it does. They know we're coming." Oddly enough, saying it made me smile. "They don't know exactly when or exactly how, but they know."

We watched the boats around us. I smoked the Erkezes down to a stub. Sierra Tres sat silent and motionless.

"I guess Sanction Four was hard," she said later.

"You guess right."

For once I beat her at her own taciturn game. I flicked the spent cigar away and fished out another two. I offered her one and she shook her head.

"Ado blames you," she told me. "So do some of the others. But I don't think Brasil does. He appears to like you. Always has, I think."

"Well, I'm a likable guy."

A smile bent her mouth. "So it seems."

"What's that supposed to mean?"

She looked away over the forward decks of the trimaran. The smile was gone now, retracted into habitual cat-like calm.

"I saw you, Kovacs."

"Saw me where?"

"Saw you with Vidaura."

That sat between us for a while. I drew life into my cigar and puffed enough smoke to hide behind.

"See anything you liked?"

"I wasn't in the room. But I saw you both going there. It didn't look as if you were planning a working lunch."

"No." Memory of Virginia's virtual body crushed against mine sent a sharp twinge through the pit of my stomach. "No, we weren't."

More quiet. Faint basslines from the clustered lights of southern Kanagawa. Marikanon crept up and joined Daikoku in the northeastern sky. As we drifted idly southward, I could hear the almost subsonic grinding of the maelstrom in full flow.

"Does Brasil know?" I asked.

Now it was her turn to shrug. "I don't know. Have you told him?"

"No."

"Has she?"

And more quiet. I remembered Virginia's throaty laughter, and the sharp, unmatching shards of the three sentences she used to dismiss my concerns and open the floodgates.

This isn't something that's going to bother Jack. This isn't even real, Tak. And anyway, he isn't going to know.

I was accustomed to trusting her judgment amid bomb blasts and Sunjet fire on seventeen different worlds, but something didn't ring true here. Virginia Vidaura was as used to virtualities as any of us. Dismissing what went on there as not real struck me as an evasion.

Certainly felt pretty fucking real while we were doing it.

Yeah, but you came out of that as pent-up and full of come as when you started. It wasn't much more real than the daydream fantasies you used to have about her when you were a raw recruit.

Hey, she was there, too.

After a while, Sierra stood up and stretched.

"Vidaura's a remarkable woman," she said cryptically and wandered off toward the stern.

● ● ●

A little before midnight, Isa cut loose of Reach traffic control and Brasil took the con from the fair-weather cockpit. By then, conventional fireworks were already bursting, like sudden green and gold and pink sonar displays, all over the Millsport skyline. Pretty much every islet and platform had its own arsenal to fire off, and across the major landmasses like New Kanagawa, Danchi, and Tadaimako, they were in every park. Even some of the boats out in the Reach had laid in stock—from several of our nearest neighbors, rockets trailed drunken lines of sparks skyward, and elsewhere rescue flares were put to use instead. On the general radio channel, against a backdrop of music and party noise, some inane presenter warbled pointless descriptions of it all.

Boubin Islander bucked a little as Brasil upped her speed and we started to break waves southward. This far down the Reach, the wind carried a fine mist of droplets thrown up by the maelstrom. I felt them against my face, fine like cobwebs, then cold and wet as they built and ran like tears.

Then the real fireworks began.

"Look," Isa said, face lit up as a bright cuff of childlike excitement showed momentarily under her wrappings of teenage cool. Like the rest of us, she'd come up on deck because she wasn't going to miss the start of the show. She nodded at one of the hooded radar sweeps. "There go the first ones. Liftoff."

On the display, I saw a number of blotches to the north of our position in the Reach, each one tagged with the alarmed red lightning jag that indicated an airborne trace. Like any rich man's toy, *Boubin Islander* had a redundancy of instrumentation that even told me what altitude the contacts were at. I watched the number scribble upward beside each blotch, and despite myself felt a tiny twist of awe in my guts. The Harlan's World legacy—you can't grow up on this planet and not feel it.

"And they've cut the ropes," the presenter informed us gaily. "The balloons are rising. I can see the—"

"Do we have to have this on?" I asked.

Brasil shrugged. "Find a channel that's not casting the same fucking thing. I couldn't."

The next moment, the sky cracked open.

Carefully loaded with explosive ballast, the first clutch of helium balloons had attained the four-hundred-meter demarcation. Inhumanly precise, machine-swift, the nearest orbital noticed and discharged a long, stuttering finger of angelfire. It ripped the darkness apart, slashed through cloud masses in the upper western sky, lit the jagged mountain landscapes around us with sudden blue, and for fractions of a second touched each of the balloons.

The ballast detonated. Rainbow fire poured down across Millsport.

The thunder of outraged air in the path of the angelfire blast rolled majestically out across the archipelago like something dark tearing.

Even the radio commentator shut up.

From somewhere south, a second set of balloons reached altitude. The orbital lashed down again; night turned again to bluish day. The sky rained colors again. The scorched air snarled.

Now, from strategic points all over Millsport and the barges deployed in the Reach, the launches began. Widespread, repeated goads for the alien-built machine eyes overhead. The flickering rays of angelfire became a seemingly constant, wandering pointer of destruction, stabbing out of the clouds at all angles, licking delicately at each transgressive vessel that hit the four-hundred-meter line. The repeated thunder grew deafening. The Reach and the landscape beyond became a series of flashlit still images. Radio reception died.

"Time to go," said Brasil.

He was grinning.

So, I realized, was I.

CHAPTeR THIRTY-ONe

The Reach waters were cold, but not unpleasantly so. I slid in from *Boubin Islander*'s dive steps, let go of the rail, and felt the jellied cool pressing me all over through the suit's skin as I submerged. It was an embrace of sorts, and I let myself sink into it as the weight of my strapped weapons and the Anderson rig carried me down. A couple of meters below the surface, I switched on the stealth and buoyancy systems. The grav power shivered and lifted me gently back up. I broke the surface to eye level, snapped down the mask on the helmet, and blew it clear of water.

Tres bobbed up a few meters away. Raised a gloved hand in acknowledgment. I cast about for Brasil.

"Jack?"

His voice came back through the induction mike, lips blowing in a heartfelt shudder.

"Under you. Chilly, huh?"

"Told you you should have laid off the self-infection. Isa, you listening up there?"

"What do *you* think?"

"All right, then. You know what to do?"

I heard her sigh. "Yes, Dad. Hold station, keep the channels clear. Relay anything that comes in from the others. Don't talk to any strange men."

"Got it in one."

I lifted an arm cautiously and saw how the stealth systems had activated the refraction shift in the suit's skin. Close enough to the bottom, standard chameleochrome would kick in and make me a part of whatever colors were down there, but in open water the shift system made me a ghost, an eyeblink twist of shadowed water, a trick of the light.

There was a kind of comfort in that.

"All right then." I drew air, harder than necessary. "Let's do this."

I took bearings on the lights at New Kanagawa's southern tip, then the black stack of Rila, twenty klicks beyond. Then I sank back into the sea, turned lazily over, and began to swim.

Brasil had taken us as far south of the general traffic as was safe without attracting attention, but we were still a long way off the Crags. Under normal circumstances, getting there would have been a couple of hours' hard work at least. Currents, sucked south through the Reach by the maelstrom, helped somewhat, but the only thing that really made the scuba approach viable was the modified buoyancy system. With electronic security in the archipelago effectively blinded and deafened by the orbital storm, no one was going to be able to pick up a one-man grav engine underwater. And with a carefully applied vector, the same power that maintained diver flotation would also drive us south at machine speed.

Like seawraiths out of the Ebisu daughter legend, we slid through the darkened water an arm's reach apart, while above us the surface of the sea bloomed silently and repeatedly with reflected angelfire. The Anderson rig clicked and bubbled gently in my ears, electrolyzing oxygen directly from the water around me, blending in helium from the ultracomp mini tank on my back, feeding it to me, then patiently shredding and dispersing my exhaled breath in bubbles no larger than fish eggs. Distantly, the maelstrom growled a bass counterpoint.

It was very peaceful.

Yeah, this is the easy part.

A memory drifted by in the flashlit gloom. Night-diving off Hirata's Reef with a girl from the upscale end of Newpest. She'd blown into Watanabe's one night with Segesvar and some of the other Reef Warriors, part of a mixed bag of slumming daddy's girls and Stinktown hardboys. Eva? Irena? All I remembered was a gathered-up rope of dark honey hair, long sprawling limbs, and shining green eyes. She was smoking seahemp roll-ups, badly, choking and wheezing on the rough blend with a frequency that made her harder-edged friends laugh out loud. She was the most beautiful thing I had ever seen.

Making a—for me—rare effort, I peeled her away from Segesvar, who in any case seemed to be finding her a drag, parked us in a quiet corner of Watanabe's near the kitchens, monopolized her all evening. She seemed to come from another planet entirely—a father who cared and worried about her with an attention I would have jeered at under different circumstances, a mother who worked part time *just so she doesn't feel like a complete housewife,* a home out of town that they owned, visits to Millsport and Erkezes every few months. An aunt who had gone offworld to work, they were all so proud of her, a brother who hoped to do the same. She talked about it all with the abandon of someone who believes these things to be entirely normal, and she coughed on the seahemp, and she smiled brilliantly at me, often.

So, she said on one of those occasions, *what do* you *do for fun?*

I, uh. I. Reef dive.

The smile became a laugh. *Yeah, Reef Warriors, somehow I guessed. Go down much?*

It was supposed to be my line, the line we all used on girls, and she'd stolen it out from under me. I didn't even mind much.

Far side of Hirata, I blurted out. *You want to try sometime?*

Sure, she matched me. *Want to try right now?*

It was deep summer in Kossuth, inland humidity had hit 100 percent weeks ago. The thought of getting into the water was like an infectious itch. We slipped out of Watanabe's and I showed her how to read the autocab flows, pick out an unfared one, and jump the roof. We rode it all the way across town, sweat cooling on our skin.

Hang on tight.

Yeah, I never would have thought of that, she yelled back, and laughed into my face in the slipstream.

The cab stopped for a fare near the Port Authority, and we tumbled off, scaring the prospective customers into a clutch of mannered yelps. Shock subsided into mutters and disapproving glares that sent us reeling off, stifling cackles. There was a hole in harbor security down at the eastern corner of the hoverloader docks—a blind spot torn by some preteen for-kicks hacker the previous year; he'd sold it to the Reef Warriors for holoporn. I got us through the gap, sneaked us down to one of the 'loader ramps, and stole a real-keel tender. We poled and paddled our way silently out of the harbor, then started the motor and tore off in a wide, cream-waked arc for Hirata, whooping.

Later, sunk in the silence of the dive, I looked up at the Hotei-toned, rippling surface and saw her body above me, pale against the black straps of the buoyancy jacket and the ancient compressed-air rig. She was lost in the moment, drifting, maybe gazing at the towering wall of the reef beside us, maybe just luxuriating in the cool of the sea against her skin. For about a minute, I hung below her, enjoying the view and feeling myself grow hard in the water. I traced the outlines of her thighs and hips with my eyes, zeroed in on the shaved vertical bar of hair at the base of her belly and the glimpse of lips as her legs parted languidly to kick. I stared at the taut muscled belly emerging from the lower edge of the buoyancy jacket, the obvious swelling at her chest.

Then something happened. Maybe too much seahemp, never a smart idea before a dive. Maybe just some fatherly echo from my own home life. The reef edged in from the side of my vision, and for one terrible moment it seemed to be tilting massively over, falling on us. The eroticism of the languid drift in her limbs shriveled to sudden, cramping anxiety that she was dead or unconscious. I kicked myself upward in sudden panic, grabbed her shoulders with both hands, and tilted her around in the water.

And she was fine.

Eyes widened a little in surprise behind the mask, hands touching me in return. A grin split her mouth, and she let air bubble out through her teeth. Gestures, caresses. Her legs wrapped around me. She took out the regulator, gestured for me to do the same, and kissed me.

"Tak?"

Afterward, in the gear 'fab the Reef Warriors had blown and set atop the reef, lying with me on an improvised bed of musty winter wet suits, she seemed surprised at how carefully I handled her.

You won't break me, Tak. I'm a big girl.

And later, legs wrapped around me again, grinding against me, laughing delightedly.

Hang on tight!

I was too lost in her to steal her comeback from the roof of the autocab.

"Tak, you hear me?"

Eva? Ariana?

"Kovacs!"

I blinked. It was Brasil's voice.

"Yeah, sorry. What is it?"

"Boat coming." On the heels of his words, I picked it up as well, the scraping whine of small screws in the water, sharp over the backdrop growl of the maelstrom. I checked my proximity system, found nothing on grav trace. Went to sonar and found it, southwest and coming fast up the Reach.

"Real-keel," muttered Brasil. "Think we should worry?"

It was hard to believe the Harlan family would run real-keel patrol boats. Still—

"Kill the drives." Sierra Tres said it for me. "Go to standby flotation. It's not worth the risk."

"Yeah, you're right." Reluctantly, I found the buoyancy controls and shut down the grav support. Instantly I felt myself starting to sink as the weight of my gear asserted itself. I prodded the emergency flotation dial and felt the standby chambers in the flotation jacket start to fill up. Cut it as soon as my descent stopped, and floated in the flashlit gloom, listening to the approaching whine of the boat.

Elena, maybe?

Green eyes shining.

The reef tipping over onto us.

As another angelfire blast cut loose, I spotted the keel of the vessel overhead, big and sharkish, and hugely misshapen on one side. I narrowed my eyes and peered in the postblast gloom, cranking the neurachem. The boat seemed to be dragging something.

And the tension drained back out of me.

"Charter boat, guys. They're hauling a bottleback carcass."

The boat labored past and faded northward on a bored drone, listing awkwardly with the weight of its prize, not even that close to us in the end. Neurachem showed me the dead bottleback in silhouette against the blue-lit surface of the water, still trailing thin threads of blood into the water. The massive torpedo body rolled sluggishly against the bow wave; the flukes trailed like broken wings. Part of the dorsal flange had been ripped loose at some point and now it flogged back and forth in water, blurred at the edges with ragged lumps and tendrils of tissue. Loose cabling tangled alongside. Looked as if they'd harpooned it a few times—whoever had chartered the boat clearly wasn't that great a fisherman.

When humans first arrived on Harlan's World, the bottlebacks didn't have any natural predators. They were the top of the food chain, magnificently adapted marine hunters and highly intelligent, social animals. Nothing the planet had evolved recently was up to killing them.

We soon changed that.

"Hope that's not an omen," murmured Sierra Tres unexpectedly.

Brasil made a noise in his throat. I vented the emergency chambers on the buoyancy jacket and snapped the grav system back on. The water seemed suddenly colder around me. Behind the automatic motions of course check and gear trim, I could feel a vague, undefined anger seeping in.

"Let's get this done, guys."

But the mood was still with me twenty minutes later when we crept into the shallows at the base of Rila, pulsing at my temples and behind my eyes. And projected on the glass of my scuba mask, the pale red route pointers from Natsume's simulation software seemed to flare in time with the ratcheting of my own blood. The urge to do damage was a rising tide inside me, like wakefulness, like hilarity.

We found the channel Natsume had recommended, eased through with gloved hands braced against rock and coral outcrops to avoid snagging. Levered ourselves up out of the water onto a narrow ledge that the software had tinted and flagged with a slightly demonic smiling face. *Entry level,* Natsume had said, shedding his monkish demeanor for a fleeting moment. *Knock, knock.* I got myself braced and took stock. Faint silvery light from Daikoku touched the sea, but Hotei had still not risen and the spray from the maelstrom and nearby wavecrash fogged what light there was. The view was mostly gloom. Angelfire sent shadows scurrying past on the rocks as another firework package burst somewhere to the north. Thunder rippled across the sky. I scanned the cliff above for a moment, then the darkened sea we'd just climbed out of. No sign we'd been noticed. I detached the dive helmet's frame from the mask and lifted it off. Shed my flippers and flexed the toes of the rubber boots underneath.

"Everybody okay?"

Brasil grunted an affirmative. Tres nodded. I secured the helmet frame at my belt in the small of my back where it wouldn't get in the way, stripped off my gloves, stowed them in a pouch. Settled the now lightweight mask a little more comfortably on my face and checked that the datafeed was still securely jacked in. Tipping my head back, I saw Natsume's route march off above us in clearly marked red hand- and footholds.

"You all seeing this okay?"

"Yeah." Brasil grinned. "Kind of spoils the fun, doesn't it? Marking it out like that."

"You want to go first then?"

"After you, Mister Eishundo."

Without giving myself time to think about it, I reached up and grasped the first indicated hold, braced my feet, and heaved myself onto the cliff. Swung up and found a grip with my other hand. The rock was wet with maelstrom mist, but the Eishundo grip held. I brought a leg across to fit against an angled ledge, swung again, and grasped.

And left the ground behind.

Nothing to it.

The thought zipped through my mind after I'd gone about twenty meters, and left a slightly manic grin in its wake. Natsume had warned me that the early stages of the climb were deceptive. *It's apeman stuff,* he said seriously. *Lots of wide swings and grabs, big moves, and your strength's good at this stage. You're going to feel good. Just remember it doesn't last.*

I pursed my lips, chimpanzee-like, and hooted gently through them. Below me, the sea smashed and gnawed restlessly at rock. The sound and scent of it came bouncing up the cliff face and wrapped me in windings of chill and damp. I shrugged off a shudder.

Swing up. Grab.

Very slowly, it grew on me that the Envoy conditioning hadn't yet come online against my vertigo. With the rock face less than half a meter in front of my face and the Eishundo muscle system thrumming on my bones, it was almost possible to forget that there was a drop below. The rock lost the coating of spray from the maelstrom as we climbed higher, the repeating roar of waves faded to distant white noise. The gecko grip on my hands made glassy, treacherous holds laughably comfortable. And more than all these factors, or maybe the culminating Eishundo touch, what I'd told Natsume seemed to be true—the sleeve knew how to do this.

Then, as I reached a set of holds and ledges whose markers the mask display labeled with a rest-point symbol, I looked down to see how Brasil and Tres were doing, and ruined it all.

Sixty meters below—not even a third of the whole climb—the sea was a blackened fleece, touched with Daikoku silver where it rippled. The skirt of rocks at the base of Rila sat in the water like solid shadows. The two big ones that framed the channel where we'd come in now looked as if they'd fit into my hand. The back-and-forth sluice of water between them was hypnotic, pulling me downward. The view seemed to pivot dizzyingly.

The conditioning came online, flattening the fear. Like air lock doors in my head. My gaze came up again to face the rock. Sierra Tres reached up and tapped my foot.

"Okay?"

I realized I'd been frozen for the best part of a minute.

"Just resting."

The marked trail of holds leaned left, an upward diagonal around a broad buttress that Natsume had warned us was pretty much unclimbable. Instead he'd lain back and moved almost upside down under the chin of the buttress, feet jammed against minute folds and fissures in the stone, fingers pinching angles of rock that barely deserved the name *hold,* until he could finally get both hands on a series of sloped ledges at the far side and haul himself back into a nearly vertical position.

I gritted my teeth and started to do the same.

Halfway there, my foot slipped, swung my weight out, and pulled my right hand off the rock. An involuntary grunt, and I was dangling left-handed, feet flailing for purchase far too low to find anything apart from empty air. I would have screamed but the barely recovering sinews in my left arm were doing it for me.

"Fuck."

Hang on tight.

The gecko grip held.

I curled upward from the waist, craning my neck to see the marked footholds in the glass of the mask. Short, panicky breaths. I got one foot lodged against a bubble of stone. Tiny increments of strain came off my left arm. Unable to see clearly with the mask, I reached up in the dark with my right hand and felt about on the rock for another hold.

Found it.

Moved my braced foot fractionally and jammed the other one in next to it.

Hung, panting.

No, don't fucking stop!

It took all my willpower to move my right hand for the next hold. Two more moves, and it took the same sickening effort to look for the next. Three more moves, a fractionally improved angle, and I realized I was almost to the other side of the buttress. I reached up, found the first of the sloping ledges, and dragged myself hyperventilating and cursing upright. A genuine, deeply grooved hold offered itself. I got my feet to the lowest ledge. Sagged with relief against the cool stone.

Get yourself up out of the fucking way, Tak. Don't leave them hanging about down there.

I scrambled up the next set of holds until I was on top of the buttress. A broad shelf glowed red in the mask display, smiling face floating above it. Rest point. I waited there while Sierra Tres and then Brasil emerged from below and joined me. The big surfer was grinning like a kid.

"Had me worried there, Tak."

"Just. Don't. Fucking don't, all right?"

We rested for about ten minutes. Over our heads, the battlement flange of the citadel was now clearly visible, clean-cut edges emerging from the chaotic angles of the natural rock it jutted above. Brasil nodded upward.

"Not far to go now, eh?"

"Yeah, and only the ripwings to worry about." I dug out the repellent spray and squirted myself liberally with it all over. Tres and Brasil followed suit. It had a thin, faintly green odor that seemed stronger in the fitful darkness. It might not drive a ripwing away under all and any circumstances, but it would certainly put them off. And if that wasn't enough . . .

I drew the Rapsodia from its holster on my lower ribs and pressed it to a utility patch on my chest. It clung there, easily at hand in fractions of a second, always assuming I could spare the hand to grab it in the first place. Faced with the prospect of meeting a cliff full of angry, startled ripwings with young to defend, I would have preferred the heavy-duty Sunjet blaster on my back, but there was no way I could wield it effectively. I grimaced, adjusted the mask, and checked the datajack again. Drew a deep breath and reached for the next set of handholds.

Now the cliff face grew convex, bulging out and forcing us to climb at a sustained backward lean of twenty degrees. The path Natsume had taken wove back and forth across the rock, governed by the sparse availability of decent holds, and even then opportunities to rest were few and far between. By the time the bulge faded back to a vertical, my arms were aching from shoulder to fingertip, and my throat was raw from panting.

Hang on tight.

I found a display-marked diagonal crack, moved up it to give the others space, and jammed an arm in up to the elbow. Then I hung there limply, collecting breath.

The smell hit me about the same time as I saw the gossamer-thin streamers of white dangling from above.

Oily, acidic.

Here we go.

I twisted my head and stared upward for confirmation. We were directly below the colony's nesting band. The whole expanse of rock was thickly plastered with the creamy webbing secretion that ripwing embryos were birthed directly into and lived in for their four-month gestation. Evidently, somewhere just above me, mature hatchlings had torn their way free and either taken wing or tumbled incompetently to a Darwinian conclusion in the sea below.

Let's not think about that right now, eh?

I cranked the neurachem vision and scanned the colony. Dark shapes preened and flapped here and there on protruding crags in the mass of white, but there weren't many of them. *Ripwings,* Natsume assured us, *don't spend a lot of time at the nests. No eggs to keep warm, and the embryos feed directly off the webbing.* Like most hardcore climbers, he was a part-time expert on the creatures. *You're going to get a few sentinels, the odd birthing female and maybe some well-fed parents secreting more gunge onto their particular patch. If you go carefully, they may leave you alone.*

I grimaced again and began to work my way up the crack. The oily stink intensified, and shreds of torn webbing began to adhere to my suit. The chameleochrome system blanched to match wherever the stuff touched. I stopped breathing through my nose. A quick glance down past my boots showed me the others following, faces contorted with the smell.

And then, inevitably, the crack ran out and the display said that the next set of holds was buried beneath the webbing. I nodded drearily to myself and plunged a hand into the mess, wriggling fingers around until they found a spur of rock that resembled the red model in the display. It seemed pretty solid. A second plunge into the webbing gave me another, even better hold and I hacked sideways with one foot, looking for a ledge that was also covered in the stuff. Now, even breathing through my mouth, I could taste the oil at the back of my throat.

This was far worse than the climb over the bulge. The holds were good, but each time you had to force your hand or foot through the thick, clinging webs until it was secure. You had to watch out for the vague shadows of embryos hung up inside the stuff, because even embryonic they could bite, and the surge of fear hormones they'd release through the webbing if you touched them would hit the air like a chemical siren. The sentinels would be on us seconds after, and I didn't rate our chances of fighting them off without falling.

Stick your hand in. Flex it about.

Get a grip. Move.

Pull clear and shake your hand free. Gag at the liberated stink. Stick your hand back in.

By now we were coated with clinging strands of the stuff and I was finding it hard to remember what climbing on clean rock had been like. At the edges of a nearly cleared patch, I passed a dead and rotting hatchling, caught upside down by the talons in a freak knot of webbing it hadn't been strong enough to break before it starved to death. It added new, sickly-sweet layers of decay to the stink. Higher up, a nearly grown embryo seemed to turn its beaked head to look at me as I reached gingerly into the gunge half a meter away.

I drew myself up over a ledge made rounded and sticky by webbing.

The ripwing lunged at me.

Probably, it was as startled as I was. Rising mist of repellent and the bulky black figure that came after, you could see how it would be. It went for my eyes with a repeated stabbing movement, punched the mask instead and jerked my head back. The beak made a skittering noise on the glass. I lost my left-hand grip, pivoted on the right. The ripwing croaked and hunched closer, stabbing at my throat. I felt the serrated edge of the beak gouge skin. Out of options, I dragged myself back hard against the ledge with my right hand. My left whiplashed out, neurachem-swift, and grabbed the fucking thing by the neck. I ripped it off the ledge and hurled it downward. There was another startled croak, then an explosion of leathery wings below me. Sierra Tres yelled.

I got another grip with my left hand and peered down. They were both still there. The ripwing was a retreating winged shadow, soaring away out to sea. I unlocked my breath again.

"You okay?"

"Can you please not do that again," gritted Brasil.

I didn't have to. Natsume's route took us through an area of torn and used-up webbing next, finally over a narrow band of thicker secretion, and then we were clear. A dozen good holds after that and we were crouched on a worked-stone platform under the main battlement flange of the Rila citadel.

Tight, traded grins. There was enough space on the platform to sit down. I tapped the induction mike.

"Isa?"

"Yes, I'm here." Her voice came through uncharacteristically high-pitched, hurried with tension. I grinned again.

"We're at the top. Better let the others know."

"All right."

I settled back against the stonework and breathed out loose-lipped. Stared out at the horizon.

"I do *not* want to have to do that again."

"Still this bit left," said Tres, jerking her thumb upward at the flange. I followed the motion and looked at the underside of the battlement.

Settlement-years architecture. Natsume had been almost scornful. *So fucking baroque, they might as well have built a ladder into it.* And the glimmer of pride that all his time as a Renouncer didn't seem to have taken away. *'Course, they never expected anyone to get up there in the first place.*

I examined the ranks of carving on the upward-sloping underside of the flange. Mostly, it was the standard wing-and-wave motifs, but in places there were stylized faces representing Konrad Harlan and some of his more notable relatives from the Settlement era. Every ten square centimeters of stonework offered a decent hold. The distance out to the edge of the flange was less than three meters. I sighed and got back to my feet.

"Okay then."

Brasil braced himself next to me, peering up the angle of the stone. "Looks easy enough, eh? Think there are any sensors?"

I pressed the Rapsodia against my chest to make sure it was still secure. Loosened the blaster in its sheath on my back. Got back to my feet.

"Who fucking cares."

I reached up, stuck a fist in Konrad Harlan's eye, and dug in with my fingers. Then I climbed out over the drop before I could think about it. About thirty hanging seconds and I was onto the vertical wall. I found similar carvings to work with and seconds later was crouched on a three-meter-broad parapet, peering down into a cloister-lined, tear-shaped ornamental space of raked gravel and painstakingly aligned rocks. A small statue of Harlan stood near the center, head bowed and hands folded meditatively, overshadowed at the rear by an idealized Martian whose wings were spread in protection and conferral of power. At the far end of the rounded space, a regal arch led away, I knew, to the shadowed courtyards and gardens of the citadel's guest wing.

The perfume of herbs and ledgefruit blew past me, but there was no local noise beyond the breeze itself. The guests, it appeared, were all across in the central complex, where lights blazed and the sounds of celebration came and went with the wind. I strained the neurachem and picked out cheers, elegant music that Isa would have hated, a voice raised in song that was quite beautiful.

I pulled the Sunjet from its sheath on my back and clicked the power on. Waiting there in the darkness on the edge of the party, hands full of death, I felt momentarily like some evil spirit out of legend. Brasil and Tres came up behind me and fanned out on the parapet. The big surfer had a heavy antique frag rifle cradled in his arms; Tres hefted her blaster left-handed to make room for the Kalashnikov solid-load in her right. There was a distant look on her face and she seemed to be weighing the two weapons for balance, or as if she might throw them. The night sky split with angelfire and lit us, bluish and unreal. Thunder rumbled like an incitement. Under it all, the maelstrom called.

"All right then," I said softly.

"Yes, that's probably far enough," said a woman's voice from the garden-perfumed shadows. "Put down your weapons, please."

CHAPTeR THIRTY-TWO

Figures, armed and armored, stepped out of the cloistering. At least a dozen of them. Here and there I could see a pale face, but most wore bulky enhanced-vision masks and tactical-marine-style helmets. Combat armor hugged their chests and limbs like extra muscle. The weaponry was equally heavy-duty. Shard blasters with gape-mouthed dispersal fittings, frag rifles about a century newer than the one Jack Soul Brasil had brought to the party. A couple of hip-mounted plasmaguns. No one up in the Harlan eyrie was taking any chances.

I lowered the barrel of the Sunjet gently to point at the stone parapet. Kept a loose grip on the butt. Peripheral vision told me Brasil had done the same with the frag rifle, and that Sierra Tres had her arms at her sides.

"Yes, I really meant *relinquish* your weapons," said the same woman urbanely. "As in put them down altogether. Perhaps my Amanglic is not as idiomatic as it could be."

I turned in the direction the voice came from.

"That you, Aiura?"

There was a long pause, and then she stepped out of the archway at the end of the ornamental space. Another orbital discharge lit her for a moment, then the gloom sank back and I had to use neurachem to keep the detail. The Harlan security executive was the epitome of First Family beauty—elegant, almost ageless Eurasian features, jet-black hair sculpted back in a static field that seemed to both crown and frame the pale of her face. A mobile intelligence of lips and gaze, the faintest of lines at the corners of her eyes to denote a life lived. A tall, slim frame wrapped in a simple quilted jacket in black and dark red with the high collar of office, matching slacks loose enough to appear a full-length court gown when she stood still. Flat-heeled shoes that she could run or fight in if she had to.

A shard pistol. Not aimed, not quite lowered.

She smiled in the dim light.

"I am Aiura, yes."

"Got my fuckhead younger self there with you?"

Another smile. A flicker of eyebrows as she glanced sideways, back the way she'd come. He stepped out of the shadowed archway. There was a grin on his face, but it didn't look very firmly anchored.

"Here I am, old man. Got something to say to me?"

I eyed the tanned combat frame, the gathered stance, and the bound-back hair. Like some fucking bad guy from a cut-rate samurai flick.

"Nothing you'd listen to," I told him. "I'm just trying to sort out the idiot count here."

"Yeah? Well, I'm not the one who just climbed two hundred meters so he could walk into an ambush."

I ignored the jibe and looked back at Aiura, who was watching me with amused curiosity.

"I'm here for Sylvie Oshima," I said quietly.

My younger self coughed laughter. Some of the armored men and women took it up, but it didn't last. They were too nervous; there were still too many guns in play. Aiura waited for the last guffaws to skitter out.

"I think we're all aware of that, Kovacs-san. But I fail to see how you're going to accomplish your goal."

"Well, I'd like you to go and fetch her for me."

More grating laughter. But the security exec's smile had paled out, and she gestured sharply for quiet.

"Be serious, Kovacs-san. I don't have unlimited patience."

"Believe me, neither do I. And I'm tired. So you'd better send a couple of your men down to get Sylvie Oshima from whatever interrogation chamber you're holding her in, and you'd better hope she's not been harmed in any way, because if she has, this negotiation is over."

Now it had grown quiet again in the stone garden. There was no more laughter. Envoy conviction, the tone in my voice, the choice of words, the ease in my stance—these things told them to believe.

"With what exactly are you negotiating, Kovacs-san?"

"With the head of Mitzi Harlan," I said simply.

The quiet cranked tight. Aiura's face might have been graven from stone for all the reaction it showed. But something in the way she stood changed and I knew I had her.

"Aiura-san, I am not bluffing. Konrad Harlan's favorite granddaughter was taken by a Quellist assault team in Danchi two minutes ago. Her secret-service detachment is dead, as is anyone else who mistakenly tried to come to her aid. You have been focused in the wrong place. And you now have less than thirty minutes to render me Sylvie Oshima unharmed—after that, I have no influence over the outcomes. Kill us, take us prisoner. It won't matter. None of it will make any difference. Mitzi Harlan will die in great pain."

The moment pivoted. Up on the parapet it was cool and quiet, and I could hear the maelstrom faintly. It was a solid, carefully engineered plan, but that didn't mean it couldn't get me killed. I wondered briefly what would happen if someone shot me off the edge. If I'd be dead before I hit.

"Crabshit!" It was me. He'd stepped toward the parapet, controlled violence raging off the way he held himself. "You're bluffing. There's no way you'd—"

I locked gazes with him, and he shut up. I sympathized—the same freezing disbelief was in me as I stared back into his eyes and truly understood for the first time who was behind them. I'd been double-sleeved before, but that had been a carbon copy of who I was at the time, not this echo from another time and place in my own lifeline. Not this ghost.

"Wouldn't I?" I gestured. "You're forgetting there's a hundred-odd years of my lifeline that you haven't lived yet. And that isn't even the issue here. This isn't me we're talking about. This is a squad of Quellists, with three centuries of grudge backed up in their throats and a useless fucking aristo trollop standing between them and their beloved leader. You know this, Aiura-san, even if my idiot youth here doesn't. Whatever's required down there—they will do. And nothing I do or say will change that, unless you give me Sylvie Oshima."

Aiura muttered something to my younger self. Then she took a phone from her jacket and glanced up at me.

"You'll forgive me," she said politely, "if I don't take this on trust."

I nodded. "Please confirm anything you need to. But please hurry."

It didn't take long for the security exec to get the answers she needed. She'd barely spoken two words into the phone when a torrent of panicked gibbering washed back out at her. Even without neurachem, I could hear the voice at the other end. Her face hardened. She snapped a handful of orders in Japanese, cut off the speaker, then killed the line and replaced the phone in her jacket.

"How do you plan to leave?" she asked me.

"Oh, we'll need a helicopter. I understand you maintain half a dozen or so here. Nothing fancy, a single pilot. If he behaves, we'll send him back to you unharmed."

"Yeah, if you're not shot out of the sky by a twitchy orbital," drawled Kovacs. "Not a good time to be flying tonight."

I stared back at him with dislike. "I'll take the risk. It won't be the most stupid thing I've ever done."

"And Mitzi Harlan?" The Harlan security exec was watching me like a predator now. "What assurances do I have of her safety?"

Brasil stirred at my side for the first time since the confrontation began.

"We are not murderers."

"No?" Aiura switched her gaze across to him like an audio-response sentry gun. "Then this must be some new breed of Quellism I was unaware of."

For the first time, I thought I detected a crack in Brasil's voice. "Fuck you, enforcer. With the blood of generations on your hands, you want to point a moral finger at us? The First Families have—"

"I think we'll have this discussion some other time," I said loudly. "Aiura-san, your thirty minutes are burning up. Slaughtering Mitzi Harlan can only make the Quellists unpopular, and I think you know they'll avoid that if they can. If that's insufficient, I give you a personal undertaking. Comply with our demands, I will see Harlan's granddaughter returned unharmed."

Aiura glanced sideways at the other me. He shrugged. Maybe he nodded fractionally. Or maybe it was just the thought of facing Konrad Harlan with Mitzi's bloodied corpse.

I saw the decision take root in her.

"Very well," she said briskly. "You will be held to your promise, Kovacs-san. I don't need to tell you what that means. When the reckoning comes, your conduct in this matter may be all that saves you from the full wrath of the Harlan family."

I smeared her a brief smile. "Don't threaten me, Aiura. When the reckoning comes, I'm going to be a long way from here. Which is a shame, because I'll miss seeing you and your greasy little hierarch masters scrabbling to get your loot offworld before the general populace strings you up from a dockyard crane. Now, where's my fucking helicopter?"

●●●

They brought Sylvie Oshima up on a grav stretcher, and when I saw her at first I thought the Little Blue Bugs would have to execute Mitzi Harlan after all. The iron-haired figure beneath the stretcher blanket was a death-white fake of the woman I remembered from Tekitomura, gaunt with weeks of sedation, pale features scorched with feverish color across the cheeks, lips badly bitten, eyelids draped slackly closed over twitching eyeballs. There was a light sweat on her forehead that shone in the glow from the stretcher's overhead examination lamp, and a long transparent bandage on the left side of her face, where a thin slash wound led down from cheekbone to jawline. When angelfire lit the stone garden around us, Sylvie Oshima might have been a corpse in the bluish snapshot light.

I sensed more than saw the outraged tension kick through Sierra Tres and Brasil. Thunder rolled across the sky.

"Is that her?" asked Tres tautly.

I lifted my free hand. "Just. Take it easy. Yes, it's her. Aiura, what the fuck have you done to her?"

"I would advise against overreaction." But you could hear the strain in the security exec's voice. She knew how close to the edge we were. "The wound is a result of self-injury, before we were able to stop her. A procedure was tried, and she responded badly."

My mind fled back to Innenin and Jimmy de Soto's destruction of his own face when the Rawling virus hit. I knew what procedure they'd tried with Sylvie Oshima.

"Have you fed her?" I asked in a voice that grated in my own ears.

"Intravenously." Aiura had put her sidearm away while we were waiting for her men to bring Sylvie to the stone garden. Now she moved forward, making damping motions with both hands. "You must understand that—"

"We understand perfectly," said Brasil. "We understand what you and your kind are. And someday soon we are coming to cleanse this world of you."

He must have moved, maybe twitched the barrel of the frag rifle. Weapons came up around the garden with a panicky rattle. Aiura spun about.

"*No!* Stand *down.* All of you."

I shot a glance at Brasil, muttering, "You, too, Jack. Don't blow this."

A soft shuttering sound. Above the long angles of the citadel's guest wing, a narrow, black Dracul swoopcopter raced toward us, nose dropped. It swerved wide of the stone garden, out over the sea, hesitated a moment as the sky ruptured blue, then came wagging back in with landing grabs extended. A shift in the engine pitch, and it settled with insect precision onto the parapet to the right. If whoever was flying it was worried by the orbital activity, it didn't show in the handling.

I nodded at Sierra Tres. She bent under the soft storm of the rotors and ran crouched to the swoopcopter. I saw her lean in and converse briefly with the pilot; then she looked back at me and gestured an *okay.* I laid down my Sunjet and turned to Aiura.

"Right, you and junior there. Get her up, bring her over here to me. You're going to help me load her. *Everybody else stays back.*"

It was awkward, but between the three of us we managed to manhandle Sylvie Oshima up from the stone garden and onto the parapet. Brasil skirted around to stand between us and the drop. I gathered the gray-maned woman under the arms while Aiura supported her back and the other Kovacs took her legs. Together we carried her limp form to the swoopcopter.

And at the door, in the chuntering of the rotors above us, Aiura Harlan leaned across the semi-conscious form we were both holding. The swoopcopter was a stealth machine, designed to run quiet, but this close in the rotors made enough noise that I couldn't make out what she was saying. I craned my neck closer.

"You what?"

She leaned closer again. Spoke directly and sibilantly into my ear.

"I said, you send her back to me whole, Kovacs. These joke revolutionaries, that's a fight we can have another time. But they harm any part of Mitzi Harlan's mind or body and I'll spend the rest of my existence hunting you down."

I grinned back at her in the noise. I raised my voice as she drew back.

"You don't frighten me, Aiura. I've been dealing with scum like you all my life. You'll get Mitzi back because I said you would. But if you really care that much about her, you'd better start planning some lengthy holidays for her offworld. These guys aren't fucking about."

She looked down at Sylvie Oshima.

"It isn't her, you know," she shouted. "There's no way for it to be her. Quellcrist Falconer is dead. Really Dead."

I nodded. "Okay. So if that's the case, how come she's got all you First Family fucks so bent out of shape?"

The security exec's shout became genuinely agitated. "Why? Because, Kovacs, whoever this is—and it's *not* Quell—*whoever* this is, she's brought back a plague from the Uncleared. A whole new form of death. You ask her about the Qualgrist Protocol when she wakes up, and then ask yourself if what I've done here to stop her is so terrible."

"Hoy!" It was my younger self, elbows crooked under Sylvie's knees, hands spread expressively wide beneath. "Are we going to load this bitch, or are you going to stand there talking about it all night?"

I held his gaze for a long moment, then lifted Sylvie's head and shoulders carefully up to where Sierra Tres waited in the swoopcopter's cramped cabin. The other Kovacs shoved hard, and the rest of her body slid in after. The move brought him up close beside me.

"This isn't over," he yelled in my ear. "You and I have some unfinished business."

I levered one arm under Sylvie Oshima's knee and elbowed him back, away from her. Gazes locked.

"Don't fucking tempt me," I shouted. "You bought-and-paid-for little shit."

He bristled. Brasil surged up close. Aiura laid a hand on my younger self's arm and spoke intently into his ear. He backed off. Raised one pistol finger and stabbed it at me. What he said was lost in the wash of the rotors. Then the Harlan security exec was shepherding him away, back along the parapet to a safe distance. I swung myself aboard the Dracul, made space beside me for Brasil, and nodded at Sierra Tres. She spoke directly to the pilot, and the swoopcopter loosened its hold on the parapet. I stared out at the other, younger Kovacs. Watched him stare back.

We lifted away.

Beside me, Brasil had a grin plastered across his face like the mask for some ceremony I hadn't been invited to attend. I nodded back at him wearily. Suddenly I was shattered, mind and body. The long swim, the unrelenting strain and near-death moments of the climb, the tight-wired tension of the face-off—it all came crashing back down on me.

"We did it, Tak," Brasil bellowed.

I shook my head. Mustered my voice.

"So far, so good," I countered.

"Ah, don't be like that."

I shook my head again. Braced in the doorway, I leaned out of the swoopcopter and stared down at the rapidly shrinking array of lights from the Rila citadel. With unaided vision, I couldn't see any of the figures in the stone garden anymore, and I was too tired to crank up the neurachem. But even over the rapidly increasing space between us, I could still feel his stare, and the unforgiving rage kindled in it.

CHAPTeR THIRTY-THRee

We picked up *Boubin Islander* exactly where she was supposed to be. Isa's seamanship, via the trimaran's pilot software, had been impeccable. Sierra Tres talked to the pilot, who seemed, on admittedly very brief acquaintance, to be a decent sort of guy. Given his status as a hostage, he'd shown little nervousness during the flight, and once he said something to Sierra Tres that made her laugh out loud. Now he nodded laconically as she spoke into his ear, maxed up a couple of displays on his flight board, and the swoopcopter fell away toward the yacht. I gestured for the spare comset again and fitted it to my ear.

"Still there, Aiura?"

Her voice came back, precise and terrifyingly polite. "I am still listening, Kovacs-san."

"Good. We're about to set down. Your flier here knows to back off rapidly, but just to underline the point, I want the sky clear in all directions—"

"Kovacs-san, I do not have the authority to—"

"Then get it. I don't believe for a moment that Konrad Harlan can't have the skies over the whole Millsport Archipelago emptied if he wants it, even if you can't. So listen carefully. If I see a helicopter anywhere above our horizon for the next six hours, Mitzi Harlan is dead. If I see an airborne trace on our radar anytime in the next six hours, Mitzi Harlan is dead. If I see any vessel at all following us, Mitzi Harlan—"

"You've made your point, Kovacs." The courtesy in her voice was fast evaporating. "You will not be followed."

"Thank you."

I tossed the comset back onto the seat next to the pilot. Outside the swoopcopter, the rushing air was murky. There hadn't been an orbital discharge since we took off, and it looked from the lack of fireworks to the north as if the light show was winding down. Thick cloud was drawing in from the west, smothering the rising edge of Hotei. Higher up, Daikoku was thinly veiled and Marikanon gone altogether. It looked as if it might rain.

The Dracul made a tight circle over the trimaran, and I saw a white-faced Isa on deck, waving one of Brasil's antique frag rifles unconvincingly. A smile touched the corners of my mouth at the sight. We backed off on the turn and dropped to sea level, then sideslipped in toward the *Boubin Islander*. I stood in the doorway and waved slowly. Isa's taut features collapsed in relief, and she lowered the frag gun. The pilot perched his craft on the corner of *Boubin Islander*'s deck and shouted to us over his shoulder.

"End of the ride, people."

We jumped down, eased Sylvie's still-semi-conscious form out after us, and lowered her carefully to the deck. Maelstrom mist coated us like the cold breath of seasprites. I leaned back into the swoopcopter.

"Thanks. Very smooth. You'd better get out of here."

He nodded and I stepped back. The Dracul ungrabbed and lifted away. The nose turned and in seconds it was a hundred meters off, rising into the night sky on a muted chatter. As the noise faded, I turned my attention back to the woman at my feet. Brasil was bent over her, peeling back an eyelid.

"Doesn't seem to be in too bad shape," he muttered as I knelt beside him. "She's running a light fever, but her breathing's okay. I've got gear below I can check her out with better."

I put the back of my hand against her cheek. Under the film of spray from the maelstrom, it was hot and papery, the way it had been back in the Uncleared. And for all Brasil's informed medical opinion, her breathing didn't sound all that good to me, either.

Yeah, well, this is a man who favors recreational virals over drugs. Guess light fever's a relative term, eh, Micky?

Micky? What happened to Kovacs?

Kovacs is back there, crawling up Aiura Harlan's crack. That's what happened to Kovacs.

The bright anger, glinting.

"How about we get her below," suggested Sierra Tres.

"Yeah," said Isa unkindly. "She looks like shit, man."

I held down a sudden, irrational flare of dislike. "Isa, what's the news from Koi's end?"

"Uh." She shrugged. "Last time I checked, fine, they were moving—"

"Last time you *checked*? What the fuck is that, Isa? How long ago was that?"

"I don't know, I was watching the radar for you!" Her voice rose with hurt. "Saw you were coming in, I thought—"

"How fucking long, Isa?"

She bit her lip and stared back at me. "Not long, all right!"

"You st—" I clenched a fist at my side. Summoned calm. It wasn't her fault, none of this was her fault. "Isa, I need you to go down and get on the comset right now. Please. Call in, check with Koi that everything's okay. Tell him we're done here, we're on our way out."

"Okay." The hurt was still in her face and tone. "I'm going."

I watched her go, sighed, and helped Brasil and Tres lift Sylvie Oshima's limp, overheated body. Her head lolled back, and I had to shift one hand up quickly to support it. The mane of gray hair seemed to twitch in places as it hung, damp with spray, but it was a feeble movement. I looked down into the pale and flushed face and felt my jaw tighten with frustration. Isa was right: she did look like shit. Not what you thought of when you imagined the flashing-eyed, lithe-limbed combat heroine of the Unsettlement. Not what you'd expect when men like Koi talked of a woken and vengeful ghost.

I don't know, she's well on her way to the ghost part.

Ha fucking ha.

Isa appeared at the top of the stern companionway just as we got there. Wrapped up in my own sour thoughts, it took me a moment to look up at her face. And by then, it was too late.

"Kovacs, I'm sorry," she pleaded.

The swoopcopter.

Faintly, the soft strop of rotors, rising out of the backdrop noise from the maelstrom. Death and fury approaching, on ninja wings.

"They're down," Isa cried. "First Family commandos tracked them. Ado's hit, the rest of them are. Half of them are. They got Mitzi Harlan."

"Who did?" Sierra Tres, eyes gone uncharacteristically wide. "Who's got her now? Koi or—"

But I already knew the answer to that one.

"Incoming!"

I screamed it. Was already trying to get Sylvie Oshima to the deck without dropping her. Brasil had the same idea, but he was moving in the wrong direction. Sylvie's body tugged between us. Sierra Tres yelled. We all seemed to be moving in mud, gracelessly slow.

Like a million furious watersprites let loose, the hail of machine-gun fire ripped out of the ocean on our stern, then up across *Boubin Islander*'s lovingly finished deck. Eerily, it was silent. Water splashed and splattered, harmlessly quiet and playful. Wood and plastic leapt out of everything in splinters around us. Isa screamed.

I got Sylvie down in the stern seats. Landed on top of her. Out of the darkened sky, hard on the heels of its own silenced machine-gun fire, the Dracul machine came hammering across the water at strafing height. The guns started up again and I rolled off the seat, dragging Sylvie's unresponsive form down with me. Something blunt smashed against my ribs as I hit the ground in the confined space. I felt the swoopcopter's shadow pass across me and then it was gone, quietened motors muttering in its wake.

"Kovacs?" It was Brasil, from above on the deck.

"Still here. You?"

"He's coming back."

"Of course he fucking is." I poked my head out of cover and saw the Dracul banking about in the mist-blurred air. The first run had been a stealth assault—he didn't know we weren't expecting him. Now it didn't matter. He'd take his time, sit out at a distance, and chew us to shreds.

Motherfucker.

It geysered out of me. All the stored-up fight that the standoff with Aiura hadn't allowed a discharge for. I flailed upright in the stern seats, got a grip on the companionway coaming, and hauled myself onto the deck. Brasil was crouched there, frag rifle cradled in both arms. He nodded grimly forward. I followed the look and the rage took a new twist inside me. Sierra Tres lay with one leg smashed to red glinting fragments. Isa was down near her, drenched in blood. Her breath was coming in tight little gasps. A couple of meters off, the frag rifle she'd brought up on deck lay abandoned.

I ran to it, scooped it up like a loved child.

Brasil opened fire from the other side of the deck. His frag rifle went off with a ripping, cracking roar, and muzzle flash stabbed out a meter from the end of the barrel. The swoopcopter swung in from the right, flinching upward as the pilot spotted the fire. More machine-gun slugs ripped across *Boubin Islander*'s masts with a pinging sound, too high to worry about. I braced myself against the gently pitching deck and put the stock to my shoulder. Lined up, and started shooting as the Dracul drifted back. The rifle roared in my ear. Not much hope of a hit, but standard frag load is proximity-fused and maybe, just maybe—

Maybe he'll slow down enough for you to get close? Come on, Micky.

For a moment, I remembered the Sunjet, dropped on the parapet as I lifted Sylvie Oshima. If I'd had it now I could have this motherfucker out of the sky as easy as spitting.

Yeah, instead, you're stuck with one of Brasil's museum pieces. Nice going, Micky. That mistake is about to kill you.

The second source of ground fire seemed to have rattled the pilot slightly, for all that nothing we were throwing into the sky had touched him. Maybe he wasn't a military flier. He passed over us again at a steep, sideslipping angle, almost snagging on the masts. He was low enough that I saw his masked face peering downward as he banked the machine. Teeth gritted in fury, face soaked with the upcast spray of the maelstrom, I followed him with frag fire, trying to keep him in the sight long enough to get a hit.

And then, in the midst of the gunsnarl and drifting mist, something exploded near the Dracul's tail. One of us had managed to put a frag shell close enough for proximity fusing. The swoopcopter staggered and pivoted about.

It seemed undamaged, but the near miss must have scared the pilot. He kicked his craft upward again, backing around us in a wide, rising arc. The silent machine-gun fire kicked in again, came ripping across the deck toward me. The magazine of the frag gun emptied, locked open. I threw myself sideways, hit the deck, and slid toward the rail on spray-slick wood—

And the angelfire reached down.

Out of nowhere, a long probing finger of blue. It stabbed out of the clouds, sliced across the spray-soaked air, and abruptly the swoopcopter was gone. No more machine-gun fire scuttling greedily at me, no explosion, no real noise outside the crackle of abused air molecules in the path of the beam. The sky where the Dracul had caught fire, flared up and then faded into the glow of an afterimage on my retina.

—and I slammed into the rail.

For a long moment there was only the sound of the maelstrom and the slap of wavelets against the hull just below me. I craned my head up and stared. The sky remained stubbornly empty.

"Got you, you motherfucker," I whispered to it.

Memory slotted. I got myself upright and ran to where Isa and Sierra Tres both lay in running swipes of spray-diluted blood. Tres had propped herself against the side of the fair-weather cockpit and was tying herself a tourniquet from shreds of blood-soaked cloth. Her teeth gritted as she pulled it tight—a single grunt of pain got past her. She caught my eye and nodded, then rolled her head to where Brasil crouched beside Isa, hands frantic over the teenager's sprawled body. I came and peered over his shoulder.

She must have taken six or seven slugs through the stomach and legs. Below the chest, it looked as if she'd been savaged by a swamp panther. Her face was still now, and the panting breaths from before had slowed. Brasil looked up at me and shook his head.

"Isa?" I got on my knees beside her in her blood. "Isa, talk to me."

"Kovacs?" She tried to roll her head toward me, but it barely moved. I leaned closer, put my face close to hers.

"I'm here, Isa."

"I'm sorry, Kovacs," she moaned. Her voice was a little girl's, barely above a high whisper. "I didn't think."

I swallowed. "Isa—"

"I'm sorry—"

And, abruptly, she stopped breathing.

CHAPTeR THIRTY-FOUR

At the heart of the maze-like group of islets and reefs wryly named El-tevedtem, there was once a tower over two kilometers high. The Martians built it directly up from the seabed, for reasons best known to themselves, and just short of half a million years ago, equally inexplicably, it fell into the ocean. Most of the wreckage ended up littered across the local seabed, but in places you can still find massive, shattered remnants on land. Over time, the ruins became part of the landscape of whichever islet or reef they had smashed down onto, but even this subliminal presence was enough to ensure that Eltevedtem remained largely unpeopled. The fishing villages on the North arm of the Millsport Archipelago, at a couple of dozen kilometers distant, were the closest human habitation. Millsport itself lay over a hundred kilometers farther south. And Eltevedtem (*I'm lost* in one of the pre-Settlement Magyar dialects) could have swallowed a whole flotilla of shallow-draft vessels, if said flotilla didn't want to be found. There were narrow, foliage-grown channels between upflung rock outcrops high enough to hide *Boubin Islander* to the mast tips, sea caves gnawed out between headlands that rendered the openings invisible except on close approach, chunks of overarching Martian tower wreckage, smothered in a riot of hanging vegetation.

It was a good place to hide.

From external pursuers, anyway.

I leaned on *Boubin Islander*'s rail and stared down into limpid waters. Five meters below the surface, a brightly colored mix of native and colonial fish nosed around the white spraycrete sarcophagus we'd buried Isa in. I had some vague idea about contacting her family once we got clear, to let them know where she was, but it seemed a pointless gesture. When a sleeve is dead, it's dead. And Isa's parents weren't going to be any less sick with worry when a recovery team cracked open the spraycrete and found that someone had carved the stack out of her spine.

It lay in my pocket now, Isa's soul, for want of a better descriptor, and I could feel something changing in me with the solitary weight it made against my fingers. I didn't know what I was going to do with it, but I didn't dare leave it for anyone else to find, either. Isa was solidly implicated in the Millsport raid, and that meant a virtual interrogation suite up at Rila Crags if she was ever retrieved. For now, I would have to carry her, the way I'd carried dead priests southward to punishment, the way I'd carried Yukio Hirayasu and his gangster colleague in case I needed them to bargain with.

I'd left the yakuza stacks buried in the sand under Brasil's house on Vchira Beach, and I hadn't expected the pocket to fill again so soon. Had even, on the voyage east to Millsport, caught myself taking occasional, momentary pleasure in the strange new lack of *carriage,* until the memories of Sarah and the habit of hatred came searing back.

Now the pocket was weighted again, like some fucked-up modern-day variant on the Ebisu-cursed trawl net in the Tanaka legend, destined forever to bring up the bodies of drowned sailors and nothing much else.

There didn't seem to be any way for it to stay empty, and I didn't know what I felt anymore.

For nearly two years, it hadn't been that way. Certainty had colored my existence a grained monochrome. I'd been able to reach into my pocket and weigh its varying contents in my palm with a dark, hardened satisfaction. There was a sense of slow accumulation, an assembly of tiny increments in the balance pan that sat opposite the colossal tonnage of Sarah Sachilowska's extinction. For two years I'd needed no purpose other than that pocket and its handful of stolen souls. I'd needed no future, no outlook that didn't revolve around feeding the pocket and the swamp panther pens at Segesvar's place out on the Expanse.

Really? So what happened at Tekitomura?

Movement on the rail. The cables thrummed and bounced gently. I looked up and saw Sierra Tres maneuvering herself forward, braced on the rail with both arms and hopping on her uninjured leg. Her usually inexpressive face was taut with frustration. Under different circumstances, it might have been comical, but from the hacked-off trousers at midthigh, her other leg was encased in transparent plaster that laid bare the wounds beneath.

We'd been skulking in Eltevedtem for nearly three days now, and Brasil had used the time as well as the limited battlefield medical gear we had would allow. The flesh beneath Tres's plaster was a black-and-purple swollen mess, punched through and torn by the swoopcopter's machine-gun fire, but the wounds had been cleaned and dusted. Blue and red tags marched down the damaged portions, marking the points at which Brasil had inserted rapid-regrowth bios. A flex-alloy boot cushioned the bottom end of the cast against outside impact, but walking on it would have required more painkillers than Tres seemed prepared to take.

"You should be lying down," I said as she joined me.

"Yeah, but they missed. So I'm not. Don't give me a hard time, Kovacs."

"All right." I went back to staring into the water. "Any word yet?"

She shook her head. "Oshima's awake, though. Asking for you."

I lost focus on the fish below me for a moment. Got it back. Made no move to leave the rail or look up again.

"Oshima? Or Makita?"

"Well, now, that really depends on what you want to believe, doesn't it?"

I nodded grayly. "So she still thinks she's—"

"At the moment, yes."

I watched the fish for a moment longer. Then abruptly I straightened off the rail and stared back to the companionway. I felt an involuntary grimace twist my mouth. Started forward.

"Kovacs."

I looked back at Tres impatiently. "Yeah, what?"

"Go easy on her. It isn't her fault Isa got shot up."

"No. It isn't."

Below, in one of the forward cabins, Sylvie Oshima's sleeve lay propped up on pillows in the double bunk, staring out of a porthole. Throughout the darting, twisting, coast-hugging sprint withdrawal up to Eltevedtem and the days of hiding that followed, she'd slept, woken only by two episodes of delirious thrashing and machine-code gibbering. When Brasil could spare time from steering and watching the radar, he fed her with dermal nutrient patches and hypospray cocktails. An intravenous drip did the rest. Now the input seemed to be helping. Some of the hectic color had faded from the feverish cheeks, and her breathing had ceased to be audible as it normalized. The face was still sickly pale, but it had expression, and the long thin scar on her cheek looked to be healing. The woman who believed she was Nadia Makita looked out of the sleeve's eyes at me and made a weak smile with its mouth.

"Hello there, Micky Serendipity."

"Hello."

"I would get up, but I've been advised against it." She nodded to an armchair molded into one wall of the cabin. "Why don't you sit down?"

"I'm fine here."

She seemed to look at me more intently for a moment then, evaluating maybe. There was a scrap of Sylvie Oshima in the way she did it, enough to twist something tiny inside me. Then, as she spoke and changed the planes of her face, it was gone.

"I understand we may have to move soon," she said quietly. "On foot."

"Maybe. I'd say we've got a few more days yet, but in the end it comes down to luck. There was an aerial patrol yesterday evening. We heard them but they didn't come close enough to spot us, and they can't fly with anything sophisticated enough to scan for body heat or electronic activity."

"Ah—so that much remains the same."

"The orbitals?" I nodded. "Yeah, they still run at the same parameters as when you—"

I stopped. Gestured. "As they always did."

Again, the long, evaluative stare. I looked back blandly.

"Tell me," she said finally. "How long has it been. Since the Unsettlement, I mean."

I hesitated. It felt like taking a step over a threshold.

"Please. I need to know."

"About three hundred years, local." I gestured again. "Three hundred and twenty, near enough."

I didn't need Envoy training to read what was behind her eyes.

"So long," she murmured.

This life is like the sea. There's a three-moon tidal slop running out there and if you let it, it'll tear you apart from everyone and everything you ever cared about.

Japaridze's homespun wheelhouse wisdom, but it bit deep. You could be a Seven Percent Angel thug, you could be a Harlan family heavyweight. Some things leave the same tooth marks on everyone. You could even be Quellcrist fucking Falconer.

Or not, I reminded myself.

Go easy on her.

"You didn't know?" I asked.

She shook her head. "I don't know, I dreamed it. I think I knew it was a long time. I think they told me."

"Who told you?"

"I—" She stopped. Lifted her hands fractionally off the bed and let them fall. "I don't know. I can't remember."

She closed her hands up into loosely curled fists on the bed.

"Three hundred and twenty years," she whispered.

"Yeah."

She lay, looking down the barrel of it for a while. Waves tapped at the hull. I found that, despite myself, I'd taken a seat in the armchair.

"I called you," she said suddenly.

"Yeah. *Hurry, hurry.* I got the message. Then you stopped calling. Why was that?"

The question seemed to floor her. Her eyes widened, then the gaze fell inward on itself again.

"I don't know. I knew." She cleared her throat. "No, *she* knew you'd come for me. For her. For us. She told me that."

I leaned forward in the seat. "Sylvie Oshima told you? Where is she?"

"In here, somewhere. In here."

The woman in the bunk closed her eyes. For a minute or so I thought she'd gone to sleep. I would have left the cabin, gone back up on deck, but there was nothing up there I wanted. Then, abruptly, her eyes snapped open again and she nodded as if something had just been confirmed in her ear.

"There's a." She swallowed. "A space down there. Like a premillennial prison. Rows of cells. Walkways and corridors. There are things down there she says she *caught,* like catching bottleback from a charter yacht. Or maybe caught like a disease? It's, it shades together. Does that make any sense?"

I thought about the command software. I remembered Sylvie Oshima's words on the crossing to Drava.

—mimint interactive codes trying to replicate themselves, machine intrusion systems, construct personality fronts, transmission flotsam, you name it. I have to be able to contain all that, sort it, use it, and not let anything leak through into the net. It's what I do. Time and time again. And no matter how good the housecleaning you buy afterward, some of that shit stays. Hard-to-kill code remnants, traces. Ghosts of things. There's stuff bedded down there, beyond the baffles, that I don't want to even think about.

I nodded. Wondered what it might take to break out of that kind of prison. What kind of person—or thing—you might have to be.

Ghosts of things.

"Yeah, it makes sense." And then, before I could stop myself, "So is that where you come in, Nadia? You something she caught?"

A brief look of horror flitted across the gaunt features.

"Grigori," she whispered. "There's something that sounds like Grigori down there."

"Grigori who?"

"Grigori Ishii." It was still a whisper. Then the inward-looking horror was gone, wiped away, and she was staring hard at me. "You don't think I'm real, do you, Micky Serendipity?"

A flicker of unease in the back of my head. The name *Grigori Ishii* chimed somewhere in the pre-Envoy depths of my memory. I stared back at the woman in the bed.

Go easy on her.

Fuck that.

I stood up. "I don't know what you are. But I'll tell you this for nothing, you're not Nadia Makita. Nadia Makita is dead."

"Yes," she said thinly. "I'd rather gathered that. But evidently she was backed up and stored before she died, because here I am."

I shook my head.

"No, you're not. You're not here at all in any guaranteed sense. Nadia

Makita is gone, vaporized. And there's no evidence that a copy was made. No technical explanation for how a copy could have gotten into Sylvie Oshima's command software, even if it did exist. In fact, no evidence that you're anything other than a faked personality casing."

"I think that's enough, Tak." Brasil stepped suddenly into the cabin. His face wasn't friendly. "We can leave it here."

I swung on him, skinning teeth in a tight grin. "That's your considered medical opinion, is it, Jack? Or just a Quellist revolutionary tenet? Truth in small and controlled doses. Nothing the patient won't be able to handle."

"No, Tak," he said quietly. "It's a warning. Time for you to come out of the water."

My hands flexed gently.

"Don't try me, Jack."

"You're not the only one with neurachem, Tak."

The moment hung, then pivoted and died as the ridiculous dynamics of it caught up with me. Sierra Tres was right. It wasn't this fractured woman's fault Isa was dead; nor was it Brasil's. And besides, any damage I'd wanted to do to the ghost of Nadia Makita was now done. I nodded and dropped the combat tension like a coat. I brushed past Brasil and reached the door behind him. Turned briefly back to the woman in the bunk.

"Whatever you are, I want Sylvie Oshima back unharmed." I jerked my head at Brasil. "I brought you these new friends you've got, but I'm not one of them. If I think you've done anything to damage Oshima, I'll go through them all like angelfire just to get to you. You keep that in mind."

She looked steadily back at me.

"Thank you," she said without apparent irony. "I will."

● ● ●

On deck, I found Sierra Tres propped in a steel-frame chair, scanning the sky with a pair of binoculars. I came and stood behind her, cranking up the neurachem as I peered out in the same direction. It was a limited view—*Boubin Islander* was tucked away in the shade of a massive, jagged fragment of toppled Martian architecture that had hit the shoal below us, bedded there, and fossilized into the reef over time. Above water, airborne spores had seeded a thick covering of creeper and lichen analogs, and now the view out from under the ruin was obscured by ropes of hanging foliage.

"See anything?"

"I think they've put up microlights." Tres put aside the binoculars. "It's too far away to get more than glints, but there's something moving out there near the break in the reef. Something very small, though."

"Still twitchy, then."

"Wouldn't you be? It's got to be a hundred years since the First Families lost an aircraft to angelfire."

"Well." I shrugged with an ease I didn't really feel. "Got to be a hundred years since anyone was stupid enough to start an aerial assault during an orbital storm, right?"

"You don't think he made four hundred meters, either, then?"

"I don't know." I played back the swoopcopter's final seconds of existence with Envoy recall. "He was going up pretty fast. Even if he didn't make it, maybe it was the vector that tripped the defenses. That and the active weaponry. Fuck, who knows how an orbital thinks? What it'd perceive as a threat. They've been known to break the rules before. Look at what happened to the ledgefruit autos back in the Settlement. And those racing skiffs at Ohrid, remember that? They say most of them weren't much more than a hundred meters off the water when it took them all out."

She shot me an amused look. "I wasn't born when that happened, Kovacs."

"Oh. Sorry. You seem older."

"Thank you."

"In any case, they didn't seem keen to put much in the sky while we were running. Suggests the prediction AIs were erring on the side of caution, making some gloomy forecasts."

"Or we got lucky."

"Or we got lucky," I echoed.

Brasil came up the companionway and stalked toward us. There was an uncharacteristic anger flickering around in the way he moved and he looked at me with open dislike. I spared him a return glance, then went back to staring at the water.

"I won't have you talking to her like that again," he told me.

"Oh *shut* up."

"I'm serious, Kovacs. We all know you've got a problem with political commitment, but I'm not going to let you vomit up whatever fucked-in-the-head rage you're carrying all over this woman."

I swung on him.

"This woman? This *woman*? You're calling *me* fucked in the head. *This woman* you're talking about is not a human being. She's a fragment, a ghost at best."

"We don't know that yet," said Tres quietly.

"Oh please. Can neither of you see what's happening here? You're projecting your desires onto a fucking digitized human sketch. Already. Is this what's going to happen if we get her back to Kossuth? Are we going to build a whole fucking revolutionary movement on a mythological scrap?"

Brasil shook his head. "The movement's already there. It doesn't need to be built, it's ready to happen."

"Yeah, all it needs is a figurehead." I turned away as the old weariness rose in me, stronger even than the anger. "Which is handy, because all you've *got* is a fucking figurehead."

"You do not know that."

"No, you're right." I began to walk away. There isn't far you can go on a thirty-meter boat, but I was going to open up as much space as I could between myself and these sudden idiots. Then something made me swing about to face them both across the deck. My voice rose in abrupt fury. "I *don't* know that. I *don't know* that Nadia Makita's whole personality wasn't stored and then left lying around in New Hok like some unexploded shell nobody wanted. I *don't know* that it didn't somehow find a way to get uploaded into a passing deCom. *But what are the fucking chances?*"

"We can't make that judgment yet," Brasil said, coming after me. "We need to get her to Koi."

"Koi?" I laughed savagely. "Oh, *that's* good. Fucking Koi. Jack, do you really think you're ever going to see Koi again? Koi is more than likely blasted meat scraped up off some back street in Millsport. Or better yet, he's an interrogation guest of Aiura Harlan. Don't you get it, Jack? It is *over.* Your neo-Quellist resurgence is fucked. Koi is gone, probably the others are, too. Just more fucking casualties on the glorious road to revolutionary change."

"Kovacs, you think I don't feel for what happened to Isa?"

"I think, Jack, that provided we rescued that shell of a myth we've got down there, you don't much care who died or how."

Sierra Tres moved awkwardly on the rail. "Isa chose to get involved. She knew the risks. She took the pay. She was a free agent."

"She was fifteen fucking years old!"

Neither of them said anything. They just watched me. The slap of water on the hull grew audible. I closed my eyes, drew a deep breath, and looked at them again. I nodded.

"It's okay," I said tiredly. "I see where this is going. I've seen it before, I saw it on Sanction Four. Fucking Joshua Kemp said it at Indigo City. *What we crave is the revolutionary momentum. How we get it is almost irrelevant, and certainly not admitting of ethical debate—historical outcome will be the final moral arbiter.* If that isn't Quellcrist Falconer down there, you're going to turn it into her anyway. Aren't you?"

The two surfers traded a look. I nodded again.

"Yeah. And where does that leave Sylvie Oshima? She didn't choose this. She wasn't a free agent. She was a fucking innocent bystander. And she'll be just the first of many if you get what you want."

More silence. Finally, Brasil shrugged.

"So why did you come to us in the first place?"

"Because I fucking misjudged you, Jack. Because I remembered you all as better than this sad wish-fulfillment shit."

Another shrug. "Then you remember wrong."

"So it seems."

"I think you came to us out of lack of options," said Sierra Tres soberly. "And you must have known that we would value the potential existence of Nadia Makita above the host personality."

"Host?"

"No one wants to harm Oshima unnecessarily. But if a sacrifice is necessary, and this is Makita—"

"But it isn't. Open your fucking eyes, Sierra."

"Maybe not. But let's be brutally honest, Kovacs. If this is Makita, then she's worth a lot more to the people of Harlan's World than some mercenary deCom bounty hunter you happen to have taken a shine to."

I felt a cold, destructive ease stealing up through me as I looked at Tres. It felt almost comfortable, like homecoming.

"Maybe she's worth a lot more than some crippled neoQuellist surf bunny, too. Did that ever occur to you? Prepared to make *that* sacrifice, are you?"

She looked down at her leg, then back at me.

"Of course I am," she said gently, as if explaining to a child. "What do you think I'm doing here?"

An hour later, the covert channel broke open into sudden, excited transmission. Detail was confused but the gist was jubilantly clear. Soseki Koi and a small group of survivors had fought their way clear of the Mitzi Harlan debacle. The escape routing out of Millsport had held up.

They were ready to come and get us.

CHAPTeR THIRTY-FIVe

As we steered into the village harbor and I looked around me, the sense of déjà vu was so overpowering, I could almost smell burning again. I could almost hear the panicked screams.

I could almost see myself.

Get a grip, Tak. It didn't happen here.

It didn't. But it was the same loosely gathered array of hard-weather housing backing up from the waterfront, the same tiny core of main-street businesses along the shoreline, and the same working harbor complex at one end of the inlet. The same clutches of real-keel inshore trawlers and tenders moored along the dock, dwarfed by the gaunt, outrigged bulk of a big ocean-going rayhunter in their midst. There was even the same disused Mikuni research station at the far end of the inlet and, not far back behind, the crag-perched prayer house that would have replaced it as the village's focal point when the project funding fell through. In the main street, women went drably wrapped, as if for work with hazardous substances. Men did not.

"Let's get this over with," I muttered.

We moored the dinghy at the beach end where stained and worn plastic jetties leaned in the shallow water at neglected angles. Sierra Tres and the woman who called herself Nadia Makita sat in the stern while Brasil and I unloaded our luggage. Like anyone cruising the Millsport Archipelago, *Boubin Islander*'s owners had laid in appropriate female clothing in case they had to put in at any of the Northern arm communities, and both Tres and Makita were swathed to the eyes. We helped them out of the dinghy with what I hoped was equally appropriate solicitude, gathered up the sealwrap bags, and headed up the main street. It was a slow process—Sierra Tres had dosed herself to the eyes with combat painkillers before we left the yacht, but walking in the cast and flex-alloy boot still forced on her the gait of an old woman. We collected a few curious looks, but these I attributed to Brasil's blond hair and stature. I began to wish we'd been able to wrap him up, too.

No one spoke to us.

We found the village's only hotel, overlooking the main square, and booked rooms for a week, using two pristine ID datachips from among the selection we'd brought with us from Vchira. As women, Tres and Makita were our charges and didn't rate ID procedure of their own. A scarfed and robed receptionist nonetheless greeted them with a warmth that, when I explained that my aged aunt had suffered a hip injury, became solicitous enough to be a problem. I snapped down an offer of a visit from the local woman's doctor, and the receptionist retreated before the display of male authority. Lips tight, she busied herself with running our ID. From the window beside her desk, you could look down into the square and see the raised platform and fixing points for the community's punishment chair. I stared bleakly down at it for a moment, then locked myself back into the present. We handprinted for access on an antique scanner and went up to our rooms.

"You have something against these people?" Makita asked me, stripping off her head garb in the room. "You seem angry. Is this why you're pursuing a vendetta against their priests?"

"It's related."

"I see." She shook out her hair, pushed fingers up through it, and regarded the cloth-and-metal masking system in her other hand with a quizzical curiosity at odds with the blunt distaste Sylvie Oshima had shown when forced to wear a scarf in Tekitomura. "Why under three moons would anybody choose to wear something like this?"

I shrugged. "It's not the most stupid thing I've seen human beings commit themselves to."

She eyed me keenly. "Is that an oblique criticism?"

"No, it's not. If I've got something critical to say to you, you'll hear it loud and clear."

She matched my shrug. "Well, I look forward to that. But I suppose it's safe to assume you are not a Quellist."

I drew a hard breath.

"Assume what you want. I'm going out."

Down at the commercial end of the harbor, I wandered about until I found a bubblefab café serving cheap food and drink to the fishermen and wharf workers. I ordered a bowl of fish ramen, carried it to a window seat, and worked my way through it, watching crewmen move about on the decks and outrigger gantries of the rayhunter. After a while, a lean-looking middle-age local wandered across to my table with his tray.

"Mind if I sit here. It's kind of crowded."

I glanced around the 'fab space. They were busy, but there were other seats. I shrugged ungraciously.

"Suit yourself."

"Thanks." He sat, lifted the lid on his bento box, and started eating. For a while, we both fed in silence; then the inevitable happened. He caught my eye between mouthfuls. His weathered features creased in a grin.

"Not from around here then?"

I felt a light tautening across my nerves. "Makes you say that?"

"Ah, see." He grinned again. "If you were from around here, you wouldn't have to ask me that. You'd know me. I know everyone here in Kuraminato."

"Good for you."

"Not off that rayhunter, though, are you?"

I put down my chopsticks. Bleakly, I wondered if I would have to kill this man later. "What are you, a detective?"

"No!" He laughed delightedly. "What I am, I'm a qualified fluid dynamics specialist. Qualified, and unemployed. Well, underemployed, let's say. These days I mostly crew for that trawler out there, the green-painted one. But my folks put me through college back when the Mikuni thing was going on. Real time, they couldn't afford virtual. Seven years. They figured anything to do with the flow had to be a safe living, but of course by the time I qualified, it wasn't anymore."

"So why'd you stay?"

"Oh, this isn't my hometown. I'm from a place about a dozen klicks up the coast, Albamisaki."

The name dropped through me like a depth charge. I sat frozen, waiting for it to detonate. Wondering what I might do when it did.

I made my voice work. "Really?"

"Yeah, came here with a girl I met at college. Her family's here. I thought we'd start a keel-building business, you know make a living off trawler repair until I could maybe get some designs in to the Millsport yacht co-ops." He pulled a wry face. "Well. Started a family instead, you know. Now I'm too busy just staying one step ahead with food and clothes and schooling."

"What about your parents? See much of them?"

"No, they're dead." His voice caught on the last word. He looked away, mouth suddenly pressed tight.

I sat and watched him carefully.

"I'm sorry," I said finally.

He cleared his throat. Looked back at me.

"Nah. Not your fault, is it. You couldn't know. It's just it." He drew breath as if it hurt him. "It only happened a year or so ago. Out of the fucking sky. Some fucking maniac went crazy with a blaster. Killed dozens of people. All old people, in their fifties and older. It was sick. Didn't make any sense."

"Did they get the guy?"

"No." Another painfully hitched breath. "No, he's still out there somewhere. They say he's still killing, they can't seem to stop him. If I knew a way to find him, I'd fucking stop him."

I thought briefly of an alley I'd noticed between storage sheds at the far end of the harbor complex. I thought about giving him his chance.

"No money for resleeving, then? For your parents, I mean?"

He gave me a hard look. "You know we don't do that."

"Hey, you said it. I'm not from around here."

"Yeah, but." He hesitated. Glanced around the 'fab, then back to me. His voice lowered. "Look, I came up with the Revelation. I don't hold with every-thing the priests say, especially these days. But it's a faith, it's a way of life. Gives you something to hold on to, something to bring up your kids with."

"You got sons or daughters?"

"Two daughters, three sons." He sighed. "Yeah, I know. All that shit. You know, down past the point we've got a bathing beach. Most of the villages have them, I remember when I was a kid we used to spend the whole summer in the water, all of us together. Parents would come down after work some-times. Now, since things got serious, they've built a wall right into the sea there. If you go for the day, they've got officiators watching the whole time, and the women have to go in on the other side of the wall. So I can't even enjoy a swim with my own wife and daughters. It's fucking stupid, I know. Too extreme. But what are you going to do? We don't have the money to move to Millsport, and I wouldn't want my kids running around the streets down there anyway. I saw what it was like when I studied there. It's a city full of fucking degenerates. No heart left in it, just mindless filth. At least the peo-ple around here still believe in something more than gratifying every animal desire whenever they feel like it. You know what, I wouldn't want to live an-other life in another body if that was all I was going to do with it."

"Well, lucky you don't have the money for a resleeve then. It'd be a shame to get tempted, wouldn't it."

Shame to see your parents again, I didn't add.

"That's right," he said, apparently oblivious to the irony. "That's the point. Once you understand you've only got the one life, you try so much harder to do things right. You forget about all that material stuff, all that deca-dence. You worry about this life, not what you might be able to do in your next body. You focus on what matters. Family. Community. Friendship."

"And, of course, Observance." The mildness in my voice was oddly un-faked. We needed to keep a low profile for the next few hours, but it wasn't that. I reached curiously inside me and I found I'd lost my grip on the cus-tomary contempt I summoned into situations like this. I looked across the table at him, and all I felt was tired. He hadn't let Sarah and her daughter die for good; he maybe hadn't even been born when it happened. Maybe, given the same situation, he'd take the same bleating-sheep option his parents had, but right now I couldn't make that matter. I couldn't hate him enough to take him into that alley, tell him the truth about who I was, and give him his chance.

"That's right, Observance." His face lit up. "That's the key, that's what underwrites all the rest. See, science has betrayed us here, it's gotten out of hand, gotten so *we* don't control it anymore. It's made things too easy. Not aging naturally, not having to die and account for ourselves before our Maker, that's blinded us to the real values. We spend our whole lives scraping away trying to find the money for resleeving, and we waste the real time we have to live this life right. If people would only—"

"Hey, Mikulas." I glanced up. Another man about the same age as my new companion was striding toward us, behind the cheerful yell. "You finished bending that poor guy's ear or what? We've got hull to scrape, man."

"Yeah, just coming."

"Ignore him," said the newcomer with a wide grin. "Likes to think he knows everyone, and if your face doesn't fit the list, he has to damned well find out who you are. Bet he's done that already, right?"

I smiled. "Yeah, pretty much."

"Knew it. I'm Toyo." A thick, extended hand. "Welcome to Kuraminato. Maybe see you around town if you're staying long."

"Yeah, thanks. That'd be good."

"Meantime, we've got to go. Nice talking to you."

"Yeah," agreed Mikulas, getting to his feet. "Nice talking to you. You should think about what I was saying."

"Maybe I will." A final twist of caution made me stop him as he was turning away. "Tell me something. How come you knew I wasn't off the rayhunter?"

"Oh, that. Well, you were watching them like you were interested in what they were doing. No one watches their own ship in dock that closely. I was right, huh?"

"Yeah. Good call." The tiny increment of relief soaked through me. "Maybe you should be a detective after all. New line of work for you. Doing the right thing. Catching bad guys."

"Hey, it's a thought."

"Nah, he'd be way too nice to them once he'd caught them. Soft as shit, he is. Can't even discipline his own wife."

General laughter as they left. I joined in. Let it fade slowly out to a smile, and then nothing but the small relief inside.

I really wouldn't have to follow him and kill him.

I gave it half an hour, then wandered out of the 'fab and onto the wharf. There were still figures on the decks and superstructure of the rayhunter. I stood and watched for a few minutes, and finally a crew member came down the forward gangplank toward me. His face wasn't friendly.

"Something I can do for you?"

"Yeah," I told him. "*Sing the hymn of dreams gone down from Alabardos's sky.* I'm Kovacs. The others are at the hotel. Tell your skipper. We'll move as soon as it's dark."

CHAPTeR THIRTY-SIX

The rayhunter *Angelfire Flirt,* like most vessels of its type, cut a mean and rakish figure at sea. Part warship, part oversize racing skiff, combining a razor-sharp real-keel center of gravity and ludicrous quantities of grav lift in twin outrigger pods, it was built above all for reckless speed and piracy. Elephant rays and their smaller relatives are swift in the water, but more importantly their flesh tends to spoil if left untreated for any length of time. Freeze the bodies and you can sell the meat well enough, but get it back fast enough to the big fresh-catch auctions in centers of affluence like Millsport, and you can make a real killing. For that you need a fast boat. Shipyards all over Harlan's World understand this and build accordingly. Tacitly understood in the same yards is the fact that some of the best elephant ray stock lives and breeds in waters set aside for the exclusive use of the First Families. Poaching there is a serious offense, and if you're going to get away with it your fast boat also needs to present a low, hard-to-spot profile both visually and on radar.

If you're going to run from Harlan's World law enforcement, there are worse ways to do it than aboard a rayhunter.

On the second day out, secure in the knowledge we were so far from the Millsport Archipelago that no aircraft had the range to overfly us, I went up on deck and stood on the left-hand outrigger gantry, watching the ocean rip past underneath me. Spray on the wind, and the sense of events rushing toward me too fast to assimilate. The past and its cargo of dead, falling behind in our wake, taking with them options and solutions it was too late to try.

Envoys are supposed to be good at this shit.

Out of nowhere, I saw Virginia Vidaura's elfin new face. But this time there was no voice in my head, no instilled trainer confidence. I wasn't getting any more help from that particular ghost, it seemed.

"Do you mind if I join you?"

It was called out over the sound of wind and keel-slashed waves. I looked right, toward the center deck, and saw her bracing herself at the entrance to the gantry, dressed in coveralls and a jacket she'd borrowed from Sierra Tres.

The gripped pose made her look ill and unsteady on her feet. The silver-gray hair blew back from her face in the wind, but weighted by the heavier strands it stayed low, like a drenched flag. Her eyes were dark hollows in the pale of her face.

Another fucking ghost.

"Sure. Why not?"

She made her way out onto the gantry, showing more strength in motion than she had standing. By the time she reached me, there was an ironic twist to her lips, and her voice when she spoke was solid in the rushing slipstream. Brasil's medication had shrunk the wound on her cheek to a fading line.

"You don't mind talking to a fragment, then?"

Once, in a porn construct in Newpest, I'd gotten wrecked on *take* with a virtual whore in a—failed—attempt to break the system's desire fulfillment programming. I was very young then. Once, not so young, in the aftermath of the Adoracion campaign, I'd sat and talked drunken forbidden politics with a military AI. Once, on Earth, I'd gotten equally drunk with a copy of myself. Which, in the end, was probably what all those conversations had been about.

"Don't read anything into it," I told her. "I'll talk to pretty much anybody."

She hesitated. "I'm remembering a lot of detail."

I watched the sea. Said nothing.

"We fucked, didn't we?"

The ocean, pouring past beneath me. "Yeah. A couple of times."

"I remember—" Another hovering pause. She looked away from me. "You held me. While I was sleeping."

"Yes." I made an impatient gesture. "This is all recent, Nadia. Is that as far back as you can go?"

"It's. Difficult." She shivered. "There are patches, places I can't reach. It feels like locked doors. Like wings in my head."

Yes, that's the limit system on the personality casing, I felt like saying. *It's there to stop you going into psychosis.*

"Do you remember someone called Plex?" I asked her instead.

"Plex, yes. From Tekitomura."

"What do you remember about him?"

The look on her face sharpened suddenly, as if it were a mask someone had just pressed themselves up behind.

"That he was a cheap yakuza plug-in. Fake fucking aristo manners and a soul sold to gangsters."

"Very poetic. Actually, the aristo thing is real. His family were court-level merchants once upon a time. They went broke while you were having your revolutionary war up there."

"Am I supposed to feel bad about that?"

I shrugged. "Just putting you straight on the facts."

"Because a couple of days ago you were telling me I'm not Nadia Makita. Now suddenly you want to blame me for something she did three hundred years ago. You need to sort out what you believe, Kovacs."

I looked sideways at her. "You been talking to the others?"

"They told me your real name, if that's what you mean. Told me a little about why you're so angry with the Quellists. About this clown Joshua Kemp you went up against."

I turned away to the onrushing seascape again. "I didn't go up against Kemp. I was sent to help him. To build the glorious fucking revolution on a mudball called Sanction Four."

"Yes, they said."

"Yeah, that's what I was sent to do. Until, like every other fucking revolutionary I ever saw, Joshua Kemp turned into a sick-fuck demagogue as bad as the people he was trying to replace. And let's get something else straight here, before you hear any more neoQuellist rationalization. This clown Kemp, as you call him, committed every one of his atrocities including nuclear bombardment in the name of Quellcrist fucking Falconer."

"I see. So you also want to blame me for the actions of a psychopath who borrowed my name and a few of my epigrams centuries after I died. Does that seem fair to you?"

"Hey, you want to be Quell. Get used to it."

"You talk as if I had a choice."

I sighed. Looked down at my hands on the gantry rail. "You really have been talking to the others, haven't you? What did they sell you? Revolutionary Necessity? Subordination to the March of History? What? What's so fucking funny?"

The smile vanished, twisted away into a grimace. "Nothing. You've missed the point, Kovacs. Don't you see it doesn't matter if I am really who I think I am? What if I am just a fragment, a bad sketch of Quellcrist Falconer? What real difference does that make? As far down as I can reach, I think I'm Nadia Makita. What else is there for me to do except live her life?"

"Maybe what you should do is give Sylvie Oshima her body back."

"Yes, well, right now that's not possible," she snapped. "Is it?"

I stared back at her. "I don't know. Is it?"

"You think I'm holding her under down there? Don't you understand? It doesn't work like that." She grabbed a handful of the silvery hair and tugged at it. "I don't know how to run this shit. Oshima knows the systems far better than I do. She retreated down there when the Harlanites took us, left the body running on autonomic. *She's* the one who sent *me* back up when you came for us."

"Yeah? So what's she doing in the meantime, catching up on her beauty sleep? Tidying her dataware? Come *on*!"

"No. She is grieving."

That stopped me.

"Grieving what?"

"What do you think? The fact that every member of her team died in Drava."

"That's crabshit. She wasn't in contact with them when they died. The net was down."

"Yeah, that's right." The woman in front of me drew a deep breath. Her voice lowered and paced out to explanatory calm. "The net was down, she couldn't access it. She has told me this. But the receiving system stored every moment of their dying, and if she opens the wrong doors down there, it all comes screaming out. She's in shock from the exposure to it. She knows that, and as long as it lasts she's staying where it's safe."

"She told you that?"

We were eye-to-eye, a scant half a meter of seawind between us. "Yes, she told me that."

"I don't fucking believe you."

She kept my gaze for a long moment, then turned away. Shrugged. "What you believe is your own business, Kovacs. From what Brasil told me, you're just looking for easy targets to take your existential rage out on. That's always easier than a constructive attempt at change, isn't it?"

"Oh, *fuck off*! You're going to hand me *that* tired old shit? Constructive change? Is that what the Unsettlement was? Constructive? Is that what tearing New Hok apart was supposed to be?"

"No, it wasn't." For the first time, I saw pain in the face before me. Her voice had shifted from matter-of-fact to weary, and hearing it, then, I almost believed in her. Almost. She gripped the gantry rail tightly in both hands and shook her head. "None of it was supposed to be like that. But we had no choice. We had to force a political change, globally. Against massive repression. There was no way they'd give up the position they had without a fight. You think I'm happy it turned out that way?"

"Then," I said evenly. "You should have planned it better."

"Yeah? Well, you weren't there."

Silence.

I thought for a moment she'd leave then, seek more politically friendly company, but she didn't. The retort, the faint edge of contempt in it, fell away behind us and *Angelfire Flirt* flew on across the wrinkled surface of the sea at almost aircraft speeds. Carrying, it dawned on me drearily, the legend home to the faithful. The hero into history. In a few years they'd write songs about this vessel, about this voyage south.

But not about this conversation.

That at least dredged the edges of a smile to my mouth.

"Yeah, now you tell me what's so fucking funny," the woman at my side said sourly.

I shook my head. "Just wondering why you prefer talking to me to hanging with your neoQuellist worshipers."

"Maybe I like a challenge. Maybe I don't enjoy choral approval."

"Then you're not going to enjoy the next few days."

She didn't reply. But the second sentence still chimed in my head with something I'd had to read as a kid. It was from the campaign diaries, a scrawled poem at a time when Quellcrist Falconer had found little enough time for poetry, a piece whose tone had been rendered crassly lachrymose by a ham actor's voice and a school system that wanted to bury the Unsettlement as a regrettable and eminently avoidable mistake. Quell sees the error of her ways, too late to do anything but mourn:

They come to me with
>Progress Reports<
But all I see is change and bodies burned;
They come to me with
>Targets Achieved<
But all I see is blood and chances lost;
They come to me with
Choral fucking approval of every thing I do
But all I see is cost.

Much later, running with the Newpest gangs, I got hold of an illicit copy of the original, read into a mike by Quell herself a few days before the final assault on Millsport. In the dead weariness of that voice, I heard every tear the school edition had tried to jerk out of us with its cut-rate emotion, but underlying it all was something deeper and more powerful. There in a hastily blown bubblefab somewhere in the outer archipelago, surrounded by soldiers who would very likely suffer Real Death or worse beside her in the next few days, Quellcrist Falconer was not rejecting the cost. She was biting down on it like a broken tooth, grinding it into her flesh so that she wouldn't forget. So no one else would forget, either. So there would be no crabshit ballads or hymns written about the glorious revolution, whatever the outcome.

"So tell me about the Qualgrist Protocol," I said after a while. "This weapon you sold the yakuza."

She twitched. Didn't look at me. "You know about that, huh?"

"I got it out of Plex. But he wasn't too clear on the detail. You've activated something that's killing Harlan family members, right?"

She stared down at the water for a while.

"It's taking a lot for granted," she said slowly. "Thinking I should trust you with this."

"Why? Is it reversible?"

She grew very still.

"I don't think so." I had to strain to pick out her words in the wind. "I let them believe there was a termination code so they'd keep me alive trying to find out what it was. But I don't think it can be stopped."

"So what is it?"

Then she did look at me, and her voice firmed up.

"It's a genetic weapon," she said clearly. "In the Unsettlement, there were volunteer Black Brigade cadres who had their DNA modified to carry it. A gene-level hatred of Harlan family blood, pheromone-triggered. It was cutting-edge technology, out of the Drava research labs. No one was sure if it would work, but the Black Brigades wanted a beyond-the-grave strike if we failed at Millsport. Something that would come back, generation after generation, to haunt the Harlanites. The volunteers, the ones who survived, would pass it on to their children, and those children would pass it on to theirs."

"Nice."

"It was a war, Kovacs. You think the First Families don't pass on a ruling-class blueprint to their offspring? You think the same privilege and assumption of superiority isn't imprinted, generation after generation?"

"Yeah, maybe. But not at a genetic level."

"Do you know that for a fact? Do you know what goes on in the First Family clone banks? What technologies they've accessed and built into themselves? What provision there is for perpetuating the oligarchy?"

I thought of Mari Ado, and everything she'd rejected on her way to Vchira Beach. I never liked the woman much, but she deserved a better class analysis than this.

"Suppose you just tell me what this fucking thing does," I said flatly.

The woman in Oshima's sleeve shrugged. "I thought I had. Anyone carrying the modified genes has an inbuilt instinct for violence against Harlan family members. It's like the genetic fear of snakes you see in monkeys, like that built-in response the bottlebacks have to wingshadow on water. The pheromonal makeup that goes with Harlan blood triggers the urge. After that, it's just a matter of time and personality—in some cases the carrier will react there and then, go berserk and kill with anything at hand. Different personality types might wait and plan it more carefully. Some may even try to resist the urge, but it's like sex, like competition traits. The biology will win out in the end."

"Genetically encoded insurgency." I nodded to myself. A dreary kind of calm descending. "Well, I suppose it's a natural enough extension of the

Quellcrist principle. Blow away and hide, come back a lifetime later. If that doesn't work, co-opt your great-grandchildren and they can come back to fight for you several generations down the line. Very committed. How come the Black Brigades never used it?"

"I don't know." She tugged morosely at the lapel of the jacket Tres had loaned her. "Not many of us had the access codes. And it'd need a few generations before something like that would be worth triggering. Maybe no-body who knew survived that long. From what your friends have been telling me, most of the Brigade cadres were hunted down and exterminated after I . . . After it ended. Maybe no one was left."

I nodded again. "Or maybe no one who was left and knew could bring themselves to do it. It's a pretty fucking horrible idea, after all."

She shot me a weary look.

"It was a weapon, Kovacs. All weapons are horrible. You think target-ing the Harlan family by blood is any worse than the nuclear blast they used against us at Matsue? Forty-five thousand people vaporized because there were Quellist safe houses in there somewhere. You want to talk about pretty fucking horrible? In New Hokkaido I saw whole towns leveled by flat-trajectory shelling from government forces. Political suspects executed by the hundreds with a blaster bolt through the stack. Is that any less horrible? Is the Qualgrist Protocol any less discriminating than the systems of economic oppression that dictate you'll rot your feet in the belaweed farms or your lungs in the processing plants, scrabble for purchase on rotten rock, and fall to your death trying to harvest ledgefruit, all because you were born poor?"

"You're talking about conditions that haven't existed for three hundred years," I said mildly. "But that's not the point. It's not the Harlan family I feel bad about. It's the poor fucks whose Black Brigade ancestors decided their political commitment at a cellular level generations before they were even born. Call me old-fashioned, but I like to make my own decisions about whom I murder and why." I held back a moment, then drove the blade home anyway. "And so, from what I've read, did Quellcrist Falconer."

A kilometer of whitecapped blue whipped past beneath us. Barely audi-ble, the grav drive in the left-hand pod murmured to itself.

"What's that supposed to mean?" she whispered at last.

I shrugged. "You triggered this thing."

"It was a Quellist weapon." I thought I could hear an edge of desperation in her words. "It was all I had to work with. You think it's worse than a con-script army? Worse than the clone-enhanced combat sleeves the Protectorate decants its soldiers into so they'll kill without empathy or regret?"

"No. But I think as a concept it contradicts the words *I will not ask you to fight, to live, or to die for a cause you have not first understood and embraced of your own free will.*"

"I know that!" Now it was clearly audible, a jagged flaw line running through her voice. "Don't you think I know that? But what choice did I have? I was alone. Hallucinating half the time, dreaming Oshima's life and . . ." She shivered. "Other things. I was never sure when I'd next wake up and what I'd find around me when I did, not sure sometimes *if* I'd wake up again. I didn't know how much time I had, sometimes, I didn't even know if I was *real.* Do you have any idea what that's like?"

I shook my head. Envoy deployments had put me through a variety of nightmarish experiences, but you never doubt at any moment that it's absolutely real. The conditioning won't let you.

Her hands were tight on the gantry rail again, knuckles whitening. She was looking out at the ocean, but I don't think she could see it.

"Why go back to war with the Harlan family?" I asked her gently.

She jerked a glance at me. "You think this war ever stopped? You think just because we clawed some concessions from them three hundred years ago, these people ever stopped looking for ways to fuck us back into Settlement-years poverty again? This isn't an enemy that goes away."

"Yeah, *this enemy you cannot kill.* I read that speech back when I was a kid. The strange thing is, for someone who's only been awake for a few weeks on and off, you're remarkably well informed."

"That's not what it's like," she said, eyes on the hurrying sea again. "The first time I woke up for real, I'd already been dreaming Oshima for months. It was like being in a hospital bed, paralyzed, watching someone you think might be your doctor on a badly tuned monitor. I didn't understand who she was, only that she was important to me. Half the time, I knew what she knew. Sometimes, it felt like I was floating up inside her. Like I could put my mouth on hers and speak through her."

She wasn't, I realized, talking to me anymore; the words were just coming up out of her like lava, relieving a pressure inside whose form I could only make guesses at.

"The first time I woke up for real, I thought I'd die from the shock. I was dreaming *she* was dreaming, something about a guy she'd slept with when she was younger. I opened my eyes on a bed in some shithole Tek'to flop-house and I could move. I had a hangover, but I was alive. I knew where I was, the street and the name of the place, but I didn't know who I was. I went outside, I walked down to the waterfront in the sun and people were looking at me and I realized I was crying."

"What about the others? Orr and the rest of the team?"

She shook her head. "No, I'd left them somewhere at the other end of town. *She'*d left them, but I think I had something to do with it. I think she could feel me coming up and she went away to be alone while it happened. Or maybe I made her do it. I don't know."

A shudder ran through her.

"When I talked to her. Down there in the cells, when I told her that, she called it seepage. I asked her if she lets me through sometimes, and she wouldn't tell me. I. I know certain things unlock the bulkheads. Sex. Grief. Rage. But sometimes I just swim up for no reason and she gives me control." She paused, shook her head again. "Maybe we're just negotiating."

I nodded. "Which of you made the connection with Plex?"

"I don't know." She was looking at her hands, flexing and unflexing them like some mechanical system she hadn't gotten the hang of yet. "I don't remember. I think, yeah, it was her, I think she knew him already. Peripherally, part of the crimescape. Tek'to's a small pond, and the deComs are always at the fringes of legal. Cheap black-market deCom gear's a part of what Plex does up there. Don't think they ever did business, but she knew his face, knew what he was. I dug him out of her memory when I knew I was going to activate the Qualgrist system."

"Do you remember Tanaseda?"

She nodded, more controlled now. "Yeah. High-level yak patriarch. They brought him in behind Yukio, when Plex told them the preliminary codes checked out. Yukio didn't have enough seniority to swing what they needed."

"And what was that?"

A repeat of the searching gaze she'd fired at me when I first mentioned the weapon. I spread my arms in the whipping wind.

"Come on, Nadia. I brought you a revolutionary army. I climbed Rila Crags to get you out. That's got to buy something, right?"

Her gaze flinched away again. I waited.

"It's viral," she said finally. "High contagion, symptomless flu variant. Everyone catches it, everyone passes it on, but only the genetically modified react. It triggers a shift in the way their hormonal system responds to a match with Harlan pheromones. The carrier sleeves were buried in sealed storage at covert sites. In the event that they were to be triggered, an assigned group would dig up the storage facility, sleeve into one of the bodies, and go walkabout. The virus would do the rest."

Sleeve into one of the bodies. The words ticked in my head, like water trickling into a crack. The Envoy harbinger of understanding hovered just out of reach. Interlocking mechanisms of intuition spun tiny wheels in the buildup to knowledge.

"These sites. Where were they?"

She shrugged. "Mainly in New Hokkaido, but there were some on the north end of the Saffron Archipelago, too."

"And you took Tanaseda to?"

"Sanshin Point."

The mechanism locked solid, and doors opened. Recollection and understanding poured through the gap like morning light. Lazlo and Sylvie bickering as the *Guns for Guevara* slid into dock at Drava.

Bet you didn't hear about that dredger they found ripped apart yesterday off Sanshin Point—

I did hear that one. Report said they ran aground on the point. You're looking for conspiracy when all you've got is incompetence.

And my own conversation with Plex in Tokyo Crow the morning before. *So how come they needed your de- and regear tonight. Got to be more than one digital human shunting set in town, surely.*

Some kind of fuckup. They had their own gear, but it got contaminated. Seawater in the gel feeds.

Organized crime, huh.

"Something amusing you, Kovacs?"

I shook my head. "Micky Serendipity. Think I'm going to have to keep that name."

She gave me an odd look. I sighed.

"Doesn't matter. So what was Tanaseda's end of this? What does he get out of a weapon like that?"

Her mouth crimped in one corner. Her eyes seemed to glitter in the light reflecting off the waves. "A criminal is a criminal, no matter what their political class. In the end, Tanaseda's no different to some cut-rate wharf thug from Karlovy. And what have the yakuza always been good at? Blackmail. Influence. Leverage to get government concessions. Blind eyes turned to the right activities, shares in the right ongoing state enterprises. Collaboration at repression for a price. All very genteel."

"But you suckered them."

She nodded bleakly. "I showed them the site, gave them the codes. Told them the virus transmitted sexually, so they'd think they had control. It does that, too, in fact, and Plex was too sloppy with the biocodes to dig any deeper than he did. I knew I could trust him to screw up to that extent."

I felt another faint smile flicker across my own face. "Yeah, he has a talent for that. Must be the aristo lineage."

"Must be."

"And with the grip the yakuza have on the sex industry in Millsport, you called it just right." The intrinsic joy of the scam sank into me like a shiver rush—there was a smooth, machined rightness to it worthy of Envoy planning. "You gave them a threat to hold over the Harlanites that they already had the perfect delivery system for."

"Yes, so it seems." Her voice was blurring again as she dropped away into her memories. "They were going to sleeve some yak soldier or other in one of the Sanshin bodies and take it to Millsport to demonstrate what they had. I don't know if he ever got that far."

"Oh, I'm sure he did. The yakuza are pretty meticulous about their leverage schemes. Man, I'd have given a lot to see Tanaseda's face when he showed up at Rila with that package and the Harlan gene specialists told him what he really had on his hands. I'm surprised Aiura didn't have him executed on the spot. Shows remarkable restraint."

"Or remarkable focus. Killing him wouldn't have helped, would it? By the time they walked that sleeve onto the ferry in Tek'to, it would have already infected enough neutral carriers to make it unstoppable. By the time it got off the other end in Millsport." She shrugged. "You've got an invisible pandemic on your hands."

"Yeah."

Maybe she heard something in my voice. She looked around at me again, and her face was miserable with contained anger.

"All right, Kovacs. You fucking tell me. What would you have done?"

I looked back at her, saw the pain and terror there. I looked away, suddenly ashamed.

"I don't know," I said quietly. "You're right, I wasn't there."

And as if, finally, I'd given her something she needed, she did leave me then.

Left me standing alone on the gantry, watching the ocean come at me with pitiless speed.

CHAPTER THIRTY-SEVEN

In the Gulf of Kossuth, the weather systems had calmed while we were away. After battering the eastern seaboard for well over a week, the big storm had clipped the northern end of Vchira around the ear and then wandered off into the southern Nurimono Ocean, where everyone assumed it would eventually die in the chilly waters toward the pole. In the calm that followed, there was a sudden explosion of marine traffic as everybody tried to catch up. *Angelfire Flirt* descended into the middle of it all like a street dealer chased into a crowded mall. She hooked about, curled in alongside the crawling bulk of the urbraft *Pictures of the Floating World,* and moored demurely at the cheap end of the starboard dock just as the sun started to smear out across the western horizon.

Soseki Koi met us under the cranes.

I spotted his sunset-barred silhouette from the rayhunter's rail and raised an arm in greeting. He didn't return the wave. When Brasil and I got down to the dock and close up, I saw how he'd changed. There was a bright-eyed intensity to his lined face now, a gleam that might have been tears or a tempered fury, it was hard to tell which.

"Tres?" he asked us quietly.

Brasil jerked a thumb back at the rayhunter. "Still mending. We left her with. With Her."

"Right. Good."

The monosyllables fell into a general quiet. The seawind fussed about us, tugging at hair, stinging my nasal cavities with its salts. At my side, I felt rather than saw Brasil's face tighten, like a man about to probe a wound.

"We heard the newscasts, Soseki. Who made it back from your end?"

Koi shook his head. "Not many. Vidaura. Aoto. Sobieski."

"Mari Ado?"

He closed his eyes. "I'm sorry, Jack."

The rayhunter's skipper came down the gangway with a couple of ship's officers I knew well enough to nod at in corridors. Koi seemed to know them all—they traded gruff arm's-length grippings of shoulders and a skein of rapid Stripjap before the skipper grunted and moved off toward the harbor-master's tower with the others in tow. Koi turned back to face us.

"They'll stay docked long enough to file for grav system repairs. There's another raychaser in on the port side, they're old friends of his. They'll buy some fresh kill to haul into Newpest tomorrow, just for appearances. Mean-time, we're out of here at dawn with one of Segesvar's contraband skimmers. It's the closest thing to a disappearing act we could arrange."

I avoided looking at Brasil's face. My gaze ranged instead over the cityscape superstructure of the urbraft. Mostly, I was awash with a selfish re-lief that Virginia Vidaura figured in the list of survivors, but some small Envoy part of me noted the evening flow of crowds, the possible vantage points for observers or sniper fire.

"Can we trust these people?"

Koi nodded. He seemed relieved to bury himself in details. "The very large majority, yes. *Pictures* is Drava-built; most of the onboard shareholders are descendants of the original cooperative owners. The culture's broadly Quellist-inclined, which means a tendency to look out for each other but mind their own business if no one's needing help."

"Yeah? Sounds a little utopian to me. What about casual crew?"

Koi's look sharpened to a stare. "Casual crew and newcomers know what they're signing on for. *Pictures* has a reputation, like the rest of the rafts. The ones who don't like it don't stay. The culture filters down."

Brasil cleared his throat. "How many of them know what's going on?"

"Know that we're here? About a dozen. Know *why* we're here? Two, both ex–Black Brigade." Koi looked up at the rayhunter, searchingly. "They'll both want to be there for Ascertainment. We've got a safe house set up in the stern lowers where we can do it."

"Koi." I slotted myself into his field of vision. "We need to talk first. There are a couple of things you should know."

He regarded me for a long moment, lined face unreadable. But there was a hunger in his eyes that I knew I wasn't going to get past.

"It'll have to wait," he told me. "Our primary concern here is to confirm Her identity. I'd appreciate it if none of you call me by name until that's done."

"Ascertain," I said sharply. The audible capitalization of *her* was starting to piss me off. "You mean *Ascertain,* right, Koi?"

His gaze skipped off my shoulder and back to the rayhunter's side.

"Yes, that's what I mean," he said.

A lot has been made of Quellism's underclass roots, particularly over the cen-turies since its principal architect died and passed conveniently beyond the realm of political debate. The fact that Quellcrist Falconer chose to build a power base among the poorest of Harlan's World's labor force has led to a curious conviction among a lot of neoQuellists that the intention during the Unsettlement was to create a leadership drawn exclusively from this base. That Nadia Makita was herself the product of a relatively privileged middle-class background goes carefully unremarked, and since she never rose to a position of political governance, the central issue of *who's going to run things after all this blows over* never had to be faced. But the intrinsic contradiction at the heart of modern Quellist thought remains, and in neoQuellist company it's not considered polite to draw attention to it.

So I didn't remark on the fact that the safe house in the stern lowers of *Pictures of the Floating World* clearly didn't belong to the elegantly spoken ex–Black Brigade man and woman who were waiting in it for us. Stern lowers is the cheapest, harshest neighborhood on any urbraft or seafactory, and no one who has a choice about it chooses to live there. I could feel the vibration from *Floating World*'s drives intensifying as we took a companionway down from the more desirable crew residences at superstructure levels over the stern, and by the time we got inside the apartment it was a constant background grind. Utilitarian furniture, scuffed and scraped walls, and a minimum of decoration made it clear that whoever did quarter here didn't spend much time at home.

"Forgive the surroundings," said the woman urbanely as she let us into the apartment. "It will only be for the night. And our proximity to the drives makes surveillance a near impossibility."

Her partner ushered us to chairs set around a cheap plastic table laid with refreshments. Tea in a heated pot, assorted sushi. Very formal. He talked as he got us seated.

"Yeah, we're also less than a hundred meters from the nearest hull maintenance hatch, which is where you'll all be collected from tomorrow morning. They'll drive the skimmer right in under the load-bearing girders between keels six and seven. You can climb straight down." He gestured at Sierra Tres. "Even injured, you shouldn't have too much trouble."

There was a rehearsed competence to it all, but as he talked, his gaze kept creeping toward the woman in Sylvie Oshima's body, then skidding abruptly away. Koi had been doing much the same thing since we brought her off the *Angelfire Flirt*. Only the female Brigade member seemed to have her eyes and hopes under real control.

"So," she said smoothly. "I'm Sto Delia. This is Kiyoshi Tan. Shall we begin?"

Ascertainment.

In today's society, it's as common a ritual as parental acknowledgment parties to celebrate a birth, or reweddings to cement newly resleeved couples in their old relationship. Part stylized ceremony, part maudlin *what about that time when* session, Ascertainment varies in its form and formality from world to world and culture to culture. But on every planet I've ever been, it exists as a deeply respected underlying aspect of social relations. Outside expensive high-tech psychographic procedures, it's the only way we have to prove to our friends and family that, regardless of what flesh we may be wearing, we are who we say we are. Ascertainment is the core social function that defines ongoing identity in the modern age, as vital to us now as primitive functions like signature and fingerprint databasing were to our premillennial ancestors.

And that's where an ordinary citizen is concerned.

For semi-mythical heroic figures, back—perhaps—from the dead, it's a hundred times more meaningful again. Soseki Koi was trembling visibly as he took his seat. His colleagues were both wearing younger sleeves and they showed it less, but if you looked with Envoy eyes the same tension was there in unconfident, overdone gestures, laughter too readily coughed out, the occasional tremor in a voice as it started up again in a dried throat. These men and this woman, who had once belonged to the most feared counterinsurgency force in planetary history, had suddenly been granted a glimpse of hope among the ashes of their past. They faced the woman who claimed to be Nadia Makita with everything that had ever mattered to them hanging clearly visible in the balance behind their eyes.

"It is an honor," Koi began, and then stopped to clear his throat. "It is an honor to speak of these things . . ."

Across the table, the woman in Sylvie Oshima's sleeve looked back at him steadily as he spoke. She answered one of his oblique questions with crisp assent, ignored another. The other two Brigade members weighed in, and she turned slightly in her seat toward each of them, offered an antique gesture of inclusion each time. I felt myself receding to the status of spectator as the initial round of pleasantries peeled away and the Ascertainment gathered momentum. The conversation picked up, moved rapidly from matters of the last few days across a long and somber political retrospective, and then into talk of the Unsettlement and the years that preceded it. The language shifted just as rapidly, from contemporary Amanglic into an unfamiliar old-time Japanese dialect with occasional gusts of Stripjap. I glanced across at Brasil and shrugged as subject matter and syntax both accelerated away from us.

It went on for hours. The laboring motors of the urbraft made dim thunder in the walls around us. *Pictures of the Floating World* plowed on her way. We sat and listened.

". . . makes you think. A fall from any of those ledges and you're offal splattered across >>*the outgoing tide?*<<. No recovery scheme, no resleeve policy, not even family death benefits. It's a >>*rage?*<< that starts in your bones and . . ."

". . . remember when you first realized that was the case?"

". . . one of my father's articles on colonial theory . . ."

". . . playing >>*?????*<< on the streets of Danchi. We all did. I remember one time the >>*street police?*<< tried to . . ."

". . . reaction?"

"Family are like that—or at least my family were always >>*?????ing*<< in a slictopus >>*plague?*<< . . ."

". . . even when you were young, right?"

"I wrote that stuff when I was barely out of my teens. Can't believe they printed it. Can't believe there were people who >>*paid good money for/ devoted seriousness to?*<< so much >>*?????*<<"

"But—"

"Is it?" A shrug. "Didn't feel that way when I >>*looked back/ reconsidered?*<< from the >>*blood on my hands?*<< basis in the >>*?????*<<."

From time to time Brasil or I would rise and make fresh tea in the kitchen. The Black Brigade veterans barely noticed. They were locked on, lost in the wash and detail of a past made suddenly real again just across the table.

". . . recall whose decison that was?"

"Obviously not—you guys didn't have a >>*chain of command/respect?*<< worth a fucking . . ."

Sudden, explosive laughter around the table. But you could see the tear sheen on their eyes.

". . . and it was getting too cold for a stealth campaign up there. Infrared would have shown us up like . . ."

"Yes, it was almost . . ."

". . . Millsport . . ."

". . . better to lie to them that we had a good chance? I don't think so."

"Would have been a hundred fucking kilometers before . . ."

". . . and supplies."

". . . Odisej, as far as I remember. He would have run a >>*?????*<< stand-off right up to the . . ."

". . . about Alabardos?"

Long pause.

"It's not clear, it feels >>*?????*<<. I remember something about a helicopter? We were going to the helicopter?"

She was trembling slightly. Not for the first time, they sheared away from the subject matter like ripwings from a rifleshot.

". . . something about . . ."

". . . essentially a *reactive* theory . . ."

"No, probably not. If I examined other >>*models?*<< . . ."

"But isn't it axiomatic that >>*the struggle?*<< for control of >>*?????*<< would cause . . ."

"Is it? Who says that?"

"Well." An embarrassed hesitation, glances exchanged. "*You* did. At least, you >>*argued?/admitted?*<< that . . ."

"That's *crabshit!* I never said convulsive policy shift was the >>*key?*<< to a better . . ."

"But Spaventa claims you advocated—"

"*Spaventa?* That fucking fraud. Is he still breathing?"

". . . and your writings on demodynamics show . . ."

"Look, I'm not a fucking ideologue, all right. We were faced with >>*a bottleback in the surf?*<< and we had to . . ."

"So you're saying >>*?????*<< isn't the solution to >>*?????*<< and reducing >>*poverty/ignorance?*<< would mean . . ."

"Of course it would. I never claimed anything different. What happened to Spaventa, anyway?"

"Umm, well—he teaches at Millsport University these—"

"*Does* he? The little fuck."

"Ahem. Perhaps we could discuss a >>*version?/view?*<< of those events that pivots less on >>*?????*<< than >>*recoil?/slingshot?*<< theories of . . ."

"Very well, as far as it goes. But give me a single >>*binding example?*<< to support those claims."

"Ahhhhhh . . ."

"Exactly. Demodynamics isn't >>*blood in the water?*<<, it's an attempt to . . ."

"But—"

And on and on, until, in a clatter of cheap furniture, Koi was suddenly on his feet.

"That's enough," he said gruffly.

Glances flickered back and forth among the rest of us. Koi came around the side of the table, and his old face was taut with emotion as he looked down at the woman sitting there. She looked back up at him without expression.

He offered her his hands.

"I have," he swallowed, "concealed my identity from you until now, for the sake of. Our cause. Our common cause. But I am Soseki Koi, ninth Black Brigade command, Saffron theater."

The mask on Sylvie Oshima's face melted away. Something like a grin took its place.

"Koi? *Shaky* Koi?"

He nodded. His lips were clamped together.

She took his outstretched hands, and he lifted her to her feet beside him.

He faced the table and looked at each of us in turn. You could see the tears in his eyes, hear them in his voice when he spoke.

"This is Quellcrist Falconer," he said tightly. "In my mind there is no longer room for doubt."

Then he turned and flung his arms around her. Sudden tear ribbons glistened on his cheeks. His voice was hoarse.

"We waited so long for you to come again," he wept. "We waited *so long*."

PART FIVE

THIS IS THE STORM TO COME

No one heard Ebisu returning until it was too late and then what had been said could not be unsaid, deeds done could not be undone, and all present must answer for themselves . . .

LEGENDS OF THE SEAGOD
Traditional

Unpredictable wind vectors and velocity . . . expect heavy weather . . .

KOSSUTH STORM MANAGEMENT NET
Extreme Conditions Alert

CHAPTeR THIRTY-eIGHT

I woke to Kossuth-grade heat and low-angle sunlight, a mild hangover and the serrated sound of snarling. Out in the pens, someone was feeding the swamp panthers.

I glanced at my watch. It was very early.

I lay for a while in sheets tangled to my waist, listening to the animals and the harsh male whoops of the feeding crew on the gantries above them. Segesvar had taken me on a tour of the place two years previously, and I still remembered the awful power with which the panthers flailed up to catch chunks of fishsteak the size of a man's torso. The feeding crew had yelled then as well, but the more you listened the more you realized that it was bravado to shore up courage against an instinctive terror. With the exception of one or two hardened swamp game hunters, Segesvar recruited pretty exclusively from the wharf fronts and slums of Newpest, where the chances of any of the kids having seen a real panther were about even with them ever having been to Millsport.

A couple of centuries back, it was different—the Expanse was smaller then, not yet cleared all the way south to make way for the belaweed monocropping combines. In places, the swamp's poisonously beautiful trees and float-foliage crept almost up to the city limits, and the inland harbor had to be redredged on a twice-yearly basis. It wasn't unheard of for panthers to turn up basking on the loading ramps in the summer heat, the chameleon skin of mane and mantle shimmering to mimic the sun's glare. Peculiar variations in the breeding cycles of their prey out on the Expanse sometimes drove them in to roam the streets closest to the swamplands, where they ripped open sealed refuse canisters with effortless savagery and occasionally, at night, took the homeless or the unwary drunk. Just as they would in their swamp environment, they sprawled prone in back alleys, body and limbs concealed beneath a mane and mantle that would camouflage to black in the darkness. To their victims, they would resemble nothing so much as a pool of deep shadow until it was too late, and they left nothing behind for the police but broad splashes of blood and the echo of screams in the night. By the time

I was ten, I'd seen my share of the creatures in the flesh, had even myself once run screaming up a wharf-shed ladder with my friends when a sleepy panther rolled over at our step-freeze-step approach, flapped one corner of its sloppy, tendriled mane at us, and treated us to a gape-beaked yawn.

The terror, like much that you experience in childhood, was transient. Swamp panthers were scary, they were lethally dangerous if you encountered them under the wrong circumstances, but in the end they were a part of our world.

The snarling outside seemed to reach a crescendo.

To Segesvar's crew, swamp panthers were the bad guys of a hundred cheap hologames and maybe a school biology class they hadn't cut, made suddenly real. Monsters from another planet.

This one.

And maybe, inside some of the young thugs who worked for Segesvar until the lower-echelon *haiduci* lifestyle inevitably took them down, maybe these monsters awoke the shivery existential understanding of exactly how far from home we all really were.

Then again, maybe not.

Someone shifted in the bed beside me and groaned.

"Don't those fucking things ever shut up?"

Recollection arrived at the same moment as the shock, and they canceled each other out. I rolled my head sideways and saw Virginia Vidaura's elfin features squashed up under a pillow she'd crushed to her own head. Her eyes were still closed.

"Feeding time," I said, mouth sticky as I spoke.

"Yeah, well, I can't make up my mind what's pissing me off more. Them or the fucking idiots feeding them." She opened her eyes. "Good morning."

"And to you." Memory of her the night before, hunched forward astride me. Beneath the sheets, I was hardening with the thought. "I didn't think this was ever going to happen in the real world."

She looked back at me for a moment, then rolled onto her back and stared up at the ceiling.

"No. Neither did I."

The events of the previous day floated sluggishly to the surface. My first sight of Vidaura, poised in the snout of Segesvar's low-profile skimmer as it held station on the roiled waters beneath the urbraft's massive load-bearing supports. The dawn light from the opening at the stern had not reached this deep into the space between hulls, and she was little more than a gun-handed, spike-haired silhouette as I came down through the maintenance hatch. There was a reassuring operational toughness to the figure she cut, but when torchglow fell briefly across her face as we boarded, I saw something else there that I couldn't define. She met my eyes briefly, then looked away.

Nobody spoke much during the skimmer ride across the early-morning waters of the Gulf. There was a solid wind out of the west and a cold gunmetal light across everything that didn't encourage conversation. As we closed on the coast, Segesvar's contraband driver called us all inside and a second hard-faced young *haiduci* swung himself up into the skimmer's gun turret. We sat in the cramped cabin in silence, listening to the engines change pitch as we slowed on approach to the beach. Vidaura took the seat beside Brasil, and down in the gloom where their thighs touched I saw them clasp hands. I closed my eyes and leaned back in the comfortless metal-and-webbing seat, running the route behind my eyes for something to do.

Off the ocean, straight up some shabby, effluent-poisoned beach somewhere at the north end of Vchira, out of sight, but barely, of the Newpest suburb skyline whose shanties supplied the poison by piped outflow. No one stupid enough to come here to swim or fish, no one to see the blunt-nosed, heavy-skirted skimmer come brazening through. Across the oil-stained mud-flats behind, through choked and dying float-foliage and then out onto the Expanse proper. Zigzag through the endless belaweed soup at standard traffic speeds to break the trail, three stops at different baling stations, each with *haiduci*-connected employees, and a change of heading after each one. Isolation and journey's end at Segesvar's home from home, the panther farm.

It took most of the day. I stood on the dock at the last baling station stop and watched the sun go down behind clouds across the Expanse like wrappings of bloodstained gauze. Down on the deck of the skimmer, Brasil and Vidaura talked with quiet intensity. Sierra Tres was still inside, trading *haiduci* gossip with the vehicle's two-man crew last time I checked. Koi was busy elsewhere, making calls. The woman in Oshima's sleeve wandered around a bale of drying weed as tall as both of us and stopped beside me, following my gaze to the horizon.

"Nice sky."

I grunted.

"It's one of the things I remember about Kossuth. Evening skies on the Expanse. Back when I worked the weed harvests in sixty-nine and seventy-one." She slid down into a sitting position against the bale and looked at her hands as if examining them for traces of the labor she was describing. "Of course, they kept us working till dark most days, but when the light tipped over like this, you knew you were nearly done."

I said nothing. She glanced up at me.

"Still not convinced, huh?"

"I don't need to be convinced," I told her. "What I have to say doesn't count for much around here. You did all the convincing you needed to back there aboard *Floating World.*"

"Do you really think I would deceive these people deliberately?"

I thought about it for a moment. "No. I don't think that's it. But that doesn't make you who you think you are."

"Then how do you explain what has happened?"

"Like I said, I don't have to. Call it the march of history if you like. Koi has what he wants."

"And you? You haven't gotten what you want out of this?"

I looked bleakly out at the wounded sky. "I don't need anything I don't already have."

"Really? You're very easily satisfied then." She gestured around her. "So no hope for a better tomorrow than this? I can't interest you in an equitable restructuring of social systems?"

"You mean smash the oligarchy and the symbology they use to achieve dominance, hand power back to the people? That kind of thing?"

"That kind of thing." It wasn't clear if she was mimicking me or agreeing. "Would you mind sitting down, it's making my neck ache talking to you like this."

I hesitated. It seemed unnecessarily churlish to refuse. I joined her on the surface of the dock, put my back to the weed bale, and settled, waiting. But then she was abruptly quiet. We sat shoulder-to-shoulder for a while. It felt oddly companionable.

"You know," she said finally, "when I was a kid, my father got this assignment on biotech nanobes. You know, the tissue-repair systems, the immune boosters? It was kind of a review article, looking at the nanotech since landfall and where it was going next. I remember he showed me some footage of the state-of-the-art stuff being put into a baby at birth. And I was horrified."

A distant smile.

"I can still remember looking at this baby and asking him how it was going to tell all those machines what to do. He tried to explain it to me, told me the baby didn't have to tell them anything, they already knew what to do. They just had to be powered up."

I nodded. "Nice analogy. I'm not—"

"Just. Give me a moment, huh? Imagine." She lifted her hands as if framing something. "Imagine if some motherfucker deliberately didn't enable most of those nanobes. Or enabled only the ones that dealt with brain and stomach functions, say. All the rest were just dead biotech, or worse still semi-dead, just sitting there consuming nutrients and not doing anything. Or programmed to do the wrong things. To destroy tissue instead of repairing it. To let in the wrong proteins, not to balance out the chemicals. Pretty soon that baby grows up and starts to have health problems. All the dangerous local organisms, the ones that belong here, that Earth's never seen, they storm aboard and that kid is going to go down with every disease its ancestors on Earth never evolved defenses for. So what happens then?"

I grimaced. "You bury it?"

"Well, before that. The doctors will come in and they'll advise surgery, maybe replacement organs or limbs—"

"Nadia, you really have been gone a long time. Outside battlefields and elective surgery, that kind of thing just doesn't—"

"Kovacs, it's an analogy, all right? The point is, you end up with a body that works badly, that needs constant conscious control from above and outside, and why? Not because of some intrinsic failing but because the nanotech just isn't being used. And that's us. This society—every society in the Protectorate—is a body where ninety-five percent of the nanotech has been switched off. People don't do what they're supposed to."

"Which is what?"

"*Run* things, Kovacs. Take control. Look after social systems. Keep the streets safe, administer public health and education. Build stuff. Create wealth and organize data, and ensure they both flow where they're needed. People will do all of this, the capacity is there, but it's like the nanobes. They have to be switched on first, they have to be made aware. And in the end that's all a Quellist society is—an aware populace. Demodynamic nanotech in action."

"Right—so the big bad oligarchs have switched off the nanotech."

She smiled again. "Not quite. The oligarchs aren't an outside factor; they're like a closed subroutine that's gotten out of hand. A cancer, if you want to switch analogies. They're programmed to feed off the rest of the body no matter what the cost to the system in general, and to kill off anything that competes. That's why you have to take them down first."

"Yeah, I think I've heard this speech. Smash the ruling class and then everything'll be fine, right?"

"No, but it's a necessary first step." Her animation was building visibly, she was talking faster. The setting sun painted her face with stained-glass light. "Every previous revolutionary movement in human history has made the same basic mistake. They've all seen power as a static apparatus, as a structure. And it's not. It's a dynamic, a flow system with two possible tendencies. Power either accumulates, or it diffuses through the system. In most societies, it's in accumulative mode, and most revolutionary movements are only really interested in reconstituting the accumulation in a new location. A *genuine* revolution has to *reverse* the flow. And *no one* ever does that, because they're all too fucking scared of losing their conning tower moment in the historical process. If you tear down one agglutinative power dynamic and put another one in its place, you've changed nothing. You're not going to solve any of that society's problems, they'll just reemerge at a new angle. You've got to set up the nanotech that will deal with the problems on its own. You've got to build the structures that allow for *diffusion* of power, not regrouping.

Accountability, demodynamic access, systems of constituted rights, education in the use of political infrastructure—"

"Whoa." I held up my hand. Most of this I'd heard from the Little Blue Bugs more than once in the past. I wasn't going to sit through it again, nice sky or no nice sky. "Nadia, this has been tried before, and you know it. And from what I remember of my precolonial history, the empowered people you place so much faith in handed power right back to their oppressors, *cheerfully,* in return for not much more than holoporn and cheap fuel. Maybe there's a lesson in that for all of us. Maybe people would *rather* slobber over gossip and fleshshots of Josefina Hikari and Ryu Bartok than worry about who's running the planet. Did you ever consider that? Maybe they're happier that way."

Scorn flickered on her face. "Yeah, maybe. Or just *maybe* that period you're talking about was misrepresented. Maybe premillennial constitutional democracy wasn't the failure the people who write the history books would like us to believe. Maybe they just murdered it, took it away from us, and lied to our children about it."

I shrugged. "Maybe they did. But if that's the case, they've been remarkably good at pulling the same trick time and again since."

"Of *course* they have." It was almost a shout. "Wouldn't *you* be? If the retention of your privileges, your rank, your life of fucking leisure and status all depended on pulling that trick, wouldn't you have it down? Wouldn't you teach it to your children as soon as they could walk and talk?"

"But meanwhile the rest of us aren't capable of teaching a functioning countertrick to our descendants? Come on! We've got to have the Unsettlement every couple of hundred years to remind us?"

She closed her eyes and leaned her head back against the weed bale. She seemed to be talking to the sky. "I don't know. Yes, maybe we do. It's an uneven struggle. It's always far easier to murder and tear down than it is to build and educate. Easier to let power accumulate than diffuse."

"Yeah. Or maybe it's just that you and your Quellist friends don't want to see the limits of our evolved social biology." I could hear my voice starting to rise. I tried to hold it down, and the words came out gritted. "That's right. Bow down and fucking worship, do what the man with the beard or the suit tells you. Like I said, maybe people are *happy* like that. Maybe the ones like you and me are just some fucking irritant, some swamp bug swarm that won't let them sleep."

"So this is where you get off, is it?" She opened her eyes at the sky and glanced slantwise at me without lowering her head. "Give up, let scum like the First Families have it all, let the rest of humanity slip into a coma. Cancel the fight."

"No, I suspect it's already too late for that, Nadia." I found there was none of the grim satisfaction in saying it that I'd expected. All I felt was tired. "Men like Koi are hard to stop once they're set in motion. I've seen a few. And for better or worse, we *are* in motion now. You're going to get your new Unsettlement, I think. Whatever I say or do."

The stare still pinned me. "And you think it's all a waste of time."

I sighed. "I think I've seen it go wrong too many times on too many different worlds to believe this is going to be very different. You're going to get a lot of people slaughtered for at best not very much in the way of local concessions. At worst, you'll bring the Envoys down on Harlan's World, and believe me, that you do not want in your worst nightmares."

"Yes, Brasil told me. You used to be one of these stormtroopers."

"That's right."

We watched the sun dying for a while.

"You know," she said. "I don't pretend to know anything about what they did to you in this Envoy Corps, but I have met men like you before. Self-hatred works for you, because you can channel it out into rage at whatever targets for destruction come to hand. But it's a static model, Kovacs. It's a sculpture of despair."

"Is that right?"

"Yes. At base, you don't really want things to get any better because then you'd be out of targets. And if the external focus for your hate ran out, you'd have to face up to what's inside you."

I snorted. "And what is that?"

"Exactly? I don't know. But I can hazard a few guesses. An abusive parent. A life on the streets. A loss of some sort early in childhood. Betrayal of some kind. And sooner or later, Kovacs, you need to face the fact that you can never go back and do anything about that. Life has to be lived forward."

"Yeah," I said tonelessly. "In the service of the glorious Quellist revolution no doubt."

She shrugged. "That'd have to be your choice."

"I've already made my choices."

"And yet you came to prise me free of the Harlan family. You mobilized Koi and the others."

"I came for Sylvie Oshima."

She raised an eyebrow. "Is that so?"

"Yes, that is so."

There was another pause. Aboard the skimmer, Brasil disappeared into the cabin. I only caught the tail end of the motion, but it seemed abrupt and impatient. Tracking back, I saw Virginia Vidaura staring up at me.

"Then," said the woman who thought she was Nadia Makita, "it would seem I'm wasting my time with you."

"Yeah. I would think you are."

If it made her angry, she didn't show it. She just shrugged again, got up and gave me a curious smile, then wandered away along the sunset-drenched dock, peering occasionally over the edge into the soupy water. Later, I saw her talking to Koi, but she left me alone for the duration of the ride to Segesvar's place.

As a final destination, the farm was not impressive. It broke the surface of the Expanse resembling nothing so much as a collection of waterlogged helium blimps sunk among the ruins of yet another U-shaped baling station. In fact, before the advent of the combines, the place had seen service as an independent belaweed dock, but unlike the other stations we'd stopped at, it hadn't sold to the incoming corporate players and was derelict within a generation. Radul Segesvar had inherited the bare bones as part payment of a gambling debt and must not have been too happy when he saw what he'd won. But he put the space to work, refitted the decaying station in deliberately antique style, and extended the whole installation across what was previously the commercial-capacity harbor, using state-of-the-art wet-bunker technology filched via a military contractor in Newpest who owed him favors. Now the complex boasted a small, exclusive brothel, elegant casino facilities, and—the blood-rich heart of it all, the thing that gave customers a *frisson* they couldn't duplicate in more urban surroundings—the fight pits.

There was a party of sorts when we arrived. *Haiduci* pride themselves on their hospitality, and Segesvar was no exception. He'd cleared a space on one of the covered docks at the end of the old station and laid on food and drink, muted music, fragrant real-wood torches, and huge fans to shift the swampy air. Handsome men and women drawn from either the brothel downstairs or one of Segesvar's Newpest holoporn studios circulated with heavily laden trays and limited clothing. Their sweat was artfully beaded in patterns across their exposed flesh and scented with tampered pheromones, their pupils blasted open on some euphoric or other, their availability subtly hinted at. It was perhaps not ideal for a gathering of neoQuell activists, but that may have been deliberate on Segesvar's part. He'd never had much patience with politics.

In any event, the mood on the dock was somber, dissolving only very gradually into a chemically fueled abandon that never got much beyond slurred and maudlin. The realities of the kidnap raid on Mitzi Harlan's entourage and the resulting firefight in the back streets of New Kanagawa were too bloody and brutal to allow anything else. The fallen were too evident by their absence, the stories of their deaths too grim.

Mari Ado, cooked in half by a Sunjet blast, scrabbling with the last of her strength to get a sidearm to her throat and pull the trigger.

Daniel, shredded by shard blaster fire.

The girl he'd been with at the beach, Andrea, smeared flat when the commandos blew a door off its hinges to get in.

Others I didn't know or remember, dying in other ways so that Koi could get clear with his hostage.

"Did you kill her?" I asked him, in a quiet moment before he started drinking heavily. We'd heard news items on the voyage south aboard the rayhunter—*cowardly slaughter of an innocent woman by Quellist murderers*—but then Mitzi Harlan could have been blown apart by an incautious commando and the shoutlines would still have read the same.

He stared away across the dock. "Of course I did. It's what I said I'd do. They knew that."

"Real Death?"

He nodded. "For what it's worth. They'll have her resleeved from a remote storage copy by now. I doubt she's lost much more than forty-eight hours of her life."

"And the ones we lost?"

His gaze still hadn't reeled in from the other side of the baling dock. It was as if he could see Ado and the others standing there in the flickering torchlight, grim specters at the feast that no amount of alcohol or *take* would erase.

"Ado vaporized her own stack before she died. I saw her do it. The rest." He seemed to shiver slightly, but that might have been the evening breeze across the Expanse, or maybe just a shrug. "I don't know. Probably they got them."

Neither of us needed to follow that to its logical conclusion. If Aiura had recovered the stacks, their owners were now locked in virtual interrogation. Tortured, to death if necessary, then reloaded into the same construct so the process could begin again. Repeated until they gave up what they knew, maybe still repeated after that in vengeance for what they had dared to do to a member of the First Families.

I swallowed the rest of my drink, and the bite of it released a shudder across my shoulders and down my spine. I raised the empty glass toward Koi.

"Well, here's hoping it was worth it."

"Yes."

I didn't speak to him again after that. The general drift of the party took him out of reach and I got pinned with Segesvar in a corner. He had a pale, cosmetically beautiful woman on each arm, identically draped in shimmering amber muslin like paired, life-size ventriloquist dolls. He seemed in an expansive mood.

"Enjoying the party?"

"Not yet." I lifted a *take* cookie from a passing waiter's tray and bit into it. "I'll get there."

He smiled faintly. "You're a hard man to please, Tak. Want to go and gloat over your friends in the pens instead?"

"Not right now."

Involuntarily, I looked out across the bubble-choked lagoon to where the swamp panther fight pits were housed. I knew the way well enough, and I supposed no one would stop me going in, but at that moment I couldn't make it matter enough. Besides, I'd discovered sometime last year that once the priests were dead and resleeved in panther flesh, appreciation of their suffering receded to a cold and unsatisfyingly distant intellectual understanding. It was impossible to look at the huge, wet-maned creatures as they tore and bit at each other in the fight pits, and still see the men I had brought back from the dead to punish. Maybe, if the psychosurgeons were right, they weren't there in any real sense anymore. Maybe the core of human consciousness was long gone, eaten out to a black and screaming insanity within a matter of days.

One stifling, heat-hazed afternoon, I stood in the steeply sloping seats above one of the pits, surrounded by a screaming, stamping crowd on its feet, and I felt retribution turning soap-like in my hands, dissolving and slipping away as I gripped at it.

I stopped going there after that. I just handed Segesvar the cortical stacks I stole and let him get on with it.

Now he raised an eyebrow at me in the light from the torches.

"Okay, then. Can I interest you in some team sports, maybe? Like to come down to the grav gym with Ilja and Mayumi here?"

I glanced across the two confected women and collected a dutiful smile from each one. Neither seemed chemically assisted, but still it felt bizarrely as if Segesvar were working them through holes in the small of each smooth-skinned back, as if the hands he had resting on each perfectly curved hip were plastic and fake.

"Thanks, Rad. I'm getting kind of private in my old age. You go on and have a good time without me."

He shrugged. "Certainly can't expect to have a good time *with* you anymore. Can't remember doing that anytime in the last fifty years, in fact. You really are turning northern, Tak."

"Like I said—"

"Yeah, yeah, I know. You half are already. Thing is, Tak, when you were younger you tried not to let it show so much." He moved his right hand up to cup the outer swell of an ample breast. The owner giggled and nibbled at his ear. "Come on, girls. Let's leave Kovacs-san to his brooding."

I watched them rejoin the main throng of the party, Segesvar steering. The pheromone-rich air stitched a vague regret into my guts and groin. I finished the *take* cookie, barely tasting it.

"Well, *you* look like you're having fun."

"Envoy camouflage," I said reflexively. "We're trained to blend in."

"Yeah? Doesn't sound like your trainer was up to much."

I turned and there was a crooked grin across Virginia Vidaura's face as she stood there with a tumbler in each hand. I glanced around for signs of Brasil, couldn't see him in the vicinity.

"Is one of those for me?"

"If you like."

I took the tumbler and sipped at it. Millsport single malt, probably one of the pricier Western Rim distilleries. Segesvar wasn't a man to let his prejudices get in the way of taste. I swallowed some more and looked for Vidaura's eyes. She was staring away across the Expanse.

"I'm sorry about Ado," I said.

She reeled in her gaze and raised a finger to her lips.

"Not now, Tak."

Not now, not later. We barely talked as we slipped away from the party, down into the corridors of the wet-bunker complex. Envoy functionality came online like an emergency autopilot, a coding of glances and understanding that stung the underside of my eyes with its intensity.

This, I remembered suddenly. *This is what it was like. This is what we lived like, this is what we lived* for.

And, in my room, as we found and fastened on each other's bodies beneath hastily disarrayed clothing, sensing what we each wanted from the other with Envoy clarity, I wondered for the first time in better than a century of objective lifetime why I had ever walked away.

●●●

It wasn't a feeling that lasted in the comedown panther snarl of morning. Nostalgia leached out with the fade of the *take* and the groggy edge of a hangover whose mildness I wasn't sure I deserved. In its wake, I was left with not much more than a smug possessiveness as I looked at Vidaura's tanned body sprawled in the white sheets and a vague sense of misgiving that I couldn't pin to any single source.

Vidaura was still staring a hole in the ceiling.

"You know," she said finally. "I never really liked Mari. She was always trying so hard to prove something to the rest of us. Like it just wasn't enough just to *be* one of the Bugs."

"Maybe for her it wasn't."

I thought about Koi's description of Mari Ado's death, and I wondered if at the end she'd pulled the trigger to escape interrogation or simply a return to the family ties she'd spent her whole life trying to sever. I wondered if her aristo blood would have been enough to save her from Aiura's wrath and what she would have had to do to walk away from the interrogation constructs in a fresh sleeve, what she would have had to buy back into to get out intact. I wondered if in the last few moments of dimming vision, she looked at the aristo blood from her own wounds and hated it just enough.

"Jack's talking some shit about heroic sacrifice."

"Oh I see."

She swiveled her gaze down to my face. "That's not why I'm here."

I said nothing. She went back to looking at the ceiling.

"Oh shit, yes it is."

We listened to the snarling and the shouts outside. Vidaura sighed and sat up. She jammed the heels of both hands against her eyes and shook her head.

"Do you ever wonder," she asked me. "If we're really human anymore?"

"As Envoys?" I shrugged. "I try not to buy into the standard tremble-tremble-the-posthumans-are-coming crabshit, if that's what you mean. Why?"

"I don't know." She shook her head irritably. "Yeah, it's fucking stupid, I know. But sometimes I talk to Jack and the others, and it's like they're a different fucking species to me. The things they believe. The *level* of belief they can bring to bear, with next to nothing to justify it."

"Ah. So you're not convinced, either."

"I don't." Vidaura threw up one hand in exasperation. She twisted about in the bed to face me. "How *can* she be, right?"

"Well, I'm glad I'm not the only one caught in that particular net. Welcome to the rational-thinking minority."

"Koi says she checks out. All the way down."

"Yeah. Koi wants this so badly he'd believe a fucking ripwing in a head-scarf was Quellcrist Falconer. I was there for the Ascertainment, and they went easy on anything it looked like she was uncomfortable answering. Did anybody tell you about this genetic weapon she's triggered?"

She looked away. "Yeah, I heard. Pretty extreme."

"Pretty much in complete defiance of every fucking thing Quellcrist Falconer ever believed, I think you mean."

"We none of us get to stay clean, Tak." A thin smile. "You know that. Under the circumstances—"

"Virginia, you're about to prove yourself a fully paid-up, lost-in-belief member of the old-style human race if you're not careful. And you needn't think I'll still talk to you if you cross over to that shit."

The smile powered up, became a laugh of sorts. She touched her upper lip with her tongue and glanced slantwise at me. It gave me an odd, electric sensation to watch.

"All right," she said. "Let's be inhumanly rational about this. But Jack says she remembers the assault on Millsport. Going for the copter at Alabardos."

"Yeah, which kind of sinks the copy-stored-in-the-heat-of-battle-outside-Drava theory, don't you think? Since both those events postdate any presence she might have had in New Hok."

Vidaura spread her hands. "It also sinks the idea she's some kind of personality casing for a datamine. Same logic applies."

"Well. Yeah."

"So where does that leave us?"

"You mean where does it leave Brasil and the Vchira gang?" I asked nastily. "Easy. It leaves them scratching around desperately for some other crabshit theory that'll hold enough water to let them go on believing. Which, for fully paid-up neoQuellists, is a pretty fucking sad state of affairs."

"No, I mean *us*." Her eyes drilled me with the pronoun. "Where does it leave us?"

I covered for the tiny jolt in my stomach by rubbing at my eyes in an echo of the gesture she'd used earlier.

"I've got an idea of sorts," I started. "Maybe an explanation."

The door chimed.

Vidaura raised an eyebrow. "Yeah, and a guest list, looks like."

I shot another glance at my watch and shook my head. Outside the window, the snarling of the panthers seemed to have settled down to a low grumble and an occasional cracking sound as they ripped the cartilage in their food apart. I pulled on trousers, picked up the Rapsodia from the bedside table on an impulse, and went through to open up.

The door flexed aside and gave me a view onto the quiet, dimly lit corridor outside. The woman wearing Sylvie Oshima's sleeve stood there, fully dressed, arms folded.

"I've got a proposition for you," she said.

CHAPTeR THIRTY-NINe

It was still early morning when we hit Vchira. The *haiduci* pilot Sierra Tres had gotten out of bed—her bed, in fact—was young and cocky, and the skimmer we lifted was the same contraband runner we'd come in on. No longer bound by the need to appear a standard, forgettable item of Expanse traffic and no doubt wanting to impress Tres as much as he impressed himself, the pilot opened his vessel up to the limit and we tore across to a mooring point called Sunshine Fun Jetties in less than two hours. Tres sat in the cockpit with him and made encouraging noises, while Vidaura and the woman who called herself Quell stayed below together. I sat alone on the forward deck for most of the trip, nursing my hangover in the cool flow of air from the slipstream.

As befit the name, Sunshine Fun Jetties was a place frequented mostly by tour-bus skimmers from Newpest and the odd rich kid's garishly finned Expansemobile. At this time of day, there was a lot of mooring space to choose from. More importantly, it put us less than fifteen minutes' walk from the offices of Dzurinda Tudjman Sklep at a pace that allowed for Sierra Tres and her limp. They were just opening when we arrived at the door.

"I'm not sure," said the underling whose job it evidently was to get up earlier than any of the partners and man the offices until they arrived. "I'm not sure that—"

"Yeah, well, I am," Sierra Tres told him impatiently.

She'd belted on an ankle-length skirt to cover her rapidly healing leg, and there was no way of knowing from her voice and stance that she was still damaged. We'd left the pilot back at Sunshine Fun Jetties with the skimmer, but Tres didn't need him. She played the *haiduci* arrogance card to perfection. The underling flinched.

"Look," he began.

"No, *you* look. We were in here less than two weeks ago. You know that. Now you want to call Tudjman, you can. But I doubt he'll thank you for getting him out of bed at this time of the morning just to confirm we can have access to the same stuff we used last time we were here."

In the end it took the call to Tudjman and some shouting to clear it, but we got what we wanted. They powered up the virtual systems and showed us to the couches. Sierra Tres and Virginia Vidaura stood by while the woman in Oshima's sleeve attached the electrodes to herself. She held up the hypnophones to me.

"What's this meant to be?"

"High-powered modern technology." I put on a grin I didn't much feel. On top of my hangover, anticipation was building a queasy, not-quite-real sensation that I could have done without. "Only been around a couple of centuries. They activate like this. Makes the ride in easier."

When Oshima was settled, I lay down in the couch next to her and fitted myself with phones and 'trodes. I glanced up at Tres.

"So we're all clear on what you do to pull me out if it starts to come apart?"

She nodded, expressionless. I still wasn't entirely sure why she'd agreed to help us without running it by Koi or Brasil first. It seemed a little early in the scheme of things to be taking unqualified orders from the ghost of Quellcrist Falconer.

"All right then. Let's get in the pipe."

The sonocodes had a harder time than usual dragging me under, but finally I felt the couch chamber blur out; the walls of the off-the-rack hotel suite scribbled into painfully sharp focus in its place. Memory of Vidaura in the suite down the corridor pricked at me unexpectedly.

Get a grip, Tak.

At least the hangover was gone.

The construct had decanted me on my feet, over by a window that looked out onto unlikely vistas of rolling green pasture. At the other side of the room by the door, a sketch of a long-haired woman similarly upright sharpened into Oshima's sleeve.

We stood looking at each other for a moment, then I nodded. Something about it must have rung false, because she frowned.

"You're sure about this? You don't have to go through with it, you know."

"Yes, I do."

"I don't expect—"

"Nadia, it's okay. I'm trained to arrive on alien planets in new sleeves and start slaughtering the natives immediately. How hard can this be?"

She shrugged. "All right."

"All right then."

She crossed the room toward me and halted less than a meter away. Her head tipped so that the mane of silver-gray slipped slowly forward and covered her face. The central cord skidded sideways down one side of her skull and hung like a stunted scorpion tail, cobwebbed with finer filaments. She looked in that moment like every archetype of haunting my ancestors had brought with them across the gulfs from Earth. She looked like a ghost.

Her posture locked up.

I drew a deep breath and reached out. My fingers parted the hair across her face like curtains.

Behind, there was nothing. No features, no structure, only a gap of dark warmth that seemed to expand out toward me like negative torchglow. I leaned closer and the darkness opened at her throat, peeling gently back along the vertical axis of her frozen figure. It split her to the crotch and then beyond, opening the same rent in the air between her legs. I could feel balance tipping away from me in tiny increments as it happened. The floor of the hotel room followed, then the room itself, shriveling like a used wipe in a beach bonfire. The warmth came up around me, smelling faintly of static. Below was unrelieved black. The iron tresses in my left hand plaited about and thickened to a restless snake-like cable. I hung from it over the void.

Don't open your eyes, don't open your left hand, don't move at all.

I blinked, possibly in defiance, and stowed the recollection.

Grimaced and let go.

● ● ●

If it was falling, it didn't feel like it.

There was no rush of air, and nothing lit to judge movement by. Even my own body was invisible. The cable seemed to have vanished as soon as I took my hand off it. I could have been floating motionless in a grav chamber no bigger than the spread of my arms, except that all around me, somehow, my senses signaled the existence of vast, unused space. It was like being a spin-drizzle bug, drifting about in the air of one of the emptied warehouses on Belacotton Kohei Nine.

I cleared my throat.

Lightning flickered jaggedly above me, and stayed there. Reflexively, I reached up; my fingers brushed delicate filaments. Perspective slammed into place—the light wasn't fire in a sky unfathomably high up, it was a tiny branching of twigs a handful of centimeters over my head. I took it gently in my hand and turned it over. The light smudged from it where my fingers pressed. I let go and it hung there, at chest height in front of me.

"Sylvie? You there?"

That got me a surface under my feet and a bedroom steeped in late-afternoon light. From the fittings, the place looked as if it might have belonged to a child of about ten. There were holos on the walls of Micky Nozawa, Rili Tsuchiya, and a host of other pinups I didn't recognize, a desk and datacoil under a window, and a narrow bed. A mirrorwood panel on one wall made the limited space seem larger; a walk-in cupboard opposite opened onto a badly hung mass of clothing that included court-style dressing-up gowns. There was a Renouncer creed tacked to the back of the door, but it was coming away at one corner.

I peered out of the window and saw a classic temperate-latitude small town sloping down to a harbor and the outlying arm of a bay. Tinge of belaweed in the water, crescent slices of Hotei and Daikoku thinly visible in a hard blue sky. Could have been anywhere. Boats and human figures moved about in dispersal patterns close to real.

I moved to the door with the poorly attached creed and tried the handle. It wasn't locked, but when I tried to step out into the corridor beyond, a teenage boy appeared in front of me and shoved me back.

"Mum says you have to stay in your room," he said obnoxiously. "Mum *says*."

The door slammed in my face.

I stared at it for a long moment, then opened it again.

"Mum says you have—"

The punch broke his nose and knocked him back into the opposite wall. I held my fist loosely curled, waiting to see if he'd come back at me, but he just slid down the wall, gaping and bleeding. His eyes glazed over with shock. I stepped carefully over his body and set off along the corridor.

Less than ten paces, and I felt her behind me.

It was minute and fundamental, a rustling in the texture of the construct, the scratch of crepe-edged shadows reaching along the walls at my back. I stopped dead and waited. Something curled like fingers over my head and around my neck.

"Hello, Sylvie."

Without apparent transition, I was at the bar in Tokyo Crow. She leaned next to me, nursing a glass of whiskey I didn't remember her having when we were there for real. There was a similar drink in front of me. The clientele boiled around us at superamped speed, colors washed out to gray, no more substantial than the smoke from pipes at the tables or the distorted reflections in the mirrorwood under our drinks. There was noise, but it blurred and murmured at the lower edge of hearing, like the hum of high-capacity machine systems on standby behind the walls.

"Ever since you came into my life, Micky Serendipity," Sylvie Oshima said evenly, "it seems to have fallen apart."

"It didn't start here, Sylvie."

She looked sideways at me. "Oh, I know. I said *seems*. But a pattern is a pattern, perceived or actual. My friends are all dead, Really Dead, and now I find it was you that killed them."

"Not this me."

"No, so I understand." She lifted the whiskey to her lips. "Somehow that doesn't make me feel better."

She knocked back the drink. Shivered as it went down.

Change the subject.

"So what she hears up there filters down here?"

"To an extent." The glass went down on the bar again. Systems magic refilled it, slowly, like something soaking through the fabric of the construct. First the reflected image, from top to bottom, and then the actual glass from base to brim. Sylvie watched it somberly. "But I'm still finding out how much we're tangled through the sensory systems."

"How long have you been carrying her, Sylvie?"

"I don't know. The last year? Iyamon Canyon, maybe? That's the first time I whited out. First time I woke up not knowing where I was, got this feeling like my whole existence was a room and someone'd been in, moving the furniture around without asking."

"Is she real?"

A harsh laugh. "You're asking me that? In here?"

"All right, do you know where she came from? How you picked her up?"

"She escaped." Oshima turned to look at me again. Shrugged. "That's what she kept saying, *I escaped.* Of course, I knew that anyway. She got out of one of the holding cells just like you did."

Involuntarily, I glanced over my shoulder, looking for the corridor from the bedroom. No sign of it across the smoky crowding of the bar, no sign it had ever existed.

"That was a holding cell?"

"Yes. Woven complexity response, the command software builds them automatically around anything that gets into the capacity vault using language."

"It wasn't very hard to get out of."

"Well, what language were you using?"

"Uh—Amanglic."

"Yeah—in machine terms that's not very complex. In fact, it's infantile in its simplicity. You got the jail your levels of complexity merited."

"But did you really expect me to stay put?"

"Not me, Micky. The software. This stuff is autonomic."

"All right, did the autonomic software expect me to stay put?"

"If you were a nine-year-old girl with a teenage brother," she said, rather bitterly, "you *would* have stayed put, believe me. The systems aren't designed to understand human behavior, they just recognize and evaluate language. Everything else is machine logic. They draw on my subconscious for some of the fabric, the tone of things, they alert me directly if there's an excessively violent breakout, but none of it has any real human context. DeCom doesn't handle humans."

"So if this Nadia, or whoever she is. If she came in speaking, say, old-time Japanese, the system would have put her in a box like mine?"

"Yes. Japanese is quite a bit more complex than Amanglic, but in machine terms the difference is close to irrelevant."

"And she'd have gotten out easily, like me. Without alerting you, if she was subtle about it."

"More subtle than you, yes. Out of the containment system anyway. Finding her way through the sensory interfaces and the baffles into my head would have been a lot harder. But given time, and if she was determined enough . . ."

"Oh, she's determined enough. You know who she says she is, don't you?"

A brief nod. "She told me. When we were both hiding down here from the Harlan interrogators. But I think I knew already. I was starting to dream about her."

"Do you think she is Nadia Makita? Really?"

Sylvie picked up her drink and sipped it. "It's hard to see how she could be."

"But you're still going to let her run things on deck for the foreseeable future? Without knowing who or what she is?"

Another shrug. "I tend to judge on performance. She seems to be managing."

"For fuck's sake, Sylvie, she could be a *virus* for all you know."

"Yeah, well, from what I read in school, so was the original Quellcrist Falconer. Isn't that what they called Quellism back in the Unsettlement? *A viral poison in the body of society?*"

"I'm not talking political metaphors here, Sylvie."

"Neither am I." She tipped back her glass, emptied it again, and set it down. "Look, Micky, I'm not an activist and I'm not a soldier. I'm strictly a datarat. Mimints and code, that's me. Put me in New Hok with a crew and there's no one to touch me. But that's not where we are right now, and you and I both know I'm not going back to Drava anytime soon. So given the current climate, I think I'm going to bow out to this Nadia. Because whoever or whatever she really is, she stands a far better chance of navigating the waters than I do."

She sat staring into her glass as it filled. I shook my head.

"This isn't you, Sylvie."

"Yes it is." Suddenly her tone was savage. "My friends are fucking dead or worse, Micky. I've got a whole planet of cops plus the Millsport yakuza looking to make me the same way. So don't tell me this isn't me. You don't know what happens to me under those circumstances because you haven't fucking seen it before, all right. Even I don't fucking know what happens to me under those circumstances."

"Yeah, and instead of finding out, you're going to stay in here like some fucking Renouncer dream of a good little girl your parents once had. Going to sit in here playing with your plug-in world, and hope someone on the outside takes care of business for you."

She said nothing, just raised the newly filled glass in my direction. I felt a sudden, constricting wave of shame pulse through me.

"I'm sorry."

"You should be. Would you like to live through what they did to Orr and the others? Because I've got it all on tap down here."

"Sylvie, you can't—"

"They died hard, Micky. Peeled back, all of them. At the end, Kiyoka was screaming like a baby for me to come and get her. You want to plug into that, carry that around with you for a while like I have to?"

I shivered, and it seemed to transmit itself to the whole construct. A small, cold thrum hung in the air around us.

"No."

We sat for a long time in silence after that. Tokyo Crow's clientele came and went around us, wraith-like.

After a while, she gestured vaguely upward.

"You know, the aspirants believe this is the only true existence. That everything outside is an illusion, a shadow play created by the ancestor gods to cradle us until we can build our own tailored reality and Upload into it. That's comforting, isn't it?"

"If you let it be."

"You called her a virus," she said pensively. "As a virus, she was very successful in here. She infiltrated my systems as if she was designed for it. Maybe she'll be as successful out there in the shadow play."

I closed my eyes. Pressed a hand to my face.

"Something wrong, Micky?"

"Please tell me you're being metaphorical now. I don't think I can cope with another hardwired believer at the moment."

"Hey, you don't like the conversation, you can fuck off out of here, can't you?"

The sudden edge on her voice kicked me back to New Hok and the seemingly endless deCom bickering. An unlooked-for smile tugged at my mouth with the memory. I opened my eyes and looked at her again. Placed both hands flat on the bar, sighed, and let the smile come up.

"I came to get you out, Sylvie."

"I know." She put her hand over one of mine. "But I'm fine here."

"I told Las I'd look after you."

"So look after her. That keeps me safe, too."

I hesitated, trying to frame it right. "I think she might be some kind of weapon, Sylvie."

"So? Aren't we all?"

I looked around at the bar and its gray speed ghosts. The low murmur of amalgamated sound. "Is this really all you want?"

"Right now, Micky, it's all I can cope with."

My drink stood untouched on the bar in front of me. I stood up. Picked it up.

"Then I'd better be getting back."

"Sure. I'll see you out."

The whiskey went down burning, cheap and rough, not what I'd been expecting.

She walked with me out onto the wharf. Here the dawn was already up, cold and pale gray, and there were no people, speeded pastiche or otherwise, anywhere in the unforgiving light. The sweeper station stood closed and deserted; the mooring points and the ocean beyond were both empty of traffic. There was a naked, stripped look to everything, and the Andrassy Sea came in and slapped at the pilings with sullen force. Looking north, you could sense Drava crouched below the horizon in similar, abandoned quiet.

We stood under the crane where we'd first met, and it hit me then with palpable force that this was the last time I'd see her.

"One question?"

She was staring out to sea. "Sure."

"Your preferred active agent up there says she recognized someone in the holding constructs. Grigori Ishii. That chime with you at all?"

A slight frown. "It sounds familiar, yes. I couldn't tell you from where, though. But I can't see how a DH personality would have gotten down here."

"Well, quite."

"Did she say it *was* this Grigori?"

"No. She said there was something down here that sounded like him. But when you faked taking down the scorpion gun, afterward when you were coming out of it in Drava, you said it knew you, something *knew* you. Like an old friend."

Sylvie shrugged. Most of her was still watching the northern horizon. "Then it could be something the mimints have evolved. A virus to trigger recognition routines in a human brain, makes you think you're seeing or hearing something you already know. Each individual it hits would assign an appropriate fragment to fit."

"That doesn't sound very likely. It's not like the mimints have had much human interaction to work off recently. Mecsek's only been in place what, three years?"

"Four." A faint smile. "Micky, the mimints were *designed* to kill humans.

That's what they were *for* originally, three hundred years ago. There's no telling if some piece of viral weaponry built along those lines has survived this long, maybe even sharpened itself a bit."

"Have you ever come across anything like that?"

"No. But that doesn't mean it's not out there."

"Or in here."

"Or in here," she agreed shortly. She wanted me gone.

"Or it could just be another personality-casing bomb."

"It could be."

"Yeah." I looked around one more time. "Well. How do I get out of here?"

"The crane." For a moment she came back to me. Her eyes switched in from the north and met mine. She nodded upward to where a steel ladder disappeared into the laced girderwork of the machine. "You just keep climbing up."

Great.

"You take care of yourself, Sylvie."

"I will."

She kissed me briefly on the mouth. I nodded, clapped her on the shoulder, and backed away a couple of steps. Then I turned for the ladder, laid hands on the cold metal of the rungs, and started climbing.

It seemed solid enough. It beat ripwing-infested sea cliff and the underside of Martian architecture, anyway.

I was a couple of dozen meters into the girders when her voice floated up to join me.

"Hey, Micky."

I peered downward. She was standing inside the crane's base, staring up at me. Her hands were cupped around her mouth. I unfastened one hand carefully and waved.

"Yeah?"

"Just remembered. Grigori Ishii. We learned about him in school."

"Learned what about him in school?"

She spread her arms.

"No idea, sorry. Who remembers shit like that?"

"Right."

"Why don't you ask *her*?"

Good question. Envoy caution seemed like the obvious answer. But stubborn mistrust came in a close second. A refusal. I wasn't buying the glorious return of Quell at the cut rates Koi and the Bugs seemed prepared to accept.

"Maybe I will."

"Well." An arm lifted in farewell. "Scan up, Micky. Keep climbing, don't look down."

"Yeah," I yelled it down. "You, too, Sylvie."

I climbed. The sweeper station shrank to the proportions of a child's toy. The sea took on the texture of hammered gray metal welded to a tilting horizon. Sylvie was a dot facing north, then too small to make out at all. Maybe she wasn't there anymore. The girders around me lost any resemblance to the crane they had once been. The cold dawn light darkened to a flickery silver that danced in patterns on the metal that seemed maddeningly familiar. I didn't seem to be tiring at all.

I stopped looking down.

CHAPTeR FORTY

"So?" she asked finally.

I stared out of the window at Vchira Beach and the glitter of sunlight on the waves beyond. Both beach and water were beginning to fill up with tiny human figures intent on enjoying the weather. The offices of Dzurinda Tudjman Sklep were eminently environment-proofed, but you could almost feel the building heat, almost hear the rising chatter and squall of tourism that accompanied it. I hadn't spoken to anyone since I came out of the construct.

"So you were right." I spared a sideways glance for the woman wearing Sylvie Oshima's body, then went back to looking at the sea. The hangover was back in place, worse it seemed. "She's not coming out. She's fallen back on childhood Renouncer crabshit to cope with the grief, and she's staying in there."

"Thank you."

"Yeah." I left the window alone, turned back to Tres and Vidaura. "We're finished here."

Nobody talked on the way back to the skimmer. We shouldered our way through brightly garbed crowds, working against the flow in silence. A lot of the time, our faces opened passage for us—you could see it in the expressions of people stepping hurriedly aside. But in the sunny warmth and enthusiasm to get to the water, not everyone was running even a surface level of attention. Sierra Tres scowled as her leg took clouts from garishly colored plastic beach implements, badly carried, but either drugs or focus kept her mouth clamped shut over any pain she suffered. No one wanted to create a memorable scene. Only once she turned to look at a particularly clumsy offender, and he practically ran away.

Hey guys. The thought ran sourly through me. *Don't you recognize your political heroes when you see them? We're coming to liberate you all.*

At Sunshine Fun Jetties, the pilot was lying on the sloping flank of the skimmer, soaking up the sun like everybody else. He sat up blinking as we came aboard.

"That was quick. You want to get back already?"

Sierra Tres glanced ostentatiously around at the bright plastic every-where in view.

"You see any reason to hang about?"

"Hey, it's not so bad. I get down here with the kids sometimes, they have a great time. 'S a good mix of people, not so fucking snooty like they are at the south end. Oh yeah, you, man. Rad's pal."

I looked up, surprised. "Yeah."

"Someone asking after you."

I paused on my way across the skimmer's flank. Cool drenching of Envoy preparedness, inked with a tiny, joyous splinter of anticipation. The hangover receded to the back of my awareness.

"What did they want?"

"Didn't say. Didn't even have your name. Described you pretty solidly, though. It was a priest, one of those northern weirdos. You know, beard and shit."

I nodded, anticipation fanning into warm, shivery little flames.

"So what'd you tell him?"

"Told him to fuck off. My woman's from Saffron, she's told me some of the shit they're getting into up there. I'd string those fuckers to a weed rack with livewire soon as look at them."

"This guy young or old?"

"Oh, young. Carried himself, too, know what I mean?"

Virginia Vidaura's words drifted back through my mind. *Sanctified solo assassins against targeted infidels.*

Well, not like you weren't looking for this.

Vidaura came up to me and put a hand on my arm.

"Tak—"

"You go back with the others now," I said quietly. "I'll take care of this."

"Tak, we need you to—"

I smiled at her. "Nice try. But you guys don't need me for anything any-more. And I just discharged my last remaining obligation back there in vir-tual. I've got nothing better to do anymore."

She looked steadily back at me.

"It'll be okay," I told her. "Rip out his throat and be right back."

She shook her head.

"Is this really all you want?"

The words chimed, real-time echo of my own question to Sylvie in the depths of the virtuality. I made an impatient gesture.

"What else is there? Fight for the glorious Quellist cause? Yeah, right. Fight for the stability and prosperity of the Protectorate? I've done both, Vir-ginia, *you've* done both, and you know the truth as well as I do. It's all so much shit on a prick. Innocent bystanders blown apart, blood and screaming and all for some final greasy political compromise. Other people's causes, Virginia, I'm fucking sick of it."

"So what instead? This? More pointless slaughter?"

I shrugged. "Pointless slaughter is what I know how to do. It's what I'm good at. You *made* me good at it, Virginia."

That took her like a slap across the face. She flinched. Sierra Tres and the pilot looked on, curious. The woman who called herself Quell, I noticed, had gone below to the cabin.

"We both walked away from the Corps," Vidaura said finally. "Intact. Wiser. Now you're just going to turn the rest of your life off like some fucking torch? Just bury yourself in a retribution subroutine?"

I summoned a grin. "I've had well over a hundred years of life, Virginia. I won't miss it."

"But it doesn't *solve* anything." Suddenly she was shouting. "It won't bring Sarah *back*. When you've done this, she'll still be gone. You've already killed and tortured everyone who was there. Does it make you feel any better?"

"People are starting to stare," I said mildly.

"I don't fucking care. You answer me. *Does it make you feel any better?*"

Envoys are superlative liars. But not to themselves or each other.

"Only when I'm killing them."

She nodded grimly. "Yeah, that's right. And you know what that is, Tak. We both do. It's not like we haven't seen it before. Remember Cheb Oliveira? Nils Wright? It's pathological, Tak. Out of control. It's an addiction and in the end, it's going to eat you."

"Maybe so." I leaned in closer, fighting to keep a lid on my own sudden anger. "But in the meantime it isn't going to kill any fifteen-year-old girls. It isn't going to get any cities bombed or populations decimated. It isn't going to turn into the Unsettlement, or the Adoracion campaign. Unlike your surf buddies, unlike your new best friend down there in the cabin, I'm not asking sacrifices of anybody else."

She looked at me levelly for a couple of seconds. Then she nodded, as if abruptly convinced of something she'd hoped wasn't true.

She turned away without a word.

● ● ●

The skimmer drifted sideways off the mooring point, spun about in a wash of muddy water, and took off westward at speed. No one stayed on deck to wave. Droplets from the fantail blew back and sprinkled my face. I watched it recede to a faint growl and a dot on the horizon, then I went looking for the priest.

Sanctified solo assassins.

I'd been up against them a couple of times on Sharya. Psychotically stoked religious maniacs in Right Hand of God martyr sleeves, peeled from the main body of fighters, given a virtual glimpse of the paradise that awaited them beyond death, and then sent to infiltrate the Protectorate power bases. Like the Sharyan resistance in general, they weren't overly imaginative—which in the end proved their downfall when faced with the Envoys—but they weren't any kind of pushover, either. We'd all developed a healthy respect for their courage and combat endurance by the time we slaughtered the last of them.

The Knights of the New Revelation, by contrast, were an easy mark. They had the enthusiasm but not the lineage. The faith rested on the standard religious pillars of mob incitement and misogyny to get its enforcement done, but so far it seemed there'd been either no time or no need for a warrior class to emerge. They were amateurs.

So far.

I started with the cheaper hotels on the Expanse-side waterfront. It seemed a safe bet that the priest had tracked me to a sighting at Dzurinda Tudjman Sklep before we left for Millsport. Then, when the trail went cold, he'd have just sat it out. Patience is a sterling virtue in assassins; you've got to know when to move but you've also got to be prepared to wait. Those who are paying you will understand this, or can be made to. You wait and you cast about for clues. A daily trip down to Sunshine Fun Jetties would feature, a careful check of traffic, especially traffic out of the ordinary. Like matte, low-profile pirate skimmers amid the bright and bloated tourist boats that habitually used the moorage. The only thing that didn't fit the pro-killer profile was the open approach to the pilot, and that I put down to faith-based arrogance.

Faint, pervasive reek of rotting belaweed, poorly kept façades, and grumpy staff. Narrow streets, sliced with angles of hot sunlight. Damp, debris-strewn corners that only ever dried out in the hours around noon. A desultory coming and going of tourists who already looked miserable and exhausted with their cut-rate attempts at fun in the sun. I wandered through it all, trying to let the Envoy sense do the work, trying to suppress my headache and the pounding hatred that surged for release underneath.

I found him well before evening.

It wasn't a hard trace to make. Kossuth was still relatively unplagued by the New Revelation, and people noticed them the way you'd notice a Millsport accent in Watanabe's. I asked the same simple questions in every place. Fake surfer speak, lifted in easily replayed chunks from the conversations around me over the last few weeks, got me inside the defenses of enough low-paid workers to trace the priest's appearances. A judicial seasoning of low-value credit chips and a certain amount of cold-eyed bullying did the rest. By the time the heat started to leach out of the afternoon, I was standing in the cramped lobby of a combined hostel and boat-and-board-hire place called the Palace of Waves. Rather inappropriately, it was built out over the sluggish waters of the Expanse on ancient mirrorwood pilings, and the smell of the belaweed rotting beneath came up through the floor.

"Sure, he checked in about a week back," the girl on reception volunteered as she worked stacking a pile of well-worn surfboards against a rack along one wall. "I was expecting all sorts of trouble, me being a female and dressed like this, y'know. But he didn't seem to fix on it at all."

"Really?"

"Yeah, got a real balance about him, too, you know what I'm saying? I thought he might even be a rider." She laughed, a carefree, teenage sound. "Crazy, huh? But I guess even up there they've got to have surfers, right?"

"Surfers everywhere," I agreed.

"So you want to talk to this guy? Leave a message?"

"Well." I eyed the pigeonhole system behind the reception desk. "It's actually something I've got to leave for him, if that's okay. A surprise."

That appealed to her. She grinned and got up. "Sure, we can do that."

She left the boards and came around to the other side of the counter. I dug around in my pocket, found a spare chargepack for the Rapsodia, and fished it out.

"There you go."

She took the little black device curiously. "That's it? You don't want to scribble him a note to go with it or something?"

"No, it's fine. He'll understand. Just tell him I'll be back tonight."

"Okay, if that's what you want to do." A cheerful shrug, and she turned to the pigeonholes. I watched her slide the chargepack in amid the dust on ledge 74.

"Actually," I said with feigned abruptness. "Can I get a room?"

She turned back, surprised. "Well, uh, sure . . ."

"Just for tonight. Just makes more sense than getting a place somewhere else and then coming back, you know."

"Sure, no problem." She prodded a display screen to life on the counter, scrutinized it for a moment, and then gave me the grin again. "If you like, you know, I could put you on the same landing as he is. Not next door, it's taken, but a couple of doors down, that's free."

"That's very kind," I said. "Tell you what then, you just tell him I'm here, give him my room number, he can come and buzz me. In fact, you can give me the hardware back."

Her brow creased with the flurry of changes. She picked up the Rapsodia chargepack doubtfully.

"So you don't want me to give him this?"

"Not anymore, thanks." I smiled at her. "I think I'd prefer to give it to him myself, directly. It's more personal that way."

Upstairs, the doors were old-style hinged. I broke into 74 using no more skill than I'd had as a sixteen-year-old street thug cracking cut-rate dive-supplier warehouses.

The room beyond was cramped and basic. A capsule bathroom, a disposable mesh hammock to save on space and laundry, storage drawers molded into the walls, and a small plastic table and chair. A variable-transparency window wired clumsily to the room's climate control system—the priest had left it dimmed. I cast about for somewhere to hide myself in the gloom and was driven into the capsule for lack of alternatives. Sting of recent antibac spray in my nose as I stepped in—the clean cycle must have run not long ago. I shrugged, breathed through my mouth, and searched the cabinets for painkillers to flatten the rolling wave of my hangover. In one, I found a foil of basic heatstroke pills for tourists. I dry-swallowed a couple and seated myself on the closed toilet unit to wait.

There's something wrong here, the Envoy sense admonished me. *Something doesn't fit.*

Maybe he's not what you think.

Yeah, right—he's a negotiator, come to talk you down. God's changed his mind.

Religion's just politics with higher stakes, Tak. You know that, you saw it in action on Sharya. No reason these people can't do the same when it comes to the crunch.

These people are sheep. They'll do whatever their holy men tell them.

Sarah seared across my mind. Momentarily, the world tilted around me with the depth of my fury. For the thousandth time I imagined the scene again, and there was a roaring in my ears like a distant crowd.

I drew the Tebbit knife and looked down at the dull, dark blade.

Slowly, with the sight, Envoy calm soaked back through me. I settled again in the small space of the capsule, letting it drench me to a chilled purpose. Fragments of Virginia Vidaura's voice came with it.

Weapons are an extension. You *are the killer and destroyer.*

Kill quickly and be gone.

It won't bring Sarah back. *When you've done this, she'll still be gone.*

I frowned a little at that one. It's not good when your formative icons start getting inconsistent on you. When you find out they're just as human as you.

The door wittered to itself and began to open.

Thought vanished like shreds in the slipstream of enabled force. I came out of the capsule, around the edge of its door, and stood braced with the knife, ready to reach and stab.

He wasn't what I'd imagined. The skimmer pilot and the girl downstairs had both remarked on his poise, and it showed in the way he spun at the tiny sounds of my clothing, the shift of air in the narrow room. But he was slim and slight, shaven skull delicate, beard an out-of-place idiocy on the fine features.

"You looking for me, holy man?"

For a moment we locked gazes and the knife in my hand seemed to tremble of its own accord.

Then he reached up and tugged at his beard, and it came away with a short static crackle.

"Of course I'm looking for you, Micky," said Jadwiga tiredly. "Been chasing you for nearly a month."

CHAPTeR FORTY-ONe

"You're supposed to be dead."

"Yeah, twice at least." Jad picked morosely at the beard prosthesis in her hands. We sat together at the cheap plastic table, not looking at each other. "Only reason I'm here, I guess. They weren't looking for me when they came for the others."

I saw Drava again as she told it, a mind's-eye view of swirling snow on nighttime black, the frosted constellations of camp lights and infrequent figures moving between buildings, hunched up against the weather. They'd come the following evening, unannounced. It wasn't clear if Kurumaya had been bought off, threatened with higher authority, or simply murdered. Behind the funneled force of Anton's command software on max override, Kovacs and his team located Sylvie's team by net signature. They kicked in doors, demanded submission.

Apparently didn't get it.

"I saw Orr take someone down," Jad went on, talking mechanically as she stared into her own memories. "Just the flash. He was yelling for everyone to get out. I was bringing carryout back from the bar. I didn't even."

She stopped.

"It's okay," I told her.

"No, it's not fucking okay, Micky. I ran away."

"You'd be dead if you hadn't. Really Dead."

"I heard Kiyoka screaming." She swallowed. "I knew it was too late, but I."

I hurried her past it. "Did anyone see you?"

A jerky nod. "Traded shots with a couple of them on the way across to the vehicle sheds. Fuckers were everywhere, seemed like. But they didn't come after me. I think they thought I was just a stroppy bystander." She gestured at the Eishundo sleeve she wore. "No trace on the net search, see. Far as that fucker Anton's concerned, I was invisible."

She'd lifted one of the Dracul bugs, powered it up, and driven right off the side of the dock.

"Had a squabble with the autosub systems getting up the estuary," she said, and laughed mirthlessly. "You're not supposed to do that, put vehicles in the water without authorization. But the clear tags worked in the end."

And out onto the Andrassy Sea.

I nodded mechanically, exact inverse of my near disbelief. She'd ridden the bug without resting, nearly a thousand kilometers back to Tekitomura and a quiet nighttime landing in a cove out of town to the east.

She shrugged it off.

"I had food and water in the panniers. Meth to stay awake. The Dracul's got Nuhanovic guidance. Main thing I worried about was keeping low enough to the water to look like a boat, not a flying machine, trying not to upset the angelfire."

"And you found me how?"

"Yeah, that's some weird shit." For the first time, something bloomed in her voice that wasn't weariness and rancid rage. "I sold the bug for quick cash at Soroban wharf, I was walking back up toward Kompcho. Coming down from the meth. And it's like I could smell you or something. Like the smell of this old family hammock we had when I was a kid. I just followed it, like I said I was coming down, running on autopilot. I saw you on the wharf, going aboard this piece-of-shit freighter. *Haiduci's Daughter.*"

I nodded again, this time in sudden comprehension as large chunks of the puzzle fell into place. The dizzying, unaccustomed sense of family longing swam back over me. We were twins, after all. Close scions from the long-dead house of Eishundo.

"You stowed away, then. It was you trying to get inside that pod when the storm hit."

She grimaced. "Yeah, creeping around on deck's fine when the sun's shining. Not something you want to try when there's heavy weather coming in. I should have guessed they'd have it alarmed up the ass. Fucking webjelly oil, you'd think it was Khumalo wetware the price they get for it."

"You stole the food out of communal storage, too, second day out."

"Hey, your ride was flying departure lights when I saw you go aboard. Left inside an hour. Didn't exactly leave me much time to go stock up on provisions. I went a day without food before I figured you weren't getting off at Erkezes, you were in for the long haul. I was fucking hungry."

"You know there was nearly a fight over that. One of your deCom colleagues wanted to brain someone for stealing it."

"Yeah, heard them talking. Fucking burnouts." Her voice took on a kind of automated distaste, a macro of opinion over old ground. "Kind of sad-case losers get the trade a bad name."

"So you tracked me across Newpest and the Expanse as well."

Another humorless smile. "My home turf, Micky. And besides, that skimmer you took left a soup wake I could have followed blindfolded. Guy I hired got your ride on the radar pulling into Kem Point. I was there by nightfall, but you'd gone."

"Yeah. So why the fuck didn't you come knock on my cabin door while you had the chance, aboard *Haiduci's Daughter*?"

She scowled. "How about because I didn't trust you?"

"All right."

"Yeah, and while we're on the subject how about I still don't? How about you explain what the fuck you've done with Sylvie?"

I sighed.

"Got anything to drink?"

"You tell me. You're the one broke into my room."

Somewhere inside me something shifted, and I suddenly understood how happy I was to see her. I couldn't work out if it was the biological tie of the Eishundo sleeves, remembrance of the month's snappish-ironic camaraderie in New Hok, or just the change from Brasil's suddenly serious born-again revolutionaries. I looked at her standing there and it was like the gust of an Andrassy Sea breeze through the room.

"Good to see you again, Jad."

"Yeah, you, too," she admitted.

●●●

When I'd laid it all out for her, it was dark outside. Jad got up and squeezed past me in the narrow space, stood by the variable-transparency window staring out. Street lighting frosted dimly in the gloomed glass. Raised voices floated up, some kind of drunken argument.

"You sure it was her you talked to?"

"Pretty sure. I don't think this Nadia, whoever she is, *what*ever she is, I don't think she could run the command software. Certainly not well enough to generate an illusion that coherent."

Jad nodded to herself.

"Yeah, that Renouncer shit was always going to catch up with Sylvie someday. Fuckers get you that young, you never really shake it off. So what about this Nadia thing? You really think she's a personality mine? 'Cause I got to say, Micky, in nearly three years of tracking around New Hok, I never saw or heard of a datamine that carried that much detail, that much depth."

I hesitated, feeling around the edges of Envoy-intuited awareness for a gist that could be stamped into something as crude as words.

"I don't know. I think she's, I don't know, some kind of spec designation weapon. Everything points to Sylvie getting infected in the Uncleared. You were there for Iyamon Canyon, right?"

"Yeah. She flaked in an engagement. She was sick for weeks after. Orr tried to pretend it was just postop blues, but anyone could see different."

"And before that, she was fine?"

"Well, she was a deCom head, that's not a job that leans toward *fine*. But all this gibbering shit, the blackouts, turning up at sites someone else had already worked, that's all post-Iyamon, yeah."

"Sites someone else had worked?"

"Yeah, you know." In the reflection of the window, the irritation flared on her face like matchglow, then guttered out as suddenly. "No, come to think of it, you don't, you weren't around for any of those."

"Any of what?"

"Ah, handful of times we zeroed in on mimint activity, by the time we got there, it was all over. Looked like they'd been fighting each other."

Something from my first meeting with Kurumaya snapped into focus. Sylvie wheedling, the camp commander's impassive responses.

Oshima-san, the last time I ramped you ahead of schedule, you neglected your assigned duties and disappeared north. How do I know you won't do the same thing this time?

Shig, you sent me to look at wreckage. *Someone got there before us, there was nothing left. I told you that.*

When you finally resurfaced, yes.

Oh be reasonable. How was I supposed to deCom what had already been trashed? We lit out, because there was nothing fucking there.

I frowned as the new fragment slid into place. Smooth and snug, like a fucking splinter. Distress radiated out through the theories I was building. It didn't fit with any of what I was starting to believe.

"Sylvie said something about it when we went to get the cleanup duty. Kurumaya ramped you and when you got to the assigned location, there was nothing but wreckage."

"Yeah, that's the one. Wasn't the only time it happened, either. We ran across the same thing in the Uncleared a few times."

"You never talked about this when I was around."

"Yeah, well, deCom." Jad pulled a sour face at herself in the window. "For people with heads full of state-of-the-art tech, we're a superstitious bunch of fuckers. Not considered cool to talk about stuff like that. Brings bad luck."

"So let me get this straight. This mimint suicide stuff, that dated from after Iyamon as well."

"Near as I remember, yeah. So you going to tell me about this spec weapon theory of yours?"

I shook my head, juggling the new data. "I'm not sure. I think she was designed to trigger this genetic Harlan killer. I don't think the Black Brigades abandoned their weapon, I don't think they got exterminated before they could set it off. I think they built this thing as the initial trigger and hid it in New Hok, a personality casing with a programmed will to set off the weapon. She believes she's Quellcrist Falconer, because that gives her the drive. But that's all it is, a propulsion system. When it comes to the crunch, setting off a genetic curse in people who weren't even born when it was conceived, she behaves like a completely different person, because in the end it's the target that matters."

Jad shrugged. "Sounds exactly like every political leader I ever heard of anyway. Ends and means, you know. Why should Quellcrist Falconer be any fucking different?"

"Yeah, I don't know." A curious, unlooked-for resistance to her cynicism dragging through me. I looked at my hands. "You look at Quell's life, most of what she did bears out her philosophy, you know. Even this copy of her, or whatever it is, even she can't make her own actions fit with what she thinks she is. She's confused about her own motivations."

"So? Welcome to the human fucking race."

There was a bitter edge on the words that made me glance up. Jad was still at the window, staring at her reflected face.

"There's nothing you could have done," I said gently.

She didn't look at me, didn't look away. "Maybe not. But I know what I *felt,* and it wasn't enough. This fucking sleeve has changed me. It cut me out of the net loop—"

"Which saved your life."

An impatient shake of her shaven head. "It stopped me feeling with the others, Micky. It locked me out. It even changed things with Ki, you know. We never felt the same about each other that last month."

"That's quite common with resleeving. People learn to—"

"Oh, yeah, I know." Now she turned away from the image of herself and stared at me. "A relationship is not easy, a relationship is work. We both tried, tried harder than we ever had before. Harder than we ever *had* to before. That's the problem. Before, we didn't *have* to try. I was wet for her just looking at her sometimes. It was all either of us needed, a touch, a look. That fucking went, all of it."

I said nothing. There are times when there is nothing you can usefully say. All you can do is listen, wait, and watch as this stuff comes out. Hope that it's a purge.

"When I heard her scream," Jad said, with difficulty. "It was like, it didn't matter. Didn't matter enough. I didn't feel it enough to stay and fight. In my own body, I would have stayed and fought."

"Stayed and died, you mean."

A careless shrug, a flinching away like tears.

"This is crabshit, Jad. It's the guilt talking because you survived. You tell yourself this but there's nothing you could have done, and you know it."

She looked at me then, and she was crying, quiet ribbons of tears and a smeared grimace.

"What the fuck do you know about it, Micky? It's just another fucking version of you that did this to us. You're a fucking destroyer, an ex-Envoy burnout. You were never deCom. You never belonged, you don't know what it was like to be a part of that. How close it was. You don't know what it feels like to lose that."

Briefly, my mind fled back to the Corps and Virginia Vidaura. The rage after Innenin. It was the last time I'd really belonged to anything, well over a century gone. I'd felt twinges of the same thing after, the fresh growth of comradeship and united purpose—and I'd ripped it up by the roots every time. That shit will get you killed. Get you used.

"So," I said, brutally casual. "Now you've tracked me down. Now you know. What are you going to do about it?"

She wiped tears from her face with hard strokes that were almost blows.

"I want to see her," she said.

CHAPTeR FORTY-TWO

Jad had a small, battered skimmer she'd hired in Kem Point. It was parked under harsh security lighting on a rental ramp at the back of the hostel. We went out to it, collecting a cheery wave from the girl on reception, who seemed to have derived a touching delight from her role in our successful re-union. Jad coded the locks on the sliding roof, clambered behind the wheel, and spun us rapidly out into the dark of the Expanse. As the glimmer of lights from the Strip shrank behind us, she tore off the beard again and gave me the wheel while she stripped off her robes.

"Yeah, why wrap yourself up like that?" I asked her. "What was the point?"

She shrugged. "Cover. I figured I had the yak looking for me at least, and I still didn't know what your end was, who you were playing for. Best to stay cloaked. Everywhere you go, people tend to leave the Beards alone."

"Yeah?"

"Yeah, even the cops." She lifted the ocher surplice over her head. "Funny stuff, religion. No one wants to talk to a priest."

"Especially one who might declare you an enemy of God for the way you cut your hair."

"Well, yeah, that too I guess. Anyway, I got some novelty shop in Kem Point to make up the stuff, told them it was for a beach party. And you know what, it works. No one talks to me. Plus." She freed herself from the rest of the robes with accustomed ease and jabbed a thumb at the mimint-killer shard gun strapped under her arm. "Makes great cover for the hardware."

I shook my head in disbelief.

"You lugged that fucking cannon all the way down here? What were you planning to do, splatter me across the Expanse with it?"

She gave me a sober look. Under the straps of the holster, her deCom T-shirt was printed with the words CAUTION: SMART MEAT WEAPON SYSTEM.

"Maybe," she said, and turned away to stow her disguise at the back of the tiny cabin.

Navigating the Expanse at night isn't much fun when you're driving a rental with the radar capacity of a child's toy. Both Jad and I were Newpest natives, and we'd seen enough skimmer wrecks growing up to throttle back and take it slow. It didn't help that Hotei was still down and mounting cloud shrouded Daikoku at the horizon. There was a commercial traffic lane for the tourist buses, illuminum marker buoys marching off into the weed-fragrant night, but it wasn't much help. Segesvar's place was a long way off the standard routes. Within half an hour the buoys had faded out of sight and we were alone with the scant coppery light of a high-flung, speeding Marikanon.

"Peaceful out here," Jad said, as if making the discovery for the first time.

I grunted and wheeled us left as the skimmer's lights picked out a sprawl of tepes root ahead. The outermost branches scraped loudly on the metal of the skirt as we passed. Jad winced.

"Maybe we should have waited for morning."

I shrugged. "Go back if you like."

"No, I think—"

The radar blipped.

We both looked at the console, then at each other. The reported presence blipped again, louder.

"Maybe a bale freighter," I said.

"Maybe." But there was a hardened deCom dislike in her face as she watched the signal build.

I killed the forward drives and waited as the skimmer coasted to a gentle halt on the murmur of lift stabilizers. The scent of weed pressed inward. I stood up and leaned on the edge of the opened roof panels. Faintly, along with the smells of the Expanse, the breeze carried the sound of motors approaching.

I dropped back into the body of the cockpit.

"Jad, I think you'd better take the artillery and get up near the tail. Just in case."

She nodded curtly and gestured for me to give her some space. I backed up and she swung herself effortlessly up onto the roof, then freed the shard blaster from its webbing holster. She glanced down at me.

"Fire control?"

I thought for a moment, then pumped the stabilizers. The murmuring of the lift system rose to a sustained growl, then sank back.

"Like that. You hear that, you shoot up everything in sight."

" 'Kay."

Her feet scuffed on the superstructure, heading aft. I stood up again and watched as she settled into the cover of the skimmer's tail assembly, then turned my attention back to the closing signal. The radar set was a bare-minimum insurance-necessity installation, and it gave no detail beyond the steadily increasing blotch on the screen. But a couple of minutes later I didn't need it. The gaunt, turreted silhouette rose on the horizon, came plowing toward us, and might as well have had an illuminum sign pasted on its prow.

PIRATE.

Not dissimilar to a compact oceangoing hoverloader, it ran no navigation lights at all. It sat long and low on the surface of the Expanse, but bulked with crude plate armoring and weapons pods custom-welded to the original structure. I cranked neurachem vision and got the vague sense of figures moving about in low red lighting behind the glass panels at the nose, but no activity near the guns. As the vessel loomed and turned broadside to me, I saw lateral scrape marks in the metal of the skirt. Legacy of all the engagements that had ended in hull-to-hull boarding assault.

A spotlight snapped on and panned across me, then switched back and held. I held up my hand against the glare. Neurachem squeezed a view of silhouettes in a snub conning tower atop the pirate's forward cabin. A young male voice, cranked tense with chemicals, floated across the soupy water.

"You Kovacs?"

"I'm Serendipity. What do you want?"

A dry, mirthless cackle. "Serendipity. Well, I just guess you fucking *are*. Serendipitous to the max from where I'm standing."

"I asked you a question."

"What do I want. Heard you. Well, what I *want,* first and foremost, I want your slim pal back there at the stern to stand down and put her hardware away. We've got her on infrared anyway, and it wouldn't be hard to turn her into panther feed with the vibe gun, but then you'd be upset, right?"

I said nothing.

"See, and you upset gets me nowhere. Supposed to keep you happy, Kovacs. Bring you along, but keep you happy. So your pal stands down, *I'm* happy, no need for fireworks and gore, *you're* happy, you come along with me, people I work for are happy, they treat *me* right, I get even happier. Know what that's called, Kovacs? That's a virtuous circle."

"Want to tell me who the people you work for are?"

"Well, yeah, I *want* to, obviously, but there's just no way I *can,* see. Under contract, not a word to pass my lips about that shit till you're at the table and doing the *something-for-you, something-for-me* boogie. So I'm afraid you're going to have to take all of this on trust."

Or be blasted apart trying to leave.

I sighed and turned to the stern.

"Come on out, Jad."

There was a long pause, and then she emerged from the shadows of the tail assembly, shard blaster hanging at her side. I still had the neurachem up, and the look on her face said she'd rather have fought it out.

"That's much better," called the pirate cheerfully. "Now we're all friends."

CHAPTeR FORTY-THRee

His name was Vlad Tepes, named apparently not for the vegetation but after some dimly remembered folk hero from precolonial times. He was lanky and pale, wearing flesh like some cheap, young shaven-headed version of Jack Soul Brasil they'd thrown out at prototype stage. Flesh that something told me was his own, his first sleeve, in which case he wasn't much older than Isa had been. There were acne scars on his cheeks that he fingered occasionally, and he trembled from head to foot with tetrameth overload. He overgestured and laughed too much, and at some point in his young life he'd had the bone of his skull opened at the temples and filled with jagged lightning-flash sections of purple-black alloy cement. The stuff glinted in the low light aboard the pirate vessel as he moved about, and when you looked at him head-on it gave his face a faintly demonic aspect that was obviously what was intended. The men and women around him on the bridge gave ground with alacrity to his jerky, meth-driven motion, and respect read out in their eyes as they watched him.

The radical surgery aside, he reminded me of Segesvar and myself at that age, so much that it ached.

The vessel, perhaps predictably, rejoiced in the name *Impaler,* and it ran due west at speed, trampling imperiously through obstacles smaller and less armored skimmers would have needed to go around.

"Got to," Vlad informed us succinctly as something crunched under the armored skirt. "Everyone's been looking for you on the Strip, and not very well is my guess, 'cause they didn't find you, did they. Hah! Anyway, wasted a fuck of a lot of time that way and my clients, they seem pushed temporally, if you know what I mean."

On the identity of the clients, he remained steadfastly closemouthed, which, on that much meth, is no mean feat.

"Look, be there soon, anyway," he jittered, face twitching. "Why worry?"

In this at least, he was telling the truth. Barely an hour after we'd been taken aboard, *Impaler* slowed and drifted cautiously broadside toward a decayed ruin of a baling station in the middle of nowhere. The pirate's coms officer ran a series of scrambled interrogation protocols, and whoever was inside the ruined station had a machine that knew the code. The coms woman looked up and nodded. Vlad stood glitter-eyed before his instrument displays and snapped instructions like insults. *Impaler* picked up a little lateral speed again, fired grapple lines into the evercrete dock pilings with a series of splintering smacks, and then cranked itself in tight. Green lights and a gangplank extended.

"Let's go then, come on." He hurried us off the bridge and back to the debarkation hatch, then through and out, flanked by an honor guard of two methed-up thugs even younger and twitchier than he was. Up the gangplank at a walk that wanted to be a run, across the dock. Abandoned cranes stood mossy with growth where the antibac had failed; chunks of seized and rusted machinery lay about, waiting to rip the unwary at shin and shoulder height. We negotiated the debris and cut a final line for an open door at the base of a dockfront supervisor's tower with polarized windows. Grubby metal stairs led up, two flights at opposed angles, and a steel plate landing between that clanked and shifted alarmingly when we all trooped across it.

Soft light glowed from the room at the top. I went uneasily in the van with Vlad. No one had tried to take away our weapons, and Vlad's cohorts were all armed with a massive lack of subtlety, but still . . .

I remembered the voyage aboard the *Angelfire Flirt,* the sense of onrushing events too fast to face effectively, and I twitched a little myself in the gloom. I stepped into the tower room as if I was going there to fight.

And then everything came tumbling down.

"Hello, Tak. How's the vendetta business these days?"

Todor Murakami, lean and competent in stealth suit and combat jacket, hair cropped back to military standard, stood with his hands on his hips and grinned at me. There was a Kalashnikov interface gun at his hip, a killing knife in an inverted pull-down sheath on his left breast. A table between us held a muffled Angier torch, a portable datacoil, and a map holo displaying the eastern fringes of the Weed Expanse. Everything from the hardware to the grin reeked of Envoy operations.

"Didn't see that one coming, huh?" he added when I said nothing. He came around the table and stuck out his hand. I looked at it, then back at his face without moving.

"What the fuck are you doing here, Tod?"

"Bit of pro bono work, would you believe?" He dropped the hand and glanced past my shoulder. "Vlad, take your pals and wait downstairs. The mimint kid there, too."

I felt Jad bristle at my back.

"She stays, Tod. That, or we don't have this conversation."

He shrugged and nodded at my newly acquired pirate friends. "Suit yourself. But if she hears the wrong thing, I may have to kill her for her own protection."

It was a Corps joke, and it was hard not to mirror his grin as he said it. I felt, very faintly, the same nostalgic twinge I'd had taking Virginia Vidaura to my bed at Segesvar's farm. The same faint wondering why I ever walked away.

"That was a joke," he clarified for Jad, as the others clattered away down the stairs.

"Yeah, I guessed." Jad wandered past me to the windows and peered out at the moored bulk of the *Impaler*. "So Micky, Tak, Kovacs, whoever the fuck you are at the moment. Want to introduce me to your friend?"

"Uh, yeah. Tod, this is Jadwiga. As you obviously already know, she's from deCom. Jad, Todor Murakami, colleague of mine from, uh, the old days."

"I'm an Envoy," Murakami supplied casually.

To her credit, Jad barely blinked. She took the hand he offered with a slightly incredulous smile, then propped herself against the outward lean of the tower windows and folded her arms.

Murakami took the hint.

"So what's all this about?"

I nodded. "We can start there."

"I think you can probably guess."

"I think you can probably drop the elicitation and just tell me."

He grinned and touched a trigger finger to his temple. "Sorry, force of habit. All right, look. Here's my problem. According to sources, seems you've got a little revolutionary momentum up here, maybe enough to seriously rock the First Families' boat."

"Sources?"

Another grin. No ground given up. "That's right. Sources."

"I didn't know you guys were deployed here."

"We're not." A little of his Envoy cool slipped from him, as if by the admission he'd lost some kind of vital access to it. He scowled. "Like I said, this is pro bono. Damage limitation. You know as well as I do, we can't afford a neoQuellist uprising."

"Yeah?" This time, I was the one grinning. "Who's *we*, Tod? The Protectorate? The Harlan family? Some other bunch of super-rich fucks?"

He gestured irritably. "I'm talking about all of us, Tak. You really think that's what this planet needs, another Unsettlement. Another war?"

"Takes two sides to run a war, Tod. If the First Families wanted to accept the neoQuellist agenda, institute reforms, well." I spread my hands. "Then I can't see there'd be any need for an uprising at all. Maybe you should be talking to them."

A frown. "Why are you talking like this, Tak? Don't tell me you're buy-ing into this shit."

I paused. "I don't know."

"You don't *know*? What kind of fucked political philosophy is that?"

"It isn't a philosophy at all, Tod. It's just a feeling that maybe we've all had enough. That maybe it's time to burn these motherfuckers down."

He frowned. "I can't allow that. Sorry."

"So why don't you just call down the wrath of the Envoys and stop wast-ing time?"

"Because I don't fucking *want* the Corps here." There was a sudden, brief desperation in his face as he spoke. "I'm *from* here, Tak. This is my home. You think I want to see the World turned into another Adoracion? An-other Sharya?"

"Very noble of you." Jad shifted against the canted windows, came for-ward to the table, and poked at the datacoil. Purple and red sparked around her fingers where they broke the field. "So what's the battle plan, Mister Qualms?"

His eyes flickered between the two of us, came to rest on me. I shrugged.

"It's a fair question, Tod."

He hesitated for a moment. It made me think of the moment I'd had to unpin my own numbed fingers from the cable beneath the Martian eyrie at Tekitomura. He was letting go of a lifetime of Envoy commitment here, and my own lapsed membership of the Corps wasn't much in the way of a justifi-cation.

Finally, he grunted and spread his hands.

"Okay. Here's the newsflash." He pointed at me. "Your pal Segesvar has sold you out."

I blinked. Then:

"No fucking way."

He nodded. "Yeah, I know. *Haiduci* dues, right? He owes you. Thing is, Tak, you got to ask yourself *which* of you he thinks he owes."

Oh shit.

He saw it hit me and nodded again. "Yeah, I know all about that, too. See, Takeshi Kovacs saved Segesvar's life a couple of centuries ago, objective time. But that's something *both* copies of you did. Old Radul's got a debt all right, but he apparently sees no reason to discharge it more than the once. And your younger, fresher self has just cut a deal on that very basis. Seges-var's men took most of your beach-party revolutionaries early this morning. Would have gotten you, Vidaura, and the deCom woman, too, if you hadn't all taken off on some crack-of-dawn errand to the Strip."

"And now?" The last stubborn fragments of clinging hope. Scour them out, and face the facts with features carved out of stone. "They've got Vi-daura and the others now?"

"Yes, they took them on their return. They're holding everyone until Aiura Harlan-Tsuruoka can arrive with a cleanup squad. Had you gone back with the others, you'd be sharing a locked room with them now. So." A rapidly flexed smile, a raised brow. "Looks like you owe me a favor."

I let the fury come aboard, like deep breath, like a swelling. Let it rage through me, then tamped it carefully down like a half-smoked seahemp cigar, saved for later. Lock it down, think.

"How come you know all this, Tod?"

He gestured, self-deprecating. "Like I said, I live here. Pays to keep the wires humming. You know how it is."

"No, I don't know how it is. Who's your fucking source, Tod?"

"I can't tell you that."

I shrugged. "Then I can't help you."

"You're just going to let it all go? Segesvar sells you out, he gets to walk away? Your friends from the beach get to die? Come *on*, Tak."

I shook my head. "I'm tired of fighting other people's battles for them. Brasil and friends got themselves into this, they can get themselves out. And Segesvar will keep. I'll get to him later."

"And Vidaura?"

"What about her?"

"She trained us, Tak."

"Yeah, us. Get on and save her yourself."

If you weren't an Envoy, you would have missed it. It was less than a flicker, some millimetric shift in stance, maybe not even that. But Murakami slumped.

"I can't do it on my own," he said quietly. "I don't know the inside of Segesvar's place, and without that I'd need an Envoy platoon to take it."

"Then call in the Corps."

"You know what that would do to—"

"Then tell me who your fucking source is."

"Yeah," said Jad sardonically, in the quiet that followed. "Or just ask him to come in from next door."

She caught my eye and nodded at a closed drop-hatch in the back of the tower room. I took a step toward it and Murakami could barely hold himself back from the blocking move he wanted to make. He glared at Jad.

"Sorry," she said, and tapped her head with a forefinger. "Dataflow alert. Pretty standard wincefish hardware. Your friend in there is using a phone, and he's moving about a lot. Pacing nervously would be my guess."

I grinned at Murakami. "Well, Tod. Your call."

The tension lasted a couple of seconds more, then he sighed and gestured me forward.

"Go ahead. You would have worked it out sooner or later anyway."

I went to the drop-hatch, found the panel, and thumbed it. The machinery grumbled to itself somewhere deep in the building. The hatch cranked upward in juddery, hesitant increments. I leaned into the space it left.

"Good evening. So which one of you's the snitch?"

Four faces turned toward me, and as soon as I saw them, four severely dressed figures in black, the pieces thumped into place in my head like the sound of the drop-hatch reaching the end of its recess. Three were muscle, two men and and a woman, and the skin on their faces all had a shiny plastic elasticity where their facial tattooing had been sprayed over. It was a short-term, daily option that wouldn't stand much professional scrutiny. But deep as they were into *haiduci* turf, it probably would save them from having to fight pitched battles on every Newpest street corner.

The fourth, the one holding the phone, was older but unmistakable by demeanor alone. I nodded my understanding.

"Tanaseda, I presume. Well, well."

He bowed slightly. It went with the package, the same groomed, old-school manners and look. He wore no facial skin decoration because at the levels he'd attained, he would be a frequent visitor in First Family enclaves that would frown on it. But you could still see the honor scars where they had been removed without benefit of modern surgical technique. His gray-streaked black hair was bound back tightly in a short ponytail, the better to reveal the scarring across the forehead and accentuate the long bones of the face. The eyes beneath the brow were brown and hard like polished stones. The careful smile he gave me was the same one he would bestow upon death if and when it came for him.

"Kovacs-san."

"So what's your end of this, sam?" The muscle bristled collectively at my disrespect. I ignored it, glanced back at Murakami instead. "I take it you know he wants me Really Dead, as slowly and unpleasantly as possible."

Murakami locked gazes with the yakuza senior.

"That can be resolved," he murmured. "Is this not so, Tanaseda-san?"

Tanaseda bowed again. "It has come to my notice that though you were involved in the death of Hirayasu Yukio, you were not wholly to blame."

"So?" I shrugged to displace the rising anger, because the only way he could have heard that little snippet was through virtual interrogation of Orr or Kiyoka or Lazlo, after my younger self helped him kill them. "Doesn't usually cut much ice with you people, who's really to blame or not."

The woman in his entourage made a tiny growling sound deep in her throat. Tanaseda cut it with a tiny motion of his hand at his side, but the gaze he bent on me belied the calm in his tone.

"It has also become clear to me that you are in possession of Hirayasu Yukio's cortical storage device."

"Ah."

"Is this so?"

"Well, if you think I'm going to let you search me for it, you can—"

"Tak." Murakami's voice came out lazy, but it wasn't. "Behave. Do you have Hirayasu's stack or not?"

I paused on the hinge of the moment, more than half of me hoping they might try to strong-arm it. The man on Tanaseda's left twitched, and I smiled at him. But they were too well trained.

"Not on me," I said.

"But you could deliver it to Tanaseda-san, could you not?"

"If I had any incentive to, I suppose I could, yes."

The soft-throated snarl again, back and forth among all three of the yakuza muscle this time.

"Ronin," one of them spat.

I met his eye. "That's right, sam. Masterless. So watch your step. There's no one to call me to heel if I take a dislike to you."

"Nor anyone to back you up when you find yourself in a corner," observed Tanaseda. "May we please dispense with this childishness, Kovacs-san? You speak of incentives. Without the information I have supplied, you would now be captive with your colleagues, awaiting execution. And I have offered to revoke my own writ for your elimination. Is this not enough for the return of a cortical stack you have in any case no use for?"

I smiled. "You're full of shit, Tanaseda. You're not doing this for Hirayasu. He's a fucking waste of good sea air, and you know it."

The yakuza master seemed to coil tighter into himself as he stared at me. I still wasn't sure why I was pushing him, what I was pushing for.

"Hirayasu Yukio is my brother-in-law's only son." Very quietly, barely a murmur across the space between us, but edged with contained fury. "There is *giri* here that I would not expect a southerner to understand."

"Mother*fucker*," said Jad wonderingly.

"Ah, what do you expect, Jad?" I made a noise in my throat. "In the end, he's a criminal, no different than the fucking *haiduci*. Just a different mythology and the same crabshit delusions of ancient honor."

"Tak—"

"Back off, Tod. Let's get this out in the open where it belongs. This is politics, and nothing even remotely cleaner. Tanaseda here isn't worried about his nephew once removed. That's just a side bonus. He's worried he's losing his grip, he's afraid of being punished for a fucked-up blackmail attempt. He's watching Segesvar get ready to make friends with Aiura Harlan, and he's terrified the *haiduci* are going to get cut in on some serious global action in return for their trouble. All of which his Millsport cousins are likely to lay pretty directly at his front door, along with a short sword and a set of instructions that read *insert here and slice sideways*. Right, Tan?"

The muscle on the left lost it, as I suspected he might. A needle-thin blade dropped from his sleeve into his right hand. Tanaseda snapped something at him and he froze. His eyes blazed at me and his knuckles whitened around the hilt of the knife.

"See," I told him. "Masterless samurai don't have this problem. There's no leash. If you're *ronin,* you don't have to watch honor sold out for political expediency."

"Tak, will you just fucking shut up," groaned Murakami.

Tanaseda stepped past the taut, rippling tension on the furious bodyguard. He watched me through narrowed eyes, as if I were some kind of poisonous insect he needed to examine more closely.

"Tell me, Kovacs-san," he said quietly. "Is it your wish to die at the hands of my organization after all? Are you *looking* for death?"

I held his eye for a few seconds, then made a tiny spitting sound.

"You couldn't even begin to understand what I'm looking for, Tanaseda. You wouldn't recognize it if it bit your dick off. And if you did stumble on it by accident, you'd just find some way to sell it."

I looked across to Murakami, whose hand rested still on the butt of the Kalashnikov at his waist. I nodded.

"All right, Tod. I've seen your snitch. I'm in."

"Then we have an agreement?" Tanaseda asked.

I compressed a breath and turned back to face him. "Just tell me this. How long ago did Segesvar cut his deal with the other copy of me?"

"Oh, not recently." I couldn't tell if there was any satisfaction in his voice. "I believe he has known that you both exist for some weeks now. Your copied self has been most active in tracing old connections."

I thought back to Segesvar's appearance at the inland harbor. His voice over the phone. *We will get drunk together, maybe even go to Watanabe's for old times' sake and a pipe. I need to look you in the eyes, my friend. To know that you have not changed.* I wondered if, even then, he'd already been making a decision, savoring the curious circumstance of being able to choose a place for his indebtedness to reside.

If so, I hadn't done myself any favors in the competition with my younger self. And Segesvar had made it plain, the previous night, almost come out and said it to my face.

Certainly can't expect to have a good time with *you anymore. Can't remember doing that anytime in the last fifty years, in fact. You really are turning northern, Tak.*

Like I said—

Yeah, yeah, I know. You half are already. Thing is, Tak, when you were younger you tried not to let it show so much.

Had he been saying goodbye?

You're a hard man to please, Tak.

Can I interest you in some team sports, maybe? Like to come down to the grav gym with Ilja and Mayumi here?

For just a second, an old, small sadness welled up in me.

The anger trampled it down. I looked up at Tanaseda and nodded.

"Your nephew is buried under a beach house south of Kem Point. I'll draw you a map. Now give me what you've got."

CHAPTeR FORTY-FOUR

"**W**hy did you do that, Tak?"

"Do what?"

I stood with Murakami under Angier glow from *Impaler*'s directional spotlights, watching the yakuza depart in an elegant black Expansemobile that Tanaseda had called in by phone. They plowed away southward, leaving a broad, churned wake the color of milky vomit.

"Why did you push him like that?"

I stared after the receding skimmer. "Because he's scum. Because he's a fucking criminal, and he won't admit it."

"Getting a little judgmental in your old age, aren't you?"

"Am I?" I shrugged. "Maybe it's just the southern outlook. You're from Millsport, Tod, maybe you're just standing too close to see it."

He chuckled. "Okay. So what's the view like from down here?"

"Same as it's always been. The yakuza handing out their ancient-tradition-of-honor line to anyone who'll listen, and meantime doing what? Working the same crabshit criminality as everybody else, but cozied up with the First Families into the bargain."

"Not so much anymore, looks like."

"Ah, come on, Tod. You know better than that. These guys have been in bed with Harlan and the rest of them since we fucking got here. Tanaseda might have to pay for this Qualgrist fuckup he's perpetrated, but the others will just make the right polite noises of regret and slide out from under. Back to the same illicit goods and genteel extortion line they've always trawled. And the First Families will welcome it with open arms because it's one more thread in the net they've thrown over us all."

"You know." The laughter was still in his voice. "You're beginning to sound like her."

I looked around at him.

"Like who?"

"Like Quell, man. You sound like Quellcrist fucking Falconer."

That sat between us for a couple of seconds. I turned away and stared out into the darkness over the Expanse. Perhaps recognizing the unresolved tensions in the air between myself and Murakami, Jad had opted to leave us alone on the dock while the yakuza were still preparing to depart. The last I saw of her, she was boarding the *Impaler* with Vlad and the honor guard. Something about getting whiskey coffee.

"All right then, Tod," I said evenly. "How about you answer me this. Why did Tanaseda come running to you to put his life right?"

He pulled a face.

"You said it yourself, I'm Millsport-born and -bred. And the yak like to be plugged in at high level. They've been all over me since I came home on my first Corps furlough a hundred and whatever years ago. They think we're old friends."

"And are you?"

I felt the stare. Ignored it.

"I'm an Envoy, Tak," he said finally. "You want to remember that."

"Yeah."

"And I'm *your* friend."

"I'm already sold, Tod. You don't need to run this routine on me. I'll take you in Segesvar's back door on condition you help me fuck him up. Now what's your end?"

He shrugged. "Aiura has to go down for breach of Protectorate directives. Double-sleeving an Envoy—"

"Ex-Envoy."

"Speak for yourself. *He's* never been officially discharged, even if you have. And even for keeping the copy in the first place, someone in the Harlan hierarchy has to pay. That's erasure-mandatory."

There was an oddly ragged edge on his voice now. I looked more closely at him. The obvious truth hit home.

"You think they've got one of you, too, don't you?"

A wry grin. "There's something special about you, you'd be the only one they copied? Come on, Tak. Does that make any sense? I checked the records. That intake, there were about a dozen of us recruited from Harlan's World. Whoever decided on this brilliant little piece of insurance back then, they would have copied us all. We need Aiura alive long enough to tell us where in the Harlan datastacks we can find them."

"All right. What else?"

"You know what else," he said quietly.

I went back to watching the Expanse. "I'm not going to help you slaughter Brasil and the others, Tod."

"I'm not asking you to. For Virginia's sake alone, I'll try to avoid that. But someone has to pay the Bugs' bill. Tak, they murdered Mitzi Harlan on the streets of Millsport!"

"Big loss. Across the globe, skullwalk editors weep."

"All right," he said grimly. "They also killed fuck knows how many other incidental victims in the process. Law enforcement. Innocent bystanders. I've got the latitude to seal this operation up afterward, marked *regime unrest stabilized,* no need for further deployment. But I've *got* to show scapegoats, or the Corps auditors are going to be all over it like livewire. You know that, you know how it works. *Someone* has to pay."

"Or be seen to."

"Or be seen to. But it needn't be Virginia."

"*Ex-Envoy heads planetary rebellion.* No, I can see how that wouldn't play too well with the Corps' public relations people."

He stopped. Stared at me with sudden hostility.

"Is that really what you think of me?"

I sighed and closed my eyes. "No. I'm sorry."

"I'm doing my best to nail this shut with a minimum of pain to people who matter, Tak. And you're not helping."

"I know."

"I need someone for Mitzi Harlan's murder, and I need a ringleader. Someone who'll play well as the evil genius behind all this shit. Maybe a couple of others to bulk up the arrest list."

If in the end I have to fight and die for the ghost and memory of Quellcrist Falconer and not the woman herself, then that will be better than not fighting at all.

Koi's words in the beached and stalled-out hoverloader on Vchira. The words and the flicker of passion around his face as he spoke them, the passion, perhaps, of a martyr who had missed his moment once before and did not intend to again.

Koi, ex–Black Brigade.

But Sierra Tres had said much the same thing while we hid in the channels and fallen ruins of Eltevedtem. And Brasil's demeanor said it for him, all the time. Maybe what they all wanted was martyrdom in a cause older and greater and weightier than themselves.

I pushed my thoughts aside, derailed them before they could get where they were going.

"And Sylvie Oshima?" I asked.

"Well." Another shrug. "As I understand it, she's been contaminated by something from the Uncleared Zones. So allowing we can salvage her from the firefight, we have her cleansed, and then hand her back her life. Does that sound reasonable?"

"It sounds untenable."

I remembered Sylvie talking about the command software aboard *Guns for Guevara. No matter how good the housecleaning you buy afterward, some of that shit stays. Hard-to-kill code remnants, traces. Ghosts of things.* If Koi could fight and die for a ghost, who knew what the neoQuellists would make of Sylvie Oshima, even after her headgear was wiped.

"Is it?"

"Come on, Tod. She's iconic. Whatever is or isn't inside her, she could be the focus for a whole new neoQuellist wave. The First Families will want her liquidated on principle."

Murakami grinned fiercely.

"What the First Families want and what they get from me are going to be two *radically* different things, Tak."

"Yeah?"

"Yeah." He slurred it, for mockery. "Because if they don't cooperate fully, I'll promise them an Envoy deployment at assault strength."

"And if they call your bluff?"

"Tak, I'm an Envoy. Brutalizing planetary regimes is what we *do*. They'll fold like a fucking deck chair, and you know it. They're going to be so fucking grateful for the escape clause, they'd have their own children queuing up to tongue my ass clean if I asked."

I looked at him then, and for just a moment it was as if a door had blown open on my Envoy past. He stood there, still grinning in the glare from the Angier spots, and he could have been me. And I remembered what it had really been like. It wasn't the belonging that came flooding back to me this time, it was the brutal power of Corps enablement. The liberating savagery that rose out of a bone-deep knowledge that you were feared. That you were whispered of across the Settled Worlds and that even in the corridors of governance on Earth, the power brokers grew quiet at your name. It was a rush that came on like branded-supply tetrameth. Men and women who might wreck or simply remove from the balance sheet a hundred thousand lives with a gesture, those men and women could be taught fear again, and the instrument of that lesson was the Envoy Corps. Was you.

I forced an answering smile.

"You're charming, Tod. You haven't changed at all, have you?"

"Nope."

And out of nowhere, the smile stopped being forced. I laughed and it seemed to shake something loose inside me.

"All right. Talk to me, you bastard. How do we do this?"

He gave me the clownish raised brows again. "I was hoping you'd tell me. You're the one with the floor plans."

"Yeah, I meant what's our assault strength. You're not planning to use—"

Murakami jerked a thumb at the bulk of *Impaler*.

"Our spiky-minded friends there? I certainly am."

"Fuck, Tod, they're a bunch of methhead kids. The *haiduci* are going to shred them."

He gestured dismissively. "Work with the tools to hand, Tak. You know how it is. They're young and angry and cranked up on meth, just looking for someone to take it out on. They'll keep Segesvar occupied long enough for us to get in and do the real damage."

I glanced at my watch. "You planning to do this tonight?"

"Dawn tomorrow. We're waiting on Aiura, and according to Tanaseda she won't get in until the early hours. Oh yeah." He tipped his head back and nodded at the sky. "And there's the weather."

I followed his gaze. Thick, dark battlements of cloud were piled up overhead, toppling steadily westward across a fragmentary, orange-tinged sky where Hotei's light still struggled to make itself felt. Daikoku had long ago drowned in a muffled glow on the horizon. And now that I noticed, there was a fresh breeze across the Expanse that carried the unmistakable smell of the sea.

"What about the weather?"

"It's going to change." Murakami sniffed. "That storm that was supposed to blow itself out in the southern Nurimono? Didn't. And now it seems it's picked up a scoop from some freak northwesterly run-on, and it's hooking. It's coming back around."

Ebisu's Eavesdrop.

"Are you sure?"

"Of course I'm not sure, Tak. It's a fucking weather forecast. But even if we don't catch the full force of it, a bit of hard wind and horizontal rain wouldn't go amiss, would it? Chaotic systems, just where we need them."

"That," I said carefully, "depends very much on how good a pilot your shaky friend Vlad turns out to be. You know what they call a hookback like this down here, don't you?"

Murakami looked at me blankly.

"No. Rough luck?"

"No, they call it Ebisu's Eavesdrop. After the fisherman host story?"

"Oh right."

This far south, Ebisu isn't himself. In the north and equatorial regions of Harlan's World, JapAmanglic cultural dominance makes him the folk god of the sea, patron of sailors, and, generally speaking, a good-natured deity to have around. Saint Elmo is cheerily co-opted as an analog or helper god, so as to include and not upset the more Christian-influenced residents. But in Kossuth, where the East European worker heritage that helped build the World is strong, this live-and-let-live approach is not reciprocated. Ebisu emerges as a demonic submarine presence to scare children to bed with, a monster that in legend saints like Elmo must do battle with to protect the faithful.

"You remember how that story ends?" I asked.

"Sure. Ebisu bestows all these fantastic gifts on the fishermen in return for their hospitality, but he forgets his fishing rod, right?"

"Yeah."

"So, uh, he comes back to get it and just as he's about to knock he hears the fishermen running down his personal hygiene. His hands smell of fish, he doesn't clean his teeth, his clothes are shabby. All that stuff you're supposed to teach kids, right?"

"Right."

"Yeah, I remember telling this stuff to Suki and Markus, back when they were small." Murakami's gaze grew distant, hazed out on the horizon and the gathering clouds there. "Got to be nearly half a century ago now. You believe that?"

"Finish the story, Tod."

"Right. Well, uh, let's see. Ebisu's pissed off so he stalks in, grabs his rod, and as he storms out again, all the gifts he's given turn to rotting belaweed and dead fish in his wake. He plunges into the sea and the fishermen have crap catches for months afterward. Moral of the tale—look after your personal hygiene, but *even more important, kids,* don't talk about people behind their backs."

He looked back at me.

"How'd I do?"

"Pretty good for fifty years on. But down here, they tell it a little different. See, Ebisu's hideously ugly, tentacled and beaked and fanged, he's a terrifying sight, and the fishermen have a hard time not just running away screaming. But they master their fear and offer him hospitality anyway, which you're not supposed to do for a demon. So Ebisu gives them all sorts of gifts stolen from ships he's sunk in the past, and then he leaves. The fishermen heave a massive sigh of relief and start talking it up, how monstrous he was, how terrifying, how smart they all were to get all these gifts out of him, and in the midst of it all back he comes for his trident."

"Not a rod, then?"

"No, not scary enough I guess. It's a massive, barbed trident in this version."

"You'd think they'd have noticed when he left it behind, wouldn't you?"

"*Shut* up. Ebisu overhears them bad-mouthing him and slips away in a black fury, only to come back in the form of a huge storm that obliterates the whole village. Those not drowned get dragged down by his tentacles to an eternity of agony in a watery hell."

"Lovely."

"Yeah, similar moral. Don't talk about people behind their backs but *even more important* don't trust those filthy foreign deities from up north." I lost my smile. "Last time I saw Ebisu's Eavesdrop, I was still a kid. It came off the sea at the eastern end of Newpest and ripped the inland settlements apart for kilometers along the Expanse shoreline. Killed a hundred people without even trying. It drowned half the weed freighters in the inland harbor before anyone could power them up. The wind picked up the lightweight skimmers and threw them down the streets as far as Harlan Park. Around here, the Eavesdrop is very bad luck."

"Well, yeah, for anyone walking their dog in Harlan Park, it would have been."

"I'm serious, Tod. If this storm does come in and your methed-out pal Vlad can't handle his helm, we're likely to find ourselves upside down and trying to breathe belaweed before we get anywhere near Segesvar's place."

Murakami frowned a little.

"Let me worry about Vlad," he said. "You just concentrate on building us an assault plan that works."

I nodded.

"Right. An assault plan that works on the premier *haiduci* stronghold in the southern hemisphere, using teenage junkies for shock troops and a hookback storm for landing cover. By dawn. Sure. How hard can it be?"

The frown again for a moment, then suddenly he laughed.

"Now you put it like that, I can hardly wait." He clapped me on the shoulder and wandered off toward the pirate hoverloader, voice trailing back to me. "I'll go talk to Vlad now. Going to be one for the annals, Tak. You'll see. I've got a feeling about it. Envoy intuition."

"Right."

And out at the horizon, thunder rolled back and forth as if trapped in the narrow space between the cloud base and the ground.

Ebisu, back for his trident, and not much liking what he'd just heard.

CHAPTeR FORTY-FIVe

Dawn was still little more than a rinsed-out gray splash thrown over the looming black mass of the storm front when *Impaler* cast off her moorings and blasted out across the Expanse. At assault speed, she made a noise as if she were shaking herself to pieces, but as we headed into the storm even that faded before the shriek of the wind and the metallic drumming of rain on her armored flanks. The forward viewports of the bridge were a shattering mass of water through which heavy-duty wipers flogged with an overworked electronic whining. Dimly, you could see the normally sluggish waters of the Expanse whipped into waves. Ebisu's Eavesdrop had delivered to expectations.

"Like Kasengo all over again," shouted Murakami, wet-faced and grinning as he squeezed in through the door that led out to the observation deck. His clothes were drenched. Behind him, the wind screamed, grabbed at the door frame, and tried to follow him inside. He fought it off with an effort and slammed the door. Storm autolocks engaged with a solid clunk. "Visibility's dropping through the floor. These guys are never going to know what hit them."

"Then it'll be nothing like Kasengo," I said irritably, remembering. My eyes were gritty with lack of sleep. "Those guys were expecting us."

"Yeah, true." He raked water out of his hair with both hands and shook it off his fingers onto the floor. "But we still trashed them."

"Watch that drift," said Vlad to his helmsman. There was a curious new tone to his voice, an authority I hadn't seen before, and the worst of his twitchiness seemed to have damped down. "We're riding the wind here, not giving in to it. Lean on her."

"Leaning."

The hoverloader quivered palpably with the maneuver. The deck thrummed underfoot. Rain made a new, furious sound on the roof and viewports as our angle of entry to the storm shifted.

"That's it," Vlad said serenely. "Hold her like that."

I stayed on the bridge for a while longer, then nodded at Murakami and slipped down the companionway to the cabin decks. I moved aft, hands braced on the corridor walls to beat the occasional lurches in the hover-loader's stability. Once or twice, crew members appeared and slid past me in the cramped space with practiced ease. The air was hot and sticky. A couple of cabins along, I glanced sideways at an opened door and saw one of Vlad's young pirates, stripped to the waist and bent over unfamiliar modules of hardware on the floor. I took in large, well-shaped breasts, the sheen of sweat on her flesh under harsh white light, short-cut hair damp on the nape of her neck. Then she realized I was there and straightened up. She braced herself with one hand on the cabin wall, folded the other arm across her breasts, and met my eyes with a tense glare that I guessed was either meth comedown or combat nerves.

"Got a problem, sam?"

I shook my head. "Sorry, mind was on something else."

"Yeah? Well, fuck off."

The cabin door sliced shut. I sighed.

Fair enough.

I found Jad looking similarly tense, but fully dressed. She was seated on the upper of the twin bunks in the cabin we'd been allocated, shard blaster stripped of its magazine and laid under the arch of one booted leg. In her hands were the gleaming halves of a solid-load pistol that I didn't remember her having before.

I swung into the lower bunk.

"What you got there?"

"Kalashnikov electromag," she said. "One of the guys down the corridor loaned it to me."

"Making friends already, huh?" An unaccountable sadness hit me as I spoke the words. Maybe something to do with the twin-sibling pheromones coming off the Eishundo sleeves. "Wonder where he stole it from."

"Who says it had to be stolen?"

"I do. These guys are pirates." I stuck a hand up to her bunk. "Come on, let me have a look at it."

She snapped the weapon back together and dropped it into my palm. I held it in front of my eyes and nodded. The Kal EM range were famed throughout the Settled Worlds as the silent sidearm of choice, and this was a state-of-the-art model. I grunted and handed it back up.

"Yeah. Seven hundred dollars, UN, minimum. No methhead pirate is going to spend that kind of money on a hushgun. He nicked it. Probably killed the owner, too. Got to watch the company you keep, Jad."

"Man, you're cheerful this morning. Didn't you get *any* sleep?"

"The way you were snoring up there? What do you think?"

No reply. I grunted again and drifted into the memories Murakami had stirred up. Kasengo, undistinguished little port town in the barely settled southern hemisphere of Nkrumah's Land, recently garrisoned with government troops as the political climate worsened and relations with the Protectorate deteriorated. Kasengo, for reasons best known to the locals, had stellar-range hypercast capacity, and the government of Nkrumah's Land were worried that the UN military might like access to that capacity.

They were right to worry.

We'd come in quietly at hypercast stations around the globe over the previous six months, while everyone was still pretending that diplomacy was a viable option. By the time Envoy Command ordered the strike on Kasengo, we were as adjusted to Nkrumah's Land as any of its hundred million fifth-generation colonists. While our deep-cover teams fomented riots on the streets of cities in the north, Murakami and I gathered a small tactical squad and disappeared south. The idea was to eliminate the garrison while they slept and seize the needlecast facilities the following morning. Something went wrong, information leaked, and we arrived to find the hypercast station heavily defended.

There was no time to draw fresh plans. The same leak that had alerted the Kasengo garrison meant that reinforcements would be on their way. In the midst of a freezing rainstorm, we hit the station in stealth suits and grav packs, sewing the sky around us with tinsel to simulate massive numbers. In the confusion of the storm, the ruse worked like a dream. The garrison were largely conscripted youngsters with a few seasoned NCOs riding herd. Ten minutes into the firefight, they broke and scattered through the rain-slashed streets in frantic, retreating knots. We chased, isolated, mopped them up. Some few went down fighting; most were taken alive and locked up.

Later, we used their bodies to sleeve the first wave of Envoy heavy assault.

I closed my eyes.

"Micky?" Jad's voice from the bunk above.

"Takeshi."

"Whatever. Let's stick with Micky, huh?"

"All right."

"You think that fuck Anton's going to be there today?"

I levered my eyes open again. "I don't know. Yeah, I guess. Tanaseda seemed to think so. Looks like Kovacs is still using him anyway, maybe as a safeguard. If no one's sure what to expect from Sylvie or the thing she's carrying, might be comforting to have another command head around."

"Yeah, that makes sense." She paused. Then, just as my eyes were sliding closed once more, "It doesn't bother you, talking about yourself that way? Knowing he's out there?"

"Of course it bothers me." I yawned cavernously. "I'm going to kill the little fuck."

Silence. I let my eyelids shutter themselves.

"So, Micky."

"*What?*"

"If Anton is there?"

I rolled my eyes at the bunk above me. "Yes?"

"If he's there, I want that motherfucker. You have to shoot him, you wreck his legs or something. He's mine."

"Fine."

"I mean it, Micky."

"So do I," I mumbled, tilting ponderously away under the weight of deferred sleep. "Kill whoever you fucking like, Jad."

● ● ●

Kill whoever you fucking like.

It could have been a mission statement for the raid.

We hit the farm at ramming speed. Garbled distress broadcasts got us close enough that any long-range weaponry Segesvar had would be useless. Vlad's helmsman ran a vector that looked like driven-before-the-storm but was actually a high-speed controlled swerve. By the time the *haiduci* realized what was going on, *Impaler* was upon them. She smashed in through the panther pens, crushing webbing barriers and the old wooden jetties of the original baling station, unstoppable, ripping loose the planking, demolishing decayed antique walls, carrying the growing mass of piled-up wreckage forward on her armored nose.

Look, I told Murakami and Vlad the night before, *there is no subtle way to do this.* And Vlad's eyes lit up with meth-fired enthusiasm.

Impaler plowed to a clanking, grinding halt amid the half-submerged wet-bunker modules. Her decks were canted steeply to the right, and down on the debarkation level a dozen collision alerts shrilled hysterically in my ears as the hatches on that side blew wide open on explosive bolts. Boarding ramps dropped like bombs, livewire security lines at their tips, writhing and shredding into evercrete for purchase. Dully through the hull, I heard the clang and whir of the major grapple lines firing. *Impaler* caught and clung fast.

It was a system once designed only for emergency use, but the pirates had rewired every aspect of their vessel for fast assault, boarding, and battery. Only the machine mind that ran it all had been left out of the loop, and still thought we were a ship in crisis.

The weather met us on the ramp. Rain and wind rushed me, slapped at my face, shoved at me from odd angles. Vlad's assault team ran bellowing into the midst of it. I glanced once at Murakami, shook my head, and then followed. Maybe they had the right idea—with *Impaler* snagged fast amid the damage she'd just created, there was no way back for anybody that didn't involve either winning or dying.

Gunfire started in the gray swirl of the storm. Hiss-sizzle of beam weapons, the boom and bark of slug guns. The beams showed pale blue and yellow in the murk. A distant ripple of thunder across the sky; pale lightning seemed to respond. Someone screamed and fell somewhere up ahead. Indistinct yelling. I cleared the end of the ramp, skidded on the bulge of a wetbunker module, gained balance with the Eishundo sleeve, and leapt forward. Down into the shallow slosh of water between modules, up the bubbled slope of the next. The surface was gritty and gave good purchase. Peripheral vision told me I was the apex of a wedge, Jad on my left flank, Murakami on my right with a plasmafrag gun.

I cranked the neurachem and spotted a maintenance ladder ahead, three of Vlad's pirates pinned down at the base by gunfire from the dockside above. The sprawled body of a comrade floated against the nearest wetbunker module, still steaming from face and chest where the blaster fire had scorched the life from its owner.

I flung myself toward the ladder with wincefish abandon.

"Jad!"

"Yeah—*go!*"

Like being back in the Uncleared. Vestiges of Slipin attunement, maybe some twin-like affinity, care of Eishundo. I sprinted flat-out. Behind me the shard blaster spoke—spiteful rushing whine in the rain—and the edge of the dock exploded in a hail of fragments. More screams. I reached the ladder about the same moment the pirates realized they were no longer pinned down. Stamped my way hurriedly up it, Rapsodia stowed.

At the top, there were bodies, torn and bloodied from the shard fire, and one of Segesvar's men, injured but still on his feet. He spat and lurched at me with a knife. I twisted aside, locked out the knife arm, and threw him off the dock. Short scream, lost in the storm.

Crouch and search, Rapsodia out and sweeping in the poor visibility, while the others came up behind me. Rain smashed down and made a million little geysers back off the evercrete surface. I blinked it out of my eyes.

The dock was clear.

Murakami clapped me on the shoulder. "Hey, not bad for a retired man."

I snorted. "Someone's got to show you how. Come on, this way."

We stalked along the dock in the rain, found the entrance I wanted, and slipped inside, one at a time. The sudden relief from the force of the storm was shocking, almost like silence. We stood dripping water on the plastic floor of a short corridor set with familiar, heavy, portholed metal doors.

Thunder growled outside. I peered through the glass of a door just to be sure, and saw a room of blank-faced metal cabinets. Cold storage for the panther feed and, occasionally, the corpses of Segesvar's enemies. At the end of the corridor, a narrow stairwell led down to the crude resleeving unit and veterinary section for the panthers.

I nodded to the stairs.

"Down there. Three levels and we're in the wet-bunker complex."

The pirates went in the van, noisy and enthusiastic. Meth-wired as they were, and not a little pissed off with having to follow me up the ladder, it would have been hard to dissuade them. Murakami shrugged and didn't try. They clattered down the stairwell at speed, and ran straight into an ambush at the bottom.

We were a flight of stairs behind, moving with undrugged caution, and even there I felt the splashback from the blasters scorch my face and hands. Cacophony of high, sudden shrieks as the pirates caught fire and died as human torches. One of them made three blundering steps back up out of the inferno, flame-winged arms raised imploringly toward us. His melted face was less than a meter from mine when he collapsed, hissing and smoking, on the cold steel stairs below.

Murakami hurled an ultravibe grenade down the well, and it bounced once metallically before the familiar chittering scream kicked in. In the confined space it was deafening. We slapped palms to ears in unison. If anybody down there screamed when it killed them, their deaths were inaudible.

We waited for a second after the grenade died, then Murakami fired the plasmafrag rifle downward. There was no reaction. I crept down past the blackened, cooling corpses of the pirates, gagging at the stench. Peered past the inward-curled, despairing limbs of the one who'd met the brunt of the fire, and saw an empty corridor. Yellow-cream walls, floor, and ceiling, brilliantly lit with overhead strips of inlaid illuminum. Close to the foot of the stairwell, everything was painted with broad swathes of blood and clotted tissue.

"Clear."

We picked our way through the gore and moved cautiously up the corridor, into the heart of the wet bunker's base levels. Tanaseda hadn't known where exactly the captives would be held—the *haiduci* were twitchy and aggressive about allowing the yakuza a presence in Kossuth in the first place. Precarious in his new role of penitent failed blackmailer, Tanaseda had still insisted, on his own admission because he'd hoped to retrieve the whereabouts of Yukio Hirayasu's stack from me by torture or extortion and thus cut his loss of face, at least among his own colleagues. Aiura Harlan-Tsuruoka, for some byzantine reason or other, agreed, and in the end it was her pressure on Segesvar that forged the diplomatic cooperation between yakuza and *haiduci.* Tanaseda had been welcomed formally by Segesvar himself, and then been told in no uncertain terms that he'd best find himself accommodation in Newpest or Sourcetown, stay away from the farm unless specifically summoned, and keep his men on a tight leash. He'd certainly not been given a tour of the premises.

But really, there was only one secure place in the complex for people you didn't want dead yet. I'd seen it a couple of times on previous visits, had once even watched some doomed gambling junkie conveyed there while Segesvar thought about how exactly to make an example of him. If you wanted to lock a man up on the farm, you put him where even a monster couldn't break free. You locked him in the panther cells.

We paused at a crossways, where ventilation systems gaped open above us. Faintly, down the conduits, came the sounds of ongoing battle. I gestured left, murmuring.

"Down there. The panther cells are all on the right at the next turn; they open onto tunnels that lead directly into the pens. Segesvar converted a couple of them for human holding. Got to be one of those."

"All right then."

We picked up the pace again, took the right turn, and then I heard the smooth, solid hum of one of the doors on the cells sliding down into the floor. Footsteps and urgent voices beyond. Segesvar and Aiura, and a third voice I'd heard before but couldn't place. I clamped down on the savage spurt of joy, flattened myself to the wall, and waved Jad and Murakami back.

Aiura, compressed rage as I tuned in.

". . . really expect me to be *impressed* by this?"

"Don't you hand me that shit," snapped Segesvar. "This is that slant-eyed yak fuck you insisted on bringing aboard. I told you—"

"Somehow, Segesvar-san, I do not think—"

"And don't fucking call me that, either. This is Kossuth, not the fucking north. Have a bit of cultural sensitivity, why don't you. Anton, you sure there's no intrusion 'cast going down?"

And the third voice slotted into place. The tall, garish-haired command head from Drava. Software attack dog for Kovacs Version Two.

"Nothing. This is strictly—"

I should have seen it coming.

I was going to wait another couple of seconds. Let them walk out into the wide, brightly lit space of the corridor, then spring the trap. Instead—

Jad surged past me like a trawler cable snapping. Her voice seemed to strike echoes off the walls of the whole complex.

"Anton, you motherless fuck!"

I came off the wall, spinning to cover them all with the Rapsodia.

Too late.

I took in a glimpse of the three of them, gaping in shock. Segesvar met my eyes and flinched. Jad stood braced, shard gun riding her hip, leveled. Anton saw and reacted, deCom swift. He seized Aiura Harlan-Tsuruoka by the shoulders and hurled her in front of him. The shard gun coughed. The Harlan security exec screa—

—and came apart from shoulders to waist as the monomol swarm ripped through her. Blood and tissue exploded through the air around us, splattered me, blinded me—

In the time it took me to wipe my eyes, they were both gone. Back through the cell they'd come out of, and the tunnel beyond. What remained of Aiura lay on the floor in three pieces and puddles of gore.

"Jad, what the *fuck are you playing at*?" I yelled.

She wiped her face, smearing blood. "Told you I'd get him."

I grabbed at calm. Stabbed a finger at the carnage around our feet. "You *didn't* get him, Jad. He's gone." Calm failed me, collapsed catastrophically before focusless fury. *"How could you be so fucking stupid. He's fucking gone."*

"Then I'll fucking catch him up."

"No, we nee—"

But she was already moving again, across the opened cell at a fast deCom lope. Ducking into the tunnel.

"Nice going, Tak," said Murakami sardonically. "Command presence. I like that."

"Shut up, Tod. Just find the monitor room, check the cells. They're all around here somewhere. I'll be back as soon as I can."

I was backing off, moving before I finished speaking. Sprinting again, after Jad, after Segesvar.

After something.

CHAPTeR FORTY-SIX

The tunnel came out in a fight pit. Steep, sloping evercrete sides, ten meters tall and torn ragged for half their height by decades of swamp panthers trying to claw their way out. Railed spectator space around the top, all open to a sky clogged with a fast-moving stampede of greenish cloud cover. It was impossible to look directly up in the rain. Thirty centimeters of thick mud in the bottom of the pit, now pounded into brown sludge by the downpour. The drainage vents in the walls couldn't keep up.

I squinted through the water in the air and on my face, spotted Jad halfway up the narrow maintenance ladder cut into one corner of the pit. Bawled at her over the sound of the storm.

"*Jad!* Fucking *wait!*"

She paused, hanging off the ladder rung, shard blaster pointing downward. Then waved and went on climbing.

I cursed, stowed the Rapsodia, and went after her up the ladder. Rain cascaded down the walls past me and drummed on my head. I seemed to hear blaster fire somewhere above.

When I got to the top, a hand came down and grasped my wrist. I jolted with shock and looked up to see Jad peering down at me.

"Stay low," she called. "They're up here."

Cautiously, I got my head above the level of the pit and looked out across the network of gantries and spectator galleries that crisscrossed the fight pits. Thick curtains of rain skirled across the view. At more than ten meters, visibility faded to gray; at twenty it was gone. Somewhere on the other side of the farm, I could hear the firefight still raging, but here there was only the storm. Jad lay flat on her belly at the edge of the pit. She saw me cast about and leaned closer.

"They split up," she shouted in my ear. "Anton's heading for the moorage space on the far side. My guess is he's looking for a ride out, or maybe the other you to give him some backup. The other guy cut back through the pens over there, looks like he wants to fight. Fired on me just now."

I nodded. "All right, you get after Anton, I'll take care of Segesvar. I'll cover you when you move."

"Done."

I grabbed her shoulder as she rolled over. Pulled her back for a moment. "Jad, you just be fucking careful. If you run into me out there—"

Her teeth split in a grin, and the rain trickled into her teeth.

"Then I'll waste him for you at no extra charge."

I joined her on the flat space of the wallwalk, drew the Rapsodia, and dialed it to tight dispersal, maximum range. I squirmed about and settled into a half-reclining crouch.

"Scan up!"

She gathered herself.

"Go!"

She sprinted away from me, along the rail, onto a connecting gantry, and into the murk. Off to the right, a blaster bolt split the curtain of rain. I triggered the shard pistol in reflex, but reckoned it wasn't close enough. Forty to fifty meters, the armorer in Tekitomura had said, but it helped if you could see what you were shooting at.

So—

I stood up. Bellowed into the storm.

"Hey Rad! You listening? I'm coming to fucking kill you!"

No reply. But no blaster fire, either. I moved warily forward, along the side of the pit gallery, trying to estimate Segesvar's position.

The fight pits were blunt oval arenas sunk directly into the silt bed of the Expanse, deeper inside than the surrounding waters by about a meter. There were nine of them pressed up against each other in rows of three, thick evercrete walls between topped with interlinked galleries where spectators could stand at the rail and watch the panthers rip each other apart at a safe distance below. Steel-mesh spectator walkways were laid corner-to-corner of each pit to provide much-needed extra space for popular fights. On more than one occasion, I'd seen the galleries packed five deep all around and the cross gantries creaking with the weight of crowds craning to see a death.

The overall honeycomb structure the nine pits formed rose about five meters out of the shallow waters of the Expanse and backed onto the low-lying bubbles of the wet-bunker complex at one side. Adjacent to this edge of the pits and crisscrossed with more gantried service walkways were the rows of smaller feeding pens and long rectangular exercise runs that *Impaler* had smashed through on her way into the farm. As near as I could make out, it was from the edge of this mangled wreckage that the blaster had fired.

"You hear me Rad, you piece of shit?"

The blaster crashed again. The beam scorched past me, and I hit the evercrete floor, splashing water.

Segesvar's voice rolled past overhead. "That's close enough, I think, Tak."

"Suit yourself," I shouted back. "It's all over but the cleaning up anyway."

"Really? Not got much faith in yourself, have you? He's over on the new dockside right now, repelling your pirate friends. He'll throw them back into the Expanse or feed them to the panthers. Can't you hear?"

I listened and caught the sounds of battle again. Blaster fire and the odd agonized scream. Impossible to know how it was going for anyone, but my own misgivings about Vlad and his methhead crew came back to me. I grimaced.

"Quite smitten, aren't we!" I yelled. "What's the matter, you and him been spending time down in the grav gym? Been poking either end of your favorite whore together?"

"Fuck you, Kovacs. At least he still knows *how* to have fun."

His voice sounded close, even in the storm. I raised myself slightly and started to crawl along the gallery floor. Get a little closer.

"Right. And that was worth selling me out for?"

"I haven't sold you out." The trawler-winch laugh rattled out at me. "I've traded you in on a better version. I'm going to do what's right by this guy instead of you. Because *this* fucking guy still remembers where he's from."

A little closer. Drag yourself a meter at a time through the hammering rain and three centimeters of standing water on the walkways. Away from one pit, around a second. Stay low. Don't let the hate and anger put you on your feet just yet. Try to push him into making a mistake.

"So does he remember you mewling and crawling in a back alley with your fucking thigh ripped open, Rad? Does he fucking remember that?"

"Yeah, he does. But you know what?" Segesvar's voice scaled upward. Must have hit a nerve. "He just doesn't *break my balls about it all the fucking time. And he doesn't milk it to take fucking liberties with my finances.*"

A little closer. I pitched my own voice amused.

"Yeah, and he's plugged you in with the First Families, too. Which is what this is really about, right? You've sold out to a bunch of fucking aristos, Rad. Just like the fucking yakuza. You'll be moving to Millsport next."

"Hey, *fuck you, Kovacs!*"

The fury came accompanied by another blaster bolt, but it was nowhere close. I grinned in the rain and dialed the Rapsodia up to maximum dispersal. Pressed myself up out of the water. Cranked the neurachem.

"And *I'm* the one who's forgotten where he's from? Come on, Rad. You'll be wearing a slit-eyed sleeve before you know it."

Close enough.

"Hey fuck—"

I rose to my feet and hurled myself forward. His voice cued me in; neurachem vision did the rest. I spotted him crouched at the far side of one of the feeding pens, part shielded by the steel-mesh side of a bridging walkway. The Rapsodia spewed monomol fragments from my fist as I ran around the oval walkway of the fight pit. No time for better aim, just had to hope that—

He yelped and I saw him stagger, clutching at an arm. Savage joy coursed through me, peeled my lips back from my teeth. I fired again and he either collapsed or dived for cover. I leapt the rail between the gallery I was on and the feeding pen beyond. Nearly tripped—didn't. Swayed back on balance and made a split-second decision. I couldn't go around on the wall. If Segesvar was still alive, he'd be back on his feet in the time it took, he'd cook me with the blaster. The walkway was a straight sprint, half a dozen meters across the top of the pen. I hit it running.

The metal beneath my feet tilted sickeningly.

Down in the pen, something leapt and snarled. The sea-and-rotting-flesh stink of the panther's breath came boiling up at me.

Later, I would have time to understand: the feeding pen had taken a glancing blow from *Impaler*'s arrival, and the evercrete on the side where Segesvar waited had fractured open. That end of the walkway hung by nothing more than bolts ripped halfway loose of their mountings. And somehow, from some similar damage elsewhere in the pen complex, one of the swamp panthers was out.

I was still two meters out from the end of the walkway when the bolts tore all the way out. Eishundo reflex threw me forward. I lost the Rapsodia, grabbed at the edge of the pen with both hands. The walkway dropped out from under me. My palms closed on rain-drenched evercrete. One hand slipped. The gecko grip in the other held me up. Somewhere below me, the swamp panther struck sparks from the fallen gantry with its talons, then fell back with a shrill howl. I scrabbled for purchase with my other hand.

Segesvar's head appeared over the lip of the pen wall. He was pale and there was blood soaking through the right arm of his jacket, but he grinned when he saw me.

"Well, fucking well," he said, almost conversationally. "My old self-righteous fucking friend Takeshi Kovacs."

I heaved sideways desperately. Got a heel hooked over the edge of the pen. Segesvar saw it and limped closer.

"No, I don't think so," he said, and kicked my foot away. I swung out again, barely retaining grip with both hands. He stood above me and stared down for a moment. Then he looked away across the fight pits and nodded with vague satisfaction. The rain hammered down around us.

"So for once I'm looking down on you."

I panted. "Oh *fuck* off."

"You know, that panther down there might even be one of your religious friends. That'd be ironic, eh?"

"Just get on with it, Rad. You're a sellout piece of shit and nothing you do here is going to prove any different."

"That's right, Takeshi. Take the fucking moral high ground." His face contorted, and for a moment I thought he was going to kick my hands away there and then. "Like you always do. *Oh Radul's a fucking criminal, Radul can't handle himself, I had to save Radul's fucking life once.* You been doing it since you slimed Yvonna away from me, and you *never fucking change.*"

I gaped up at him in the rain, the drop below me almost forgotten. Spat water out of my mouth.

"What the fuck are you talking about?"

"You know fucking well what I'm talking about! Watanabe's that summer, Yvonna Vasarely, with the green eyes."

Memory flared with the name. Hirata's Reef, the long-limbed silhouette above me. A sea-wet, salt-tasting body on damp rubber suits.

Hang on tight.

"I." I shook my head numbly. "I thought she was called Eva."

"You see, you fucking *see.*" It came seething up out of him like pus, like poison contained too long. His face distorted with rage. "You *didn't* give a shit about her, she was just another nameless fuck for you."

For long moments, my past swept back over me like surf. The Eishundo sleeve took over and I hung in a lit tunnel of kaleidoscope images from that summer. Out on the deck at Watanabe's. The heat, pressing down from a leaden sky. Scant breeze across the Expanse, not enough to stir the heavy mirrored wind chimes. Flesh slick with sweat beneath clothing, beaded with it where you could see. Languid talk and laughter, the acrid aroma of sea-hemp on the air. The green-eyed girl.

"That's two hundred fucking years ago, Rad. And you weren't even *talking* to her most of the time. You were snorting meth out of Malgazorta Bukovski's cleavage, as per fucking usual."

"I didn't know how to. She was." He locked up. "I fucking *cared about her,* you *cunt.*"

At first I couldn't identify the noise that came out of me. It could have been a choked cough with the rain that forced its way down my throat every time I opened my mouth. It felt a little like a sob, a tiny wrenching sense of something coming loose inside. A slippage, a loss.

But it wasn't.

It was laughter.

It came up through me after the first spluttering cough like warmth, demanding space in my chest and a way out. It blew the water out of my mouth, and I couldn't stop it.

"Stop laughing, you fuck."

I couldn't stop. I giggled. Fresh energy curled up my arms with the unlooked-for hilarity, into my gecko hands, new tensile strength down the length of every finger.

"You stupid bastard, Rad. She was Newpest money, she wasn't ever going to waste herself on street like us. She went off to study in Millsport that autumn and I never saw her again. She *told* me I'd never see her again. Said not to get hung up about it, we'd had fun but it wasn't our lives." Barely conscious of what I was doing, I found I'd started to heave myself up to the lip of the pen while he stared at me. The hard evercrete edge of it against my chest. Panting as I talked. "You really think. You'd ever have gotten *near* someone like that, Rad? Thought she'd have your. Babies, and sit on Spekny Wharf with the other gang wives? Waiting for you to come home. Fried from Watanabe's at dawn? I mean." Between grunts, the laughter came bubbling up again. "How fucking desperate would a woman, *any* woman, have to be for that?"

"Fuck you!" he screamed, and kicked me in the face.

I suppose I knew it was coming. I was certainly pushing him hard enough. But it all seemed suddenly very distant and unimportant alongside the glittery bright images of that summer. And anyway, it was the Eishundo sleeve, not me.

My left hand lashed out. Grabbed his leg around the calf as it swung back from the kick. Blood gouted from my nose. The gecko grip locked. I yanked back savagely, and he did a ridiculous little one-legged jig at the edge of the pen. He looked down at me, face working.

I fell, and dragged him down.

It wasn't far to fall. The sides of the pen sloped the same way as the fight pits, and the fallen walkway had jammed itself halfway down the evercrete wall, almost on an even keel. I hit the meshed metal and Segesvar landed on top of me. I lost the air in my lungs. The walkway juddered and scraped down another half a meter. Below us, the panther went crazy, flailing at the rail, trying to tear it down to the floor of the pen. It could smell the blood streaming from my broken nose.

Segesvar squirmed around, fury still in his eyes. I threw a punch. He smothered it. Snarling monosyllables through gritted teeth, he got his injured arm across my throat and leaned on it. It ripped a cry out of him, but he never eased the pressure for a moment. The panther slammed into the side of the fallen gantry, blasting the stink of its breath through the mesh at my side. I saw one raging eye, obliterated by sparks as the talons tore at the metal. It shrilled and slobbered at us like something insane.

Maybe it was.

I kicked and flailed, but Segesvar had me locked down. Nearly two centuries of street violence stored up, he didn't lose this kind of fight. He glared down at me and the hate fed him strength to beat the pain of the shard-blast damage in his arm. I got one arm free and tried again to punch him in the throat, but he had that covered, too. An elbow block and my fingers barely grazed the side of his face. Then he held my arm locked there and settled his weight harder onto the injured arm that was choking me.

I raised my head and bit through the jacket into the shredded flesh of his forearm. Blood welled up in the cloth and filled my mouth. He screamed, and punched me in the side of the head with his other arm. The pressure on my throat began to tell—I couldn't breathe anymore. The panther battered at the metal gantrywork, and it shifted. I slipped fractionally sideways.

Used the shift.

Forced my open palm and fingers flat against the side of his face. Dragged downward hard.

The gecko-gene spines bit and gripped the skin. Where the pads at the tips and the base of my fingers pressed hardest, Segesvar's face tore open. Street-fighter instinct had screwed his eyes shut as I grabbed him, but it did no good. The grip on my fingers ripped the eyelid from the brow downward, scraped the eyeball, and tugged it out on the optic nerve. He screamed, gut deep. A sudden spray of blood squirted red against the gray of the rain, splattered warm on my face. He lost his hold on me and reeled backward, features maimed, eye hanging out and still pumping tiny spurts of blood. I yelled and came after him, hooking a punch into the undamaged side of his face that threw him staggering sideways against the walkway rail.

He sprawled there for a second, left hand raised dizzily to block me, right fist curled tight despite the damage the arm had taken.

And the swamp panther took him down.

There and gone. It was a blur of mane and mantle, forelimb slash and beakgape. Its claws hooked into him at shoulder height and hauled him down off the walkway like a rag doll. He screamed once, and then I heard a single, savage crunch as the beak snapped closed. I didn't see, but it probably bit him in half there and then.

For what must have been a full minute I stood swaying on the canted walkway, listening to the sound of flesh being torn apart and swallowed, bones being snapped. Finally, I staggered to the rail and made myself look.

I was too late. Nothing in the carnage around the feeding panther looked like it had ever been remotely associated with a human body.

Rain was already sluicing the worst of the blood away.

●●●

Swamp panthers aren't very bright. Fed, this one showed little or no interest in my continuing existence over its head. I spent a couple of minutes looking for the Rapsodia, couldn't see it, and so set about getting out of the pen. With the multiple fractures *Impaler*'s arrival had put in the evercrete wall, it wasn't too difficult. I used the widest crack for leverage, jammed in my feet, and hauled myself up hand-over-hand. With the exception of a bad scare when a chunk of evercrete came away in my hand at the top, it was a swift and uneventful climb. On the way up, something in the Eishundo system gradually stopped my nose bleeding.

I stood at the top and listened for the sounds of battle. Heard nothing above the storm, and even that seemed quieter. The fighting was either done or down to skulk-and-stalk. Apparently I'd underestimated Vlad and his crew.

Yeah, or the haiduci.

Time to find out which.

I found Segesvar's blaster in a pool of his blood near the feeding pen rail, checked it for charge, and started to pick my way back across the fight-pit gantries. It dawned slowly on me, as I went, that Segesvar's death had left me with no more than a vague sense of relief. I couldn't make myself care much anymore about the way he'd sold me out, and the revelation of his bitterness at my transgression with Eva—

Yvonna.

—Yvonna, right, the revelation just reinforced an obvious truth. Despite everything, the only thing that had held the two of us together for nearly two hundred years was that single, involuntarily incurred back-alley debt. We'd never really liked each other after all, and that made me think that my younger self had probably been playing Segesvar like an Ide gypsy violin solo.

Back down in the tunnel, I stopped again every few paces and listened for gunfire. The wet-bunker complex seemed eerily quiet, and my own footfalls echoed more than I liked. I backtracked up the tunnel to the hatch where I'd left Murakami and found Aiura Harlan's remains there with a surgically neat hole where the top of her spine used to be. No sign of anyone else. I scanned the corridor in both directions, listened again, and picked up only a regular metallic clanging that I reckoned had to be the confined swamp panthers, smashing themselves against the cell hatches in fury at the disturbances outside. I grimaced and started to work my way down the line of faintly clanging doors, nerves cranked taut, blaster cautiously leveled.

I found the others half a dozen doors along. The hatch was down, the cell space within unmercifully lit. Tumbled bodies lay sprawled across the floor; the wall behind was painted with long slops of blood, as if it had been thrown there in buckets.

Koi.

Tres.

Brasil.

Four or five others that I recognized but didn't know by name. They'd all been killed with a solid-load weapon, and then they'd all been turned face to the floor. The same hole had been hacked in each spine, the stacks were gone.

No sign of Vidaura, no sign of Sylvie Oshima.

I stood amid the carnage, gaze slipping from corpse to tumbled corpse as if searching for something I'd dropped. I stood until the quiet in the brightly lit cell became a steady whining hum in my ears, drowning out the world.

Footsteps in the corridor.

I snapped around, leveled the blaster, and nearly shot Vlad Tepes as he poked his head around the edge of the hatch. He jolted back, swinging the plasmafrag rifle in his hands, then stopped. A reluctant grin surfaced on his face, and one hand crept up to rub at his cheek.

"Kovacs. Fuck, man, I nearly killed you there."

"What the fuck is going on here, Vlad?"

He peered past me at the corpses. Shrugged.

"Beats me. Looks like we got here too late. You know them?"

"Where's Murakami?"

He gestured back the way he'd come. "Over the far side, up on the parking dock. He sent me to find you, case you needed help. Fighting's mostly done, you know. Just mopping up and some good old piracy to do now." He grinned again. "Time to get paid. Come on, this way."

Numbly, I followed him. We crossed the wet bunker, through corridors marked with the signs of recent battle, blaster-charred walls and ugly splashes of shattered human tissue, the odd sprawled corpse and once an absurdly well-dressed middle-age man sitting on the floor staring in catatonic disbelief at his shattered legs sticking straight out in front of him. He must have been flushed from the casino or the brothel when the raid started, must have fled down into the bunker complex and gotten caught in the crossfire. As we reached him, he raised both arms weakly toward us, and Vlad shot him with the plasmafrag. We left him with steam curling up from the massive hole through his chest and climbed up an access ladder into the body of the old baling station.

Out on the parking dock, there was similar carnage. Crumpled bodies were strewn across the wharf and in among the moored skimmers. Here and there, small flames burned where blaster fire had found something more readily flammable than human flesh and bone. Smoke drifted through the rain. The wind was definitely dying down.

Murakami was by the water, knelt beside a slumped Virginia Vidaura and talking urgently to her. One hand cradled the side of her face. A couple of Vlad's pirates stood around, arguing amiably, with their weapons slung over their shoulders. They were all drenched but apparently unharmed.

Across the forward carapace of a green-painted Expansemobile moored nearby, Anton's body.

He lay head-down, eyes frozen open, rainbow command-head hair trailing down almost to the water. There was a hole you could have put your head through where his chest and stomach had been. It looked as if Jad had gotten him dead-center from behind with the shard blaster's focus dialed up to tight. The blaster itself lay discarded on the dock amid pools of blood. Of Jad, there was no sign.

Murakami saw us coming and let go of Vidaura's face. He picked up the shard blaster and held it out to me in both hands. The magazine was ejected, the breech clear. It had been fired empty, then discarded. He shook his head.

"We've looked for her, but there's nothing. Col here says he thinks he saw her go into the water. Shot from the wall up there. Could be she was only winged but in this shit." He gestured at the weather. "No way to tell till we sweep for bodies. Storm's moving out westward, dying off. We can look then."

I stared down at Virginia Vidaura. I couldn't see any obvious injuries, but she looked to be semi-conscious, head lolling. I turned back to Murakami.

"What the fuck is—"

And the shard blaster butt came up and hit me in the head.

● ● ●

White fire, disbelief. A brand-new nosebleed.

Wha—

I staggered, gaped, fell down.

Murakami stood over me. He tossed the shard blaster away and pulled a neat little stunner from his belt.

"Sorry, Tak."

Shot me with it.

CHAPTeR FORTY-SeVeN

*A*t the end of a very long, darkened corridor, there's a woman waiting for me. I'm trying to hurry, but my clothes are waterlogged and heavy, and the corridor itself is canted at an angle and almost knee deep in viscous stuff that I'd think was congealing blood except it stinks of belaweed. I flounder forward on the submerged, tilted floor, but the open doorway doesn't seem to be getting any closer.

Got a problem, sam?

I crank the neurachem, but something's wrong with the bioware because what I can see is like an ultradistant sniperscope image. I only have to twitch and it dances about all over the place, hurting my eyes when they try to keep focus. Half the time the woman is Vlad's well-endowed pirate comrade, stripped to the waist and bent over the modules of unfamiliar equipment on the floor of her cabin. Long, large breasts hanging like fruit—I can feel the roof of my mouth aching to suck in one of the blunt, darkened nipples. Then, just when I think I've got a grip on the view, it slides away and becomes a tiny kitchen with hand-painted blinds that block out the Kossuth sunlight. There's a woman there, too, also stripped to the waist, but it isn't the same one because I know her.

The scope wobbles again. My eyes stray to the hardware on the floor. Matte-gray impact-resistant casings, lustrous black disks where datacoils will spring up when activated. The logo on each module is inscribed in ideographic characters that I recognize, though I don't currently have a reading knowledge of either Hun Home or Earth Chinese. TSENG PSYCHOGRAPHICS. It's a name I've seen around battlefields and psychosurgical recovery units in the recent past, a new name. A new star in the rarefied constellation of military brand names, a name and a brand that only very well-funded organizations can afford.

What you got there?

Kalashnikov electromag. One of the guys down the corridor loaned it to me.

Wonder where he stole it from.

Who says it had to be stolen?

I do. These guys are pirates.

Abruptly, my palm is full of the rounded, voluptuous weight of the Kalashnikov butt. It gleams up at me in the low light of the corridor, and it's begging to be squeezed.

Seven hundred dollars, UN, minimum. No methhead pirate is going to spend that kind of money on a hushgun.

I thrash forward another couple of steps as an awful sense of my own failure to grasp the facts soaks into me. It's as if I'm sucking up the viscous stuff in the corridor through taproots in my legs and waterlogged boots, and I know that when I'm full it's going to clog me to a violent stop.

And then I'll swell and explode with it, like a bag of blood squeezed too hard.

You come in here again, boy, and I'll crush you till you fucking pop.

I feel my own eyes widen with shock. I peer through the sniperscope again and this time it's not the woman with the hardware, and it's not the cabin aboard Impaler.

It's the kitchen.

And it's my mother.

She's standing, one foot in a bowl of soapy water, and leaning over to swab her leg with a blob of cheap farm-cultured hygisponge. She's wearing a thigh-length wraparound weed gatherer's skirt that's split down one side and she's naked to the waist, and she's young, younger than I can normally remember her. Her breasts hang long and smooth, like fruit, and my mouth aches with a trace memory of tasting them. She looks sideways and down at me then, and smiles.

And he slams into the room from another door that fleeting recall tells me leads out onto the wharf. Slams into the room, and slams into her like something elemental.

You cunt, you conniving fucking cunt.

With the shock of it, again, my eyes crank, and I'm suddenly standing at the threshold. The sniperscope veil is gone, this is now and real. It takes me the first three blows to move. Backhander with full swing, it's a blow we've all had from him at one time or another, but this time he's really letting go—she's catapulted back across the kitchen into the table and falls, she gets up and he punches her down again and there's blood, bright from her nose in a stray beam of sunlight through the blind, she struggles to get up, from the floor this time, and he stamps with a booted foot on her stomach, she convulses and rolls on her side, the bowl goes over and soapy water laps out toward me, over the threshold, over my bare feet, and then it's as if a ghost of myself stays at the door while the rest of me runs into the room and tries to get between them.

I'm small, probably not much more than five, and he's drunk so the blow falls inaccurately. But it's enough to knock me back out the door. Then he comes and stands over me, hands braced clumsily on his knees, breathing heavily through a slack mouth.

You come in here again boy, and I'll crush you till you fucking pop.

He doesn't even bother to close the door as he goes back to her.

But as I sit there in a useless heap, beginning to cry, she reaches out across the floor and shoves at the doorjamb with her hand, so it swings closed on what's about to happen.

Then only the sound of blows, and the closed door receding.

I flounder through the canted corridor, chasing the door as the last light squeezes through the crack, and the weeping in my throat modulates upward toward a ripwing scream. A tidal rage is rising in me, and I'm growing with it, I'm older with every passing second, soon I'll be old enough and I'll reach the door, I'll get there before he finally walks out on us all, disappears out of our lives and I'll make him disappear, I'll kill him with my bare hands, there are weapons in my hands, my hands are weapons, and the viscous slop is draining away and I hit the door like a swamp panther, but it makes no difference, it's been closed too long, it's solid and the impact reverberates through me like a stunblast and—

Oh, yeah. Stunblast.

So it's not a door it's—

—the dockside, and my face was crushed against it, sticky in a little pool of spittle and blood where I'd apparently bitten my tongue as I went down. It's not an uncommon outcome with stunners.

I coughed and choked on a throatful of mucus. Spat it out, took a rapid damage inventory, and wished I hadn't. My whole body was a jarring assemblage of trembling and ache from the stunblast. Nausea clawed at my bowels and the pit of my stomach; my head felt light and filled with starry air. The side of my face throbbed where the rifle butt had hit me. I lay for a moment getting it all back under some kind of control, then peeled my face away from the dock and heaved my neck up like a seal. It was a short, abortive movement. My hands were locked behind my back with some kind of webbing, and I couldn't see much above ankle height. Warm throb of active bioweld around my wrists. It gave so as not to maim hands held cuffed for long periods, it would dissolve like warm wax when you poured the right enzyme on it, but you could no more wriggle out of it than you could pull your own fingers off.

Pressure on my pocket brought home an expected truth. They'd taken the Tebbit knife. I was unarmed.

I retched and brought up the thin leavings of an empty stomach. Fell back and tried hard not to get my face in it. I could hear blaster fire from a long way off and, faintly, what sounded like laughter.

A pair of boots splashed past in the wet. Stopped and came back.

"He's coming right back around," someone said, and whistled. "Tough little motherfucker. Hey, Vidaura, did you say you trained this guy?"

No reply. I heaved up again and succeeded in rolling onto my side. Blinked dazedly up at the form standing over me. Vlad Tepes looked down out of a clearing sky that had almost given up on rain. The look on his face was serious and admiring, and he stood absolutely still as he watched me. No trace of his former methhead twitchiness to be seen.

"Good performance," I croaked at him.

"Liked it, huh?" He grinned. "Had you fooled, right?"

I ran my tongue around my teeth and spat out some blood mingled with vomit. "Yeah, I thought Murakami had to be fucking cracked to use you. So what happened to the original Vlad?"

"Ah well." He made a wry face. "You know how it is."

"Yeah, I know. How many more of you are there? Apart from your gorgeous-breasted psychosurgical specialist, that is."

He laughed easily. "Yeah, she said she caught you looking. Beautiful piece of meat, isn't it? You know, the last thing Liebeck wore before that was a Limon cable athlete's sleeve. Flat as a board. A year down the line and she still can't make up her mind if she's pleased or pissed off about the change."

"Limon, huh? Limon, Latimer."

"That's right."

"Home of cutting-edge deCom."

He grinned. "All starting to make sense, is it?"

It isn't easy to shrug when you're cuffed behind your back and flat to the floor. I did my best. "I saw the Tseng gear in her cabin."

"Damn, so you *weren't* looking at her tits."

"No, I was," I admitted. "But you know how it is. Nothing peripheral is ever lost."

"That is the fucking truth."

"Mallory."

We both looked toward the shout. Todor Murakami was striding along the dock from the direction of the wet bunker. He was unarmed apart from the Kalashnikov at his hip and the knife on his chest. Soft rain fell around him with a sparkle in it from the brightening sky.

"Our renegade's sitting up and spitting," said Mallory, gesturing at me.

"Good. Now, since you're the only one who can get that crew of yours to do anything in a coordinated fashion, why don't you go and sort them out. There are still bodies at the brothel end with stacks intact, I saw them on my way through. There may even be living witnesses hiding down there for all I know. I want a final sweep, no one left alive, and I want every stack melted to slag." Murakami gestured disgustedly. "Jesus fuck, they're *pirates*, you'd think they could manage that. Instead of which, most of them are playing at setting the panthers loose and using them for target practice. Just listen to it."

The blaster fire was still in the air, long undisciplined bursts laced with excited shouting and laughter. Mallory shrugged.

"So where's Tomaselli?"

"Still setting up the gear with Liebeck. And Wang's waiting for you on the bridge, trying to make sure no one gets eaten by accident. It's your boat, Vlad. Go get them to stop fucking about, and when they've finished the sweep, bring *Impaler* around to this side for loading."

"All right." Like a ripple over water, Mallory adopted the Vlad persona and started to pick twitchily at his acne scars. He nodded down at me. "See you soon as I see you, eh, Kovacs. Soon as."

I watched him to the corner of the station wall and around it, out of sight. Flicked my gaze back to Murakami, who was still staring away toward the sounds of the postop merriment.

"Fucking amateurs," he muttered, and shook his head.

"So," I said bleakly. "You're deployed after all."

"Got it in *one*." As he spoke, Murakami crouched and hauled me up into an ungainly sitting position with a grunt. "Don't hold it against me, huh? Not like I could have told you last night and appealed to your sense of nostalgia for help, is it?"

I looked around from my new vantage point and saw Virginia Vidaura, slumped against a mooring post, arms bound back. There was a long darkening bruise across her face, and her eye had swollen. She looked dully at me, and then away. There were tears smeared in the dirt and sweat on her face. No sign of Sylvie Oshima's sleeve, dead or alive.

"So instead you played me for a sucker."

He shrugged. "Work with the tools to hand, you know."

"How many of you are there? Not the whole crew, apparently."

"No." He smiled faintly. "Just five. Mallory there. Liebeck, whom I understand you've met, sort of. Two others, Tomaselli and Wang, and me."

I nodded. "Covert deployment strength. I should have known there was no way you'd be just hanging around Millsport on furlough. How long have you been on the ground?"

"Four years, near enough. That's me and Mallory. We came in before the others. We bagged Vlad a couple of years ago, been watching him for a while. Then Mallory brought the others in as new recruits."

"Must have been awkward. Stepping into Vlad's shoes like that."

"Not really." Murakami sat back on his heels in the gentle rain. He seemed to have all the time in the world to talk. "They're not overly perceptive, these methhead guys, and they don't really forge meaningful relationships. There were only a couple of them really close enough to Vlad to be a problem when Mallory stepped in, and I took them out ahead of time. Sniperscope and plasmafrag." He mimed the act of tracking and shooting. "Bye-bye head, bye-bye stack. We tumbled Vlad the week after. Mallory'd been sitting on him for the best part of two years, playing pirate groupie, sucking his dick, sharing pipes and bottles with him. Then, one deep dark night in Sourcetown, bop!" Murakami slapped fist into palm. "That portable Tseng stuff is beautiful. You can do a de- and resleeve in a hotel bathroom."

Sourcetown.

"You've been watching Brasil all this time?"

"Among others." Another shrug. "The whole Strip, really. It's the only place on the World there's any serious insurgency spirit left. Up north, even in most of Newpest, it's just crime, and you know how conservative criminals are."

"Hence Tanaseda."

"Hence Tanaseda. We like the yakuza, they just want to snuggle up to the powers that be. And the *haiduci,* well, despite their much-vaunted populist roots, they're really just a cut-rate no-table-manners version of the same disease. By the way, did you get your pal Segesvar? Forgot to ask before I dented you out there."

"Yeah, I did. Swamp panther ate him."

Murakami chuckled. "Outstanding. Why the hell did you ever quit, Tak?"

I closed my eyes. The stunblast hangover seemed to be getting worse. "What about you? Did you solve my double-sleeving problem for me?"

"Ah—no, not yet."

I opened my eyes again, surprised.

"He's still walking around somewhere?"

Murakami made an embarrassed gesture. "Apparently. Looks like you were hard to kill, even at that age. We'll get him, though."

"Will you," I said somberly.

"Yeah, we will. With Aiura down, he's got no handler, nowhere to run. And sure as fucking lightspeed no one else in the First Families is going to want to pick up where she left off. Not if they want the Protectorate to stay home and let them keep their oligarch toys."

"Or," I said casually, "you could just kill me now you've got me, then let him come in and cut a deal."

Murakami frowned. "That's not funny, Tak."

"Wasn't meant to be. He's still calling himself an Envoy, you know. He'd probably jump at the chance to get back in the Corps if you offered."

"I don't fucking care." There was anger in his tone now. "I don't know the little fucker, and he's going down."

"Okay, okay. Cool off. Just trying to make your life easier."

"My life's easy enough," he growled. "Double-sleeving an Envoy, even an ex-Envoy, is pretty much irrevocable political suicide. Konrad Harlan is going to shit when I turn up in Millsport with Aiura's head and a report on all this. Best thing he can hope to do is deny knowledge of everything and pray I let it go at that."

"You get a stack out of Aiura?"

"Yeah, head and shoulders pretty much intact. We'll interrogate her, but it's a formality. We won't use what she knows directly. In situations like this, we tend to let the local presidential scum keep their deniability intact. You remember the drill: minimize local disruption, maintain a seamless authority front with the Protectorate, hang on to the data for future leverage."

"Yeah, I remember." I tried to swallow some moisture back into my mouth. "You know Aiura might not crack. Family retainer, she'll have some pretty heavy loyalty conditioning."

He grinned unpleasantly. "Everybody cracks in the end, Tak. You know that. Virtual interrogation, it's crack or go insane, and these days we can even bring them back from that." The grin faded out to something harder and no less unpleasant. "Anyway, it doesn't matter. Our beloved leader-in-perpetuity Konrad will never know what we do or don't get out of her. He'll just assume the worst and cringe to heel. Or I'll call in an assault force, torch Rila Crags around him, and then feed him and his whole fucking family to the EMP."

I nodded, looking out across the Expanse with what felt like half a smile on my mouth. "You sound almost like a Quellist. That's what they'd like to do, too, near enough. Seems a shame you can't come to some arrangement with them. But then, that's not really what you're here for." Abruptly, I switched my gaze back to his face. "Is it?"

"Sorry?" But he wasn't really trying, and the grin lurked in the corner of his mouth.

"Come on, Tod. You turn up with state-of-the-art psychographic gear; your pal Liebeck was last deployed on Latimer. You've taken Oshima away somewhere. And you say this gig has been running for about four years, which ties in rather too neatly with the start of the Mecsek Initiative. You're not here for the Quellists, you're here to keep an eye on the deCom technology."

The grin crept out. "Very sharp. Actually, though, you're wrong. We're here to do both. It's the juxtaposition of cutting-edge deCom *and* a residual Quellist presence that's got the Protectorate really shitting their pants. That, and the orbitals of course."

"The orbitals?" I blinked at him. "What have the orbitals got to do with it?"

"At the moment, nothing. And that's the way we'd like it to stay. But with deCom tech, there's just no way to be sure of that anymore."

I shook my head, trying to dislodge the numbness. "Wha—? Why?"

"Because," he said seriously. "The fucking stuff appears to work."

CHAPTeR FORTY-eIGHT

They brought Sylvie Oshima's body out of the baling station on a bulky gray grav sled with Tseng markings and a curving plastic shield to keep the rain off. Liebeck steered the sled with a handheld remote, and another woman I assumed was Tomaselli brought up the rear with a shoulderborne monitor system, also Tseng-logo'd. I'd managed to lever myself to my feet as they came out, and oddly Murakami seemed content to let me stay that way. We stood side by side in silence, like mourners at some premillennial funeral procession, watching the grav bed and its burden arrive. Looking down at Oshima's face, I remembered the ornate stone garden at the top of Rila Crags, the stretcher there, and it struck me that, for the crucible of a new revolutionary era, this woman was spending a lot of time strapped unconscious to conveyances for invalids. This time, under the transparent cover, her eyes were open but didn't seem to be registering anything. If it hadn't been for the vital-signs display on a built-in screen beside her head, you could have believed you were looking at a corpse.

You are, Tak. You're looking at the corpse of the Quellist revolution there. This was all they had, and with Koi and the others gone, there's no one going to bring it back to life.

It wasn't really a shock that Murakami had executed Koi, Brasil, and Tres; I'd been expecting it at some level from the moment I woke up. I'd seen it in Virginia Vidaura's face as she slumped against the mooring post; when she spat out the words, it was no more than confirmation. And when Murakami nodded matter-of-factly and showed me the fistful of freshly excised cortical stacks, all I had was the sickening sensation of staring into a mirror at some kind of terminal damage to myself.

"Come on, Tak." He'd stuffed the stacks back in a pocket of his stealth suit and wiped his hands together dismissively, grimacing. "I had no choice, you can see that. I already told you we can't afford a rerun of the Unsettlement. Not least because these guys were always going to lose, and then the Protectorate boot comes down, and who wants that?"

Virginia Vidaura spat at him. It was a good effort, considering she was still slumped against the mooring post three or four meters away. Murakami sighed.

"Just fucking *think* about it for a moment, will you, Virginia? Think what a neoQuellist uprising is going to do to this planet. You think Adoracion was bad? You think Sharya was a mess? That's nothing to what would have happened here if your beach-party pals had raised the revolutionary standard. Believe me, the Hapeta administration aren't fucking about here. They're hard-liners with a runaway mandate. They'll crush anything that looks like a revolt anywhere in the Settled Worlds, and if it takes planetary bombardment to suppress it, *then that is what they'll use.*"

"Yeah," she snapped. "And that's what we're supposed to accept as a model of governance, is it? Corrupt oligarchic overlordship backed up with overwhelming military force."

Murakami shrugged again. "I don't see why not. Historically, it works. People like doing what they're told. And it's not like this oligarchy is so bad, is it? I mean, look at the conditions people live in. We're not talking Settlement-years poverty and oppression anymore. That's three centuries gone."

"And *why* is it gone?" Vidaura's voice had gone faint. I began to worry that she was concussed. Surfer-spec sleeves are tough, but they don't design them to take the facial damage she'd incurred. "You fucking moron. It's because the Quellists kicked it in the head."

Murakami made an exasperated gesture. "Okay, then, so they've served their purpose, haven't they? We don't need them back again."

"That's crabshit, Murakami, and you know it." But Vidaura was staring emptily at me as she spoke. "Power isn't a structure, it's a flow system. It either accumulates at the top or it diffuses through the system. Quellism set that diffusion in motion, and those motherfuckers in Millsport have been trying to reverse the flow ever since. Now it's accumulative again. Things are just going to go on getting worse, they'll keep taking away and taking away from the rest of us, and in another hundred years you're going to wake up and it *will* be the fucking Settlement years again."

Murakami nodded all through the speech, as if he were giving the matter serious thought.

"Yeah, thing is, Virginia," he said when she'd finished, "they don't pay me, and they certainly never trained me, to worry about a hundred years from now. They trained me—*you* trained me, in fact—to deal with present circumstance. And that's what we're doing here."

Present Circumstance: Sylvie Oshima. DeCom.

"Fucking Mecsek," Murakami said irritably, nodding at the prone figure in the grav bed. "If it was my call, there's no way local government would have had access to this stuff at all, let alone a mandate to license it out to a bunch of drugged-up bounty-hunter dysfunctionals. We could have had an Envoy specialist team deployed to clean up New Hok, and none of this would ever have happened."

"Yeah, but it would have cost too much, remember?"

He nodded glumly. "Yeah. Same fucking reason the Protectorate leased the stuff out to everybody in the first place. Percentage return on investment. Everything's about fucking money. No one wants to make history anymore, they just want to make a pile."

"Thought that was what you wanted," Virginia Vidaura said faintly. "Everyone scrabbling for cash. Oligarchical caretakers. Piss-easy control system. Now you're going to fucking *complain* about it?"

He shot her a weary sideways look and shook his head. Liebeck and Tomaselli wandered off to share a seahemp spliff until Vlad/Mallory showed up with *Impaler*. Downtime. The grav sled bobbed unattended, a meter from me. Rain fell softly on the transparent plastic covering and trickled down the curve. The wind had dropped to a hesitant breeze, and the blaster fire from the far side of the farm had long ago fallen silent. I stood in a crystalline moment of quiet and stared down at Sylvie Oshima's frozen eyes. Whispering scraps of intuition scratched around at the barriers of my conscious understanding, seeking entry.

"What's this about making history, Tod?" I asked tonelessly. "What's going on with deCom?"

He turned to me, and there was a look on his face I'd never seen before. He smiled uncertainly. It made him look very young.

"What's going on? Like I said before, what's going on is that it *works*. They're getting results back at Latimer, Tak. Contact with the Martian AIs. Datasystem compatibility, for the first time in nearly six hundred years of trying. Their machines are talking to ours, and it's this system that bridged the gap. We've cracked the interface."

Cold-taloned claws walked briefly up my spine. I remembered Latimer and Sanction IV, and some of the things I'd seen and done there. I think I'd always known it would be pivotal. I just never believed it would come back to claim me.

"Keeping it kind of quiet, aren't they," I said mildly.

"Wouldn't you be?" Murakami stabbed a finger at the supine figure on the grav sled. "What that woman's got wired into her head will talk to the machines the Martians left behind. In time it might be able to tell us where they've gone, it might even lead us *to* them." He choked a laugh. "And the joke is she's not an archaeologue, she's not a trained Envoy systems officer or a Martian specialist. No. She's a fucking bounty hunter, Tak, a borderline psychotic mercenary machine killer. And there are fuck knows how many more like her, all wandering around with this stuff active in their heads. Do you get any sense of how badly the Protectorate has fucked up this time? You were up there in New Hok. Can you imagine the consequences if our first contact with a hyperadvanced alien culture happens through these people? We'll be lucky if the Martians don't come back and sterilize every planet we've colonized, just to be on the safe side."

I felt suddenly like sitting down again. The trembling from the stunblast came rolling back over me, up from the guts and through my head, leaving it light. I swallowed the nausea and tried to think straight over a clamor of suddenly recalled detail. Sylvie's Slipins in laconic, murderous action against the scorpion gun cluster.

Your whole system of life is inimical to ours.

Yeah. And besides which, we want the fucking land.

Orr and his wrecking bar, stood over the dysfunctional karakuri in the tunnel under Drava. *So we going to switch it off or what?*

DeCom bravado aboard *Guns for Guevara,* vaguely amusing for its ludicrous presumption, until you gave it a context that might mean something.

Anytime you come up with a way to deCom an orbital, Las, just let us know.

Yeah, count me in. Bring down an orbital, they'd make Mitzi Harlan give you head every morning for the rest of your life.

Oh fuck.

"You really think she could do that," I asked numbly. "You think she's capable of talking to the orbitals?"

He bared his teeth. It was anything but a grin. "Tak, for all I know she already *has* been talking to them. We've got her sedated right now, and the Tseng gear is monitoring her for transmissions, that's part of the brief, but there's no telling what she's already done."

"And if she starts?"

He shrugged and looked away. "Then I've got my orders."

"Oh great. Very constructive."

"Tak, what fucking choice do we have?" Desperation edged his voice. "You know the weird shit that's been going down in New Hok. Mimints doing things they're not supposed to, mimints built to specs no one remembers from the Unsettlement. Everyone thinks that's some kind of machine evolution, basic nanotech all grown up, but what if it's not? What if it's deCom that's triggering this? What if the orbitals are waking up because they've got a whiff of the command software, and they're doing something to the mimints in response? That stuff was designed to appeal to Martian machine systems, as near as we understand them, and the word out of Latimer is that it works. So why wouldn't it work here?"

I stared at Sylvie Oshima, and Jad's voice echoed back through my head.

—all this gibbering shit, the blackouts, turning up at sites someone else had already worked, that's all post-Iyamon—

—handful of times we zeroed in on mimint activity, by the time we got there, it was all over. Looked like they'd been fighting each other—

My mind went spinning off down the avenues Murakami's own Envoy intuition had opened for me. What if they hadn't been fighting each other? Or what if—

Sylvie, semi-conscious on a bunk in Drava, muttering. *It* knew *me. It. Like an old friend. Like a—*

The woman who called herself Nadia Makita, lying in another bunk aboard *Boubin Islander.*

Grigori. There's something that sounds like Grigori down there.

"Those people you've got in your pocket," I said quietly to Murakami. "The ones you murdered for the sake of a more stable tomorrow for us all. They all believed this was Quellcrist Falconer."

"Well, belief is a funny thing, Tak." He was staring away past the grav sled, and there was no humor in his tone at all. "You're an Envoy, you know that."

"Yeah. So what do *you* believe?"

For a couple of moments he was silent. Then he shook his head and looked at me directly.

"What do I believe, Tak? I believe that if we're about to decode the keys to Martian civilization, then the Really Dead coming back to life is going to seem like a small and relatively unremarkable event."

"You think it's her?"

"I don't care if it's her. It doesn't change a thing."

A shout from Tomaselli. *Impaler* came forging around the side of Segesvar's devastated farm like some huge thuggish cyborg elephant ray. At the risk of throwing up again, I worked the neurachem gingerly and made out Mallory standing in the conning tower with his coms officer and a couple of other pirates I didn't recognize. I stood closer to Murakami.

"I've got one other question, Tod. What are you planning to do with us? Virginia and me?"

"Well." He rubbed vigorously at his cropped hair so fine spray flew out of it. The hint of a grin surfaced, as if the return to practical topics of conversation was some kind of reunion with an old friend. "That's a little problematic, but we'll sort something out. Way things are these days back on Earth, they'd probably want me to bring you both in, or wipe you both out. Renegade Envoys don't profile well under the current administration."

I nodded wearily. "And so?"

The grin powered up. "And so fuck 'em. You're an Envoy, Tak. So is she. Just because you lost your clubhouse privileges doesn't mean you don't belong. Just walking away from the Corps doesn't change what you are. You think I'm going to write that off because a greasy little gang of Earth politicians are looking for scapegoats?"

I shook my head. "That's your employers you're talking about there, Tod."

"Fuck that. I answer to Envoy Command. We don't EMP our own people." He caught his lower lip in his teeth, glanced at Virginia Vidaura and then back at me. His voice dropped to a mutter. "But I'm going to need some cooperation to swing this, Tak. She's taking the whole thing too hard. I can't turn her loose with that attitude. Not least because she's likely to put a plasmafrag bolt through the back of my head as soon as I turn around."

Impaler drifted in sideways toward an unused section of the dock. Her grapples fired and chewed holes in the evercrete. A couple of them hit rotten patches and tugged loose as soon as they started to crank taut. The hover-loader backed off slightly in a mound of stirred-up water and shredded belaweed. The grapples wound back and fired again.

Something behind me wailed.

At first, some stupid part of me thought it was Virginia Vidaura finally venting her pent-up grief. A fraction of a second later I caught up with the machine tone of the sound and identified it for what it was—an alarm.

Time seemed to slam to a halt. Seconds turned into ponderous slabs of perception; everything moved with the lazy calm of motion underwater.

—Liebeck, spinning away from the water's edge, lit spliff tumbling from her open mouth, bouncing off the upper slope of her breast in a brief splutter of embers—

—Murakami, yelling at my ear, moving past me toward the grav sled—

—The monitor system built into the sled screaming, a whole rack of data-coil systems flaring to life like candles along one side of Sylvie Oshima's suddenly twitching body—

—Sylvie's eyes, wide open and fixed on mine as the gravity of her stare drags my own gaze in—

—The alarm, unfamiliar as the new Tseng hardware, but only one possible meaning behind it—

—And Murakami's arm, raised, hand filled with the Kalashnikov as he clears it from his belt—

—My own yell, stretching out and blending with his as I throw myself forward to block him, hands still bound, hopelessly slow—

And then the clouds ripped open in the east, and vomited angelfire.

And the dock lit up with light and fury.

And the sky fell in.

CHAPTeR FORTY-NINe

Afterward, it took me a while to realize I wasn't dreaming again. There was the same hallucinatory, abandoned quality to the scene around me as the childhood nightmare I'd relived after the stunblast, the same lack of coherent sense. I was lying on the dock at Segesvar's farm again, but it was deserted and my hands were suddenly unbound. A faint mist lay over everything, and the colors seemed bleached out of the surroundings. The grav sled stood patiently floating where it had been, but with twisted dream-logic it was Virginia Vidaura who now lay on it, face pallid on either side of the massive bruise across her features. A few meters out into the Expanse, patches of water were inexplicably burning with pale flames. Sylvie Oshima sat watching them, hunched forward on one of the mooring posts like a ripwing and frozen in place. She must have heard me stumbling as I got up, but she didn't move or look around.

It had stopped raining, finally. The air smelled scorched.

I walked unsteadily to the water's edge and stood beside her.

"Grigori fucking Ishii," she said, still without looking at me.

"Sylvie?"

Then she turned, and I saw the confirmation. The deCom command head was back. The detail of how she held herself, the look in her eyes, the voice had all shifted back. She smiled wanly.

"This is all your fault, Micky. You gave me Ishii to think about. I couldn't leave it alone. Then I remembered who he was, and I had to go back down there and look for him. And dig through the paths he came in on, the paths *she* came in on, too, once I started looking." She shrugged, but it wasn't an easy gesture. "I opened the way."

"You're losing me. Who *is* Grigori Ishii?"

"You really don't remember? Kids' history class, year three? The Alabardos Crater?"

"My head hurts, Sylvie, and I cut a lot of school. Get to the point."

"Grigori Ishii was a Quellist jetcopter pilot with the fallback detachment at Alabardos. The one who tried to fly Quell out. He died with her when the angelfire cut loose."

"Then . . ."

"Yeah." She laughed, barely, a single small sound. "She is who she says she is."

"Did?" I stopped and looked around me, trying to encompass the enormity of it. "Did she do this?"

"No, I did." A shrugged correction. "They did, I asked them to."

"You *called down* the angelfire? You hotwired an orbital?"

A smile drifted across her face, but it seemed to catch on something painful as it passed. "Yeah. All that crabshit we used to talk, and I'm really the one that swings it. Doesn't seem possible, does it?"

I pressed a hand hard against my face. "Sylvie, you're going to have to slow down. What happened to Ishii's jetcopter?"

"Nothing. I mean, everything, exactly what you read about in school. The angelfire got it, just like they tell you when you're a kid. Just like the story." She was talking more to herself than to me, still staring away into the mist the orbital strike had created when it vaporized *Impaler* and the four meters of water beneath. "It's not the way we thought, Micky. The angelfire. It's a blast beam, but it's more than that. It's a recording device, too. A recording angel. It destroys everything it touches, but everything it touches has a modifying effect on the energy in the beam as well. Every single molecule, every single subatomic particle changes the beam's energy state fractionally, and when it's done it carries a perfect image of whatever it's destroyed. And it stores the images afterward. Nothing's ever lost."

I coughed, laughter and disbelief. "You've got to be fucking kidding me. You're telling me Quellcrist Falconer has spent the last three hundred years inside a fucking Martian database?"

"She was lost at first," she murmured. "She wandered for such a long time among the wings. She didn't understand what had happened to her. She didn't know she'd been transcribed. She had to be so fucking *strong.*"

I tried to imagine what that might be like, a virtual existence in a system built by alien minds, and couldn't. It made my skin crawl.

"So how did she get out?"

Sylvie looked at me with a curious gleam in her eyes. "The orbital sent her."

"Oh please."

"No, it's." She shook her head. "I don't pretend to understand the protocols, only what happened. It saw something in me, or in the combination of me and the command software, maybe. Some kind of analogy, something it thought it understood. I was the perfect template for this consciousness, apparently. I think the whole orbital net is an integrated system, and I think it's been trying to do this for some time. All that modified mimint behavior in New Hok. I think the system's been trying to download the human personalities it has stored, all the people the orbitals have burned out of the sky over the past four centuries, or whatever's left of them. Up to now, it's been cramming them into mimint minds. Poor Grigori Ishii—he was part of the scorpion gun we took down."

"Yeah, you said you knew it. When you were delirious in Drava."

"Not me. *She* knew it, she recognized something about him. I don't think there was much left of Ishii's personality." She shivered. "There's certainly not much left of him down in the holding cells; it's a shell at best by now, and it's not sane. But something tripped her memories of him, and she flooded the system trying to get out and deal with it. It's why the engagement fell apart. I couldn't cope, and she came storming up out of the deep capacity like a fucking bomb blast."

I squeezed my eyes shut, trying to assimilate.

"But why would the orbitals do that? Why start downloading?"

"I told you, I don't know. Maybe they don't know what to do with human personality forms. It can't be what they were designed for. Maybe they put up with it for a century or so, and then started looking for a place to put the garbage. The mimints have had New Hok to themselves for the last three hundred years; that's most of our whole history here. Maybe this has been going on all the time, there's no reason we'd know about it before the Mecsek Initiative."

I wondered distantly how many people had lost their lives to the angelfire over the four hundred years since Harlan's World was settled. Accidental victims of pilot error, political prisoners cut loose on grav harnesses from Rila Crags and a dozen other such execution spots around the globe, the few odd deaths where the orbitals had acted out of character and destroyed outside their normal parameters. I wondered how many dissolved into screaming insanity inside the Martian orbital databases, how many more went the same way as they were stuffed unceremoniously into mimint minds in New Hok. I wondered how many were left.

Pilot error?

"Sylvie?"

"What?" She'd gone back to staring out over the Expanse.

"Were you aware when we pulled you out of Rila? Did you know what was going on around you?"

"Millsport? Not really. Some of it. Why?"

"There was a firefight with a swoopcopter, and the orbitals got it. I thought at the time the pilot miscalculated his rate of rise or something, or the orbitals were twitchy from the fireworks. But you would have died if he'd kept strafing us. You think . . . ?"

She shrugged. "Maybe. I don't know. It's not a reliable link." She gestured around her and laughed, a little unsteadily. "I can't do this sort of thing at will, you know. Like I said, I had to ask nicely."

Todor Murakami, vaporized. Tomaselli and Liebeck, Vlad/Mallory and his whole crew, the entire armored body of the *Impaler* and the hundreds of cubic meters of water she floated on, even—I looked at my wrists and saw a tiny burn on each—the bioweld cuffs from my and Virginia's hands. All gone in the microsecond unleashing of a minutely controlled wrath from the sky.

I thought about the precision of understanding necessary for a machine to achieve all that from five hundred kilometers above the surface of the planet, the idea that there could be an afterlife and its guardians circling up there, and then I remembered the tidy little bedroom in the virtuality, the Renouncer tract peeling away at one corner from the back of the door. I looked at Sylvie again and I understood some of what must be happening inside her.

"What does it feel like?" I asked her gently. "Talking to them?"

She snorted. "What do you think? It feels like religion, like all my mother's crabshit pontifications suddenly coming home to roost. It's not talking, it's like." She gestured. "Like sharing, like melting down the delineation that makes you who you are. I don't know. Like sex, maybe, like good sex. But not the . . . Ah fuck it, I can't describe it to you, Micky. I barely believe it happened at all. Yeah." She grinned sourly. "Union with the godhead. Except people like my mother would have run screaming out of the Upload center rather than *really* face something like that. It's a dark path, Micky, I opened the door and the software knew what to do next, it *wanted* to take me there, it's what it's for. But it's dark and it's cold, it leaves you. Naked. Stripped down. There are things like wings to cover you, but they're cold, Micky. Cold and rough and they smell of cherries and mustard."

"But is it the orbital talking to you? Or do you think there are Martians in there, running it?"

Out of somewhere, she came up with another crooked grin. "That'd be something, wouldn't it? Solving the great mystery of our time. Where are the Martians, where have they all gone?"

For a long moment, I let the image soak through me. Our bat-winged raptor predecessors hurling themselves into the sky by the thousands and waiting for the angelfire to flash down and transfigure them, burn them to ash and virtual rebirth above the clouds. Coming, maybe, from every other world in their hegemony in pilgrimage, gathering for their moment of irrevocable transcendence.

I shook my head. Borrowed imagery from the Renouncer school, and some trace element of perverse Christian sacrifice myth. It's the first thing they teach cub archaeologues. Don't try to transfer your anthropomorphic baggage onto what is nothing like human.

"Too easy," I said.

"Yeah. What I thought. Anyway, it's the orbital that's talking, it feels like a machine the same way the mimints do, the same way the software does. But yes, there are still Martians in there. Grigori Ishii, what's left of him, gibbers about them when you can get any verbal sense out of him at all. And I think Nadia's going to remember something similar when she gets enough distance on it. I think when she does that, when she finally remembers how she walked out of their database and into my head, she's going to be able to *really* talk to them. And it's going to make the link I've got look like Morse code on tom-toms by comparison."

"I thought she didn't know how to use the command software."

"She doesn't. Not yet. But I can teach her, Micky."

There was a peculiar tranquility on Sylvie Oshima's face as she spoke. It was something I'd never seen there before, in all the time we spent together in the Uncleared and after. It reminded me of Nikolai Natsume's face in the Renouncer monastery, before we came and spoiled it all for him—sense of purpose, confirmed beyond human doubt. A belonging to what you did that I hadn't known since Innenin, and that I didn't expect to feel again. I felt a wry envy curl through me instead.

"Going to be a deCom *sensei*, Sylvie? That the plan?"

She gestured impatiently. "I'm not talking about teaching in the real world, I'm talking about *her*. Down in the capacity vault, I can crank up the real-time ratio so we get months out of every minute, and I can show her *how to do this*. It's not like hunting the mimints, that's not what this stuff is for. It's only now I realize that. All the time I spent in the Uncleared, it feels like I was half asleep by comparison with this. *This*, it feels like I was born for."

"That's the software talking, Sylvie."

"Yeah, maybe. So what?"

I couldn't think of any answer to that. Instead, I looked across at the grav sled where Virginia Vidaura lay in place of Sylvie. I moved closer, and it felt like something was tugging me there by a cable wired into my guts.

"She going to be okay?"

"Yeah, I think so." Sylvie pushed herself wearily off the mooring post. "Friend of yours, huh?"

"Er—something like that."

"Yeah, well, that bruising on her face looks bad. Think the bone might be cracked. I stuck her in there as gently as I could, kicked the system on, but all it's done so far is sedate her, on general principles I think. Haven't gotten a diagnosis out of it yet. It'll need re—"

"Hmm?"

I turned to prompt her and saw the gray-cased canister at the top of its arc. There was no time to get to Sylvie, no time to do anything except fling myself, tumbling, over the grav sled and into the scant shadow its covered length offered. Tseng military custom—at a minimum it had to be battlefield-hardened. I hit the ground on the other side and flattened myself to the dock, arms wrapped over my head.

The grenade blew with a curiously muffled crump, and something in my head screamed with the sound. A muted shock wave slapped me, dented my hearing. I was on my feet in the blurred humming it left, no time to check for shrapnel injuries, snarling, spinning to face him as he climbed out of the water at the edge of the dock. I had no weapons, but I came around the end of the grav sled as if my hands were filled with them.

"That was fast," he called. "Thought I'd get you both there."

His clothes were drenched from his swim, and there was a long gash across his forehead that the water had leached pink and bloodless, but the poise in the amber-skinned sleeve hadn't gone anywhere. The black hair was still long, tangled messily to his shoulders. He didn't appear to be armed, but he grinned at me just the same.

Sylvie lay crumpled, halfway between the water and the sled. I couldn't see her face.

"I'm going to fucking kill you now," I said coldly.

"Yeah, you're going to try, old man."

"Do you know what you've done? Do you have any fucking idea who you just killed?"

He shook his head, mock-sorrowful. "You really are getting past your sell-by date, aren't you? You think I'm going to go back to the Harlan family with a *corpse* when I can take a live sleeve? That's not what I'm getting paid for. That was a stun grenade, my last one unfortunately. Didn't you hear it crack? Kind of hard to mistake if you've been anywhere near a battlefield recently. Ah, but then maybe you haven't. Shock wave knockout and inhaled molecular shrapnel to keep everyone that way. She'll be out all day."

"Don't lecture me on battlefield weaponry, Kovacs. I fucking *was* you, and I gave it up to do something more interesting."

"Really?" The anger sparked in the startling blue eyes. "What was that, then? Low-grade criminality or failed revolutionary politics? They tell me you've had a crack at both."

I stalked forward a step and watched him draw into a combat guard.

"Whatever they *tell* you, I have seen a century more sunrises than you. And now I'm going to take them all away from you."

"Yeah?" He made a disgusted sound in his throat. "Well if they're all leading up to what you are now, you'd be doing me a favor. Because whatever else happens to me, the one thing I never want to be is you. I'd rather blow my own stack out the back of my head than end up standing where you are now."

"Then why don't you do that. It'll save me the trouble."

He laughed. It was meant to be contemptuous, I think, but didn't quite make it. There was a nervousness to it, and too much emotion. He made a displacement gesture.

"Man, I'm almost tempted to let you walk away, I feel so sorry for you."

I shook my head. "No, you don't understand. I'm not going to let you take her back to Harlan again. This is over."

"It certainly fucking is. I can't believe how totally you've fucked up your life. Just fucking look at you."

"You look at me. It's the last face you're ever going to see, you stupid little fuck."

"Don't get melodramatic on me, old man."

"Oh, you think this is melodrama?"

"No." This time he got the edge on the contempt about right. "It's too fucking pitiful even for that. It's *wildlife.* You're like some lame old wolf that can't keep up with the pack anymore, has to hang around on the fringes and hope it can grab some meat no one else wants. I can't *believe* you fucking quit the Corps, man. I can't *fucking* believe it."

"Yeah, well, you weren't fucking there," I snapped.

"Yeah, because if I had been, it never would have happened. You think *I* would have let it all go down the drain like that? Just fucking walked away, like Dad did?"

"Hey, *fuck you!*"

"You left them just the same, you fuck. You walked out on the Corps and you walked out of their lives."

"You don't know what the fuck you're talking about. They needed me in their lives like a fucking webjelly in a swimming pool. I was a *criminal.*"

"That's right, you were. What do you want, a fucking medal for it?"

"Oh what would *you* have done? You're an ex-Envoy. You know what that means? Barred from holding public office, military rank, or any corporate post above menial level. No access to legal credit facilities. You're so fucking smart, what would you have done with that hand?"

"I wouldn't have quit in the first place."

"You weren't fucking there."

"Oh, okay. What would I have done as an ex-Envoy? I don't know. But what I do fucking know is that I wouldn't have ended up like you after nearly two hundred years. Alone, broke, and dependent on Radul Segesvar and a bunch of fucking *surfers.* You know I tracked you to Rad before you got here yourself. Did you know that?"

"Of course I did."

He stumbled for a moment. Not much Envoy poise in his voice; he was too angry.

"Yeah, and did you know we've plotted just about every move you've made since Tekitomura? Did you know I set up the ambush at Rila?"

"Yes, that bit seemed to go especially well."

A new increment of rage twisted his face. "It didn't fucking matter, because we had Rad anyway. We were covered from the start. Why do you think you got away so fucking easily?"

"Uh, because the orbitals shot down your swoopcopter, and the rest of you were too fucking incompetent to track us into the Northern arm perhaps?"

"Fuck you. You think we looked hard for you? We knew where you were going, man, right from the start. We've been on you right from the fucking start."

Enough. It was a hard pellet of decision in the center of my chest, and it drove me forward, hands raised.

"Well, then," I said softly. "All you've got to do now is finish it. Think you can manage that all on your own?"

There was a long moment when we stared at each other, and the inevitability of the fight dripped down behind our eyes. Then he rushed me.

Shattering blows to throat and groin, unwrapping from a tightly gathered line of attack that drove me back a full two meters before I could contain it. I turned the groin strike on a sweeping block downward with one arm and dropped low enough to take the throat chop on the forehead. My own counter exploded at the same time, directly up and into the base of his chest. He staggered, tried to hook my arm with a favorite aikido move I recognized so well that I nearly laughed. I broke free of it and stabbed at his eyes with stiffened fingers. He swept a tight, graceful circle out of reach and unleashed a side kick into my ribs. It was too high, and it wasn't fast enough. I grabbed the foot and twisted savagely. He rolled with it, took the fall, and kicked for my head with his other foot as momentum rolled him through the air. His instep cracked me across the face—I was already backing off, rapidly, to avoid the full force of the kick. I lost my hold on his foot, and my vision flew briefly apart. I staggered back against the grav sled as he hit the ground. It bobbed on its fields and held me up. I shook my head to get the airy lightness out of it.

It wasn't quite as savage as it should have been. We were both tired and relying inevitably on the conditioned systems in the sleeves we wore. We were both making mistakes that under other circumstances might have been lethal. And perhaps, we were neither of us really sure what we were doing here in the quiet, mist-tinged unreality of the empty dock.

The aspirants believe . . .

Sylvie's voice, brooding in the capacity vault.

Everything outside is an illusion, a shadow play created by the ancestor

*gods to cradle us until we can build our own tailored reality and Upload
into it.*

That's comforting, isn't it.

I spat and drew breath. Got off the curve of the grav sled cover.

If you let it be.

Across the dock, he climbed back to his feet. I got in fast, while he was
still recovering; summoned everything I had left. He saw it coming and
twisted to meet me. Kick-turned off a raised and crooked leg, fists brushed
aside on a pivoting double-handed block across his head and chest. I lunged
past on deflected momentum and he followed me around, elbow hooking
into the back of my head. I went down before he could do more damage,
rolled and flailed in an attempt to knock his feet out from under him. He
danced aside, took the time to snarl a grin, and came back in, stamping.

For the second time that morning, my time sense dissolved. Combat
conditioning and the jacked-up Eishundo nervous system slowed everything
to a crawl, blurry motion scrawled around the approaching strike and behind
it the bared teeth of his grin.

Stop laughing, you fuck.

Segesvar's face, long decades of bitterness contorting to rage and then
despair as my taunts sheared through the armor of illusions he'd built up for
himself over a lifetime of violence.

Murakami, fistful of bloody excised stacks, shrugging back at me like a
mirror.

Mother, and the dream and—

*—and he stamps with a booted foot on her stomach, she convulses and rolls
on her side, the bowl goes over and soapy water laps out toward me—*

—tidal rage, rising—

*—I'm older with every passing second, soon I'll be old enough and I'll
reach the door—*

*—I'll kill him with my bare hands, there are weapons in my hands, my
hands are weapons—*

—a shadow play—

His foot came down. It seemed to take forever. I rolled at the last moment, into him. Committed, he had nowhere to go. The blow landed on my
upturned shoulder and unbalanced him. I kept rolling and he stumbled.
Luck put one of his heels against something lying on the dock. Sylvie's motionless form. He toppled backward over her.

I came upright, hurdled Sylvie's body, and this time I caught him before
he could regain his feet. I put a brutal kick into the side of his head. Blood
jumped in the air as his scalp tore. Another, before he could roll. His mouth
tore and spilled more blood. He slumped, propped himself groggily up, and
I landed hard on his right arm and chest with all my weight. He grunted and

I thought I felt the arm snap. I lashed down with open palm to his temple. His head rolled, his eyes fluttered. I drew up for the chop to the throat that would crush his larynx.

—a shadow play—

Self-hatred works for you, because you can channel it out into rage at whatever targets for destruction come to hand.

It's a static model, Kovacs. It's a sculpture of despair.

I stared down at him. He was barely moving; he'd be easy to kill.

I stared at him.

Self-hatred—

Shadow play—

Mother—

Out of nowhere, an image of hanging beneath the Martian eyrie at Tekito-mura from a grip welded shut. Paralyzed and suspended. I saw my hand clamped on the cable, holding me up. Keeping me alive.

Locking me in place.

I saw myself unhinge the grip, one numbed finger at a time, and move.

I got up.

I got off him and stepped back. Stood staring, trying to work out what I'd just done. He blinked up at me.

"You know," I said, and my voice jammed rustily. I had to start again, quietly, wearily. "You know, fuck you. You weren't at Innenin, you weren't on Loyko, you weren't at Sanction Four or Hun Home. You've never even been to Earth. What the fuck do you know?"

He spat out blood. Sat up and wiped his smashed mouth. I laughed mirthlessly and shook my head.

"You know what, let's see *you* do it better. Think you can sidestep all my fuckups? Go on then. Fucking try." I moved aside and waved at the moored ranks of skimmers by the dock. "Got to be a few of those that weren't shot up all that badly. Choose your own ride out of here. No one's going to be looking for you, get moving while you're ahead."

He picked himself up a fraction at a time. His eyes never left mine; his hands trembled with tension, floating at guard. Maybe I hadn't broken his arm after all. I laughed again, and it felt better this time.

"I mean it. Let's see you steer my fucking life better than I have. Let's see you not end up like I have. *Go on.*"

He stepped past me, still wary, face grim.

"I will," he said. "I don't see how I could do much worse."

"Then fucking *go. Get the fuck out of here.*" I grabbed at the fresh anger, the urge to knock him down again and finish it. I cranked it back down. It took surprisingly little effort. My voice came out even again. "Don't fucking stand here bitching to me about it, *let's see you do better.*"

He gave me one more guarded look, and then he walked away, to the edge of the dock and toward the less damaged skimmers.

I watched him go.

A dozen meters away, he paused and turned back. I thought he started to lift one hand.

And a liquid gout of blaster fire splashed out from across the dock. It caught him in the head and chest and torched away everything in its path. He stood for a moment, gone from the chest up, and then the smoking ruins of his body collapsed sideways, over the edge of the dock, bounced off the nose carapace of the nearest skimmer and slid into the water with a flat splash.

Something tiny stabbed up under my ribs. A small noise came seeping up through me and I locked it down behind my teeth. I spun, weaponless, in the direction the blast had come from.

Jadwiga stepped out of a doorway in the baling station. From somewhere she'd gotten hold of Murakami's plasmafrag rifle, or one very like it. She held it propped upright on her hip. The heat haze still shimmered around the muzzle.

"I take it you've not got a problem with that," she called across the breeze and the dead quiet between us.

I closed my eyes and stood there, just breathing.

It didn't help.

ePILOGUe

From the deck of Haiduci's Daughter, *the coastline of Kossuth fades to a low charcoal line astern. Tall, ugly clouds are still just visible farther south where the storm blunders about the western end of the Expanse, losing force in the shallow waters and dying. The forecasts are for calm seas and sunshine all the way north. Japaridze reckons he could get us to Tekitomura in record time, and he'd happily do it for the money we've paid him. But a sudden sprint north from an aging freight hoverloader would probably just get us noticed, and that's not what we need right now. The slow, commonplace commercial rhythm of the stopping route up the western coast of the Saffron Archipelago makes a far better cover. And timing is the key.*

Somewhere, I know, there's an investigation ripping through the corridors of power in Millsport. The Envoy ops auditors have been needlecast in and are picking over the scant debris of Murakami's covert operation. But like the fading storm on the Expanse, it isn't going to touch us. We've got time; if we're lucky, all the time we need. The Qualgrist virus is creeping steadily through the global population, and the threat it poses will drive the Harlan family out of their aristo flesh and back into the datastacks with their ancestors. The power vacuum their withdrawal creates at the center of things will suck the rest of the First Families oligarchy into a political maelstrom that they'll handle badly, and then things will begin to fall apart. The yakuza, the haiduci, *and the Protectorate will circle like bottlebacks around a weakened elephant ray, waiting for outcome and watching each other. But they won't move yet, any of them.*

That's what Quellcrist Falconer believes, and though sometimes it sounds a little too slick, like Soseki Koi's march-of-history rhetoric, I'm inclined to agree with her. I've seen this process on other worlds, in some places I've worked to bring it about, and there's the ring of truth to her projections. Plus she was there for the Unsettlement, and that makes her a bigger expert on political change on Harlan's World than any of us.

It's strange, being around her. Bad enough that you know you're talking to a centuries-old historical legend—that knowledge is a fluctuating thing, sometimes vague, sometimes eerily immediate. But beyond it, there's the increasing fluidity with which she comes and goes, switching places with Sylvie Oshima the way Japaridze changes watch on the bridge with his first officer. Sometimes you'll see it happen, and it's like a flash of static across her face—then she blinks it away and you're dealing with a different woman. At other times, I have moments when I'm not sure which of them I'm talking to. I have to watch the way the face moves, listen to the cadences of the voice again.

I wonder if, in the decades to come, this slippery new kind of identity is going to become a common human reality. From what Sylvie tells me when she's up, there's no reason why not. The potential in the deCom systems is almost unlimited. It'll take a stronger kind of human to deal with it, but that's always been the case, with every major step in knowledge or technology that we take. You can't get by on past models, you have to keep moving forward, building better minds and bodies. Either that or the universe moves in like a swamp panther and eats you alive.

I try not to think too much about Segesvar and the others. Especially the other Kovacs. Slowly, I'm talking to Jad again because in the end I can't blame her for what she did. And Virginia Vidaura, the night we pulled out of Newpest harbor aboard Haiduci's Daughter, *gave me an object lesson in learning to let these things go. We fucked, gently, careful of her slowly healing face, and then she wept and talked to me about Jack Soul Brasil all night. I listened and soaked it up, the way she trained me a century ago. And in the morning, she took my waking erection in her hand, pumped it and mouthed it and slid it inside herself and we fucked again, and then got up to face the day. She hasn't mentioned Brasil since, and when I did, inadvertently, she blinked and smiled, and the tears never made it out of her eyes onto her face.*

We are all learning to put these things away, to live with our losses, and to worry instead about something we can change.

Oishii Eminescu once told me there was no point in toppling the First Families because it would only bring the Protectorate and the Envoys down on Harlan's World. He thought Quellism would have failed if the Envoys had existed during the Unsettlement. I think he was probably right, and even Quell herself has a hard time arguing it any other way, though when the sun is going down over a burnished evening ocean and we sit on deck with tumblers of whiskey, she likes to try.

It doesn't really matter. Because down in the capacity vault, stretching minutes into months, Sylvie and Quell are learning to talk to the orbitals. By the time we get to Tekitomura, Sylvie at least thinks they'll have it down. And from there she thinks they can teach the same trick to Oishii and maybe some other like-minded deComs.

And then we'll be ready.

The mood aboard Haiduci's Daughter *is quiet and grim, but there's an undercurrent of hope to it whose unfamiliar edges I'm still feeling my way around. It isn't going to be glorious, it isn't going to be bloodless. But I'm beginning to think it can be done. I think, given the circumstances and a little angelfire, we may be able to bring down the First Families, chase out the yakuza and the* haiduci *or at least bring them to heel. I think we may be able to warn off the Protectorate and the Envoys, and then, if there's anything left, we'll maybe give Quell's demodynamic nanotech a shot.*

And I can't help believing—hoping, maybe—that an orbital platform that can reach down and wipe out at one and the same time a hoverloader full of people and the minute bindings on two individual humans' hands, that can destroy and record at the same time, that can decant whole minds back into datasystems on the ground—I can't help believing that the same system may be able someday to look down at the fringes of the Nurimono Ocean and find a pair of decades-abandoned weed-grown cortical stacks.

And bring back to life what they hold.

ABOUT THe AUTHOR

RICHARD K. MORGAN always wanted to travel and write. He managed to get the traveling part down long before the writing part came. Following graduation from Queens' College, Cambridge University, Morgan moved to London, where he states that his dreams of being a successful novelist were "cut down to size." Morgan says, "About the only worthwhile thing I did in London that year was cultivate a taste for Thai and Japanese cuisines, Jack Daniel's on ice, and Islay single malts. None of which I could really afford. It was time to leave." After four weeks of training as an English-language teacher, he found himself in Istanbul. Then it was back to London, then Madrid, and finally Glasgow, where he secured a university post. Fourteen years after his initial foray to London, his first novel, *Altered Carbon,* was purchased for publication. Shortly thereafter, Hollywood optioned the book for the movies. He is now a happy, full-time writer with the means to write and travel when he wants to (which is usually). *Woken Furies* is Morgan's fourth novel and features the return of Takeshi Kovacs, the imperfect protagonist from *Altered Carbon* (winner of the 2003 Philip K. Dick Award) and *Broken Angels.* His third book, *Market Forces* (a standalone novel), was nominated for the Arthur C. Clarke Award in 2005.

ABOUT THE TYPE

This book was set in Bulmer, a typeface designed in the late eighteenth century by the London type-cutter William Martin. The typeface was created especially for the Shakespeare Press, directed by William Bulmer; hence, the font's name. Bulmer is considered to be a transitional typeface, containing characteristics of old-style and modern designs. It is recognized for its elegantly proportioned letters, with their long ascenders and descenders.